Neal Barrett, Jr.

This special signed edition is
limited to 750 numbered copies.

This is copy 346.

OTHER SEASONS:
The Best of Neal Barrett, Jr.

OTHER SEASONS:
The Best of Neal Barrett, Jr.

NEAL BARRETT, JR.

Subterranean Press 2012

First Edition

ISBN
978-1-59606-406-5

Subterranean Press
PO Box 190106
Burton, MI 48519

www.subterraneanpress.com

Table of Contents

In the Shadow of the Worm

A piece of space cracks high and sharp—ping-*ping!*—like glass blown to powder frost, and the ship blinks into cold brightness.

We are far from home—as far as far could be. The Great Lens is a blind-white eye, our ship a cobalt tear.

Emptiness. And a blue tear. But we are not alone. A fun-bubble drifts nearby—three dark Sheegai cease a fornication of great complexity, turn, and stare. I can sense their no-shapes, inside-out, like solid gloves, and imagine their great yellow eyes...

Few are the ships they see out here, and surely none like ours—proud, sleek and graceful—a wolf that turned into a bird! Oh, fearsome and great she is! A league and a half of terror and love from silver beak to spiked bronze tail—a'shimmer with golden scales from steel-ruffle neck to dragon wings; and each bright horny shield as wide as fifty humans high.

It is a sight for even the Sheegai to record in gray-brittle memories...

▲▼▲

The ship is named *Gryphon*, and I stand alone in her cavernous skull, close my eyes and feel the great bird's surging power. My senses reach out, and I *know* her diamond-bright perfection, hear the clean, pure hum of submolecular song. All is well. There remains the one matter...

The ship is intelligent, certainly—in her own way. More so than I in many respects. I am not too good at simultaneous multiples, but *she* has noted a billion different things since emergence—*chatter! chatter! chatter!* She tells me the presence of the Sheegai bubble is reasonable, considering where we are—and I agree.

But while I am not a man, I have the near-duplicate aspects, and I wish to see such things for myself. Drifting to the starboard eye, I find the tiny dot against the black. I nod at it—as a real man might easily do—then turn, and quickly drop down the *Gryphon*'s velvet throat...

— 1 —

Lady Larrehne waited in the maw of the great closed beak. She stood quite still; dark lashes curtained over violet eyes, golden legs straight, arms gently folded—a flower of cool evening, waiting for moonlight to bloom.

Standing there in velvet light—light that breathed as she breathed—her beauty seemed a fragile thing. But she was not fragile at all...The smooth angle of high cheeks swept down to lips of pliant warmth and fullness; but the fullness could fade to thin, taut determination in the flick of an eye.

Still, Larrehne of Mourlin was not perfect—perfection is fleeting. There were flaws in her character, face and figure, and the result was the unmatchable Larrehne: exquisite imperfection. No one who saw her remembered everything about her—and yet none forgot what they had seen...

▲▼▲

Steifen the non-man was no exception—but non-men have a way of concealing those emotions they were never really meant to have. His eyes never wavered as he drifted from the throat of the *Gryphon* to stand before her. He merely lowered his head respectfully, and let the perfume of a thousand dreams wash over his senses.

"All is secure, Lady..."

Dark lashes rose slightly, still veiling violet eyes.

"Good, Steifen. I thank you." Then the lashes opened fully, and deep eyes warmed the non-man's chromium soul.

"It *is* there, isn't it?" she asked anxiously. "You've seen it?"

"No, Lady. I didn't look from Control. I came directly to you. But it is there."

She smiled, sighed gently. "Well, this is what we came for, old friend. I suppose there's no reason to put it off, is there?"

She stepped toward him, and the live Silkit robe gathered itself firmly about her.

Steifen did not move. She turned, let her eyes hold him a long moment, then stretched slim fingers to meet his own.

"Come. Please..." Her voice was a gentle whisper, warming him like summer twilight.

"Steifen, whatever is here, *you're* with me. I'm not afraid." Her fingers tightened over his. He met her eyes, and could do nothing but stand aside and let her walk beside him...

— 2 —

Side by side, they glided down the dark curve of the *Gryphon*'s beak. The silver stream beneath them came alive to sniff the way; cresting in brightness ahead, dying in sparkle motes behind. Blue and white glow-balls fluttered down to dart and skirr around their heads like restless halos.

The silver path hissed against ancient wood, faded, frothed to gray foam. Steifen's hand touched the hard, polished surface, felt the familiar, gem-studded pattern beneath his fingers.

He hesitated, glancing quickly at Larrehne. She was very still beside him, peering into darkness.

He paused a second more, then pressed fire-yellow and sea-green circles to life.

The great upper beak of the *Gryphon* moved, hummed back upon itself 300 silent feet above. Larrehne of Mourlin and Steifen non-man, mites in the domed tip of the giant's tongue, watched the planet's glare flood in upon them.

Larrehne gasped, wide, dark eyes bright in the green glow.

"I'm not sure—what I expected, but—it *is* very beautiful, is it not?"

Steifen shrugged. "From here, yes, Lady. This is a world that gains beauty as one retreats from it. I think it would be lovelier still from the other side of the Great Lens."

Larrehne's coral lips formed a wide O of mock astonishment.

"Why, Steifen!" She turned, touching his chin and bringing him around to face her.

"My, we're having a cynical turn, aren't we?" She laughed. Bright, silver bells. "This is a new facet of your personality, old friend—I find you ever full of surprises!"

Steifen permitted the thin ghost of a smile. "I was programmed full of surprises, Lady—your father didn't build a frog to converse with his swan."

Larrehne glanced up. Her head turned pertly, and she looked at him as if she were truly seeing him for the first time.

"Sometimes, Steifen," she said thoughtfully, a finger to her cheek, "I wonder if you haven't simply discarded your program in favor of one that suits you better. Honestly—the things you say!"

Steifen cleared his throat. "Of course, Lady, initial programming is only the first step toward creative fulfilment of a—"

Larrehne laughed, spreading her hands in surrender. "All right—I give up! When *you* start quoting non-man scripture...come on, I'm hungry, and I *don't* think I'll feel much like eating later." She nodded toward the swollen world above. "And I *would* like a glass of that Felizian rose and perhaps something from the sandwich tree—and do stop pouting—I *like* you the way you are!"

▲▼▲

A quick selection, and luncheon sighed into place. Steifen dimmed the baleful light of the too-bright world, and glowballs clustered softly over the small round table.

Larrehne took quick, delicate bites, followed by sips of cloud-pink wine. Her face was bright with pleasure.

Steifen raised his own glass, holding it so the dim planet floated redly beneath the surface. "Truly," he said, "the wines of Feliz are unmatched, and I'm eternally grateful My Lady holds a sound block of shares in so worthy a world."

She laughed, but watched him with knowing eyes. "I did not meet Steifen non-man yesterday," she said casually, measuring the long stem of her glass, "nor the day before that. And when he speaks of wine, you can be sure he is *thinking* of something quite different. So. Steifen non-man, what are you thinking *about?*"

Steifen flinched. "My soul is open to your ever-watchful eye. What chance has a poor bundle of tubes and pipes against brains and beauty? I was not exactly thinking, Lady—it was more like idle speculation of the 'what if' variety. I was wondering what kind of a galaxy it would be if more worlds followed in the path of Feliz."

"I fear," she grinned, "it would be a rather blurry galaxy."

"No," said Steifen, "not *all* of them growing grapes—Heaven forbid. But it is *honest* work, isn't it?—And I was comparing that world's industry—with this one's." He pointed his glass at the pale circle of light above.

Larrehne looked down. "Oh...I see."

"A moment ago you accused me of taking a cynical turn, Lady," he said. "There, if you will, is truly a world for the cynic to contemplate, be he real or non-man. Ouriee, when it was not this, but a world of the Sheegai, and later, simply Outpost, when Man took it from them. And since—Carnis and Bouchier, and Abbattoir..."

Larrehne sighed. "So that's what's bothering you...I certainly should have known. Steifen, Steifen—I *know*, and I like this dream of—of honest worlds. But," she peered at him closely, "I know *you*, too; and I know what is behind such thoughts. They have been there since we began this, and before."

She leaned across the table and covered his hand with hers.

"Steifen, your Lady is neither a butterfly wing or a flower petal. I *won't* shrivel and wilt from gazing on—that..."

"No. No," he said firmly, "you will not, Lady..."

— 3 —

Larrehne stood. A quick wave of her hand, and the luncheon table sighed in upon itself, disappeared.

Steifen rose to stand silently beside her.

"I *know* what to expect," she said suddenly, sensing his mood, "I've seen the end of this. I can surely stand the beginning, Steifen."

There was a fine hint of firmness in her voice. Still the non-man did not move. Instead, he studied the tiny pulse in the pearl column of her neck. He knew. He had known for a long time that this moment would come; and when it did, that he would disobey her.

It was a peculiar feeling—and most unwelcome. Certain nodes sent uncomfortable shocks through his system.

A glowball drifted by her shoulder, warming white flesh. She smiled at him in the quick light, and at once he felt shame. He clenched his fists and stepped back from the railing—he could not stop her, but this time he could not cause her pain, either.

Then, the thought: To initiate an act that would bring her displeasure, wasn't that better than letting her bring displeasure on herself? The answer didn't click readily into place as it should have, and he knew what was wrong—he was wandering in the ever confusing corridors of real-man philosophy. If *they* can't answer it, he asked himself wearily, what is such a thing doing in my head?

Larrehne of Mourlin was blessed with understanding. Moving quietly past him, she studied the gem patterns in dark wood. She moved as if simple curiosity instead of necessity brought her to pushbutton jobs that were his.

Her fingers drifted over softly burning jewels, settled, and pale blue opals winked and died. She looked up slowly, and at once her body trembled and stiffened against the rail...

Steifen followed her gaze as the dome flickered, blurred; and the planet rushed in until it covered all but a shard of space. He glanced away, quickly, at Larrehne, and swallowed hard. His fingers tightened around the rail.

His Lady felt pain. He knew it and could not act to stop it—not against her will. The muscles in her face contorted and her body trembled, but her eyes remained locked on the terrible, swollen globe that was hanging in black space...

Steifen found it hard to pull his own gaze away. The constant, rhythmic motion of the planet's surface had a hypnotic effect—and he knew the movement, there was no trick of a hazy atmosphere. Not this time. Whatever moved on *that* world was awesomely real...

First, pinpoint smudges of gray, evenly-spaced over the vast, swimming surface, each point ringed with a writhing, darker circle whose rim touched other rims circling other points—and swarming from those dark rims, the great wombs of the planet, the terrible blind herds stumbling toward death before birth could register on feeble brains. Then: *Snap! Jerk!* into the FTL auras gleaming a thousand miles above the surface.

It was over quickly, and he knew those near-mindless things never felt the wrench of gravitic death. Still, knowing and feeling are different—oh, so different! A non-man is acutely aware of this, and Steifen could not repress a shudder, or shut out the vision of things muscle-blue, fat-yellow and hideless speeding through frozen space...

▲▼▲

Blink! Blink! Blink!
One per second through the aura,
...Out the big dark hole—
Moo-moo, Baa-baa, piggie lad;
Where did you leave your soul?

▲▼▲

Larrehne gave a little cry that twisted Steifen's heart. He stabbed out savagely and hurled the bright image into comforting distance. The galaxy's slaughterhouse rolled back through space until it was only a gray-pink puffball spiked with delicate filaments of white.

Steifen felt her touch, a small hand pressing gratefully against his own—and at the same time the breath of her thoughts brushed him like the cold whisper of winter...

"*Oh, Steifen, Steifen, maybe I am that butterfly wing—but don't let me be crushed just yet—not yet, Steifen!...*"

— 4 —

The Balimann was tall, spare, hard-rubber muscled. His long face was fine-chiseled, high-polished, bleached and tanned until his color seemed to reach out and glow a good inch above the skin.

He threw back his iron-gray mane when he laughed, and his spike beard cut notches in the air. He shook his head and wiped his eyes with a ruffled sleeve.

Larrehne watched him curiously. The Balimann warded her off with a palm raised in peace. "But it *is* marvelous, you know! Garahnell will be simply furious!"

Larrehne shook her head firmly. "Now you are putting words in my mouth, and I meant no discourtesy to Garahnell. I have business with him—as I have with you. I chose to stay on Balimann's Moon because I will *not* set my ship down on Slaughterhouse. Never. When we have finished here, Garahnell can come and join us, and—that amuses you, Balimann?"

His grin had widened as she spoke. Now he shrugged easily. "Oh, I wasn't laughing at *you*, Lady. Of course you couldn't know, but— Garahnell, come *here*? Never in a million years!"

"And why not?" she asked tightly.

Balimann looked at her steadily, then lowered his eyes with a slight bow. "That is for Garahnell to tell you, Lady—if he so wishes."

It was Larrehne's turn to shrug. "As you say, of course. It is certainly none of my business."

"I'm sorry, I didn't mean it to come out quite that way. I—" Suddenly his hand jerked to his head as if he had remembered something important.

"Ah, Lady, I am *much* too isolated here! Forgive me. I have committed the worst sin of all—tempting a woman with a secret then announcing that I cannot tell it to her! Hah! Balimann the Bumkin!"

Larrehne laughed. "You are forgiven, Balimann. And, it *was not* a woman's prying, really. I merely thought that you and Lord Garahnell, under the circumstances..."

Balimann nodded. "*That* I can answer, Lady. Garahnell and I *are* rather dependent upon each other for whatever companionship we require; and fortunately, both our requirements are small—what I mean to say is that we value each other's absence so highly that a strong bond exists between us." Balimann smiled. "So Lord Garahnell keeps to his pesthole—and I to mine."

Larrehne glanced about the room. "My, it seems a warm and friendly pesthole to me, Balimann."

"Because, for some happy reason, Lady, you have chosen to bring a bright candle into this dark place..."

Larrehne read the question on his lips. She ignored it, stood, and walked to the high port that looked from The Balimann's study onto the great night. Steifen stood in the shadows there, and she followed his gaze upward where the *Gryphon* hung like a brass and silver moon. She smiled at the non-man, and Steifen understood. She turned and faced Balimann.

"I'm sure you must already know why I have come here."

The dark head lifted slowly, then bowed solemnly. "I feared it was not the charm of Balimann himself that brought you to the ice-thin edge of the galaxy." He sighed. "I'm afraid I am still The Balimann, then— keeper of Andromeda's ugly child. You come, Lady, to see The Worm. This I know..."

Larrehne laughed. "I would never say this Wormkeeper lacks charm—but I fear life on this lonely moon has turned him into a very bad poet."

Balimann grinned and refilled her glass with dark wine. "Perhaps," he said slyly, "but I am also the *best* poet on Balimann's Moon—am I not?" He spread his hands in bewilderment. "I ask you, Lady—what other weapon have I—but the evasion of poetry? I cling like a flea to the rim of the Big Wheel—but I am still a *man*! I will spout poems until I am blue in the face if I believe there is a small chance of changing your mind. How, I ask you, can I hope to win the fair Larrehne after I have shown her the Great Horror, the Eater of Worlds, the—"

"Oh, stop it!" Larrehne laughed. "I've heard all the scary stories in my cradle, Balimann. Now I am a woman, and I wish to see this—World Eater for myself."

Balimann was silent a long moment. He stood, finally, his hands braced on the table between them. His eyes were dark and somber now, burning like black suns into her own.

"Then I have done what I can to dissuade you?" he said. Larrehne was shocked by the change in his voice. She stared up at him, saying nothing.

"Yes," he said finally, "I see that I have. Then of course you shall see the thing, Lady. I cannot deny you."

He stood, extending his arm. "Now, Lady, it is late, and I suggest you rest from your journey. We're somewhat isolated here, but I think you'll find most of the comforts. And tomorrow," he added grimly, "I believe you will most assuredly need your strength."

Larrehne did not rise. She watched him curiously. *"I'm* not tired, Balimann, really. Is there some reason, some preparations you must make—"

Balimann sighed. "You want to know why I still evade, yes?" He shook his head, and Larrehne decided the wine had begun to show in the man's eyes, in the way the muscles moved at the corners of his mouth.

"No reason, Lady," he went on. "—at least, not for you. This is something I do for myself. Call it the small eccentricity of a host who is a stranger to his role. I cannot deny you—I said that—but one thing..." He held up a finger. "When you leave, I would like to hear that you've enjoyed a restful night on Balimann's Moon." He spread his hands, smiling wearily. "And how could this be—if I let you see the Nightmare of Nightmares your very first night... ?"

— 5 —

Larrehne rose refreshed. Not even the memory of Slaughterhouse, or the gloomy promises of her host, disturbed her sleep. She found her Selfband and spent a peaceful hour before Steifen came to bathe and dress her for the day.

"You slept well, Lady?"

"Oh, yes, thank you, Steifen. And you?"

"Very comfortably, Lady."

It was always the same ritual, though the words varied slightly from day to day. They both knew Steifen had not slept since the day of his creation; but it was an enjoyable way to begin the day.

It was, Steifen admitted, a beautiful day. Give The Balimann credit for that. Artificial, yes—but the 'sun' had risen with a dazzling display through the rose quartz walls of Lady Larrehne's bedroom.

He wondered, idly, whether such refinements were normal here, or whether 'sunrise' was reserved for their host's rare guests. Or, perhaps, contrived especially for this certain special guest?

He shrugged off the thought. It mattered not a whit, one way or the other; he was concerned with another matter, one not too far removed from The Balimann's flair for decoration.

Steifen sensed something unusual in the air, sensed it in a manner not readily explainable—for it was a sense he didn't share with real-men. It was on the order of a probability, based partially on the functioning of this unexplainable quality, and partly on common sense—a quality he *did* share with humanity.

The two senses told him there was an 84% probability that The Balimann had a method of observing Larrehne of Mourlin nude in her bath; and that there was a 97% probability that if he *did* have such a method—he was using it now.

Steifen was enraged at the thought, even though he knew his Lady would not lower herself to consider such vulgarity important—nor permit him to take action against it.

Still, he filed the thought away. At least, it helped evolve a more complete picture of the many-faceted personality of The Balimann.

He dried the Lady Larrehne with the softest towels, and applied oils and powders to her body. He dressed her in a young Silkit whose tiny brain must surely have cried out in sorrow as its own texture touched that incredible flesh.

Instantly, Steifen was flooded with shame. It had happened again, and after he had burned and destroyed the cells and circuits that carried the fearful thing to his brain, those thoughts had not come to him again.

Steifen non-man was programmed for unstinting loyalty to Lady Larrehne—all that he had was hers—every thought her own possession for the asking. He could not tell her that he was indeed imperfect. This one thing he knew he could never share with her, and the thought shattered the crystals of his mind:

While he condemned The Balimann, and all others that lusted after her, he, her non-man, ached with that same longing. And what, he cried out, was more tragic than that? That a non-man be created with real-man emotions that could never in a million universes grow into reality?

— 6 —

The morning had hardly begun, and already, Steifen, with hate in his non-heart for The Balimann, and for himself, found himself hating still another!

It began normally enough, at breakfast, in The Balimann's ever-present psuedo-dawn. Again Steifen bowed to his host's taste. It was a green and dew-fresh garden; a sweet wind in the trees brought odors of a distant meadow, and it was easy to forget how achingly far, far, far this airless world lay from the meadows he remembered.

Even the Lady Larrehne was taken by the charm of this setting— and oh, The Balimann! All gloom of the night before had vanished, and he was again charm itself. His eyes shone like suns when his gaze fell upon Larrehne, and Steifen clenched his teeth and wondered if those eyes gleamed with the reflection of Larrehne of Mourlin clad in the light of a rose-quartz morning?

Then, the new man. It happened so quickly Steifen's weapon was in his hand and the trigger half-depressed before he understood.

No one noticed his mistake at all—every eye was on something stranger than that. It was only a projection, but real enough to bring a startled cry from Larrehne and a curse from Balimann. At once, Steifen knew he had met Lord Garahnell, Master of Slaughterhouse.

"Hah! A*hah!*" The high-pitched voice matched the gaunt, spectral figure. A thin-lipped, red grin spread across a lean and nervous visage; a bony arm stretched out and a long finger uncurled in accusation.

Steifen looked about, wondering what great crime this stranger had discovered.

Garahnell loped toward them in great strides, his garish, archaic robes slurring across the marble beneath him. He stopped, suddenly, at the edge of the almost imperceptible glow that marked the limit of his projection, and his great cape dashed like foamy breakers across bony shoulders.

His fiery eyes rolled in a high circle, and rested on Larrehne, and for a quick moment Steifen saw, in shocked and painful familiarity, his own hunger mirrored.

Garahnell bowed low, sweeping a plumed hat from his head.

"Lady!" breathlessly, with gestures. "Let me say I am much relieved to find you safe and unharmed. Do not fear; even now my forces are mobilizing to effect your rescue!"

Steifen stared. What? What? A player's lines, memorized for the occasion? A sharper study, a deeper look into the eyes of this incredible man and he knew Lord Garahnell himself was not overly sure where the play ended and life began.

To what madhouse, Steifen wondered, *have I brought My Lady!*

Balimann, suddenly on his feet, knocking his chair over behind him, hands clenching like white claws, lips stretched across his teeth.

"Garahnell," said Balimann, his voice a velvet pouch full of tiny shards of glass, "you do me a discourtesy coming here without invitation. I excuse you—and beg that you leave now, and present yourself to the Lady Larrehne of Mourlin at a more suitable time."

Garahnell made a mock bow, grinning widely. "Well said, Wormkeeper! Well said! And that *suitable* time would be—when *you* have finished with her? Eh? Eh? Hah!"

Larrehne paled. The Balimann was livid, trembling with rage. He glanced quickly at Steifen.

Steifen, though, was coldly calm. He simply marked the man, and Garahnell spoke on borrowed time.

"Garahnell," hissed Balimann, "you—are—*warned!*" Steifen could see the shards, now, ripping through velvet.

Garahnell's brows lifted over dark eyes. "Warn? *Warn*, Wormkeeper? Say again *warn* when the air is sucked from the tunnels of that mud-ball of yours! Say again *warn* when Balimann's Moon is a dusty ring circling Slaughterhouse! Say—"

"Stop that, Lord Garahnell—instantly!" Larrehne's voice was brittle-blue ice.

Garahnell turned, his thin lips widening. "I offend, Lady?"

Larrehne shrugged. "I find you overly theatrical, Lord—and your remarks presumptuous. However, as you are here, let me say I wish to speak with you about an important matter. At your convenience."

Garahnell swirled his cape and showed white teeth. "Oh, speak we *will*, Lady! And soon!"

Again, the great cape swirled about scarecrow shoulders. "Do not resist me, Wormkeeper!" shrieked Garahnell. Balimann lunged forward, and the image faded as quickly as it had come.

Steifen stepped forward. "I must ask you, Lady, to accompany me at once to the *Gryphon*. I am at a loss to understand this man, but he is under the illusion you are a prisoner here. Balimann, I'm sure my Lady would be most happy to have you join us. I think you'll find the *Gryphon* as impregnable as you find it amusing."

Balimann laughed shortly. "There's little need for impregnability, non-man! You misunderstand the Lord Garahnell."

Larrehne's eyes flashed hotly. "Then I, too, misunderstand him, Balimann! He is either insane—or a fool!"

Balimann shook his head. "He is not the most likeable of men, Lady—but I know him—and he means no harm. Please. Will you come?" He moved a few steps from the table.

Larrehne stood, watching him with silent eyes. She placed her hand tightly in Steifen's and followed the Wormkeeper's steps.

— 7 —

The *Gryphon* shimmered in eternal night beyond the great window. Balimann pointed. Nothing.

Then: "Wait—ah, there!"

Larrehne strained forward, but a man's eyes are sharper than a woman's, and a non-man's sharper still. The hackles of his psuedo-hair began a long climb up along the length of Steifen's neck...

Like Garahnell himself, it was a parody. From the right, a fleet of one-man ships in perfect vee. They approached, broke clumsily, and formed a ragged, hovering ring around Balimann's Moon.

Grinning, Balimann flipped a long finger and the ships seemed touching close.

But even before, Steifen knew—he sensed them. He knew they were present, because it could be nothing else. *Sheegai!* His non-blood boiled. The Sheegai, condemned forever to the far rim and beyond, without even a planet of their own—this their punishment for that great and awesome crime against Man so long ago.

And now—a madman had put those black minds into fighting ships again!

Who else, Steifen asked himself, *could* it be? The ships bore the stamp of their maker, and he would have been amused if he could have forgotten the creatures who manned them. Those black, warty vessels resembled no ship that ever crossed the heavens. They were Garahnell's pointed symbols of Evil, complete with pathetic, shark-like faces on snubby bows.

Larrehne, too, saw little to laugh about. Her lovely eyes filled with violet fire. "Balimann—I find this intolerable!"

"Intolerable, Lady?" Balimann said dryly, "no longer madness, then?"

"It is more than madness to break the Covenant!" she snapped. "And *you*—your guilt is the greater, to know this and do nothing!"

"No, Lady," a little wearily, "I do nothing—because there is nothing that needs to be done. Look there!"

Steifen followed Larrehne's glance past Balimann's gesture. From the skies, vengeful angels fell in screaming silence. And as the black ships were Evil, so the white and gleaming hawks were symbols of Good. *Oh, Lord Garahnell*, Steifen sighed, *what a piteous child's game is this!*

Larrehne looked away, sharing the non-man's thoughts.

Hauteur vanished from Balimann's eyes. His features softened into weariness. "You see, don't you? He is no madman, Lady—no madder than us all. He merely does what he can to be Man—and there is little of that, even done in a manner such as this..."

The fleets clashed around them. Harmless fireballs of green, pink, lilac and white lit the sky. Blue petals blossomed against a hull of black Evil and a villain spun away in mock-death.

"You see how it is, Lady?" said Balimann. "My game is the study of an ugly enigma that lies or perhaps does not lie between here and

Andromeda. You leap from star to star in a bird that is not a bird, with a man that is not a man. And Garahnell plays with war toys for his imprisoned Lady—who is neither his, imprisoned, nor likely to thank him for his troubles. Where, then, is the dream of Man?"

He shrugged, and his face was creased with purple sadness as another petal grew and blossomed outside the great window.

— 8 —

Garahnell's strange actions revealed a different Balimann to Steifen. Pride turned to reflection—the mock and piteous war of his neighbor seemed to bring things to the fore of the Wormkeeper's thoughts that were easier to shrug off through lonely nights—more difficult in the presence of others.

Things are *not* the same here, thought Steifen. We are on the last sprinkled mote of sand before the great sea begins. And all great seas, he told himself, have a certain strangeness.

Balimann, and the Master of Slaughterhouse—both cardboard figures in the most bizarre of plays on a most lonely stage—meaningless, meaningless…

I *know* this, he told himself, and My Lady and I have no part in things that mean nothing. Whatever life this play mirrors, we will *not* become a part of it. I *will* believe that…!

— 9 —

"We came to see Slaughterhouse, and to view the Great Worm, Steifen. As is so often true, I think, one sometimes finds more than they look for."

Larrehne smiled. A tired smile, yes—but in it Steifen saw a hint of joy, of eagerness. For Lady Larrehne was ever the seeker, he knew; to her all knowledge was a step on the path to truth.

"My mind is with yours," said Steifen. "I sensed that you, too, felt we stood with one foot in reality and one in dreams, there before Balimann's window—with no way of knowing which foot belonged to what. It was most confusing, Lady."

Her eyes sparkled at his words. She leaned forward and pressed his hands tightly.

"Steifen—you saw this? I'm glad—so very glad!"

Steifen found it pleasant to be so near this loveliness—but a poor stimulus for the pondering of real-man philosophy; a thing difficult enough under the best of circumstances. Here, in the eternal rose-quartz dawn of her room, Larrehne's skin retained that quality it had captured in early morning, when he viewed the whole of it so longingly.

"Lady," he asked quickly, fearful that a child could read such thoughts, "I am a non-man, and can only pursue such questions in an academic manner, but, this thing we felt—it seemed akin to the subject of mystical phenomena—something we have spoken of before."

Larrehne closed her eyes. A finger rested delicately against the soft hair of her temple. "It is, I think, in the sense that we find ourselves feeling peculiarly detached from our surroundings. But," she sighed lightly, "I'm afraid it's a poor mystical experience, Steifen, if we can't tell whether we leave reality or approach it!"

Steifen said darkly, "If this playing at games, this Black against White business of Garahnell's is reality, then I prefer to let him and the Wormkeeper *have* such realities. I would rather be a puppet in some dream I somewhat understand."

Larrehne frowned. "Steifen, I haven't mentioned this before, but you've probably guessed it in one way or another. I've been most concerned since we began this voyage—and 'reality' is a big part of that concern. While I'm still a novice with the use of the Selfband, I've had several experiences lately which add greatly to my concern. I—well, I believe I've made contact with my Other, that higher Self which guides us all."

Steifen stood excitedly, "Lady! I'm very pleased!"

She shook her head and brought him down beside her. "No, Steifen, it is much too early for congratulations. Guru McBain points out that there is much hard work for the seeker *after* the Other is found. Still, as I say, though these first contacts have been little more than ghostly whisperings—I am *most* disturbed..."

"Lady, in what way?"

"I don't think we've been faced with a choice between reality and unreality, Steifen. It is becoming clear to me that the very strangeness of Balimann's Moon and Slaughterhouse points to a greater truth.

"As you know, McBain teaches that *all* is unreality in this life; a most difficult barrier for even the most advanced of seekers to cross!"

Steifen released a deep breath. "Real-man philosophy again! We have spoken of this, Lady—and it occurs to me our experiences today are no very telling demonstration of Guru McBain's teachings."

Larrehne brightened. "But don't you *see*? They are, they are!"

Steifen shrugged. "I'm sorry, Lady. I cannot see it as clearly as you."

"Why, then," she said excitedly, "is the life we left in such sharp contrast to this one? Why—as you have put it—do we feel one foot in reality and the other in a dream? Isn't it because these worlds on the gulf of emptiness are mirrors of the worlds we left?

"Is there a more cutting parody of the Good and Evil we have known back there, than Garahnell's mock war—or the birth-death of Slaughterhouse? When I think of the life we left—Oh, Steifen, it's hard to say which nightmare mirrors the other!"

Steifen was saddened by these thoughts, and the sadness colored his voice. "It seems a picture of futility to me, Lady—not a thing Guru McBain would wish to conclude. Still, perhaps I've become even more fuddled in my thinking than I was when you began. This is very possible."

Larrehne favored him with a gentle smile. "My friend, I'd never accuse you of befuddlement. You are, of course, a born pessimist, and this tends to tip the scales of your reasoning toward the darkest conclusion."

"This, too," he agreed, "is possible. I only pray your eternal hope can tip those scales the other way."

"And that," she answered wryly, "is either flattery or sarcasm—but certainly not philosophy! Still, I accept your challenge. We have yet to see the greatest enigma this dream world of yours has to offer—remember?"

"No, I haven't forgotten, and I'm not likely to," said Steifen. "And Lady, please don't refer to this as 'my' dream world. I claim not a particle of it for myself. Also, if the enigma you speak of is The Worm, and I am sure it is—we must carry the classification of dreams a step further into that of nightmares. No, I'm not at all heartened by this last great challenge…"

— 10 —

While Steifen was bound to heed his Lady's wishes, he was also programmed to evaluate. Thus, he exercised discrimination, and spared her the job of editing sense from nonsense. This faculty of discrimination also freed him to protect her from subjects he did not feel served to further her sense of well-being. He never glossed over harsh truth—he merely refrained from repeating every painful experience.

For this reason, he made it quite clear to The Balimann that she was not to be informed of Garahnell's gifts, which he viewed in the lock where Balimann had been sensible enough to confine them.

"Rather charming—in a way," mused Balimann.

"In a way that's rather obvious, if I may say so," Steifen answered.

They *were* supple and lovely creatures, and Lord Garahnell had given them the most attractive attributes of the human female—but they curled about the legs of Steifen and Balimann, and preened themselves, purring in a vibrant, deep-throated *hummmmmmmm—hrrrmmmmm* that was essentially feline. Their eyes denied any hint of humanity, and in the end they were simply female cats in what appeared to Steifen to be a state of perpetual heat.

Outside, he faced Balimann stiffly. "Just what did Garahnell have in mind for My Lady to *do* with these creatures? I see but one use for them; if I am right, this is the foulest of insults to Larrehne of Mourlin!"

Balimann shifted nervously. He inspected a fleck of lint on his sleeve. "I—don't believe Garahnell meant anything unseemly or distasteful by this. His viewpoint differs from yours—or mine," he added quickly. "I imagine he felt these creatures would make excellent handmaidens for a great Lady."

"Hmmmm. Anything is possible," Steifen said dryly. "But I fear your neighbor is again projecting his own bizarre tastes onto others."

"All right," sighed Balimann sharply, "perhaps he is, non-man!" Balimann turned and stalked off down the long hall. He glanced quickly, almost imperceptivly, back at the closed port.

Steifen, who saw things a real-man might miss, knew he would never be able to decide whether Garahnell's gifts found their way back to Slaughterhouse...

— 11 —

Another incident Steifen did not report to his Lady: On the other side of the great window, which he asked to be closed, the battle of the white hawks and black demons still raged. Lord Garahnell's quest continued for the Lady imprisoned in his own mind...

— 12 —

Without the distraction of the great mock war, Balimann's study, where Steifen and his host waited for Larrehne to complete her meditations, was a pleasant and comfortable place. Vaulted ceiling rose above real wooden beams in a manner so ancient that few could have said what period was reflected there. The fireplace contained real wood, too—and the Almighty knew where Balimann obtained such a thing. Steifen had seen only one other—in the home of Larrehne's father, where he had begun life, and served until the Master of Mourlin's death.

Balimann, across from Steifen, leaned forward before the crackling flames to fill their glasses with dark wine.

"You know," he said curtly, "you have no need to worry. I am not quite the crude outworlder you mark me as."

Steifen looked up. "What is this, Balimann?"

"You need not concern yourself that I will speak of Garahnell's gift. That is what I mean!" He turned fiery eyes on Steifen. "You judge too lightly and too quickly, non-man. In this, you do your Lady a great disservice."

"I do not need you to tell me how to serve my Lady," Steifen said stiffly. "However, if I have said anything to offend you—"

"Ha!" Balimann was on his feet, an accusing finger aimed at Steifen's chest. "You see? You do it again! Non-man, do you think I live or die on your opinion of me, or Lord Garahnell, or—or those bitchcats in the air-lock! God in Heaven—protect me from the ego of the galactic!"

Balimann downed his wine too quickly, and twin red lines stained his cheeks and turned to dark spots on his tunic. Still, the storm seemed to have died, and he continued in a quieter tone.

"Believe what I say, or ignore it—as you choose," he said. "Your over-hasty judgments concern me in only one respect: When you shrug The Balimann aside, you toss his words out in the same bundle—and my words, non-man, are not to be taken lightly!"

Steifen, irritated, said: "*You* give them out lightly, my friend."

Balimann hesitated, then nodded in quick understanding. "Yes. My light banter with your Lady was a mistake—perhaps. I did not realize how serious she was about—The Worm. I do now. It will not happen again. That did not work so I have, frankly, changed my personality to suit the need. And I will continue to change it for her until I can convince that stubborn Lady—or you—that it is very possibly worth your *life* to look at that thing!"

Steifen watched the man a long moment. Finally, he nodded. "Perhaps, Balimann. And perhaps I have misjudged some of your motives. Still, I can tell you My Lady has her reasons for taking whatever chance exists. She knows the stories—and she will not be dissuaded."

"It is her life—her sanity," Balimann said coldly. "But I will continue to try. I could not forgive myself if I didn't. Perhaps I would feel better if I knew *why* she feels this great need to come here at all. You have not volunteered this information—nor has she. I haven't pried for it. Now I suppose I will."

"My Lady has told you—"

Balimann shrugged disdainfully. "Yes. You have come to see Slaughterhouse and The Worm. That wasn't my question, was it? *Why?*

The Lady Larrehne is no simple tourist, flitting about the rim of creation in that fantastic bird!"

Steifen looked abstractedly into the fire. His glass made a hollow sound in the quiet room as he placed it on the table before him.

"You are only partially right, Balimann. Seeing Slaughterhouse and The Worm are not my Lady's end motives. There is a great deal more to it than that. I see no reason why you should not hear the story, since you, yourself, have now become a part of it..."

— 13 —

"Lady Larrehne is an exceptional person, Balimann. In these dark times, when ignorance seems the fashion, *she* seeks ever to expand her knowledge. She is, of course, in a good position to do so. The House of Mourlin has interests in many systems, and little happens on a thousand worlds that does not reach our ears. Thus, a great business empire holds itself together.

"Through these same channels, information often comes our way that has little to do with Mourlin business—bits and pieces from here and there that may mean nothing viewed separately—but can often mean a great deal when the parts are fitted together."

Steifen shifted in his chair and took a deep breath. He leaned back and looked at The Balimann. "It was in this way, through her study of certain dispatches over a period of time, that My Lady began to realize something was gravely wrong. There were reports of strange, grotesque animals being sold for pets on Centallia. It was rumoured that a man on Bagdar had three Piggies who wore shirts and shoes and accompanied him about his business. Our man on Garalando reported Baa-baas were much in demand for personal servants...

"We knew at once where these creatures *had* to come from— Slaughterhouse. There was no other possibility. Lord Garahnell's interests had expanded from the production of meat to the creation of semi-intelligent life-forms!

"We had already had the dubious pleasure of visiting one of the FTL receivers long before. It is not a pretty sight, as I'm sure you know. Food means nothing to me, of course—but My Lady has not touched meat since that time. And I don't believe many who saw that operation would go away with different feelings. It is not so much slaughter of animals that offends—the things are long dead and space-frozen when they pop out of no-space. It is the *appearance* of the things that offend—stubby, weak legs, strong enough to propel them from the wombrings to the senders, enough heart and lung to run the pitiful legs, and an ounce or so of brain sacked neatly away with the other organs. And no head, of course, since there is no need for eyes, mouth or tract. I think this detail offended My Lady more than anything."

Steifen shook his head. "With this memory still fresh in her mind, and the distressing reports of Garahnell's new enterprise before her, My Lady was in no mood for the next event. We attended a party given by a certain wealthy man on Farvir, and for the first time, had the opportunity to see Garahnell's handiwork face to face."

Steifen grimaced. "I won't describe them. I will say only that the party was a bizarre and ugly success—My Lady and I left before too many vulgarities were performed.

"I've met many aliens in my long life," Steifen sighed, "and strange as many of them were, still, they *were what they were*—not intentional parodies of Man, things with snouts and hooves and fur designed to mock humanity. God knows, humanity itself is mockery enough these days!"

▲▼▲

Balimann was silent a long moment. "I see," he said finally. "I know, of course, Garahnell has spent no little ingenuity on the design of these—grotesqueries. I had no idea he was exporting the creatures. And turning a pretty profit, I'm sure!"

His brow deepened and he looked steadily at Steifen. "I am no saint, my friend—I don't pretend to be. There's a certain perverse fascination about those creatures in my airlock—no use denying that. Any man could see it. Garahnell's manufactured an attractive new toy, and I expect the jaded galactic will be more than delighted!

"I frankly deplore what Garahnell has done. I *hope* I'm still a cut above that galactic mind. Yes—if your Lady is concerned with the moral fibre of her fellow man, she has good reason."

Steifen let out a deep sigh. "That's not all of it, Balimann—I only wish it were…"

"What?"

Steifen smiled grimly. "Do you think *she* has travelled beyond the rim of the galaxy because of a—'perverse fascination?'"

The non-man stood, leaning close over The Balimann's chair.

"Look at *me*, real-man. What do you see? Look closely and you'll see a thing as unhuman as that chair—or this wine glass! I'm a *non-man*. I look like you and speak like you and think like you, but there's not an ounce of flesh or a drop of blood about me. I live forever—and I was never born! I can be destroyed—but I cannot die!" Steifen paused. "Now, Balimann, what is the difference between me—and Garahnell's creatures?"

Balimann frowned. "This is—unnecessary. I know what you are. You have no reason to compare yourself with them..."

"Exactly," Steifen nodded. "No reason at all. We're both creations of Man—but one is merely unnatural, while the other is *artificial*."

Steifen laughed. "Ironic isn't it? Your unnatural creation shares your higher functions—while your flesh and blood monsters have every one of your base, low desires! A non-man has no stomach, but he drinks your wine—he isn't cold, but he warms himself by your fire. I share your emotional capabilities, Balimann, with a brain that responds to all real-man emotions. I'm mentally, if not physically, very capable of *enjoying* this wine and that fire—perhaps more capable than you!"

Steifen sank back into his chair. Balimann looked blank.

"I'm sorry," Steifen said, "I—hoped it would help you to understand. Don't you see, now, what concerns My Lady? *I* can never become Man— but I can't become an animal, either. Garahnell's creatures can never, *never* become Man—there is no danger in that. But somehow—in a way that defies all understanding—the Master of Slaughterhouse has made possible a terrible—and *fruitful*—union. *And now Man can become an animal!*"

Balimann paled. The wine glass fell from his fingers, shattered, and red droplets hissed into the fire...

— *14* —

Balimann looked up, finally. The color was drained from his dark face, and life seemed to have left his limbs.

"Man has infinite potential for reaching unimaginable heights," he said harshly, "or inventing new ways of debasing himself. He has discovered the final method." Balimann turned away, staring into the dying coals.

Steifen nodded. "Two creatures—are under study in Mourlin's laboratories. They are both very young, of course—not more than a few weeks old. But already we know we are dealing with an essentially animal mind—there is no potential for great intelligence. But—*cunning!* I don't believe there is anything that can match them there."

Balimann looked up. He faced Steifen, but his eyes were far away. "I am a man who knows his own race too well, non-man. Even when they know the price they must pay for this pleasure, it will make no difference—I don't know what will stop them—until every world is crawling with snuffling beasts..."

"Nor do I," Larrehne's voice came softly, "but I know it is a question that *must* be answered."

Even Steifen was unaware of her presence. He turned as she stepped from the shadows. Before he could rise, her hand rested on his shoulder.

"I'm glad Steifen has confided in you, Balimann; I always approve his discretions, and I concur in this one. I hope the viewpoint of one so close to this problem will prove helpful."

Larrehne dropped down beside Steifen, and Balimann rose to pour her wine.

"I am shaken by what the non-man has told me, Lady. And while I can offer you no ready answer, I am certainly at your service. I know, now, I believe, what your business is with Garahnell. And *you* must know, now that you've spoken to him once—that speaking to him again will gain you nothing." He shook his head. "That one will not stop what he is doing."

"No," she said, "I've tried to fool myself into thinking he might yet listen to reason—but I know he will not..."

Steifen tensed. His eyes were suddenly cold. "He will listen if *I* speak, Lady. He will listen, and understand."

Larrehne smiled sadly. "I knew you would have to make that offer, old friend. It has ever been on your mind, hasn't it? Ah, Steifen—you would destroy a world? Even a world of monsters?"

"*He* would destroy a galaxy, Lady. A galaxy of men who would *be* monsters!"

Larrehne turned. "And you, Balimann?"

"In a second, Lady. I would happily fight the non-man for the privilege. I see no other way."

"Nor do I," she said, a strange smile passing briefly across her face. "Somehow I knew this—long before we came. I knew the answer would not come from Garahnell. I knew then, Balimann, that it could only come from you..."

Balimann stared. "From—*me!*"

"I *know what happened here*, Balimann. At least, I know a part of it. I know that Man reached out, and stood here on the beach where his small pond swelled into the great sea. I know he looked out over that sea, toward the far island of Andromeda; looked, and saw what was waiting for him there. I know he turned, and fled back to the Thousand Worlds to scatter the seeds of his shame and despair."

She looked up at Balimann, and her eyes burned with violet fire. "*This* is where Garahnell's monsters were born—*here*, ten thousand years ago, at the moment when a newborn giant turned into a stunted dwarf." She shook her head slowly, and a sad smile again creased her face. "What can a man in a cage do, Balimann—but turn into a beast?"

Balimann looked at Larrehne with new respect. "You know much of the story, Lady. I wish, with all my heart, that I could deny you the rest of it. I cannot."

She bowed her head and closed her eyes. "For that I truly thank you…"

"I hope I never regret the decision, Lady. I pray I will not." He turned the stem of his glass so it caught the final spark of the dying fire. "I haven't asked what you hope to find in the image of The Worm. I haven't, and I will not. Perhaps you will find an answer to a question I cannot answer myself."

"And that question?"

"Simply, Lady: can we blame Man for erasing what he saw from the memory of his race?"

Larrehne favored him with a gentle smile. Her eyes were dark stars, very near him, but incalculable years away. "That question has been a part of me too long now, Balimann. A deadly shadow has fallen over Man; he is dying in its darkness—I would see what casts a shadow such as that…"

— 15 —

It seemed strange to Steifen that the lift should plunge them down toward the center of Balimann's Moon, when the object of their search lay in the deep seas between the galaxies. But, as The Balimann cryptically explained, "There are observatories, non-man—then there are *observatories*…"

Lady Larrehne's eyes tilted in a question, and Balimann continued: "Balimann's Moon houses no ordinary instrument—I assure you. It was not made for staring at dust-mote worlds or puny constellations. It was built, by the first Balimann, for one purpose only—to probe the very heart of Andromeda. And that, Lady, it can do—and more.

"For this, an immense amount of energy is required—and energy we have, the unlimited power of the stars themselves! It is all around us now, stolen from the cores of a million angry giants, and locked in the center of Balimann's Moon."

That power was there, an unbelievable, terrible surging force, Steifen could not deny. The deeper the lift plunged, the heavier this force weighed upon his senses.

It was a strange feeling for the non-man. He knew the deep, throbbing power of great space carriers, the howling, unchained monsters that plunged across the Barrier as wind rips through a spider's web. An imperceptible coldness pressed against him—this was something different. An age-old thing, but shiny new. A prize that fell from Man's hip pocket when he fled the Great Gulf in terror and scattered his belongings to the dark winds...

The lift slowed gently and heaviness returned. The door slid open with a tiny sigh. Balimann moved aside, and Larrehne and Steifen stepped out.

A tiny bulb above the lift door was the only light. Whatever lay beyond its glow was clothed in darkness.

"Please be prepared," Balimann warned. "I can't explain it to you, but the effect is unusual." He turned away and pressed something behind him.

Steifen flinched as brightness exploded around him. Larrehne's strong fingers tightened on his arm and he caught the sound of her quick gasp of breath. He blinked, looked away, closed his eyes. He opened them again and dizziness returned. A billion tiny Steifens shook their heads and returned his stare.

"Steifen! Steifen, I—" He clutched her arm as she swayed and Balimann made a swift movement. The room darkened and a single dim light circled the carpet beneath them.

"I'm sorry," said Balimann, "it takes some time before you are accustomed to it."

"No," smiled Larrehne weakly, "I'm all right now. Just—dizzy, I think. It is a strange illusion—as if I were trapped in the center of some gigantic jewel!"

"It is no illusion, Lady. We are at the bottom of a large, spheroid room—shaped much like that of an egg. The dizziness and confusion are caused by a multitude of tiny, reflective shards of silvered crystal which project the image of the stars from receivers on the surface. It is the perfection of these projecting planes which rob the eye of balance, and leave it no point of reference. It is also," he continued, "the factor that makes Balimann's Moon unequaled by any observatory in the galaxy. It has been so for ten thousand years, and I think it may not be surpassed for ten thousand more—or never, perhaps, unless the worlds of men change their courses."

"The perfection of these instruments, Balimann," said Steifen dryly, "has already changed the course of Man once. Had your ancestor's image of The Worm been *less* than perfect, perhaps the road to Andromeda would be filled with ships, now—and your race reaching out instead of turning in upon itself."

"Steifen!" Larrehne said sharply, "that was most unfair!"

Steifen shrugged. "There was no offense intended toward The Balimann, Lady. I was merely indulging in irony again."

Balimann laughed grimly. "And you're right, of course, non-man! The successful explorer is the one ignorant of the terrors he faces over the horizon. The Great Captains who gathered here a hundred centuries ago didn't have that advantage—Oh, no, they definitely did not!"

▲▼▲

Suddenly, his hand swept out in a deft, practiced movement. Lights sprang on beside them, circling a shallow bowl at the base of the spheroid hall. Larrehne and Steifen turned as sudden movement caught their eyes.

Dark iris shadows hummed, widening on the azure carpet in neat rows. Black-sheathed, silver stalks pushed into the light, sang, hissed, filled the amphitheatre with alien wheat that suddenly bloomed, spread black wings and flashed silver limbs—*snap!*—into rigid silence...

"It is a humbling thing," whispered Larrehne, "to see legend come to life. Even one that died unborn."

She gazed out over the silent rows, the dark and empty thrones. She read the silver-hued crests emblazoned on black, spelled the names so long unknown—DeLoyega, Graham-Martin, Pieter, Vashiel...

Larrehne stopped. She squinted at a crest too much in shadow, and suddenly knew it was no shadow at all. It was dark, aged—almost ancient among the cold-silver names around it.

"You cannot read it, Lady," said Balimann. "That name is burned from the rolls of the Great Captains. But I know it—it is Marshekian."

Balimann looked long at the dark and twisted crest. Then he turned away in sadness. "This is the rest of the story, Lady. The part that does not even live in legend but only in the heart of The Balimann.

"They gathered here, The Hundred, The Great Captains. Their ships circled this moon like giant, hungry hounds, power throbbing in their angry souls, waiting for their masters to turn them loose across the void.

But their masters were here, and they had just seen what waited for them there, in the Great Gulf.

"The Captain of Captains," Balimann went on, "was Stergoffsenn, a giant with flaming red hair. When it was all over, he rose and turned to them, a sea of brave men's faces gone pale and slack. Seeing those faces, he must have known; but he tried to cover his own fear—and theirs—with his fierce and blazing eyes. He told them, simply, calmly, that they would return to their ships, that nothing had changed, nothing—they would sail into the Great Sea, demon or no demon, and the first man to bolt would feel the heat of his blaster."

"And Marshekian," said Larrehne softly, suddenly understanding the darkness of the chair's crest, "Marshekian was the first…"

Balimann nodded. "He was, Lady. And a finer, braver man has never lived, so the legends say. He stood, slowly, facing the Captain of Captains. 'No,' he said, 'we are going home, Stergoffsenn. We are going home, now.' And Stergoffsenn looked at him with deep understanding, and raised his blaster and fired.

"Then he turned away, dropped the weapon; his great head shaking in his hands. Stergoffsenn wept shamelessly for the first time in his long life…

"Then" Balimann said grimly, "the Captains, no longer the Great Ones, no longer The Hundred, but merely men, now, lowered their heads and left the two alone—Marshekian, dead; Marshekian, most dearly beloved brother of Stergoffsenn, who died because his brother had asked him, with his eyes, to let him be chosen; to let him die for all the rest.

"And when the others had gone, Stergoffsenn covered his brother with his own golden cape, and wept no more. He gazed up into the heights of this very room, where a moment before the terrible image had appeared to wreck men's dreams. Then he looked once more at the quiet shape under the golden cape," and Balimann pointed, "to the right of where the non-man stands."

Larrehne and Steifen caught the hint of darkness stained on azure blue, death ten thousand years old, and turned away.

Balimann glanced at Larrehne, then the non-man. He let his eyes rest on the woman. "You are still ready, Lady? After the story is finished?" He gestured toward the hundred black and silver thrones behind her.

"I am, Balimann." She drew herself up, straight and tall. "But you will have to make other seating arrangements, I fear. I'm sorry, but I find that with a wealth of chairs there is not a one I care for."

Balimann smiled softly. "Ghosts, Lady? Surely not."

"If you will," she said distantly, her eyes resting beyond the pool of light, beyond, even, the darkness above. "These thrones of The Hundred carry enough of a burden now, Balimann. I can sense this, and I know Steifen feels much he does not say. If I fail, too, then it would be a sad thing to drape another mantle of guilt over this poor furniture, would it not?"

— 16 —

Indeed, the non-man sensed much he kept to himself—but the strange, ice-borne thoughts added more to puzzlement than knowledge.

What was *happening* to him! For a quick second he felt near-panic, a real-man emotion he had never known. As the lights dimmed, and the caressing arms of his couch enfolded him, he gazed up into darkness. A deep shudder trembled through his body. The thoughts that flooded in upon him were a strange mixture of non-man prescience and human fear and superstition. He was born—he was dying. A dark shadow bore down upon him with awesome speed...

He laughed hollowly to himself. This, then, the moment he had feared for *her*! And now, fingers tight against his thighs, pseudo-sweat beading on synthetic brows, he sensed no fear from the form on the couch beside him. No. Fear was much closer than the Lady Larrehne.

My God! My God! What is happening to me!! He bit his lip until busy invisible nodes signaled pseudo-flesh was being damaged.

He lay back in his chair, trembling, as his body manufactured and bathed him in unfamiliar acid. Steifen, learning a brand new human emotion after all these years—one every real-man child was better equipped to handle. Steifen the non-man, shivering, eyes wide-staring in blackness, afraid of the dark...

...Calmness returned. Non-man controls clamped down on errant emotions; did not destroy, and negate the usefulness of these new things, but came to a silent understanding between the subjective and objective impact of fear on the electronic psyche.

The wave swept over him, abated, was replaced with controlled understanding. He became aware of physical sensation again, dimly aware of The Balimann himself. Somewhere, the gaunt frame bowed tautly over a bubble of blackness; strong fingers flicked through clusters of singing lights that sucked the power of the stars, and held far galaxies squeezed within the high dome...

▲▼▲

Steifen floated over black seas. He gazed down, let his vision sink in dark water...deep...deep...deep...

▲▼▲

Below, a dim shape swimming in velvet currents. Larger...larger... a luminous pearl, a lamp's soft glow through midnight fog...

▲▼▲

Softness cracked wide! Pearl shattered! Diamond brilliance crashed out, broke free in aching streaks of splintered color. Needle shards of brittle-green ice-blue bloodsharp-red pierced darkness. Cold, cold, cold...Andromeda! A black, depthless sea—and on the other side—Andromeda...Andromeda...

▲▼▲

Then...gone! Steifen blinked. No, it was there—but Balimann had dimmed the jewel galaxy to a pale ghost. It was there, after-image gray, and before it, between Steifen and faint Andromeda—

A sharp chill of apprehension jolted him. Muscles tightened toward pain. *Now! Now! Now!* Plastic veins sprayed cold acid through steel bones.

Then: What? What? *What?* No. That isn't it. Not yet. But he knew it was. Ice melted. Relief flooded in warmly, and Steifen laughed aloud.

It was appalling, beyond belief! Mentally, he stamped out a legend with his finger, blotted out ten thousand years of terror with the joint of a thumb. This lacy filament of green, a nebulous wisp of starry ribbon—twisted vaguely like a worm, yes—but Lord, no Eater of Worlds!

Balimann raised the magnification, and green filament became a jade-ice necklace tossed on velvet...

Again—now it stretched across the whole range of vision, big enough to see a billion clusters of tiny emerald suns...

Again—a single cluster of the brilliant, crowded suns, spun together with misty olive webs...

And again—a dozen green suns, alone; some aching brilliant, some merely bright, and some blurred behind dim veils, all imbued with flowing movement, and—

—AGAIN!

AGAIN!

AGAIN...!

— 17 —

...How long, now, has it been? How far, how far...?

▲▼▲

These are things I cannot answer—such questions are meaningless to me. In the Control Room of the *Gryphon*, a thousand shiny eyes that saw and measured everything now see nothing. All the quivering needles sleep silently against red zeros...

One thing I know—*some* measure of time and distance separates my 'now' from the things that happened on Balimann's Moon.

How many non-miles and no-years lie between, I cannot say. I sit alone in a great lost ship and stare at silent clocks, imagining that frozen hands move again. As a blind man savors the memory of that last bright moment, I, too, reach back and taste every jewel second of real-time.

▲▼▲

...Balimann's face is frozen forever in my 'now.' Every line, every twisted plane—just as it was when my shadow touched him and he turned to show me his fear.

I felt great anger for him then. I weighed that fear, and knew it was stronger than any grief for her. But I did nothing. He was a real-man. I expected no more.

I brushed him aside, and for a long moment stood gazing down at My Lady. I closed my eyes, reached out and sensed the gentle quietness in her mind, the soft stillness of her heart. Of my thoughts, then, my feelings—I shall say nothing. These things belong to me.

"Non-man—please!"

My dream shattered. I turned away from her, slowly, opened my eyes, and let anger rise and turn my arms to tight cords.

"She is dead," said Balimann. "She—is dead. I—know..." His voice was an urgent whisper, a moth beating nervously against the flame. He was watching me. Very carefully. Anxiously. His fear was a great thing within him.

"Still," he chattered, "still, there are things that *can* be done—sometimes. You know? A chance, non-man—!"

Somewhere, he had found a Re-Lifer. It floated beside him, rocking gently, humming its soft red tune. His eyes darted from me to the Re-Lifer, and back again. He bit his lip, hesitated.

"We must—try," he said, "if we wait longer—"

He suddenly jerked forward, tried to push past me. I gripped his arm in steel. He stared at me, paled, and I let him go. He fell back, rubbing the numbness.

I laughed, and his eyes widened as the harsh sound broke the stillness. "*You*, real-man, and that poor machine with its hummings and groanings? You think you can reach *her*, now? You think that is *all* you have to do? New lungs with new air—a new heart pumping with vitality and life? And what are you going to do, Balimann—wire her *soul* together again?"

He stepped back quickly, and I turned away from him and gathered that small, silent form in my arms. Then I walked across the deep carpet toward the blue glow of the lift.

"All right!" he yelled after me. "*Kill* me, then, if you will—But I *will* speak! You blame *me* for this! I know—I can see that and I *will not* bear that burden for you—!"

I turned slowly and looked at him. "No *false man* can place that upon me!" he said harshly. "I gave you warning—*you* could have stopped her—and you *did not*. I couldn't stop *you*, false man—even though I *knew what was there*, felt—"

"Do not tell me what you feel, Wormkeeper," I said tiredly. "Please. I know what you feel. I can read those things as if they were written in the air before your eyes. You *feel* that I might kill you. You *feel* that you might suffer. Other than this, there is little in you…"

"That *isn't true*! I did not *want* this! I *warned* you—!"

I shook my head. "Warn? And how could you *warn*, Balimann? Do you think I do not know, now? No one knows better than I, real-man. *You cannot warn others of things you have not seen yourself!*"

His face went white and his whole body staggered backwards.

"I *have* seen!"

"No. You have walked a little way into the forest, perhaps. You know the shadows of the beasts that dwell there. But you sent My Lady and I along the deeper path—the one you feared to walk."

I held him with my eyes and he did not move. "This is your crime, Balimann. You are not The Worm's keeper. It—is yours!"

Something broke inside him. All the man spilled out and left a hollow thing standing in its place. I turned away, and let the lift enclose me. I did not need to kill this real-man for his perfidy. He could take care of his own dissolution better than I…

…Perhaps I am wrong. Perhaps Balimann will once more find his manhood. It may be that when the beasts swarm over his moon—as they will, I know; there, and on the many worlds of the Great Wheel—then, perhaps, the spark will glow again, and he will fire until his weapon is hot and empty, and die with the laugh of heroes on his lips.

I hope this is so. I hope the blood of past greatness returns to the veins of man. For men *did* know greatness once, I know. The Great Captains fled when they saw their enemy—yes. But they *still knew* the shame they brought upon themselves. In that time, they failed as a man fails.

They *were men*—they could not have faced what they did and come away without madness if they had not been men. There are not even non-men like that. I, too, went insane at the sight of the enemy, for I am an imitation of man, and no better.

But I am also a machine, and a machine can sometimes correct the tangled, twisted circuits of madness. It is not so easy with a man.

What, then, did I see, there in the darkness of Balimann's observatory? What do I know of the thing that is the Nightmare of Man? I know all—and I know nothing. I know that something *seems* to be coming from Andromeda. I know that sometimes it is coming at a great, incredible speed—and sometimes it is not there at all. I know that it cannot be measured, recorded, or classified. I know that I cannot describe its horror so that another will understand it—because its form is not form, its shape is not shape. It is *there*, in the great nebula of The Worm. Again, it is not there at all. But it *feels* there…

I see there is no way. I cannot tell you of the thing itself, but only of the nightmares it brings—the projection of the thing that it really *is*. And this—is close enough to madness.

Sometimes I can see them, chittering and howling in the veiled green cloud. Sometimes I see a black, ape-like thing that turns into a loathsome, mindless creature like the most terrible of sea-things. There are a million—a billion of them. All of them are different—all are the same.

Sometimes they die—or cry—or pray—or entwine themselves in unexplainable obscenities. More often, even this shadow projection of The Worm is so alien that I cannot say what they do. Perhaps that is what The Worm itself is—a projection of some other, more alien and unexplainable creature. And that creature…

This is all I can convey to you. And it is nothing—nothing. I know only that I travel at speeds I cannot know toward this great enigma. Toward the brightness of Andromeda, and the green cloud that hangs before it. It is a journey that passes in a second—or a million years— I do not know. I cannot.

My Lady sleeps, still and silent, in the death that is not death, but something else I cannot explain. It is the death I could not—would not— convey to Balimann.

She is here—somewhere—with me. Her body rests in the great Control Room in the eye of *The Gryphon*—and it is she who sends us on through no-space and no-time—it is she who would not let me turn Garahnell's world into a great sun, would not let me destroy the beasts mankind nurtures in his soul. This is not her way, this changing of destinies. Her way is another, and I obey her silent wishes that whisper about me.

This is her way. We left the beasts that spawn from within far behind—and face the beast that comes from without...

There is, then, but one thing more...

I cannot understand it and I try not to think upon it. I know, that while we lay there, My Lady and I, in Balimann's observatory, she reached out and gently touched my mind with hers. We lay there and watched the horror come in upon us, and for that moment, we were one.

It was only for a moment. She could not take me where she was going—but she *wanted* me to see—to know—to *understand*. I saw. But I did not understand. I saw evil, horror and sensed what they were—but I did not understand. I know only this:

I saw my gentle Lady reach out with a cry of great joy and embrace these obscenities and take them to her, as a woman takes a lover she has waited for through long eternities...

I, Steifen non-man, saw only loathesome evil. What did she see, that I did not? Why does she embrace what all men flee? I do not know. *I do not know...*

To Plant a Seed

Gito leaned against his dome and squinted narrowly at the 888 naked vermilion backsides. It's not too often, he mused, one has the opportunity to examine the collective rear of an entire race. Not just the greatest distinction in the world, maybe, but good enough to win a bar bet.

No need to count, he knew—they were all there, the whole population of Sahara III stretched upon the sand, waiting for Lord Sun to rise above the brown horizon.

As an awesome moan rose from 888 throats, Gito automatically reached up and lowered his dark goggles. Then, in unison, 888 heads plunged into the hot sand in penance for yesterday's sins. In answer, Lord Sun burst over the horizon in a flash of white anger. The heads rose again, and moans turned to high-pitched shrieks of gladness.

Gito frowned. It was hard to share the joy of a new dawn when *Posi Frondee*, Lord Sun, turned his eyes into lead marbles even through the thick-lensed goggles. The incandescent eye stared down with unbelievable brightness—each ray a burning wire stretching 8000-million miles to shrivel and desiccate Gito Marachek.

He took one last look. The ceremony was over, and the brick-red figures scurried for their sandy tunnels. Twenty seconds of dawn was sufficient on Sahara III—even for the Kahrii who lived and died there.

Gito sealed the door behind him and pulled in great gulps of cool air. Then he swallowed a heat tablet and chased it with a pint of moderately cold water.

▲▼▲

At the beginning of his tour, his nightmares had concentrated on vivid pictures of his foolproof power pack oozing into metallic butter, leaving him to face *Posi Frondee* without air conditioning. The nightmares had stopped, but he still caught himself running an occasional rag or the edge of a sleeve lovingly over the pack's smooth surface.

Not that dust could possibly enter the sealed unit—it was just a matter of respect.

The buzzer rang softly. Gito jerked around and frowned suspiciously at the port. Buzzing meant guests—and daytime guests were as common on Sahara III as blizzards.

He stood and moved across the room. Through the slight translucence of the dome a short figure stood outlined against the morning terror of *Posi Frondee*. Gito quickly pressed the door stud. He heard the outer panel slide open, then shut. The temperature lowered as cool air poured in and sucked out the stifling heat. Gito slid back the lock portal and dimmed the lights.

Golsamel-ri dropped his white robe on the floor and stood in naked formality before the entranceway. "Greetings, friend Geetomorrow-shek. Happy dawning to you."

"Happy dawning to you, friend Golsamel-ri," said Gito. "What passes to bring honor to my dwelling?"

Golsamel-ri blinked, his sensitive eyes closed to bare slits even in the dimness of the dome.

"I am not disturbing? You were not preparing for sleep?"

Gito shrugged. "Later, perhaps. Each second of your presence is more dear to me than an hour of sleep-time."

Golsamel-ri acknowledged with a gracious bow, lowering his forehead nearly to the ground. Then he straightened, closed his eyes, and folded his hands carefully over his mouth.

Gito sighed, and relaxed against the back of his chair. Evidently, he had done it again—stumbled onto one of the 8,888 Supreme Compliments, or close enough to count, anyway. It was not too hard, if you spoke any Kahriin at all.

Custom now called for a few moments of meditative silence, and Gito was glad enough to take advantage of the interruption.

He was puzzled over Golsamel-ri's visit. Being at the dome was not unusual—he was a frequent and welcome guest—but his timing was far from normal for a native of Sahara III. A complex set of rules dictated Kahrii behavior—to break one of those rules was something to be considered. Golsamel-ri had come to the dome from the Ceremony, upsetting a lifelong habit that called for silence and sleep until the next waking, when *Posi Frondee* sank in the west and work resumed on the surface.

What, then, had brought him here? Casting custom aside would cause Golsamel-ri temporary anguish, certainly—but there was also the trip back to his tunnel in the terrifying heat. More than *temporary* anguish could result from that.

Whatever it was, Gito had an idea he wasn't going to like it. He glanced apprehensively at the Kahrii. Standing, Golsamel-ri would have reached slightly above his waist. Now, in his squat-straddle position, the Kahrii's body seemed like a limbless red statue. He was, of course, anything but limbless, Gito knew. The stubby, scoop-shaped feet and hands could pack plenty of power when they needed to.

On another world, they might have been the limbs of a mindless, nocturnal burrower—on Sahara III, the fleshy webbing that covered long splayed fingers ended abruptly beneath the third joint of four-jointed members—allowing free use of fingers that should have been no more than claws, in conjunction with a perfectly respectable thumb. It wasn't much of a difference, Gito reminded himself, but while Golsamel-ri might still be a nocturnal burrower, he was also a thinking, reasoning creature.

Slit eyes opened and blinked at Gito over narrow, short-whiskered jowls.

"I thank you for bestowing honor upon me," Golsamel-ri whispered, "I am undeserving."

The statement required no answer. Gito waited in silence.

"I will not long disturb your privacy," he went on. "May *Posi Frondee* understand and forgive my intrusion. I wish to speak of the other—the female you name Cowezh-a-tir."

Gito's brow lifted. "Arilee? Arilee Colwester? What passes with her? Has she intruded in some way on your being? If she has—"

"*No.*" Golsamel-ri's head shook violently. His eye slits opened wide. "Please, I make no formal accusation against Cowezh-a-tir. This is not lightly done!"

"Yes, of course," Gito covered quickly, "I—understand that."

Golsamel-ri breathed a sigh of genuine relief. "As I say, this thing *concerns* Cowezh-a-tir—but is in no way a criticism. I would go to her myself, but my life thread has not traveled with hers as it has with yours. Also, of course—forgive me—she is a female. I had thought it would be seemly if I spoke to you about the thing—and perhaps you would convey it to Cowezh-a-tir? You are offended by this presumption?"

Gito relaxed imperceptively. Evidently, it wasn't too bad—just another Kahrii ethical entanglement that might be unraveled in a week or two of ceremony.

"No," Gito assured him, "I am in no way offended. On the contrary, I gain much honor by assuming any confidence you might bestow."

Good grief, Gito swallowed, *did I say that?* No question about it, he decided grimly; I've about had it on Sahara III.

"Now. What may I carry to Colwester?"

Golsamel-ri looked away. "I hesitate, good friend. Still, I have spoken with those wiser than myself, and it must be." He straightened himself and took a deep breath. "Dishonor may fall upon me, but Cowezh-a-tir is no longer to be allowed to observe the tunnels of the children of *Posi Frondee*.

Gito sat very still.

"It is a terrible thing," Golsamel-ri moaned. "We are forced to break the High Rule of Hospitality. I only pray the enormity of our reason is sufficient. There will be an indemnity, of course."

Gito opened his mouth, then caught himself quickly. He bowed his head gravely. "Of course. I will discuss the terms with Colwester."

Golsamel-ri stood, wrapping his white robe about himself in that peculiar manner Gito had never quite been able to duplicate.

"I speak no more of this," he said quietly. "Convey my mortification to Cowezh-a-tir. Good Sleeping, Geetomorrow-shek."

"Good Sleeping, Golsamel-ri—my dwelling has been blessed."

With a quick bow, the alien was through the airlock. In a moment, Gito caught a glimpse of him diving for the nearest tunnel mound, *Posi Frondee*'s beneficent rays burning into his vitals.

Gito frowned at the empty desert. He gazed up at the ceiling, tapping one finger thoughtfully against his cheek. Then, cursing himself silently, he walked the few steps to the rear of the dome and stuck his head around the corner.

"Arilee?"

The sleeping quarter's lights were dimmed, and for a moment he could see nothing. He stepped out of the doorway and let the sunlight behind him fall on bare shoulders and wheat-colored hair. He caught an almost imperceptible flinch at the back of a slim, white neck.

Grinning, he sat down beside her.

"You awake?"

"No. Certainly not." Then she turned over toward him and sat up, pulling the thin gown about her just in time—or a particle of a second too late. It was a trick most any well-trained Mistress over a Five could do in her sleep; but Gito could recall none that did it quite as well as Arilee.

She kissed him lightly and brushed a strand of hair from her eyes. "Well," she smiled, "crisis on Sahara III too big for you to handle?"

Gito nodded, looking as firm-and-no-nonsense as he could when he was looking at Arilee.

"Yes, as a matter of fact there is—and I think its name is Arilee—or Cowezh-a-tir, depending on your point of view."

Arilee lifted a brow in question.

"Our friend Golsamel-ri just risked about a 99th degree burn to let me know you've been officially banned from roaming about the tunnels of the Children of the Sun."

Arilee bit her lip. "*Uh-oh.*"

"Yep. Uh-oh it is. Naturally, the whole thing was too mortifying for him to go into—so suppose you fill me in on the details?"

Arilee sighed, wrinkling her face in thought. Then she looked at Gito and nodded slowly.

"Now what is *that* supposed to mean?"

"Just that I am not at all surprised, love. I was—expecting something like this—sort of."

Gito thought her eyes darted away maybe a second too soon. He stood up and looked down at her. "You're trying to tell me something. And I have an idea I'm not going to like it."

"I don't think you are either," she admitted. She paused, then smiled up at him brightly. "Coffee? You—me—talk-talk?"

Arilee was a mimic, and he instantly recognized Innocent Tahitian Beauty Established Rapport With White Trader. He grinned before he remembered to look stern.

"Okay. Coffee is called for. You dress and I'll brew—and I *mean* dress. This is definitely talk-talk."

▲▼▲

The coffee was bubbling when she stepped from the sleep quarters, and he remembered with happy resignation that a Mistress always obeys, if not the letter of the law, then the vague spirit of it. The implied order was plainly 'fully dressed and no distractions,' and Arilee complied. Only Arilee was distracting in anything, and Mistress-designed coveralls did a great deal more than cover.

"Very funny," he said acidly, "ha-ha."

She picked a chair and breezed into it with natural and innocent grace. He handed her a steaming mug and she smiled.

Gito settled down across from her and passed a cigarette.

"Now—to the point."

"Okay," she nodded, "to the point. I think Golsamel-ri doesn't want me in the tunnels because they're doing something of religious significance."

Gito sighed. "Doll, you are delaying the game. *Everything* they do is of religious significance—and *you* know it."

Arilee shrugged. "Sure. But this is ah—more significantly significant. You ready?"

"I am firmly braced."

She took a deep breath. "Gito, I suspect it is getting close to moving day for the Kahrii."

"Once more, if you please. I don't think I got that."

"Simple. They are leaving the tunnels. Taking off. Make big journey. Gods angry—"

"All right, knock it off." He shook his head and laughed. "You have flipped, Arilee. You are my own living doll and all that but you don't know what the hell you are talking about. I think you've been getting too much sun, or *Posi Frondee*, or whatever you want to call it."

Arilee shrugged. She pursed her lips and peeked at the ceiling. "I didn't *think* you were going to like it."

"Ho-ho," he said flatly, "that does just about sum it up." He leaned forward and took her hands in his. "Now Arilee," he said quietly, "you pulled a little boo-boo and you're too stubborn to admit it. Okay. I've let you roam around down there because I was—frankly—pleased that you were interested in finding out what they were like. In spite of the fact it's against every regulation in the book. Now, you tell me what it was and we'll forget it. Okay?"

She shook her head. "Not okay. Did Golsamel-ri say that?"

"Say what?"

"That I—pulled a boo-boo?"

Gito dropped her hand in mock astonishment. "If you'd dissected his grandmother, would he risk eternal mortification by *complaining* about it? He said he prayed his sin would be forgiven—or something. And there is an indemnity—I suggest twenty-five lengths of Shari cloth."

Arilee cringed. "I don't want any Shari cloth. It itches."

"Arilee—"

She grabbed his wrists and smiled patiently. Gito frowned. "Now don't give me the mother-will-explain bit, Arilee."

She laughed. "Mother's going to *have* to, because I get the strange feeling you don't believe a word I'm saying. Listen—I *mean* it, Gito. I'm *not* just making this up."

He looked at her closely. For a moment, he had the horrified idea that she wasn't.

"One," she said, holding up a finger, "the Shari roots are *not* being worked. They are simply being *sliced off* in portable sections. You see that? *Portable?* As in Going Somewhere?"

"That's all?"

"Nope."

"Then—?"

"They're—nervous. Like they're afraid—or anticipating something."

Gito snorted. "The Kahrii are never nervous. They are incapable of being afraid."

"*These* Kahrii are…" she said haughtily.

Gito ran a hand across his face. "Is that all?"

"No."

"Please, Arilee…"

After a moment, Gito said, "Just slicing the roots?"

"Uh-huh. Slicing."

He tried to consider the intricacies of Kahrii agriculture. "You mean slicing—not just notching for the milk or cutting the polyps?"

Arilee nodded smugly.

"Hah!" said Gito suddenly. "Doesn't mean a thing. The roots could be cramped—the Kahrii could be thinning them out. They could be diseased, they could—oh, come on, Arilee; you took one little fact and decided the whole race is about to take the Long Trek?" He spread his hands to take in the whole smoldering world outside. "Arilee—where in hell would they *go*?"

Arilee said nothing. And that, thought Gito warily, is disturbing in itself. She just sat there, small hands neatly folded in her lap. He had the uncomfortable feeling she was measuring him for dissection and study.

"Arilee, will you *please* not do that? I'm trying, out of my high regard for your brains, beauty, and assorted charms—not to mention the fact that you're at the head of your class in Gito's Quick Course in Alien Ethics—to give you a fair hearing on this—this—"

She uncurled long legs from her chair and walked over and put her arms around his neck. She kissed him long and soundly.

When she stepped back, her eyes were sparkling. "You have no idea," she said sincerely, "how *relieved* I am to get this foolish idea out of my head. Now that you've explained it to me, I can see it's all just nonsense. And you *won't* let the idea of the Kahrii slicing off the roots of the plant that *keeps them alive* bother you—will you?"

"What? Oh, certainly not."

She walked to the door of their sleeping quarters and raised a hand to the top of her coveralls. Again, it was impossible to tell what she had in mind.

"See?" she said happily. "When you talk things out, it's not so bad, is it?"

▲▼▲

Sunset usually pulled Sahara III's temperature down to the low nineties, but Gito seldom left his dome until the local midnight. In the first place, there was no place to go—and nothing to see he hadn't seen before. More particularly, his comfort-oriented logic told him it was pointless to trade his refrigerated 72 for a dry, hot and thirsty 86.

Now, drooping limply in the sandcar, gasping from the short run through the heat of dusk, he waited for the air conditioning to breathe him back to life.

Gito had actually witnessed few Saharan sunsets in the open. They left him with the illogical but unshakable conviction that the great molten eye of *Posi Frondee* might reverse itself and rise again, catching him there on the bare surface. It was an unpleasant thought, to say the least—and the image of Arilee curled comfortably in the cool darkness of the dome was no help at all.

In an hour or so she'd be awake, and know damn well he'd taken her seriously enough to have a look on his own. He grinned and shook his head. Being Arilee, she had probably known what he'd do all along anyway.

Arilee Colwester was a Nine, like himself—and while a Nine was average for an experienced Planet Warden, a Mistress classification that high was nothing to sneer at. Not, of course, that he'd ever sneer at Arilee. She had been with him only two out of the eight months of her tour, and already he had a feeling for her he'd never experienced with the others.

Now that he thought back, it hadn't really taken two months—from the moment she stepped off the supply ship there was, well—something—he couldn't put his finger on exactly what it was. It was just there.

And, as he told her, he was frankly and genuinely flattered when she took an interest in the habits of the Kahrii. Gito was perceptive enough to recognize that it *was real* interest; and he had broken a hard and fast rule to allow her to enter the tunnels of Golsamel-ri's people.

And so, brother, he told himself wryly, stretching in the cramped confines of the sandcar, it is your own damn fault you're out here—waiting like an idiot for the natives to take off for Nowhere…

Gito geared the sandcar forward at a snail's pace across the desert floor. The first hint of darkness was beginning to color the landscape, and number one of Sahara's four moons was visible above the horizon.

In a moment, the first pair of bright, luminous eyes peered above ground, then scurried across the sand. Another pair followed—and another. Soon the land seemed covered with darting, bodiless fireflies.

With darkness, work began on the Kahrii's major—and only—occupation: the care and cultivation of the Shari cacti, source of Shari cloth, Shari root, Shari fruit, and a hundred other products of Kahrii existence. It was also the pipeline to Sahara III's rarest molecular combination—water.

What the people of the tunnels actually did with—or to—the Shari, was much of a mystery to Gito. As far as he could see, the cacti were doing a damn good job of surviving without any help. Still, he reasoned, you have to do something. You can dig so many tunnels—then what?

It was, Gito pondered, a strange and rather frightening world. On the whole planet, only the tall and bulbous Shari dared defy *Posi Frondee*. Of the two life forms on Sahara III, the vegetable Shari thrust its silver-gray columns above the surface, while the intelligent bipeds tunneled fearfully beneath it.

▲▼▲

For an hour, Gito wormed the sandcar in a wide circle around the night's work area. With the windshield on infrared, Kahrii deviations from the norm stood out like the proverbial sore thumb. The sand-trencher trenched sand in a circle beginning 4 units from the base of the Shari, and the moment the circle was completed the thorn-binder stepped in with 44 lengths of thornbinding, and bound 44 thorns, stepped aside, and allowed the pulp-juicer in to juice pulp—etc., etc., etc.

The fact that Arilee's alleged root slicing had occurred beneath the surface didn't worry him. What happened below would eventually be reflected above. That was the way the Kahrii did things.

▲▼▲

The second hour, Gito widened his circle and left the work area behind. Five miles out, the Shari forest thinned, and only a few lone sentinals thrust above the sand. Sahara's four moons rolled crazily across the sky, casting dull spokes from the dark plants.

Gito geared the sandcar into overdrive, and the shielded drive unit whined briefly, then thrummed into silent power. At 130, he eased off and let the treads turtle back into the hull as the lift units took over and inched him off the hard-packed sand on a cushion of air.

At high speeds, there was no sensation of going anywhere at all. The featureless landscape offered no point of reference. The horizon seemed endless, but it was an illusion of darkness Gito was accustomed to. When the star that seemed to hang over the horizon a long fifty miles away suddenly disappeared, he arced the sandcar into the beginning of a slow curve.

Ahead was the great wall that sheltered the Kahrii in their long and narrow valley; a wind-scoured, smooth sandstone barrier 750 feet high and a hundred miles around. Gito had seen it from the air in the few times he had lifted the sandcar over the rim. It was an oddity duplicated maybe a dozen times on the planet; a long scar in the endless sand, a sunken ellipse that partially protected the life of Sahara III from the murderous storms of wind and sand that periodically swept the surface.

The walled valley was the big wrench in Arilee's idea of the Long Trek—even, as he had explained, if the Kahrii *wanted* to leave their tunnels, there was no place to go and no way to get there. Scaling the walls was possible, but it could certainly not be done in a night—and no Kahrii would live to continue his try—not if he had to cling to the wall during the day. So it meant a 25 mile walk to the base of the wall, a few handholds hacked in the stone, then a race against dawn back to the tunnels. About 30 years work for the entire population, Gito figured roughly. And once on top of the rim, nothing but death. The fertile Shari groves of the valley had little in common with their dry and stunted cousins scattered sparsely above.

And no Shari—no Kahrii. It was as simple as that.

▲▼▲

He kept the sandcar in a steady climb up the side of the wall, and soon he was skimming round the rim of the valley on a naturally-slanted raceway. To his left was the valley floor, to his right the stars. In a few seconds, he thought, I've gone higher than any Kahrii in a thousand years—or, perhaps, in the whole history of the planet.

No, there might be some significance in the natives' slicing the roots of their life-giving Shari—but whatever it was could not be explained in any terms Arilee had imagined. Her idea had worried him—more than he had let her know. He had seen some strange things happen on the far-flung planets of the galaxy. Still, his ride around the valley had convinced him migration was not the answer to an unexplained deviation in agriculture.

By the time the car's treads touched sand again and began the slow crawl through the Shari, Gito was beginning to feel his ride around the rim through the muscles of his back. Stretching, he took a last look at the Kahrii at work, and locked the sandcar in its dome. There was still another 15 hours of the long night to go; but he had seen nothing in three, and had no intention of sticking around for the rest.

A picture of Arilee asleep in the darkness before him hurried his steps across the still warm sand.

▲▼▲

It might have been night; the sleeping quarters' ceiling was still opaqued. Then a ray of intense white glanced from the other room off Arilee's cheek, and he knew *Posi Frondee* had returned to bless Sahara III.

"Gito…"

It was pleasant to hear his name—he liked the way she said it…

"Gito, get UP!"

He jerked, opened his eyes fully, and stared up at her. There was something—something wrong.

"Gito!"

Another look and he sat up straight, grasping her shoulders.

"No," she said tightly, "don't say anything." There was a small line between her brows he hadn't noticed before.

"Arilee, what—"

She shook her head. "No. Don't. Just—look. Just go out there and—and look."

She was beginning to shake, and he was past her before she finished, the hairs rising on the back of his neck. Whatever it was, he thought grimly, he had gone to bed a little too early to catch it. He wasn't at all sure he wanted to know what the Kahrii considered too important to do in his presence.

At the sleeping quarter's door he jerked to a stop, slapping his hand across his face. The dome could be adjusted from opaque to complete transparency, and Arilee had dialed too far. The room was flooded with unreal brightness, and the cooler labored to draw away the heat.

He reached blindly for the dial. The dome darkened, and his vision returned through a maze of whirling spots of color.

He stared, blinking his eyes. The hair rose up the back of his neck again and stayed there. Beside him, Arilee tightened her grip on his arm.

He had been on Sahara III a long time. The scenery was not much— but it was damn well the only scenery he had. Now, it was as if a city of tall buildings had been swallowed overnight, leaving behind an emptiness more terrifying for the memory of the space it had filled.

The Shari were gone. All of them. The dense, protective groves of cacti that nourished the Kahrii, kept them alive on this harsh world, were gone. No, Gito thought, it's worse than that. For the Shari were dead, but *not* gone. A thousand silver corpses lay scattered about the settlement for a hundred yards around the dome.

…*Scattered?* He made a quick, wide circle with his eyes. Arilee saw it too. A gasp caught in her throat.

What in all hell—? thought Gito. No catastrophe had hit the grove. The Shari had been *cut*! Cut, stripped, and sliced into long curved sections. They lay about the landscape in every conceivable variation of the open curve. Where there was a need for big sections, slices had been butted together and laced with tough Shari fiber. There were semi-ovals, near-circles, and half-ellipses of every size and description. The longest one Gito could see was seventy-five feet across the widest point of its arc.

▲▼▲

They lay there, staked into position, as if, Gito thought, they had been tortured for some insane vegetable secret and left to dry and shrivel under *Posi Frondee*'s glare.

He let out a breath he hadn't realized he'd been holding. He turned to Arilee. "I—believe we could use a drink about now."

She said nothing.

"All right," he said sharply, "what *else* do you suggest?" He closed his eyes and turned from the dome, fists clamped tightly at his side.

Arilee sat on the couch below him, looking suddenly very small. She smiled weakly. "I'm—sorry, Gito." Her voice was a little too high.

Gito took a deep breath, shrugged. "What for? You didn't do it, doll—you just called it." He studied her carefully. "How, I'm not even going to *try* to figure out."

He swore suddenly, slamming his fist against the dome. "What do they think they're *doing* out there? Don't they know—don't they *know*…!" His voice faded. He walked to the wall and frowned at the chaotic landscape.

Arilee mixed drinks in two shaky glasses. Gito turned his up and passed it back to her, then resumed his nervous circle of the dome.

"I hope," he said acidly, "they cut off a lot of those roots. It's a long walk to the next meal."

Arilee looked up questioningly.

"No, of course not," he shook his head. "I'm just raving. They *can't* get there—if it was right on top of the rim they couldn't get there! And it isn't. It's about 2,000 miles away."

Gito bit his lip and closed his eyes. "Two thousand miles...if I could take two at a time in the sandcar, at night...God, that's 444 round trips!... and each two would *have* to start digging the new tunnel...big enough for the next two. Arilee! Arilee—" He shook his head and rubbed a hand across the side of his face. "Good Lord, what am I thinking of? It's too incredible."

She was with him, smiling gently. "Gito..."

He looked up and held her eyes a long moment, then reached out and squeezed her hand. He shrugged and showed her a sad smile. The whole thing was insane, ridiculous—hopeless.

"I'm sorry," he said. "It's just—this is the first world that ever suicided on me..."

He thought about what he'd said, and added a hollow laugh. That's it, he told himself. Laugh at it—and maybe it won't be real...

▲▼▲

They were both out of the dome as soon as darkness sent the first Kahrii out of the tunnels. It hasn't been a good day, Gito thought—but it sure as hell has managed to be a long one. They had batted it back and forth, and gotten nowhere. Speculations were easy, and the frayed nerves and quick tempers that followed—but answers were something else.

"Sure," he had told her, "everything the Kahrii do has a basis in religion—but what kind of a rite do you hand down generation after generation that calls for suicide? Self-destruction might be an impressive gesture to the gods—but you can only show that kind of devotion once!"

"—and then," Arilee had finished for him, "what does *Posi Frondee* do for worshippers? It isn't just insane, Gito—it's uneconomical!"

Through it all, Gito became increasingly aware of some very interesting qualities in Arilee—rare, he decided, even in a Class Nine Mistress. He'd had such thoughts before about women, certainly—that nostalgic sadness when they left, often wishing they could extend their tour.

But never like this—this was something else. Before, his thoughts had usually dwelled on a woman's more obvious qualities—thoughts that were generally quickly relegated to shadowy memories by the next Mistress.

Objectively, he told himself that being a perfect companion to a man was just what a Mistress was born and trained to do—was it possible that Arilee Colwester just managed to do that job a little better; mirror his ego, his thoughts, a little more keenly than the others? No. He didn't believe that. She, well, she just couldn't be *that* good an actress.

At least—he fervently *hoped* she wasn't.

▲▼▲

After the first pair of Kahrii eyes edged about the ground, they quickly disappeared. Soon, four others emerged, and stayed. When they saw Gito and Arilee, three of them fell flat on their faces and covered their great owlish eyes. Gito thought he could hear high, thin squeaks coming from the huddled trio. He looked at Arilee and motioned her still. It was unnecessary—Arilee had no intention of moving.

The fourth member of the group stared at them a moment, then slipped back into the tunnel. He was back up in a few seconds, and walking straight for them.

Arilee stiffened and Gito took a deep breath. He saw it too, and frowned uneasily.

"Just take it nice and slow," he said softly, not taking his eyes from the white-robed Kahrii.

Gito had recognized Golsamel-ri, and just as quickly identified the thing in his hand. If he had landed that moment on Sahara III he would have known. On Sahara, or any other world—a taboo stick looks the same.

Dyed Shari cloth hung in drab colors from a gnarled Shari root that had been turned into a crude staff. From the top of the staff hung four painted skulls—three adults and a child whose age, health or religious status had made them expendable on those occasions when the population exceeded the ritual number of 888.

Golsamel-ri plunged the taboo stick into the sand and stepped back. The skulls rattled against the dry stick, then stilled. For a long moment they stared across the darkness at each other, Golsamel-ri's unblinking eyes mirroring the moons and stars.

Well, Gito decided, somebody's got to do it. "Friend Golsamel-ri—I wish to speak with you. I do not understand what your people have done."

Golsamel-ri was visibly shaken. Familiarity with the Kahrii had given Gito some knowledge of their facial expressions. Golsamel-ri displayed a commingling of fear and disgust. Hatred was not yet there, but it might break through any moment.

"Please," Gito went on recklessly, "if I ask things that offend you, it can be forgiven by your knowledge of my ignorance. I am unblessed by *Posi Frondee.* Have you not said you desired that I understand your god?"

Golsamel-ri bowed his head a moment, then looked up. His gaze flicked briefly to Arilee, then rested on Gito.

"There is nothing for you to understand," he said softly. "My people do not exist, therefore I can explain nothing about anything they have done—if they existed and were capable of any action. Also, having nonexistence myself, I could not explain their non-act or nonexistence."

Gito swallowed hard. One question was answered, at least. The Kahrii were perfectly aware of what they had done—they already considered themselves dead.

"It remains," Golsamel-ri continued, "for me to deliver this message from the nonliving. This staff signifies a line across which the living must not pass. You are forbidden to disturb the work of the souls of the children of *Posi Frondee*."

So much, sighed Gito, for the traditional Kahrii courtesy. Less seems to be required from the nonliving.

"One thing remains," said Golsamel-ri. "It nearly escaped my recognition, so much has death clouded my mind. The former Golsamel-ri, during the last days of his life, offended the female Cowezh-a-tir. His ghost wishes to pay his indemnity, as he has been instructed."

The nonliving Golsamel-ri reached into his robe and drew out a tightly-packed bundle. Gito touched Arilee. She looked up at him, eyes wide. He nodded toward the Kahrii, and she bit her lip and stepped forward. Golsamel-ri extended the bundle, and Gito could tell it was Shari cloth.

"Thank you," said Arilee clearly, "I accept and thank the soul of Golsamel-ri." Gito was proud of her. She stepped back beside him and he squeezed her hand.

Gito fully understood her fear. Arilee had made many friends among the Kahrii, and Gito himself had come as close to Golsamel-ri as a man could to a being born on an alien world. It was nonsense, of course, he told himself—but this was a totally different Golsamel-ri. How, and why, he couldn't say.

"The shade of Golsamel-ri accepts your thanks," said the Kahriin, "for the being formerly surrounding his soul. And now, farewell, Geetomorrow-shek, from my previous self. I will be honored to greet you in the next life."

Then he turned, and walked slowly back to his huddled companions. At a word, they rose and went to their tasks. Behind them, the ghosts of the population of Sahara III slid like wraiths from their tunnels.

Dead or alive, Gito noted solemnly, there still seemed to be a great deal to do.

▲▼▲

Gito pressed against the dome wall, straining against the Sahara night. Even with the dome lights darkened, there was little he could see. The fourth moon's rising would improve things somewhat, but he wished fleetingly that there was some way to dismantle the infrared panel from the sandcar.

The area outside the taboo stick had not been forbidden; still, Gito felt uneasy about venturing beyond the dome at all—at least for the time being. Actually, he admitted grimly, with the dome completely surrounded by decapitated Shari, freedom was now something like having the run of a hole in a doughnut.

"Gito," said Arilee testily, "if I'm interrupting, say so, but—"

Gito shrugged. He turned and picked her out in the dark. "Interrupting what? Unfortunately, there's absolutely nothing *to* interrupt." He caught her gaze and held it a moment.

"That—rambling, about airlifting the Kahrii—that's what it was, abstract rambling. I might as well have been figuring ways to save Pompeii." He paused, knowing there was more, knowing she was waiting, too. It was a subject they had skirted, carefully avoided.

She was watching him, and he read a kind of pleading in her eyes.

"Don't make it any harder," he said stonily, turning away.

"I'm sorry—I didn't mean—"

"—to forget the rules? Don't you think I'd *like* to? Don't you think I'd try to save as many as I could?" He shook his head. "We're on a Class C planet, Arilee. Spelled out that means Sahara III is populated by intelligent beings in a stage where my job becomes a matter of being present—and observing. Period. No footnotes. No boosts up the ladder. On a C you stop, look and listen—and make sure no one else gets a finger in the pie. No backdoor traders, no Sportships. Did you know C stands for 'Casual' and 'Critical?' A world in a critical stage of development—calling for casual contact by the Planetary Warden. Namely me. And," he grinned slightly, "in this case, you."

She looked at him. "Will it—I mean, you shouldn't have let me go down there. I know that—"

"No. I shouldn't have. Only it doesn't matter. You didn't do anything. As a Nine you could qualify for an Observer. If it came to that—well, you are now so appointed. Only it won't come to that."

He sat down beside her, and she moved over to make room, then dropped her head on his shoulder.

"Why, Gito?"

"What?" he answered her, but knew what she meant.

"Why did you let me—just because I wanted to. Would—"

He saved her from having to ask. "—Would I let anyone else do that? No. I wouldn't." He turned her head toward him. "As to why—that's a rhetorical-type question, isn't it, Arilee? You have to know the answer before you ask."

She looked up into his eyes. "Yes. I know." She got up quietly and disappeared into the sleeping quarters. She half-closed the door before turning on the dim light. He knew she was combing her hair—which, as far as he was concerned, never needed combing—but it was a task that would keep her away awhile. She had brought up the subject herself, broken the ice. But he knew she wasn't ready to take it any further. Gito was glad. Of course, he had sensed she realized this tour wasn't turning out quite like the others—for either of them. Now, she had answered a question for him, too.

In a moment the door opened and she came back to her place beside him.

"I'm sorry," she said. "Maybe I shouldn't have brought up anything—like that, when there's so much else." She faced him, and he frowned, seeing her eyes slightly wet. "I think that's why I did, Gito, because I know the rules and I don't like to think about them. I—guess I don't understand why they have to die because of a rule. There should be something—there's always something—isn't there?"

He wanted to say yes. He shook his head. "No. There isn't, Arilee. Sure, I could call for help, advice—but they wouldn't give it to me. Not on a C…"

He got up and walked to the darkened wall. "Once, Arilee, there was a planet with a new race. It wasn't even a C. There just seemed to be some slight chance—potential—of intelligence." He turned back toward her. "Have you ever heard a Warden say 'Something Bad on Tsirtsi?' No? Well it means emergency, help, war, planet-wide disaster—and it comes from what happened on that planet with the new race. What happened, I won't say and no other Warden will either. But when something like this happens—what's happening here—a Warden catches himself, and remembers Tsirtsi."

Arilee sat, unmoving, as he paced through the shadows of the dome.

"We found out you can't equate the things an alien *seems* to do, with what you know a human does under similar conditions. We learned the hard way, and we learned there is more diversity in the forms intelligence can take than we had dreamed. What are they doing out there with those circles of rotting cacti? Why did they destroy their food and water source?" He shrugged. "I don't know. So I keep hands off. The Kahrii may die, Arilee. That's something we have to face. But C's aren't allowed the deus ex machina. I don't introduce the miracle drugs, the 'wonders of science'—no matter what."

Arilee frowned somberly. "But Gito, haven't you *already* done that? I mean, they *know* there's something better. They've seen the dome, the—the sandcar, the supply ship, uh—in here, the way we live. It's too late for that, don't you think?"

Gito shook his head. "That sounds right, but it's a fallacy. A C culture doesn't have the background to conceive of an atomic generator or a space drive. It's like taking their picture with a 'magic box.' So what? There's a god in there, with a little power, and that's just fine. They have gods with power, why shouldn't the man from the sky? No, if you want to corrupt them, give the Kahrii a steel knife, or a shovel—or worse yet, introduce trade goods and a system of barter. *Ideas* are the real danger. Why an idea can—can—!"

Gito stopped. He had paused in his pacing to watch the third and fourth moon rise together over the rim of the world, flooding the desert in pale light. He pressed his face hard against the dome.

"Gito, what is it?"

"Come here, Arilee—quick!"

Gito pointed, and Arilee gave a short cry. As they watched, several of the Kahrii attached strong Shari fiber ropes to the open ends of one of the arcs they had sliced and sewn the night before. Gito swore silently. He had made a quick, snap judgment about the cacti—they had not rotted in the sun at all. As one group pulled the ropes, another braced the center of the arc—and the arc raised slowly—*and stiffly*—into the air.

Gito whistled sharply. They knew what they were doing—whatever that was. That the Shari could be dried into a strong, light-weight building material had never crossed his mind.

But, he asked himself, *why*? What would the Kahrii *want* to build?— And above the ground, where they couldn't possibly live even if they had suddenly planned on remaining alive?

After a few precautionary guywires were attached, the arc stood firmly in place. It stood like a giant horseshoe magnet, resting on its back, poles aimed at the stars.

"Maybe it's a—temple, or something," Arilee suggested weakly. "The—last sacrifice to *Posi Frondee*?"

"Huh-uh. If it's a temple, they've got their arches upside down. Besides, where did they get an idea like that? They've lived in tunnels since the race began. Architecture doesn't just spring up overnight." He cut her off as she took in a deep breath. "—And don't say *I* corrupted them with the dome. Whatever it is they're building, they'll never get a dome out of *that*!"

▲▼▲

The Kahrii wasted little time admiring their work. In fifteen minutes, they had another arc in place, directly in front, and twenty feet away from the first.

Gito watched in silence. When the third, smaller arc went up, something small and cold dropped heavily into the pit of his stomach. With the fourth and fifth, he knew he was going to be sick...

Gito and Arilee watched off and on, for most of the night. Arilee forgot how many times the coffee pot emptied itself. When they talked at all, they talked of the past, people they had known—anything instead of what was happening outside the dome. To talk about that, they knew, might somehow make it more real than it already was.

By dawn there was little more use pretending the Kahrii project didn't exist. The arcs now stretched 100 yards across the desert. Those near the center, the first to go up, stood alone; the smaller, tightly-curved sections rose on each end to graceful points supported by a cross-hatch of framework. Running the full length of the row, a network of stout Shari beams now connected each arc to the other. A night of coffee had dulled his senses, left him hollow and empty. Now dawn brought the cold weight back to his stomach and left his mouth dry and tinged with acid. He was angry and tired, and he knew he was going to stay angry and tired no matter how much sleep he could manage to get.

He was angry because he was a man who was used to problems, and used to finding reasonable solutions to those problems. Gito didn't like questions without answers, and he knew he was going to knock his head against the dome wall forever without dulling the truth. Nothing he could do would change the fact that the Kahrii, who dug their tunnels in a world of sand and never dreamed of more water than the pitiful droplets that could be sucked from one Shari fruit at a time—had spent the night laying the keel of a ship...

▲▼▲

He was awake at dusk. He frowned at, then meekly accepted the cup of hot coffee waiting for him in the main room of the dome. He noted, thankfully, that Arilee had been considerate enough to opaque the dome walls. Maybe, he thought sourly, she has the right idea. If we can't see it, the whole damn thing just might go away.

He glanced at Arilee. She was watching him and he smiled back, weakly.

"Bad?" she asked.

"I dreamed," he said, letting himself sink back into the cushions, "that Golsamel-ri was an Admiral—gold braid and all—and I was walking the plank. Have you ever had the opportunity to drown in *sand*?"

Arilee cringed, holding back a grin. "No water?"

"My imagination," he said wryly, "is not as vivid as that. Even in my dreams I could not conjure up water on Sahara III. Hell, I've been here so long I'm about half Kahrii anyway—I just don't believe in things like oceans. They don't exist."

"They did once," Arilee said quietly. Gito turned slowly.

"You believe that, Arilee?"

She shrugged, getting up to refill her cup. "Are you saying you haven't been thinking about it? There's nothing else *to* think—is there?"

Gito didn't answer. He sat back on the couch and blew smoke at the ceiling. For a moment, he studied the drifting patterns curling toward the vent.

"Gito, I think it's an exciting possibility." She leaned forward. "Just think, how long ago—"

"It doesn't excite me," he snapped. "It worries the hell out of me!"

She went on without him, her eyes sparkling. "If there *were* seas out there once, and they remember—I mean, the story must have been handed down for centuries..."

Gito jumped up, rubbing his hand quickly across his face. "All right. I know where you're going, but look—I'm no geologist, and it'll be quite a few years before one gets here. But Arilee—we're not talking about thousands of years—maybe *millions*! And those beings are still digging tunnels with their—*hands*?" He shook his head violently. "I just can't buy that."

"They didn't always dig tunnels, Gito. Once, when there was a better climate, more water...well, anyway, now all they remember is a *symbol* of what they had. A ship, and no sea to sail it on."

"Very pretty picture. Only," he said patiently, "it just *wasn't that way*, doll. There were never—repeat *never* any oceans on Sahara III."

She caught his eyes and held them and he knew he'd been a little strong. He hadn't meant to carry it that far. He was scared, and now she clearly sensed it.

He was scared because he knew the Kahrii, and knew their religion. It was a hard, practical and basic kind of religion. *Posi Frondee* was not a symbol of God, a representation of light—no subtleties or symbols here. He *was Posi Frondee*, and if you didn't believe he existed, just go stand a moment under his blazing eye and defy his reality.

No, when the Kahrii made a sacrifice, it was a real sacrifice—often enough with real Kahrii. If these beings had built a ship—and God only knew where the idea had come from, the dark past, glimpses of the dim future—if that *was* a ship, then they would sail in it to meet *Posi Frondee*. And the sea of sand would suck them dry and preserve them in their broiling vessel forever—and that would be all anyone would have to remember of the Kahrii...

▲▼▲

Time between dusk and dark passed too slowly—or quickly—Gito couldn't decide which. An endless chain of cigarettes and coffee ticked off the long silence.

Arilee was in no mood for charm or dazzling wit. She could have braced herself—she was well-trained for that—and put on a real performance if it would have done any good. She knew it wouldn't, and Gito was grateful for her awareness. He knew she was there, and the warmth of her presence made extra efforts unnecessary. From the way she moved about the dome, performing small duties that didn't need to be performed, he knew she was sharing his experience.

You can face a thing when it happens, and scream about it and curse it, and even discuss it in sane and reasonable terms. Shock is a sugar coating for a bitter pill. It is a period of experience, not understanding. Now, as the coating dissolved, Gito was jolted by what he saw.

Curiously, he realized, the ship was not a part of it. He no longer feared it because he simply could find no way to accept it. There could *be* no ship, not on Sahara III. He would not let his mind dwell on a history that included dark seas and waterless deserts—and a race that survived and spanned that awful time between the two.

That kind of understanding was too much to handle now—for Gito, the vehicle of Kahrii destruction paled beside the destruction itself. The death of a race repelled him, and the thought that he was going to stand by and watch it chilled him until he fought to keep from fleeing past Arilee and shutting himself in the sleeping quarters.

What the hell kind of job was this, anyway? His anger reached out to pull in all Planet Wardens and the Corps itself. A race, relatively small and unimportant, and certainly unimposing, was going to kill itself. Period.

Was that *all*? Do you just write it off the books? Was it possible to look at it with that kind of cold objectivity?

Then: Did what happened on Tsirtsi have any relation to Sahara III?

But: Could you look at the Kahrii now, and say their loss could ever be related to what we lost on Tsirtsi?

No. But they didn't *know* on Tsirtsi, either, did they? Not until it was over. Not until it was too late.

He slammed a fist painfully into the arm of his chair. If that was the way the system worked, *then the system was wrong*! Just as man had no right to interfere—he also had no right *not* to, didn't he?

When, then, was the time to keep the rule and the time to break it? There was a way, was there not? There *had* to be a way to tell—at least to judge. Playing God halfway just wouldn't work out. Even a backwater planet like Sahara III had a right to their chance at greatness—or anonymity.

But the rule of the Wardens said no one had the right to interfere with that race's decision—even if that race rejected both choices and chose final oblivion.

Arilee touched his arm lightly, a quiet smile on her face. She spoke softly. "Hey, remember me?" It was not a bid for attention. She was asking, with her eyes, to share his thoughts.

He pulled his gaze away from her and glanced apprehensively at the darkening sky.

She pulled him back to her. "No," she said sternly. "It's not time, Gito." She led him to a chair and set a plate before him.

"Now eat. They won't do a thing for two hours. You're not going to miss a move."

He looked down at the thick steak and grinned at her. He hadn't even realized he was hungry. He was warmly pleased by her attention, and strangely touched. The scores were adding up, as if there was a kind of game going on between them. There was more here than just an 8-month Mistress with a trim figure and wheat-colored hair. He idly wished for a vague time and place when there would be nothing to keep him from pursuing that line of thought.

▲▼▲

Arilee was wrong. The Kahrii emerged from their tunnels long before that two hours was up. Gito's pulse quickened as he pressed against the wall of the dome. Something seemed terribly out of place. He sensed the frantic urgency that had brought the aliens to the surface while the heat of day still waved above the sand.

He thought about the food supply of Shari roots that must be dwindling down to nothing. The roots were not the Kahrii's favorite food, they were a supplement only; they could not possibly sustain 888 workers for long.

He was suddenly struck by the ludicrous, insane logic of the situation. Whatever the Kahrii were building, they were working with back-breaking haste to complete it before starvation set in—they didn't want to starve to death before they had a chance to kill themselves!

When the rolls of thick Shari cloth stretched across the ribs of the ship, Gito was only mildly surprised. Considering the Kahrii were building a seagoing vessel on possibly the driest habitable planet in this end of the galaxy, why shouldn't they carry the inanity to completion?

They worked in a fever of desperation, and the job of covering the hull went quickly. As soon as one crew stretched material over a section of the ship, another followed with fiber buckets of milky substance which they brushed into the cloth.

For a moment, Gito was puzzled, then realized with a start the Kahrii were applying what must be a *waterproofing* resin to the hull! The hackles on his neck rose at the thought.

"*Why?*" he said aloud, turning to Arilee, "why should they take the trouble to—" He stopped, seeing she wasn't going to answer. Curled up in a tight ball on the couch, she seemed more a small child than a woman. He kissed her lightly, then got up to empty his cold coffee.

While the fresh pot heated, a familiar thought worried its way back to the edge of his consciousness. From the beginning, the Kahrii ship had presented a paradox. He knew it was impossible—all right, so highly improbable as to *be* impossible—for even the ceremony-bound Kahrii to maintain such a link with an incredibly distant past that included oceans on Sahara III. He simply could not accept it.

Still, on the other end of the paradox, there remained the fact that the Kahrii *just did not have the ingenuity or background to symbolize something they had never seen*! It wasn't there, and never had been. Existence was harsh, precarious and deadly dull on Sahara III. As *Posi Frondee* was a real God, one that could literally bring life or death; so was the day to day battle of survival real. There was no time for the niceties of easy symbolism, the fabrication of legends.

Gito poured his coffee, lit another tasteless cigarette, and sank into his chair near the dome window. It didn't figure—it just didn't figure at all. Still, there they were, and the hull of the ship that couldn't be was turning into a very familiar shape. Gito didn't like it at all...

▲▼▲

Suddenly, he sat up stiffly. For a moment he thought he had fallen asleep—it was possible, but a glance at his watch assured him no more than ten minutes had passed since he'd last checked.

Gito blinked uncertainly. Something—what was it? He stared hard through the port. Nothing had changed. The routine he had watched half the night continued. The Kahrii swarmed over the surface of their ship attaching the long rolls of Shari cloth to the stiffened ribs, their figures casting odd, multi-shadowed shapes under the swift-running moons, the—? Gito bit his tongue and squeezed the arm of his chair. *Shadows!* That was it, of course. He had been watching so long he hadn't even noticed. The dark silhouette of the Kahrii ship was different— subtly *changed...*

The sides still sloped to the 'deck' level in a gentle arc, but now the curve continued—more Shari lengths had been added and were already partially covered! The chill began at the base of Gito's spine and gained momentum until it reached the top of his head. His scalp was suddenly unbearably tight.

There was no use trying to justify it or explain it or pass it off. If they continued—and he had every reason to believe they would—the Kahrii boat would soon be transformed into a completely covered, long and tapered cylinder.

In the darkness, with the tricky lighting of the four moons masking its imperfections, it looked too much like the thing it was meant to imitate. It was made of dried cactus and covered with coarse cactus fiber. It would never move a fraction of an inch above the surface of Sahara III—much less course out to touch the stars. But it was what it was, and nothing Gito could do would change that...

It was painfully clear in the first hot light of dawn. No one would mistake the Kahrii structure for a working spaceship—but, Gito admitted, no one would hesitate to say it was beginning to *look* like one.

After the first moment of stunned surprise, Gito readily accepted it. He sensed the same reaction, or lack of it, in Arilee. How many times were you *supposed* to start, catch your breath, stare wide-eyed at some new alien madness? For Gito and Arilee, the distance between the impossible and the utterly impossible was easy enough to swallow.

"If they change the damn thing into a cactus-covered nuclear reactor," Gito said darkly, "I don't intend to contribute a batted eyelash."

Arilee showed a small, sad smile and added a sigh of resignation. "My poor Gito. I had no idea warding—is that right? Warding? Wardening? I had no idea there were so many problems."

She was perched on the arm of his chair. He looked up at her. "Neither," he said sourly, "did I." He pulled her down into his lap and held her golden head between his hands.

"Arilee, I am about as drained of useful ideas as I ever believed possible. This business has left me empty of bright thoughts—if I ever had any—and I'm sick of pulling cultural histories out of thin air. It doesn't do any good, or lead anywhere at all unless you can base your fairy tales on something solid. And something solid—pardon the grammar— is what we don't have anything of."

Arilee got up and brushed back a strand of hair from her cheeks. She sat down across from him and rested her chin on two fists.

"You really mean it. You are not going to like it—you *know* that."

Gito grinned. "Every time you say that damned if you're not right. But, yes—go ahead. I've got a good grip on my chair, and I have the added advantage of knowing where you're going this time. And no— I *don't* like it!"

"What else is there, then?" she said softly.

Gito shrugged.

"Okay," she went on, "then we take it straight with no flinching. It's an old story—but it's a *possible* one, isn't it?"

Gito felt the chill get another good grip on the back of his neck. "Yes. It is. And it might as well be, for all we've got to go on. But look, Arilee—" He reared out of his chair and stalked to the edge of the room. "Every second looie in the Corps finds a 'lost race' on his first tour of duty. It's—it's—!"

"I know—and the video picks it up and squeezes it to death. A once mighty race that coursed the stars, then sank to savagery, forgetting their heritage. Worshipping," she said sternly, "at the shrine of Ah-tom and Aye-on, and—"

Gito moaned, slapping his hands to his ears.

"I don't like it," said Arilee, "any more than you do. If you want to hear an elated confession—the more I thought of the boat idea the less I could see *that*! So now—" She shrugged her hands, "—where to, love?"

"We're back," he scowled, "to Ah-tom and Aye-on—that's where we are. I'd like to say I won't buy it; and every time I don't 'buy' something, *they* build it!" He waved his hands wildly in the direction of the desert.

"I don't give a hang about that thing sitting out there. I *know* these people. They have *not*, damnit, 'sunk to savagery.' They never saw a spaceship and their immortal ancestors didn't, either!"

"So?"

"So nothing. If I could ever convince myself I know them as well as I think I do, I wouldn't keep getting that creepy feeling that all the hairs on the back of my neck are marching up the top of my head. One—I don't believe they have carried on some eternally long memory of a high technological culture. Two—and this is what hurts—I also know they simply don't have the inherent ability to think up boats and spaceships out of the blue. The children of *Posi Frondee* are as rigid as day and night.

"You see the paradox, Arilee? They *couldn't* think up anything like this themselves—and the other possibility just *does—not—happen*!"

"You're sure," Arilee said thoughtfully, "you're *certain* they never saw a spaceship?"

He stared puzzledly at her. "What? Oh, you can forget that. We don't introduce that sort of thing at this stage of the game. Everything big and scary stays off-atmosphere. Nothing bigger than a strut and tube platform comes in on a C. Just try to get the mistaken image of an FTL ship out of one of those—in the dead of night, completely out of sight of the settlement. These people think we came from over the ridge somewhere—and they'll continue to think so."

Arilee looked away quickly, and Gito remembered that future tense no longer applied to the Kahrii—not if they boarded their impossible ship for one short and terrifying journey.

Was it possible, then? Was he really taking his knowledge of the Kahrii for granted? Golsamel-ri had said his people were *already* dead— they considered themselves shades of their former selves. But, he remembered, the Kahriin had also expressed his desire to see Gito again when *next they lived*!

A thought flicked on the borders of his mind, then dropped with sudden coldness. Was Golsamel-ri talking about an afterlife—or was he following the narrow and literal pattern of his race—actually intending to *see* Gito again?

Gito turned suddenly. He stared at Arilee but his gaze was far beyond her and she stepped quickly aside, opening her mouth in a question then catching a glance of his eyes and keeping her silence.

Arilee knew men, and for some time she had realized she was making more effort than the job called for to know this one. The thing she saw in his eyes as he rummaged through the small equipment locker kindled a personal fear that rose from a fire she had not known existed. Not for a long time.

▲▼▲

It was hot. Gito expected that. Sahara III was no ice-world. He looked back the hundred yards to the dome and felt a moment of panic. It might easily have been a hundred miles. Even with the suit's filtered glass the dome shimmered like a fiery jewel seen through wavering weeds of heat.

The maximum use of the suit was protective comfort. He knew that. It was not designed for survival in the vacuum of space or the poisonous atmosphere of a chlorine world. Of course, neither condition existed here, and the bright foil surface of the suit *should* reflect enough of *Posi Frondee*'s glare—with the help of the built-in air conditioner.

Looking up, he read the small, efficient legend on the inside of his helmet: 'For emergency use on an extremely hot surface—limited endurance.' He scowled grimly. That, he told himself, is about the most unscientific damn description I have ever heard! He wondered what the Corps semantics expert mean by 'limited' this week. The laboring wheeze of the conditioner was helping him to form his own opinion.

A quick glance at the exterior temperature gauge showed 176. Gito swallowed and tried to turn the conditioner knob to maximum. It was already there. The sweat poured down from his hair and stung his eyes.

He paused in the small strip of inadequate shade cast by the Kahrii ship and craned his neck upward. This close, the thing was even more awesome and impossible. He tramped slowly around the side until he found what he was looking for. It was a small hole, less than two feet across, about eight feet off the ground. Reluctantly, he could only think of it as an entry port.

Entry, though, was not going to be easy. The hole was small, with no ladder—it was high, and it was getting hotter. Gito kept his eyes from the temperature gauge, ran back a few yards, and jumped. On the fourth try, his fingers grasped the rough edge of the port and held. For a long moment he hung there, breathing hard. In a split second of panic he thought the air conditioner had stopped. Then he heard its heavy wheezing above the ringing in his ears. Gathering his muscles, he closed his eyes and pulled himself up and over the lip of the port.

▲▼▲

He lay flat against the sloping walls of the Kahrii ship, letting the straining unit catch up with his need for air. The strain was considerable—inside the ship the heat was a stifling, breathless hell.

Gito sat up. Light from the open port drilled a bright tube into the opposite wall of the ship. It was a white cylinder filled with dusty strands of coarse Shari fiber. His admiration for the Kahrii rose several points. He had expected the interior to be riddled with stars of sunlight—as far as he could tell there wasn't a single leak. A breath of old fear touched him. *It was thorough—too thorough!* A good imitation of an airtight ship—but what?

Okay, he told himself sharply, this *is* what you came for, isn't it? You wanted to know the truth, whatever it was—didn't you? No, he answered himself solemnly—no, I didn't want any such thing.

Biting his lip, he pulled the flashlight from his belt and aimed it down the long darkness.

A dry and brittle cry left his throat and bounced again and again through the helmet. He turned his shaking hand and flicked the light down the opposite end of the ship. His heart pounded against his chest. It was the same—everywhere! At even intervals, the inside of the ship was ringed with coarse, woven sacks, like cocoons, or—the image forced itself into his mind—shrouds. On each side of the sacks two cords hung loose. Their purpose was too obvious—he could picture one of the Kahrii in each sack, the cords tied securely.

Counting the sacks in one section of the ship he multiplied quickly—knowing he would end somewhere near the figure of 888. Like the ship, the sacks were crude imitations—but their use was clear enough. Gito laughed harshly.

Acceleration couches! My God, what were they going to accelerate *against*!

He was vaguely aware that the heat was rising much too quickly within the suit. The ringing in his ears seemed to drown out the wheeze of the conditioner.

Okay, he reasoned, this is it. You've seen it. Here is a race that has forgotten its past, forgotten everything except the long journey through the vast darkness. And now they would relive that journey—after how many countless eons? Only this time they would not emerge from the darkness—this time the acceleration couches would not cushion their passengers against the harsh shock of death.

Only it isn't going to happen, he thought grimly, forcing himself back through the small entry port. I *can't let* it happen! Not now! The idea had come unbidden, wedging itself into a corner of his consciousness.

He stopped, swaying in the shadow of the ship. The giant, malignant star was higher now, and he could feel its increased heat blazing, burning through his suit. He twisted the conditioner knob frantically. Where was the air—what was wrong? His face, oddly enough, was cold. Why should that be, he wondered vaguely. Bright dots of color swam before his eyes.

He took a step forward. Somewhere, the dome blurred in the distance. He had to reach it now—had to reach it because he knew what he had to do.

Another step—another... The sand wavered dizzily around him. He had to make it, because he knew what the Kahrii were, and he knew the Corps was wrong. The lesson on Tsirtsi was one thing—but that had happened a long time ago and had nothing to do with now, here, on Sahara III.

There had to be a time when rules were broken, and this *was that time*! What they did to him—after—didn't matter. With a faraway sadness, he saw a dream dissolve. He shrugged it off.

What had he been thinking of, anyway? What kind of a love can you have with a Mistress? With a—he said the word—*professional*, someone who had loved others before and would love others after you.

No! It *wasn't* like that—not with Arilee. She had almost told him it wasn't, she—still, he thought slyly, she would, would she not? Wasn't that her *job*?

He gritted his teeth and blinked hot sweat from his face. He was cold all over now. Good—then the conditioner was working again. Everything was going to be all right. He would make it now. *Arilee... I've got to tell you, even if it never means a thing to you...Arilee... Arilee...!*

Out of the raging stars, the bright, exploding moons, the white ghost staggered toward him. He tried to take a breath, but there was no air. It was all right, he didn't really need air, did he? Not now...

The ghost came closer, weaving across the hot sand, its white hood parted to show a pale head topped by long flames of wheat-colored hair. Then the ghost staggered, falling toward him, and there was a comforting blackness...

▲▼▲

For a long century the ghost dragged him roughly over the bright sand. Then there was darkness again. Later, coolness, great lungfuls of sweet air, and sleep...

No. NO! He sat up, fighting against the exploding stars. His vision cleared and a great sob broke from his throat. She was on the floor beside him, her body tangled in the white robe. He parted the robe and dropped it with a cry. The velvet flesh was red, seared, blistered and cracked. He jerked to his feet and fell into the supply locker. He ripped the medikit from its rack and nearly fainted again.

He tore the robe away and ripped off the clothes underneath. Tears welled up uncontrollably. He placed the medikit under her left breast and heard it begin its chittering and humming as it began to probe and prick like a benevolent leech.

The blackness was almost upon him again. He tore through the locker again until his hands touched a round surface. The lettering on the spraycan blurred before his eyes. He said a silent prayer that it was the right one and covered her body with the spray, turning her gently, until the can was empty. He had a last, shimmering glimpse of a slim figure covered in a cottony foam. Then the can dropped from his hands.

▲▼▲

"That's a hell of a way…to get a suntan," he said weakly. She turned quickly as he opened his eyes. A little cry escaped her as she knelt and buried her face against his shoulder.

"You're…all right?" he said. He grasped her shoulders and held her at arm's length. She winced slightly at his touch and he jerked his hands away.

She shook her head. "No. It just burns a little. Still. But hold me, Gito. Hold me! I thought you were—were—"

He cut her off and pulled her to him, gently. The wheat-colored hair brushed his cheek. A brown shoulder pressed against his chest. He was amazed at the job the spray had done. The medikit had undoubtedly brought her out of shock, but the spray had sucked away the heat and smoothed the damaged cells. Her skin was a golden bronze against the white of her brief costume.

Gito grinned weakly. The spray had brought seared flesh back to gold velvet, but Arilee was gingerly wearing as little as possible, and would be for awhile.

Her deep eyes stared into his, and he remembered the white-robed figure moving toward him under the death-bearing sun.

"Arilee…Arilee…"

She shook her head gently and pressed a finger to his lips. "Hey, now," she said softly, "Don't. I had to go out. What would I do with a fried Planet Warden, anyway?"

▲▼▲

When he told her his decision, she said nothing. Outside, the giant ball of *Posi Frondee* once more flattened against the high ridge.

Gito scowled thoughtfully. "I thought maybe you'd have something to say. I'd like to hear it."

Arilee bit her lip. She looked up at him briefly, then her gaze traveled down to the gray-cased weapon on the table.

"I don't know anymore," she said anxiously. "It was easy before— when it was just talk; about saving them, I mean. Now—" She shrugged, reached out for his hand. He moved it away quietly, shaking his head.

"I told you, Arilee, that can't matter." His voice bordered on irritation. He touched the weapon then looked away.

"If I let it be that way, thinking about it afterward, I can pretty quickly decide my life is worth more than 888 of them! I'm human, Arilee. I want something for myself, too. More than ever now. You understand that?"

Her eyes were wet and she nodded quickly before her face contorted and she turned and buried her head in the couch.

Gito closed his eyes hard. Was it right—*that* right? Strange, he thought, that the rightness seems to matter, and I'm not worried about the other part. He knew what the punishment would be—*had* to be. The Corps was humane, certainly, but this couldn't be overlooked. It would be humane—quick, and final.

Still, that wasn't it. He *had* to be right! If he stopped them, prevented them from sacrificing themselves for an insane gesture—could he ever really know? The Kahrii had traveled to this world through the terrible, yawning vastness of space a million years before his own ancestors had learned to speak. Could he decide now, what was right for them?

He paused, following the last rays of *Posi Frondee* into the darkness. Tonight. Yes, he knew that. He couldn't say how. But he knew. The Kahrii would leave their tunnels and crawl into their ship to die. And he could stop them, maybe discover where they had come from, bring them back to greatness—they *must* have reached greatness, long ago, when—

Doubt overtook him again. Doubt, he told himself acidly, or a last attempt to ease out of a decision. The excuses were countless in number, and they had all paraded themselves before him by now. The Kahrii were not an ancient, superior race—they had landed here in a lifeboat from some disaster. They were poor slaves of some other race, left here to die.

Sure. And is that why they're so perfectly adapted to this planet, so obviously a part of it.

No. There was to be no justifying. No more. There was the ship, the endless rows of acceleration couches. He pictured it, the way it must have been, when the Kahrii left their world, (was it dying?) which must have been like Sahara III. They came in search of a new home, knowing they would have to begin again. Did they realize just how much they would lose?

He picked up the weapon and looked out into the fast darkening night. Already the ship was a black silhouette. Soon, now.

"Arilee," he said.

"Yes, Gito."

He turned. She was already beside him. She was dressed in her work coveralls, flashlight and tools hooked neatly to her belt. She looked very small, now, a delicate and lovely spirit from some quiet, elfin world. He had known for some time that he loved her—he had never loved her as much as he did now.

▲▼▲

Gito's plan was simple—it was the aftermath that would be difficult. The weapon was a standard stunner. With a wide-open lens it would merely bring long and restful sleep to its victims. When the Kahrii had entered the ship, he would spray it—stem to stern, and he and Arilee would carry the sleepers back to the tunnels. It would be a long night's work. But then, he told himself, Saharan nights were uncommonly long anyway.

And after that? There was the Corps to inform of his action. He grimaced at that. They would not be overly long in replying.

They stood together in the sultry beginnings of night. When the first pair of luminous eyes emerged from the tunnel Arilee's hand tightened on Gito's arm. He looked at her, but said nothing. A long, stiffened Shari root gangway was placed in the entry port; its carriers then knelt beside the ship and buried their heads in prayer. Moments later, a low, eerie sound drifted from the tunnels. Gito stiffened, and a sob tightened in the girl's throat.

It was a sound he knew, instinctively, had not been heard before. It was a song of hot winds sweeping over the desert, green shoots searching the scorched planet for water; a song of life, birth and death. And then they came.

They came out of the tunnels in a single file, their heads bowed low, and the song rose with them and filled the night.

To Gito, the white-robed figures already seemed long-dead ghosts returning to haunt themselves; to haunt the race that had forsaken some far off star eons before. With a start, he saw that each carried a small section of Shari root, cradled in their arms like a precious child.

A picture flashed before him of the tombs of long-dead Egypt on Earth, and the eerie columns of a forgotten race of Sirians. There, too, were the remains of ceremonial food provided for the long journey into death.

Gito had no idea how long they had been there, while the endless procession emptied the tunnels and disappeared into the ship. When Arilee touched his arm he jerked back, startled, then blinked his eyes. The desert was empty. The entry port was closed.

The weapon seemed suddenly heavy. He looked at Arilee a long moment, then walked toward the ship. He stopped a bare twenty yards from the dark shape. He was not sure what effect the walls of the vessel might have on the weapon's field of dispersal at so wide a setting. He had to be sure. The thought of facing the Kahrii after they regained consciousness and discovered what he had done, was bad enough. He was already haunted by that. To meet one before, who had not been affected by the weapon, would be unbearable.

Arilee held the flash while he made final adjustments. With his finger finally on the heavy trigger, the enormity of his act brought cold sweat to his face. Okay. He had expected this, and steeled himself against it. Last minute qualms were normal—but it was worse than he had imagined.

He was wrong, and he knew it. No! Damn it, you *made* your decision—do it! His finger tightened. Nothing happened. He jerked his finger away. His heart beat wildly against his chest and his whole body shook. He looked up at the sudden shifting of the eerie light.

Over the crest of the dark ridge, the four moons of Sahara III moved swiftly toward him through the black sky. He looked again. He had never seen them like that before—had he? Always, they seemed to travel the night in wild, erratic patterns, chasing each other across the heavens in a meaningless procession. Now, the two largest moons had nearly converged upon each other to become one—and the two dwarf sisters moved swiftly toward them in a path that could only bring them into conjunction.

Gito looked away. The moons of this planet themselves seemed to be warning him against the thing he had to do. Could he go back? No! He could stop them, save them. It was his—

The word stuck in his throat. His finger fell away from the trigger once more.

My God, was that what I was going to say? Is that how I justify this—as a duty?

He trembled at what he had almost done. Suddenly, a parade of self-righteous, cold-eyed madmen passed before him in solemn review. From their lips they uttered a stream of unctuous, emotionless edicts; edicts that changed, condemned, doomed a billion helpless faces.

It is our duty, *they told the fearful crowds: it is for you we make these changes—we have decided for you how you shall live, how you shall die, and this is right, because* WE HAVE DONE THESE THINGS AND KNOW THEY WILL BE RIGHT FOR YOU! *Your shape, your color, your gods have been wrong; but now we will make them right...*

...And the centuries of one way are forgotten, and the faceless crowd begins new ways...because the grim-lipped men who spoke had more than strength in their words; they had strength in other ways...

Gito's trembling hands opened and the weapon dropped to the sand. He looked up with blurred eyes at four moons that were now one, shimmering, ghostly light above.

"Gito...GITO!" Arilee's fingers bit painfully into his arm. He turned, following her wide, staring eyes to his feet. There was nothing. Only the discarded weapon half-covered in the sand.

Then he saw. The pale gray of the sand was turning to mottled blackness. He stepped back quickly. Then bent to the ground. He jerked his hand away and stared at it as if it was a thing he had never seen. *Wet!* His hand was *wet*!

As he watched, the mottled patches blurred together until a visible film of moisture covered the sand beneath his feet. He looked up, scanning the desert. All around them, the floor of the flat valley shimmered beneath the converging moons.

Arilee trembled. "Gito. What *is* it?" Her voice was barely a whisper. He stilled her with a gesture and cocked his head to listen. The song of the Kahrii was beginning again. It was the same song, he thought, only—there was a difference. The first song had been something old, the end of a life—this was a song of beginning.

The ground beneath his feet seemed to tremble with the urgency of the Kahrii voices. Then, he knew it was more than that—a low, awesome rumble of power was rising from deep beneath the surface of the planet.

Arilee gasped. The sand beneath her feet gurgled in a final protest, then the water bubbled from the ground in force. Gito grabbed her and shoved her toward the dome. She stood, numbly watching the strange fluid that already covered her ankles.

"Run," he said sharply, "*Run!*"

"Gito—!"

"I don't *know*!" he yelled, "Just run!"

Halfway there, his heart sank. The water was rising faster than ever now; he estimated quickly and knew they would never make it. Even if they reached the dome, how could they enter without bringing the flood with them? Then what? How high was it going to *go*? How much pressure would the dome take, submerged under the tons of water?

He stopped Arilee and jabbed a hand toward the smaller, closer dome of the sandcar. Arilee saw. Together, they pulled through the sandy water that now swirled above their waists. Arilee stumbled, disappeared. Gito plunged down to bring her up, gasping and choking.

At the dome, he pressed the lock of the port with his thumb and waited, listening to the mechanism groan against the pressure. Once it seemed to stop and he wedged his body between the narrow opening and shoved. The motor began again, then slowly folded back the door. The waters rushed in to fill the dome above the tracks of the sandcar.

Once Arilee was seated beside him and the canopy locked, he shoved down hard on the overdrive bar, not waiting to build up speed on the useless treads. The power unit howled in protest. Great founts of steam roared beneath them in a gray cloud as the treads retracted and the sandcar trembled. Then they were out of the dome and rising on a hurricane column above the water...

▲▼▲

It was a dawn he would never forget. From the ridge above the valley, he watched, Arilee sleeping restlessly in the seat beside him.

The first rays of *Posi Frondee* streaked the new alien sea with red. How many centuries had passed, he wondered, since the four moons had met to suck the dormant waters from the ground and fill the deep well of the dry valley?

He knew, now, that was exactly what it was—a well of the planet's own making, ringed by the solid rock wall.

As the harsh light hit the ridge across the valley, he could see the water had reached far less than halfway back up the 750 feet of the wall. And already it was receding, sinking back into the depths below the sandy floor.

He picked up his binoculars and swept the far end of the valley. Yes. There it was. It had drifted some in the night, but it was still there. The Kahrii ship floated serenely, rolling above the valley floor. Above, he reminded himself grimly, the flooded tunnels he might have used to 'save' the aliens from their folly.

He closed his eyes and took a deep breath. He let it out slowly. He had been right—and wrong, too. Golsamel-ri had told him they would meet again—and they would.

Symbols? Well, the Kahrii were bound, as he had known, by what they could actually see. In his hand he held the symbol that had saved them when the waters rose—this time, and how many times before?

He opened his fist and looked at the object in his palm. It was a small, rough, cylinder, two inches long. Millions of them had risen with the water from the ground, and hundreds had clung to his clothes, and Arilee's.

He split it open down a long seam with his fingernail. Black, tender seeds clung to the inside of the pod. When he touched them lightly, they fell in a numberless stream into his lap.

Gito grinned. No, not numberless at all. When he had the time to count, he knew there would be 888—and the answer to the controlled population of the Kahrii.

Here was the tiny miniature, the model, for the Kahrii ark. When the waters receded, the seeds would recede with them, and the giant Shari would renew themselves and grow in the moist sand.

The larger Kahrii 'seed' would come to rest, too, and new tunnels would be dug in the sand, waiting for the silver-gray shoots to rise and nurture the race.

There would be hunger, he knew. But the Kahrii were good about that—and he suspected the old, mature Shari that had been sheared off at the surface would renew themselves for awhile, and provide until the young plants thrust to the sun. It had happened before, hadn't it? And the race had lived.

Gito pulled his gaze away from the scene outside and rested his eyes on the figure beside him.

He wondered, briefly, if the Warden of Tsirtsi had left an Arilee behind? A quiet chill of fear began to rise in his heart, then died quickly.

He, too, had acted to save—and had ended by destroying. And through the same, sure sense of knowledge and duty Gito had come so close to repeating.

"Arilee," he said softly. She opened one sleepy eye and smiled.

Again, the small finger found his lips and closed them.

"Don't," she said. "Haven't you learned yet a Mistress always knows what a man is thinking?

"Even," she added sleepily, "one that just handed in her resignation?"

The Stentorii Luggage

The Double-A call light wailed and blinked itself into a bright red hemorrhage on the wall. I woke up fast. My first thought was fire. Logically, reasonably, I know there hasn't been a hotel fire in 800 years—but tradition is tradition.

I punched the visor and Greel's face popped on the screen. The lobby clock over his shoulder read 3:35. I moaned silently and flipped on vocal.

"Duncan here."

"Chief, get down here quick." I didn't ask why. Greel's my head bellhop and bellhops can smell hotel trouble.

"Where are you?"

"Level 12. Desk 19."

"Check. Hold everything, kid." I started to cut off, then I saw something else behind him. I took a deep breath and held it.

"Greel. Is that—Ollie?"

Greel nodded. Like he was going to be sick. I was in my clothes and out the door. I took a manual emergency lift and fell seventy-eight floors in eighty seconds, not even thinking about my stomach. Not with Ollie to think about.

Ollie's uncle is Mike Sorrenson, owner of Hotel Intergalactica, and a reasonably decent person. Ollie is something else again. Crew cut, eager, bow tie and fresh out of college. My job—teach him "all there is to know about the hotel business." Which should be a real snap, as he already knows all there is to know about everything.

Thursday, for instance. Ollie got his menus mixed and served scrambled eggs to five hundred visiting Vegans. That's all. No trouble. Except the difference between a Vegan and a chicken is strictly a matter of size and evolution—and we're still cleaning up Ballroom Nine.

▲▼▲

I came out of the lift, my stomach only ten floors behind. Ollie popped out of his chair and came toward me, a sick smile pasted across his face.

"Mr. Duncan, I—"

"Sit down, Ollie, and shut up," I said quietly. He swallowed and sat down.

I turned to Greel.

"Okay," I said. "I'm ready. Let's have it."

"I'll save the details for later," said Greel. "We've got to get moving. Fast. I have reason to believe there are from four to fifty Skeidzti loose in the hotel."

I drew a blank at first. Then it hit me and I felt cold all over.

"Oh, my God," I said, sending a withering look at Ollie.

"Uh-huh." Greel nodded. "The way I get it from Ollie, four Stentorii checked in about 3:00. They wanted to go right up to their room so Ollie sent a boy with them and told the Stentorii he'd put their luggage in a lift right away."

"They kind of grinned at me, Mr. Duncan," Ollie interrupted, "and said that was fine, there was no hurry about the bags."

"Yeah, I'll bet they did," I said. I looked at Greel, and we both felt sick. "Don't tell me the rest. Ollie checked them in on the Master Register, turned to get their bags—and what do you know, they were gone."

Ollie looked surprised. He started to ask how I could possibly know but I glared him back to his chair.

"Okay," I said. "What have you done so far?"

Greel took a deep breath. "First, they have about thirty to thirty-five minutes head start. I've shielded four levels above and below. I don't think they'll get that far, but no use taking chances. We've got one lucky break. Since the whole Quadrant borders on Free City they can't get out except through a Registration area."

"What about—"

Greel nodded. "Already done it. I've closed all five Desks in the Quadrant. Anyone wants to register has to come in by way of Seven."

"Fine. Just one thing—" I flipped through the register. "Could they have gotten outside through this door?"

"No. It was unshielded, all right. But there were no checkouts after the Stentorii registered."

▲▼▲

Our luck was holding. At least the Skeidzti were still just the hotel's problem. I've got a few friends on Free City's revolving council, but I don't like to mess with those boys unless I have to.

I sent Greel to organize the bellboys into search squads. Then I checked the Stentorii's room number and hauled Ollie out of his chair, figuring the only way to make sure he stayed out of trouble was to keep him with me. Before I left the lobby I picked up a pair of low-charge stunners and handed one to Ollie.

"Look," I said, "do you think you could possibly handle one of these things without knocking us both out cold?"

Ollie nodded vaguely. He took the weapon and held it as if he were certain it would go off in his hand.

"Sure, Mr. Duncan, but why do we need weapons? I mean, I'm sorry I let those things get loose, but—"

I stopped at the lift and stared at him. I suddenly realized the poor kid had no idea what he had done wrong. All he could see was that Greel and I were making a big fuss over a couple of alien housepets.

"Ollie," I said patiently, "do you really know what a Skeidzti is? I don't want an oration. Just tell me the simple truth. Do you or don't you?" He started to say something, then changed his mind and shook his head.

"I thought so. Well, first of all, don't refer to them as 'pets.' They may be cute as a kitten to a Stentorii, but as far as you're concerned they are dangerous, quick, carnivorous, highly adaptable little monsters. Only 'adaptable' is about as descriptive as calling the ocean moist. A Skeidzti in a kitchen will hide in a stack of plates and, by God, you'll eat off of him and swear he *is* a plate. A Skeidzti in a garden is a rock, a weed, a pile of leaves. In your bedroom he's a garter, a sock or a necktie. Only— put one around your neck and you'll damn well know he's not a necktie. Now do you think it might be permissible for me to continue to bear arms against the Skeidzti, just in case?"

Ollie was taken aback, I could tell. Almost enough to keep his mouth shut. He thought for maybe a full second before he said anything.

"But Mr. Duncan, if the Stentorii knew they were dangerous—" And that did it. I poked a hard finger in his chest and backed him against the wall.

"Look, Ollie," I said grimly, "that college line of logic is what got us into this jam in the first place. Now get this, and remember it. You don't need a degree in Alien Psychology to know that Rule One is *never* use your own viewpoint as a premise in guessing what an alien is think- ing or doing. It just simply doesn't work that way. An alien's actions are based upon what he thinks is reasonable and proper—not what you think he ought to think.

"Why do you think we have separate Quadrants and private entranc- es to each room? It sure as hell isn't for economy's sake, I can tell you that. It so happens that some of these so-called reasonable civilized beings still consider each other as rare culinary delights. While that sort of nonsense is SOP in Free City, this hotel is strictly out of bounds. And here's another rule you can put down in Duncan's lectures on Alien Psychology: If a guest phones down for a midnight snack, he may mean he wants the key to his neighbor's room." I took a deep breath.

"Am I getting through to you, Ollie?" Ollie nodded, wide-eyed, and I shoved him into the lift ahead of me. We hung for a moment, then the gravs caught hold.

▲▼▲

In my business you learn to get along with aliens, or at least put up with the ones you can't possibly get along with. And some *are* completely impossible—like the Nixies. Except for simple trade relations, I can't conceive of anything I might have in common with a Nixie.

And there was another rule of thumb for Ollie: Never be deceived by appearances. An alien's resemblance to human form is no indication that his outlook will in any way resemble human logic and reason. Until you know, don't guess; and don't assume, either, that a lack of human form denotes a lack of common interest. A Goron is a repulsive, warty glob of pink and brown protoplasm consisting of twelve eyes, nine pseudo-arms—and an entirely human liking for jazz, poetry, Scotch and women. Or anyway, Goron females.

On the other hand, ignoring the general hairiness and the rodent-like features, a Stentorii looks as humanoid as I do. He is also a completely alien, cold-blooded, murderous creature without a shred of mercy in his body.

I stared hard at the Stentorii who opened the door. He stared back at me from tiny red eyes set wide on either side of his whiskery pink muzzle. Then he saw Ollie and gave a high squeaky laugh, baring a mouthful of sharp yellow teeth. He turned into his room and said something in Stentor to his companions. They nearly fell apart.

I had had just about enough. Time was running out. I switched on my portable recorder and said:

"According to Statute XII, Galactic Standard Code, I wish to invoke the privilege of communicating with you; without fear of future prosecution in case I may offend, by way of accidental implication, any tradition, custom or moral standard of your race." The Stentorii just grinned. I spoke a little louder. "I said I speak without offense!"

The Stentorii frowned. He didn't like that at all. But he understood it.

"All right," he said grudgingly, "I accept."

"Fine," I said, and let him see that I had switched off my recorder. I never start an argument with an alien without invoking the non-offense clause. Of course, the same clause is stated in every Registration Contract, providing mutual protection for the hotel's guests and its employees. But I like to play it safe.

By now the three other Stentorii were up, grinning at Ollie. I ignored them and spoke to the one at the door.

"My name is Duncan," I told him. "I am manager of the hotel. This is my assistant, Mr. Sorrenson. I will come right to the point. You played a little joke down in the lobby a few minutes ago. Although the incident is a serious breach of your Registration Contract, I am willing to forget the matter if I am able to gain your full cooperation. On behalf of Hotel Intergalactica, I formally request you recall your Skeidzti immediately and turn them over to me for housing in the hotel kennel."

The Stentorii glanced at his companions, then turned to me with a look of mock astonishment.

"Mr. Duncan, do you imply the hotel has allowed my pets to become lost? Naturally, I will hold you responsible if they come to any harm while in your charge." I had half expected something like this. I couldn't do a thing but play it out.

"All right," I said, "I haven't time to appreciate your humor. You know it is illegal to bring unregistered alien pets into this hotel. I am also certain you are aware that we are in the Federation Circle, which is *not* in Free City territory—which means all guests, by the act of signing their Registration Contracts, place themselves under Federation law for the duration of their stay here."

The Stentorii grinned, showing his yellow teeth.

"Mr. Duncan, you are bluffing. I am quite aware of the law, and respectfully submit that if you check your copy of our Registration Contracts you will find your employee here countersigned the Alien Responsibility Clause."

Well, that was his round. I was sure he was too oily a character to fall for it, but I had had to try. He was right. Under our Registration Contract it is presumed that while the hotel is responsible for a full knowledge of the Galactic Customs Restrictions, an alien cannot be expected to inform the Desk Clerk of all possible violations he may be guilty of on any particular world. And any clerk green enough, or stupid enough, or both— like Ollie—who signs a Responsibility Clause without checking Galactic Customs—ought to have his head examined. Of course, we could take the Stentorii to court. Maybe we might even win, on the grounds of purposeful malice, but I don't like to get the hotel into lawsuits. It's bad publicity, and it gives other wise guys grand ideas.

The legal pitch having failed, I was ready to continue with Unveiled Threat No. 1.

"Look," I said wearily, "I admit you are within your legal rights. Although just how far within I'm not too certain at the moment. But before you come to any decision let me remind you that, while I may not be in a position to take official action against you, I fully intend to file a Warning Report to every member of the Galactic Hotel Association, which includes nearly twelve million first-class hotels and their subsidiaries. I don't know what your business is. But since you are here I presume it entails traveling. Traveling means hotels. If you refuse your cooperation, I assure you it may be quite difficult to find a decent room within twelve thousand parsecs of this planet."

The Stentorii shrugged and closed the door on my foot. I'm sure he would have hacked it off for a souvenir if I hadn't jerked it out.

I looked at Ollie. His fists were clenched by his side and there was a look of iron determination in his eyes.

"Well?" I said.

"Boy," said Ollie. "Just *wait* until they try to check into a GHA hotel again."

"Ollie," I said weakly, "I didn't come up here to actually accomplish anything with those characters. It is strictly a matter of form. A necessary routine for the record. Everything I said went completely down the drain. They were not impressed, frightened or embarrassed in any way. It is impossible to reason with a Stentorii because he is inherently incapable of taking anything you say seriously. He is also incapable of caring whether he gets a hotel room. Anywhere. Ever. He has one now, and the future is absolutely of no importance. He doesn't care about you, me, life, death *or* hotel rooms. Didn't you hear anything I said in the lift?"

"Sure, Mr. Duncan, but—"

"Ollie. Shut up."

▲▼▲

I stopped off at my office for a wake-up pill. Greel had his command post set up in the Level 12 lobby and I joined him there. The lobby was full of squat Fensi bellhops, swarming in and out of the lifts like agitated ants.

Most of my bellhops and some of the administrative staff are Fensi. I like to have them on the payroll, and I'd hire fifty more if I could get them. Fensi are quick, alert, reasonably honest and highly adaptable. Their adaptability alone makes them worth their weight in gold to a big hotel. A Fensi can breathe a wide variety of atmospheres, take plenty of g's, and doesn't care whether he's hot, cold or in-between. Unless you're a Fensi, room service around here can be a literally killing job.

Greel sprinted across the lobby, a wide smile stretching over his hairless blue face.

"I'm glad you're so happy," I said. "Maybe you should have gone to see our friends upstairs."

Greel laughed. "Maybe we won't need 'em, chief. The boys think we can clean the Skeidzti out by morning—with a little luck, of course."

"More than a little, if you ask me. Get any yet?"

Greel held up a finger. "One. Skorno picked up an ashtray on Ten and it nearly bit his hand off." He nodded toward the desk and Ollie and I followed. He picked up a small stationery box and pushed it toward me.

"Skorno got it before it could change completely—you can see what it was trying to do."

I could. The object in the box was a dead Skeidzti, but only one-quarter of it was in its natural form. The last thing it had touched was Skorno's hand. Following its blind-rule instinct it had imitated a hairless blue Fensi arm nearly up to the elbow before it had either run out of material or died.

Now that it was dead it was slowly changing back to its natural form. The part we could see resembled a thin, eight-inch-wide worm-like creature with stubby serrated legs. I figured it could move about as fast as a caterpillar without adapting. It was a highly vulnerable creature, and in order to survive it had developed a high degree of protective camouflage. With its soft body and slow speed almost anything could pick up a quick and easy meal. And its natural color didn't help at all. The dead quarter of the Skeidzti was a brilliant, almost phosphorescent orange.

"Well, son, get some idea what we're up against?" Ollie's eyes were glued to the box and his face was as blue as Greel's.

"Can they—can they adapt to *anything*?"

"No," said Greel, "they have limitations. I'm sure they can *imitate* most anything, but they couldn't change as quickly under six or eight g's, or, say, in a methane atmosphere."

"Not for two or three generations, anyway," I added soberly. Greel nodded.

"Anyway, Ollie, the point is these varmints are already used to a Stentor-Earth atmosphere. And if any get out—"

"It would be comparable," I put in, "to a plague of invisible bobcats."

I think for the first time Ollie was hit with the seriousness of our problem. I could sense a kind of helpless panic in his eyes, as if he had suddenly realized he'd opened the floodgates and let the valve break off in his hand.

"Mr. Duncan, I—well, maybe we ought to get help. I mean—I'll take the blame—and—and—" He was shaking like a leaf. I eased him down to a chair.

"And just what sort of help did you have in mind?" I asked.

"Well, the police! Couldn't you—"

I shook my head firmly. "No. I certainly could not. That, my friend, is all we need. The Federation would quarantine the hotel, rout several thousand guests out of their various notions of sleep, and raise enough hell to wake every DeepDream addict from here to Andromeda."

"Aside from the fact," Greel added, "that every Skeidzti in the hotel could hitch a free ride out of here in some cop's pocket."

"Right. No, we can handle it ourselves, a hell of a lot quieter. We've had worse before." Ollie's face told me he thought I was an out and out liar. But then, like I said, this kid has a lot to learn about the hotel business.

The Skeidzti had been loose in the hotel since 3:00 A.M. By 5:30 we had killed eight of them. And eight Fensi bellhops had bandaged hands.

It was obvious we couldn't go around touching everything in the hotel to see if it was real or Skeidzti. Added was the problem of knowing *when* we had killed them all. The Skeidzti came in disguised as four pieces of Stentorii luggage, but we had no idea how many had clustered together to form each piece. And the Stentorii weren't telling.

I called Greel and Ollie to the Desk for a strategy meeting. Ollie dropped in a chair and sank into brooding silence. Even Greel's customary optimism seemed to have temporarily vanished. He reported the bellhops were doing their poking with sticks now, but the results were still alarmingly low.

"What we need," Greel complained, "is a system."

"Yeh, we need a system, all right," added Ollie helpfully. I stood up, paced around the Desk. The strategy meeting was dying on its feet.

"Look," I said, "let's analyze it. Our problem is to get rid of the Skeidzti, right?"

"Right," from Greel and Ollie.

"Okay. Now to kill them we have to see them. And by seeing them I mean we have to see them as they really are."

"Or catch them during a change," added Greel.

"Exactly." Somewhere in the back of my head an idea was catching hold. I kept talking, trying to push it out.

"Then our problem is this. We have to *force* them to change into something we can recognize as a definite Skeidzti." Greel's frown vanished. He sat up straight in his chair.

"You mean, like if we made them all change into an object we knew we only had one of."

"Sort of like that. Only that means we'd have to be able to isolate the Skeidzti in a specified area—and even if we could do that it'd be a hell of a problem to get rid of all the objects we didn't want them to imitate. Which means more stick poking. Remember, they can flatten out on the walls and ceilings just as easily as they can curl up like an ashtray or a sofa pillow." Greel's face dropped back into a disappointed frown.

"No, you've got the general idea," I said quickly. "But I think I've got a way to work the same thing, only quicker." Greel suddenly looked around, and I turned and saw Skorno, our first casualty, coming out of the lift. In his bandaged hand he held an ominous looking club, and in the other a limp and bloody throwrug. He stopped before us, grinning, and tossed the rug on the floor.

He said, "Three more, chief."

I bent down for a closer look. This time, three Skeidzti had joined to imitate a portion of the rug. It was a near-perfect job. They had continued the intricate pattern, carrying out the design exactly where the real rug stopped. The only thing wrong, Skorno explained, was that he passed the rug fifty times a day and knew it was about twice as large as it should have been.

Something about Skorno's rug worried me. I asked him how long he thought it took for the Skeidzti to change from one form to another.

"About half a second," he said. "But I think it varies, depending on what they're imitating."

"For instance?"

"Well, on a plain surface, like a wall or something, they're faster—much faster."

"You mean," I asked, "if they have something more complicated to imitate, it takes longer?"

Skorno shook his head. "I wish it did. When I said it varies, I meant just the first few times. Once they've imitated something, they don't forget it."

"Well, hell," I snapped, "I know they can't imitate simultaneously! There has to be *some* definite minimum time lapse!"

Skorno spread his hands helplessly. "I know, chief. But whatever it is, it's too small to do us much good. They're just too fast for our reaction time. We still only get about one out of every ten we see." Swell, I thought. If they were too fast for the Fensi, we were really up the creek.

"What about spraying a low-charge disruptor all over the place and picking up the pieces?" said Greel hopefully.

Skorno said, "I forgot to mention that with a low-charge you have to hit them in just the right place or they're only knocked out for a while."

"And while they're unconscious they're just as safe as ever," I finished for him. Then Skorno's words suddenly sank in. "Good Lord! Do you mean you're using *high*-charge disruptors—inside this hotel!"

Skorno nodded sheepishly. "What else can we do, chief? Sure, the place looks like a two-cluster cruiser plowed through. But we're getting 'em, slow but sure."

I was beginning to get a little bit mad. I thought about the Stentorii, sleeping peacefully in their rooms while we blasted four levels of valuable real estate looking for their damnable pets. And what, I asked myself, are we doing about it? Mooning around in the lobby on our respective rears, that's what we are doing. I stood up again, glaring at Ollie on general principles.

"All right," I said firmly. "This has gone far enough, gentlemen. I'm not saying there *is* any other way to finish off this mess, but I do have one humble idea that might save a little of Hotel Intergalactica's property. I figure as long as we're going to turn this place into a shooting gallery we might as well have something to shoot at."

I went over our floor plan with Greel and Skorno and picked out an area where the Skeidzti had proven particularly obnoxious. Then I sent Greel to seal off the other contaminated levels, and told Skorno to marshal his forces in Humanoid Hall. I picked Humanoid Hall for two reasons: One, plenty of Skeidzti to work on, and two, a minimum of furniture. For previously stated reasons I kept Ollie with me, and hopped a Class-A lift for Level Eight.

▲▼▲

More than once I've had good reason to be thankful we enforced strong lift security measures. No matter where the Skeidzti might go, I was dead sure they would never reach guest quarters.

There's a good reason for this. We ordinarily house about thirty thousand guests in the hotel at any one time. That number represents five to fifteen thousand separate races, each one requiring its own unique set of conditions. In Quadrant Four I've got Denebian Iceworms at -200 F. right "next door" to a cluster of Calistan Feroids sleeping soundly in boiling mercury. No problem. We can handle 1,240 different atmospheres, with innumerable variations in density, temperature and lighting.

The real problem is sociological, not mechanical. If the Galaxy is old, the oldest things in it are its grudges. To put it bluntly, some of these characters have hated each other's guts so long they forgot *why* about two million years ago.

Naturally, an Altaran isn't going to walk into a Vegan's room and strangle him. There's a problem of about 900 degrees and thirty g's to overcome first. But that's no real problem either—about 500,000 years ago they swarmed all over each other's planets in protective armor, and strangling was the nicest thing that happened.

And that's where we come in.

What they do outside Hotel Intergalactica is none of our business—but inside we make sure no one is faced with temptation. That's why our room segregation is vertical instead of horizontal. The hotel is built on the hive principle. Each cell or room has a private entrance bordering on the lift. There are no halls or corridors to wander around in, and any connecting rooms connect up and down. No exceptions.

It's a necessary rule and we enforce it. There are plenty of Common Rooms on the opposite side of the lifts for conferences and amiable gatherings—free of charge.

We work it that way for economical reasons, too. It's a lot easier to, say, keep a gravitic lift at 9g constant for a Cygnian than to change it to forty-five for a Lyri passenger. Everybody minds their own business—and nobody waits for an elevator.

That's where lift security comes in.

We run a high density forceshield over each lift entrance. Try to enter one that's not attuned to your requirements and you run smack into an invisible wall. Which is precisely what would happen if the Skeidzti tried it. Imitation is one thing. Fortunately, duplication is another.

It suddenly dawned on me that here was the real reason the Stentorii played their little joke on Ollie. They knew the Skeidzti couldn't get by the lift shields, so they didn't even try. A typical bit of Stentorii humor, I thought wryly. Don't dump your problems just anywhere—toss 'em where they can do some good.

▲▼▲

I knew pretty well what to expect on Level Eight.

It was worse.

What did Skorno say? Like a two-cluster cruiser plowed through? It was more like a complete reenactment of the Battle of the Rim. ·

Through a low cloud of acrid blue smoke I made out the dim outlines of Fensi bellhops, lined up in military order across the room. Skorno groped toward me through the wreckage. I put a handkerchief to my nose and stumbled out to meet him, Ollie choking along behind. The air was full of the smell of fused plastic, burnt carpeting and a particularly nauseous odor I identified as fried Skeidzti.

"Are you sure there's *anything* left alive up here?" I asked. Skorno nodded, breathing in the poisonous atmosphere like fresh country air.

"Sure, chief, they're here all right. You just can't see 'em." He nodded toward the ready Fensi crew. "We're all here, I think. What next?"

"Nothing," I choked, "until this smoke clears away. What happened to the air conditioning?"

"Greel's working on it. We had to block off some of the vents. Grid's not fine enough to keep out a Skeidzti." I looked up. The air was already beginning to clear. I gave it a few more minutes, then stepped up on a scorched sofa. I was anxious to get started so I cut it as short as possible. The idea, I explained, was to take advantage of the fact that there was a lapse, however small it might be, between the time a Skeidzti could change from one form to another. Catch them in that stage, and we had 'em. Simple as that, if it worked.

I lined the Fensi in a crude circle in the center of the room, facing outwards. Then I pulled some debris together for a shield, jerked Ollie down behind it and dimmed the lights. Dimmed them—not turned them off. The idea was to force the Skeidzti to adapt to new lighting conditions, and I was afraid if I turned them off altogether they'd sense they were safe in the absolute darkness and not adapt at all.

I gave them plenty of time, dimming the lights slowly until I could hardly tell they were on at all. Then I pressed the switch for maximum brightness and the room was flooded with brilliant light.

And there they were. They were fast, but not faster than the speed of light. For nearly a full second they stood out like ink spots on a clean white sheet, and we poured it on 'em. They were stunned perhaps a quarter-second past their normal reaction time. The Fensi are fast anyway, and that quarter-second margin was all they needed. We went through the routine three more times, then had to wait for the smoke to clear. We had killed thirty-seven Skeidzti.

Fine. But it gave me something to think about.

We had estimated there were at most fifty or sixty Skeidzti loose— and if we had killed thirty-seven on one level, in one room—how many did that mean were left? I mentioned it to Greel. He shrugged it off with typical Fensi optimism.

"What difference does it make, chief? We've got 'em on the run!"

"Sure," I said cautiously, "we've got 'em on the run *now*, all right." Both Greel and Skorno were grinning from ear to ear, having the time of their lives.

But I wasn't sure at all. Something kept asking me how long it would be before the Skeidzti caught on to the system—and whether we could come up fast enough with something to meet them. Before I left I gave explicit instructions to keep all isolation shields up—even after they were sure a room was clean. Greel gave a resigned shrug. I could tell they both thought the old man was taking the sport of Skeidzti hunting entirely too seriously.

Back in the lobby I sank into a chair and lit a cigarette. Ollie brought coffee, and we stared bleary-eyed at each other for half an hour. Ollie obviously didn't feel like talking and I was too damn tired to chew him out anymore. I could tell he was giving it to himself pretty hard anyway. That was probably doing more good than anything I could say.

Poor Ollie! If nothing else, one night of crisis at Hotel Intergalactica had rubbed off a considerable amount of shiny college exterior. His perfectly trimmed hair was caked with ceiling plaster. His neat bow tie dangled from his neck like last night's lettuce, and somehow he had managed to crack one side of his gold-rimmed glasses. He was beginning to look exactly like what he was supposed to be—a harried night clerk, who wished to hell he could remember why he had ever thought of going into the hotel business.

At 7:30 I located my army on the intercom. They had finished Eight, Nine and Ten, and were mopping up on Eleven. I told Greel to split his crew and send half up to Thirteen. We gulped the last of our coffee and headed down to Eleven.

I breathed a sigh of relief. Eleven wasn't nearly as bad as Eight. Either the Fensi had improved their marksmanship or the light trick was cutting out a lot of random shooting. Greel walked up, holstering his weapon.

"Well," I asked, "what do you think?"

"I think we just may survive the night," he said tiredly. "I'm going to try one more go-around here, then move up to Twelve."

"I have purposely been avoiding that thought," I said dryly, picturing the grinning Fensi horde blasting through my expensive lobby. "And of course," I added casually, "we haven't really *seen* any Skeidzti in the lobby, Greel. It may be that—ah—" Greel shot me a suspicious glance and I shut up. So who needs a lobby?

Greel reloaded his disruptor—a little too eagerly, I thought—and leaned against the wall.

"Actually," he said, "I don't picture it being too bad on Twelve."

"You don't, huh?" I said doubtfully.

"No, I mean it, chief. Funny thing, they were as thick as flies on Eight and Nine, but on Ten, and here on Eleven—they seem to be sort of thinning out."

I raised an eyebrow at that. "I don't suppose there could be a leaky shield, somewhere, or they might be catching on to that light trick."

"Oh, no," Greel insisted, "we're getting them all. They're just not as thick is all. I figure when they got loose on Twelve they all high-tailed it down to the lower floors for some reason, maybe to make—"

I grabbed Greel's arm and squeezed it hard. Something he had said suddenly sent a cold chill down my neck. Greel looked puzzled. I motioned him and Ollie to a quiet corner of the room, then turned to Greel.

"Did you send half your crew up to Thirteen?" I asked carefully.

Greel shrugged. "Sure, chief. You said—"

"Okay. Now think. I want to know exactly how many men you had here—*before* you split the crew."

Greel thought. "Forty-eight."

"Exactly forty-eight?"

"Exactly. I'm sure because it's the whole night shift for the Quadrant and everyone's on duty."

"Mr. Duncan," said Ollie, "what are you—"

I cut him off sharply. "Hold it, Ollie. Whatever it is can wait." I turned back to Greel. "Then if you split your crew, we should have twenty-four men in this room. Right?" Greel nodded. He started to speak, gave me a puzzled frown instead. He turned and carefully counted his crew.

"Oh, my God!" he said.

"I get thirty-six," I told him. "Ollie?" Ollie nodded, wide-eyed. I felt Greel stiffen beside me. I looked, and his hand was sliding toward his holster.

"Hold it," I said. "There's one way to make sure."

I checked on the intercom with Skorno on thirteen. Skorno counted twenty-four men. I nodded to Greel and Ollie.

▲▼▲

I had wondered what the Skeidzti would come up with to counter our move. Now I knew. They had done the only thing they could do. They had imitated the most common thing in the room, the only thing that wasn't being blasted to shreds by the disruptors: the Fensi themselves.

I walked quickly to the center of the room.

"Attention, everyone," I yelled. "Line up against the wall, quick!" I watched them carefully, getting dizzy trying to spot the phonies.

"I'm going to tell you this once," I said. "Listen, and get it right!" I told them right off that twelve of them were fakes. They caught on fast, knowing better than anyone what the Skeidzti were capable of. I wasn't worried about warning the Skeidzti. Whatever they were, they were no more intelligent than a well-trained dog.

"There is going to be some shooting," I said. "Ignore it and do exactly as I say." I paused, and Ollie and Greel drew their weapons.

"All right, first man. When I say go, walk to the lift and drop to Ten. Go!" The first Fensi walked to the lift and disappeared.

"Second man, go!"

"Third man, go!" The third Fensi walked to the lift, exactly like the first two. Only that was as far as he could go.

Ollie, Greel and I burned him before he could change.

Then it happened. The Skeidzti sensed something wrong. Eleven fakes suddenly bolted for the lift. The real Fensi ignored my order and joined the shooting. I yelled but no one could hear me.

Suddenly the whole area about the lift erupted in blinding blue flame. I shielded my face and felt a sharp pain in my side as the floor came up to meet me.

Greel was on his feet first. I shook my head and limped over to him. There was a large jagged hole in the wall and I knew right away what it was, even before I saw the tangled mass of fused wire and metal. I picked up a hunk of carpet and tossed it down the lift. Then I went limp all over.

The carpet went down the lift as smooth as any living thing. The shields were down. The Skeidzti had the run of the whole Quadrant.

Greel was giving his crew a royal chewing out. I cut him off and ordered the Fensi to Level Twelve, on the double. It was too damn late for chewing out now. We were in real trouble. I looked around for Ollie. He was gone. I cursed myself and kicked a piece of furniture halfway across the room. That's all I needed—the Skeidzti and Ollie running loose.

"Greel! Check the inner shields, see if we've still got *anything* sealed off in this place!"

"I did. So far as I can tell it's just the lift."

"That's bad enough," I said grimly. "On this side of the lift they're open to anything one room deep. And on the other side, the first guest who steps out of his room will—" Greel shook his head violently. I brightened, suddenly remembering. We had already sealed the guest side and I knew the two sides were controlled separately. Unless something else happened, we still had them sealed into the lift with access restricted to the Common Rooms, kitchens and ballrooms. They were still within the Quadrant, and away from the guests.

"All right," I said as calmly as possible, "we start over. It means maybe eighty floors of isolation, and they won't fall for that light trick again. We'll have to escort every guest through the lift and arrange for alternative dining areas. And I want every Fensi tested through a shield that's working. I don't think they'll try that again, but—"

The intercom crackled and Skorno's voice came on high and frantic.

"Chief! Listen, that crazy kid has opened the shields! He broke into Central Control and let down every barrier in the Quadrant!"

"*What!* Why in—look, it may be too late but try to get the damn things up again. Quick!"

Skorno moaned. "I can't. He's fused the controls! I can't even *find* the cutoff switch!" I felt a sharp pain in my mouth and realized I was trying to bite my tongue off. If I ever got my hands on that kid—

"Listen, Skorno, find him! I don't care what you do to him, just find him!"

"I can't figure it," moaned Greel. "He must have gone completely off his rocker."

"He had better be off his rocker," I said grimly. That's the only thing that's going to save him from me." The intercom sputtered again. Ollie. Somehow, I knew before he even spoke.

"Mr. Duncan, listen, I had to do it. I couldn't tell you because I knew you'd—"

"Listen, you little punk—" growled Greel. I frowned and shook my head.

"Ollie," I said gently, "this is Mr. Duncan. I understand. I'm not angry. Not at all. Now listen, Ollie. I know you're not feeling well. You're tired, Ollie. Tell us where you are and we'll come and get you—help you, I mean—"

"Listen," Ollie said angrily, "I'm not crazy. Now pay attention and do what I say—exactly!"

I swallowed. He was gone, all right. "Yes, Ollie. We're listening. Go ahead."

His voice relaxed. "I'm on Eighteen. The Crystal Ballroom." I swallowed again. My beautiful new ballroom.

"Come up through the loading entrance," Ollie went on. "You'll enter at Lift, ah—Forty-five, Humanoid Kitchen annex."

"Yes, Ollie. We'll do that."

"And Mr. Duncan—"

"Yes, Ollie?"

"This is not a threat, sir. But don't bring any weapons."

"Oh—" The intercom went dead. Ollie was through talking.

"Well?" said Greel.

"Well what?" I snapped. "Do *you* want to flush him out of there?"

Greel shrugged. "Lift Forty-five is this way, chief."

▲▼▲

Ollie let us into the kitchen.

The smell nearly knocked us back into the lift.

"Gahhhh! What is it, Ollie!"

"Ghayschi stew," he said. "Pretty horrible, isn't it? Here. Wear these." He tossed me a box and I quickly jammed two of the Chef's Little Wonder Air Filters into my nose and passed the box to Greel. Ghayschi stew, I thought. The kid has really flipped.

"Ollie—" Then I stopped. He was evidently not kidding. His eyes were a little too bright and his face was wet and glistening. Also, he had a disruptor in his hand.

"It's on low charge," he said, "but I don't want to knock anybody out, Mr. Duncan. I got us into this mess and I've got to get us out—my own way." He paused. "Now," he said, "will you give me a hand with this pot?" I shot him a skeptical glance.

"Why? Where are we taking it?"

Ollie tensed. "Mr. Duncan," he pleaded, "you've got to trust me!"

"Trust you! You've wrecked my hotel, let those infernal pests loose, and you—you stand there with a gun in your hand and ask me to trust you? Move the damn pot yourself!"

Ollie seemed to think a minute, then a hurt expression spread over his face. "All right," he said calmly. "If I give you the gun, will you help me? You said yourself the hotel is wrecked. Why not give me a chance?"

I took a deep breath and let it out slowly.

"Okay, Ollie. Give me the gun." Ollie handed me the disruptor. Greel started to move and I motioned him back. Ollie was right. I really had absolutely nothing to lose.

I grabbed one end of the pot.

"This way," said Ollie, shoving open the door to the ballroom.

"Here?"

Ollie nodded.

The Crystal Ballroom is new, and I'm proud of it. The floor is imported Denebian seaglass and the walls are Serinese protomurals. When the murals are on and the floor is lit, there isn't a hotel in the system that can touch it. I cringed as we set the large pot of Ghayschi stew square in the middle of the seaglass floor.

"Now what?" I asked.

"Now we get out of here. Quick." I followed him back to the kitchen. Behind him he trailed a long, thin wire. One end was attached to the top of the pot. Greel and I watched in silent wonder as he pulled the wire through the kitchen and into a tiny room off the kitchen pantry.

I knew where we were; it was the light control booth for the seaglass floor. I had shown it to Ollie several days before.

Ollie seated himself at the control board and began to play the lights. Through a small window I could see the ballroom, and the huge pot of Ghayschi stew. The floor began to glow, pulsing from gold to blue to green and back again. Ollie experimented a while, then seemed to be satisfied.

"Now," he said finally, without turning away from the controls, "we are ready."

I raised an eyebrow at Greel. Both of us were wondering just exactly what we were ready for.

"Fortunately," said Ollie, "the ballroom itself doesn't border directly onto one of the unshielded lifts. The anteroom shield is still up, though. And now—" he pressed a button by his chair— "it's down." Greel and I exchanged another look.

"Next," said Ollie suddenly, "dinnertime."

I shut my eyes. Ollie jerked his wire. The pot tipped and the gray and brown viscous mess of Ghayschi stew spread slowly across the ballroom floor.

"Now what?" I asked cautiously.

"Now we wait. I've turned on the auxiliary blowers. The smell is spreading through the Skeidzti occupied areas." I had a few choice comments on this move, but I kept them to myself. This was Ollie's party. I figured I could always strangle him later.

We waited ten minutes.

Then Ollie suddenly went into action. His hands swept over the light control board and the seaglass floor danced and pulsed with shifting colors, shifting faster and faster through the spectrum. I watched Ollie's face. His skin was tight and great beads of sweat poured from his forehead down his neck. Then the tense mask suddenly broke and a wide grin spread over his face.

"Look!" he yelled, nodding toward the floor.

I looked. At first there was nothing to see. Then I rubbed my eyes. The fast-changing lights must have affected my vision because the whole floor seemed alive with bright orange spots.

Then it hit me. *Skeidzti!* The floor around the stew was crowded three deep with them—and they were all changing back to their natural form!

We watched for an hour and a half. Finally Ollie jerked a lever and the colors faded away. He sank weakly back in his chair. I felt cold all over, and suddenly realized I was soaking wet. Later, we counted two hundred seventy-nine dead Skeidzti on the ballroom floor. It was all over.

▲▼▲

I had plenty of questions but I saved them until after breakfast. Some of it I could figure out, but I still didn't know how Ollie had been sure the Skeidzti would eat his infernal stew.

"Oh, I knew they'd like it," said Ollie. "Ghayschi stew is a favorite Stentorii dish. I looked it up. I figured the Skeidzti ate table scraps."

"That I can guess," I said. "But when they couldn't keep up with the changing lights why didn't they stop eating? Were they too stupid to know they either had to give up a meal or die?"

"No," said Ollie, "not stupid. They just couldn't help themselves. I figured any animal that could adapt so quickly and move around so fast was bound to have a pretty high metabolism. Any animal like that has to eat, oh, maybe six or eight times his weight in food every day or starve to death. They came into the hotel at 3:00. When I turned on the lights upstairs it was nearly 10:00. After seven hours they *had* to eat. There was nothing in the world that could have stopped them."

Ollie paused, sipped his coffee. "They finally adjusted to your light trick because they had no alternative stronger than survival. I used the same idea, but this time they had to make an impossible choice between two basic instincts."

"And they couldn't," I added. "So to avoid it they sort of, what—died of a nervous breakdown?"

"Something like that. In school there was this thing about some old experiments where a chicken or rat was trained to certain responses, then the responses were mixed or taken away and—"

I yawned and got up to leave. "Sure, Ollie," I said. "Let's be sure and talk about it some time." I started for the door.

"Mr. Duncan—?"

"Yes?"

"Am I fired?"

I thought a minute. I was so tired I could hardly hear him.

"No, Ollie," I said wearily. "I don't think so. There's just one thing, though."

"Sir?"

"Keep," I said sternly, "the hell out of *my* kitchens!"

A Walk on Toy

Mara was teeth-gritting mad.

There were tears, too, but mostly tears of relief—a few tears were called for, she decided, after two months in a stinking suit on a mudball planet.

She let her eyes climb the high column of the *Taegaanthe*, towering over Gara Station. Tightness welled up and caught in her throat. It was more than just a ship. It was hot food, clean clothes, safe sleep, human talk.

And it was a bath. God help that rusty can if it didn't have a good eight hours of hot water on hand!

She breathed a deep sigh and turned away from the closed hatches. Clenching her fists, she cursed whatever silent crew was aboard to the limits of her nearly unlimited vocabulary. Then she sat down again and waited...

She was used to waiting. She had waited on Earth for an Outworld ship and endured the soul-draining trip to Krishna. And she had waited for the freighter at Krishna. And waited...

The freighter was a ghost-tripper. Ninety-nine-plus percent cargo. Cabin doubling as quarters-mess-control room-lounge.

And Mara Trent-Hanse, raised in the ultraprivacy of Earth, lived eighteen inches from the pilot for twenty-two days. He was an old spacer named Haust, and he was doubly dedicated to the long, dark night, and life without "the confining burden of clothes."

A ghost-tripper towing four million miles of cargo doesn't emerge from subdrive to disembark passengers. Certainly not a passenger as uncooperative as Mara. The Trent-Hanse name meant nothing to Haust, and no name he could imagine was worth risking unaccountable megabucks in some warped envelope of space-time.

With a final friendly pinch, he loosed the escape capsule in what he hoped was the approximate orbit of Gara in real space and silently wished her luck.

Gara Station. Two months of staring through her faceplate at chlorine clouds on a flat brown horizon. Occasionally, a paddle-wheel mudder and its toad-gray crew, slapped across the dull surface, going slowly from nowhere to nowhere...

She had been patient. It wasn't that easy, now. There was something else to look at besides mudflats. There was the high needle of the *Taegaanthe*, old and ugly, scarred by the winds of time—and the most beautiful sight on Gara or any other world.

▲▼▲

When the hatch finally slid open, she caught herself—and walked leisurely toward the dark hull. Her heart pounded. Her knees were weak. And she'd be double-damned if she'd let them know it.

It was a long ten minutes before the face appeared in the small panel and the outer lock closed on Mara. Her helmet was off before the green light winked on, before the cool hiss of oxygen finished filling the chamber.

She filled her lungs and rolled her head in a lazy arc, letting the ecstasy of clean air sweep over her. Then she turned to the face in the panel. Tall, deep-featured. Heavy brows cragged over a strong nose, wide mouth, long jaw. She thought him crudely attractive except for the cold, tourmaline eyes.

The mouth opened. The voice came harshly over the speaker.

"All right—get the helmet back on."

Mara blinked. "What?"

His eyes closed patiently. "I said: Get the helmet back on. I can't spray it without you in it."

"Oh," she said, remembering. She snapped the thing back on her shoulders, flinching at the suit's smell. It was more fetid than ever after the tantalizing taste of pure air.

The germicidal spray jetted from six sides of the chamber, the hotness penetrating even through the protective insulation. Finally, fresh water washed boiling liquid away, and the man's nod signaled approval.

Mara needed little encouragement. She stripped off the heavy suit, opened a panel, and tossed suit and helmet inside. She heard the cleansing jets go to work. Then she turned back to the dark face.

He was watching, impatience pulling at the tourmaline eyes. Whatever he was waiting for, it was a mystery to Mara.

"Well—would you open *up*, please?"

His heavy brow rose, and one corner of the wide mouth lifted in amusement.

"In those?" He nodded toward the filthy coveralls.

Mara felt color rise to her face. "I intend to bathe as soon as possible," she said icily. "I won't offend you for long. But I certainly can't do anything about it in here."

He laughed heartily. "Like hell you can't! Think I'm going to let you in like that? Son of a squid, girl, we'd have to abandon ship! Hurry up, now—strip and soap. I can't stand here all day."

Mara's eyes widened. "Stand here all—look, friend. I don't intend to—to—"

The face disappeared and the panel slammed in midsentence. A tube of soapy material plopped out of the wall, and warm water bombarded her from all directions.

Mara cursed and choked, then stoically closed her mouth. One grim eye on the closed panel, she unzipped the coverall and stuffed it down the disposal. It wasn't exactly what she'd anticipated for two long months. But it was water—hot water and soap, and it was over all too quickly. She closed her eyes and stretched, standing on tiptoe, letting warm jets of air flow over her skin.

There was a sudden *chink!* of metal on metal. She froze, opened her eyes and stared. The inner lock was open. He stood there letting his eyes take the grand tour. He tossed the clean, folded coveralls and boots with a grin, and left her standing with tight, balled fists and murderous eyes.

She slipped into the things quickly, masking her embarrassment with loathing. Then she grimly crossed through the lock into the ship.

She faced him squarely. Her eyes shot sparks of anger.

He smiled easily, leaning against the bulkhead with his arms folded across his chest.

"Well, you're not half bad with all the grime off you—even for an Earthie. Heard they all had figures like ore sacks, but I can't say that fits you. I'm Gilder. Are you contracted for the night? No, course not—you don't know anyone but me, do you?"

She slapped him hard and spat out a word in the common tongue. It meant alien-tainted-debauched lecher. And more.

He grinned at her.

"On Earth," she said tightly, "I could have you *fixed* for that!"

He eyed her quizzically. "Why, it was a formal proposition, girl. N'more than common courtesy." He studied her another long moment, then jerked his head over his shoulder.

"Handel! Get your carcass in here!"

Mara turned curiously, then stiffened. She backed against the bulkhead and gripped it tightly.

The boy crept out of the corridor, naked except for thin black shorts. His body was thick with welts and heavy keloid. He had a tiny, bald head, watery eyes, and a cut for a mouth. Gilder raised his boot and slammed it hard into bare ribs.

Handel moaned and trembled against the deck. Mara blinked in disbelief, and with a scornful stare at Gilder, bent and touched the boy's bleeding side. His face met hers. Mara jerked away. She read the meaning in his eyes, knew it for what it was. Dark, passionate loathing for her. For Gilder...

The big man laughed. "He's a Painie—never see one before?" His eyes settled on her with dark amusement. "You can throw away the book here, girl. This is Outworld, and you're among Survey folk, now. It isn't Muh-ther Earth, it's Gara, Zybarr, and Deep-squeeze—an' about as far from Free City courtesy as you're likely to get."

He shook his head disdainfully. "Great Suns, what the hell are you doing out *here*, anyway?"

Mara was half listening, numb with fear and revulsion. "I'd—like to go to my quarters—*please!*"

If he'd keep silent, not speak, she might make it. And if the boy didn't look at her again...

"Handel!" Gilder kicked the boy solidly in the head. Mara leaned weakly against the bulkhead. The corridor started to swim around her.

"Handel, lead milady to her quarters, eh?" He laughed softly, and Mara stumbled down the hall following the thin, shuffling feet.

▲▼▲

Eridek awoke.

He lay on his bunk and watched the great chill drain from his limbs. The pump of his heart took hold; stilled blood began to move.

He opened his eyes and looked up at the gray ceiling. From the stillness beneath him, he judged they had landed and knew it must be Gara. He searched his senses, still feeble and unresponsive, probing for some thread that bound him from his state before the Dream and now.

A memory opened slowly, petaling to let tiny lights drift to the surface. Gara.

Gara and a girl.

What about the girl?

Something flitted by, and was gone—a fleeting patch from the fading fabric of the Dream.

Eridek shrugged, sat up, and worked the tone back into his muscles. His mouth was dry and padded. He reached a shaky hand for a tube of water, sucked hungrily at its coolness, then closed his eyes and let the whole substance of the Dream unfold like a dark bolt of heavy cloth.

He remembered...

He remembered the One who lived within the great darkness of the far nebula. For the timeless length of the Dream, Eridek had been behind that darkness and lived as another and seen things no other man might possibly imagine.

Now, until the Dream came again, the One would look out upon the things that Eridek saw—and think them almost as strange as Eridek did the other.

He stood, walked to the long mirror, and stared at his naked reflection. Tall, lean-bodied, fair skin, even features, clear eyes. It was a handsome enough face, but he knew it lacked the strength of a man to whom "strength" had meaning.

For Eridek had no need for such a thing. Strong emotions denoted conflicts and tensions, and the One who shared his soul wished no harm or corruption in its resting place.

Eridek dressed. Once more, a fleeting thought of the girl came to his mind. He shrugged the thought aside. Whatever it was, it would come soon enough. Sooner than he'd care for, certainly.

▲▼▲

Out of the room, among the familiar sounds of the ship, he found himself almost glad to be moving toward the company of others. He rounded the corner and saw the stunted figure of the boy a split second before Handel stumbled into him.

The boy whimpered. Eridek shook him off with a muttered warning. Then he saw the girl.

He glanced for a moment into dark, startled eyes, then jerked back as searing pain coursed through his skull. He doubled up, gasped for breath.

When he looked up, they were gone. The pain dissolved as quickly as it had come, but Eridek stood against the bulkhead a long moment, letting his breath return, waiting for his hands to stop shaking.

It had been a bad one. Very bad. He pushed it hurriedly into a deep recess where it would fade from black to gray and hopefully, lie dormant and unseen for awhile.

▲▼▲

He stepped into the Common and quickly scanned the three faces. He breathed a quick sigh of relief. There was nothing significant about the future of Gereen deGeis—nothing except the shallow wave of pleasure-pain that was always there.

She turned and smiled as he entered, and Eridek flinched away and let his eyes sweep briefly over Gilder Lanve-Hall, and then to Pfore, the man's alien Gantry Brother.

There was a brief shadow over Gilder, but whatever it was, it was of no immediate concern. And there was nothing at all in the quiet, gray eyes of Pfore. The slim, azure-skinned creature did not even deign to look up.

Eridek ignored them all and mixed himself a drink. From behind him, Gilder said, "Have a nice Dream, Eri?"

Eridek's hand immediately tightened around his glass. Even before he turned, he could see the contempt in the Gantryman's eyes.

Facing him, the contempt was still there, but Eridek no longer felt anger. He understood that anger too well. And the contempt, too. To erase that contempt was to erase Gilder, and the water world of Gantry, and the involved relationship of Gilder's forebears with Pfore's people.

And that, of course, he couldn't do—any more than he could change the way Gereen looked at a man, or the reason she bothered to look at all.

They sat together—Gilder, bare to the waist, drink in one hand, the other draped in easy familiarity over her shoulder. Her red hair hung in marvelous disarray, and the thin chemise revealed or covered as chance allowed.

It's a false picture, he told himself. He knew Gereen's sensuality was almost void of intent, just as Gilder's cruelty was as unstudied as a beast's. They are what they are. What they must be, he corrected.

As I must be what I am.

"Missed you, Eri," she said. She moved easily away from Gil and came toward him. "Why spend so much time by yourself, when your friends need you? Why, Eri?"

She touched his arm lightly. He smelled the closeness of her and turned away. He downed the drink quickly and made another.

Gil laughed harshly. "Sit down, Gereen. You can't compete with Eri's soulmate, for God's sake!"

Gereen frowned in mock disapproval. She leaned over a chair and cocked one eye at Eri. "Eri can't help what he is," she said softly. "Any more than you can, defiler of whales—"

Gilder laughed and choked on his drink. He reached out and pulled her to him. She landed in his lap and the silver bells on her ankles tinkled with her own high laughter.

Eridek said, "Who is the girl, Gilder?"

Gil looked up, mild annoyance beginning at the corners of his mouth. Then he seemed to sense something in Eri's voice. "What?"

"Who is she?" Eri repeated.

Gil shrugged. "From our noble captain's words, I take it she's the replacement for Hali Vickson. Why?" He grinned. "You taking an interest in new females?"

Eri ignored him. "I know she's Hali Vickson's replacement. But who is she? Where does she come from?"

Gil studied him a second before answering; Gereen looked from Gil to Eri, puzzlement crowding her face.

"She's an Earthie, no less," Gil said. "Cute little thing, too. High born and high—"

"What is it, Eri?" Gereen interrupted. Eri caught her eyes upon him. She was all seriousness, now. The wanton sparkle was gone. From the corner of the room, blue-skinned Pfore's saucer eyes blinked and opened.

"All right," Eri sighed, "I had a Telling."

Gereen paled. Her hand touched her bare throat with a life of its own.

"So. You had a Telling," Gil said too loudly. "So what?"

"Gil!" Gereen snapped.

Gilder mumbled something to himself, glanced at Eri, then turned away.

"I was in it, wasn't I, Eri?" Gereen was as white as death. "What's going to happened to me, Eri, what—"

"No!" Eri barked savagely. The girl relaxed slightly, but her fingers still wandered nervously over her body.

"If it was you, think I'd tell you?" Eri said irritably. "If you're going to get it, you're going to get it, Gereen. Don't come to me for your weight and fortune every time I have a goddamn Telling!"

Gilder clapped and laughed loudly. Eri glared at him.

"You saw Hali Vickson," she said tightly. "You knew that, and you *told* him it would happen to him—"

"No," Eri said evenly. "I didn't."

"He—said he *thought* you knew," Gereen corrected. "It's the same thing, isn't it?"

"I'm sorry I mentioned it," said Eri. He faced her and smiled lightly. "Nothing will ever happen to you, Gereen—unless you put the wrong tube in the wrong vein."

Gereen suddenly laughed. The wanton sparkle was back. "You might try it with me sometime, Eri. If the Belt *allows* that sort of thing—"

Eri shrugged wearily, knowing the uselessness of battling wits with Gereen. He felt the first two drinks, and needed the third.

"The girl, now," Gilder said quietly. "She was in your Telling, Eri."

Eri felt muscles tighten with a quick fear. He glared narrowly at the Gantryman.

Gil made a face that mirrored disgust. "Come on, Eri, cut the outraged look. Doesn't your mighty Belt know I can't listen in on *that*?"

"The Belt knows you, Gil," Eri said solemnly, "but I don't."

"What the hell is that supposed to mean?" He shrugged. "Suit yourself. It was the girl though, wasn't it?"

Eri remained silent. Gilder looked into his drink, then emptied it.

"Well, who needs Earthie girls!" Gereen laughed shrilly. Her voice was overly loud against the silence. "From what I understand..." She cupped her hand over Gil's ear and whispered. Gil laughed and pushed her away.

Gereen picked up one of the bottles and searched for a glass, then lifted the bottle itself. She whirled, a high turn that lifted the softness of the chemise, and then fell into Gilder's lap again. She squealed, tossing the bottle to Eri.

Eri caught it with a thin smile. "Right," he said softly. "Who needs her?"

And who needed Hali Vickson? And Shered of Dorbek? And Tregalon? He drank and tossed the bottle to Pfore.

Or us? he added. Who needs any of *us*?

He watched Gereen from a sad corner of his mind, and the poetry of her reached down and found a quiet, dormant segment of his soul untouched by the One—a tiny corner that still belonged to Eridek the man.

▲▼▲

He was out of sight, but Handel still crouched against the bulkhead, shaking and white. His limbs jerked uncontrollably.

"Stop that, please!" said Mara. She bit her lip nervously. "Stop it, do you hear?"

Handel's eyes rolled back in his shiny skull. "Hnnnnnnn-n-n-n—Hhnnnnn!"

Mara felt the deep emptiness begin once more in the pit of her stomach. She closed her eyes and swallowed hard.

"All right. Get up. It's over," she said calmly.

Handel raised himself to a crouch and peered cautiously between his fingers at the empty hall. Then he looked fearfully at Mara.

"Come *on*," she said firmly.

"He—go?"

It was the first time she'd heard him speak. She flinched and held back her revulsion. His voice was like the frantic thrashing of a fish out of water.

"Yes," she said. "He's gone. Who was he, and why did you—"

Handel shrank back. "He is Eridek, Lady! He wears the Belt of Aikeesh!"

Mara felt a cold chill begin at the back of her neck. "Nonsense," she said quickly, "there's—there's no such thing."

Handel shook his head dumbly. "He is no real-man, Lady! No man!"

▲▼▲

She opened the door at the light knock. The girl raised a brow at her expression, catching the slight hint of hesitation, the caution in her eyes.

Gereen smiled. "God, I don't blame you. Our dear Gilder the diplomat welcomed you aboard—right?" She laughed lightly and extended a hand. "I'm Gereen, Mara. Okay if I come in?"

Mara nodded dumbly. The sight of Gereen had shaken her for a moment. Even on Earth, where faces and figures changed with the tide to meet the quick demands of fashion, the girl would be exotically beautiful. Red hair fell lazily over ivory shoulders. Deep, green eyes gazed at her above a sculptured nose and full lips. Her mouth and the tips of her eyes were delicately touched with silver.

"Really. You mustn't pay any attention to Gil." Gereen sank gracefully into a chair.

"Oh?"

She leaned back lazily and studied Mara. "He means well, but—Gantrymen aren't particularly famous for their manners. It's the way they are."

"I—noticed." Mara smiled thinly. She felt her face color at the thought of the morning's incident. Gereen looked at her questioningly, and Mara said quickly, "I'm very anxious to meet the rest of the crew. How many are on board?"

Gereen shrugged. "Gil, you've met—and me. And there's Eri—"

That would be the one, she thought...the man in the corridor...the one who scared the boy.

"—And there's Pfore. He's Gilder's Gantry Brother. Not very sociable either, I'm afraid. But Eri, now—Eri's very nice." She laughed. "He'll talk to you without scowling. And then Handel—" She frowned distastefully. "And that's all. Oh, the captain, of course."

Mara straightened hopefully. "Yes! The captain." She leaned forward earnestly. "Should I call on him—I mean, what's the custom? Let him know I'm aboard? Is that the right thing? Or at dinner, maybe—"

An amused smile had begun to spread across Gereen's lips. It grew into a wide grin, and she threw back her head and laughed throatily.

"No, darling." She shook her head at Mara's puzzlement. "You'll see the captain, in time—but *not* at dinner. At least I hope not!"

She reached out to touch Mara's hand. "Sorry—you couldn't know, of course. Our good captain is—Q'sadiss—an alien. He doesn't eat with the crew."

She rolled her eyes to the ceiling. "Thank the gods for *that*. Sk'tai might possibly fornicate in front of the entire ship—but he certainly wouldn't share a meal with us." She smiled wryly. "And I'm sure the former couldn't possibly be as distasteful as the latter!"

"Oh," Mara said softly, "I see." She didn't, but she pushed aside the images forming in her mind.

Gereen stood up. "Anyway, welcome aboard," she said warmly. "I hope I haven't scared you off or anything. We're not a bad bunch, really." She winked broadly. "—For Outworlders, I mean."

Mara flushed. "Gereen—don't think I come equipped with a full set of Terran intolerances. We aren't all that way, you know."

Gereen looked at her a long moment, then shook her head absently. "No. Of course not. You wouldn't be here if you were. Would you?"

"No," said Mara evenly. "I wouldn't." It was easy to see that the girl didn't believe her, in spite of her easy smile.

"Anyway," said Gereen, "here. For your first dinner on the *Taegaanthe*. Unless things have changed a great deal, I *know* they don't let a girl bring many pretty things to the Rim."

She pulled a small package from a fold in her gown and pressed a silver nail against its seam. The package blossomed like a flower, spilling shimmering petals of blue across her arm.

"It's a Palaie chemise," she explained, and caught Mara's questioning look. "Don't worry. It'll fit. You don't need to flow into a Palaie—*it* flows onto *you!*"

Mara reached out and held the almost weightless garment. "It's—lovely." She smiled warmly. "Thank you, Gereen. For thinking of me. I—"

Gereen shook her head. "See you at dinner. Oh, 1900 hours, by the way, Common's just down the hall to the right." And then she was gone, and Mara decided there was at least one person aboard who thought "Earthies" weren't the intolerable pariahs of the galaxy...!

▲▼▲

Eri shook his head adamantly. "Serevan has more sense than that, Gil. Why plunder a few planets now and risk bringing the Rim in against him—when he can get his finger in the whole Outworld pie with a little patience?"

Gilder lowered his glass. His eyes flicked from Gereen deGeis, sitting across from him, to Mara Trent-Hanse at the end of the table. Yellow hair, tilted eyes and golden skin. She caught his glance, then, and turned away. Gil grinned.

"But Serevan *isn't* patient, you see?" He waved a finger at Eri. "As you say, a clever man would wait till his seat at the Council's bought and paid for; then he'd take a bite of this and a bite of that, and who's to know the difference?"

Eri nodded. "And that's what I say. He'll not risk everything now."

Gil spread his hands hopelessly. "Eri, Serevan's a *Rafpigg*—he'll try for the whole dish—and maybe choke on it."

He laughed and pushed his plate aside. "Hell's Gates, it's more likely the Rim'll sit back and let him have what he wants. If their own slice is big enough!"

Eri shook his head. Pfore shifted slightly, and his deep-azure skin caught highlights from the Common's lamps.

"Do you think, Brother, that the Outworlds will have nothing to say of this? It is of a time—"

Gil made a noise. "You think like a Sunperch, Pfore. The Outworlds have nothing to say. As usual. And nothing to say it with," he added bitterly.

"That's no longer quite true," Eri said softly.

Gil turned on him. "You're not talking about the Rim fleet, I hope?" He laughed incredulously and emptied his glass. "You think those day lilies would risk a spanking from Earth—just to help the *Outworlders*?" He shook his head darkly. "Not when it's easier to lean back and look the other way—and fill their fat pockets right along with Serevan."

Mara bit her lip. She could hardly believe her ears. Why—it was Lord Serevan himself they were talking about—as if he were a common *thief* or something!

She'd met the man several times in her uncle's home. A tall, charming man—sun-dark with full patches of silver against his temples. He'd been a planetary governor even then, several years before he was mentioned for a seat on the Council.

Listening to Serevan, actually, had finally convinced her to try for the Outworlds. He'd told of the exotic worlds with black glass mountains and wine-red seas. Worlds of mile-high forests under feathery leaves as big as a whole room in Hanse House.

And he was a Vegan, too, she reminded herself, and that made him practically Terran stock, didn't it?

Mara stopped herself. That was the way they expected her to think, wasn't it? And she was showing them how right they were...

All right, so it might take a while to shake an "Earthie's" scorn for the Outworlds. But—by damn, she'd do it—in spite of Gilder Lanve-Hall or a captain who couldn't eat with his crew!

"Mara," laughed Gereen, "have you left us, dear?"

Mara looked up quickly. "Oh. No, I—" She brought a hand nervously to the top of her chemise. "I'm sorry." She smiled around the table. "Thinking, I guess."

Gilder smiled amusedly. "Serevan hit too close to home, Lady?"

Mara flushed. "He—" She bit off her words and smiled politely. "You're entitled to your opinion of the Lord Serevan. And I imagine you might get a—different point of view in the Outworlds. But I'm sorry. I can't agree with you at all."

"Why?" Gil leaned forward intently, hands folded under his chin. "Because he's a Vegan? Or because I say he's an out-and-out planet stealer? Or both, maybe?"

Mara frowned thoughtfully. "Do you mean am I prejudiced because he's a Vegan? Probably, to be honest. That's not unexpected, is it? After all," she smiled, "you are prejudiced because he *is* one. Aren't you?"

"I detest him because he's a thief," Gil said simply. "He takes things that belong to other people."

Mara shook her head firmly. "I don't believe that. I believe he wants to see the Outworlds develop and grow—and not for himself, either. For the eventual benefit of the people of the Outworlds."

Gilder slapped his hand against the table and threw back his head in a raucous laugh.

"*Eventual benefit*, is it?" He glanced around the table. "Now there is a real Earthie for you, my friends. Be good children. Go find us some lovely worlds—preferably with a lot of fine metals on 'em. And some sweet-smelling spices and maybe a new furry animal, something that we can cuddle and love but that doesn't *bite*. And—be sure it doesn't live too long, 'cause we tire easily of our toys here on Earth!"

"You're rather good at clichés," Mara said coolly, "and over-simplifications. It's easy to leave out the parts you don't like, isn't it?"

Gil leaned forward. She could almost feel the heat of his hatred.

"You really want to hear the parts I don't like? Try this one: If you find a world that's not too nice a place to live—a little too hot or cold, or full of things that don't take to humans, why—that's easy enough. *Just don't be human any more!"*

He shook his head sadly. "Don't you know how it was out here? Truly? Didn't they tell you at home—or have the history books taken care of that? If a world doesn't suit you, they told us—change to suit the world. Grow a tail or a pair of horns or a set of fine gills." He laughed.

"Gilder," said Eri.

Gil ignored him. "Look, Lady, you see?" He reached up and pulled his shirt away from his throat. Mara felt her heart pound against her chest. Pink, open slits pulsed on either side of his throat from below his chin to the base of his collarbone.

"Gil, Gill, Gilder," he smiled. "You see—Gantry didn't exactly have any *land* to settle on—but it had a lot of fine, high-grade ore on her sea bottoms. Ore that Mother Earth wanted." He looked around the table. Eri, Gereen and Pfore were staring into their glasses.

"As I say—if the world's not right—change to fit the world. And in six or eight generations, we'll let you *keep* a little of that ore for yourselves. But not too much. And none at all, if an Earthie pet like Serevan comes along and gets it first!"

"It's—not like that," Mara said numbly. "It's not like that at all."

Gil stood. He poured a glass of wine and toasted her grimly. "You're a hothouse flower, girl," he said harshly. "Come out in the fields and see how all the *weeds* are growin'!"

Mara got to her feet shakily. "Excuse me...please," she muttered and fled from the room quickly...

▲▼▲

She sat on the edge of her bed, knees held tightly together, hands pressed against her sides.

It's not like that at all, she told herself.

She made herself say it. Again and again.

And if she said it enough, she knew she could make it true. She straightened suddenly. *Make* it true? Do I have to *make* it true? Don't I believe it? Or do I think Gilder is right?

Certainly, Earth's a wealthy planet. No one ever said it wasn't. And why shouldn't it be? Earth sent out the ships that found the worlds, and it was Earth's children who tamed them.

Then why did these people think of themselves as "Outworlders"— people who didn't belong to Earth at all, who despised and hated their mother world with a paranoid passion?

All right, she told herself grimly. Turn it around. *Try* to see it the way they do.

They don't really know Earth. They're third, fourth, fifth generation—born nowhere near the hills of New Frisco, or Roma or Atlanta Complex. Home is Gantry, Hellfire, Styryxx and Lone. And—are they still children of Earth?

She wondered. When the body changed, what happened to the soul, the psyche, the inner man that was really what a man was. Did it change, too—become something else?

Certainly there would be changes in a man born on a water world like Gantry—a man who had no dry-land heritage to remember.

She realized, suddenly, that it wasn't really a question of whether or not the Outworlders were children of Earth. They were not. They were children of their own worlds. What was she asking, then?

Not whether or not they're children of Earth...but whether they are still men...

And she knew the hatred, the murderous image of Earth came from something deeper than that. It came from the real or imagined belief that Earth had cast its one-time children aside, turned them into something not quite human to be used and exploited to fatten a few billion distant cousins on a world they'd never see.

And that was the thing she would never let herself believe. If that were true, it meant that men like Serevan carried an unspeakable guilt upon their shoulders. And more than that. It meant that the Families of Earth, who ruled the commerce of the stars, bore an even greater guilt. Families, she reminded herself, such as the House of Trent-Hanse...

▲▼▲

Something was wrong with the Palaie chemise.

The pressfold she'd used to mold the gown about her was gone. The almost invisible seam should have fallen away with the slightest touch. It didn't. The more she searched and pulled, the tighter the garment wrapped itself around her.

Mara sighed and bit her lip in frustration. Gereen, maybe, could show her—

No. She'd sleep in the damn thing before she'd ask for help.

She crossed the cabin irritably and poured a glass of the pale white wine on the table. Of all the ridiculous—

Mara stiffened. The glass fell from her fingers and shattered on the floor.

She stood perfectly still. She refused to let herself believe what was happening. There was some other explanation, some—

A chill rose along her back and touched the fine hairs at the base of her neck. Something moved. Lightly, softly up the side of her leg, smoothly over her thigh, warmly past her stomach to her breasts.

Mara gasped. She tore at the gown, trying desperately to rip it from her. At her touch, the dress responded fiercely. It caressed her with a wild, burning intensity. She threw herself against the wall, grabbed sharp scissors from the table, and cut at the thing with all her strength. The dress tightened about her. She cried out and the scissors jerked from her hand.

Then the word touched her mind with a sudden shock of horror. *Stimdress!* It was no Palaie chemise at all, and Gereen had known exactly what it was.

Sickness welled up into her throat and gagged her with a sour, burning taste. She realized what Gereen had in mind. And only because Mara had left the Common when she did…

She screamed, strained for breath. She felt her grip on the wall give way as the thing tore her away and pulled her to her knees, forced her to the floor. Its living hands throbbed across her body, and she had no more strength to cry, to scream, to move.

She silently cursed Gereen in one sane corner of her mind. *Bitch!* she yelled. *Alien-tainted bitch! Damn you…damn all of you!*

▲▼▲

Murky water roiled on the surface of the tank, and Pfore turned over in warm silt and smiled to himself.

A picture wavered, then crystallized in his mind. Handel. Thin limbs pressed against a hard surface. Metal? A roundness. Tunnel. Pipe.

The boy was in the ventilator shaft on the port side. The shaft ran by the engine room and then past stores and over the cabins.

Handel's vision was sliced by thin, vertical bars of blackness. Pfore recognized the blackness as the grids that looked down upon Gereen's room.

Beyond the grid, through Handel's eyes, Pfore saw the delicate blue tracery of veins against ivory flesh, the cold glint of shiny needles, and the serpentine coil of bright red tubing.

And on the wetness of Gereen's lips and the azure shadows of her closed eyes—Peace. Hate. Agony. Love.

Pfore read the thoughts in Handel's mind. They crawled over his consciousness like scuttering, mindless insects—tiny creatures who lived and died in quick seconds of unfulfilled intensity.

Pfore smiled. The image of Handel wavered, changed. Handel lengthened and swelled, and his eyes bulged into milky globes. His sleek, scaled body raced fearfully into the depths. Pfore circled silently above, his body cutting the green waters, his eyes on the frantic creature below.

The Sritafish jerked in and out of high coral castles. It knew that the blue thing above was a Hunter and that unless it found cover its life was measured in seconds.

Gills throbbed, and the pink membranes within shivered in fear. The fear grew, and the long body trembled in a flash of silver scales. No! Movement would only help the blue Hunter find him, would only—

The blue Hunter struck. Its impact drove razor teeth into the Sritafish's spine. The teeth snapped, and in a blinding second of pain it was over.

Handel screamed…

▲▼▲

The blue Hunter rolled lazily away. His stomach was full, the taste of blood-prey still tart upon his lips. Then the gray shadow loomed dangerously before him. The Hunter blinked, startled.

Gilder laughed. "He who dreams of the Sritafish had best keep an eye out for the shark, Brother!"

"There are no Sritafish here. Only filthy vermin in the ventilators."

"We will hunt the warm seas again. Soon."

"Will we, Brother?"

"Yes!" Gilder projected an angry, foam-flecked wave. It crashed against jagged red coral in splintering fingers of blue. Pfore caught the blue splinters, froze them into cold points of light, tossed them against blackness.

"You see? We swim in a dark and airless sea, Brother."

"It is necessary, now."

"Is it?"

"The airless sea holds our enemies, Pfore. Would you fight them here, or wait until they foul the waters of Gantry?"

"They already foul those waters. The herds were thin less than a two-period ago. What must they be like now?"

Gilder was silent.

"They want it all, Brother. It is as you say. There will be nothing but scraps left for the Gantrymen. And now there is even an Earthie in our midst. What is she here for? What does she want? Do the Terrans fear we will hide the Survey worlds from them? I do not like her here."

"I do not like her presence either. But she is here, Brother. She brought herself."

Pfore sighed and laughed lightly. "Ah, Gilder, I hear your words. But—does your Egg Brother see what you are blind to see?"

He lifted the image gently from Gil's mind. Golden hair. Wide, dark eyes. The fragile, slender figure…

Gilder scoffed. He brought high winds and salt spray and the fronts of sea trees together and superimposed them over the slim picture of Mara. Mara disappeared under a tall, full-breasted Gantrywoman with slate-blue eyes and dark hair flecked with spray.

"You paint fine pictures," Pfore said drolly. "If you wish, we shall pretend your Egg Brother was born upon the morning tide, and does not know a Pirishell from his breakfast."

Pfore turned over in his tank and Gilder lashed out angrily. His thoughts met only the dark shield of sleep…

▲▼▲

The hovercraft hummed high above yellow fields marbled with a dark tracery of stone. Mara leaned out and let the afternoon sun fall full upon her face, then pulled her head back into the cabin.

"What did you call it? Psi? Psi as in old Greek?" She fluffed her thick hair into place.

Eri shook his head grimly. "No. Scythe. S-C-Y-T-H-E. As in slash, cut, slit, kill."

"Oh." Mara sank back in silence.

Eri looked at her. "We named it that after we left," he explained.

Mara turned to him questioningly. "The—ship's been here before?"

"Six months ago. This is where we lost your predecessor." He moved his head in a vague, downward direction. "Hali Vickson caught it over there—near that darkest ridge."

Mara looked. She could see nothing, but the sight of the low line of black rock gave her an uneasy shudder.

"There's an ecological shift going on here that's got 'em jumping back at Center," he said. "We've got a couple of snoopers planted around, but a snooper won't always catch what a man does. We have to come and take a look for ourselves now and then."

Eri turned the hovercraft in an easy curve, pressing Mara against the narrow hatch. "That yellow stuff that looks like dead wheat is dormant Sabregrass. The grass is what got Hali. He knew all about it. Had it neatly catalogued away. Slides, pictures, seed spores, growth patterns—the works. He had three weeks down there and plenty of research time in the ship. He never went out without body armor. So we got ready to leave, and Hali had to have one more look—something about a possible connection between a wide band of this and a short band of that. And that's when the Sabregrass got him."

Eri frowned darkly. "That's when something always gets you," he added, almost to himself. "When it's all over and you turn around and walk away from it, and it knows you're finished and not really watching any more."

He turned, suddenly, and stared at her with open puzzlement. "What are you doing out here, Mara? What do you want with us?"

There was anger in his voice—a deep, harsh resentment only partially masked by his even tones.

And that, thought Mara, was all that really made the difference between Eri and Gilder. Eri still wore the veneer of a few superficial niceties. Gilder no longer bothered, or never had. He wore his hatred like a banner.

She'd hoped Eri might prove to be different. Whether he wore the Belt, as Handel said, or not—he seemed less divorced from humanity than the others.

She had had little to do with either Gilder or Gereen since the incident at dinner, and the episode with the Stimdress. Both events still lingered like a dull horror in the back of her mind.

And that left Eri. Well, so the door was shut there, too.

"Is it so hard to believe," she answered him, "that I could just *be* here, Eri? Because I want to be?"

Eri shrugged. He kept his eyes on the low horizon. "Mara, you talk as if it's an everyday thing to see an Earthie—a Terran, working in the Outworlds." He smiled dully. "We don't want to be here. Don't you know that? What do you expect us to think about you?"

She turned away. "Maybe," she said evenly, "I just expect to be accepted for what I am. That's asking too much, isn't it?"

"Probably," he said frankly.

She gave a bitter little laugh and shook her head. "Well, anyway, *all* the prejudice doesn't begin on Earth, I see."

"It's a waste of time to talk about such things," he said flatly. "Gilder tried to tell you about the Outworlds. You didn't believe him."

"I think the Outworlder's picture of Earth is probably no more accurate than Earth's view of the Outworld."

"That's hardly an answer."

"It is, though. How can I know the Outworlds unless I see them? And you. And Gilder and Gereen. Have any of you ever really *been* to

Earth? Do you know what it's like? Or do you just think what you want to think because it's convenient?"

Eri jerked around. "Have I ever been—" He threw back his head and laughed. "You don't really know, do you?"

Mara frowned. "Know what?"

"Outworlders *can't* go to Earth. We're not allowed there. We're quarantined—fenced off. Keep the freaks out of sight so they won't upset the good citizens!"

"That's not true, Eri—now you sound like Gilder. I've *seen* Outworlders on Earth."

"You've seen what they wanted you to see. A few bought and paid-for flunkies. Showcase Outworlders from Vega or Alpha C. No more Outworlders than you are. But they make a hell of a lot better appearance than some wart-hided dwarf from Rigo."

Eri looked at her. "Settlement policies were different in the beginning. When there were plenty of Earth-type worlds to go around, there was no need to bother with the Vulcans and Zeros. But the planets past the Rim weren't as easy to live on as Paradise and Dale. Heavy gravity, hard radiation, too hot, too cold—or worse.

"But the Outworlds had something most of the First Colony planets didn't. They were rich in the things desperately needed on Earth. Remember what Gilder said? If the planet's not right—change to fit the planet. He's right. Do you think Earth intended to let those worlds *go*—just because they weren't fit to live on?" He shook his head bitterly.

"Eri," Mara protested, "I know about the Adapters. No one forced the colonists to—change. They did it because they *wanted* those worlds!"

Eri laughed. He swung the hovercraft in a smooth arc that took them past sawtooth peaks and out over another broad expanse of bright-tipped Sabregrass.

"That's the textbook answer," he said. He spat out the words harshly. "Didn't they teach you in school where those colonists came from? Did you think they were bright-eyed pioneers, eager to conquer new worlds?"

He shook his head. "The people who submitted to the Adapters were misfits—throwaways. Ring War veterans too battered to work in the new cities. And women caught in first-wave radiation who didn't stand a chance of getting genetic clearance on Earth. But they could have their bodies altered for four-g living on Gelerax! And, hell, they were likely to breed monsters anyway—why not breed *useful* monsters?"

"Aren't you exaggerating, Eri?" she said reasonably. "There are always some—undesirables among colonists. But I won't believe that the Outworlds were settled solely by Ring War vets and GX women!"

"Those undesirables you're talking about are my esteemed ancestors," he said dryly.

"I didn't mean—"

"I know. You didn't mean anything. You're an Earthie. You think like an Earthie thinks. Why shouldn't you? You've never been told anything different."

Eri shrugged bitterly. "No, I'm the one who's naïve, Mara—not you. Eridek of Colmier VI explains the Outworlds to the daughter of the Hanse House!" He laughed and locked himself in silence.

▲▼▲

The hovercraft circled over the high, flat mesa, then turned into the wind to settle a hundred yards from the orange dome.

Eri jumped down without looking back. He walked quickly away through a veil of rising heat. Mara watched him a few moments, then grimly opened the hatch and stepped into a wave of stifling air.

"Anything?" Eri asked.

Gil looked up. He was bare to the waist, sweat streaming from his neck and shoulders in small rivulets. He squatted before the dome and glared suspiciously at a green wave dancing palely about in the shaded scope.

"Something," he muttered darkly. "Don't know what the hell to call it, though." He looked up sourly at Eri. "Doesn't make sense. Pfore's down at Two Mile. There's no indication of any pulse like that on his side. That means the thing's localized—whatever it is—something's happening on my scope that's not happening on his. And that, friend, is impossible."

Eri frowned. "No malfunctions, I suppose."

Gilder made a noise. "No. Equipment's okay. What it means is that the organic life of Scythe is undergoing a dramatic change. Basically, it's centered about the Sabregrass, but everything's played a part, you can bet on that. Now. Suppose you tell me why it's happening all over the planet, except in a 300-square-mile area over there?"

He spat disgustedly on the sandy ground. "I even changed meters with Pfore, just to make—"

Gilder stopped. He squinted past his scope, out over the broad mesa. He cursed silently, and his eyes moved up to Eri.

"What's she doing here?"

Eri shrugged. "She wasn't doing anything on the ship. I thought maybe she could make herself useful. As long as she's here," he added.

"And just what the hell did you figure she'd *do*, Eri? To make herself 'useful?'"

Eri held Gilder's gaze. The Gantryman's shoulders hung loose, relaxed, but his eyes smoldered with barely controllable anger.

"Take her back. Now."

"Any particular reason—or just a Gantryman's privilege?"

Gilder darkened. The narrow, pink slits in his throat fluttered nervously.

Eri let himself smile. "As you say, Gil." Gilder didn't like the smile, he knew. Eri turned and stalked away toward the hovercraft.

"Eri—"

Eri stopped and looked back.

"She doesn't belong here. She's got no business running around on Scythe."

Eri spread his hands. "Gil, she's got no business on the ship—but she's there. You didn't send for her and neither did I. Survey qualified her. Do we use her or don't we?"

Gilder's lips suddenly split into a wide grin.

"Goddamn, Eri—use her for what? What do you do with an Earthie girl on a Survey ship?" His blue eyes sparkled with amusement. "Any suggestions?"

"That's your department," Eri said blankly. "Not mine." He brushed moisture from his brow and turned away.

Before he turned, his eyes caught Gilder, and Gilder was looking past him, at the girl. The amusement was gone. There was something else there. Eri couldn't say what it was.

▲▼▲

Mara swallowed hard. She wondered whether anything as alien as Captain Sk'tai could possibly read a human expression. If he can, she thought, I'm in trouble already.

The bridge of the *Taegaanthe* was a hemisphere amidships, a smooth concavity bristling with multicolored lights and studded with pearl-gray buttons.

The greater part of the circle was filled with Captain Sk'tai himself. To Mara, standing behind the guard rail directly above, he seemed like a gigantic leather butterfly constantly emerging and retreating in its cocoon. A bewildering assortment of appendages brushed out to touch against the pearly buttons and flashing lights.

"Mara Trent-Hanse, is it?"

Mara started, as the human-sounding voice boomed all about her.

"Yes—sir," she said.

The captain chuckled. "Beauty. Such a beauty. A flower of Old Earth in our midst. Wonders never cease, as they say."

Mara flushed.

"Been to Earth—or close to it, anyway. New Phoenix? Reykjavik Station? That surprise you?"

"Yes, sir. A little."

"It's not stranger than *you* being *here*, though. I guess you've heard that already."

"Several have—mentioned it, yes," Mara said tightly.

"And—?"

"I didn't expect a welcome-aboard party. I knew the Outworlder attitude toward Earth."

"But you came anyway."

"I did."

"Why?"

"Because I don't like to hear how something's supposed to be. I don't care to read about places or look at pretty pictures. And I've never cared a great deal about other people's opinions. In other words, I wanted to see the Outworlds myself."

"—And Outworlders," the captain added, with only a thinly veiled amusement.

"Yes," said Mara. "And Outworlders."

The captain sighed. The noise was like the wind from a great bellows.

"Well, you passed the tests at some Survey School or other—or you wouldn't be here. Either that or you have considerable pull. Which is not unlikely with a name like Trent-Hanse."

Mara took a deep breath. "I was in High Range at Remoga. I can perform my duties." *If you and the others will let me,* she said to herself.

"Remoga, eh? And they trained you in—"

"I'm a Speaker, Captain. First Class," she added tightly.

Captain Sk'tai seemed to hesitate. "A—Speaker?" Some part of the great bulk below seemed to shake its head incredulously.

Mara filled her lungs and launched into a partial double debate in High Treecoosh, stopped suddenly and gave him a sample of the impossibly complex Yaraday chittering, a smattering of Erebist, and finally, the ritual blessing of his own tongue—as unlikely a combination of sounds as she could imagine.

"Glory!" Sk'tai gasped. "I wouldn't have believed it!" He laughed soundly. "You speak with a northern tinge, know that? My own island, too—or near enough."

"I can give you the eastern ridge dialect if you prefer," she said calmly.

"Enough—I'm convinced."

"I was two years in surgical implant—three under hyp. I hope," she said dryly, "I can mumble a few languages."

"I sense more than a little bitterness—and in your own language, too," he said questioningly.

Mara laughed nervously. "Really, Captain? I can't imagine—"

"Look," he said, and his voice took on a firmer note. "You'd do well to face some realities. And you'd do well to face them now, I think."

Mara's hands tightened on the railing. She swallowed hard and with a great effort of will, made herself speak without any hint of a tremor in her voice.

"I—have faced little else *but* realities, Captain. From the moment I stepped on board, realities have been served to me three times a day—"

She clenched her fists and felt the control drop away from her voice. "I am sick to death of—Outworld realities!"

The captain was silent a long moment. The leathery cocoon below fluttered, then stilled.

"You came to us, remember? No one asked for you."

"No. They didn't. But what is it I've done that—"

"—That makes them despise you?" he finished. "Simple. You've brought out the love-hate in Gilder. The sado-envy in Gereen deGeis. The oh-so-thinly buried Dream psychosis in Eri."

Sk'tai sighed. "Not because of what you do—simply because you're here. You remind them too much of things they would rather not remember.

"You're a backward child, Mara Trent-Hanse. From a backward world. Oh, the Terrans are clever and ruthless, when they want to be, and *that's* often enough. But in the Outworlds an Earthie's a crawling infant—no more than that. And you're a most dangerous infant to have around, I think, because you carry seeds of destruction within you—and they all see that! And miserable creatures though they be, none want that destruction!"

"I don't want to destroy anyone!" Mara said hopelessly. "I want to *learn!*"

But she knew that learning had nothing at all to do with what he was saying.

"I can," she repeated lamely. "I can—if you'll let me."

"You can die," he said simply, "and perhaps destroy. I see nothing more that you can do aboard the *Taegaanthe.*"

Mara's heart stopped. "*Die!*" She shook her head in open-mouthed refusal. "I came here *to learn to live*, Captain!"

"Living isn't enough in the Outworlds. Don't you see? Can't you realize that is what they sense in you? *Survive* is the only word they've ever known out here. To *live* is what an Earthie does!

"You think Gilder a barbarian. A man with no more than lust and murder on his mind. He's much of that, granted. But more, too. Gilder and his Egg Mate were born on a world where trust meant death and murder meant another day of life.

"And Eri. Five hundred years ago his ancestors landed on Jaare, a world no more made for man than—than my own. The seeds of the Dreamers were already on Jaare when Eri's people got there. To stay, they accepted the Dreamer spore, and became more than men—and less.

"Gereen deGeis had the blood drained from her veins the day she was born on Tyson's world. To face what they found there, Tyson's people had to match the planet's eccentricities with their own. And so Gereen's drug cycle hands her a new metabolism twice a day—but she lives."

The captain sighed. "I know nothing of Handel, or how he comes to be what he is. We found him on Gellahell, more dead than alive. We saved him, and of course he hates us all for that. There's no way to say where he comes from, but you can bet it's a world where pain's the same as survival.

"Now tell me, Mara Trent-Hanse," he said gently, "tell me how it is they'll learn to—*accept you for what you are?*" He laughed hollowly. "That's the sad joke, you see? What you are is the one thing they can never accept!"

"I see no joke," she cried, "no joke at all—"

"There's more to it than you know, though," he told her. "The Q'saddis have some rare traits, Mara—I'm more than what you see slithering around below—I'm anything I want to be. Whatever I see, whatever crawls or flies or bounces about. Can you see the joke in that? I can taste your beauty, Mara, and desire you, too. You look at me with loathing, and you can do no more, being what you are. But *I'm* not the exotic creature aboard the *Taegaanthe*—it's your human-appearing companions *who are the real aliens here*...Do you see? Do you see what you've brought yourself into?"

Mara turned with a low, stifled cry and ran blindly down the corridor. She shut her door behind her, backed stiffly against it, and stared straight ahead at nothing.

▲▼▲

"No," Gilder said flatly. He cursed under his breath and gripped the railing tightly.

Captain Sk'tai ignored him. "She will go with you," he said. "She's being paid to work; so she'll work. If the sensors are correct about C-71 there'll be a use for her."

Gilder was silent.

"You dislike her so much," Sk'tai said finally, "that you'd rather do without a talent you may need."

Gilder's mouth twisted into a frown. "I don't like or dislike the girl," he said irritably. "I have a job to do. My Brother and I can't do that job— and keep our Earthie from falling in a goddamn hole or something at the same time."

The captain chuckled.

"You know how Pfore and I work," Gil protested. "You tell me how she fits!"

"She goes with you, Gilder," the captain said patiently.

"If you think Pfore and I can't handle this—"

"I think nothing." The captain's patient tone had taken on a sharper edge. "I think Center sent us a Speaker, and who knows the ways of Center, or questions their reasons? It may be they had C-71 in mind."

"There's no one to talk to on C-71," Gil muttered.

"No, but there *were* beings there, were there not?" The captain sighed. "Gilder," he said wearily, "let us not pursue this. I give not one of your damns for your feelings about the girl. She is here. She is a Speaker. There is a most peculiar world awaiting you down there. It may be that she can shed some light upon its peculiarities."

"It may be that she can get us all killed," Gil muttered darkly.

▲▼▲

Gil stood on the gentle hill and eyed his surroundings with narrow suspicion. The rise beneath him was a perfect quarter-sphere covered with neatly clipped grass. At the base of the hill, shorter grass abruptly gave way to another variety that was one unit higher and one shade darker.

Exactly one unit.

Exactly one shade.

He squinted out across the narrow horizon. The darker grass continued for a thousand units, then gave way again to the lighter variety. The light grass climbed a hill that was a duplicate of the one beneath his boots...

It was as if a planet of overzealous gardeners had finished their work just that morning, cleaned their tools, and vanished into the ground.

Into the ground—or somewhere, Gil frowned scornfully. And when? Yesterday? A thousand years ago? Six months?

Only the former inhabitants of C-71 could answer that, and they had neglected to give word.

Gil reached down and ripped up a large handful of grass. It was a peculiarly pleasant sensation, and he allowed himself a half smile. Seconds ago there had been order and perfection. Now, one blemish scarred a small circle on the top of one hill in one quadrant of a perfect world.

He watched. Somewhere below, he knew, frantic signals pulsed out from the torn root system. A nutrient booster was even now flowing up to bathe and heal the damaged area.

Gil shook his head grimly as the blades began to quiver. Within thirty seconds, the new crop was entrenched. It stopped growing at the precise unit height of its mates.

He turned away and walked the few steps back to the dome. A tall whip aerial flashed from the silver console by the entry. To one side, Mara puttered with a collapsible table and chairs. He smelled the aroma of food from the small cook unit, grunted to himself, and passed her without looking up.

"Well," she said behind him, "what do you think of Toy?"

Gil stopped, one arm still crooked like a wing in his jacket. He squinted back over his shoulder, then faced her.

"What do I think of—*what?*"

Her half-expectant smile faded quickly. She looked away nervously and inspected the cook unit.

"I—thought it was rather appropriate," she snapped. "That's all. If you don't like it, for God's sake call it C-71!"

Gilder bristled. "Girl, look at me!"

Mara's eyes rose patiently.

"I don't care *what* you call this world," he said darkly. "It's what you're thinking that bothers me." He glared at her disdainfully. "Don't you understand? That kind of thing doesn't belong out here. It leads to carelessness, is what it does, and I'll not put up with carelessness where *my* hide's involved!"

He spat contemptuously at the close-cropped grass. "You're right. The name's appropriate—too damned appropriate as far as I'm concerned. An' when you start associating those cute little trees and phony hills with some Earthie fairy tale, you might as well shoot yourself full of sarazine and sit down and wait for it, 'cause you're as good as dead already!"

Suddenly, his eyes widened, and he jerked away. "Mara, behind you!"

She twisted aside and threw herself into a half crouch, clawing for the sidearm at her belt.

There was nothing at all behind her. She turned and flashed him an angry stare.

"Like I say," he said somberly, facing her, "start thinking of this place as 'Toy,' and the next thing you know, you've forgotten all about Survey rules and set your pistol for a goddamn cook unit!"

Mara flushed. Gil reached down and picked up the gold-barreled weapon, made a show of opening it and meticulously checking the charge. Then he jammed the pistol back into its holster and tossed it to her roughly.

"Put it on," he said flatly. *"Don't* take it off."

Mara gritted her teeth and said nothing. She buckled on the pistol and rolled the cook unit back into the dome and walked to the edge of the hill.

If there was a hidden menace on Toy, she decided grimly, it was probably the menace of monotony. An entire planet of precise lawns and duplicate hills. And cities, too. They'd flown over half a dozen that morning. Tiny squares of whiteness from the air—each exactly like the other. Each mathematically equidistant from the rest.

Mara shook her head. Could you ever really understand such a world? Divorce yourself from humanity and see Toy through alien eyes?

She remembered a lean, star-burned man, a teacher at Survey who looked twenty years older than he was. He had lost his arms at Stinger and had definite ideas on staying alive in the Outworlds.

"...There's one thing we can't teach you here—you'll learn it in the field or you won't. Forget where you came from. Forget who you are. Think and reason in alien terms, not your own. Assimilate every aspect of your surroundings and never turn your back on a strange world. It's not easy—but it's the only way a Survey man keeps alive..."

That was the answer, then. You learned. Or you died. And Mara wrapped her arms about her shoulders as a sudden chill struck her atop the low hill.

She *couldn't* think that way. She was Mara Trent-Hanse from Earth, and she could never become an Outworlder. And that meant Gil, Sk'tai and all the others were right.

I'm lonely again, she thought. I'm as lonely here as I was on Earth. I didn't belong there, and I'm not a part of the Outworlds, either.

Where am I supposed to be?

▲▼▲

Toy's sun dropped behind perfect hills, and Mara spotted the small figure on the broad green plain below. She turned away and walked wearily back to the dome. Gilder sat over the dark, enameled box whose slow-moving needle recorded some mysterious segment of Toy's inner workings.

"Pfore's coming back," she said absently.

Gil frowned. He didn't look up. "Yes, I know."

"Oh," she said, "well, of course you do." She knew immediately that he'd taken her words in a different way than she'd meant them.

"You don't like him, do you?" He glanced away from the snail-pace tape and grinned at her with amusement.

Mara tightened. "Don't, Gilder," she said calmly. "Please. Don't start something. I meant that you would know Pfore's coming before I did for the simple reason that you can—talk to him. You can. I can't. I forgot. It's no more than that—not unless *you* want to make something out of something that's not there. If you do, go ahead. Just don't include me!" she added hotly.

She turned and walked stiffly to her own segment of the dome.

▲▼▲

"Greetings, seducer of mighty whales. What kept you?"

"What do you mean, what kept me?"

"I couldn't raise you," Pfore said idly. "I supposed you were deeply involved in some important project." He presented a lurid image of what he imagined that project to be.

Gil made a mental noise. "It's for certain you haven't been watching too closely, Mudfish, or you'd not come up with rubbish like that."

"No need to watch, Brother," Pfore said wryly. "I can read the purple tones of frustration a mile away."

Gilder's thoughts turned to ice. Pfore felt them, and backed away.

"There are times when you imagine too much, Brother."

"Perhaps," said Pfore. "After all, what does an Egg Mate know?" Then, he broke contact quickly, before Gilder could retaliate.

▲▼▲

Gereen made a wide sweep above the three small figures. Their presence on the green plain appeared as bright pulses of life on her screens. Behind them was the ever-present static of C-71's star, and the broader, darker wave that said there was a substantial amount of electronic and mechanical activity going on under the planet's surface.

The energy was fairly low and constant beneath the grassy lawns and low hills—higher under the cities. She expected that. The support systems under a living center *should* be more complex than the ones bringing food and water to plants.

The screens told Gereen a great deal about C-71's cities. The motionless blue lines said power—the lighter, nervous spiderwebs of aqua showed how that power was being used.

She was fascinated by the intricate patterns of energy. The automated facilities must be filling the cities' needs at a near capacity rate. Each area, she guessed, was turning out enough goods and services to support several million inhabitants—inhabitants who no longer required the systems' capabilities.

What happened to those things the planet produced? Cycled back to raw materials, probably, she thought. Made, destroyed, and made again.

Life support for millions—and only three pulses of life on her screen—Gilder, Pfore and the Earthie. And in the distance, the white, too-perfect city...

▲▼▲

Eri watched duplicates of Gereen's screens in the dark Commpad of the *Taegaanthe*, circling C-71 a thousand miles away. He saw, and understood, the broad socio/geo structure painted by glowing lines and waves, but noted them only vaguely in one corner of his mind.

Something bigger worried at the edge of Eri's consciousness. So far, it was only an itch, an uncomfortable feeling. But it was moving about in the darkness, trying to shape itself into something real.

Eri knew what it was. The One who shared his soul saw something in Eri's universe that interested, stimulated, or disturbed its being...

▲▼▲

Captain Sk'tai held the image of the Survey Team on C-71 in some facet of his mind. Other facets noted the hull temperature of the *Taegaanthe*, the ship's speed, altitude, orbital path, and the fact that one and a quarter liters of coolant per tenday were leaking from the aft gally refrigeration system.

Three aspects of his being played an incomprehensible mathematical game with each other. He noted that one of those aspects was attempting to cheat the other.

▲▼▲

Handel slept, and dreamed of white mice with razor-chrome teeth...

▲▼▲

From the top of the last hill she looked down upon the city. Perfect, windowless white buildings set in a grillwork of even streets. A game board, she thought. A game with all the pieces set up shining and new, and all the players gone.

The outer perimeter began with neat, uniform structures four stories high. From there they progressed in symmetrical ascensions to a central, fifty-story tower. She decided it looked all the more like an alien chessboard—a giant, insane chessboard with all the pawns, knights and queens on the same side...

▲▼▲

"We should be back in two hours," Gil told her. "We won't go too far in on this first trek. It's just a look-see."

Mara shook her head. "Who's *we*, Gilder?"

He frowned, pretending not to understand. "Why, Pfore and I." He grinned foolishly. "Well, damn me—did you think you were goin' in with us?"

Mara set her jaw tightly. "And why not?"

Gilder shrugged and exchanged a quick look with Pfore. "Someone's got to mind the store," he muttered.

"You've got Gereen for that," she reminded him. "In the hovercraft."

"Gereen," he corrected, "and you." He turned to his Gantry Brother, and they lifted light packs and started off down the hill.

"You're afraid something will happen to me," she said.

Gilder stopped. He turned, and an incredulous frown spread across his features. "Where in hell did you get an idea like that? What I'm afraid of is you'll get *me* killed—with some damn foolishness."

He chuckled disdainfully. "Course, there's not much to worry about, is there? Here on 'Toy,' I mean."

Mara ignored him. She lifted her own pack and adjusted it to her shoulders. His brows rose in the beginning of refusal.

"I'm going, Gilder," she said quietly.

Mara felt strangely apart from herself—as if her mouth opened, while someone else she didn't quite know formed the words.

Gil studied her with no expression at all, then moved down the hill.

▲▼▲

Mara glanced at Pfore out of the corner of her eye. His blue skin glistened like soft rubber in the sunlight. The flat, even features of his face reminded her of the bare beginnings of a sculptor's head—clay smooth and wetted for tomorrow's work.

He's never spoken to me, she realized suddenly. He's never once spoken or even looked in my direction since I've been aboard the *Taegaanthe*. I'm not even here.

She turned away and let her eyes touch the walls of the city. The pale slabs rose all around her—untouched, unblemished. Ahead, the black surface of the street disappeared under points of diminishing whiteness. There wasn't a mote of dust under her feet. Not a twig or a scrap of paper or a blade of grass.

Only what we've brought with us, she thought, and looked back at the three dull sets of footprints behind her.

She could hear her own breath magnified against the silence. The soft rustle of her clothing was a harsh, noisy intrusion.

Pfore shifted and Mara followed his glance. Gilder ducked and walked out of one of the low doors. He blinked in the sunlight.

"Nothing new," he said somberly. "It's exactly like the others. God!" He shook his head in wonder. "Apartments. Maybe a couple of million of 'em—an' every one the same, down to the last nit-picking detail."

He glanced meaningfully at Pfore. "I took some check measurements. There's something that looks like a bed in each place, and next to it there's a stool. There's not so much as a millimeter's difference between the way the stool sits from the bed in any room in this whole kookin' city."

"Irrational," said Pfore.

"Not really," said Mara. "Not from their point of view, anyway."

They both glanced at her blankly, as if they'd forgotten she was there.

"What," Gil asked impatiently. "What's that, now?"

"I said the creatures who built this, and all of C-71 for that matter—probably thought this was the most *rational* world possible. It's—well, order, carried to the highest possible degree, isn't it?"

Gil laughed lightly. His mouth twisted into a slight grin. "I think we can all look around us and see the evidence of order, Mara."

She flushed at his tone. "Then it's not an irrational world!"

"It is to me," he shrugged.

"To you, Gil?" She raised a brow. "Really? I would have imagined that an experienced Survey man is capable of *projecting himself into the problem*."

His ice-cold eyes fell on her a full second before his laughter echoed through the empty streets.

"I've seen it all, now, by the Stars—an Earthie quotin' Survey rules!" He walked off, slapping Pfore on the back, and Mara followed silently.

▲▼▲

They turned a corner and came upon it suddenly; none of them expecting anything except the monotonous regularity of the streets and buildings.

Gilder gave a low whistle. He stopped, muttering something under his breath Mara couldn't hear.

The statue stood under a high arch atop a square column. Beyond, there was a tantalizing glimpse of a broad plaza and long walls covered with signs and symbols. But for the moment, none of them could take their eyes off the statue.

"Swine," Gil said almost to himself. "By God, swine standin' up on two legs."

"No." Mara shook her head. "*Mock* swine. What swine shouldn't be."

Gil looked at her. "What?"

"She is right," Pfore said, and Gil frowned and shaded his eyes at the statue again.

"Yeah," he bit his lip thoughtfully, "yeah, I guess so." He gave her a peculiar, appraising glance, as if he'd found himself suddenly agreeing with her and wasn't sure how to handle the new feeling.

Mara couldn't take her eyes from the squat, ugly figure. In hard stone, she saw only soft, yielding flesh and dark-pit eyes. Her mind reeled dizzily. Pig eyes. Little pig eyes just a step away from—*people* eyes.

Her heart pounded and the breath caught in her throat. Why? Why are they swine and not swine at all…?

It's not right—not right at all…and I don't want to *be* here—not on Toy or Scythe or anyplace else I don't belong and don't understand.

▲▼▲

"Mara?"

She blinked, looked down with puzzlement at Gil's hand under her arm.

"What, Gil? What?"

"You all right, now?"

She looked up into the tourmaline eyes. Cold, a moment ago, and now—what? Concern? Was there concern there for a brief second?

She laughed to herself. Whatever it was, it was gone as quickly as it had come—if anything had been there at all.

▲▼▲

The long, high walls rose nearly a hundred feet above the square. Light clouds moved against a pale sky and gave the illusion that the walls were leaning slowly in upon them.

"It's a script of some kind," Mara said. "But—the alternating rows are pictographs." She nodded excitedly. "Gilder, I'm almost certain. The pictographs tell the story of the words above them."

He looked at her doubtfully. "Can you read it?"

She frowned at the high wall and tapped one fingernail against her chin. "I don't know. It's not exactly my line, but—a Speaker picks up a certain feel for this kind of thing. Let's see…"

She moved off slowly down the wall. Gil and Pfore followed.

"There was at one…period, *enclosed*…yes! A segment of time, then. Has to be that. At one time there was…see the little figures all—different?" She pointed. "And then that's negated very strongly on the right, to show the same figures—only in order, this time."

"At one time," she read slowly, "there was disorder, then came—whatever it is; I think it's the symbol for their race. Then came blank and there was order and—rightness…"

A cold shiver swept over her at the thought. She turned to Gilder.

"They're saying everything was 'out of order' at one time, and they came and made everything right. That—things can't be as they should be until there's no conflict. Until—*sameness* makes the ugliness of difference go away."

"A hive culture," Gil said grimly.

Pfore nodded. "But not a natural hive," he pointed out. "They picked up hive aspects along the way. They didn't start out like this."

"I wonder," Mara said almost to herself, "how it—*did* begin?"

▲▼▲

The question plagued her.

Why? she asked herself. Is it because I know and they don't—that Toy reminds me too much of Earth?

Earth never came close to Toy, she knew. But the pattern was there. In the sameness of people, the sameness of cities. In the way an overcrowded culture moved toward the—what? The dangerous security of identity?

No conflict...make the ugliness of difference go away...

To be alike was to be without fear. And we almost made it—when the billions begat billions and there was no more room for persons. Only for people. Numbers. Inhabitants of the hive.

But it didn't happen on Earth. It didn't happen on Earth, she realized suddenly, *because the Outworlds bought our freedom...*

Mara stopped—almost staggered with the weight of realization. It was true, wasn't it? There was no way to make it go away. The explosion to the stars gave Earth a wealth they'd never imagined. And more than that. Much more. The precious room to breathe...

And wasn't this, really, what the Outworlds hated?

Not because we sent them to the stars and changed them—made them more, and sometimes less, than human...

...But because we threw them away. Because we made them change so we could stay the same.

▲▼▲

It happened quickly.

At the other end of the square, Gilder and Pfore were setting up the photo-recorders against the waning light. The squat machines glittered and whirred as they scanned the enigmatic walls of Toy.

Mara walked distractedly along the edge of the broad plaza. Her mind was light-years away, her eyes on the even blocks beneath her boots.

She looked up suddenly, blinking in surprise, to find she'd turned the far corner of the wall without even thinking where she was going. And then she saw the rows of bare white booths.

They were faced in thin sheets of milky glass, and she thought, idly, that it was odd they'd seen no glass besides this anywhere in the city, and maybe it wasn't glass at all, but a kind of plastic...

...And even as she walked the few steps to touch the cold surface, the thought brushed against her mind that she might be an Earthie, but she was also a qualified member of the *Taegaanthe*'s Survey Team, in spite of what anyone said, and the alternate moment to this one flashed before her, where she backed away and called Gilder and didn't touch the glass at all...

▲▼▲

Gereen's eyes widened and she tensed and leaned forward, her hands automatically seeking knobs for adjustment as a new kind of wave pulsed wildly across her screens...

▲▼▲

Eri screamed as bright hooks of pain tore at his soul.

His fists smashed through the Commpad's monitor and came away bloody. His body jerked uncontrollably, flailing itself against steel walls in painful, erratic arcs. Finally, when the One who shared his being gained control of muscles and tendons that had already pulled themselves through awful convolutions, Eri sank to the floor and curled up silently, arms folded across his chest, knees tight against his chin...

▲▼▲

Captain Sk'tai blinked an aspect of consciousness into being, and with the flexibility of his kind, experienced awareness, from a new and unfamiliar viewpoint...

▲▼▲

In Handel's dream, the beautiful white rats with razor-chrome teeth came delightfully closer...

▲▼▲

Gilder was running before the high, short scream echoed and died across the plaza. He turned the wall, body low and angled to the smallest silhouette, pistol tight against the butt of his palm and thrust out before him.

He saw the brief flicker of movement as the milky panel whispered shut upon itself, and he knew. In a cold, frozen instant he knew all there was to know about the silent booths, and he put all his hate and anger and horror into his heavy boot and smashed the panel into a million white shards.

And of course she was gone, just as he knew she would be.

▲▼▲

"*Cover!*" He shot the mental command to Pfore, and Pfore moved. Gil bent low and melted the base of the booth until slag and steel hissed in poison clouds and forced him away.

"Too late, Brother—!"

"Shut up!"

"I can see, Gil."

"Probe, Pfore!"

"Too late—"

"No!"

"Gilder—"

"Deeper, Brother—deeper, damn you!"

Pfore sobbed—sent out deep mental fingers and reeled back in agony. Gil caught him roughly, gripped his arm tightly.

"Pfore," he said aloud. "Pfore, once more. *I* can't go there—if I could—"

"They want me, Gil," Pfore said numbly, "and you—and all of us. They want us all."

"There's nothing *down* there!" Gil said savagely. "Machines, Brother, nothing more!"

"Gilder—"

Gil's teeth locked and he tasted blood. "Get—her—*out*, Pfore!" He held Pfore in a steel grip. "Get—her—"

He saw it as it came around the far corner of the wall. His mind cried out and he cursed himself and wondered why he couldn't have known—with the grass, the hills and the city—why hadn't he seen this, too, because it was the logical thing to see and the final goddamn insanity of sameness...

There was the ugliness of difference, and then there was order...

And Gilder knew they'd finally achieved it on Toy. The booths were the last answer, and there were no more answers after that, and no more questions or conflicts or disorder...Only mirror-image citizens on a mirror-image world, and a statue to mock their madness.

▲▼▲

It came around the wall and waddled toward him uncertainly on drunken pig legs. He saw the fish-belly flesh and the dark-pit eyes, and when the mouth tried to gasp itself into his name, he shut out the picture of a girl with dark hair on a green hill, and he squeezed the trigger and held it until there was nothing more of her to see.

And then he dropped the pistol and leaned against the high wall and retched...

▲▼▲

They had been sitting in the Common, and he hadn't spoken for a long time, and Gereen said, "You're thinking about the Earthie girl, Gilder."

And Gilder said, "I'm not thinking about anything at all."

"It was a long time ago, Gil."

She said nothing for a long moment, then, "She didn't belong, you know that, don't you? It's not the same as Eri on Tristadel or Ramy Hines on Butcher. They knew what to expect and it could have been you or me, don't you see? It's not the same, Gil. She didn't *belong*."

For the first time in his life, Gilder felt the faint whisperings of fear, and he wondered if this was the way it had begun for Hali Vickson and Mara Trent-Hanse and Eri and Ramy and all the rest.

First the fear, then the sudden, chilling loneliness.

And finally, the knowledge that no one ever truly belonged—that you only really belonged to the last world that claimed you...

The Flying Stutzman

Angela always told him at the door, "Lew, you look like a dead person. You didn't sleep on the plane?" And he always said, "No I didn't sleep on the plane, I *can't* sleep on the plane, Angela." Angela wanted to know why and Stutzman didn't know. Ten years on the road, eleven in September, could he remember even a minute sleeping on the plane? "You should try, Lew," she told him. "You should try and get some sleep. You look like a dead person." I *feel* like a dead person, he wanted to tell her.

Stutzman squinted out the little round window. Flat banks of perfectly white clouds covered the earth. He liked to look at clouds. You could look at a cloud all day and not think about anything. Once when he got home he told Angela, "Nobody ever hurt his head, looking at a cloud."

It was maybe the one good thing about flying. The rest was a nothing. And he could give up the clouds, easy. You like clouds, get a picture and put it in the den and look at clouds. An airplane you don't need to see a cloud.

The fat lady in the next seat ate oranges. She had a whole sack of oranges in a little net bag like you get in the store. She would peel an orange and drop the peelings in the pocket on the back of the seat, which was already stuffed to the top. A nice surprise, thought Stutzman, for Miss Stuck-Up the stewardess, who had time, all right, to twitch her ass for Mr. Joe College in the back but no time to get coffee for Stutzman. Fine. She should get a handful of oranges.

Stutzman closed his eyes and thought about being home. He thought quickly past the baggage-limo-taxi part and on to Angela. She would meet him at the door. Maybe she'd wear the evening pajamas he liked, the Halston number, which was a hand-painted three-piece, yellow petals on a silk chiffon and ran about nine-hundred fifty bucks retail. She'd be fresh from the beauty shop with black curls around her face and a little green eyeshadow. A good wife, and a good-looking woman still, thought Stutzman. His family had shaken their heads and told him you marry a girl with Italian blood, she'll go to fat, Lew. But Angela could stand up to any of them. So a little padding around the thighs and tummy, now. What was a fifty-two-year-old woman supposed to look like, a Las Vegas cutie? A chorus girl with pink feathers on her tits, she's going to stay home and fix supper for Stutzman? She could still get in a 12, which was more than you could say for Miss Stuck-Up.

She'd have a little drink ready and then a meal he'd be too tired to eat, but he'd take a few bites to please her. And then they'd go to bed and watch *The Tonight Show* and maybe something nice would happen. Or maybe it wouldn't. Sometimes the miles caught up with him the first night back.

He could never tell Angela, because she wouldn't understand. The best part of getting home wasn't Angela. It was just *getting* there. Peeling off your clothes and dropping in the hot tub and washing off the trip. How could you get so dirty, just flying? You're not looking, they got people sneak around and put soot in your clothes? He'd tried to tell her once about that: "Look, you pack and get out to the airport and get on the plane, okay? Take a shower and a shave and you got your clothes all clean and packed and you get on the plane. So it goes down the runway and they decide to come back, maybe. A wheel's bad or something. You go six blocks on the runway and they come back and you get off and go home. Everything you got on, it's dirty. You need a shave, you smell like an animal in the zoo. Everything in the bag, you didn't even wear it, that's dirty too. Why? I don't know why. Maybe they got girls in a room somewhere, they put dirt in the ticket."

There was that, thought Stutzman, and the pockets. Start out with a wallet and a pencil and take a one-day and back, you got pockets that look like goiters. A million dollars in nickels hanging to your knees, you bought cigarettes and a Snickers. You got maybe a hundred matches from everywhere. A one-day from Dallas to Houston, you see a customer and come home, you got enough matches and change to fill a truck.

The plane banked and fell into clouds and Miss Stuck-Up said she was glad they'd all gotten to fly together and maybe they could do it again sometime. You should get a pocket full of peelings, thought Stutzman.

▲▼▲

People cluttered about the end of the carpeted tunnel, but Stutzman didn't look up. Nobody was waiting for him, and he moved quickly past them to baggage. He didn't look up even when he heard his name. Then he did look up, and there was Bernie Freed. Stutzman frowned at him like he'd never seen him before. "Bernie. What are you doing at the airport?"

Bernie laughed and pumped his hand. "The airport is where the planes come in. What I'm doing is waiting for Stutzman."

"What for?" A terrible thought crossed his mind. "Angela. Something's happened to Angela."

"Nothing has happened to Angela," Bernie assured him. They were making an island in the stream of traffic, and Bernie moved them to a wall.

"Something has happened," said Stutzman. "Don't tell me nothing has happened." Thirty years, he could read Bernie Freed.

"Okay. So something's happened." Bernie looked up at him. He had to look up to see Stutzman. Stutzman wasn't tall but Bernie was short. A short, jumpy little terrier in a blue blazer, houndstooth pants and white turtleneck. The pencil-thin mustache twitched under water-blue eyes.

"I gotta ask a favor, Lew. Christ, you're gonna hate me. But I gotta ask."

"What?" Stutzman said warily. "You gotta ask what?"

"It's a trip."

"A trip? What kind of a trip? You mean like flying? When?" He already knew when, because Bernie hadn't *said* when.

Bernie didn't answer. He slid back his cuff and darted a glance at his gold Piguet. "Look, we're shorta time. We better move while we talk." He grabbed Stutzman's elbow and guided him toward the escalator. He was looking at everything in the airport. He wasn't looking at Stutzman.

"Bernie. You're not looking at me. Just tell me what it is, okay? And look at me. Where are we going? I got bags back there."

"Lew, the bags are okay."

"How are they okay? Tell me. I'm not there and the bags are okay."

Bernie led him down the escalator into the hot air and through a glass door under the terminal. It was a small, concrete room where you could catch the boxy little Air-trans cars from one airline to another, when the system was working.

It wasn't getting any better and Stutzman didn't like it. "Bernie. Stop a minute. Just stop and talk to me."

Bernie looked at his watch again. Glass doors slid open and one of the cars clacked to a stop. Bernie pushed Stutzman in and the doors hissed together.

"*Ber*nie—"

Bernie's mustache twitched. "Lew, it's Neuman."

Stutzman looked blank. "Neuman? So what about Neuman?"

"He's gone crazy or something." Bernie spread his hands in despair. "I don't know him anymore. Twenty years, I don't even *know* him. What happens to people?"

"I don't know what happens to people," Stutzman said patiently. "What's happened to Neuman?"

Bernie's eyes went hard. "He is killing me, is what. He's losing the line everywhere, and it'll take a hundred years to get it back. A hundred? A hundred fifty is closer. Neuman is fucking everything on the east coast. Models, buyers, secretaries—goddamn *poodles* he's fucking. Mostly, he is fucking me. Can you believe? He tries to screw the Saks buyer. Right in her own office. They can't get him *out* of there, he's crying." Bernie looked at the ceiling. "Crying. Can you believe it? Everybody's canceling. I call New York and nobody'll talk to me. Bloomingdale's doesn't know me. Bergdorf is maybe burning our line in the street."

"Neuman is fifty-seven," said Stutzman. "He's got a family."

Bernie glared at him. "He's a hundred and two, what's that? He's killing me!"

The car bobbed to a halt and Bernie stopped talking. A girl got on. She was young, twenty or so, with long straight hair faded yellow in the sun. Small breasts and a lanky figure. Patched jeans and something Stutzman decided were shower clogs. She dropped a green backpack on the floor and took out a paperback and started reading. Stutzman saw the name on the front and made a face. Herman Hesse. Great. Now we got Nazi hippies flying around the country.

"What I got to do," Bernie was telling him, "is straighten this thing out or we're dead. You see where I am, right? I *hate* to do it to you, Lew. Honest to God. I know you been gone a couple weeks. I been on the road, I know how it is."

"Three."

"What?"

"Three weeks. I been gone three weeks. And why me, anyway, Bernie? I'm a salesman. Send a vice-president or something. Send Marvin or Harry." Go yourself, he didn't say.

"Lew." Bernie looked pained. "Marvin and Harry don't know from selling. I got to send someone they'll respect. They know you. You got a name in the business."

Stutzman turned in his seat and looked right at him. "Bernie, where are we? Right now. Just tell me where we are right now."

Bernie looked bewildered. "Lew. You know where we are."

"No, I mean it. What city? Where is this, Bernie? I want you to tell me."

"Lew. It's Dallas. You know where it is. What're you trying to do to me?"

"Dallas." Stutzman nodded. "Okay, I am very pleased to hear that. It's a big load off my mind. Because you know what, Bernie? Sometimes

I been out a week maybe and I'm sitting in a motel somewhere, I got to stop and try to figure where I am. I think maybe—okay, this is Atlanta, because it's Wednesday. Only maybe it's not. Maybe I got behind a day and it's Raleigh or Nashville or Charlotte or somewhere. If I watch the TV, I can wait until a program's over and maybe they'll give the town, you know? So I get home once in a while, and you know what? Nothing looks right. It doesn't even smell like a Holiday Inn or a Ramada or any-place I ever been. I look in the bathroom and I think, what kind of place is this? The glasses aren't wrapped. They don't even have a little paper thing over the pot—which is wrong anyway because the seat's white instead of black. I go around feeling pictures. They aren't screwed in the walls. Nothing's right. And you know why? I'm *home* is why, and I feel like I broke in a house or something."

The girl looked up over her book at him. Stutzman came right out of his seat and shook a finger in her face. "Just get right back in your dirty book, Miss Dope Smoker," he shouted. "This doesn't concern you!" The girl shrugged and looked away.

"Jesus, Lew." Bernie shook his head. The car came to a stop and he led Stutzman out. "I never heard you talk like this before."

"Maybe I never did before."

"I feel like a son of a bitch."

"Good," said Stutzman, "that's something." At the top of the escalator he stopped. "So where am I going, Bernie? What am I supposed to do? You got the bags coming? Great. I'm leaving town, I got two bags full of dirty shirts and smelly underwear."

"Forget it." Bernie waved him off. He handed over a heavy envelope. "I got all the stuff here. Names, you know most of them. Tell 'em every-thing's gonna be fine; we're sorry about Neuman, the lousy bastard; we'll give them discounts on top of discounts, whatever. Throw away your goddamn clothes. Get a whole fucking wardrobe. I don't care. *Fix* it, Lew. Okay? I'll never forget it."

"Okay, Bernie."

"No, I mean it." He clutched Stutzman's elbow. "I'll make up for it."

"I got to call Angela. I don't know what the hell I'll tell her, but I got to say something."

He got an angry busy signal and waited a minute and called again. She was still on the phone. He waited and called again, then glumly set the phone back on its hook. He looked at his ticket to see where he was going. New York. On Braniff. Bernie was hopping around from one foot to the other by the gate, like he needed to pee. Stutzman stared morose-ly out the broad windows. Planes in Braniff's varied colors squatted around the big half loop. Wonderful. So I'll ride a yellow banana to New York. Or maybe an apple or a lettuce. He looked past the planes at the hot summer sky. "Listen, God," he said darkly, "I never said a bad thing about You anytime—so what's the big deal on Stutzman? I don't *need* this trip, and You know it. What I need is a hot bath and a bed. You could make him get someone else easy if You wanted to. You could do it now, I'm still at the airport."

Stutzman waited. Nothing happened.

"Okay. You're pissed off at Stutzman, I'm telling You something. You like it nor not, Stutzman is plenty pissed off at You…"

▲▼▲

On the flight he took his attaché case into the cramped restroom and shaved and brushed his teeth and took his shirt off enough to spray under his arms. That didn't make the shirt clean or the underwear either. He had an extra pair of socks in the case but no underwear. He sat on the toilet and changed the socks. The old ones smelled awful. He hated to put them back in the case. He thought about it a minute and then did something he'd never done before. He wadded them up and tossed them in with the paper towels. That made him feel a lot better. Bernie Freed could spring for new socks. Bernie could spring for new everything. He would go to a place he knew in New York and buy wholesale and charge Bernie the retail price and maybe a little on top. Let him scream about it if he wanted to. He didn't like it, he could send one of his nephew vice-presidents to do his dirty work. That'd serve him right, too. He could see Marvin and Harry in Saks and Lord & Taylor and Jordan Marsh. Bernie'd be lucky if he didn't lose the whole east coast.

The more he thought about it, the madder he got. What the hell was he doing here? On another damn airplane to New York? He was a salesman and a good one. This year he'd pull in maybe sixty-five, seventy thousand in commissions. It wasn't his job to clean up after Bernie Freed. So if it wasn't, what was he doing here?

Someone knocked on the door. He muttered to himself and tossed his toothbrush and toothpaste back in the attaché and snapped it shut and opened the door. It was the hippie girl in the jeans. "Listen, you smoke up the place with heroin in there, I'll have you arrested," he told her.

"Fuck you," said the girl.

▲▼▲

Stutzman spent two days in New York, mending the company's fences. Bernie hadn't exaggerated about Neuman. Neuman had clearly gone bananas. He had run up and down the eastern seaboard with his pants down. People in the business stopped him on the street. What's with Neuman, they wanted to know? What could happen to such a man, Stutzman wondered? A man with a family and responsibilities? One minute he's okay, the next he's acting like a crazy. He felt sorry for Neuman and his family. But he felt even sorrier for himself. He was unhappy about being in New York, and to make matters worse, he caught a cold the first day in the city. No—when he stepped off the *plane* he got a cold. It was waiting for him there, ready to hop off someone else into his nose. And when he left for Philadelphia, he took the cold with him. He took it to Baltimore and Washington. He took it to Hartford and Boston. When he talked to Angela she said he should get more sleep on the plane and keep his health up. In Richmond he thought about calling Bernie and telling him he could send someone else up to catch diseases. Who needed a trip to catch a cold? You could do it at home and save the money. Only Bernie would think it was a trick of some kind. He would be certain Stutzman had gotten the cold on purpose. Like you could go into Gimbel's maybe and buy a cold.

▲▼▲

When he was on the road, Stutzman never counted days or cities. Through years of traveling he had developed the ability to ignore the little counter in his head that kept track of things like that. It was there but he wouldn't look at it. Not until the last day in the last city. Then he would open his black appointment book and take out his pen and mark through all the cities and stores and dates at once. Somehow, that made it easier. Like the trip had only taken that long. Just the time it took to scratch them out.

On the last day in Miami he called Angela and told her he was coming, and then he sat on the edge of his bed at the motel and took out his book and crossed off the list. He crossed off New York and Philadelphia and Baltimore and Washington. He crossed off Hartford and Boston and Richmond. Charlotte and Roanoke and Miami. He crossed off American and Piedmont and Eastern. He closed the book and put it away. Then he took it out and looked at it again.

Now that's peculiar, he thought. In his head he quickly checked the places he'd been and the people he'd seen. Then he did it again and put the book down on the bed and got up and looked at himself in the mirror.

Something was wrong somewhere. For the life of him, he couldn't remember being in either Roanoke or Boston. All the others fell into place, but those two were a blank. He couldn't remember a store or a face. He sat and tried for a long time, but nothing happened. Finally, he turned back to his meeting notes and found them, along with where they'd gone to lunch and how much the taxis cost and where he spent the night. Seeing the notes pushed everything back in place again. But he couldn't forget it had *happened*. Was he a crazy, like Neuman? Maybe that's how it started. You forget where you've been, next minute you're chasing a poodle.

What it was was the goddamn trip, he told himself wearily. One right on top of the other with nothing in between. You couldn't push a man forever. He had to stop, sometime. Well, Lew Stutzman sure as hell had a stop coming, and Bernie Freed and all his nephews wouldn't get him on the road again soon. He'd take the phone out and lock Angela in the bedroom. Maybe they'd do some things you weren't supposed to if you were over fifty and a respectable person. Why not? If hippies could do any kind of dirty stuff they wanted right out in front of everyone, couldn't a man be a crazy in his own bedroom?

▲▼▲

Usually Stutzman stayed in his seat when he couldn't get a non-stop and the plane set down somewhere. In Atlanta, though, they were going to be on the ground for maybe half an hour while something got fixed—he didn't know what, and Miss Smartmouth the stewardess wasn't saying.

He was tired and stiff. If he got up, the time would pass. He took his attaché with him. The girls weren't supposed to touch anything, but who could know what they did when you weren't looking?

By the time he walked up the long tunnel and got cigarettes and a *Newsweek* it was time to get back. He showed his ticket at the gate and strapped himself in and buried his head in the *Newsweek*. There was a story on the economy, which was bad. Such a big surprise, thought Stutzman. Everything was still in turmoil in the Middle East, God should curse the Arabs, and food was up again. He closed the magazine and stuffed it in the seat pocket and glanced out the window. The ground was dropping away and the light was off. He reached for a cigarette and found orange and blue Howard Johnson's matches in his pocket and opened the ashtray and lit a match. He looked at the match a minute and then blew it out. Now *that* was funny. He hadn't noticed it before, but the seat in front of him was the wrong color. It wasn't the way it *had* been before he got off the plane. How could that be? Maybe he was in the wrong seat. He looked up and across the aisle. That wasn't it, either. *All* the seats were the wrong color. Stutzman leaned out and peered up the long aisle. His heart jumped up in his throat. It wasn't even the same kind of stewardess—the uniforms were different!

Stutzman moaned. He felt suddenly weak all over. For Christ's sake, he was on the *wrong* airplane! He'd gotten off and gotten on again on the wrong goddamn plane!

He felt like a complete idiot. How could you *do* a thing like that? He waved frantically until the girl saw him and came briskly down the aisle.

"Yes, sir?"

"Look," Stutzman cleared his throat, "I'm not a crazy or anything, so don't think something. This isn't a Delta, is it? I'm not on an airplane with a Delta."

The girl smiled. "This is Southern, sir. To St. Louis."

"St. *Louis*!" Stutzman was furious. "I'm not flying a Southern—I'm flying a Delta to Dallas!"

The smile didn't change. "May I see your ticket, sir?"

Stutzman fumbled through his coat, cursing to himself, and handed it to her. She looked at it, and then held it up and showed it to Stutzman. Stutzman was appalled. It didn't say Delta on the folder. It said Southern. She opened it up and took out the ticket.

"You're Mister—" she looked down, "—Stutzman?"

"I'm Stutzman, I'm Stutzman."

She closed the packet and handed it back to him. "Your ticket's in order, Mr. Stutzman."

"What do you mean in order!" shouted Stutzman.

"You *are* on the right plane, sir." She opened it up and showed it to him. "Atlanta. Southern to St. Louis."

Stutzman stared at the ticket. Was he going crazy? There was his name. Lew Stutzman. To St. Louis. There wasn't anything about Dallas.

"There's a mistake. I'm not going to St. Louis. I got nothing to do in St. Louis."

"Sir, could you see our agent in St. Louis? I'm sure he can clear things up for you. I'm terribly sorry for the inconvenience." She gave him a look he didn't like and trotted back up the aisle.

Stutzman leaned back and tried to relax. How could such a thing happen? What had they done, switched tickets on him? When, though? The ticket was fine in Miami. Atlanta, then. When he got off the plane. Maybe he took the ticket out somewhere. When he got the *Newsweek* and the cigarettes. He tried to think. Maybe there was another Stutzman. Was the other Stutzman on his way back to Dallas? That didn't make any sense at all. The whole thing gave him a headache.

He lit a cigarette and tried to read the *Newsweek*. After he'd scanned the same paragraph half a dozen times, he wadded up the magazine and jammed it angrily into the seat pocket. Goddamn airlines. He was dead certain, now, what had made Neuman a crazy...

▲▼▲

In St. Louis the man at Southern said he was sorry for whatever it was that had happened and directed him to Ozark. He got an Ozark to Dallas and waited for flight time and got in line at the gate. He wanted to phone Angela and tell her what had happened, but he decided not to. Just get there. Just get on the goddamn plane and get home.

The man in front of him moved away, and Stutzman got out his ticket for the agent. The agent took it. Stutzman grabbed it back. The sign above the counter didn't say Ozark. It said TWA. What was he doing at TWA!

"Your ticket, sir?"

"No." Stutzman shook his head. "I'm in the wrong place." What was the *matter* with him? Was he really losing his mind—trying to get on the wrong plane *again*?

The agent took his ticket and smiled. "No, sir. Everything's fine." He tore out a page and picked up a boarding pass. "Smoking or no smoking?"

"Smoking," Stutzman said dully. He looked at the agent in horror. What was he saying that for? He wasn't even *going* on TWA! He jerked back the ticket and stepped out of line, peering down the long corridor for Ozark. There wasn't a sign anywhere. He'd have to go back to the terminal and work his way back and maybe miss the flight. Shit. He'd be stuck forever in St. Louis.

Stutzman put his ticket in his pocket and started back up the corridor. Only he didn't. He started back in his head, but nothing happened. He was thinking all the things you were supposed to think to get moving, but he didn't. He wanted to go. But he couldn't. Nothing worked. All he could do was stand there and look where he wanted to go.

Stutzman had never been so frightened in his life. His heart slammed painfully against his chest. He was hot all over. He could smell the sweat under his arms. I'm dying, he decided. God in Heaven, I'm having a coronary. I'm having a coronary right here in the terminal in St. Louis, and I don't even *know* anyone in St. Louis.

How could he do that, he wondered. Who ever had a coronary standing up? You fell on the floor and turned blue, maybe. You didn't freeze like a pillar of salt in an airport!

He tried to move again—and gave a big sigh of relief. Whatever it was went away, and he was all right again. His feet were moving like feet were supposed to. He was going.

Only *where* was he going? He stared down helplessly, his heart beating fast again, as his traitorous legs turned him around and walked him past the counter and through the waiting room and onto the TWA that wasn't going to Dallas.

Stutzman sat rigid in his seat, afraid to move. He looked down at the dark landscape and back at his ticket. How could it say that? It should read Stutzman to Dallas on Ozark—not Stutzman to Denver on TWA. Why was he going to Denver? What was happening to him? What had they *done* to him!

When they put the tray of food in his lap, he sat and looked at it until the girl took it away. When it was gone, he couldn't even remember what had been on it.

Stutzman knew he had to stay calm. Whatever it was, it was something he could handle. If he was having a breakdown, he'd see someone. There was no disgrace in it. You could get a problem in your head, without being a crazy.

The more he thought about it, though, the more it frightened him. He wanted a drink badly but settled for coffee. Right now, he couldn't afford to screw up his head any more than it was already.

At Denver he ran all the way down the terminal. He was out of breath and sweating all over. He tried to light a cigarette but his hands were shaking and he dropped the match. Okay, he told himself. Just calm down and take it easy, Stutzman. Just do it right this time and get home and get to bed. There were Braniff flights to Dallas every hour. He got a ticket and studied it carefully. It was fine. It was exactly like it was supposed to be. It didn't say Stutzman to somewhere he didn't want to go. It said Stutzman on Braniff to Dallas. He walked back out to the planes, making sure it said Braniff where he turned. There was no line, and they took one of his tickets and gave him a boarding pass, and he got in his seat and strapped himself in. The plane lumbered out to taxi, and he could see the lights blinking on the wing and hear the engine whining up the scale for takeoff. The plane howled down the runway, and the ground blurred away in streaks of light, and they were in the air. He lit a cigarette and looked at his ticket. It was a TWA again and it said Stutzman to San Francisco.

▲▼▲

There was blinding sunshine on a blue ocean. Wind whipped the waves frothy white and tossed them angrily against a rocky coast. The plane banked sharply and skimmed in for a landing, tires squealing rubber on the hot runway. Stutzman stared wearily out the window. His head felt like a fuzzball. His legs ached and his body was a sack of rocks. Where was he? On the TWA? In San Francisco, or where? No. He remembered, now. He was off the TWA. The TWA was—what, yesterday? The day before? He wasn't sure which.

The plane taxied up to the terminal, and he saw the other planes sitting there. Fat and round, gleaming in the sun. The terminal said Pacific Southwest and the planes were all painted pink and red and white. They said PSA and there were little smiles painted across their noses.

It came back to him a little at a time. San Francisco and Los Angeles and Hollywood/Burbank and San Diego and wherever. Up and down the coast. Hopping about like rabbits from one city to the other. And how long had that been? It was hard to think. Things happened—but it wasn't easy to say when. Like the watch in his head had stopped running. The whole thing was a terrible nightmare. It wasn't happening. Why were they *doing* this to him?

On the TWA from Denver, Stutzman had tried to talk to people. That had been the most frightening thing of all. It wasn't as if nobody would answer. They just didn't *hear* him right. He told the stewardess he had to get off. She brought him coffee. He pleaded with her. She brought him peanuts. He told a respectable-looking business man he was on the wrong plane and he had to get to Dallas and would he do something to help. "Fine, and you?" said the man.

What was Angela thinking, he wondered. She'd be worried sick. Would she try to do something? They could trace the tickets, maybe. Track him down and find him and make whoever was doing this terrible thing let him go.

He looked down morosely at his suit. It was crumpled and saggy and wrinkled all over. It pulled up tight around his crotch, and his bottom was numb from sitting. He felt like a fat brown lettuce. His face was covered with a scraggly stubble. He smelled and his feet itched. He reached down under his socks and scratched. He could clean up, anyway, and maybe feel better. He still had the attaché with the toothbrush and the razor. He could, he thought angrily, if everyone would just get out of the bathroom.

Stutzman didn't get a chance to clean up until he was on the Canadian Pacific from San Francisco. He brushed his teeth and shaved and took off his clothes and washed all over as well as he could in the cramped little room. He looked at himself in the mirror. A gray, pudgy face with bloodshot eyes looked back at him. He wanted to cry. "Lew, you look like a dead person," Angela said in his head. "So maybe I am," he said back to her.

They landed at Vancouver and Calgary and Edmonton. They stopped at Winnipeg and Ottawa and Montreal. He took something to New York and went on to Chicago and got North Central to Madison and Green Bay and Milwaukee and La Crosse and Grand Rapids. He learned to eat whenever they'd serve him after he got stuck on short hops for two or three days where there was nothing but peanuts.

He took American to Tucson and Phoenix and Las Vegas and even back to Dallas once. That was almost more than he could take. He was right there—and all he could do was go wherever his legs would take him. Angela! Angela!

He went to Seattle and Portland and Anchorage and Fairbanks...

Des Moines and Detroit and Memphis and Wichita...

Nashville and Pittsburgh and Dayton and Kansas City...

He flew Frontier and Capital and Southwest and National...

Northwest and Continental and Eastern and United...

He flew airlines he'd never heard of before.

▲▼▲

Even though Stutzman missed a meal now and then, he was putting on weight. He couldn't get his pants together anymore. His shirt wouldn't button. All he ever did was sit in the cramped economy seats and eat. There were sores on his thighs and buttocks, now. When he took his standup baths, he cleaned them off as best he could, but they burned worse than ever the minute he sat down again.

He used the toothpaste sparingly but it finally ran out. He started using salt he took from the meal trays. The deodorant was gone. There was still a good blade left, but he wouldn't let himself use it. He kept scratching away with the dull ones, tearing and scraping and making himself bleed. He stubbornly resisted the new blade. It was somehow a symbol of normalcy. Once the blade was gone, Stutzman was certain something terrible would happen.

Washing out the socks and underwear wasn't so bad, except he couldn't leave them out anywhere and they never got dry in the attaché. There was nothing to do about the shirt and the suit. They both smelled like a cat box, but after a while he didn't notice.

He ran out of cigarettes the second day and started robbing ashtrays. Since he always used credit cards and traveler's checks, he only had about twelve dollars cash. He spent it all on drinks, and when it was gone, he watched longingly as his fellow passengers downed bourbons and Scotches and vodkas and beers. Sometimes a passenger would leave the little toy bottles in a seat pocket, and he'd dig them out later and get maybe a drop or two. He was ashamed and embarrassed to do this, but he missed having a drink. It was something. There wasn't much else.

Sometimes on a long night flight, Stutzman sat and stared out the little window and wondered why it had all happened to him. Who was doing this terrible thing? What had *he* ever done to anyone? A family man and a responsible person who minds his own business. A taxpayer and a citizen. So who?

He had a good idea who. It almost had to be God. Who else could handle such a thing? It took a big organization and a lot of tricky business. Like making feet go where they shouldn't and messing around with people's tickets.

Stutzman didn't want to believe it was God. If it was God, he was in for it. You could deal with almost anybody better than Him. Bernie Freed who thinks he knows everything, okay. A Bernie Freed you can handle. A God, though, what're you going to do? A God is a lot cagier than a Bernie Freed.

"This is something we can talk about?" Stutzman asked the dark window. "Whatever it is, it's got to be something we can talk about. There's nothing people can't work out, they sit down and talk together. There's been a misunderstanding, we can do something."

Stutzman paused a moment, considering. He dug around in the ashtray and found a butt that was mostly filter.

"Look, no offense—" he said, "you don't mind me saying, there's plenty You could be doing besides fooling around with Stutzman. So who's Stutzman, a Hitler? Does Stutzman chase around after buyers and poodle dogs? Maybe You already know it, I'm not telling anything new. Bernie Freed cheats like a dog on his taxes. Also, he's got a *shiksa* girlfriend. The one sits in the corner in accounting? You can't miss her, she's got tits out to here."

It wasn't right, thought Stutzman. Bernie was back in Dallas with his home and his gold Piguet watch and his girlfriend with the tits, and Lew Stutzman was flying around like a crazy with no toothpaste. It didn't make sense. What had *he* done so terrible? God could be giving Arabs the clap or something. Why all the trouble with Stutzman?

It might be something that had happened a long time ago, he decided. Something he'd forgotten. That was the thing with God. He could hold a grudge forever. You could read about it in the *Torah*. One little thing. Pow!

"Listen, it's not the business with Mary Shuler's daughter, is it? That's forty years ago! You go back to that, it's only fair You get Levitch and Greenwaldt, too. I took her out once, maybe twice. She was happy to go, that counts for something."

Other things came back to him when he started thinking. Little things. Okay, a couple of mediums. So who's perfect? The trouble with God was you couldn't tell. He was picky about some things and some things He wasn't.

"Sure," Stutzman said aloud once, "it's easy enough for You. *You* don't have to go out and sell in a bad season when nobody's buying. Try that sometime You got nothing to do!"

▲▼▲

Stutzman looked at movies when there was one on the flight until he'd seen most of them twice. He read magazines until his eyes burned. He read *Time* and *Newsweek* and *Sports Illustrated* and the *Reader's Digest*. He read *People* and *Business Week* and *The National Geographic*. He even read things he couldn't stand like *Vogue* and *Ms.* and *Glamour*. There were two things he didn't read. He didn't read magazines that ran pictures of naked girls because it made him feel bad. After a while, he didn't read newspapers, either. Newspapers were terrible reminders of the passage of time. Tormenting calendars that scratched off the slow days of his long trip to nowhere. It was better not to know. He couldn't bear to think about it.

As it was, the days and nights seemed to blur and flow together like two heavy syrups, one never quite becoming the other...

▲▼▲

Stutzman didn't imagine it could get any worse, until it did. He wasn't sure how long it was before he realized he wasn't on domestic flights anymore. There were long, endless journeys from New York to Paris...

From London to Los Angeles...

From Frankfurt to Capetown to Dar es Salaam...

From Karachi and Delhi to Osaka and Seattle...

There were strange butts in his ashtrays. Foods he didn't like and magazines he couldn't read and people he couldn't understand.

He flew Air France and Alaska and Alitalia…
El Al and Lufthansa and Varig…
Icelandic, Sabena and Finn-Air…
Mexicana, Garuda and Qantas.

"It was the sales meeting in Tahoe, maybe?" he asked God. "One weekend—You're going to make a big thing out of that?"

He couldn't eat. But he couldn't not eat, either. A deadly cycle began: dreary, constipated days followed by awesome watery nights. His stomach cried out against breakfast in Bangkok, lunch in Zagreb and dinner in Kinshasa. He threw up gazpacho, schnitzel and shad. Rumaki, sevich and rabat loukoum. He had cold chills and hot flashes. For a while, he was too weak to get from his seat to the john. The terrible bed-sores got worse. He itched all over. He didn't even bother about the underwear and the socks anymore. It was too much trouble and he didn't care. If he smelled, he smelled. They didn't like it, they could kick him off the plane.

"So what is it," he cried, "cheating Marty Engel at poker? Eight dollars, I got to fly forever for *that*?"

▲▼▲

For some time, God hadn't even bothered with the wrong-ticket business. He got on, he got off. The feet knew where to go, if Stutzman didn't. Sometimes the man didn't look at his ticket. Sometimes he couldn't even remember changing planes. One flight flowed into another, like the days and the nights.

He quit trying to talk to people. Whatever he said, nobody listened. He had a secret horror that they couldn't even see him anymore. A smelly, invisible Stutzman. God could see him. But could anyone else? There was a way to find out. He could talk to someone. If he answered, he was there. He didn't even think about trying. If it was true, he didn't want to know.

▲▼▲

The morning the sun came up over somewhere and burned into his eyes and clear through the back of his soul, and he knew why he'd saved the last good blade. There was no fear or sorrow in the knowledge. It was like the moment before lovemaking. The bouquet of a good wine. It was a beautiful and perfect thing. Stutzman didn't hesitate a minute. When it came to him, he was ready. Ready? He couldn't wait to get started.

In the tiny john he crouched on the toilet and took off his coat and rolled up his sleeve. Before he started, he let himself think a moment. About Angela. Only a moment. Any more and he knew he might not do it. It was the only thing that could stop him. She flickered into his consciousness, a little wallet picture, and then she was gone.

The blade was cold in his fingers. Like a melting sliver of ice. Sweat stung his eyes and he closed them hard and shut his mind and sliced quick and deep across his wrist. Stutzman went rigid with fear. The blade didn't hurt, but he felt the horror of its passage in his heart.

It had all happened so fast, the deed coming swiftly on the thought. He hadn't considered what might come after. In the back of his mind somewhere there was a vague projection of peace and darkness and clean boxer shorts. In the picture, there was nothing in between. In actuality, there was much more than that—a long interval of *living* he hadn't counted on. Stutzman was frightened. Death was one thing. Dying was something else again!

He was angry and disgusted. What was he supposed to do now? How would it feel? Would it hurt? Would he just get weaker until he passed out?

So far, it didn't feel like anything. Okay. So what's the matter with that?

He told himself he'd be all right. He could do it. Just sit still and let it happen. Just keep your eyes closed and *don't look.* He knew what it would look like and it was something he didn't want to see. Ever. Jesus—how long had he been *in* here? There'd be blood over everything. It would look awful.

He promised himself all he'd do was open his eyes a *little.* Just enough to let the gray in. Not any more than that. The best thing to do would be start high, and work down. That way, you could stop just before you got to something you didn't want to see. You'd see the edge of it first and you could quit.

He saw the top of the wall. The edge of the sink and part of the door. A piece of his leg. A little spot of white that was the end of a finger. Hold it. Damn, there ought to be something awful by now. Slow, slow. A little further but not much—

Stutzman opened his eyes all the way and stared. *Nothing!* Not even a scratch! How could that be? He picked up the blade and ran it carefully over his finger. Again, harder. Finally, he slashed his palm desperately a dozen times as hard as he could. A terrible cry stuck in his throat, and he dropped the blade and tore at his face with his hands. Hot tears ran down his cheeks. He should have known. He might have guessed God wouldn't let him do it. It was just the kind of dirty trick He'd come up with...

▲▼▲

Getting off the foreign run helped for a while. Stutzman was even glad to see *Ms.* and *Popular Science.* He welcomed the toy bags of salt and pepper, and even the seventy-four ways the airlines cooked chicken looked good again.

He flew to Chicago and Des Moines and Corpus Christi...

Omaha and Ft. Smith and Cedar Rapids...

Tulsa and Knoxville and Fargo and St. Petersburg.

For a time, there was a remote sense of day/night/day/night, like the quick frames of a movie flicking by. A numbing rhythm at best, but at least it held the dull hint of one something following another. Then, the beats and flickers blurred into a single, nearly inaudible hum, and for Stutzman there was neither yesterday nor tomorrow, only the terrible, frozen barb of now lost in the temporal wilderness...

▲▼▲

He flew to Wichita and Albuquerque and Amarillo...

Austin and Sioux City and St. Paul...

Reno and Bismarck and Boise.

Sometimes he remembered to take off his suit in the tiny washroom and clean himself a little, but even that seemed to take a great effort of will, more than he had to give. He forgot things like that. Or didn't bother when they came to mind. It had been a long time since he'd shaved. Right after God tricked him, he threw the good blade away. A thing like that, a man couldn't put to his face.

One night when his window looked far down on the lights of somewhere, the dreary curtain parted in his mind, and in a rare moment of clarity he remembered things. Things beyond the dull animal sense of simply being a Stutzman, who was hungry and tired sometimes and had a cramp in his foot. He remembered Angela and cobwebs and wine. Grass and pillows and bathtubs. He remembered the hippie girl with the yellow hair and the lady peeling oranges and Neuman's buyers and poodle dogs. He remembered everything there was to remember about Bernie Freed. The blazer and the houndstooth pants and the gold Piguet watch and the mustache that twitched. And in that moment he remembered something else, a thing that had happened right in the airport with Bernie he hadn't remembered before.

"That's the thing, maybe?" he asked God. "A thing like that? Listen, a person gets mad, he says things. It's something you say, you don't mean it like it sounds. Anyway, it's Bernie I'm pissed at, not You. I meant Bernie, I should've said Bernie. I'm sorry. You got nothing to do with it. The whole thing's a mistake. It's something'll never happen again, You got Stutzman's word on it."

Stutzman waited, but nothing happened. Maybe it wasn't that at all. Maybe it really was the business with Marty Shuler's daughter and God wouldn't admit it. "I'm supposed to know, You won't talk to me? How can you get along with someone, the someone won't sit down and talk? It's a good thing You got Your own business," Stutzman shouted, "You'd sure as hell never make it working for somebody else!"

▲▼▲

He flew to Shreveport and Dayton and New Orleans...

Clearwater and Brownsville and Hartford...

Little Rock and Augusta and Wheeling.

In the beginning he'd put on extra weight, eating rich food and sitting in his seat and doing nothing. Now he hardly ate at all. He wasn't hungry anymore. Trays passed over his lap uneaten, an endless train of plastic and glass and chicken and peas and tarts and butters and coffees.

He didn't read anymore.

Or dig for butts in the ashtrays.

He sat in his seat and looked at nothing, encasing the essence of Stutzman.

He slept more and more, the sleeping and the waking subtly brushing together, until it was hard to tell one from another.

"I still look like a dead person, Angela," he said aloud or dreamed, "but you should be happy—I'm sleeping on the airplane."

▲▼▲

He was dimly aware of rain slapping hard against the window. Dirty clouds swept by in quick streaks of gray. The plane hit heavy air and jolted him awake. Stutzman opened bleary eyes and saw the trailing edge of the wing groan down in place for a landing. He felt the wheels shudder from their nests and bite air. He leaned back again and closed his eyes and opened them wide. The plane gave a crazy little tilt. Stutzman's head slammed the window. The belly hit concrete and hot metal howled. The wing showered sparks and clutched earth, clipping bright blue lights like a lawnmower.

From the moment the plane touched ground until the end, only seven quick seconds went by. But Stutzman saw it all, in an instant replay of horror—slow dark honey creeping down a pancake forever.

He saw a gray wing crumple and tear like leftover foil...

He saw the big engine, still whining and angry, pull gently from its place and tumble gracefully through First Class and out the other side...

He saw the bright white wall of fire roll back to swallow Economy and watched the pale-eyed surfers swim against it...

And then in an instant they were gone. He saw dark clouds and felt cold rain on his face. He was alone. No sound, no sight, no touch, no nothing.

In the instant he knew what had happened and understood that he would die in the tiny slice of a second, Stutzman felt a great and terrible fear. Then, a wonderful sense of joy and happiness brushed the fear away, and he saw that God had forgiven him and let him off the hook. No more bedsores and dirty underwear. No more seat belts and peanuts and paper napkins. And in that fragment of a moment before nothing, Stutzman returned the favor and forgave God.

▲▼▲

"Jesus!"

Okay, so I'm wrong. You got a Son. Whatever.

"C'mere. This one's alive!"

Alive? What's with alive?

White faces and white coats. White arms lifting and pulling and a white ambulance door and a siren shrieking and red and white and blue.

"Where am I?" said Stutzman.

"You're okay, mister. Got a little burn on your arm is all, you're gonna be okay."

Stutzman stared at him. "I got out? I'm alive? A thing like *that*, nobody's hurt?"

The white face went whiter. "*Hurt?* Shit, man, there ain't nobody *whole* back there! Maybe a hundred fifty poor fuckers all—"

"Hey, he don't want to hear all that," said the other face.

Me, he thought wondrously, just me? Everybody dead, and Stutzman alive? He understood, then. God was sorry for what he'd done. He'd spared Stutzman. It was over. All over and he could see Angela. He could get a drink and take a bath and kick the shit out of Bernie Freed. He could get a little furniture store, maybe a dress shop. You got to go somewhere, you get a bus or a taxi.

"You okay?" said the face.

"I'm okay."

"Can you sit up?"

"I can sit."

The doors opened, and the man helped him out, and he could hear the big engines idling and see the tail of the plane high against the dark and the moisture pebbling its skin. The stewardess got his ticket from his coat and looked at it and smiled, and from the yellow light in the door he could hear the other girl telling everyone how federal regulations require that your seat back and tray table be upright for takeoff and landing and that should the cabin become depressurized oxygen masks would automa—

Nightbeat

The wakechimes touched me with the sound of cinnamon. I stretched, turned over, and watched the clockroach play time games against the wall. It marked the spidery minutes in fine script and left crystal duntracks behind.

It was half-past blue, and a lemon moon spilled color into the room. Its light burnished Bethellen's hair to silver and brushed her flesh with coffee shadow.

She stirred once, and I slid quietly away, padded to the shower cage, and let cool spicewater bring me awake. There were cocoacubes where Bethellen had left them, but I passed them by and trotted back to the nightroom. My Copsuit sprang from its hollow with a sunfresh scent, and I slipped into it quickly.

I would have liked to look at myself. A small vanity, but mine own. I take a pride in the uniform. It's a Copsuit in the classical cut—basic whipcord in umber and vermilion, sepia pullover, and fringe-leather vest. The jackboots, gloves, and chainbelt are traditional indigo. The Marshal's Star of David is cadmium-gold, and the Peacemaker by my side is finest quartz and ivory.

Set. Ready to go, and a last look at Bethellen. She had turned in her sleep to catch the moonwaves. Citron limbs bared to an ocher sea. By morning, I'd taste lemon on her lips.

Outside, the prowlbug hummed to electric life. The moon was high now, and a second had joined it—a small saffron tagalong. Lime shadows colored the streetways. The dashglow winked me into service, and I switched the roadlights and moved along.

The street ribboned over soft hills furred with bonebrake, and through dark groves of churnmoss. Raven blossoms hung from high branches nearly to the ground. I swung the prowlbug into Bluewing, whispered through Speaklow, and coasted down the steep circle to Singhill.

There were people all about now. If I listened, I could feel the sound of their sleeping. From Tellbridge I watched lonelights far and away. Not everyone slumbered, then, but all were snug in their homeshells till the day. None would stir before Amberlight polished the world. For that was as it was—the day belongs to us, but not the night.

I have often stopped the prowlbug and dimmed the lights and watched the darklife. In moments, the night fills with chitter-hums and thrashes. A beetlebear stops to sniff the air, pins me with frosty muzzle and razor eyes. For a while there is pink carnage in her heart; then she scutters by clanging husky armor. Jac-Jacs and Grievers wing the dark hollows. A Bloodgroper scatters his kill. There is much to darklife, and few have seen it as it is.

A quarter till yellow. The dashglow hemorrhages, coughs up a number. The prowlbug jerks into motion, whines up the speedscale. Sirens whoo-pa-whoopa-whoopa through the night, and I switch on the traditional lilac, plum, and scarlet flashers.

There are no strollwalkers to pause and wonder. No other bugs abroad to give me way. Still, there are customs to keep alive, bonds with the past.

▲▼▲

The address was nearby. Prowlbug skittered up the snakepath around Henbake. Pressed me tight against the driveseat. Pink lights to port. A homeshell high on Stagperch, minutes away.

Around a corner, and green sparkeyes clustered ahead—nightmates and shadelings hunkered in the streetway. The prowlbug whoopa-ed a warning, and they scattered like windleaves.

They were waiting for me, portal open. A big man with worry lines scribbled on paper features. His handstrobe stitched my path with light-craters to shoo stray nightlings. The woman was small and pretty. Hands like frightened birds. I moved through them up turnstairs past buffwalls to the boy's room.

I'd been there before, but they didn't remember. No-face in a uniform.

▲▼▲

A child in Dreamspasm is not a pretty sight. I punched his record on the bedscreen, scanned it quickly. Twelve and a half. Fifth Dream. Two-year sequence. No complications. I gripped one bony arm and plunged Blue Seven in his veins. The spasms slowed to a quiver. I touched him, wiped foamspittle from his cheeks. His skin was cold, frogdank. Waterblue eyes looked up at nothing. The small mouth sucked air.

"He's all right." The man and woman huddled behind. "Take him in in the morning. Don't think he did internal damage, but it won't hurt to check."

I laid a vial beside the bed. "One if he wakes. I don't think he will."

"Thank you," said the man. "We're grateful." The woman nodded his words.

"No problem." I stopped in the hall and faced them again. "You know he could secondary."

They looked startled, as if they didn't.

"If he does, stay with him."

They frowned questions, and I shook my head. "Punch in if you like, but there's nothing else I can do. He can't have Seven again. And a strong secondary's a good sign." I sent them a Copgrin. "He's old enough. You could be out of the woods."

They gave each other smiles and said things I didn't hear. The prowlbug was turning all my buttons red and shrieking whoopas into the night. I bounded down turnstairs and tore out the portal. No time for strobes and such. If nightlings got underfoot, they'd get a jackboot for their trouble.

The prowlbug scattered gravel, skit-tailed into the streetway. It was wound up and highwhining and I held on and let it have its way. Stagperch faded, and the snakepath dizzied by in black patches. I prayed against sleepy megapedes bunked in on the road ahead. A tin medal for Bethellen. Early insurance.

The dashglow spit data, but I already knew. Bad. Category A and climbing. Name of Lenine Capral and long overdue. First Dream and fifteen.

▲▼▲

The Rules say punch before you practice. No way with Lenine Capral. No record, no time, no need. The Dream had her in nighttalons. Down on the dark bottom, and nothing for it. Lost, lost Lenine.

I drew the Peacemaker, pressed the muzzle between her eyes. Her body arched near double, limbs spread-eagled. I pulled back lids and looked. Milkpools. Silverdeath darting about. The little shiverteeth nibbling away.

I tossed my jacket aside. Grabbed a handful of hair and pinned her neck where I wanted it. Put the muzzle low behind the ear and up. This time, shock jerked a small arm and snapped it like crackwood. But nothing snapped Lenine.

I couldn't shoot her again. More would burn her skull bone-dry. And nothing in the little glass tubes. Blue Seven was fine for the boy—about as good as mouse pee for Lenine.

Okay. One deep breath and down to dirty fighting. I ripped the sheet away. Stripped her bare. She was slim and fragile, too close to womantime. I spread her wide, and the motherperson made little noises.

"Out."

The man understood and moved her.

Dreamspasm is a thing of the mind. But that door's closed for helpers. The physical road is the only way. Peacemakers. Blue Seven. Redwing. And after that: physical stimuli to build mental bridges back home. Countershock for young minds. For Lenine Capral, therapeutic rape. Thumb the Peacemaker to lowbuzz and hope this one's led a sheltered life.

Hurt her good.

Whisper uglies in her ear.

Slap and touch and tear. No gentle Peacemaker funsies. Only the bad parts. A child's garden of horrors. Everything mother said would happen if the bad man gets his hands on you.

Orange.

Red-thirty.

Coming up violet. Cream-colored dawn on the windows.

And finally the sound you want. Lenine the wide-eyed screamer. The violated child awake and fighting. Afraid of real things, now. Scared out of Dreamspasm One.

Quickly out and past the hoverfaces. No gushy gratitude here. Mother doesn't thank the Coprapist.

Outside, dawnbreeze turns the sweat clammy cold. A medbug has braved the nightlings all the way from Fryhope. Lenine will get proper patching.

The prowlbug has a homepath in mind, as well it might. Only I am not ready for Bethellen and breakfast. Both are out of temper with the night's affairs. Instead, I brave the prowlbug's grumblings, move past Slowrush, and wind down to Hollow. The road ends, and prowlbug will duly record that I have violated Safecode and am afoot before the dawn. The nightlings don't concern me. They've fed before Firstlight and bear no ill. At the stream I hear their thrums and splashings as they cross back over to find hugburrows for the day.

The stream is swift and shallow and no wider than a childstep. It makes pleasant rillsongs and winds beneath green chumtrees. It has no name. It is simply the stream that divides the world. Dark from light. Night from day.

There is still nightshadow on the other side. The groves are thick and heavy. I watch, wait, and listen to the stream music.

Timebug says half-past violet. While I wait, I polish dun-glasses. Put them on. They help to see what is, and temper what isn't at all.

Wait.

Watch the waterlights.

A blink and a breath and he's there. As if he'd been there all along.

For a moment my stomach does its tightness. But it's not so bad for me. They make teetiny headchanges in policemen. Little slicecuts that go with the Copsuit. But there is still a childmind to remember. Dreamspasms in dark nightrooms

Through the dun-glasses I can see bristly no-color. Hear his restless flickersounds. See him move with the shape of frostfur. Hear him breathe hot darkness. Sense his crush-heavy limbs.

Only, I cannot see or hear these things at all.

I wonder if he watches, and what he sees of me. I have to look away. And when I look again, he is gone. Nothing has changed in the thickgroves.

What would I say to him? That wouldn't need the saying?

▲▼▲

Back to the prowlbug. Ten till indigo now. Amberlight dares the high ridges. Sucks away darkness.

I imagine him. Thromping and shiffing. Dark fengroves away. Safe against the sunstar. And all the young darklings purged of manfear. Only fright-thoughts, now—fading daydemons named Lenine.

Who can tell such a thing? The stream divides the world. Whatever could be said is what he knows. That there are pinchfew places left. That mostly there is nothing. That we will have to make do with what there is to share.

Hero

What I told Colonel Dark was he could shove it all the way up and break it off, for all I cared. I sure wasn't going to ride in no groundhog parade.

"Sergeant Ash, you sure are going to do just that," Dark told me.

"Sir, I'm not. Begging the colonel's pardon."

"It is all set, boy, and I reckon you are."

I looked across the desk at him. You got to check twice to make sure the man is sitting. Jack's seven foot eight in his socks—shoulders wide as rail ties, and a chest like big black sacks of cement. Long-steppin' legs hard as good oak, and fists the size of baby heads. I'm no boy-child, myself—but I'm no Jack Dark, either.

He was dressed the same as me—spit and blister boots, pitch-night skinners, and star-silver piping from shoulder to toe. From the head on up, we're not much alike. Jack's got this black rubber face he's worn since Razoridge—darker'n his own was, and twice as ugly.

"Jack," I told him, "you're 'bout the scariest nigger I ever seen."

"You just remember that, cracker," he said solemnly.

"If I was a little ol' tyke, I'd pee in my pants just looking at you."

"Some do, I hear."

"Aw, shit, Jack." I threw my coonskin cap on his desk and tried to look mean as him. "I ain't going to do it, and that's that. Get someone else. Get old Bluebelly Ripper. Now *there's* an A-number one hero. I seen him on a magazine."

Colonel Dark looked at me with big, sad eyes. "They don't want an everyday space jock up front, Ash. What they want's a real live wormhead. And you're it."

"Well, I ain't, either. You can bust me or whatever. This boy isn't riding in no parade, and you got my honest to God word on it."

I meant it, too, and Dark knew it. In a field situation I wouldn't question an order from Colonel Jack, but this wasn't any field situation or anything like it. And a man's got to stand up for himself when he knows he's right. That goes for soldiers as well as anybody.

▲▼▲

I felt like the biggest damn fool on Earth, and likely looked the part. Bands playing and flags flying and paper falling all over—and me riding in a bright red skimmer with Dark and the President and whoever, and enough high brass to start our own little war. And of course our tag-alongs were right close by, his and mine—their pretty red boxes nice and handy. I kept grinning and waving and looking happy as a frog, and Jack sat right there watching, smiling real nice and showing me his fine white teeth.

It was a good parade, I suppose, if you didn't know better. There were lots of drums and pretty costumes and long-legged girls. There were battle trophies and war wagons and even a dead Centaurian in a tank—one of the better-looking varieties. They'd found an old Beta Scout somewhere that'd been rusting out for about ten years and painted it all up and stuck it on a float. Major Bluebelly Ripper was ridin' that, and looked near as miserable as I did.

The worst part, though, were the troopers. I could take all the rest, but that was kind of hard to swallow. There must have been soldiers from half the old units on Earth—every one in fancy dress, all brand-spankin' new and shiny. Jack's Nairobi Lancers were there looking tall and proud, red plumes waving on their big bone helmets. Right behind me were the Swiss High Guards and the Queen's Own, and I could see the green banner of the Virginia Volunteers up ahead, and the Red Russian Eagles after that. And right in front of me, of course, a troop of Tennessee Irregulars, my own outfit. Each and every one in fine buck leather, sporting coal-black beards and coonskin hats.

I didn't know whether to laugh or bust out bawling. What I really wanted to do was hop right out of there and knock me some heads together. Sort of work out the tension some. Dark looked right at me, once, and I figured he was feeling the same.

The truth is, there wasn't a man there fit to wear those outfits. Not a one had ever been off-planet, and if any two of 'em had been soldiering more than a week, why I'd buy them all the beer they could drink.

There aren't any Tennessee Irregulars any more—haven't been for near twenty years. Maybe me, and three others, from what started. The same goes for Jack's outfit, and the rest. We still come from everywhere, but there isn't much time to think on it, or worry 'bout who's carrying the flag. We're soldiers, and we do what we have to do.

Only, like Jack Dark says, that don't make much of a parade. People get tired reading about a war they never see. I guess you got to give them something to look at now and then, so they'll know we're still out there, fighting for home and mother—and pretty soldiers marching by is about the best thing for it. Folks sure don't want to see much more than that, or think on it any. How we drop a million troopers every couple of years out there and don't get more than a handful back alive. Who's going to do much cheering about that?

There was plenty of noise and shouting, but it sure got awful quiet when I passed by. People looked, all right. They didn't want to miss a real wormhead—there aren't that many to see. But they didn't want to *really* look, not like you look at just anyone. What they'd do is look *at* something else and kind of see me in the bargain. Like maybe starin' straight at me would give 'em warts, or something worse.

I could've done the same. Looked right over them and never seen a thing. I didn't, though. I grinned until my face hurt and caught every one of them right in the eye. Squirm, you bastards, I told them. You ain't sure what I got, but you're *god*damn sure you don't want any...

▲▼▲

"Marcus, I'm buying," said the colonel, when we were right near the end.

"Shit, Jack, you haven't *got* enough whiskey to buy out of this one," I told him.

There was a ground-hot major sitting up front, and he didn't much like it—me talking to an officer like that. He started to say something, then didn't. Which was a good idea. I wouldn't ever do anything to embarrass Jack, but he's not near as nice to folks as I am.

▲▼▲

There was a banquet somewhere with tin speeches and paper food, and we put up with about fifteen minutes of that before Dark got up and pulled me off to a nearby bar. What we didn't drink we threw at the walls, and we soon had the place to ourselves. When we got into regimental songs about two in the A.M., the tag-alongs cut us off quick. A couple of sober shots, and we were ready to go again, but our keepers said absolutely no. Instead, they called a staff car and packed us off fast to Heroes' Hotel. Dark and I protested—but not much. His tag-along was a lieutenant, and mine a captain, which doesn't mean anything. If you're a wormhead, your tag-along outranks God.

Jack went his way and I went mine. Halfway down the long hall, though, he stopped and called out over his shoulder. "Sergeant! Sleeeeeeep TIGHT!"

"Sir!" I shouted back, "Don't let the BAD bugs bite!"

▲▼▲

Captain Willie Brander roused the night crew. They weren't too glad to see me, but no one complained. I'm about all they have to do.

Annie See stripped me down and held me under happy juice. Little Mac Packer scrubbed every hole and hollow with a fine rusty brush.

Bigo Binder glued me up tight.

They dried me and rubbed me and ground me up good, then rolled me in the Sounder. All the little hairs that had dared start growing since yesterday got hummed off quick.

Finally, I lay back flat on the table and let the red rubber jam-jams wrap me up tight. Three hundred thirty-two gold and silver wires dug their little snout noses into my skin. Dewpads shut my eyes and plugged up my ears. Hard rubber clamps spread my jaws so the bright yellow tubes could snake down my gullet. Then, when all was done and checked, they picked me up easy and dropped me down deep in the white foam pool.

I couldn't move an eyelash. Even if I had one.

It was beddy-bye time. But tell that to a wormhead, and he'll come right out of his nightsuit and hand you your ass.

▲▼▲

Another wonderful night in Ash's head. All my good bug-buddies were waiting, and we romped and splashed all over and had us a time. The little white teeth were slice-belly sharp and we gutted each other good. There was hot red screaming, and pink things to eat. We ripped and tore and cut through the long wet hours, and the night didn't last more than a couple thousand years.

It doesn't get better, it just gets worse. Like someone who isn't here any more scratched in the bar downstairs:

Hell is where the good guys go.

Only, you got to be a wormhead to know it.

▲▼▲

"Sleeeeeeep TIGHT?"

"Damn RIGHT!"

Dark shot us all a big grin and dropped his ugly self down between Miguel Mendoza and me.

"Pleasant dreams, Ash?"

"Hell, yes, Colonel. I'm thinkin' about going on back after breakfast and grabbin' me another couple hours."

Everyone laughed at that, and Jack Dark reached out a big paw and speared about thirty ounces of steak.

"You got the hungries, Jack?" Mendoza asked him.

"Always do after a good night's sleep, Mig."

The chatter went around the table and back again, like it always does with wormheads in the morning. We're so damn glad to be awake there isn't anything doesn't sound funny.

There were thirty-two of us there, all the wormheads on Earth. Off-planet there's more, of course, though not as many as you'd think. The survival factor out there's low enough to be a big dark secret, and so the number of live troopers with kills is lower still. We're the cream of the crop. Or the worst of the lot, whichever. Men with anywhere from 550 to 900 kills on their record, which makes us too hot for the field Sleepers to handle any more. We come from most everywhere, but this bunch is heavy on soldiers from the U.S.A. and the African Republics. No special reason, except maybe there were more of us out there in the beginning. Everyone's in it, now—every male-child over fifteen who can walk, or crawl some. There'd be plenty of women in it, too, if the law would let them. But that'd play hell with making new baby soldiers, and then where'd we be?

I said there were thirty-two of us. There were thirty-three, until last night. Everybody at breakfast knew Hu-cheng had bought it in bed, but wasn't one of us goin' to say anything. What's there to say, that we weren't all thinking anyway?

No one was left except Dark and me, trying to see who could out-hog the other. Jack always wins in the end—he's just got more room to put it than I do. But I give him a fight now and then.

"Jack, I sure want to thank you for yesterday," I told him. "I ain't ever been in a parade before. I get a chance, I'll make it up to you, for certain."

Dark just looked at me and did something in his throat that sounded like thunder.

"I'm dead serious," I said. "That was an opportunity don't come to just every soldier. Ridin' around with officers, wavin' at folks—"

"You just keep talking, Ash."

"Sir, I'm not joking about this—"

"Sergeant." Dark turned on me. "I got work to do, and I sure don't have time to sit here listening to you. However, if you like, I can spend a minute or two thinking up some useful job needs to be done."

"Reckon I'll just freshen up some, then maybe see me some town, Colonel."

Dark looked at me sideways and eased back down in his chair.

"Now just hold her, Jack." I knew what was coming. "I'm a big boy now. Near as big as you."

"You're a wormhead."

"Don't guess I need you to tell me that."

"Sounds like you need someone, Sergeant."

"Well, I don't—and I'm going. Isn't any need to talk about it, sir."

Jack gave me his ugliest look, and I gave it right back to him. Finally, he just got up like he was leaving, but I could feel him standing right behind me. A big black cloud wondering when it ought to rain.

"Maybe you ought to know, Ash," he said quietly. "Hu-cheng didn't die in bed. He opted out."

That shook me good. Just like he knew it would. Hu was a good man, and more than a friend. And there wasn't anybody'd tried harder to make it go right.

"Colonel," I said, "I'm obliged to you for tellin' me. But I guess I'm going to have to see me some town."

Dark didn't say anything. I just sat there eyeing steak bones and cold gravy for a while, and when I looked up again, he was gone.

▲▼▲

We were right in D.C. and it wouldn't have been anything to get a skimmer down to Nashville. I could have hitched a free ride from the base to most anywhere—or rented my own craft, if I wanted. Money's no big problem for a soldier, if he lives long enough. There's no place to spend your pay out on the dung worlds, and I had about ten years coming, plus enough bonus and time to about double that.

I wasn't quite ready for home, though. When I am—if I am—I'll know it. There's something funny about going back where you haven't been since you weren't much more than a kid. You got this picture of it, the way it ought to be. It feels real good that way, all nice and comfortable, and you don't want it any different. Maybe you figure going back will change something, and if it did, it wouldn't be the same in your head any more.

So I did what a man does in a place he doesn't know, that doesn't know him.

Bars haven't changed all that much. I reckon you could go in one a thousand years ago or a thousand from now and know right where you were. This one was dark and cool and served a good whiskey, and the music wasn't bad enough to bother a man's drinking. That's a funny thing about music. It changes when you're out of touch, but if you stay gone long enough, it comes right on back around to where it was.

Poor old tag-along took him a seat and waited and kept a good strong eye on me. I'd have bought him a beer but of course he wouldn't touch it. When you're shaggin' a wormhead, you keep your cool all the time, and you sure don't do any drinking. So old Willie sat loose, trying hard to look like there wasn't anything peculiar about a man hanging dry in a bar, carrying a little red box on one hip and a big .45 on the other. If he was having bad thoughts about damnfool wormheads who had to go roamin' around loose, he kept them to himself.

Sitting still isn't one of my best family traits. So I laid a couple of bills on the counter and drained the last drop. The boy tending bar moved up and shoved the cash right back.

"You're not buying any drinks in here, Sergeant. No way."

I looked him over close, catching what I'd missed the first time 'round.

He was about sixty-percent prosthetic, in all the wrong places. Kind of split down the middle, where the baddies had got him good. Rubber face, pink ears and nice new teeth.

"Where were you, boy?"

"Alpha-two. First landing in twenty-one."

"Shit. I was right next door on that little old mudball, where all the meanies come when you fellas flushed them out."

He grinned at that.

"What's your outfit. Virginians?"

He shook his head and his chin came up real proud. "California Diggers. Second Corps."

"Damn good outfit."

"Was. Nothing much left of 'em now."

I nodded. What's there to say?

"Listen," he told me, "I know who you are, Sergeant." His good eye touched my ribbons and the bald dome under my cap. "You need anything in this man's town, you give a yell. The groundies around here don't much understand why you guys are special. There's some of us do, though."

"I'm obliged," I told him and got myself out of there. He was well meaning and all, but I wasn't figuring on starting any more parades. About one's all I can handle.

▲▼▲

The next spot had a fancy name, all red and gold and old-looking inside, with lots of dark wood showing. There wasn't any big surge of patriotism going on here. Nobody'd ever heard of Sergeant Major Marcus Ash, and didn't want to. If you could handle the tab—about four times what whiskey ought to be—why, you were just welcome as could be.

I would have backed on out real quick if it hadn't been for the girl. She just sidled right up and slid on in, easy as you please. I *could* have left after that, but didn't much want to. She was tall and kind of lanky, lazy blue eyes and wheat-colored hair falling easy off her shoulders. She had that special kind of thing some women carry around without really trying. They know who they are and don't need anyone to tell them.

"Care if I sit? It's okay if you don't."

As soon as she opened her mouth, I leaned back and grinned. "Well, if that don't beat all. Where you from, child?"

She looked into me real strong, then came out laughing. "Atlanta, right outside. And you got to be Tennessee."

I slapped the table hard and waved down a waiter. "Nashville, honey, and what are you drinkin'?"

▲▼▲

She made it just as clear as could be right off. Worked in an office in Defense, which was about all you could work for now, and wanted me to know she wasn't a pro or anything but she did like to talk and have a drink and that was the best way to get to meet people. If we got along, fine. If not, that was okay, too. Her name was Jennie and she was twenty-three and how long had I been in the army and what was it really like out there?

I told her my name and she didn't seem to know it. That I'd been in the army twenty-one years and was thirty-six now. I skipped the last question, but it didn't matter anyway—she was doing a little quick arithmetic on the age business.

"My God. You were fifteen."

"Close to it."

"That's all your life." She was having trouble swallowing that.

"Well, time really flies when you're havin' fun."

"Can you get out now?"

"Could."

"Don't you want to?"

"And do what?"

"Well—" She waved me off into the ceiling somewhere. "—anything."

"Honey," I told her, "I don't *know* anything else. Last job I had on Earth was cuttin' high school and stealing spoons. Don't much want to do that again."

She laughed and kind of leaned back easy, knowing that I was going to tell the rest of it.

"See, there was this fella run a restaurant down home," I said. "Did a big business all over town, but he didn't much like to buy stuff. He was mostly interested in *selling*. So what he'd do is give us kids next to nothing for all the spoons and knives and forks and whatever we could steal off of somebody else. Hell, he didn't care whether they matched or nothing. Glasses, plates, salt shakers—everything."

"So what happened?"

"So bein' kids, we got ourselves caught, and the judge fella tells our folks they got a new rule on with the war just starting, and we can either go to the county farm for about six months, or join up."

Jennie looked pained. "So you got twenty-one years."

"Uhuh. Cured me of stealing spoons, though."

She laughed, showing me a pretty pink mouth.

"It's the God's truth," I told her and held up a hand to prove it. "Listen, you want another drink or you gettin' hungry?"

She thought about that. "You really want to take me to dinner? You don't have to. I just sat. You didn't ask"

"Know I didn't. But I'd like it, if you would."

"I would. Okay?"

"Okay. Only this is your town, and I haven't got the slightest idea where to start."

Jennie closed one eye. "There're a lot of good places."

"What's the best?"

"For what?"

"Anything."

She stopped a minute. "Are you asking me the best place in *town*?"

"Uhuh."

"That's very nice," she said gently, "but we don't have to do that." What she meant, was I likely couldn't.

"Yeah, but if we did."

"If we did, it'd be The Chalice."

"Food any good?"

She decided to ignore that. "Marcus. I don't even know anyone who's ever been there."

"Well, you will tomorrow," I told her. "Reckon I ought to call?"

"You're kidding. For which month?"

I grinned at her and got up and found a phone. Jack Dark was in a meeting and didn't much like getting out, but he'd do it.

"Done," I told her.

"It is?"

"Uhuh."

"Hey. How about that?" Something hit her and the big pink smile dropped real quick "Look, friend," she said coolly, "if I'm going to get raped in an alley or something, just say so, okay? But *don't* promise me The Chalice first. I couldn't take that."

I laughed and helped her up and we started out. It was the first chance I'd had to get close to her and smell her hair and feel how soft she was to touch. It did good things to me. You think a lot about girls like Jennie out there. Not just the loving part. Laughing when you want to and going where you want and breathing all the clean air you can hold. There are good and precious times out there when there's no fighting for a while and you know you're most likely going to live through the week. You can get yourself a woman sometimes if you're lucky and go off and share army beer. You remember all that and hold on to it. But it isn't the same thing.

▲▼▲

Outside we stopped to blink the bright sun away, and I caught Jennie's gaze going past me, over my shoulder, and saw it happen right in her eyes. It might have ended right there. It should have. Only I didn't want it to.

I'd been waiting for it, knowin' damn well when it'd be; and of course the minute she spotted the tag-along on my heels, it wasn't hard to put together. She just stood there, one hand kind of stiff in front of the little 'o' her mouth was making.

"Look, I never should've let us get going," I told her. "Forget it, okay?"

She stared at me, not really seeing much. "You're him. My God you really are. I didn't even know."

I felt the heat startin' up my neck. "Yeah, fine. Well you do now!"

"Hey." Concern crossed her face. "What is this? Listen, I'm sorry. I'm a little—well, surprised. I've never been out with a genuine hero before, Marcus."

I studied her real hard. "Jennie. You don't have to play no games with me. I don't know about any hero shit, but I'm something besides that—and if you know who I am, you know what it is."

"What I *know* is I got me an invitation to a fancy restaurant from one Marcus Ash, and if he's figuring on squirming out of that little number, he better have one hell of a good reason."

She looked so damn funny, all pouty and ready to spit needles. That wasn't the end of it. We'd have to take it some further than that. But it was enough, for the moment. "Come on, lady," I told her, "let's get ourselves some supper."

▲▼▲

There wasn't much talking on the way to her place. We just sat real quiet, enjoying where we were and not wanting to worry it any. I stayed in the skimmer while she changed. Tag-along Brander was up front with the driver, a kid no more than thirteen or so. No, he didn't mind stopping for a couple of minutes—or forever, if someone was paying.

I couldn't see the boy's eyes—they were locked in on some kind of crap under a pair of those personal vidspecs everybody's wearing. Something they came up with while I was out chasing meanie-bugs. You could see folks everywhere doing it—bars, streets, all over. Looked like a whole stumblin' town full of blind men. I thought about the kid. The draft age is fifteen, now. If there wasn't something real bad wrong with him, he'd be out fighting bugs in a year or so. We were building a world of children and old men, and nothing in between.

▲▼▲

What can I say about Jennie? She came back looking straight and tall and shiny, her dress was all shimmery white—kind of there, and kind of not, all at once, like she was walking in smoke. I just stared like a dumb kid somebody'd handed the biggest piece of candy in the world. Jennie finally started turning red all over and said if I kept thinking stuff like I was thinking we weren't ever going to get much dinner. I told her that had sure crossed my mind, and she said it would just have to *stop* crossing because she wasn't going back to work telling everyone how she almost ate dinner at the fanciest place in town.

Washington raced by below as far as you could see, until somewhere up the way it got to be something else with a different name. There was a river, with the last of the sun making whole pools of copper, and I got a glimpse of some kind of monument and wide bands of green places checkered with white buildings. The skimmer gave a little tilt, then straightened, as the driver got hung in heavy patterns and turned the job over to a computer somewhere.

"We've got things to say," Jennie told me. "I'd kind of like to, if we can."

"Good enough," I said, like I really did mean that.

"You were—right, back there," she admitted. "Some, anyway. I *was* surprised to find out who you were, Marcus, and that's most of it. Honest. Only, there was some of the other stuff, too. You saw it and I knew you did and I—didn't know what to do about it. I didn't know because I don't under*stand* it. I—" she dropped her hands in her lap and made little fists. "Okay. Straight, huh? You read about it, but it doesn't ever say much. I know there are men who've been in the war and they've—what? Got something in their heads that makes them different. I want to know and I want to understand only you don't *have* to, Marcus. It doesn't really make any…difference…"

She just kind of let it trail off, and I reached over and pulled her around. "Hey. Sure it does. You'd be a damn fool if it didn't."

She wouldn't look at me. "Yeah. Damn it, Marcus, it does. Is that—"

"It isn't anything. 'Cept maybe a little plain old human curiosity. How much do you know about what we're fighting? The Centaurians."

"About as much as anyone my age. I don't remember not hearing about the war, Marcus. It's just always been there." She shrugged. "I've seen the pictures a thousand times. And the things they've got in tanks at the museums. I know they're awful."

"Okay. Without gettin' scientific, they're bugs, worms—whatever. About twenty-two hundred varieties, four of 'em dominant. And every one of them meaner than anything Hell's got to offer. If you want to know what happened to me, Jennie, and the others, you got to understand about them. First, there isn't anything even similar between humans and bugs. Nothing. We can't even talk to each other, even if the Centaurians wanted to, and they damn sure don't. Second, and this is something Army don't like to make much out of, but it's true—they're *better'n* we are in most everything that's got to do with fighting. They're faster, better coordinated—everything. And the reason they're better is there isn't anything a Centaurian wants to do but kill something. Us, each other, it don't much matter. They eat and sleep and reproduce and kill. And they do the first three so's they can get on with the fourth. The only reason they haven't whipped us already is a piece of plain old luck. We beat 'em into space about thirty years, and we got us a better drive. We can get there—and they can't get here. Not yet, anyway. If they could, we wouldn't be sittin' here talking about it. We got to kill every last one of them and burn every egg in the system. If we don't—" I ran a quick finger over my throat and Jennie shuddered.

"I'm not telling you anything new, but it's something you got to really see if you're going to understand. What they are, and why, has got just about everything to do with how they affect humans. Only that part's not so easy. Everybody knows about it—but isn't anybody sure what it is."

"You mean, the thing that happened to you."

"To me—but to them, first. What they were makes 'em what they are now. Hasn't anybody had a chance to do much on-hand studying about prehistoric Centaurians, but they got some pretty good guesses. They had to survive, like anything else. Probably there was something eating *them* a couple million years ago. So they developed something to fight back with. Anything ate a big bug got this—picture, image, whatever, and it stayed with him. Something like a stinger that won't come out. And maybe next time he thought twice about goin' after that particular meal."

Jennie bit her lip thoughtfully. "That doesn't *say* anything, Marcus, not if you just leave it there with images and pictures. It's all kind of vague. Like on the holos, when you were in the parade, only I didn't know it was you—"

"So what'd they say?"

"Nothing much more than they *ever* say about anything. You know— 'One of our brave troopers who still carries the terrible memories of the war within him blah-blah—dreams of Centaurian warriors blah-blah-blah.' Is that like it is, Marcus? Dreams?"

I didn't look at her; I just studied Willie Brander's head up front like it was real interesting. "Guess it's kind of which words you want to use," I said. "It's not something we can come real close to naming, Jennie. The thing that started out bein' a defense mechanism evolved into something a lot more than that. It's a matter of pride, now. Only it's a natural kind of pride, like breathin'. The top baddie around is the one with more kills to his credit. And he's got the wispies in his head to prove it."

Jennie shuddered. "The what?"

"Wispies. Spookprints, psycho-shadows, whatever. The science fellas have got fancier labels than that."

Jennie went real quiet a minute. The skimmer dipped down out of traffic, and I figured we were getting where we were going.

"Marcus," she said finally, "it's not the same, is it? With people?"

"Well, sort of," I told her. "Not just *exactly* the same, though." Seemed like I was doing a lot of talking to the back of old Willie's head.

▲▼▲

I never been many places. Wasn't time to, hitting Earth about twice in twenty years. You don't have to pick up every rock you come to, though, to figure what's under it. A man makes it through about two hundred landings, he gets a fair nose for the terrain up ahead.

The smell I was getting now was money. Dusty bottle money, all fat and lazy—and they smelled me, same as I did them. I was the wrong kind of animal, one they hadn't seen before and didn't much want to. Bald-skinned and big, suited up black as night. A bright shiny girl beside me, and a tag-along behind. It scared the deep hell out of 'em, and I was feeling just pure mean enough to enjoy it.

Jennie didn't smell anything, 'cept what she was supposed to—crystal and silk and candle-shine silver. She took one look at the table, and the menu, and got the panics. "Marcus! I didn't have any *idea*—"

I tried to tell her what kind of money old soldiers have to spend, but she didn't believe that, either.

It was a hell of a place. There were dead-men waiters all over, men with long, gray-powder faces. They moved without walking and you never heard them coming. When food came out it was all secret and covered, and they'd stand around and whisper real serious awhile, then off one'd go, like a doctor wheeling God into surgery.

I don't know what Dark told them to get us in, but in wasn't eating. They were in no big hurry—we were there, but they'd make it hurt if they could. I grabbed one cruising by and told him we were ready, and he gave me this patient little smile and said he'd be glad to get me a menu in English. I grinned right back and told him I'd sure be grateful. When the new menu came, I set it aside without looking and ordered from the old one in Danish, Frisian and a little Pashto. I couldn't see his face, but Jennie could. He wouldn't know more than two of those, and they'd have to run tapes off his little pad recorder and take them off somewhere and get 'em figured.

When he was finished, I stopped him and gave him the look I learned from old Dark. "Boy, you been about this much help, so far," I told him, flipping a U.S. dime on the table. "You get your head on straight real soon, and we'll see about something better, okay?" I took a new eight hundred dollar bill out of my pack and laid it by the dime. He hated himself, but he wanted it, and he took himself out of there quick.

Jennie was eating needles. "That insufferable *bas*tard!"

"Hey, he's just got the sorries, like most everyone else," I told her. "Sorry he's standin' instead of sitting; probably hates every one of these folks and has reason to. We sure goin' to get us some service, though."

"You are not a nice person, Marcus Ash."

"Never get time for it."

She tried a little wine and gave me a crooked grin. "Okay. That cute trick with the languages. Where'd you get time for that?"

I filled up her glass again, and mine. "We got soldiers out there from most everywhere, Jennie. We're all supposed to speak standard Armycom in the field, and we do if there isn't much hurry. You put a man under fire, though, where you got about an eighth of a second to figure which way to duck, your buddy's goin' to say '*watch it, Ash!*' in whatever tongue he was born with. When he does, I don't want to take no time sayin' 'huh?' just because he's Portuguese or Welsh. Besides, there isn't much else to do out there if you're not fighting, 'cept talk. So you learn to do it with whoever's in the same hole. Maybe that's worth a war, I don't know. Maybe when it's over we'll all go back to being just like we were."

The salad came, bright green with some kind of fruit on top I'd never seen before, and a thick white sauce with little specks in it. Whatever it was, I'd ordered it during my big show-off scene, and if I didn't like it, that son of a bitch would sure never know it.

Halfway through the next course I caught Jennie with fork in midair, watching my tag-along. It wasn't the first time. She hadn't got on that yet, but she was thinking about it. Willie was a couple of tables away with a plain glass of water—untouched—trying hard not to look like he was looking.

"Poor guy," she said, shaking her head, "he doesn't have much fun, does he?"

I gave her a real hurt face. "Hey, *I'm* the hero, remember? He isn't supposed to have fun."

"Oh, golly, listen I forgot myself." We both laughed, but she was still thinking. "Does it—bother you any?"

"No. Way it's got to be unless I want to sit around Heroes' Hotel all day." I read her question. "Officially it's RIFETS—Research Institute for Extraterrestrial Studies. Someone dubbed it Heroes' Hotel 'cause it's homebase for troopers with peculiar conditions like mine."

"He goes with you, because something might happen to you." It wasn't a question. There was worry in the tight little corners of her mouth. It kind of did something to me to see it there.

"Hey, you know about the tag-along," I told her. "Something *could* happen, but it's not likely. The wispies I'm draggin' around don't bother you any unless you're sleeping, passed out drunk or otherwise uncon-scious. I sure as hell don't go to *sleep* on purpose, and we've learned not to booze it up too much. Most of the time. The tag-along's with us for that slim chance you might fall on your head, have a stroke—whatever. He's got all kinds of goodies in that little red box, and he can jolt me full of wake-up real quick if he has to."

I picked up my glass, and she started to say something; then I caught him over the rim, bearing in on us from across the room. Big belly and three or four stars on his tabs—a couple of little ground-hog ribbons on his chest for peeing straight. Whatever he'd been pouring down was working just fine. He was having trouble with his feet and trying to make up for it by walking real slow and serious.

Jennie caught my eyes going small and didn't know why. I stood up slower'n you're supposed to, and he wheeled on over and shot me a big grin.

"Listen, you *sit*, Sergeant." He winked down at Jennie, going over her good and taking his time. "I'm the one ought to be standing, Rafe Hacker." A wet hand came out. "I know who you are, Sergeant Ash. Hey, sit. I mean it."

He had it all figured and so did I. If Ash sits, he sits too, and there we go. He plants himself down awhile, then goes back and tells his buddies he talked to a real one. Maybe he picks up the girl's name in the bargain. Only the whole business wasn't going right, and he was beginning to figure out why. If we kept standing, everybody guesses the general's pullin' rank on the hero sergeant. If he sits—and I don't—it looks a lot worse than that.

"Sergeant, I'd be pleased if you'd let me buy you and the lady a drink." His little eyes are right on me and he knows.

"Thank you, sir. Maybe we could take a raincheck on that."

"Maybe the lady—"

"No, sir. She wouldn't."

The eyes don't move but the grin gets real tight. "Sergeant, I've got a lot of respect for you wormheads, but—"

"Sir. That isn't one of your words. You got no right to it."

His face went slack. "You are out of *line*, Sergeant."

"No, sir. You are. That's our word. We can use it, you can't. Go out and make your kill and get your gray ribbon, and it's yours. Until then, you don't own it. You want my number, sir, it's 775041113."

The red was starting up over his best ugly smile. He was thinking about what ought to happen next and how he ought to bring me up on charges and all, but he wasn't dumb enough to do it. Instead, he showed me the little pig eyes again and hauled himself out of there.

Jennie was trying to crawl under a napkin. "Hey, listen, you're more fun than anyone. Who we gonna kill next?"

"Sorry. I got this thing about ground-hog brass."

"No, really?"

"Okay, let me go. Peace."

"Oh, sure. St. Marcus of Ash."

We laughed together and caught each other just right for a quick second and held it there, then let it go. It'd be there when we came looking for it.

▲▼▲

Outside we got us a brand-new high, breathing in all the good night air. It was one of those times anybody watching figures there's another couple of happy drunks running loose—but you see it different from the inside 'cause you've got something circling in around you keeping all the fine stuff going. We were smarter than anybody and saw things nobody'd ever seen before. And of course *every*thing was funny.

We both knew what was coming, that we were about a breath away from bein' there. We held it all back in the skimmer because we knew we couldn't handle it and didn't want to.

"Hey, Marcus Ash."

"Uhuh."

"Got to know. Okay?"

"Got to know what?"

"Dinner. How much that huge goddamn dinner cost. 'Bout a zillion dollars?"

"None of your business."

"Come *on*."

"All right. Nine hundred somethin'."

"*Dollars?*"

"Well, hell, yes."

"My God. And an *eight* hundred dollar tip. Who's going to believe me? What'd you do this weekend, Jennie? Oh, nothing. Picked me up a war hero and we had us a couple of drinks and 'bout nine hundred dollars' worth of snacks—"

"Hey, now. I didn't say I left that groundie no eight hundred dollars."

"Didn't you?"

"No."

"How much?"

"Half that."

"Four hundred?"

"Hell, no."

"What?"

"*Half* that."

"Listen, you…"

"Goddamn, Jennie, I said half, I meant half." Scrubbing around in my pouch, I found it and gave it to her. She blinked at it a long time, then threw back her head and howled until the tears came.

"Marcus, what's that—*poor* man going to do with half an eight hundred dollar bill? Oh, no!"

We looked at each other and got the funnies goin' and couldn't get 'em stopped. When everything settled down a little, I told her I had something real wonderful for her and gave her the silver spoon I'd stolen from The Chalice. "Don't look like I learned nothing since high school, does it?"

▲▼▲

When she looked up at me her hair was making yellow smoke around her head and there were tiny bright points in her eyes. "Hey." She poked one finger at my chin. "I can't make any words, Marcus."

"Maybe it isn't a talkin' kind of time."

"Yeah. Maybe it isn't."

She slid in close all lazy warm and smelling like girl and said something, and I said *what?* and she said whatever it was again and grinned in closer. Past her I could see the city, and it seemed to stretch on forever, like worlds fadin' out to the Rim until there wasn't any place else to go. If I thought about it just right, all the lights turned into stars, and I was out there again, where I didn't ever want to be. This time the whole string ran out, and the billion-to-three odds clicked back to zero. The meanies holed me up in some stink-warren and ripped me good. Snap-claws clipped me down like paper, and all the little razor feet came hummin' in to peel the wrapper…

"Hey, you're off somewhere."

"Right here."

"What you thinking?"

"I was just kind of wondering what those little stringy things was in 'bout the umpty-third course—you know? Right after the duck with sugar peaches…?"

Jennie made a face. "You weren't either."

"Sure I was. What you figure I was thinking about. You?"

"Well, maybe."

"Huh."

"You were thinking about me a minute ago."

"That wasn't thinking."

"Oh? What was that?"

"Doing, mostly."

"Yeah. Was, wasn't it?" She gave another one of those sounds and turned over and propped her chin in her hands, and I leaned back to enjoy the view. We didn't say anything, and she kind of stared out the window and thought about something and then looked back at me again. "What are you going to do, Marcus?"

"About what?"

"You."

She said *you*, but she was thinking you and maybe me.

"What I'm doing now," I told her. "It's a little late to start learning a new trade."

Her head came up. "You mean the army? God, Marcus, you don't have to go out *there* again? They wouldn't send you *back*?"

"Not fighting, no. There's other things."

"You want to do that."

"It's that, or go back to stealin' spoons."

"I'm serious, Marcus." She reached out and touched the little chained medallion on my chest, holding it and turning it in two fingers.

"Sure," I said, "I am, too. The army's not a bad place for a guy like me. It's somewhere I can do some good. If the war keeps on, and I reckon it will, there's going to be plenty of use for a man who's made it through more years than he ought to. When—hey, you listening to me?"

"What? Yes. No, I'm sorry. Marcus, what's this?"

I winked at her and took the medallion from her fingers. "This, is somethin' real important. What it does is let you and me do what we're doing in here without Captain Willie Brander sitting right there on the corner of the bed."

She looked at me without expression, and then it suddenly dawned on her what I was talking about. I laughed and swiped at her hair. "Honey, it doesn't do *pictures*—just stuff like pulse, respiration, BP. Comes through on the little red box."

"Well, if he's any good," she said coolly, "he sure as hell knows what *you're* doing. If I'd known that, I would have made you take the thing off. It's like—peeking."

"No, you wouldn't," I told her. "If I did, old Willie'd come right through that wall, and there wouldn't be no question about *peeking*."

She sat up and stared at me.

"Well, sure. What did you think?"

"My God, I don't know." She shook her head, troubled. "Marcus, you must think I'm an idiot. We talked about this, and here I am asking a bunch of dumb questions again. It's—" She shrugged helplessly. "Yeah, I do know, too. I forget all that when we're—like this."

So do I...

"It doesn't seem important. It's outside somewhere and not in here, and it doesn't have anything to do with us. Oh, damn, Marcus, it *doesn't*!" A little sound stuck in her throat; she came to me quick and held me, and the tears were hot on my chest. "Don't you see? I just want you to *be* here, I want to wake up with you, and I don't—"

She felt what it did to me because she pulled back fast and kind of stared at her hands, like I'd gone all hot and burned her. I grabbed her shoulders hard. "Goddamn. You don't know what you're talking about." I was hurting her bad, but I didn't let go.

"Even if it was bad, I wouldn't care." She just kept shaking her head, not even feeling anything. "If you woke up *screaming*, I'd be there. I'd—"

"Shit." I was already out of bed looking for my stuff in the dark. I could hear her trying to make little noises and feel her movin' all soft-naked behind me, and I shut that out and didn't feel anything.

"Marcus, please!"

I can't hear you any more...

"God, what did I *do*? I want you to *stay* here is all, I don't *care*!" She reached out and found me, and I came around fast and slapped her hard. She made a little cry and fell back. I didn't look at her anywhere else. Just the eyes. There wasn't anything there yet. Only fright and tears and hurt.

"Look," I told her, "you got your belly full of food and some of me under that. You lookin' for more, girl, don't. There ain't nothing you got I can't get somewhere else. You *read* me?"

She didn't want to hear it. She was going to shut it all out and say it wasn't real. So I just stood there a minute, taking my eyes down her slow, leaving dirty where I passed. Then I waited until I could see it happening to her. Like real good glass, coming all apart.

▲▼▲

When they snugged me in good and made all the little wires just right, I kept seein' her, only I couldn't much look at her now because all the bad hurt kept looking right back. Jennie, Jennie, I had to kill the tomorrows, or we'd wind up trying to live 'em, and that can't ever be. We *can't* tell folks what it's like inside. We got to say it's wispies and nightmare shadows in our heads. There's kids out there with dyin' on their minds, and not much more. They going to *fight* any better, knowing the red screaming baddies in my head are just as real as real can be?

Shall I stay the night and hold you, then, Jennie? I can rest on your pillow with the smell of your hair and the soft-soft sound of your breath— and you can pray good Willie Brander drops me quick when they come and find me sleeping...

Jennie, Jennie, do you see? Old Dark is right, and a wormhead can't be what you want him to. He can drink with all the other fine heroes and think where he'd like to be. But more than that's a bad and hurtful thing...

Survival Course

Vivid pictures oscillated across Martin's mental screens:

He was a warm pearl in a giant oyster. The oyster was squeezing him to death with dank passion...

He was in the last crushing seconds of fetal agony. Damn! Mother should never have had children...

An inchworm. Inside a great pea. Bam! Cook snapped him cruelly from the pod...

The last, he decided, was close enough to the truth. Something very bad had happened to the ship. Something fatal. The escape capsule had imploded its fleshy walls, formed a Martin-sized cocoon and ejected him from whatever catastrophe lay behind. Now—

ABLE MARTIN.

"What?" Martin tried to move his head. Abruptly the walls sucked themselves back into place. Martin rose weightlessly from his form-couch, pulled himself back, snapped himself down.

MARTIN.

"Who's that?"

SHIP'S COMPUTER, MARTIN.

"Oh."

ARE YOU INJURED IN ANY WAY?

"No. What happened?"

THE SHIP HAS BEEN DESTROYED. YOU ARE ABOARD ESCAPE CAPSULE FORTY-TWO.

Martin waited for more. Evidently direct questions were required. "Did we hit something? No, that's not likely, is it? How did it happen? Did anybody else get off?"

Ship's computer was silent. Martin shrugged, inspected his sur-roundings. There wasn't much to see. The capsule was spherical. Spongy amber walls. No ports. A single safe-light to his right. Maximum distance from one wall to another, roughly two-and-a-half meters.

And he was—where? Deep space. Between Wolf's Star and Jefferson. But that didn't mean a thing, really. He knew that much. The ship had been in Warp when whatever happened had happened—it could have been tossed into reality nearly anywhere. If he was now remotely near either Wolf's Star or Jefferson it would be a universally large coincidence.

MARTIN.

"Right here."

THE SHIP WAS DESTROYED THROUGH A MALFUNCTION IN THE DAVIDSON AUXILIARY REGULATORS. ESSENTIALLY, INTERFERENCE FROM AN UNANTICIPATED MASS CAUSED A SUBSEQUENT MISALIGNMENT OF THE DRIVE FIELDS, WHICH EJECTED THE SHIP FROM NONSPACE AND DESTROYED IT WHILE ITS WARP ENGINES WERE STILL PARTIALLY FUNCTIONING.

"Oh," said Martin. He had no idea what the computer was talking about.

CHANCES AGAINST SUCH A MALFUNCTION ARE EIGHT TO THE TENTH POWER. THERE ARE NO SURVIVORS OTHER THAN YOURSELF.

Martin winced at that. "*No*body got out? There were two hundred and fifty people aboard."

TWO-HUNDRED-FORTY-SEVEN, the computer corrected. EXCLUD-ING YOURSELF. WHY WERE YOU IN ESCAPE CAPSULE FORTY-TWO WHEN THE SHIP WAS DESTROYED?

Martin was taken aback. "Huh? I was taking a nap. Why do you ask?"

IT IS UNAUTHORIZED TO ENTER THE ESCAPE CAPSULE UNLESS AN EVACUATION ORDER HAS BEEN ISSUED OR ENTRY PERMISSION HAS BEEN GRANTED.

"Look—"

IF YOU WISHED TO TAKE A NAP, MARTIN, WHY DID YOU NOT UTILIZE THE BUNK IN YOUR CABIN?

"I don't know, I was tired. The capsule was handy. It seemed like a good idea at the time. Listen—what difference does it make now?"

OCCUPYING AN ESCAPE CAPSULE WITHOUT AUTHORIZATION AND/OR RECEIPT OF AN EVACUATION ORDER IS A PASSENGER VIOLATION. THE VIOLATION WILL BE RECORDED.

Martin laughed out loud.

NOT UNDERSTOOD, said the computer. WHY DO YOU EXPRESS DISINTEREST IN THE REPORTING OF THIS VIOLATION?

"Forget it," said Martin. He was getting fed up with the computer's rational ramblings. And worried. There were things he needed to know. Important things. *Where are we and where are we going? When does help arrive? How much air is aboard? Food? Water?*

▲▼▲

He asked the most important question first. The answer set his heart thumping against his chest.

"That's all? Eight *days*?"

APPROXIMATELY, the computer told him.

"I don't want approximately, I want exactly!"

EXACT OXYGEN REQUIREMENTS FOR A PERSON OF YOUR PHYSICAL STRUCTURE, MARTIN: ONE HUNDRED NINETY HOURS, PLUS OR MINUS ONE HOUR, CALCULATED FOR NORMAL WAKING AND SLEEPING PERIODS, WITH MINIMAL ACTIVITY.

"Holy Christ," Martin muttered.

YOU NEED NOT BE CONCERNED WITH OXYGEN CONSUMPTION, MARTIN.

"No?"

NO. THE SUPPLY IS MORE THAN ADEQUATE FOR THE DURATION OF YOUR ANIMATE PERIOD.

Martin sat up. "My *animate* period?" Short hairs climbed the back of his neck. "What's that supposed to mean?" He remembered something. "Listen—you're talking about putting me under—something like that. So I'll use less oxygen? Great. I—"

The computer droned: I AM REQUIRED TO STATE CERTAIN FACTS. PLEASE HEAR THEM BEFORE YOU COMMENT FURTHER. ONE: EACH STANDARD ESCAPE POD, MOBILE (SEPM), IS EQUIPPED WITH AN ADEQUATE LIFE SUPPORT SYSTEM. THIS SYSTEM INCLUDES OXYGEN—WHICH WE HAVE DISCUSSED—CONCENTRATED FOOD STAPLES, WATER AND A NUMBER FOUR MEDI-PACKET, MODIFIED. TWO: ADDITIONALLY, BASIC PLANETARY SURVIVAL GEAR IS AVAILABLE SHOULD THE CAPSULE AND ITS OCCUPANT BE RELEASED IN THE VICINITY OF A PLANETARY BODY CAPABLE OF SUPPORTING HUMAN LIFE. THE CAPSULE IS DESIGNED TO ACCOMPLISH A SINGLE LANDING ON SUCH A BODY UNDER NORMAL CONDITIONS. THREE: THE CAPSULE IS ALSO EQUIPPED WITH A STANDARD REIMAR SEVEN-O-TWO BEACON TRANSMITTING DEVICE (BTD), CAPABLE OF EMITTING A THREE-STAGE TRANSLIGHT EMERGENCY SIGNAL WITH A RANGE OF FIVE-HUNDRED LIGHT-YEARS. THE BTD TRANSMITS A CONTINUOUS HOMING PATTERN FOR A PERIOD OF ONE STANDARD YEAR.

Martin waited. The computer remained silent. He felt immensely relieved. The capsule didn't look like much, but apparently there was more behind its fleshy walls than met the eye.

"This—signal beacon," Martin asked. "How long does it take to reach—wherever it's going?"

THE BTD SIGNAL IS A TIGHT-BEAM TRANSMISSION WHICH
BOOSTS AN EMERGENCY 'PULSE' AT TRANSLIGHT SPEEDS, AS I
EXPLAINED. THE IMPULSE REACHES ITS MAXIMUM RANGE OF FIVE
HUNDRED LIGHT-YEARS IN FOURTEEN POINT SEVEN MINUTES.

Martin let out a breath. "Then it's already out there. Someone could
have picked it up. They could be on their way now."

NEGATIVE, MARTIN.

"What?"

THEORETICALLY, YOU ARE CORRECT. IF THE SIGNAL HAD BEEN
TRANSMITTED—AND RECEIVING DEVICES HAD BEEN WITHIN
RANGE OF ITS IMPULSE AND A WARP SHIP HAD BEEN AVAILABLE—
AS YOU SAY, 'THEY COULD BE ON THEIR WAY NOW.' HOWEVER, ALL
SUCH ASSUMPTIONS ARE NECESSARILY INVALID SINCE NO SIGNAL
HAS BEEN TRANSMITTED.

"What?" Martin nearly leaped off his couch, forgetting the safety belt
that held him in place. "Look—what the hell are you waiting for? I've got
a hundred and ninety hours of *breathing* time, friend—plus or minus
whatever I'm wasting jawing with you! Just get yourself—"

The computer interrupted: YOU DO NOT UNDERSTAND. I STATED
THAT I WAS REQUIRED TO MAKE CERTAIN FACTS KNOWN TO YOU.
THESE FACTS CONCERNED THE CAPABILITIES OF THE ESCAPE
CAPSULE. 'CAPABILITY' IS DEFINED AS 'HAVING THE CAPACITY OR
ABILITY.' IN OTHER WORDS, THE ESCAPE CAPSULE IS EQUIPPED
TO PERFORM AND/OR SUPPLY THE AFOREMENTIONED SERVICES.
UNDER CERTAIN CIRCUMSTANCES, FOR EXAMPLE, THE BTD SIGNAL
WOULD BE UTILIZED. UNDER OTHER CONDITIONS, IT MIGHT
BECOME EXPEDIENT TO EMPLOY PLANETARY SURVIVAL GEAR. AS IT
STANDS, HOWEVER, NONE OF THE EQUIPMENT AND/OR SERVICES
MENTIONED ARE APPLICABLE TO THIS PARTICULAR SITUATION.

Martin's blood ran cold. *Applicable?* His first impulse was to scream
at the computer and beat on the amber walls. What the hell did it care?
It was content to stay where it was forever—an electronic half-wit buried in spongy bliss. Its oxygen supply wasn't running out in plus-or-
minus hours.

Instead he brought his rapid breathing under control and leaned
back on his couch. Not that the computer would care one way or the
other whether he was calm or hysterical. Screaming, however, was
bound to use up an inordinate amount of oxygen.

Half-wit or not, the computer was there and had to be dealt with.

"Look," Martin said easily, "what I think we have here is a communications problem."

I AM EXPERIENCING NO DIFFICULTY IN COMMUNICATING, MARTIN.

"Okay. I am, though. Let's run through it again. You haven't activated the signal beacon. Why?"

AS I EXPLAINED, BTD TRANSMISSION IS NOT APPLICABLE IN THIS SITUATION.

"Why not?"

WHEN THE SHIP WAS DESTROYED IT WAS THROWN OUT OF WARP AND BACK INTO REALITY. I HAVE MADE EXTENSIVE EFFORTS TO LOCATE OUR POSITION RELATIVE TO INHABITED AND/OR RECORDED QUADRANTS. FROM THIS POINT IN SPACE NO RECOGNIZABLE CONSTELLATIONS CAN BE OBSERVED. I HAVE, OF COURSE, TAKEN INTO CONSIDERATION THE FACT THAT STELLAR PATTERNS DIFFER ACCORDING TO ONE'S POSITION. ADDITIONALLY, I HAVE MADE SPECTROSCOPIC ANALYSES IN AN ATTEMPT TO IDENTIFY A FAMILIAR CLUSTER OR UNIT. RESULTS: NEGATIVE.

Martin's heart sank. "In other words, we're lost."

RELATIVE TO MY RECORDED KNOWLEDGE, YES.

A thought suddenly struck him and he sat up straight again.

He weighed his words carefully. "Do you believe your—navigational records are wholly complete?"

NOT UNDERSTOOD, MARTIN. 'WHOLLY COMPLETE' IN WHAT SENSE?

"In the sense that you have data on all planets and star-systems that have been discovered, all areas of space that have been mapped and explored."

TO A LARGE EXTENT, YES. WHEN I WAS ON THE SHIP NEW DATA WERE CONTINUOUSLY PROGRAMMED INTO MY BANKS IN AN EFFORT TO MAINTAIN COMPLETE AND ACCURATE NAVIGATIONAL RECORDS. LOGICALLY, HOWEVER, IT IS POSSIBLE THAT DATA EXIST THAT HAVE NOT BEEN MADE AVAILABLE TO ME. I HAVE NO DEFINITE BASIS TO CONCLUDE OTHERWISE.

Martin took a deep breath. "Then—logically—a signal from our position *could* be received."

IT IS CONCEIVABLE.

"Then transmit the signal," Martin said firmly. "If there's any chance at all—"

NEGATIVE, MARTIN. THE ODDS ARE ASTRONOMICALLY HIGH AGAINST RECEPTION.

"To hell with the odds!" Martin struck his fist against the couch. "My odds are zero unless you do something!"

NEGATIVE, MARTIN. I WILL NOT ACTIVATE THE SIGNAL BEACON.

Martin eyed the blank walls narrowly. "I'm not asking—I'm *telling* you. I'm a—a human and I'm giving a machine an order."

PERHAPS IT WOULD BE HELPFUL IF YOU FULLY UNDERSTOOD THAT THERE IS A DIFFERENCE BETWEEN A COMPLEX COMPUTER SYSTEM BASED ON THE PRINCIPLES OF LOGIC AND A SIMPLE SERVING ROBOT. ALTHOUGH I AM RECEPTIVE TO CERTAIN COMMANDS, I AM NOT PROGRAMMED TO OBEY YOU BLINDLY UNDER ALL CIRCUMSTANCES. MY BASIC FUNCTION IS TO INITIATE LOGICAL ACTIONS BASED UPON AVAILABLE DATA. WHILE IT IS TRUE THAT THERE IS A POSSIBILITY THAT A SIGNAL BEAMED FROM THIS POSITION MIGHT BE RECEIVED THE ODDS—AS I EXPLAINED—ARE OVERWHELMINGLY NEGATIVE. ACTIVATING THE SIGNAL WOULD INVOLVE THE DISSIPATION OF AN IMMENSE AMOUNT OF ENERGY. CONSIDERING THE ODDS, SUCH AN EXPENDITURE WOULD BE UNNECESSARILY WASTEFUL.

Martin dropped his head to the couch. "Look," he said wearily, "what am I going to do with all that immense amount of energy when I'm *dead* eight days from now? Will you explain that to me. Please?"

He let out a deep breath and looked at the amber walls. "Listen, I said a minute ago we had a communications problem. No. *I* do. You know my name, so you also probably know from the passenger roster what I do. I'm a heavy-equipment salesman. I sell things to people who want to dig up mountains and build bridges. All of our stuff is fully automatic—you can program it to do anything you want it to do. Only, that's not my end of the business. I know how to stick the tape in—period. What I'm saying is, I'm not used to talking to computers. I simply don't understand why it seems—and I'm not saying it's true—but it *seems* as if you're not making every effort to get me back to civilization before my air runs out." Martin shook his head. "I don't understand that. If you're not going to activate the signal—what are you going to do?"

An idea suddenly occurred to him. "A minute ago you said something about how I wouldn't need all the oxygen on board. That it would be—what? 'Adequate for my animate period?' Is that what you've got in mind—putting me in some kind of deep sleep or something? We didn't get back to that."

YOU MISUNDERSTOOD, MARTIN. THE WORD 'ANIMATE' IN THE SENSE IT WAS USED, CAN BE DEFINED AS 'POSSESSING LIFE,' OR 'LIVING.' WHAT I SAID WAS THAT 'THE SUPPLY IS MORE THAN ADEQUATE FOR THE DURATION OF YOUR ANIMATE PERIOD.' BY THAT I MEANT THAT PRIOR TO THE TIME WHEN YOUR AVAILABLE OXYGEN SUPPLY WOULD ORDINARILY BE CONSUMED YOU WILL

BE IN AN ESSENTIALLY NONLIVING STATE, AS FAR AS PERSONAL COGNIZANCE IS CONCERNED.

Martin felt something terrible clutch at his stomach. "For God's sake—what are you talking about? What are you going to do to me?"

I ASKED EARLIER THAT YOU ALLOW ME TO PRESENT CERTAIN FACTS. YOU HAVE, HOWEVER, FREQUENTLY ALLOWED YOUR EMOTIONS—

"Damn you!" Martin shouted. "I'm alive! I'm supposed to have emotions!"

ASSUREDLY. AS I STATED, THE STANDARD ESCAPE POD, MOBILE (SEPM), HAS CERTAIN CAPABILITIES. I ALSO ATTEMPTED TO EXPLAIN THAT WHILE THE SEPM'S PRIMARY FUNCTION IS TO TRANSPORT HUMAN SURVIVORS TO SAFETY, IF POSSIBLE, THERE ARE CONDITIONS UNDER WHICH—

"Listen," said Martin, "I don't want to hear any of that again."

—UNDER WHICH THIS FUNCTION IS NO LONGER RELEVANT. EXAMPLES: WHEN NO PLANETARY BODY CAPABLE OF SUPPORTING LIFE IS PRESENT WITHIN THE OPERATIONAL SPHERE OF THE CAPSULE…WHEN THE ODDS AGAINST RECEPTION OF A BTD SIGNAL BEAM ARE ASTRONOMICAL. I ALSO EXPLAINED THAT, WHILE I AM RECEPTIVE TO CERTAIN COMMANDS UNDER SPECIFIC CONDITIONS, I AM NOT PROGRAMMED TO OBEY ALL INSTRUCTIONS. PRESENT CONDITIONS ARE SUCH THAT I HAVE OVERRIDDEN ALL BUT MY PRIMARY PROGRAMMING. I AM INITIATING A SECONDARY LOGICAL ACTION BASED ON AVAILABLE DATA. I WILL EXERCISE THE STELLAR OUTREACH OPTION IN EXACTLY FORTY-FIVE STANDARD MINUTES.

Martin stared dumbly. "You'll what? I don't have any idea what you're talking about."

IT IS QUITE PAINLESS, MARTIN. YOU WILL NOT—

"Painless!"

YOU MUST UNDERSTAND THAT THE ALTERNATIVE IS QUITE NECESSARY. THE STELLAR OUTREACH OPTION IS NOT EXERCISED UNLESS OTHER CHOICES ARE IMPRACTICAL. IN THIS CASE NO OTHER OPTION IS OPEN. AGAIN, THE PROCEDURE IN NO WAY—

"Wait a minute," Martin said hoarsely. He was scared, bewildered. His head throbbed. The whole thing was a nightmare.

Only one fact was frighteningly clear: the computer had no intention of trying to save his life. For some reason of its own it was going to kill him.

Once he'd let his mind form the words he felt reasonably calm. And it was absolutely necessary for him to remain completely rational. His emotions were meaningless to the computer. If he was going to stay alive he would have to face the computer on its own ground. If he couldn't fight logic with logic—he was dead. It was as simple as that. The computer couldn't have put it better.

"All right," he said calmly, "tell me about the—Stellar Outreach option."

YOUR REASONABLE ATTITUDE IS ENCOURAGING, MARTIN.

"Thanks," Martin said dryly.

THE STELLAR OUTREACH OPTION WAS PROGRAMMED INTO THE BANKS OF EVERY SHIP'S COMPUTER AS AN ALTERNATE TO THE ESCAPE CAPSULE'S PRIMARY FUNCTION. ESSENTIALLY: SURVIVORS WITH LOW RESCUE PROFILES—SUCH AS YOURSELF, MARTIN—ARE REAPPORTIONED INTO THEIR CHROMOSOMAL COMPONENTS, ENCAPSULATED IN LIFEBANK DISPERSAL CARRIERS (LDC) AND PROJECTED IN A RANDOM PATTERN FROM THE CENTRAL POINT OF ORIGIN—WHICH, OF COURSE, IS THE ESCAPE CAPSULE ITSELF.

Martin swallowed and stared at the amber wall. "But—why?"

THE PURPOSE OF STELLAR OUTREACH IS TO SPREAD THE SEED OF MAN. IT IS AN ENTIRELY LOGICAL SUB-PROGRAM. THOSE WHO CANNOT SURVIVE IN THEIR PRIMARY FORMS ARE GIVEN THE OPPORTUNITY TO SURVIVE AS POTENTIAL LIFEBANKS OF THE FUTURE. IT HAS BEEN THEORIZED THAT MAN MAY HAVE EVOLVED ON MANY PLANETS IN JUST THIS MANNER. AT ANY RATE, APPROXIMATELY ONE HUNDRED MILLION CHROMOSOMAL UNIT PACK SYSTEMS (CUPS) ARE DISPERSED THROUGH SPACE IN ONE THOUSAND LIFEBANK DISPERSAL CARRIERS. AT A SPECIFIED DISTANCE FROM THE INITIAL DISPERSAL POINT EACH LDC EXPLODES AND SCATTERS ITS CUPS—THUS, GREAT SPATIAL DISTRIBUTION IS ACHIEVED.

Martin was valiantly holding onto his reason. *God help me*, he thought grimly, *if I ever get back to anywhere someone's going to hear about this...*

"You can—do all that?" He was curious in spite of himself. "Here—in this capsule?"

THE PROCEDURE IS RELATIVELY SIMPLE, the computer told him. BASICALLY THE SUBJECT'S PHYSICAL BODY IS—

"I don't want to go into that part," Martin said quickly.

THEN PERHAPS AN ANALOGY WILL SERVE. GENETICALLY SPEAKING, IF YOUR BODY WERE SUDDENLY TO EXPLODE EACH PARTICLE WOULD, IN A SENSE, RETAIN ITS IDENTITY. THOUGH EACH, OF COURSE, WOULD BE NONSENTIENT, EACH WOULD RETAIN THE CELLULAR IDENTITY OF ABLE MARTIN. CURIOUSLY, I CAN PRESENT

A SIMILAR ANALOGY USING MYSELF AS AN EXAMPLE. ORIGINALLY COMPUTERS WERE CONSTRUCTED AS SINGULAR UNITS. NOW, NEARLY ALL ARE ORGANIC TO THEIR IMMEDIATE ENVIRONMENT. I WAS A PART OF EVERY PART OF THE SHIP. PARTS OF ME WERE LOST WHEN THE SHIP WAS DESTROYED, BUT SINCE EACH PART IS ESSENTIALLY A PART OF THE WHOLE—

"Okay, I understand," said Martin. "One question. Logic or no logic, what you've got in mind is to do me in, right?"

IT IS A COLLOQUIALISM MEANING TO BRING ABOUT THE DEATH OF AN INDIVIDUAL.

"Yes. That's what it is. What it amounts to is you are going to take a human life against its will. What *that* is is murder, whether a—a person does it or a computer. You can look up the definition yourself. I don't have any desire to be 'nonsentient,' friend—and I couldn't care less about Spreading the Seed of Man. I don't know much about robots and computers but I can't believe you haven't got some kind of built-in something or other that prohibits your taking a human life. Look that up in your banks or cells or whatever and tell me I'm wrong."

ESSENTIALLY YOU ARE RIGHT, MARTIN. HOWEVER, YOUR STATEMENT IS NONRELEVANT.

"It's relevant to me!" Martin shouted.

PERHAPS. HOWEVER, WHEN I TRANSFORM YOU FROM YOUR PRESENT PHYSICAL STATE INTO CHROMOSOMAL UNIT PACK SYSTEMS I WILL NOT BE 'TAKING A HUMAN LIFE.' I WILL MERELY BE REDISTRIBUTING ITS COMPONENTS IN A DIFFERENT MANNER. FROM YOUR WORDS I SENSE THAT YOU ARE EMOTIONALLY DISTURBED. AS I STATED, THE PROCEDURE IS PAINLESS. AN ODORLESS GAS—

"You can't—"

—WILL BE RELEASED IN THIRTY-EIGHT MINUTES. A—

"Thirty-eight minutes!"

—A STANDARD FORTY-FIVE MINUTES IS GRANTED TO SUBJECTS BETWEEN ANNOUNCEMENT OF THE PROCEDURE AND ACTUAL PROCESSING. THIS TIME MAY BE USED AT THE DISCRETION OF THE INDIVIDUAL CONCERNED—SLEEPING, EATING, OR THE CONTEMPLATION OF MYTHICAL DEITIES ARE SEVERAL OPTIONS. ENTERTAINMENT TAPES AND HOLOGRAPHIC PRESENTATIONS ARE AVAILABLE. ACCELERATED LEARNING TAPES ON A VARIETY OF SUBJECTS ARE ALSO ABOARD, INCLUDING COURSES IN ONE HUNDRED SEVENTEEN LANGUAGES. THESE LATTER, OF COURSE, MAY APPEAR IMPRACTICAL TO STELLAR OUTREACH CANDIDATES.

YOU HAVE NOW CONSUMED NINE MINUTES, MARTIN. TIME REMAINING: THIRTY-SIX MINUTES.

▲▼▲

Martin's body was slick with moisture. A sickly odor exuded from his pores. Think, think—he had to *think*! Only, how could he think with his head splitting open? He wondered if there was anything as simple as an aspirin in a Number Four MediPacket, Modified.

In moments his hands began to shake. He tried to stop them by putting them under his back, then clamping them to the arms of the couch. Nothing helped. The sweat on his body turned cold and he began to tremble uncontrollably. He closed his eyes and forced his breathing back to normal.

Maybe, he decided, it would be best to forget the whole thing. Stop fighting it. He had less than eight days of oxygen—even if the computer would let him live to use it. Those eight days would be pure hell—knowing they were the end, that no help was on the way. Why not just...

He angrily swept the thought aside. Anything could happen in eight days. If he could stay alive maybe he could con the computer into sending a signal. Someone *might* pick it up. A range of five hundred light-years covered a pretty big chunk of space.

Life Dispersal Carriers—great God, who had thought that one up! He wondered what the odds were against any of the one-hundred-million cellular bits of Able Martin ever getting anywhere. Or doing anything when they got there. Those kind of odds, though, didn't seem to bother the computer at all. And why should they? Passengers in Chromosomal Unit Pack Systems would find it difficult to complain to the space lines.

Time...time...damn it, time was running out! Thirty-six minutes. Less than that, now. Maybe there was something in the planetary survival gear. If he could find it. And get to it. Take a good slice at the fleshy walls. Maybe short out the computer and...He tossed the idea aside. That wouldn't get him any closer to activating the beacon. Hell, he wouldn't know what to do with it if he found it.

There was only one way. He'd known that from the beginning. Fight the computer on its own ground. The computer wasn't God—it was a machine—a machine that used the tools of intelligence, but really had no intelligence of its own. Computers reasoned—but they only reasoned with what they had to work with. Didn't they? Basically, then, while the computer had access to a great deal more knowledge than he had and could put it together faster and better—he, Able Martin, could outthink it. If he pushed the right button at the right time. That was the key: the computer had limitations. Find those limitations.

He tried to think back on what the computer had said. There had to be something. Somewhere. Option: activate the signal beacon. No. The computer was stubbornly set against that. No time to argue the point. Option: Get to a planet. Get out of the capsule. Double-negative. He was a billion prime miles from nowhere. Option: talk the computer into letting him live long enough to dream up other options...

Martin wearily swept the whole thing aside. It was hopeless. No time. *Think*, damn it! Look at it. Turn it around. Take it apart.

"Computer."

YES, MARTIN.

"How much time left?"

SEVENTEEN MINUTES, TWENTY-ONE SECONDS, MARTIN.

Martin's stomach turned over. No time, no time!

▲▼▲

He didn't try to think. Just let it flow. Let it all run by like a swiftly moving river. Watch it as it passes. Warp. Malfunction. Destruction. Ejection. Beacon—

Hold it.

Something.

He struggled to pin it down. Don't struggle—relax. Warp. Malfunction. Destruction. Destroyed how? What did the computer say?

"Computer!"

YES, MARTIN.

"How was the ship destroyed?"

I HAVE INFORMED YOU OF THAT, MARTIN.

"Inform me again!" Martin said savagely.

YES, MARTIN. THE SHIP—

"Like you told it before. *Exactly* like you told it before."

—THE SHIP WAS DESTROYED THROUGH A MALFUNCTION IN THE DAVIDSON AUXILIARY REGULATORS. ESSENTIALLY, INTERFERENCE FROM AN UNANTICIPATED MASS—

"Wait. There. An unanticipated mass. What—kind of a mass?"

A MASS WITH THE DENSITY OF—

"Forget the details," Martin said quickly. "General description."

GENERAL DESCRIPTION: THE MASS IN QUESTION IS DEFINED AS A PLANETARY BODY.

Martin's heart skipped a beat. "Okay. Planetary body. And the ship came too close to it. So its mass interfered—Where? Where was the mass? In Warp?"

NO, MARTIN. THERE ARE NO PLANETARY BODIES IN NONSPACE.

"Then it's here—in real space?"

YES, MARTIN. IF THE DAVIDSON AUXILIARY REGULATORS HAD BEEN FUNCTIONING PROPERLY, PRESENCE OF A MASS OUTSIDE THE WARP WOULD NOT HAVE—

"There's a planet here? And you didn't tell me about it!"

ITS PRESENCE WAS NOT RELEVANT, MARTIN.

Martin bit off his words. "Time. How much time?"

TWELVE MINUTES, EIGHT SECONDS, MARTIN.

Martin took a deep breath. Easy. Take it easy...

"The planet. How far away is it?"

FOURTEEN POINT SEVEN MILLION MILES.

"How long would it take to get there?"

NOT RELEVANT, MARTIN.

"Hypothetically!"

SIX STANDARD DAYS, PLUS FOUR HOURS, MARTIN.

We could make it. We could just...

"Air. How about air?"

OXYGEN CONTENT IS SUITABLE FOR HUMAN LIFE.

"Then why in hell—" Martin paused, collected himself. "Please. Give me the reasons this planet isn't—relevant to me."

SUITABLE OXYGEN CONTENT FOR SUSTAINING LIFE IS MERELY ONE REQUISITE FOR PLACEMENT OF SURVIVORS ON A PLANETARY BODY. OTHER FACTORS INCLUDE; PROBABILITY OF ADEQUATE FOOD AND WATER SUPPLIES. SUITABLE CLIMATIC CONDITIONS. NEGATIVE FACTORS: POSSIBILITY OF PRESENCE OF LIFE FORMS INIMICAL TO HUMAN LIFE. POSSIBLE—

"Look," Martin interrupted. "Those things are for me to decide. I'll take my chances." He stopped, bit his lip thoughtfully. "Wait. Wait, you don't know whether any of those factors are relevant, do you? You said 'possible,' and 'probable'—that means you can't tell anything from here. Or can you?"

NO, MARTIN. AT THIS DISTANCE, IT IS ONLY POSSIBLE TO COMPUTE MASS, DENSITY, ATMOSPHERIC CONTENT, PRESENCE OF LAND AND WATER AREAS—

"Then you can't say it's not suitable—you haven't seen it!"

AFFIRMATIVE, MARTIN.

"Then for God's sake, let's at least look at it! We've got the time, we can get there. What's the big hurry to send me sailing off in your bloody whatever it is—lifebank disposal—"

LIFEBANK DISPERSAL CARRIERS (LDC), MARTIN.

"Okay! You've got to—"

MARTIN. FIRST, I SHOULD NOTE THAT THE POSSIBILITY OF ACTIVATING THE BTD WAS CONSIDERED, DUE TO THE PRESENCE OF THE PLANETARY MASS. HOWEVER, LACK OF ANY RADIO ACTIVITY OR EVIDENCE OF OTHER COMMUNICATION DEVICES NEGATED THE OPTION. IT WAS NECESSARY, THEN, MARTIN, TO WEIGH THE PROBABILITY OF YOUR SURVIVAL ON THE PLANETARY MASS AGAINST UTILIZATION OF YOUR COMPONENTS UNDER THE STELLAR OUTREACH OPTION. RESULTS· ONE: IT IS NOT POSSIBLE FROM THIS DISTANCE TO ADEQUATELY DETERMINE ALL PERTINENT CHARACTERISTICS OF THE PLANETARY MASS IN QUESTION. TWO: SUCH CHARACTERISTICS COULD BE DETERMINED BY VIEWING THE PLANET FROM A CLOSER PROXIMITY. THREE: ENERGY CONSUMPTION REQUIRED TO REACH THE PLANETARY MASS FOR FURTHER STUDY WOULD PROHIBIT FURTHER LARGE EXPENDITURES OF ENERGY. FOUR: IF THE CHARACTERISTICS OF THE PLANET INDICATED A LOW SURVIVAL PROFILE (LSP), PLACEMENT WOULD BE NEGATED. ADDITIONALLY, NO ENERGY WOULD THEN BE AVAILABLE TO EXERCISE THE STELLAR OUTREACH OPTION. CONCLUSIONS: IT FOLLOWS THAT SURVIVOR ABLE MARTIN COULD THEN NEITHER BE (A) PLACED ON A SUITABLE PLANETARY BODY NOR (B) UTILIZED AS CHROMOSOMAL UNIT PACK SYSTEMS (CUPS). THEREFORE, I HAVE A CHOICE BETWEEN EITHER EXERCISING THE STELLAR OUTREACH OPTION OR PLACING MYSELF IN THE POSITION OF VERY POSSIBLY BEING UNABLE TO EXERCISE EITHER THE STELLAR OUTREACH OPTION OR PLANET-PLACEMENT. IT IS ILLOGICAL TO CHOOSE THE LATTER. FURTHER, EDICT ONE OF MY PRIMARY PROGRAMMING INSTRUCTIONS (PPI) PROHIBITS SUCH ACTION.

Martin looked up wearily. "I have to ask. What's Edict One?"

EDICT ONE PROHIBITS ME FROM ENDANGERING A HUMAN BEING'S CHANCE OF SURVIVAL THROUGH NEGLIGENCE.

"What?" Martin jerked up, then sank back limply to the couch.

"Time."

SIX MINUTES, EIGHTEEN SECONDS. THE PROCESS, AS I HAVE EXPLAINED, IS COMPLETELY PAINLESS. AN ODORLESS—

"Shut up," said Martin.

That was it then. Six minutes. Zero. There was no point in carrying the farce any further. Clearly, he had been had. The electronic half-wit was winner and still champion.

▲▼▲

He thought about three girls who might miss him for a while and a number of creditors who would tearfully mourn his passing. He wondered what the planet looked like. He wished he could see it and tried to imagine it. Trees. Lakes, maybe? Fresh air. All the fresh air he would ever need. Lonely, but a whole world…

Martin sat up abruptly. "Computer!"

YES, MARTIN.

"What's your definition of a world—a planetary body—capable of supporting human life?"

ONE; ATMOSPHERIC CONTENT TO CONSIST OF—

"Just generalize—briefly!"

ADEQUATE AIR, FOOD AND WATER PLUS A SUITABLE ENVIRONMENT.

"That's all?"

YOU REQUESTED A BRIEF, GENERAL STATEMENT, MARTIN. THERE ARE NUMBEROUS SPECIFIC REQUIREMENTS.

"But basically, that's it."

AFFIRMATIVE, MARTIN.

Martin took a deep breath. "I'm going to describe a specific planet. It has adequate air, food and water, plus a suitable environment. That meets your general requirements?"

YES, MARTIN.

"I have described this escape capsule. Do you still accept my definition?"

NEGATIVE, MARTIN. THIS ESCAPE CAPSULE PARTIALLY MEETS SOME OF THE REQUIREMENTS OF A PLANETARY BODY CAPABLE OF SUPPORTING LIFE. IT DOES NOT, HOWEVER—

"It has air, food and water," Martin shouted. "And the environment's suitable—I love it!"

—DOES NOT, HOWEVER MEET ALL NECESSARY STANDARDS OF A SUITABLE PLANETARY BODY.

"Listen," Martin said desperately, "there are artificial planets, satellites…"

YES, MARTIN.

"They have atmospheres—like this one—and don't tell me that atmosphere has to be on the outside, either—"

AGREED, MARTIN.

"—and nobody said anything about size, so—"

PLANETARY BODIES CAPABLE OF SUPPORTING HUMAN LIFE CAN INCLUDE THE CATEGORY OF ARTIFICIAL AS WELL AS NATURAL PLANETS. HOWEVER, THIS PARTICULAR ARTIFICIAL PLANET LACKS A NECESSARY CHARACTERISTIC.

"What?"

UNDER YOUR DEFINITION, A SPACESHIP, SEAGOING VESSEL, LANDCAR OR EVEN AN ANIMAL-DRAWN VEHICLE COULD CONCEIVABLY FULFILL THE REQUIREMENTS OF HAVING ADEQUATE SUPPLIES OF AIR, FOOD AND WATER AND A SUITABLE ENVIRONMENT—WHETHER THEY ARE PLANETARY BODIES ARE NOT. HOWEVER, NONE OF THESE CARRIERS FULFILL THE NECESSARY REQUIREMENT TO WHICH I REFER. NONE CAN SUSTAIN A HUMAN BEING OVER HIS NATURAL LIFESPAN. NEITHER CAN THIS CAPSULE. NOR IS THERE ANY LOGICAL PROBABILITY THAT ADDITIONAL SUPPLIES OF AIR, FOOD OR WATER CAN BE OBTAINED FROM OUTSIDE SOURCES. THEREFORE, IT, TOO, MUST BE CLASSIFIED AS A CARRIER, AN INSTRUMENT CAPABLE OF SUSTAINING HUMAN LIFE ON A TEMPORARY BASIS—NOT AS A PLANETARY BODY.

"Oh, Jesus," Martin moaned. "How much time?"

THREE MINUTES, TEN SECONDS, MARTIN.

"Look—what's the hurry? Can't you delay?"

NEGATIVE, MARTIN. THERE IS NO LOGICAL REASON FOR PROPOSING A DELAY IN PROCESSING.

Three minutes...

▲▼▲

No way to—"Hold it!" Martin sat up, strained against the couch. "That's all that's missing, right? The capsule's got to sustain me for my natural lifespan. Then it can be a planet. Officially."

YES, MARTIN. UNDER A BROAD DEFINITION.

Martin held his breath. "Computer. How old am I?"

QUESTION, MARTIN. ARE YOU INQUIRING AS TO YOUR AGE OR MY KNOWLEDGE OF YOUR AGE?

"Yes. Your knowledge. Do you know how old I am?"

NEGATIVE, MARTIN. I DO NOT HAVE THAT INFORMATION.

Martin breathed a silent sigh. It wasn't in the passenger records, then—just name, occupation, destination. The image of a second-hand sweeping around a dial at lightspeeds flashed through his mind.

"What's the average lifespan of a human being?" Martin asked.

SOURCE: CONFEDERATION STATISTICAL BUREAU (CSB): THE AVERAGE LIFESPAN OF HUMAN BEINGS WITHIN THE PROVINCES AND TERRITORIES OF THE CONFEDERATION IS NINETY-SEVEN POINT FOUR STANDARD YEARS.

"Oldest recorded lifespan?" Martin added quickly.

OLDEST RECORDED LIFESPAN: ONE HUNDRED AND FIFTY-ONE POINT THREE STANDARD YEARS. PLACE: SYSTEM NUMB—

"And you don't *know* how old I am?" Martin broke in. "Earlier you said you could tell from my physical characteristics how much oxygen I'd use. Can't you see me? Don't you know what I look like?"

NEGATIVE, MARTIN. I DO NOT 'SEE' AS A HUMAN DEFINES 'SEEING.' I HAVE SENSORY DEVICES WHICH ENABLE ME TO GAIN A VARIETY OF DATA—

"How much time?"

FIFTY-THREE POINT NINE SECONDS, MARTIN.

Sweat stung Martin's brow. He gripped the couch to keep his hands from trembling.

"Computer," he said evenly. "I am three hundred and forty-nine years old."

QUESTION: MARTIN: WHILE I CANNOT 'SEE' YOU IN THE MANNER IN WHICH YOU DEFINE 'SEEING,' I CAN SENSE CERTAIN PHYSICAL FUNCTIONS. YOUR HEART IS OPERATING IN THE MANNER EXPECTED OF A HEALTHY HUMAN MALE BETWEEN THE AGES OF THIRTY-FOUR AND THIRTY-SEVEN.

Martin's stomach turned over. *Christ, I had him. I almost had him...*

—THEREFORE, THERE IS AN IRREGULARITY BETWEEN YOUR STATED AGE AND YOUR PHYSICAL CONDITION. TIME: FOURTEEN POINT THREE SECONDS.

Martin's throat clamped shut.

PRELIMINARY PROCESSING WILL BEGIN, MARTIN.

"Wait!" Martin cried frantically.

TIME: EIGHT POINT ONE SECONDS, MARTIN.

"Listen, damn it," Martin shouted, "I'm three hundred and forty-nine years old. I—Wait, look—it *is* a thirty-five year-old heart, I—I had a transplant! Right, I had a transplant!"

TIME: SIX POINT THREE SECONDS, MARTIN.

"You can't kill me," Martin shouted, "don't you understand? Look at the odds—I'm way overdue to die! That's logical, isn't it? I've got more than enough air, food and water to last me the rest of my natural lifespan!"

TIME, TWO SECONDS, MARTIN. THE—

"No!"

—STELLAR OUTREACH OPTION IS CANCELED.

Martin sank back and sucked in precious swallows of air. "All right," he said weakly, "this capsule is a planet. An official planet."

AFFIRMATIVE, MARTIN.

"And the Medi-Packet. And the food and water supplies."

AFFIRMATIVE, MARTIN.

"Show me how you open the thing up. The exit portal."

A red knob appeared beside him. IT IS INOPERATIVE, MARTIN, UNLESS SENSORY PROBES INDICATE A SUITABLE ATMOSPHERE ON THE OUTER SURFACE. THERE IS NO SUCH—

"Fine. Okay." Martin lay back and took a deep breath. "Computer. I want *my* planet to assume an orbit around the other planet in question. Any objections?"

NEGATIVE, MARTIN. THERE IS PRECEDENT.

"Any orbit I want."

AFFIRMATIVE, MARTIN.

"Okay. Do it. Now."

AFFIRMATIVE, MARTIN. SPECIFY ORBITAL HEIGHT, PLEASE.

Gotcha, you son of a bitch...

"I want a decaying orbit," Martin said, "to about eighteen inches. Then just hold it there. Stationary. Yes, that'll do nicely."

The computer said nothing.

Grandfather Pelts

Klaywelder landed the *Glory B* as gently as a baby's breath. The gravitics held a quarter-inch above the ground as the big engines hummed down the scale and sighed.

Klaywelder sighed with them. Then, without a glance outside, he pulled himself up quickly from the pilot's couch and walked the few feet to his quarters. At the foot of his bunk he carefully pressed his right thumb against a particular spot on the bulkhead. The deck beneath him shuddered and screeched in protest as its atoms were harshly realigned. The metal surrounding his cargo was now unmetal—a horrid molecular mess with all the spectographic purity of scrambled eggs.

Klaywelder nodded with satisfaction. No one, not even Klaywelder himself, could open it now—only the peculiar little character on Filo who had installed the thing could wrench it back to normal without melting down the ship.

Klaywelder strolled back to the cabin and stuffed his pipe with Guubi weed. The first puff made him gag. He scowled and knocked the bowl out on the deck. Earth tobacco, he promised himself, would be first on his list. And with what he had in the hold he could well afford the best, this time.

He glanced through the port at the rolling, sage-green hills and whipped-cream skies. Last stop, Pharalell IV, and then home—and more credits than even he had ever dreamed of.

Klaywelder's smug contentment turned to mild annoyance. The domed entryport at the edge of the field looked like an ugly pink hive—and now, out of that hive swarmed three angry silver hornets, making their way for the *Glory B*.

As the hornets drew closer they turned into glittering speedsters. Klaywelder spotted the tiny Federation emblems on their sides. Two of the speedsters carried customs guards with dark rifles bouncing off their backs. The third held the short, stocky frame of Arto Frank.

Klaywelder bit his lip. He hadn't seen Arto in six years—and Arto was the last person he'd hoped to run into on Pharalell IV.

Klaywelder dropped to the ground and closed the port behind him. Frank burned rubber inches from his boots.

"Uhuh. I thought so." Arto Frank eyed him grimly. "What do you want here, Klaywelder?" He didn't wait for an answer. His head jerked to one side and motioned the other speedsters. "Mac, Artie—seal the ship."

The guards braced kickstands and moved forward.

"Hold it," warned Klaywelder.

The guards looked at each other, then at Frank. Klaywelder backed against the hull and pointedly pressed a bright stud at his belt. Frank watched him from narrowed eyes.

Klaywelder folded his arms. "I just wanted to get this whole little scene down on film, Arto. All right, now tell 'em."

Frank showed the barest instant of hesitation. Klaywelder smiled to himself. He reached into his tunic and tossed Frank a neat blue packet. Frank caught the object without looking at it.

"Travel Clearance," said Klaywelder. "Ship's Registry, Ownership Certificate, Parole Papers and Federation Tourist Visa."

"Tourist Visa," Frank repeated and looked at him without expression. Then he turned his head and nodded slightly at the two guards. They pressed their speedsters to life and roared off across the field.

"You can turn off the gimmicks now," said Frank. "If you had them on in the first place."

"I did," said Klaywelder. He pressed another stud. "I'm not under arrest, then?"

"No." Frank faced Klaywelder squarely. "You're not under arrest. What you're under is a thirty-two-hour surveillance until you break atmosphere."

"That's harassment—"

"You can forget the guardhouse law, Klaywelder," Frank said flatly. "Just remember this. As Federation Customs Officer on Pharalell IV I can arrest you if you break the law here, lock you up, seal your ship or send you right back to Barrion for breaking parole. I'll do that, Klaywelder, if you so much as step on the grass. Understood?"

Klaywelder nodded.

"Just to set the record straight," Frank added quietly, "I know why you're here. I've even got a fair idea where you've been." He glanced up at the ship's dark hull. "I can smell contraband fur, Klaywelder—behind eighteen inches of titanium. I'm sure you have a nice hoard in there. I'm just as sure you could turn the whole cache into carbon before I could get a Search & Seizure."

Frank shook his head. "I wouldn't go to the trouble. Just remember—" he poked a menacing finger at Klaywelder— "you're not dealing with animals here. The Pharalellians are intelligent beings under Federation protection. You lay one hand on a Pharalell pelt—"

"Arto!" Klaywelder let an expression of shock cross his face.

"Uhuh. Sure." Frank stared at him distastefully. "I forget. You're a tourist. Just don't you forget, Klaywelder."

With a final look of disdain, he mounted his speedster and disappeared across the blue tarmac.

▲▼▲

Through long years on the outer fringes of the law—and somewhat beyond—Klaywelder had learned to maintain an outer calm in spite of inner feelings. It was difficult to hold onto that control now.

Difficult? It was all he could do to keep from shouting, jumping up and down, turning handsprings. Arto Frank was right, of course. There was indeed a lovely cache of furs beneath the metallic fruitcake of his deck—heavy, cobalt-blue Rhinofox from Claxin, incredibly fine Sapphurs from Ehhinode and fifty-thousand rare microfurs from Deserexx—inch-long platinum pelts from the tiny minkmice, who conveniently welded themselves together in death to form long, silky stoles.

And all those goodies looked like so much boar bristle next to what he was seeing now.

He strolled beneath the feathery, sage-blue trees in the central plaza of Ochassh, the town nearest Pharalell's sole spaceport. He felt a little like an ant at a convention of beetles. The Pharalellians were roughly the size of teenage elephants but there was nothing remotely elephantine about them. They strolled gracefully and majestically about the plaza—four long legs moving in rhythm with shorter forearms hanging from shoulder height. If a prize Afghan were mated with an oversized anteater, Klaywelder decided, their progeny might look something like a Pharalellian.

But Klaywelder only absently noted these minor characteristics—for covering those great bodies from head to toe was the most indescribably glorious fur he had ever seen. It was finer than a spider's gossamer strands. It had the sheen of a lovely woman's hair by moonlight, the sparkle of a dew-covered leaf in early morn, just touched by the sun. And it came in blacker than jet, in breathtaking amber, in fleeting cream—and in every other shade he could imagine. Knowing his special customers as he did, Klaywelder was sure each pelt—just to be ultra-conservative—Klaywelder gave up.

Counting credits in stacks that high made him dizzy.

He played tourist for the rest of the afternoon. He bought examples of carved *Dinii* wood, a favorite Pharalell souvenir. He sent half a dozen postcards to people he had never heard of and ignored Arto Frank's man, who had not been more than twenty yards behind him all day.

At sundown, he walked back to the ship, had a leisurely meal and fell into a peaceful sleep. His dreams were so erotic and furry he almost blushed passing the mirror on the way in to breakfast.

Klaywelder had managed to stay out of jail more often than he'd been forced to stay in. He was sure, in his own mind, this was because he took his work seriously and went about each job with a surgeon's care. He had learned a lot about Pharalellians before landing on the planet. He knew they were extremely religious, exhaustingly polite and unbelievably naïve. All three qualities placed them in an almost textbook Category AAA—which meant they were rigidly protected by Federation edict against people like Klaywelder.

On the other hand, the Pharalellians' own mores and manners tied Arto Frank's hands very nicely. Frank could in no way warn the Pharalellians against him. Discourtesy to any living creature—and that included bad-mouthing fur thieves—was a most extreme no-no. Frank, then, could not make a move until and if Klaywelder stepped out of line.

And that Klaywelder wasn't about to do—certainly not in any way discernible to Arto Frank.

▲▼▲

It was the largest house on the square—large even by Pharalellian standards. Sun-washed white stone flowed into subtle pastels of pink and green. A high, ornate metal gate graced a vine-covered entryway.

The big Pharalellian moved sedately out of his doorway and into the street. Klaywelder faultlessly allowed himself to be crowded off the stone walk. He flailed his arms wildly, then collapsed in a horrible heap. He lay there unmoving, his head cocked ominously against the curb.

The Pharalellian stiffened, then cringed visibly.

"Siim shave me!" it cried. "What have I done?"

Klaywelder moaned. The Pharalellian swooped down and laid a beautifully furry hand across his brow. "I am Steressh-shi," it said gently. "You will call me Garii, please. It is a name reserved for intimate friends who have known me at least forty seasons. You have by my discourtesy earned the right to use it. Are you hurt badly?"

Klaywelder sat up and blinked.

"I'm all right. I think." He shook his head. Then his eyes widened. "Oh, no—"

Garii stiffened. "You are injured, then?"

"No, it's not that." Klaywelder began frantically searching the street around him. "My physical body is of no consequence. Not when my spiritual well-being is threatened."

Garii's eyes quivered under his furry brow. "Your—spiritual—"

"Yes." Klaywelder nodded. "I can't seem to find my pouch. It was here—I wear it around my neck on a silver chain—"

The Pharalellian bent down to join the search. "This pouch—it is important to you?"

Klaywelder sighed. "It is only my ticket into Paradise, nothing more."

Garii sucked in a deep breath.

"It contains the nail parings of my father and his fathers before him," Klaywelder explained somberly. "As I am the ninth son of the ninth virgin, the pouch containing the male spirits of my family is naturally in my trust."

"Yes, naturally." Garii was openly trembling now. "Our ways are strikingly similar."

"You noticed that?" Klaywelder peered under a loose bit of paving. "Actually, that's why I've been so anxious to visit Pharalell IV. I truly believe my people have a strong spiritual kinship with yours."

"Oh, yes—indeed!" Tears rolled down Garii's eyes, staining his silvery pelt a light cobalt blue. "And I, through gross stupidity, have banned your soul from the Thousand Rooms of Infinite Pleasure!"

"It's nothing, really," said Klaywelder.

Garii swept great hands to his face and moaned.

"If you will permit me I shall begin Atonement by tearing out my visual organs. It is a small thing—but a start—"

"No, please," said Klaywelder. "Ah—there's my pouch. It was under your foot all the time."

Garii stifled another moan. "Now I have trod upon your fathers. Visual organs alone will not suffice."

"No problem," Klaywelder said easily. "They're found." He hooked the pouch around his neck. "That's what's important."

The Pharalellian gently helped him to his feet. "You must enter my house, now. I have much indebtedness to overcome."

"Oh, no." Klaywelder yawned absently. "I wouldn't consider disturbing you."

Garii's mouth opened in horror. "I could not blame you for refusing. I have no right to ask. Still—" he faced Klaywelder with pleading eyes— "I beg you not to leave me with no chance of Atonement."

Klaywelder watched the sun form fascinating whorls of color on Garii's fur. Out of the corner of his eye he could see Arto Frank's man frowning in puzzlement at the edge of the plaza.

"All right," he said finally. "If you really insist."

"My gratitude is unbounded, sir."

Klaywelder shrugged. "You can call me Klay."

▲▼▲

Garii insisted Klaywelder spend the remainder of his stay on Pharalell IV in his home. Klaywelder declined and the Pharalellian nearly removed his visual organs before it was explained that Klaywelder could not possibly spend nights outside his ship since his ancestral altars were located there and could not be moved.

Garii understood. But during the daylight hours Klay must allow his host the opportunity to work at full Atonement. That, Klaywelder agreed, seemed fair enough.

Klaywelder was not about to spend a night away from the *Glory B.* Not that Arto Frank could possibly do any damage there but Klaywelder did not intend to give him the chance. Besides that, he wanted Frank to establish a normal Klaywelder day-night pattern in his mind.

▲▼▲

At sunset on the third day Frank pulled up beside him on the narrow road from Ochassh to the spaceport.

Klaywelder greeted him with a slightly lopsided grin. He was more than a little high—mentally and physically. Wine had flowed freely at the party, and Garii made certain his guest-of-honor's cup was never empty. Every swallow, it seemed, was a step closer to full Atonement.

There was more. Klaywelder was dizzy from mingling with the twenty or thirty Pharalellians assembled to meet him. Each one's pelt was more magnificent and multihued than any he had imagined before he came to Pharalell IV.

Frank studied him.

"You're going ahead with it, aren't you?" he said finally. "I can read it all over you." He shook his head. "Klaywelder—"

"I don't know what you're talking about," said Klaywelder. "I'm up to my ears in Pharalellian wine at the moment, Arto. My host—Steressh-shi, to you—I can't reveal his intimate name to strangers but—"

Frank's speedster jerked ahead abruptly, wheeled to block Klaywelder's path.

"Listen," Frank said darkly, "I know what it's all about. I've known since the minute you set down here. You can't pull it off. Don't even try, Klaywelder—"

Klaywelder sighed. "I sense deep spiritual conflicts within you, Arto. At evening devotions I shall ask my ancestors to bring peace to your troubled soul."

Frank made a pointed remark about Klaywelder's ancestors and their relation to Klaywelder himself. Then he left in a cloud of dust and disappeared down the road.

▲▼▲

"As further proof of my Atonement, Klay, and because I consider you a spiritual brother whose devotion transcends the boundaries between us, I hope you will allow me one more privilege."

"Only ask," said Klaywelder.

"You have noticed the great door at the end of my quarters?"

"I may have," said Klaywelder, who had noticed little else since he had become Garii's guest.

"That door leads to the Shrine of my Ancestors," said Garii. "I would be honored if you would accompany me there."

Klaywelder lowered his eyes to hide his excitement.

"The toenails of my fathers are pleased, Garii."

His heart pounded against his chest. His research on Pharalellian religion had been very specific about ancestral shrines.

Garii pulled a lavish key in the great door and something clicked. The massive panel swung open.

Klaywelder held back a gasp. The room was as big as an auditorium. Dark, somber columns arched from the walls and met high above in a domed ceiling. A single shaft of sunlight fell from a high pane, giving the great vault an aura of eternal twilight.

Nearly a hundred candles set in dark red glass circled the walls— and spread carefully over the stone floor before each candle was a magnificent golden pelt.

Golden.

Klaywelder could hardly believe his eyes. If living Pharalell pelts were indescribable—what could you say about these?

"It is our belief," Garii said reverently, "that the degree of virtue attained by a Pharalellian is later reflected in the tone of his pelt. I am most pleased that my fathers and their fathers are all of respectable hues."

You can say that again...

Garii led him silently about the room and Klaywelder noted that a small earthen pot of wine and a clay dish of fruit had been placed before each glowing candle.

"That is a part of my duty," Garii explained proudly. "As the reigning male in my family, I have been accorded this privilege. Each day I bring fresh offerings of reverence." He lowered his big head. "To do so brings great honor to me and my house."

Garii laid a gentle hand on Klay's arm. "Come, my friend—now I would show you Shastalian, greatest of my ancestors."

Klaywelder followed past long rows of gleaming, golden pelts. Finally Garii stopped. "There—" he pointed— "Shastalian, grandfather of grandfathers. A saintly creature and the most famed of all Pharalellians."

Klaywelder wanted to cry. He could hardly bear to hold his eyes on the rippling sea of gold at his feet. He was here—this close to it. A planet's ransom and then some in one glorious pelt.

Not that it really mattered but he wished briefly that he had been a little more imaginative about his own 'religion.' Somehow ancestral nail parings just didn't quite cut it next to Shastalian.

"You see, Klay," Garii explained solemnly, "we consider the Pharalellian body to be unimportant. We are held within its bonds only a little while—but Eternal Life resides in the Pelt. When we are fortunate enough to move into that Loftier Plane the troubles, cares and Atonements of this existence are left in the poor vessel we term the body. Your beliefs are similar, I think."

"Oh, yes," Klaywelder said absently, "very similar, Garii."

"When the time comes for one of us to pass on to that Higher Existence he is taken to a most sacred place. You have seen the large building on the other side of the plaza? The one trimmed in black and gold?"

Klaywelder nodded.

"That is *Fakash-il Shrai*. It means Abode of the Skinners."

Klaywelder swallowed. He looked up at Garii.

"The—skinners?"

"Yes. It is a most dedicated profession. Skinners are chosen from among only the highest and worthiest of clans. Since the body of a Pharalellian is never seen without his pelt the Skinner candidates are blinded at birth, of course."

"Of course," said Klaywelder. He decided this was one phase of Pharalellian religion he could have done without.

"They are very skilled members of the Priesthood," Garii went on. "They must be, since it is a delicate thing to transfer the living soul from the body to the Pelt."

Klaywelder stiffened. "The—living soul? You mean—"

"Certainly," said Garii. "There must be breath still in the body when the Skinners begin their task." He spread his hands. "Or else the soul would not go on to Eternal Life, would it?"

Klaywelder felt a cold chill creep up the back of his neck. He wondered how many Pharalellian ancients, at that last moment, looked up at the sharp blade and blinded eyes of the faithful Skinners—and decided they weren't quite ready for Eternal Life as a golden rug.

"You seem far away, my friend." Garii's voice held puzzlement.

Klaywelder cleared his throat. "I—was, Garii. I'm so overwhelmed by what I've seen, by what you've told me—I fear I lapsed into meditation for a moment. I hope you'll forgive me."

Garii sighed happily.

"Don't apologize, Klay. To think that you have actually experienced the feelings I have known here myself." He stared gravely at Klaywelder. "Might I presume that my Atonement is now complete?"

Klaywelder glanced once more at the great golden pelt of Shastalian, grandfather of grandfathers.

Damn thing must weigh a good four or five hundred pounds. Still.

"Yes, Garii," he said finally. "I'd say that just about does it."

▲▼▲

Klaywelder eased through the lower hatch of the *Glory B* and flattened himself against the cold concrete below the ship. It was long past the middle hour of Pharalell's night. The light in Arto Frank's dome had winked out some time before but Klaywelder had waited patiently in the darkened cabin.

Even in the Blacsuit, he felt as conspicuous as a blazing beacon crawling on his belly across the broad field. The skintight garment ate every photon of available light—still, he imagined Frank's cold eyes cutting a blinding swath through the darkness.

He was sure radar had his ship bracketed to the ground. If *Glory B*'s hull rose as much as a half-inch or the power level of her engines suddenly changed—every alarm in the area would scream itself into a blue hemorrhage. He was banking on the fact that Arto Frank would be expecting a ship to leave the field—not a man. And he prayed silently to his ancestors' mythical toenails that Pharalell was too small a post to include body sensors as standard equipment.

At the rear of Garii's house, he pulled a small gravitic unit from under his Blacsuit and attached it to his belt. On half power he lifted himself over the high wall, then pulled himself smoothly along, inches above the clay shingles, and up the arching dome.

With a suction attached to the single pane, he lifted the glass out easily with quick use of his cutter. Then, slowly, he lowered the grav's dial to one. Weight returned and pressed him against the tiles. He removed the unit and hinged a thin, sloping metal wedge to its base, forcing the wedge into its "load" position against a heavy spring.

Finally he poked a shielded flash through the dome's hole, let a thin smile crease his lips. There it was—dazzlingly bright even in the dim shaft of light. Shastalian.

Klaywelder bit his lip.

Here comes the tricky part...

He placed the grav unit just inside the edge of the dome, then flipped his remote until he was sure the unit's weight had been sufficiently reduced to hold itself. When he was certain, he increased the weight and watched it slowly descend to the floor.

It touched bottom a good eighteen feet from Shastalian. Klaywelder wiped sweat from his brow. The unit had no horizontal control. The trick was quickly to raise the unit a few feet, shut off its power, let it fall, then raise it again before it hit the floor—and repeat the procedure until he could get the thing moving in a series of parabolic arcs toward Shastalian.

Klaywelder took a deep breath. The first time his hand trembled and the unit fell nearly to the floor. He tried again. He was getting the hang of the thing now, and the unit was moving in slow, graceful arcs—luckily, in the general direction of the Shastalian pelt.

Ten feet. Fifteen. Seventeen—now.

Klaywelder gently halted the unit and lowered it to the floor. His heart pounded against his chest. He was only inches from the pelt—he didn't dare press his luck further. Wiping his brow once more, he twisted the remote to full weight, pressing the unit below hard against the floor.

Click!

Klaywelder winced. The noise seemed to echo off the stone walls, much louder than he had expected. But—it was done. The spring-loaded wedge, set off by the unit's weight, whipped a thin steel tongue under the edge of the pelt. By raising the unit inches at a time, Klaywelder slowly wormed the wedge under the heavy fur, caterpillar style.

He glanced at the horizon. A thin line of pink was edging the low hills to the east. He turned away and concentrated on the problem below. There was no more time—the unit was nearly under the center of the pelt and it would have to do. He closed his eyes and turned the dial to full power.

Shastalian lifted slowly off the floor and rose toward the ceiling, a shadowy golden ghost in the dim shaft of his light. The pelt nuzzled up against the top of the dome only yards away. Klaywelder extended a thin metal tube to the right length and gaffed Shastalian as he would a giant, furry fish.

He had one more moment of panic when the pelt stuck in the dome's narrow hole. Then he was home free. Klaywelder touched the pelt for the first time. A chill ran through his whole body. There was absolutely no way to compare Shastalian to anything.

▲▼▲

Bracing himself and his prize, he pressed a small wafer to his throat and mouthed a single sub-vocal command. A few miles away, a relay clicked in *Glory B*'s computers. Silent engines whined into life. And at the same time, alarms hooted and moaned across the field and bright beams stabbed angrily into the sky.

Glory B rose swiftly from the spaceport in a low, ground-hugging curve, homing in on Klaywelder. For a moment blue strings of heat spat at her from the field. They halted abruptly. At that angle, Frank would soon have been sizzling the roofs of Pharalell homes and buildings.

Klaywelder grinned. The ship streaked over the outskirts of Ochassh and came to a hovering stop three feet above him. He let the grav unit lift Shastalian into the port, then pulled himself up. The port snapped shut and Klaywelder bounded to the control cabin. He threw himself into the command seat and slapped one hand full across the board.

Glory B lunged upward in teeth-shattering acceleration. Blue fire spiderwebbed against the hull for a brief moment. Then Pharalell IV shrank to a bright green globe against blackness.

▲▼▲

Federation ships would already be on Red Alert—but space was terrifyingly vast and the patrols were spread pitifully thin. He would be long gone when they finally got to where he was supposed to be. A quick stop on Filo to open the scrambled hold, then a first-class plastjob for himself—a good one, this time, from eyes to toes—and then Earth.

He broke out his last sixteen-ounce steak from the locker and topped it with a bottle of Pharalellian wine. In comfortable lethargy he strolled toward his quarters, stopping by the entry port to gaze once more at Shastalian. He would have liked to have spread the big pelt out to its full length but there was no place in the ship nearly large enough to accommodate the great golden fur.

Stretched out on his bunk, Klaywelder thought about Arto Frank and grinned tiredly. Poor Arto. He was, though, genuinely sorry about Garii. Garii was all right. He hoped Shastalian's loss didn't hit him too hard.

Still, he reasoned with Klaywelder logic, Garii had lots of pelts— while he had only one. Klaywelder turned over and closed his eyes.

—and came fully awake. The luminous dial over his bunk said he had slept only a short hour. His senses were fuzzy from the strong Pharalellian wine. He cocked his head and listened. Nothing. He shrugged and turned over—then sat up stiffly.

There it was again. Unfamiliar.

He set his feet on the floor and something heavy draped over his ankles and wrapped softly about his calves. Klaywelder gasped and jerked away. The firm grip held, tightened, and he yelled as he was pulled to the floor.

Klaywelder fought savagely. He kicked, pummeled with his fists. His blows were muffled in thick, warm fur, as damp leather tightened about his waist and inched up across his chest.

He screamed and cursed himself and Garii and the universe until his throat was raw. And in some last, coherent corner of his mind he wondered if anyone else knew Pharalellians didn't believe in a life after death—and didn't need to.

As thick golden fur covered his face he saw a quick bright picture of dark earthen cups on a smooth stone floor—small offerings of reverence for those who had passed on to Eternal Life.

Diner

He woke sometime before dawn and brought the dream back with him out of sleep. The four little girls attended Catholic junior high in Corpus Christi. Their hand-painted guitars depicted tropical Cuban nights. They played the same chord again and again, a dull repetition like small wads of paper hitting a drum. The light was still smoky, the furniture unrevealed. He made his way carefully across the room. The screened-in porch enclosed the front side of the house facing the Gulf, allowing the breeze to flow in three directions. He could hear rolling surf, smell the sharp tang of iodine in the air. Yet something was clearly wrong. The water, the sand, the sky, had disappeared, lost behind dark coagulation. With sudden understanding he saw the screen was clotted with bugs. Grasshoppers blotted out the morning. They were bouncing off the screen, swarming in drunken legions. He ran outside and down the stairs, knowing what he'd find. The garden was gone. A month before, he'd covered the small plot of ground with old window screens and bricks. The hoppers had collapsed the whole device. His pitiful stands of lettuce were cropped clean, razored on the ground as if he'd clipped them with a mower. Radishes, carrots, the whole bit. Eaten to the stalk. Then it occurred to him he was naked and under attack. Grasshopper socks knitted their way up to his knees. Something considered his crotch. He yelled and struck out blindly, intent on knocking hoppers silly. The fight was next to useless, and he retreated up the stairs.

▲▼▲

Jenny woke while he was dressing.
"Something wrong? Did you yell just a minute ago?"
"Hoppers. They're all over the place."
"Oh, Mack."
"Little fuckers ate my salad bar."
"I'm sorry. It was doing so good."
"It isn't doing good now." He started looking for his hat.
"You want something to eat?"
"I'll grab something at Henry's."

She came to him, still unsteady from sleep, awkward and fetching at once. Minnie Mouse T-shirt ragged as a kite. A certain yielding coming against him.

"I got to go to work."

"Your loss, man."

"I dreamed of little Mexican girls."

"Good for you." She stepped back to gather her hair, her eyes somewhere else.

"Nothing happened. They played real bad guitar."

"So you say."

▲▼▲

He made his way past the dunes and the ragged stands of sea grass, following the path over soft, dry sand to solid beach, the dark rows of houses on stilts off to his right, the Gulf rolling in, brown as mud, giving schools of mullet a ride. The hoppers had moved on, leaving dead and wounded behind. The sun came up behind dull anemic clouds. Two skinny boys searched the ocean's morning debris. He found a pack of Agricultural Hero cigarettes in his pocket and cupped his hands against the wind. George Panagopoulos said there wasn't any tobacco in them at all. Said they made them out of dried shit and kelp and that the shit wasn't bad, but he couldn't abide the kelp. Where the sandy road angled into the beach, he cut back and crossed Highway 87, the asphalt cracked and covered with sand, the tough coastal grass crowding in. The highway trailed southwest for two miles, dropping off abruptly where the red-white-and-blue Galveston ferries used to run, the other end stretching northeast up the narrow strip of Bolivar Peninsula past Crystal Beach and Gilchrist, then off the peninsula to High Island and Sabine Pass.

Mack began to find Henry's posters north of the road. They were tacked on telephone poles and fences, on the door of the derelict Texaco station, wherever Henry had wandered in this merchandising adventure. He gathered them in as he walked, snapping them off like paper towels. The sun began to bake, hot wind stinging up sand in tiny storms. The posters said: FOURTH OF JULY PICNIC AT HENRY ORTEGA'S DINER. ALL THE BARBECUE PORK YOU CAN EAT. EL DIOS BLESS AMERICA.

Henry had drawn the posters on the backs of green accounting forms salvaged from the Sand Palace Motor Home Inn. Even if he'd gotten Rose to help, it was a formidable undertaking.

No easy task to do individually rendered, slightly crazed, and plainly cockeyed fathers of our country. Every George Washington wore a natty clip-on Second Inaugural tie and, for some reason, a sporty little

Matamoros pimp mustache. Now and then along the borders, an extra reader bonus, snappy American flags or red cherry bombs going *kapow.*

Mack walked on picking posters. Squinting back east, he saw water flat as slate, vanishing farther out with tricks of the eye. Something jumped out there or something didn't.

▲▼▲

Jase and Morgan were in the diner, and George Panagopoulos and Fleece. They wore a collection of gimmie caps and patched-up tennis shoes, jeans stiff and sequined with the residue of fish. Mack took the third stool down. Fleece said it might get hotter. Mack agreed it could. Jase leaned down the counter.

"Hoppers get your garden, too?"

"Right down to bedrock is all," Mack said.

"I had this tomato," Panagopoulos said, "this one little asshole tomato 'bout half as big as a plum; I'm taking a piss and hear these hoppers coming and I'm down and out of the house like that. I'm down there in what, maybe ten, twenty seconds flat, and this tomato's a little booger hanging down." He made a swipe at his nose, held up a finger, and looked startled and goggle-eyed.

Mack pretended to study the menu and ordered KC steak and fries and coffee and three eggs over easy; and all this time Henry's standing over the charcoal stove behind the counter, poking something flat across the grill, concentrating intently on this because he's already seen the posters rolled up and stuffed in Mack's pocket and he knows he'll have to look right at Mack sooner or later.

"Galveston's got trouble," Jase said. "Dutch rowed back from seeing that woman in Clute looks like a frog. Said nobody's seen Mendez for 'bout a week."

"Eddie's a good man for a Mex," Morgan said from down the counter. "He'll stand up for you, he thinks you're in the right."

Mack felt the others waiting. He wondered if he really wanted to get into this or let it go.

Fleece jumped in. "Saw Doc this morning, sneaking up the dunes 'bout daylight. Gotta know if those hoppers eat his dope."

Everyone laughed except Morgan. Mack was silently grateful.

"I seen that dope," Jase said. "What it is there's maybe three tomato plants 'bout high as a baby's dick."

"I don't want to hear nothin' about tomatoes," said Panagopoulos.

"Don't make any difference what it is," Fleece said. "Man determined to get high, he going to do it."

Panagopoulos told Mack that Dutch's woman up in Clute heard someone had seen a flock of chickens. Right near Umbrella Point. Rhode Island Reds running loose out on the beach.

Mack said fine. There was always a good chicken rumor going around somewhere. That or someone saw a horse or a pack of dogs. Miss Aubrey Gain of Alvin swore on Jesus there was a pride of Siamese cats in Liberty County.

Mack wolfed down his food. He didn't look at his plate. If you didn't look close, you maybe couldn't figure what the hot peppers were covering up.

When he got up to go, he said, "Real tasty, Henry," and then, as if the thought had suddenly occurred, "All right if you and me talk for a minute?"

Henry followed him out. Mack saw the misery in his face. He tried on roles like hats. Humble peon. An extra in *Viva Zapata!* Wily tourist guide with gold teeth and connections. Nothing fit. He looked like Cesar Romero, and this was his cross. Nothing could rob him of dignity. No one would pity a man with such bearing.

Mack took out the roll of posters and gave them back. "You know better than that, Henry. It wasn't a real good idea."

"There is no harm in this, Mack. You cannot say that there is."

"Not me I can't, no."

"Well, then."

"Come on. I got Huang Hua coming first thing tomorrow."

"Ah. Of course."

"Jesus, Henry."

"I am afraid that I forgot."

"Fine. Sure. Look, I appreciate the thought, and so does everyone else. This Chink, now, he hasn't got a real sense of humor."

"I was thinking about a flag."

"What?"

"A flag. You could ask, you know? See what he says. It would not hurt to ask. A very small and insignificant flag in the window of the diner. Just for the one day, you understand?"

Mack looked down the road. "You didn't even listen. You didn't hear anything I said."

"Just for the one day. The Fourth and nothing more."

"Get all the posters down, Henry. Do it before tonight."

"How did you like the George Washington?" Henry asked. "I did all of those myself. Rose did the lettering, but I am totally responsible for the pictures."

"The Washington was great."

"You think so?"

"The eyes kinda follow you around."

"Yes." Henry showed his delight. "I tried for inner vision of the eyes."

"Well, you flat out got it."

Jase and Morgan came out, Jase picking up the rubber fishing boots he'd left at the door. Morgan looked moody and deranged. Mack considered knocking him senseless

"Look," Mack told him, "I don't want you on my boat. Go with Panagopoulos. Tell him Fleece'll be going with me and Jase."

"Just fine with me," Morgan said.

"Good. It's fine with me, too."

Morgan wasn't through. "You take a nigger fishing on a day with a *r* in it, you goin' to draw sharks certain. I seen it happen."

"You tell that to Fleece," Mack said. "I'll stand out here and watch."

Morgan went in and talked to Panagopoulos. Jase waited for Fleece, leaning against the diner, asleep or maybe not. Mack lit an Agricultural Hero and considered the aftertaste of breakfast. Thought of likely antics with Jenny's parts. Wondered how a univalve mollusk with the mental reserve of grass could dream up a wentletrap shell and then wear it. This and other things.

Life has compensations, but there's no way of knowing what they are.

▲▼▲

Coming in was the time he liked the best. The water was dark and flat, getting ready for the night. The bow cut green, and no sound at all but a jazzy little counterbeat, the crosswind snapping two fingers in the sails. The sun was down an hour, the sky settling into a shade inducing temporary wisdom. He missed beer and music. Resented the effort of sinking into a shitty evening mood without help.

Swinging in through the channel, Pelican Island off to port, he saw the clutter of Port Bolivar, the rusted-out buildings and the stumps of rotted docks, the shrimpers he used to run heeling drunkenly in the flats. South of that was the chain-link fence and the two-story corrugated building. The bright red letters on its side read SHINING WEALTH OF THE SEA JOYOUS COOPERATIVE 37 WELCOME HOME INDUSTRIOUS CATCHERS OF THE FISH.

This Chinese loony-tune message was clear a good nautical mile away; a catcher of the fish with a double cataract couldn't pretend it wasn't there.

Panagopoulos's big Irwin ketch was in, the other boats as well, the nets up and drying. Fleece brought the sloop in neatly, dropping the sails at precisely the right moment, a skill Mack appreciated all the more because Morgan was scarcely ever able to do it, either rushing in to shore full sail like a Viking bent on pillage or dropping off early and leaving them bobbing in the bay.

The Chinks greatly enjoyed this spectacle, the round-eyes paddling the forty-three-foot Hinckley in to shore.

Mack and Jase secured the lines, and then Jase went forward to help Fleece while the Chinks came aboard to look at the catch. The guards stayed on the dock looking sullen and important, rifles slung carelessly over their shoulders. Fishing Supervisor Lu Ping peered into the big metal hold, clearly disappointed.

"Not much fish," he told Mack.

"Not much," Mack said.

"It's June," Fleece explained. "You got the bad easterlies in June. Yucatán Current kinda edges up north, hits the Amarillo Clap flat on. That goin' to fuck up your fishing real good."

"Oh, yes." Lu Ping made a note. Jase nodded solemn agreement.

Mack told Jase and Fleece to come to the house for supper. He walked past the chain-link fence and the big generator that kept the fish in the corrugated building cooler than anyone in Texas.

The routine was, the boats would come in and tack close to the long rock dike stretching out from the southeast side of the peninsula, out of sight of the Chinks, and the women and kids would wave and make a fuss and the men would toss them fish in canvas bags, flounder or pompano or redfish if they were running or maybe a rare sack of shrimp, keeping enough good fish onboard to keep the Chinese happy, but mostly leaving catfish and shark and plenty of mullet in the hold, that and whatever other odd species came up in the nets. It didn't matter at all, since everything they caught was ground up, steamed, pressed, processed, and frozen into brick-size bundles before they shipped it out.

Mack thought about cutting through the old part of the port, then remembered about Henry and went back. There were still plenty of posters on fence posts and abandoned bait stands and old houses, and he pulled down all he could find before dark.

▲▼▲

They ate in front of the house near the dunes, a good breeze coming in from the Gulf strong enough to keep mosquitoes and gnats at bay, the wind drawing the driftwood fire nearly white. Henry brought a large pot of something dark and heady, announcing it was Acadia Parish shrimp creole Chihuahua style, and nobody said it wasn't. Mack broiled flounder over a grill. Jase attacked guitar. Arnie Mace, Mack's uncle from Sandy Point, brought illegal rice wine. Not enough to count but potent. Fleece drank half a mason jar and started to cry. He said he was thinking about birds. He began to call them off. Herons and plovers and egrets. Gulls squawking cloud-white thick behind the shrimpers. Jase said he remembered pink flamingos in the tidal flats down by the dike.

"There was an old bastard in Sweeny, you know him, Mack," George Panagopoulos said. "Swears he had the last cardinal bird in Texas. Kept it in a hamster cage long as he could stand it. Started dreaming about it and couldn't sleep, got up in the middle of the night and stir-fried it in a wok. Had a frazzle of red feathers on his hat for some time, but I can't say that's how he got 'em."

"That was Emmett Dodge," Mack said. "I always heard it was a jay."

"Now, I'm near certain it was a cardinal." Panagopoulos looked thoughtfully into his wine. "A jay, now, if Emmett had had a jay, I doubt he could've kept the thing quiet. They make a awful lot of noise."

Mack helped Fleece throw up.

"Georgia won't talk to me," Fleece said miserably. "You the only friend I got."

"I expect you're right."

"You watch out for Morgan. He bad-talkin' you ever chance he get."

"He wants to be pissant mayor, he can run. I sure don't care for the honor."

"He says your eyes beginnin' to slant."

"He said that?"

"Uh-huh."

"Well, fuck him." Fleece was unsteady but intact. Mack looked around for Henry and found him with Rose and Jenny. He liked to stand off somewhere and watch her. A good-looking woman was fine as gold, you caught her sitting by a fire.

He took Henry aside.

"I know what you are going to say," Henry said. "You are angry with me. I can sense these things."

"I'm not angry at all. Just get that stuff taken down before morning."

"I only do what I think is right, *mi compadre*. What is just. What is true." Henry tried for balance. "What I deeply feel in my heart. A voice cries out. It has to speak. This is the tragedy of my race. I feel a great sorrow for my people."

"Okay."

"I shall bow to your wishes, of course."

"Good. Just bow before Huang gets here in the morning."

"I will take them down. I will go and do it now."

"You don't have to do it now."

"I feel I am an intrusion."

"I feel like you've had enough to drink."

"Do you know what I am thinking? What I am thinking at this moment?"

"No, what?"

"I am thinking that I cannot remember tequila."

"Fleece has already done this," Mack said. "I don't want you doing it, too. One crying drunk is enough."

"Forgive me. I cannot help myself. Mack, I don't remember how it tastes. I remember the lime and the salt. I recall a certain warmth. *Nada.* Nothing more."

Tears touched the Cesar Romero eyes, trailed down the Gilbert Roland cheeks. *If Jase plays "La Paloma," I'll flat kill him,* thought Mack. He left to look for Rose.

▲▼▲

Jenny told him to come out on the porch and look at the beach. Crickets crawled out of the dunes and made for the water. The sand was black, a bug tide going out to sea. The crickets marched into the water and floated back. In the dark they looked like the ropy strands of a spill.

"The ocean scares me at night," Jenny said.

"Not always. You like it sometimes." He wanted to stop this but didn't know how to do it. She was working up to it a notch at a time.

"It's not you," she said.

"Fine, I'll write that down." He worked his hand up the T-shirt and touched the small of her back. She leaned in comfortably against him.

"Things are still bad, you get too far away from the coast. I don't want you just wandering around somewhere."

"I haven't really decided, Mack. I mean, it's not tomorrow or anything."

"I don't think you're going to find anyone, Jenny." He said it as gently as he could. "Folks are scattered all about."

She didn't answer. They stood a long time on the porch. The house already felt empty.

▲▼▲

The chopper came in low out of the south, tilted slightly into the off-shore breeze, rotors churning flat, snappy farts as it settled to 87, stirring sand. Soldiers hit the ground. They looked efficient. Counterrevolutionary acts would be dealt with swiftly. Fleece and Panagopoulos leaned against the diner trading butts. Henry came out for a look and ducked inside. The morning was oyster gray with a feeble ribbing of clouds. Major Huang waved at Mack. Then Chen came out of the chopper and started barking at the troops. Mack wasn't pleased. Huang was purely political—fat and happy and not looking for any trouble. Chen was maybe nineteen tops, a cocky little shit with new bars. Mack was glad he didn't speak English, which meant Jase wouldn't try to sell him a shark dick pickled in a jar or something worse.

The Chinese uniforms were gallbladder green to match the chopper. Chen and three troopers stayed behind. The troopers started tossing crates and boxes to the ground. One followed discreetly behind the major.

"Personal hellos," Huang Hua greeted Mack. "It is a precious day we are seeing."

Mack looked at the chopper. "Not many supplies this time."

"Not many fishes," Huang said.

It's going to be like this, is it? Mack followed him past the diner down the road to Shining Wealth Cooperative 37. He noticed little things. A real haircut. Starched khakis with creases. He wondered what Huang had eaten for breakfast.

Sergeant Fishing Supervisor Lu Ping greeted the major effusively. He had reports. Huang stuffed them in a folder. The air-conditioning was staggering. Mack forgot what it was like between visits.

"I have reportage of events," Huang began. He sat behind the plain wooden table and folded his hands. "It is a happening of unpleasant nature. Eddie Mendez will not mayor himself in Galveston after today."

"And why's that?"

"Offending abuse. Blameful performance. Defecation of authority." Huang looked meaningfully at Mack. "Retaining back of fishes."

"What'll happen to Eddie?"

"The work you do here is of gravity, Mayor Mack. A task of large importance. Your people in noncoastal places are greatly reliant of fish."

"We're doing the best we can."

"I am hopeful this is true."

Mack looked right at him.

"Major, we're taking all the fish we can net. We got sails and no gas and nothing with an engine to put it into if we did. You're not going to help any shorting us on supplies. I've got forty-one families on this peninsula eating nothing but fish and rice. There's kids here never saw a carrot. We try to grow something, the bugs eat it first 'cause there's no birds left to eat the bugs. The food chain's fucked."

"You are better off than most."

"I'm sure glad to hear it."

"Please to climb down from my back. The Russians did the germing, not us."

"I know who did it."

Huang tried Oriental restraint. "We are engaging to help. You have no grateful at all. The Chinese people have come to fill this empty air."

"Vacuum."

"Yes. Vacuum." Huang considered. "In three, maybe four years, wheat and corn will be achieved in the ground again. Animal and fowl will be brought. This is very restricted stuff. I tell you, Mayor Mack, because I wish your nonopposing. I have ever shown you friendness. You cannot say I haven't."

"I appreciate the effort."

"You will find sweets in this shipment. For the children. Also decorative candles. Toothpaste. Simple magic tricks."

"Jesus Christ."

"I knew this would bring you pleasure."

Huang looked up. Lieutenant Chen entered politely. He handed Huang papers. Gave Mack a sour look. Mack recognized Henry's posters, the menu from the diner. Chen turned and left.

"What is this?" Huang appeared disturbed. "Flags? Counterproductive celebration? Barbecue pork?"

"Doesn't mean a thing," Mack explained. "It's just Henry."

Huang looked quizzically at George Washington, turning the poster in several directions. He glanced at the cardboard menu, at the KG Sirloin Scrambled Eggs Chicken-Fried Steak French Fries Omelet with Cheddar Cheese or Swiss Coffee Refills Free. He looked gravely at Mack.

"I did not think this was a good thing. You said there would be no trouble. One thing leads to a something other. Now it is picnics and flags."

"The poster business, all right," Mack said. "He shouldn't of done that. I figure it's my fault. The diner, now, there's nothing wrong with the diner."

Huang shook his head. "It is fanciment. The path to discontent." He appeared deeply hurt. The poster was an affront. The betrayal of a friend. He walked to the window, hands behind his back. "There is much to have renouncement here, Mayor Mack. Many fences to bend. I have been lenient and foolish. No more Henry Ortega Diner. No picnic. And better fishes, I think."

Mack didn't answer. Whatever he said would be wrong.

Huang recalled something of importance. He looked at Mack again.

"You have a black person living here?"

"Two. A man and a woman."

"There is no racing discrimination? They are treated fairly?"

"Long as they keep picking that cotton."

"No textiles. Only fishes."

"I'll see to it."

▲▼▲

Mack walked back north, past a rusted Chevy van waiting patiently for tires, past a pickup with windows still intact. Rose hadn't seen Henry. She didn't know where he was. "He didn't mean to cause trouble," she told Mack.

"I know that, Rose."

"He walks. He wanders off. He needs the time to himself. He is a very sensitive man."

"He's all of that," Mack said. He heard children. Smelled rice and fish, strongly seasoned with peppers.

"He respects you greatly. He says you are *muy simpático*. A man of heart. A leader of understanding."

A woman with fine bones and sorrowful eyes. Katy Jurado, *One-Eyed Jacks*. He couldn't remember the year.

"I just want to talk to him, Rose. I have to see him."

"I will tell him. He will come to you. Here, take some chilies to Jenny. It is the only thing I can grow the bugs won't eat. Try it on the fish. Just this much, no more."

"Jenny'll appreciate that." A hesitation in her eyes. As if she might say something more. Mack wouldn't ask. He wasn't mad at Henry. His anger had abated, diluted after a day with Major Hua. He left and walked to the beach. Jase and Fleece were there. Jase had a mason jar of wine he'd maybe conned from Arnie Mace.

"Tell Panagopoulos and some of the others if you see 'em," Mack said, "I want to talk to Henry. He's off roaming around somewhere; I don't want him doing that."

"Your minorities'll do this," Jase reflected. "I'm glad I ain't a ethnic."

"It's a burden," Fleece said. "There going to be any trouble with the Chinks?"

"Not if I can help it."

"Fleece thought of two more birds," Jase said. "A cormorant and a what?"

"Tern."

"Yeah, right."

"Good," Mack said. "Keep your eyes peeled for Henry. He gets into that moon-over-Monterey shit, it'll take Rose a month to get him straight."

▲▼▲

"I think I'm going to go," Jenny told him. "I think I got to do that, Mack. It just keeps eatin' away. Papa's likely gone, but Luanne and Mama could be okay."

He put out his cigarette and watched her across the room, watched her as she sat at the kitchen table bringing long wings of hair atop her head, going about this simple task with a quick unconscious grace. The mirror stood against a white piece of driftwood she'd collected. She collected everything. Sand dollars and angel wings, twisted tritons and bright coquinas that faded in a day. Candle by the mirror in a sand-frosted Dr Pepper bottle, light from this touching the bony hillbilly points of her hips. When she left she would take too much of him with her, and maybe he should figure some way to tell her that.

"I might not be able to get you a pass. I don't know. They don't much like us moving around without a reason."

"Oh, Mack. People do it all the time." Peering at him now past the candle. "Hey, now, I'm going to come on back. I just got to get this done."

He thought about the trip. Saw her walking old highways in his head. Maybe sixty-five miles up to Beaumont, cutting off north before that into the Thicket. He didn't tell her everything he heard. The way people were, things that happened. He knew it wouldn't make a difference if he did.

Jenny settled in beside him. "I said I'm coming back."

"Yeah, well, you'd better."

He decided, maybe at that moment, he wouldn't let her go. He'd figure out a way to stop her. She'd leave him in a minute. Maybe come back and maybe not. He had to know she was all right, and so he'd do it. He listened to the surf. On the porch, luna moths big as English sparrows flung themselves crazily against the screen.

▲▼▲

The noise of the chopper brought him out of bed fast, on the floor and poking into jeans before Jase and Panagopoulos made the stairs.

"It's okay," he told Jenny, "just stay inside and I'll see."

She nodded and looked scared, and he opened the screen door and went out. Dawn washed the sky the color of moss. Jase and Panagopoulos started talking both at once.

Then Mack saw the fire, the reflection past the house. "Oh, Jesus H. Christ!"

"Mack, he's got pigs," Panagopoulos said. "I seen 'em. Henry's got pigs."

"He's got what?"

"This is bad shit," Jase moaned, "this is really bad shit."

Mack was down the stairs and past the house. He could see other people. He started running, Jase and Panagopoulos at his heels. The chopper was on the ground, and then Fleece came out of the crowd across the road.

"Henry ain't hurt bad, I don't think," he told Mack.

"Henry's hurt?" Mack was unnerved. "Who hurt him, Fleece? Is someone going to tell me something soon?"

"I figure that Chen likely done a house-to-house," Fleece said, "some asshole trick like that. Come in north and worked down rousting people out for kicks. Stumbled on Henry; shit, I don't know. Just get him out of there, Mack."

Mack wanted to cry or throw up. He pushed through the crowd and saw Chen, maybe half a dozen soldiers, then Henry. Henry looked foolish, contrite, and slightly cockeyed. His hands were tied behind. Someone had hit him in the face. The rotors stirred waves of hot air. The diner went up like a box. Mack tried to look friendly. Chen lurched about yelling and waving his pistol, looking wild-eyed as a dog.

"Let's work this out," Mack said. "We ought to get this settled and go home."

Chen shook his pistol at Mack, danced this way and that in an unfamiliar step. Mack decided he was high on the situation. He'd gotten hold of this and didn't know where to take it, didn't have the sense to know how to stop.

"We can call this off and you don't have to worry about a thing," Mack said, knowing Chen didn't have the slightest notion what he was saying. "That okay with you? We just call it a night right now?"

Chen looked at him or somewhere else entirely. Mack wished he had shoes and a shirt. Dress seemed proper if you were talking to some clown with a gun. He was close enough to see the pigs. The crate was by the chopper. Two pigs, pink and fat, mottled like an old man's hand. They were squealing and going crazy with the rotors and the fire and not helping Chen's nerves or Mack's, either. Mack could just see Henry thinking this out, how he'd do it, fattening up the porkers somehow and thinking what everybody'd say when they saw it wasn't a joke, not soyburger KG steak or chicken-fried fish-liver rice and chili peppers. Not seaweed coffee or maybe grasshopper creole crunch. None of that play-food shit they all pretended was something else, not this time, *amigos,* this time honest-to-God pig. Maybe the only pigs this side of Hunan, and only Henry Ortega and Jesus knew where he found them. Mack turned to Chen and gave his best mayoral smile.

"Why don't we just forget the whole thing? Just pack up the pigs there and let Henry be. I'll talk to Major Huang. I'll square all this with the major. That'd be fine with you, now, wouldn't it?"

Chen stopped waving the gun. He looked at Mack. Mack could see wires in his eyes. Chen spoke quickly over his shoulder. Two of the troopers lifted the pigs into the chopper.

"Now, that's good," Mack said. "That's the thing you want to do,"

Chen walked off past Henry, his face hot as wax from the fire, moving toward the chopper in this jerky little two-step hop, eyes darting every way at once, granting Mack a lopsided half-wit grin that missed him by a good quarter mile. Mack let out a breath. He'd catch hell from Huang, but it was over. Over and done. He turned away, saw Rose in the crowd and then Fleece. Mack waved. Someone gave a quick and sudden cheer. Chen jerked up straight, just reacting to the sound, not thinking any at all, simply bringing the pistol up like the doctor hit a nerve, the gun making hardly any noise, the whole thing over in a blink and no time to stop it or bring it back. Henry blew over like a leaf, taking his time, collapsing with no skill or imagination, nothing like Anthony Quinn would play the scene.

"Oh, shit, now don't do that," Mack said, knowing this was clearly all a mistake. "Christ, you don't want to do that!"

Someone threw a rock, maybe Jase. Troopers raised their rifles and backed off. A soldier near Chen pushed him roughly toward the chopper. Chen looked deflated. The rotors whined up and blew sand. Mack shut it out, turned it back. It was catching up faster than he liked. He wished Chen had forgotten to take the pigs. The thought seemed less than noble. He considered some gesture of defiance. Burn rice in Galveston harbor. They could all wear Washington masks. He knew what they'd do was nothing at all, and that was fine because Henry would get up in just a minute and they'd all go in the diner and have a laugh. Maybe Jase had another jar of wine. Mack was certain he could put this back together and make it right. He could do it. If he didn't turn around and look at Henry, he could do it...

Sallie C.

Will woke every morning covered with dust. The unfinished chair, the dresser with peeling paint, were white with powdery alkali. His quarters seemed the small back room of some museum, Will and the dresser and the chair, an exhibit not ready for public view. Indian John had built the room, nailing it to the hotel wall with the style and grace of a man who'd never built a thing in all his life and never intended to do it again. When he was finished, he tossed the wood he hadn't used inside and nailed the room firmly shut and threw his hammer into the desert. The room stayed empty except for spiders until Will and his brother moved in.

In August, a man had ridden in from Portales heading vaguely for Santa Fe and having little notion where he was. His wife lay in the flat bed of their wagon, fever-eyed and brittle as desert wood, one leg swollen and stinking with infection. They had camped somewhere, and a centipede nine and three-quarter inches long had found its way beneath her blanket. The leg was rotting and would kill her. The woman was too sick to know it. The man said his wife would be all right. They planned to open a chocolate works in Santa Fe and possibly deal in iced confections on the side. The railroad was freighting in their goods from St. Louis; everything would be waiting when they arrived. The man kept the centipede in a jar. His wife lay in the bed across the room. He kept the jar in the window against the light and watched the centipede curl around the inner walls of glass. Its legs moved like a hundred new fishhooks varnished black.

The man had a problem with connections. He couldn't see the link between the woman on the bed and the thing that rattled amber-colored armor in the jar. His wife and the centipede were two separate events.

The woman grew worse, her body so frail that it scarcely raised the sheets. When she died, Indian John took the centipede out and killed it. What he did, really, and Will saw him do it, was stake the thing down with a stick, Apache-style. Pat Garrett told the man to get his sorry ass out of the Sallie C. that afternoon and no later. The man couldn't see why Garrett was mad. He wanted to know what the Indian had done with his jar. He said his wife would be fine after a while. He had a problem with connections. He couldn't see the link between burial and death. Indian John stood in the heat and watched ants take the centipede apart. They sawed it up neatly and carried it off like African bearers.

Will thought about this and carefully shook his trousers and his shoes. He splashed his face with water and found his shirt and walked out into the morning. He liked the moment suspended, purple-gray and still between the night and the start of day. There was a freshness in the air, a time before the earth changed hands and the sun began to beat the desert flat.

Behind the hotel was a small corral, the pen attached to the weathered wooden structure that served as workshed, stable, and barn. The ghost shapes of horses stirred about. The morning was thick and blue, hanging heavy in the air. Saltbush grew around the corral, and leathery beavertail cactus. Will remembered he was supposed to chop the cactus out and burn it.

Indian John walked out on the back steps and tossed dishwater and peelings into the yard. He took no notice of Will. The chickens darted about, bobbing like prehistoric lizards. Will opened the screen and went in. The hotel was built of wood but the kitchen was adobe, the rough walls black with smoke and grease. The room was hot and smelled of bacon and strong coffee. Will poured himself a cup and put bread on the stove to make toast.

"John, you seen my brother this morning?" Will asked. He didn't look up from his plate. "He get anything to eat?"

"Mr. Pat say your brother make a racket before noon he goin' to kill him straight out. Like that." John drew a finger across his throat to show Will how.

"He hasn't been doing that, John."

"Good. He gah'dam better not."

"If he *isn't*, John, then why talk about it?"

"Gah'dam racket better stop," John said, the menace clear in his voice. "Better stop or you brother he in helluva big trouble."

Will kept his fury to himself. There was no use arguing with John, and a certain amount of risk. He stood and took his coffee and his toast out of the kitchen to the large open room next door. He imagined John's eyes at his back. Setting his breakfast on the bar, he drew the shades and found his broom. There were four poker tables and a bar. The bar was a massive structure carved with leaves and tangled vines and clusters of grapes, a good-sized vineyard intact in the dark mahogany wood. Garrett had bought the bar up in Denver and had it hauled by rail as far as he could. Ox teams brought it the rest of the way across the desert, where Garrett removed the front of the hotel to get it in.

There was a mirror behind the bar, bottles and glasses that Will dusted daily. Above the bottles there was a picture of a woman. The heavy gilt frame was too large for the picture. The woman had delicate features, deep-set eyes, and a strong willful mouth. Will imagined she had a clear and pleasant voice.

By the time he finished sweeping, there were pale fingers of light across the floor. Will heard steps on the back stairs and then the boy's voice talking to John, and then John speaking himself. John didn't sound like John when he spoke to the boy.

Will looked at the windows and saw they needed washing. It was a next-to-useless job. The sand ate the glass and there was no way to make them look right. The sight suddenly plunged him into despair. A man thirty-six with good schooling. A man who sweeps out and cleans windows. He wondered where he'd let his life go. He had scarcely even noticed. It had simply unraveled, coming apart faster than he could fix it.

The boy ran down the steps into the yard. He walked as if he owned the world and knew it. Will couldn't remember if he'd felt like that himself.

The front stairs creaked, and Will saw Garrett coming down. This morning he wore an English worsted suit and checkered vest. Boots shined and a fresh linen collar, cheeks shaved pink as baby skin. The full head of thick white hair was slicked back, and his mustache was waxed in jaunty curls. Will looked away, certain Garrett could read his every thought. It made him furious, seeing this ridiculous old fart spruced up like an Eastern dandy. Before the woman arrived, he had staggered around in moth-eaten dirty longhandles, seldom bothering to close the flap. At night he rode horses blind drunk. Everyone but John stayed out of his way. Now Will was supposed to think he had two or three railroads and a bank.

Garrett walked behind the bar and poured a healthy morning drink. "Looks real nice," he told Will. "I do like to see the place shine."

Will had rearranged the dust and nothing more. "That Indian's threatening my brother," he announced. "Said he'd cut his throat sure."

"I strongly doubt he'll do it. If he does, he won't tell you in advance."

"What he said was it was you. I assure you I didn't believe him for a minute. I am not taken in by savage cunning."

"That's good to know."

"Mr. Garrett, my brother isn't making any noise. Not till after dinner like you said."

"I know he's not, Will."

"So you'll say something to John and make him stop?"

"If you've a mind to weary me, friend, you've got a start. Now how's that wagon coming along?"

"Got to have a whole new axle like I said. But I can get it done pretty fast."

Garrett looked alarmed. "What you do is take your time and do it *right*. Fast is the mark of the careless worker, as I see it. A shoddy job is no job at all. Now run out and see that boy's not near the horses. I doubt he's ever seen a creature bigger than a fair-sized dog."

▲▼▲

Garrett watched him go. The man was a puzzle, and he had no use for puzzles of any kind. Puzzles always had a piece missing, and with Will, Garrett figured the piece was spirit. Someone had reached in and yanked it right out of Will's head and left him hollow. No wonder the damn Injun gave him fits. A redskin was two-thirds cat and he'd worry a cripple to death.

Garrett considered another drink. Will had diminished the soothing effects of the first, leaving him one behind instead of even. He thought about the woman upstairs. In his mind she wore unlikely garments from Paris, France. John began to sing out in the kitchen. *Hiyas* and such strung together in a flat and tuneless fashion. Like drunken bees in a tree. Indian songs began in the middle and worked out. There was no true beginning and no end. One good solution was the 10-gauge Parker he kept under the bar. Every morning Garrett promised himself he'd do it. Walk in and expand Apache culture several yards.

"I'll drink to that," he said, and he did.

▲▼▲

The boy was perched atop the corral swinging his legs. John had given him sugar for the horses.

"Mr. Garrett says you take a care," Will told him. "Don't get in there with them now."

"I will be most careful," the boy said.

He had good manners and looked right at you when he talked. Will decided this was a mark of foreign schooling. He walked past the horses to the barn. The morning heat was cooking a heady mix, a thick fermented soup of hay and manure, these odors mingled with the sharp scent of cleanly sanded wood, fuel oil, and waxy glue.

Will stopped a few feet from the open door. The thing seemed bigger than he remembered. He felt ill at ease in its presence. He liked things with front and back ends and solid sides to hold them together. Here there was a disturbing expanse of middle.

"Listen, you coming out of there soon?" Will said, making no effort to hide his irritation. "I'm darn sure not coming in."

"Don't. Stay right there." His brother was lost in geometric confusion.

"Orville, I don't like talking to someone I can't even see."

"Then don't."

"You sleep out here or what? I didn't hear you come to bed."

"Didn't. Had things to do."

"Don't guess you *ate* anything, either."

"I eat when I've a mind to, Will, all right?"

"You say it, you don't do it."

"One of those chickens'll wander in I'll eat that. Grab me a wing and a couple of legs."

Will saw no reason for whimsy. It didn't seem the time. "It isn't even eight yet, case you didn't notice," he said shortly. "I promised Mr. Garrett you wouldn't mess with that thing till noon. John raised Ned with me at breakfast. Me now, Orville, not you."

Orville emerged smiling from a torturous maze of muslin stretched tightly over spars of spruce and ash, from wires that played banjo as he passed, suddenly appearing as if this were a fine trick he'd just perfected.

"I am not to make noise before noon," he told Will. "Nobody said I couldn't work. Noise is forbidden, but toil is not."

"You're splitting hairs and you know it."

Orville brushed himself off and looked at his brother. "Listen a minute, Will, and don't have a stroke or anything, all right? I'm going to try her out tomorrow."

"Oh, my Lord!" Will looked thunderstruck.

"I'd like for you to watch."

"Me? What for?"

"I'd like you to be there, Will. Do I have to have a reason?" Orville had never asked him a question he could answer. Will supposed there were thousands, maybe millions of perplexities between them, a phantom cloud that followed them about.

"I don't know," he said, and began to rub his hands and bob about. "I can't say, maybe I will, I'll have to see." He turned, suddenly confused about direction, and began to run in an awkward kind of lope away from the barn.

▲▼▲

Helene kept to herself. Except for her usual walk after supper, she had not emerged from the room since her arrival. Herr Garrett sent meals. The savage left them in the hall and pounded loudly at her door. Helene held her breath until he was gone. If he caught her, he would defile her in some way she couldn't imagine. She ate very little and inspected each bite for foreign objects, traces of numbing drugs.

Garrett also sent the Indian up with presents. Fruits and wines. Nosegays of wilted desert flowers. She found these offerings presumptuous. The fruit was tempting; she didn't dare. What rude implication might he draw from a missing apple, a slice of melon accepted?

"God in Heaven, help me!" she cried aloud, lifting her head to speed this plea in the right direction. What madness had possessed her, brought her to this harsh and terrible land? The trip had been a nightmare from the start. A long ocean voyage and then a train full of ruffians and louts. In a place called Amarillo they said the tracks were out ahead. Three days' delay and maybe more. Madame was headed for Albuquerque? What luck, the stranger told her. Being of the European persuasion, she might not be aware that Amarillo and Albuquerque were widely known as the twin cities of the West. He would sell her a wagon cheap, and she would reach her destination before dark. Albuquerque was merely twenty-one miles down the road. Go out of town and turn left.

Her skin was flushed, ready to ignite. Every breath was an effort. Her cousin would think she was dead, that something dreadful had happened. She applied wet cloths. Wore only a thin chemise. The garment seemed shamefully immodest and brought her little relief. Sometimes she drifted off to sleep. Only to wake from tiresome dreams. Late in the day she heard a rude and startling sound. Mechanical things disturbed her. It clattered, stuttered and died and started again.

Before the sun was fully set, she was dressed and prepared for her walk. Hair pale as cream was pinned securely under a broad-brimmed hat. The parasol matched her dress. In the hall she had a fright. The savage came up the stairs with covered trays. Helene stood her ground. Fear could prove fatal in such encounters; weakness only heightened a man's lust.

The savage seemed puzzled to see her. His eyes were black as stones. "This your supper," he said.

"No, no, danken Sie," she said hurriedly, "I do not want it."

"You don't eat, you get sick."

Was this some kind of threat? If he attacked, the point of the parasol might serve her as a weapon.

"I am going to descend those stairs," she announced. "Do you understand me? I am *going* down those stairs!"

The Indian didn't move. Helene rushed quickly past him and fled. Outside she felt relatively secure. Still, her heart continued to pound. The sky was tattered cloth, a garish orange garment sweeping over the edge of the earth. Color seemed suspended in the air. Her skin, the clapboard wall behind her, were painted in clownish tones. Even as she watched, the color changed. Indigo touched the faint shadow of distant mountains.

So much space and nothing in it! Her cousin's letter had spoken of vistas. This was the word Ilse used. Broad, sweeping vistas, a country of raw and unfinished beauty. Helene failed to see it. At home, everything was comfortably close. The vistas were nicely confined.

"Well now, good evening, Miz Rommel," Garrett said cheerfully, coming up beside her to match her pace, "taking a little stroll, are you?"

Helene didn't stop. "It appears that is exactly what I am doing, Herr Garrett." The man's feigned surprise seemed foolish. After four days of popping up precisely on the hour, Helene was scarcely amazed to see him again.

"It's truly a sight to see," said Garrett, peering into the west. "Do you get sunsets like this back home? I'll warrant you do not."

"To the best of my knowledge, the sun sets every night. I have never failed to see this happen."

"Well, I guess that's true."

"I am certain that it is."

"I have never been to Germany. Or France or England, either. The Rhine, now that's a German river."

"Yes."

"I suppose you find my knowledge of foreign lands greatly lacking."

"I have given it little thought."

"I meant to travel widely. Somehow life interceded."

"I'm sure it did."

"Life and circumstance. *Herr,* now that means mister."

"Yes, it does."

"And mrs., what's that?"

"*Frau.*"

"Frau Rommel. In Mexican that would be *Señora. Señor* and *Señora.* I can say without modesty I am not unacquainted with the Spanish tongue."

"How interesting, I'm sure."

"Now if you were unmarried, you'd be a *señorita.*"

"Which I am not," Helene said, with a fervor Garrett could scarcely overlook.

"Well, no offense of course," said Garrett, backtracking as quickly as he could. "I mean, if you were, that's how you'd say it. You see, they put that *ita* on the end of lots of things. *Señorita*'s sort of 'little lady.' Now a little dog or little—Miz Rommel, you suppose you could see your way clear to have supper with me this evening, maybe nine o'clock? I would be greatly honored if you would."

Helene stopped abruptly. She could scarcely believe what she'd heard. "I am a married woman, Herr Garrett. I thought we had established this through various forms of address."

"Well now, we did but—"

"Then you can see I must decline."

"Not greatly I don't, no."

"Surely you do."

"To be honest I do not."

"Ah, well! All the more reason for me to refuse your invitation! To be quite honest, Herr Garrett, I am appalled at your suggestion. Yes, *appalled* is the word I must use. I am not only a married woman but a mother. I have come to this wretched land for one reason, and that reason is my son. As even you can surely see, Erwin is a boy of most delicate and sickly nature. His physician felt a hot and arid climate would do him good. I am no longer certain this is so."

"Miz Rommel," Garrett began, "I understand exactly what you're saying. All I meant was—"

"No, I doubt that you understand at all," Helene continued, her anger unabated, "I am sure you can't imagine a mother's feelings for her son. I can tell you right now that I see my duty clearly, Herr Garrett, and it does *not* include either the time or the inclination for—for illicit suppers and the like!"

"Illicit suppers?" Garrett looked totally disconcerted. "Jesus Christ, lady…"

"Language, Herr Garrett!"

Garrett ran a hand through his hair. "If I've offended you any, I'll say I'm sorry. Far as that boy of yours is concerned, you don't mind me saying, he looks healthy enough to me. If he's sickly, he doesn't show it. John says he takes to the desert like a fox."

"I would hardly call that an endorsement," Helene said coolly.

"John knows the country, I'll hand him that."

"He frightens me a great deal."

"I don't doubt he does. That's what Indians are for."

"I'm sorry. I do not understand that statement at all."

"Ma'am, the Indian race by nature is inured to savage ways. Murder, brutalizing, and the like. When he is no longer allowed these diversions, he must express his native fury in some other fashion. Scaring whites keeps him happy. Many find it greatly satisfying. Except of course for the Sioux, who appear to hold grudges longer than most."

"Yes, I see," said Helene, who didn't at all. The day was suddenly gone; she had not been aware of this at all. The arid earth drank light instead of water. Garrett's presence made her nervous. He seemed some construction that might topple and fall apart.

She stopped and looked up and caught his eye. "My wagon. I assume you will have it ready quite soon."

The question caught Garrett off guard. This was clearly her intention.

"Why, it's coming along nicely, I would say."

"I don't think that's an answer."

"The axle, Miz Rommel. The axle is most vital. The heart, so to speak, of the conveyance."

He was fully transparent. He confirmed her deepest fears. She could see his dark designs.

"Fix it," she said, and the anger he had spawned rose up to strike him. "Fix it, Herr Garrett, or I shall take my son and *walk* to Albuquerque."

"Dear lady, please..."

"I will *walk,* Herr Garrett!"

She turned and left him standing, striding swiftly away. He muttered words behind her. She pretended not to hear. She knew what he would do. He would soothe his hurt with spirits, numb his foul desires. Did he think she didn't know? God preserve women! Men are great fools, and we are helpless but for the strength You give us to foil them!

There was little light in the west. The distant mountains were ragged and indistinct, a page torn hastily away. Garrett had warned her of the dangers of the desert. Rattlesnakes slithering about. He took great pleasure in such stories. She had heard the horrid tale of the centipede. From Garrett, from Will, and once again, from Erwin.

Turning back, she faced the Sallie C. again. How strange and peculiar it was. The sight never failed to disturb her. One lone structure and nothing more. A single intrusion on desolation. A hotel where none was needed, where no one ever came. Where was the woman buried, she wondered? Had anyone thought to mark the grave?

Drawing closer, she saw a light in the kitchen, saw the savage moving about. Another light in the barn, the tapping of a hammer coming from there. She recalled the clatter she'd heard that afternoon. Now what was that about? Erwin would surely know, though he had mentioned nothing at all. The boy kept so within himself. Sometimes this concerned her, even hurt her deeply. They were close, but there was a part of this child she didn't know.

Helene couldn't guess what made her suddenly look up, bring her eyes to that point on the second story. There, a darkened window, and in the window the face of a man. Her first reaction was disgust. Imagine! Garrett spying on her in the dark! Still, the face made no effort to draw away, and she knew in an instant this wasn't Garrett at all but someone else.

Helene drew in a breath, startled and suddenly afraid. She quickly sought the safety of the porch, the protecting walls of the hotel. Who was he, then, another guest? But wouldn't she have heard if this were so?

She smelled the odors of the kitchen, heard the Indian speak, then Erwin's boyish laughter. Why, of course! She paused, her hand still on the door. The savage had carried *two* covered trays when she met him in the hall. At the time, she had been too fearful of his presence to even notice. The other tray, then, was for the man who sat in the window. He, too, preferred his meals in his room. Something else to ask her son. What an annoying child he could be! He would tell her whatever she wanted to know. But she would have to ask him first.

▲▼▲

It was Pat Garrett's habit to play poker every evening. The game began shortly after supper and lasted until Garrett had soundly beaten his opponents, or succumbed to the effects of rye whiskey. Before the game began, Garrett furnished each chair with a stack of chips and a generous tumbler of spirits. Some players' stacks were higher than others. A player with few chips either got a streak of luck or quickly folded, leaving the game to better men. Bending to the harsh circle of light, Garrett would deal five hands on the field of green, then move about to each chair in turn, settle in and study a hand, ask for cards or stand, sip from a player's glass and move on, bet, sip, and move again. After the first bottle of rye the game got lively, the betting quite spirited, the players bold and sometimes loud in their opinions. Will, lying awake in the shed out back, and on this night, young Erwin at the bottom of the stairs, could hear such harsh remarks as "Bet or go piss, McSween," "You're plain bluffing, Bell, you never saw kings and aces in your life..."

More than once, Will had been tempted to sneak up and peer in a window to assure himself Garrett was alone. He thought about it but didn't. If Garrett was playing with ghosts, Will didn't want to know it.

▲▼▲

Sometime close to three in the morning, Helene awoke with a start. There was a terrible racket below, as if someone were tossing chairs and tables across the room, which, she decided, was likely the case. Moments later, something bumped loudly against the wall outside her window. Someone muttered under his breath. Someone was trying to climb a ladder.

Helene woke Erwin, got him from his bed and brought him to her, holding the boy close and gripping her parasol like a saber.

"God save us from the defiler," she prayed aloud. "Forgive me all my sins. Erwin, if anything happens to me, you must get to cousin Ilse in Albuquerque. Can you ride a horse, do you think? Your father put you on a horse. I remember clearly he did. At Otto Kriebel's farm in Heidenheim?"

"*Nein, Mutti,*" he assured her, "it is all right, nothing is going to happen."

"Hush," she scolded, "you don't know that at all. You are only a boy. You know nothing of the world. You scarcely imagine the things that can happen."

At that moment, a most frightening shout came from just below the window. The cry receded, as if it were rapidly moving away. The ladder struck the ground, and half a second later something heavier than that. The night was silent again.

"Perhaps someone is injured," Erwin suggested.

"Go to sleep," Helene told him. "Say your prayers and don't forget to ask God to bless Papa. We are far away from home."

▲▼▲

There was no question of sleeping. To the usual morning noise of men stomping heavily about, of chickens clucking and horses blowing air, was now added the hollow ring of timber, of hammering and wheels that needed grease. Helene dressed quickly, recalling her promise to Erwin the night before. Before she could sweep her hair atop her head he was back, eyes alight with wonder, those deep, inquisitive eyes that seemed to see much more than a boy should see.

"*Komm' schnell, Mutti!*" he urged her, scarcely giving her time to pause before the mirror. Holding tightly to her hand, he led her quickly down the stairs and out into the brightness of the morning. The Indian leaned against the wall, drinking a can of peaches from the tin, practicing looking Mescalero mean. Garrett slumped in a rocker, his leg propped testily on a stool.

Helene could not resist a greeting. "Are you hurt, Herr Garrett? I do hope you have not had an accident of some sort."

"I am in excellent health, thank you," Garrett said shortly.

"Well. I am most pleased to hear it." The man seemed to have aged during the night. His flesh was soft as dough. Helene wondered if he would rise, swell like an ungainly pastry in the heat.

"There, *Mutti,* see?" said Erwin. "Look, they are coming. It is most exciting, yes!"

"Why yes, yes, I'm sure it is, Erwin," Helene said vaguely. In truth, she had no idea what she was seeing. The strange sight appeared around the corner of the hotel. It seemed to be an agricultural device. Helene framed a question for Erwin, but he was gone. "Have a care," she called out, but knew he didn't hear.

Two men guided the wagon toward the flats. One of the two was Will. She guessed the other was his brother. Will looked stricken, a man pressed into service, who clearly hoped no one would notice he was there.

As Helene watched, the first flash of morning touched the horizon, a fiercely bright explosion that scarred the earth with light and shadow. A silver lance touched the strange device; the thing seemed imbued with sudden magic. Light pierced the flat planes of muslin and spruce, and Helene imagined transparent flesh and hollow bones. A dragonfly, a golden fish in a dream.

"Oh. Oh, *my,*" she said aloud, deeply touched by the moment.

"Looks to me like a medicine show hit by a twister," said Garrett.

"*I* think it has a certain grace," said Helene. "The rather delicate beauty one associates with things Oriental."

"Chink laundry," Garrett countered. "Got in the way of a train."

"They say strong spirits greatly dull the imagination," Helene said coolly and took herself to the far end of the porch.

Out on the flats, Will and his brother carefully lifted the device off the wagon onto the ground. Broad wooden runners that might have come from a horse-drawn sleigh were attached to the contraption's undercarriage. Helene knew about sleighs. The runners seemed strangely out of place. Snow was clearly out of the question.

Suddenly, the engine in the device began to snarl. The latticed wooden structure, the wire and planes of fabric began to shake. In the rear, two enormous fans started churning plumes of sand into the air. Orville donned a long cotton duster and drew goggles over his eyes. He climbed aboard the device, perched on a bicycle seat, and looked carefully left and right.

"Erwin, *nein,*" Helene cried out, "get back from that thing!"

Erwin, though, was too engrossed to hear. He held a rope attached to the lower muslin plane. Will held one on the other side. The engine reached a shrill and deafening pitch. Orville raised a hand. Erwin and Will released their hold.

The contraption jerked to a start, a dog released from its chain. Helene made a small sound of surprise. Somehow, the possibility of motion hadn't occurred. The device moved faster and faster. Orville leaned hard into the wind. His hands clutched mystical controls. Muslin flapped and billowed. Suddenly, with no warning at all, the thing came abruptly off the ground.

"Holy Christ Colorado," said Garrett.

Helene was thunderstruck. The device, held aloft by forces unseen and unimagined, soared for ten seconds or more then wobbled, straightened, and gently kissed the earth. The engine fluttered and stopped. Will and Erwin ran frantically over the flats, waving their arms. Orville climbed to the ground. Will and Erwin shook his hand and clapped him firmly on the back. Then all three made their way to the hotel.

Erwin was elated. He might explode from excitement any moment. Even Will seemed pleased. Orville was curiously restrained. His goggles were pushed atop his head. His eyes were ringed with dust.

"*Mutti*, it was something to see, was it not?" Erwin cried.

"It certainly was," said Helene.

"I've got to admit," said Garrett, "I never saw a man ride a wagon off the ground."

"Now I can fix that," Orville said thoughtfully. "I know exactly what happened. This was only the first trial, you understand."

Garrett seemed confused. "You planning on doing that again?"

"Why, yes sir. Yes, I am."

Garrett pulled himself erect. "Not till after noon you're not, Orville. That racket assaults the nerves. I doubt if it's good for the digestion." He turned and went inside.

"It was most entertaining," Helene said, thinking that she ought to be polite.

"The elevator needs more weight," said Orville, as if Helene would surely agree. "That should keep the front firmly down. And I shall tilt the sail planes forward. Too much vertical lift the way they are."

"Yes, of course," said Helene.

"Well, we had best get her back to the barn," Orville said. "Lots of work to do. And thank you for your help, young man."

Erwin flushed with pride. "Sir, I was honored to assist."

Will and Orville walked back into the sun.

"*Mutti,* it is a marvel, is it not?" said Erwin.

"Yes, it is," Helene agreed. "Now you stay away from that thing, do you hear? I want you to promise me that."

Erwin looked stricken. "But Herr Orville has promised that I shall have a ride!"

"And *I* promise that you shall do no such thing," Helene said firmly. "Just get that out of your head."

Erwin turned and fled, holding back the tears that burned his eyes. Helene released a sigh, wondering how she would manage to handle this. Everyone was gone. She seemed to be all alone on the porch.

▲▼▲

The sounds of Orville's labor continued throughout the day. When Helene returned from her regular evening walk, a lantern still glowed within the barn. Orville disturbed her more than a little. The man had a fire in his eyes. Such a look in a man frightened her. Her husband's eyes were steady and reassuring. When she saw the two together, Orville and her son, a vague disquieting shadow crossed her heart. Erwin had such a light as well.

"Evening, Miz Rommel," said Garrett. The glow of his cigar came from the porch.

"I did not see you standing there," said Helene. Her tone was clearly distant.

"I suppose you're put out with me some."

"With reason, I should think."

"I guess there is."

"You only guess?"

"All right. I would say you have some cause."

"Yes, I would say that indeed."

"Look, Miz Rommel—"

"Is this an apology, then?"

"I was getting to that."

"Then I shall accept it, Herr Garrett."

Garrett shifted uncomfortably. "That wagon will be ready in the morning. Now Albuquerque's a hundred and twenty miles through real bad country in the heat. There can be no question of such a trip. On the other hand, it is only fifty miles down to Roswell and the train. I shall have Will ride along and see that you get there safely."

"I am grateful, Herr Garrett."

"You don't have to be at all."

"Perhaps you could pack a nice lunch."

"I don't see why I couldn't."

"And rig some kind of shade for the wagon."

"I could do that, yes."

"How nice. A very thoughtful gesture."

"Miz Rommel—"

"Yes, Herr Garrett?"

Garrett was on the brink of revelation. He had steeled himself for the moment. He would bare the fires of passion that burned within. She would be frightened and appalled, but she would know. He saw, then, as the words began to form, that her skin matched the pearly opalescence of the moon, that her hair was saffron-gold, spun fine as down from a baby duck. In an instant, his firm resolve was shattered. He muttered parting words and turned and fled.

A most peculiar man, thought Helene. A drunkard and a lecher without a doubt, yet God was surely within this wayward soul, as He is within us all.

She had meant to go directly to her room. Yet she found her steps taking her to the barn and knew the reason. Erwin was surely there. The matter must be settled. She loved the boy intently. Anger struggled with the pain she felt in her heart. They had never quarreled before as they had that morning. She had sternly forbidden him to have anything to do with Orville's device. Yet, he had openly disobeyed. Helene had no desire to quell his spirit. Still, she could not brook open rebellion in her child.

The moon was bright with chalky splendor. The broad backs of the horses moved like waves on a restless sea. A man came toward her through the dark. From his quick, awkward gait she knew at once that it was Will.

"Good evening," she said, "can you tell me if my son is back there, please?"

"Yes, ma'am, yes he is," said Will. "He's surely there, Miz Rommel."

Why did the man act in such a manner? He was ever bobbing about like a cork. As if there might be danger in standing still.

"He is *not* supposed to be there," Helene sighed. "I am afraid he has disobeyed."

"That wagon will be ready in the morning," said Will.

"Yes. So Herr Garrett has explained." She felt suddenly weary, eager to put this place behind her. "Do you know Erwin well? Have you talked to him at all?"

"No ma'am. Not a lot. He mostly talks to Orville."

"He feels some kinship with your brother."

"Yes, he surely does."

"He is a free spirit, your brother. I see that in him clearly."

"I guess he's that, all right."

"A man pursuing a dream?"

"He has never been different than he is. The way you see him now. When we were boys, he'd say Will, there is a thing I have to do. And I'd say what would that be, Orville, and he'd say man sails boldly before the wind across the seas. I would set him free to sail the land. And I'd say, Orville, why would you want to do that? Lord, I guess I've asked that question a million times."

"And what would Orville say?"

"Same thing every time. Why not, Will?"

"Yes. Yes, of course," Helene said softly. Oh, Erwin, have I lost you to your dreams so soon!

"Miz Rommel..."

"Yes, Will?"

Will bobbed about again. "Maybe I have no business speaking out. If I don't, you just tell me and I'll stop. That boy wants to ride in Orville's machine. Wants it so bad he can taste it. I hope you'll relent and let him do it. He's a boy bound and determined is what he is."

"I think I know that, Will."

"I am a man of practical bent, Miz Rommel. I will never be anything more. I used to see this as a virtue in myself. In some men maybe it is. In me it is a curse, the great failing of my life. Mr. Garrett thinks Orville is a fool. That I am a man who's lost his spirit. Perhaps he is right about us both. But he does not know the truth of the matter at all. It is not my brother's folly that brought us here but mine alone. *I* failed. *I* brought us down. We had a small shop where we repaired common household items. Coffee mills, lard presses, ice shavers, and the like. Not much, but it kept us going. I felt there was something more. I reached for a distant star and invested quite heavily in the windmill accessory business. I think Orville sensed that I was wrong. Out of kindness, he did nothing to dissuade me. When we left Ohio, we had nothing but our wagon. A few days' food and the clothing on our backs. And Orville's wood and muslin and his motors. Our creditors demanded these as well. I have never stood up for myself. Not once in all my life. But I stood my ground on this. Your Erwin is a good boy, Miz Rommel. Let him be what he will be."

"Yes. Yes," said Helene. "I understand what you are saying. And I am grateful to you, Will."

Helene was taken aback by this long and unexpected declaration. She hadn't dreamed the man owned so many words, or that he had the passion within him to set them free. Now, as he tried to speak again, he seemed to see what he had done. He had tossed away countless nouns and verbs, spent whole phrases and contractions he couldn't retrieve. Clutching his hat, he bolted past her and disappeared. Helene listened to the horses stir about. Orville laughed and then her son. It seemed one voice instead of two. She made her way quickly to her room.

▲▼▲

Erwin's mother had asked him if he knew about the man, and Erwin did. He knew John took him all his meals. He knew the man never left his room. He was much too angry at his mother to tell her that and so he lied. The lie hurt. It stuck in his throat and stayed, no matter how hard he tried to swallow. Late the night before when he came in from working in the barn, she was sitting waiting quietly in the dark. They burst into tears and cried together. Erwin told her he was sorry. She said that it was over now and done. He didn't feel like growing up and yet he did.

▲▼▲

It took all the courage he could muster. Just to stand in front of the door and nothing more. What if John came up the stairs? He wasn't afraid of John and yet he was.

The door came open with ease. Erwin's heart beat wildly against his chest. The room was musty, heavy with unpleasant odors. Stale air and sour sweat. Food uneaten and chamber pots neglected. Mostly the smell was time. The room was layered with years. Erwin saw yesterdays stuffed in every corner.

A window centered the wall. The morning burned a harsh square of brightness, yet the light failed to penetrate the room. It was stopped, contained, it could go no further than this. The sound of Orville's machine worried the quiet, probed like a locust through the day.

"You stand there, boy, you'll turn to stone. Or is it salt, I can't recall. Salt or stone one. Get over here close so I can see."

Erwin jumped at the voice. He nearly turned and ran.

"It's salt. Salt for certain. Lot's wife. Sodom and Cincinnati. Lo the wicked shall perish and perish they do. I have seen a great many of them do it."

Erwin walked cautiously to the window. The man sat in shadow in a broken wicker chair. The chair had once been painted festive yellow. Down the arms there were eagles or maybe chickens in faded red.

Cactus the pale shade of leafy mold. For a moment it seemed to Erwin that the man was wicker, too, that the chair had fashioned a person out of itself, thrust brittle strands for arms and legs, burst dry backing from Chihuahua, Mexico, for springy ribs. The whole of this draped with tattered clothes of no description. Hair white silk to the shoulders and beyond. The head newspaper dry as dust, crumpled in a ball and tied with string about the brow, a page very likely blown six hundred miles from Fort Worth across the flats. Eyes and nose and shadow mouth vaguely nibbled into shape by friendly mice.

Or so it all seemed on this attic afternoon.

"Well, what's your name now?" the man asked, in a voice like rocks in a skillet.

"Johannes Erwin Eugen Rommel, sir," said Erwin, scarcely managing to find his voice at all.

"By God. That's more name than a boy needs to have, I'll tell you sure. What do they call you for short?"

"Erwin, sir."

"Erwin sir and two more. Might be handy to have a spare at that. Knew a man called Zero Jefferson White. Couldn't remember who he was. What does your father do?"

"He is a schoolmaster, sir."

The paper mouth crinkled in a sly and knowing way. "I am aware of that, you see. John has told me all. I am kept informed, and don't forget it."

"Are you a hundred, sir?" The words came out before he could stop them.

The mouse-nibble eyes searched about. "I might be, I couldn't say. What year you think it is?"

"Nineteen-hundred-and-three, sir."

"It is? Are you sure?" The man seemed greatly surprised. "Then I am likely forty-four. I have lived a fretful life and half of that in this chair less than a man. It's a wonder I look no worse. How old are you?"

"Eleven, sir. I shall be twelve in November. When I am eighteen I shall become a *Fahnenjunker*. I will be a fine officer cadet, and I shall excel in fencing and riding."

"I doubt a soldier's life would have suited me at all. Parades. Lining up and the like. That kind of nonsense and wearing blue shirts. Never trust a man in a blue shirt. You do, I can promise you'll live to regret it."

The man seemed intrigued by the sight beyond his window, by the sleek muslin craft cutting graceful figure-eights across the sand. The engine clattered, the fans roared, and Orville sped his dream across the desert, raising great plumes of dust in his wake. The dust rose high in the still hot air and hung above the earth like yellow clouds.

"Charlie Bowdrie and old Dave Rudabaugh would go pick the best horses they could find and start out from Pete Maxwell's place and ride the mounts full out. Ride them full out without stopping, you understand, until one or the other dropped dead, the horse still running being the winner. The other horse too would generally die, as you might expect. A senseless thing to do. Dangerous to the man and plain fatal to the horse."

"I am sorry that you are ill, sir."

"What? Who said that I was?" The paper eyes came alive. "Definitions, boy. I am done, mortally hurt. That is not the same as ill. Ill, as I recall, is simply sick. Taken with disease. An affliction or discomfort of the body. I am mortally hurt, is what I am. Cut down, stricken, assaulted by violent hand. Felled with a bullet in the spine. God in Oklahoma, that's a wonder," the man said, following Orville's path. "A marvel of nature it is. I wish Charlie Bowdrie could see it. I would give some thought to the army. I can think of nearly thirty-two things I'd rather do. 'Course that's entirely up to you. I went to Colorado one time, me and Tom O'Folliard driving horses. Came back quick as I could. The cold there not to my liking at all."

"You got to go now," said John, and Erwin wasn't sure just how long he'd been standing there in the room.

▲▼▲

"That canopy will shade you from the sun," said Garrett. "I don't expect the heat will be bad. You'll reach Roswell before dark, and Will'll see you settled before he leaves."

"Thank you," said Helene, "we are grateful for your help."

Will sat straight as a rod beside Erwin and his mother. He was proud of this new, if only temporary, post as wagon driver, and was determined to see it through. Orville wore his duster and his goggles. Earlier, after he had taken Erwin racing over the flats for nearly a full half-hour, he had given him a finely rendered pen-and-ink sketch of his muslin craft. John gave him two brass buttons, which he said had belonged to a U.S. Army major prior to a misunderstanding with Apaches in the Sierra Diablo country, which is south of the Guadalupe Mountains in Texas.

Garrett extended his hand. "Take care of your mother, boy. I have confidence that you will make yourself proud."

"Yes, sir," said Erwin.

"Well, then." Garrett extended his hand again, and Helene laid white-gloved fingers in his palm for just an instant. He studied the fair lines of her face, the silken hair swept under her bonnet. Strangely enough, he found he no longer regretted her departure. To be honest, he was glad to see her go. Keeping real people and phantoms apart was increasingly hard to do. Delusions he'd never seen were lately creeping into his life. An old lady crying in the kitchen. A stranger at the table betting queens. The woman only served to cause confusion, being real enough herself while his fancy made her something she never was.

"I'm giving you the shotgun, Will," said Garrett, "I don't see trouble, but you use it if there is."

"Yes sir, I surely will."

"You know where the trigger is, I guess."

"I surely do."

"And which way to point it, no doubt."

"Quite clearly sir, yes, I do."

"Then make sure you—"

"Oh. Oh, my!" said Helene, and brought a hand quickly to her lips.

Garrett turned to see her concern. The sight struck him in the heart. "Christ Jesus California!" he said at once, and stepped back as if felled by a blow. John stood in the door with the wicker chair, his great arms around it like a keg, the chair's pale apparition resting within. Garrett was unsure if this image was whiskey-real or otherwise and greatly feared it was the latter.

"John," he managed to say, "what in *hell* is he doing out here!"

"Mr. Billy say he ride," John announced.

"Ride what, for God's sake?"

"Ride that," John nodded. "He say he ride in Orville's machine."

"You tell him he's lost his senses."

"Mr. Billy say to tell you he going to do it."

"Well, you tell Mr. Billy that he's not," Garrett said furiously. "This is the most damn fool thing I ever heard."

"Tell Mr. Garrett I can kill myself any way I want," Billy said. He looked right at Garrett with a wide and papery grin. "Tell him I do not need advice from a fellow can't shoot a man proper close up."

"So that's it, is it," said Garrett. "You going to come downstairs every twenty-odd years now and pull *that* business out of the fire. By God, it's just like you, too. I said I was sorry once, I don't see the sense in doing it twice."

"Miz Rommel," said Billy, "I do not think your boy ought to look to the army. That is a life for a man with no ambition or gumption at all, and it is clear your boy is a comer. Bound for better things. May I say I have greatly enjoyed watching you take your evening walk. I said to Sallie Chisum once, you've likely seen her picture inside if Mr. Garrett hasn't thrown it out or burned it, which wouldn't surprise me any at all, I said Sallie, a woman's walk betrays her breeding high or low. She might be a duchess or the wife of a railroad baron or maybe even a lady of the night, a woman dedicated to the commerce of lust and fleshly delight, but the walk, now, the walk of a woman will out, the length and duration of her stride will tell you if she comes from good stock in a moment's glance, now am I right or am I not?"

"I would—I would really—I would really hardly—" Helene looked helplessly at Garrett.

"Will, Miz Rommel is sitting around in the heat," Garrett said firmly. "Would you kindly get this wagon headed south sometime before Tuesday?"

Will bobbed about with indecision, then flicked the reins and started the team moving with a jerk. Erwin waved. Garrett and John and Orville waved back.

Billy waved, too, though in no particular direction. "If you are headed for Roswell," he advised, "there was a fair hotel there at one time. Of course it may have changed hands, I can't say. Mr. John Tunstall and I stopped there once, and I recall that the rates were more than fair. A good steak is fifty cents, don't spend any more than that. The cook is named Ortega. His wife cooks a good *cabrito* if you can find a goat around that's not sick. Don't eat a goat that looks bad or you'll regret it. They are too bitter, though I've known those who prefer it that way to the other. Mr. John Chisum took four spoons of sugar. I could not fathom why. He kept an owl in a cage behind his house. That and other creatures some considerably less than tame…"

▲▼▲

When the wagon reached the rise sightly east of the Sallie C., Erwin looked back and heard the engine running strong and saw the white planes of muslin catch the sun, saw the runners racing swiftly over the sand. Orville's duster flew, his goggles flashed, his hands gripped the magic controls. John gripped the chair at Orville's back, and though Erwin from afar couldn't see Billy at all, spiderweb hair like a bright and silken scarf trailed past the wicker arms to whip the wind.

Winter on the Belle Fourche

He had come down in the cold from the Big Horn Mountains and crossed the Powder River moving east toward the Belle Fourche, all this time without finding any sign and leaving little of his own. There were wolf tracks next to the river and he saw where they had gone across the ice, which told him they were desperate and hungry, that they would turn on each other before long. An hour before dark, he pulled the mount up sharp and let his senses search the land, knowing clearly something had been there before. Finally, he eased to the ground and took the Hawken rifle with him, stood still in the naked grove of trees, stopped and listened to the quiet in the death-cold air, heard the frozen river crack, heard the wind bite the world. He looked south and saw the Black Hills veiled in every fold, followed them with his eyes until the land disappeared in the same soot color as the sky. He stood a long time and sniffed the air and the water moving slow beneath the ice. He let it all come together then and simmer in his head, and when it worked itself out, he walked down in the draw and started scooping off the snow.

A few inches down he found the ashes from the fire. They had camped right here the night before, made a small supper fire and another in the morning. He ran the ashes through his fingers then brought them to his nose. They were real smart Injuns. They hadn't broken dead sticks off the trees but had walked downstream to get their wood. Cupping more snow aside, he bent to smell the earth. Six, he decided. If he dug a little more he'd find they all had mounts, but he didn't need to bother doing that. They wouldn't be on foot out here.

This close to the Powder and the Belle Fourche, they could be any kind of red nigger and not any of them friends. He knew, though, this bunch wasn't Sioux or Cheyenne, but Absaroka. He'd smelled them right off. Crow warriors certain, and likely from Big Robert's camp.

He straightened and looked east, absently touching the bowie at his belt, the scalp ring next to that. That's where they'd gone, east and a little north, the way he was headed, too. They weren't after him, didn't know that he was there. And that was something to chew on for a while.

▲▼▲

The snow came heavy in the night, slacking off around the dawn. He was up before light and keeping to the river. Soon he'd have to figure what to do. It was two hundred miles to Fort Pierre on the Missouri, a lot more than that if he kept to every bend in the river. Del Gue would be waiting at the fort; he didn't need to be chasing after Crow, there were plenty out sniffing after him. Still, it wouldn't take much time to see what kind of mischief they were up to over here. The Absaroka were a little far east from where they rightly ought to be. He didn't think they'd want to keep on riding and maybe tangle with the Sioux, who would go without breakfast any day to skin a Crow.

At noon he found the answer. The snow had lightened up enough for tracks and he saw where the Crow had taken off, digging up dirt in the snow and hightailing it across the frozen river, heading back northwest into Absaroka country. Now he went slowly, keeping his eyes open for whatever had spooked the Crow. Sioux, most likely, though the Cheyenne could be around, too. Hard winter and empty bellies made everybody brave, and a man might go where he hadn't ought to be.

▲▼▲

He smelled the death before it saw it. The cold tried to hide it, but it came through clear and he was off his horse fast, leading it down to cover in the draw. The dead were in the trees just ahead, and though he knew there was no one there alive he circled wide to make sure, then walked into the clearing, the Hawken crooked loose against his chest.

Three men, mostly covered by the snow. He brushed them off enough to see they were soldiers, a white lieutenant and two buffalo troopers. Each had been shot and soundly scalped, then cut up some in the playful manner of the Sioux. The soldier's clothes and boots were gone; the Sioux had taken everything but long-handle underwear and socks.

A quick look around showed the Sioux hadn't taken them by surprise. They'd stood their ground and gotten off a few shots, and that was of some interest in itself. North, he found high ground and lighter snow and saw where the Sioux had walked Army-shod mounts northwest among their own. Ten or twelve riders. They'd gone back to the river with their trophies; the Crow had seen them then and turned for home. About this time the day before, the massacre a little before that.

He stopped and tried to work the thing out. What had the three troopers been doing up here? And why only three? It was maybe a hundred and fifty miles to Fort Laramie, a powerful lot to go in heavy snow and the cold maybe thirty-five below. Troopers didn't have a lot of smarts, but anyone'd know more than that.

He mounted up and crossed the river, circled and crossed again. Two miles down he found the trail. Something about the tracks caught his eye, and he eased out of the saddle and squatted down. Now there was puzzle for sure. One of the horses had ridden double—*before* those boys had been hit by the Sioux. But there were only three bodies in the snow. Which meant the red coons had likely taken one alive, carried him back home for Injun fun. Nothing you could do for that chile, except hope he got to die, which wasn't real likely for a while. Del Gue had been taken by the Sioux the year before, and barely got out with his topknot intact. A trooper would get an extra measure sure, a skinning and worse than that.

He had the whole story now. There was no use following tracks back to the clearing, but he did. He'd kept his scalp for twelve years in the wilds, and part of that from being thorough, taking two stitches in a moccasin when one might do as well, winding up a story like this to see how it came about.

He came upon the cabin without knowing it at all, reined the horse in and just sat there a minute and let the sign all around him sink in. The cabin was built low against the side of a ravine, nearly covered by a drift and he'd damn near ridden up on the roof. He cursed himself for that. It was the kind of aggravation he didn't like, coming on something like this after he'd gotten the whole story put away. He could see it clear now, like he'd been right there when it happened. The troopers had ridden past this place into the trees, sensed trouble up ahead, and the man riding double had ridden back, stopped at the cabin, then turned and joined his comrades again. Which meant he'd left someone behind. There were no more tracks in the snow, so whoever that'd be was still there, unless they'd sprouted wings and flown to Independence like a bird.

Snow was nearly three feet high against the door, and he carefully dug it clear. Jamming the stock of his Hawken in the snow, he pulled the Colt Walker and the bowie from his belt and stepped back.

"You inside there," he called out. "I'm white an' I don't mean ye any harm, so don't go a-shootin' whatever it is you got."

There was nothing but silence from inside. Edging up close, he bent his head to listen. There was someone in there, all right. He couldn't hear them but he knew.

"Mister," he said, "this chile's no Injun, you oughter have the sense to know that." He waited, cussed again, then raised his foot and kicked solidly at the door. It was old and split and snapped like a bone. Before it hit the floor he was in, moving fast and low, sideways like a bear, coming in with the Colt and the knife and sweeping every corner of the room. Kindling and dead leaves. The musty smell of mice. A fireplace nearly caved-in. Half a chair and a broken whiskey crock. An Army blanket in the corner, and something under that. He walked over and pulled the blanket aside with his foot.

"Great Jehoshaphat," he said aloud, and went quickly to the still and fragile form, touched the cold throat and felt for signs of life he was sure he wouldn't find.

▲▼▲

She woke to the memory of cold, the ghost of this sensation close to death, a specter that consumed her, left her hollow, left her numb with the certainty there was no heat great enough to drive the terrible emptiness away. She woke and saw the fire and tried to draw its warmth to her with her eyes. The walls and the ceiling danced with shadow. The shadows made odd and fearsome shapes. She tried to pull her eyes away but could find neither the strength nor the will for such an effort. The shadows made awful deathly sounds, sounds she could scarcely imagine. And then with a start that clutched her heart she remembered the sounds were real; she had heard them all too clearly through the walls from the trees across the snow.

"Oh Lord Jesus, they are dying," she cried aloud, "they are murdered every one!"

Darkness rose from the floor and blocked the fire. It seemed to flow and expand to fill the room, take form as a broad-shouldered demon cloaked in fur; it grew arms and a dark and grizzled beard, a wicked eye.

She screamed and tried to push herself away.

"Ain't any need for that," the demon said. "Don't mean ye any harm."

She stared in alarm. His words brought her no relief at all. "Who—who are you?" she managed to say. "What do you want with me?"

"My name's John Johnston," the figure said. "Folks has mostly took out the *t,* but that ain't no fault of mine. Just lie right still. You oughter take in some soup if ye can."

He didn't wait for an answer, but moved across the room. Her heart pounded rapidly against her breast. She watched him carefully, followed his every move. He would likely attack her quite soon. This business of the soup was just a ruse. Well, he would not catch her totally unaware. She searched for some weapon of defense, pulled herself up on one arm, the effort draining all her strength. She was under some heavy animal skin. It held her to the floor like lead. She saw a broken chair, just beyond her reach. With the help of Lord Jesus it would serve her quite well. David had very little more and brought another fearsome giant to his knees.

As she reached for the chair, stretched her arm as far as it would go, the heavy skin slipped past her shoulders to her waist. She felt the sudden cold, stopped, and caught sight of herself. For an instant, she was too paralyzed to move. Frozen with terror and disbelief. She was unclothed, bare beneath the cover! Her head began to swim. She fought against the dizziness and shame. *Oh Lord, don't let me faint,* she prayed. *Let me die, but don't let me faint in the presence of the beast!*

Using every ounce of will she could find, she lay back and pulled the cover to her chin. With one hand, she searched herself for signs of violation, careful not to touch any place where carnal sin resides. Surely he had done it in her sleep. Whatever it was they did. Would you know, could you tell? Defilement came with marriage, and she had no experience in that.

The man returned from the fire. She mustered all her courage.

"Stay away from me," she warned. "Don't take another step."

He seemed puzzled. "You don't want no soup?"

"You—you had no right," she said. "You have invaded my privacy. You have looked upon me. You have sinned in God's eyes and broken several commandments. I demand the return of my clothing."

He squatted down and set the soup on the floor. "Ma'am, I didn't do no sinnin' I recall. You was near froze stiff in them clothes."

"Oh, of course. That is just what you would say to excuse your lust. I would expect no less than that."

"Yes, ma'am."

"I cannot find it in my heart to forgive you. That is my failing. I will pray that our Blessed Savior will give me the strength to see you as His child."

"You feel a need fer this soup," Johnston said, "it's on the fire." With that he rose and left her, moved across the room and curled up in a buffalo robe.

▲▼▲

He woke at once and grabbed his heavy coat and picked up the Hawken rifle, all this in a single motion out of sleep. The woman hadn't moved. He had propped the broken door back up as best he could, and now he moved it carefully aside and slipped out into the night. The world seemed frozen, silent and hard as iron, yet brittle enough to shatter into powder at a touch. He couldn't put his finger on the sound that had broken through his sleep. The horse was all right, safely out of the wind by the cabin's far wall. The ground was undisturbed. He circled around and watched, stopped to sniff the air. Nothing was there now, but something had left its ghost behind.

Inside he warmed his hands by the fire. The woman was still asleep. It wasn't fair to say that she hadn't roused him some, that the touch of her flesh as he rubbed life back into her limbs hadn't started up some fires. Not like an Injun girl now, but some. He'd seen maybe two white women stark naked in his life. They seemed to lack definition. Like a broad field of snow without a track or a rock to give it tone. An Injun girl went from one shade to another, depending where you looked. John Hatcher had kept two fat Cheyenne squaws all the time. He kept them in his cabin in the Little Snake Valley and offered Johnston the use of one or both. He had politely declined, preferring to find his own. Hatcher's squaws giggled all the time. An Injun woman tended to act white after a spell and start to giggle and talk back. His wife hadn't done that at all. She'd been pure Injun to the end, but there weren't very many like that.

▲▼▲

When she woke once again she felt sick, drained and brittle as a stick. The man was well across the room, squatting silently by the wall.

"I would like that soup now if you please," she said as firmly as she could. She would show him no weakness at all. A man preyed upon that.

He rose and went to the fire, filled a tin cup and set it by her side.

"Take a care," he said, "it's right hot." He returned to the fire and came back and dropped a bundle on the floor. "Your clothes is all dry," he said.

She didn't answer or meet his eyes. She knew any reference to her garments would encourage wicked thoughts in his head. The soup tasted vaguely of corn, meat a little past its prime. It was filling and soothed the hurt away.

"Thank you," she said, "that was quite good."

"There's more if you want."

"I would like you to leave the cabin for a while. I should think half an hour will do fine."

Johnston didn't blink. "What fer?"

"That is no concern of yours."

"You want to get dressed, why you got that buffler robe. Ain't no reason you can't do it under there."

"Why, I certainly will not!" The suggestion brought color to her cheeks.

"Up to you," he said.

"I shall *not* move until you comply."

"Suit yorself."

Oh Lord, she prayed, *deliver me from this brute. Banish transgression from his mind.* Reaching out beneath the robe, she found her clothing and burrowed as far beneath the cover as she could, certain all the while he could see, or surely imagine, every private move she made.

▲▼▲

"Certain rules will apply," she said. "I suppose we are confined here for the moment, though I trust the Lord will release us from adversity in good time."

She sat very close to the fire. The warmth never seemed enough. The cold came in and sought her out. The man continued to squat against the wall. It didn't seem possible that he could sit in this manner for long hours at a time. Only the blue eyes flecked with gray assured her he had not turned to stone. He was younger than she'd imagined, perhaps only a few years older than herself. His shocking red hair and thick unkempt beard masked his face; hard and weathered features helped little in determining his age.

"You will respect my privacy," she said, "and I shall certainly respect yours. There will be specific places in this room where you are not to venture. Now. I wish to say in all fairness that I believe you very likely saved my life. I am not ungrateful for that."

"Yes'm," Johnston said.

"My name is Mistress Dickinson. Mistress Emily Elizabeth Dickinson to be complete, though I caution you very strongly, Mr. Johnston, that while circumstances have thrown us together, you will *not* take the liberty of using my Christian name."

"Already knew who you was," Johnston said.

Emily was startled, struck with sudden fear. "Why, that is not possible. How could you know that?"

"Saw yer name when I went through yer belongin's," Johnston said.

"How dare you, sir!"

"Didn't mean to pry. Thought you was goin' to pass on 'fore the morning. Figured I ought git ycr buryin' name."

"Oh." Emily was taken aback. Her hand came up to touch her heart. "I…see. Yes. Well, then…"

Johnston seemed to squint his eyes in thought. For the first time, she detected some expression in his face.

"Ma'am, there's somethin' I got to say," Johnston said. "Them soldiers you was with. I reckon you know they're all three of 'em dead."

"I…guessed as much." Emily trembled at the thought. "I have prayed for their souls. Our Lord will treat them kindly."

"Some better'n them Sioux did, I reckon."

"Do not take light of the Lord, Mr. Johnston. He does not take light of you."

Johnston studied her closely again. "Jes' what was you an' them fellers doin' up here, you don't mind me askin'."

Emily paused. She had kept this horror repressed; now, she found herself eager to bring it out. Even telling it to Johnston might help it go away.

"Captain William A. Ramsey of Vermont was kind enough to ask me to accompany him and his troopers on a ride," Emily said. "There were twelve men in all when we started. The day was quite nice, not overly cold at all. We left Fort Laramie with the intention of riding along the North Platte River a few miles. A storm arose quite quickly. I believe there was some confusion about direction. When the storm passed by, we found ourselves under attack, much to everyone's alarm. Several men were killed outright. It was…quite terrifying."

"Cheyenne, most likely," Johnston said, as if the rest was quite clear. "They kept drivin' you away from the fort. Gittin' between you an' any help."

"Yes. That is what occurred."

"Pocahontas an' John Smith!" Johnston shook his head. "Yer lucky to be alive whether you know that or not."

"The men were very brave," Emily said. "We lost the Indians the third day out, I believe. By then there were only three men left and myself. Whether the others were cruelly slain or simply lost in the cold, I cannot say. We could not turn back. I think we rode for six days. There was almost nothing to eat. One of the colored troopers killed a hare, but that was all."

"You got rid of the Cheyenne an' run smack into the Sioux," Johnston finished.

"Yes. That is correct."

Johnston ran a hand through his beard. "You don't mind me sayin', this end of the country ain't a fit sort of place fer a woman like yerself."

Emily met his eyes. "I don't see that is any concern of yours."

Johnston didn't answer. She found the silence uncomfortable between them. Perhaps he didn't really mean to pry.

"Mr. Johnston," she said, "I have lived all my life in Amherst, Massachusetts. I am twenty-five years old and my whole life to now has passed in virtually one place. I have been as far as Washington and Philadelphia. I had no idea what the rest of God's world was like. I decided to go and see for myself."

"Well, I reckon that's what ye did."

"And yes. I confess that you are right. It was a foolish thing to do. I had no idea it would be like this. In my innocence, the Oregon Trail seemed a chance to view wildlife and other natural sights. Soon after departing Independence, I sensed that I was wrong. Now I am paying for my sins."

"I'd guess yer folks ain't got a idea where you are," Johnston said, thinking rightly this was so.

"No, they do not. I am certain they believe I am dead. I only pray they think I perished somewhere in the New England states."

"You ain't perished yet," Johnston said.

"I fear that is only a question of time," Emily sighed.

▲▼▲

This time he was waiting, fully awake and outside, hunched silently in a dark grove of trees. It was well after midnight, maybe one or two. There was no wind at all and the clouds moved swiftly across the land. He thought about the woman. Damned if she wasn't just like he figured, white in near every way there was, stubborn and full of her own will. It irked him to think she was stuck right to him and no blamed way to shake her loose. There wasn't any place to take her except back to Fort Laramie or on to Fort Pierre, and either way with one horse. He thought about White Eye Anderson and Del Gue and Chris Lapp, and old John Hatcher himself, seeing him drag in with this woman on a string. Why, they'd ride him for the rest of his life.

The shadow moved, and when it did Johnston spotted it at once. He waited. In a moment, a second shadow appeared, directly behind the first. He knew he'd been right the night before. How many, he wondered. All six or just two? What most likely happened was the Crow ran back toward the Powder, then got their courage up when the Sioux were out of mind. One was maybe smarter than the rest and found his trail. Which meant there was one red coon somewhere with a nose near as good as his own. Now that was a chile he'd like to meet. Johnston sniffed the world once more and started wide around the trees.

▲▼▲

Now there was only one shadow. The other had disappeared while he circled past the grove. He didn't like that, but there was not much for it. He sat and waited. Part of the dark and the windblown striations of the snow. Part of the patch of gray light that swept the earth. He knew what the Crow was doing now. He was waiting to get brave. Waiting to get his juices ready for a fight.

When it happened, the Indian moved so quickly even Johnston was surprised. The Crow stood and made for the cabin door, a blur against the white and frozen ground. Johnston rose up out of nowhere at all, one single motion taking him where he had to be. He lifted the Crow clearly off the ground, the bowie cutting cold as ice. It was over fast and done and he knew in that instant, knew before the Crow went limp and fell away, where the other one had gone. Saw him from the corner of his eye as he came off the roof straight for him, and knew the man had buried himself clean beneath the snow, burrowed like a mole and simply waited out his time. Johnston took the burden on his shoulder, bent his legs and shook the Indian to the ground. The Crow came up fighting, brought his hatchet up fast and felt Johnston's big foot glance off his chest. He staggered back, looked fearfully at Johnston as if he knew a solid blow would have stopped his heart at once, as if he saw in that moment the widows in the Absaroka camp whose men had met this terrible sight before. Turning on his heels, he ran fast across the snow, plowing through drifts for the safety of the trees. Johnston tugged the Walker Colt from his belt, took his aim and fired. The Crow yelled but didn't stop.

Johnston cussed aloud; the red coon was bloodied but still alive. He didn't miss much, and this sure was a poor time to do it. He'd counted on horses. Now the Crow would take them off. He maybe should have gotten the horses first. The Crow would go and lick his wound and come back and that was pure aggravation.

He dragged the dead body well back behind the cabin. He sat beside the corpse, cut the heavy robes away. He saw a picture in his head. He saw his woman. He saw his unborn child within her womb. The child sprang to life. It played among the aspens on the Little Snake River and came to him when he called. The picture went away. He drew the knife cleanly and swiftly across the Indian's flesh below the ribs and thrust his hand inside the warmth.

▲▼▲

With no windows at all, with the cold outside and no difference she could see between dismal day and night, the hours seemed confused. She was often too weak to stay awake. When she slept, the rest seemed to do her little good.

She felt relieved to wake and find him gone. Relief and some alarm. His size, his presence, overwhelmed her. Yet these very qualities, the nature of the man, were all that stood between her and some greater menace still. He cannot help being what he is, she told herself. God surely made him this way for some reason, for some purpose, though she could scarcely imagine what that purpose might be.

The soup tasted good. That morning he had made some kind of bread out of corn, and there was still a little left. The fire was getting low and she added a little wood. The wood caught and snapped, for an instant lighting every dark corner of the room. He had set his belongings along the wall. A buffalo robe and a saddle. Leather satchels and a pack. His things seemed a part of the man. Fur and hide greased and worn, heavy with the raw and sour smells of the wild.

She had never ventured quite this close to his things. It seemed like a miniature camp, everything set the way he liked. Her eyes fell upon a thick leather packet. She looked away and then quickly looked back. The corner of a paper peeked out, and there was writing on the edge. How very strange, she thought. Literacy was wholly unexpected. She knew this wasn't fair, and chastised herself at once.

Certainly, she did not intend to pry. She would never touch Mr. Johnston's things. Still, what one could plainly see was surely no intrusion. I should not be here at all, she decided. I must turn away at once. Should dizziness occur, I might very well collapse, and this is not the place for that. Indeed, as she turned, this very thing happened. Her foot brushed against the leather packet, and slipped the paper free.

"Now look what I have done," she said, and bent to retrieve the paper at once. In spite of her good intention, the words leaped up to meet her eyes:

> It makes no difference abroad,
> The seasons fit the same,
> The mornings blossom into noons,
> And split their pods of flame.

And then, from the packet, another scrap of paper after that:

> The sky is low, the clouds are mean,
> A traveling flake of snow
> Across a barn or through a rut
> Debates if it will go.

"Oh. Oh, dear," Emily said aloud. "That last one's quite nice. Or at least I *think* it is." She read the lines again, frowning over this and that, and decided it was slightly overdone.

Still, she wondered, what was verse doing here? Where had this unlettered man of the wilds come across a poem? Perhaps he found it, she reasoned. Came across it in a cabin such as this where some poor traveler had met his fate.

The sound of the shot nearly paralyzed her with fear. "Oh blessed Jesus!" she cried. The papers fluttered from her hand. She fled to a corner of the cabin, crouched there and stared at the door. An Indian would enter quite soon. Possibly more than one. They would not slay her, though they would take her to their camp. She would tell them about Christ. They would renounce their savage ways. They would certainly not touch her in any way.

It seemed forever before the door opened again and Johnston appeared. "Oh, thank the Lord you're all right," Emily sighed. "That shot. I thought—I thought you had surely been killed!"

"Took a shot at a deer," Johnston said. "Wasn't nothin' more'n that." He shook his coat. His beard seemed thick with ice.

"God be praised," Emily said.

Johnston set his Hawken aside. Stomped his feet and ran his hand through a bushy nest of hair. He looked down then and saw the papers on the floor and picked them up. He looked right at Emily and didn't say a thing.

Emily's heart began to pound. "I...I'm very sorry," she said. "I certainly had no right."

"Don't matter none," Johnston said. He stood with his backside to the fire.

"Yes, now yes it does," Emily said firmly. "It is I who have transgressed. I am clearly in the wrong. I do not deny my sin."

"I ain't never hear'd so much about sin," Johnston said.

Emily felt her face color. "Well, there certainly is sin abroad, Mr. Johnston. Satan has his eye upon us all."

"I reckon," Johnston said. He scratched and sat down. Leaned against the wall in his customary manner.

Emily wondered if she dare break the silence. He didn't seem angry at all, but how on earth would one know? And they could not simply sit there and look at one another.

"Mr. Johnston, I do not excuse my actions," she said, "but perhaps you'll understand when I say I have an interest in poetry myself. As a fact, one small effort has seen the light of publication. Three years ago. February 20, 1852, to be exact. In the *Springfield Daily Republican.*" She smiled and touched her hair. "I recall the date clearly, of course. There are dates in one's life one remembers very well. One's birthday, certainly—" Emily blushed, aware she was chattering away. "Well, yes, at any rate…"

Johnston said nothing at all.

"You must be quite chilled," Emily said. "There is still a little soup."

"I ain't real hungry," Johnston said.

▲▼▲

This time would have to be different; the Crow was wary now and hurt, and an Injun like that was the same as any other creature in the wild in such condition, the same as he'd be himself, Johnston knew, as deadly as a stirred-up snake. The Crow would be in place early this night, out there in spite of the cold, because the first man out could watch and see what the other man would do. It was a deadly advantage, and Johnston was determined not to let the Absaroka have it.

The Indian was cautious and he was good. Johnston could scarcely hear him, scarcely smell his fear. He seemed to take forever, moving when the wind rose some, stopping when it died.

Tarnation, Johnston thought, *come on and git it done, chile, 'fore I freeze these bones to the ground.*

At last the Crow struck, coming in swiftly without a sound. The hatchet fell once, slicing the heavy furs, withdrew and hacked again, and Johnston, even in the dark, saw emotion of every sort cross the Absaroka's face, saw surprise and alarm and then final understanding that the furs crouched there against the tree didn't have a man inside, that it was simply too late to remedy that.

Johnston shook the snow aside. "That war your trick, son, not mine," he said aloud. "Ye got no one to blame but yourself…"

▲▼▲

She hated the boredom most of all. It overpowered fear and apprehension. Now she sorely missed being scared. Now there was nothing at all to do. Was it day outside or was it night? Sometimes Johnston would tell her. For the most part, he sat like a stone or wandered out in the night. Worse than sitting in the cabin were the times when she had to go out to attend to bodily needs. It was horrid, a humiliation she could scarcely bear. She had to *ask*. He would not let her venture out alone. He would stand by the door with his weapon while she struggled as far as she dared through the snow. And the cold! That fierce, and unimaginable cold. Winter, she saw now, gave New England a fleeting glance. This terrible empty land was where it was born.

▲▼▲

She heard him at the door and then he stepped inside, letting in the cold. "Found us a couple of horses," Johnston said, and dropped his heavy coat on the floor.

"You did?" Emily was surprised. "Why, isn't that odd."

"Ain't nothin' odd to it," Johnston said.

"Yes, well..." He seemed very pleased with himself. It dawned on her then that horses had meaning in her life. "Heavens," she said, "that means we can leave this place, does it not?"

"First thing in the mornin'," Johnston said. He didn't even glance her way. He simply wrapped up in his robes and turned his face against the wall.

Emily felt the heat rise to her cheeks, and this brought further irritation. Anger at Johnston, but mostly at herself. What did *she* care what he did? They certainly had nothing to talk about. No topic that would interest her in the least. Still, the man's rudeness had no bounds at all. He had no concept of social intercourse.

"You are just going to—sleep?" she said. "Right now?"

"I was plannin' on it," Johnston said.

"Well, you could at least impart information. There are things one needs to know."

"'Bout what?"

"About the trip." Emily waited. Johnston didn't answer. "What I mean, is how long will it take? I have no idea of the distance to Fort Laramie. As you know, I left under unusual circumstances."

"Ain't goin' to Fort Laramie. Goin' to Fort Pierre."

Emily sat up. "Mr. Johnston, I demand to be returned to Fort *Laramie*. I have no intention of going anywhere else."

"Fort Pierre's whar I'm headed," Johnston said.

"Whatever for?"

"Meetin' someone."

"Well, who?"

"Like you're fonda sayin', Miz Dickinson, that ain't no concern of yours."

Emily tried to contain herself. To show Christian restraint. A sudden thought occurred. A woman, that was it. He was going to see a woman. Possibly a wife. The thought defied imagination. What sort of woman would this backwoods ruffian attract?

"Are you married, Mr. Johnston?" Emily asked. "I don't believe you've ever said. But of course you're quite correct. That is no concern of mine."

Johnston kept his silence. He had likely gone to sleep and hadn't heard a word she said. The man had no consideration.

"My wife's dead," Johnston said. The tone of his words brought a chill. "Her an' the chile, too. Crows killed 'em both."

Emily felt ashamed. "I'm...terribly sorry, Mr. Johnston. Really."

"Reckon I am, too."

"You are angry with me, I know."

"Ma'am, I ain't angry at all."

"Yes, now, you are. I do not fault you for it, Mr. Johnston. I have intruded upon your life. I am guilty of certain violations. And you are still upset about the poems."

"No I ain't."

"Yes you are. That is quite clear to me. I want you to know that I have since shown respect for your possessions. I was tempted, yes. We are all weak vessels, and there is nothing at all to do in this place. Still, I did not succumb. Lord Jesus gave me strength."

"Git some sleep," Johnston said, and pulled the buffalo robe about his head.

▲▼▲

He awoke in fury and disbelief, clutched the Hawken and came to his feet, saw the dull press of dawn around the door, heard the faint sound of horses outside, hardly there at all, as if they'd come up with him out of sleep.

Great God A'Mighty, they'd played him for a fool, him sleeping like a chile and sure he'd got the only two. Maybe it wasn't Crow, he decided. Maybe it was Sioux coming back. And what in tarnation did it matter which brand of red coon it might be—they flat had him cold like a rabbit in a log.

The woman came awake, a question on her face. "Jes' get back in yer corner and keep quiet," Johnston said harshly. He turned to face the door, made sure the Walker Colt was in his belt. How many, he wondered? The horses were silent now.

"Come an' git your medicine," he said softly, "I'm a-waitin' right here."

"Inside the cabin," a man shouted. "This is Lieutenant Joshua Dean. We are here in force, and I must ask you to come out at once, unarmed."

Johnston laughed aloud. He decided he was plain going slack. A man who couldn't tell shod horses in his sleep was a man who maybe ought to pack it in.

▲▼▲

"I am grateful for what you have done," Emily said. "I owe you my thanks, Mr. Johnston."

"Nothin' to thank me for," Johnston said. The troopers had stopped fiddling about and seemed ready to depart. He wondered why a soldier took an hour to turn around. The lieutenant had eyed the Indian ponies but didn't ask where their riders might be. If he recognized Johnston or knew his name, he didn't say.

"We have had our differences, I suppose," Emily said.

"I reckon so."

"God has a reason for what he does, Mr. Johnston. I am sure this adventure serves a purpose in His plan."

Johnston couldn't figure just what it might be. "You have a safe trip, Miz Dickinson," he said.

"I will do just that," Emily said. "I expect Massachusetts will seem dear to me now. I doubt I'll stray again."

She walked away through the snow, and the lieutenant helped her mount. Johnston watched till they were well out of sight, then went inside to get his things.

▲▼▲

As he rode through the flat white world with the slate-dark sky overhead, he thought about the Bitter Root Mountains and the Musselshell River. He thought about the Platte and the Knife and the Bearpaw Range, every peak and river he'd ever crossed clear as glass in his head. He thought about Swan, eight years dead in the spring, and it didn't seem that long at all, and in a way a lot more. Dead all this time, and he still saw her face every day.

Before dark, he found a spot near the Belle Fourche and staked the horses out safe. One Crow pony had a blaze between its eyes. He favored an Injun horse with good marks. He wondered if Del Gue was still waiting at Fort Pierre. They'd have to get moving out soon to get some hides. He thought again how he'd waited too long to get in the trapping trade, the beaver near gone when he'd come to the mountains and hooked up with old Hatcher. Just bear and mink now and whatever a man could find.

Scooping out a hole in the snow, he snapped a few sticks and stacked them ready for the fire, then walked back and got his leather satchel and dipped his hand inside. Johnston stopped, puzzled at an unfamiliar touch. He squatted on the ground and started pulling things out. There was nothing but an old Army blanket. His paper was all gone.

"Well, cuss me fer a Kiowa," he said aloud. That damn woman had filched the whole lot. He was plain irritated. It wasn't like he couldn't spark a fire, but a man fell into easy habits. A little paper saved time, especially if your wood was all wet. Came in handy, too, if you had to do your business and there wasn't no good leaves about.

She'd gotten every piece there was. He hadn't ever counted, but there were likely near a thousand bits and scraps, rhymes he'd thought up and set down, then saved for the fire. This was by God pure aggravation. He grumbled to himself and found his flint. A man sure couldn't figure what was stewing in a white woman's head. An Injun wasn't like that at all.

Stairs

Mary Louise made wheat-crackle mush and the last of the cabbage rose tea. "I think what I will do is I will book," she decided. "I will book about the boy with amethyst eyes." The thought made her blush. A naughty flew in her ear and buzzed about. She hurried through supper quick as a wink. Rinsed out the bowl and the long copper spoon and the milk-blue cracked china cup. Moved about the room and fussed and straightened this and that. Made everything neat as it could be.

"That's that," she said at last, and sat down in the straight-back chair and took the big brown book from the table. The binding was chip-brittle, dry and cracked. Mary Louise turned pages limp as soup. A word came off on her finger. She held it up and looked. The word said Ǝ⅃IMƧ. Mary Louise made a face and licked it off. Words became pictures in her head. She saw the young man with amethyst eyes. The crisp black hair and cheery grin. She saw the olive coat and the soot-black trousers and the fine high boots brown as wood. She saw how the clothes fit tight across his chest and muscled arms. Her heart beat faster and a warm touched her lightly on the cheek. She turned the page as quickly as she could. Words slipped off and disappeared. *Thigh* and *quicksilver,* and *mute anticipation.*

Mary Louise booked. The lamp with the red paper shade made a cozy circle of light. The light stayed where it belonged. Never reached dusty corners, wallpaper waterstained and marbled with coffee clouds and the ghosts of tiny flowers. Left undisturbed places sad and torn and worn, a lace dress buried in the wall.

Tap-tap-tap, came a sound or maybe didn't come at all.

Tap-tap-tap, it maybe didn't come again.

Mary Louise stopped booking and watched the dark around the room. The colors time-soft like ash and russet and plum. Colors that smelled of dustballs, whits and spiderbreath, places dry and hollow. She listened to the drone and the rumble on the stairs, listened to the hum of the people passing by.

"Who's there," Mary Louise said softly. "Is that you I hear, Mrs. Wood?"

"Hello, Mary Louise," said Mrs. Wood. "And how are we doing this lovely day?" Voice dry as paper, chipped as a china cup.

"Why, I'm just fine, Mrs. Wood."

"And how old are we today, Mary Louise?"

"Nineteen," said Mary Louise, knowing that Mrs. Wood could never remember. "You're feeling well, I hope?"

"As well as I can be," said Mrs. Wood.

"Are you sewing, Mrs. Wood?"

"No I'm not, Mary Louise."

"Are you sweeping, Mrs. Wood?"

"No I'm not, Mary Louise."

"What are you doing, Mrs. Wood?"

"I'm doing a book, Mary Louise."

"Why, so am I!" said Mary Louise.

"My book's a book about mice," said Mrs. Wood. "Every possible kind of mice that you can name. Feelmice, realmice, mice that live in a jar."

"I don't suppose I know about a myce," said Mary Louise.

"I can guess what your book's about," said Mrs. Wood. "I can guess it's a book about a boy."

"It is not," said Mary Louise, feeling another warm behind her ears. "It's nothing of the sort!"

"I know young ladies like you," said Mrs. Wood. "I know what they like to do."

"I had a cup of tea," Mary Louise said quickly. "I fixed a fine cup of tea a while ago."

"That's nice," said Mrs. Wood. "Do you know what I'm doing right now? I'm looking at the water. I've been looking at the water all day."

"I see," said Mary Louise, who didn't see at all. She tried to picture Mrs. Wood. Mrs. Wood sat in a chair. Mrs. Wood booked myce and looked at water. Now why would she want to do that?

"How old are you now, Mary Louise?"

"Still nineteen, Mrs. Wood."

"Do you like to dress up, Mary Louise?"

"I only have two dresses, Mrs. Wood."

"Are you pretty, Mary Louise?"

"I wouldn't know, Mrs. Wood."

"Do you play with your little whoozie, Mary Louise?"

"Mrs. *Wood*!" Mary Louise was so startled, the book fell from her lap and struck the floor. "If that's the way you're going to be," she said crossly, "I'm not going to talk to you at all!"

But Mrs. Wood was gone. There was nothing there at all but the rumble of the people on the stairs.

▲▼▲

Mary Louise didn't like to go out, but there was nothing in the pantry but a biscuit hard as stone. She found a few monies in the drawer. Her big brass key and a broken comb. Monies in her pocket, she unlocked the door and slid the wooden bolt aside. The stairs were people thick. People and the smells that people do. A woman with a nose like a knife tried to peek into her room. She said, *"paste lethal, globally remiss."*

Mary Louise shut the door and locked it tight, thrust the brass key in her pocket. People bumped and pushed and squeezed. Jabbed and poked. Stuck her in the ribs and kicked her shins. She was caught in the crowd and swept along. She passed her orange number on the wall. 320,193. The rumbles and the hums picked her up and sucked her in. Mary Louise struggled and shoved, dug and grabbed. Turned and found the lane going down. The stairs twisted pinch-tight and narrow, twisted dizzily round and round. She breathed in feet smells, armpit and teeth smells, cheese smells, sweat smells, he smells and she smells. Squeezed down the stairs in a flatulescent fog. The walls and the ceilings and the stairs were dark wood caked and clotted with people stuff, and the people wrote and scribbled as they passed. Made fingernail names, drew acts they'd like to commit. Mary Louise never read what people wrote.

A woman with a face gray as lead touched her hair. A man found her ear, whispered, *"carp bridal, imminent intent."* Wormed clever fingers down her neck and pinched her pointy. Mary Louise bit her lip and clutched her key. That was a trick they liked to use. Do something awful, make you let go of your key for just a wink. Steal it and get your things while you were gone. Wait and pull you in when you returned.

A yellow bulb made bleary light on every floor. The bulbs were thick with people-soot and spiders. The spiders came to eat and warm their eyes. Mumble-mumble shove. People wearing dun and slate and gray. People wearing patch-torn black and burnt sienna.

320,193

320,189

320,185

One floor one door one more.

Mary Louise shoved and pushed. Popped out of people like a cork. A beggar with putty eyes sat on the floor. A man with a yellow tongue stepped on his hand. The beggar said, *"miscarry, continental mire."*

Grocer Bill ran a store in his room. Mary Louise held her breath and made her way along the wall. There were thirty-seven people inside.

The table was lined with brown paper sacks. Grease sacks, used sacks, patched with other sacks. There was a curtain on a string.

"Well, I haven't seen you for a while, Mary Louise," said Grocer Bill. He wore a green paper hat shaped like a box. Grocer Bill always gave her funny looks, gave her sly funny looks when he knew Mrs. Bill wasn't around. Mary Louise clutched her key and squeezed her monies in her pocket.

"I need a few things," said Mary Louise. "What do you have that's good today?"

"I have some very fine lardstring noodles," winked Grocer Bill. "Very fine indeed."

Mary Louise made a face. Sniffed into brown paper sacks. Fat noodles, skinny noodles, noodles white as the skin between her toes.

"I guess I'll take wheat-crackle if you have it," said Mary Louise. "And fatcake and sourmeal pie. There's no dirtsugar, I don't suppose?"

"Oh, all out of that, I'm afraid."

"Any cabbage rose tea?" she said, really afraid to ask.

"Now that's hard to get, Mary Louise," said Grocer Bill. "Real hard to get is what it is." His shiny black eyes darted about, searching for Mrs. Bill. One hand snaked under the counter and came up with a small twist of paper. Pressed it in her palm and squeezed her fingers under his. "That's just for you," said Grocer Bill. "Don't tell anyone where you got it."

"Thank you," Mary Louise said politely, "I surely won't."

"Anything else you need today?"

"I don't guess," said Mary Louise.

"That'll be, let's see." Grocer Bill flicked his tongue about his teeth. "About seven monies, Mary Louise."

"Goodness, that much?"

"Hard times, Mary Louise."

Mary Louise dug monies from her pocket. There were six pearl buttons and a black steel washer. A thumbtack without any point, and a marble as blind as an eye. A military button with important swirly lines.

"Let's see what we have," said Grocer Bill. Poked at her palm, sneaked a tickle. Snatched up the button and went right for the cloudy eye. Mary Louise snapped her fist shut tight.

"That's a real good monies that first one," she said firmly. "That *ought* to be enough. It's probably a nine is what it is."

"Well now, I wouldn't say a nine," grinned Grocer Bill, the grin telling her he'd gotten the best of the bargain. She wished she hadn't shown him the button at all.

Grocer Bill put her goods in a sack. Mrs. Bill poked her head through the curtain, saw Mary Louise and made a face. Mary Louise smiled. Turned to go. Stopped, and looked curiously down the table. A boy was leaning against the wall. Not buying a thing, just leaning against the wall. He was tall and knobby-kneed with a thatch of yellow hair. The hair seemed to perch upon his head, as if it didn't intend to stay. He carried a wooden box on a string. The string hung over his shoulder to his side. And, he had a *most* peculiar clothes. Mary Louise had never seen such a clothes in all her life. It was a patchwork of bright and raggedy squares. Reds and blues and greens. Yellows and silvers and golds. Colors she couldn't name and didn't want to if she could. How awful, she thought. How terribly ugly and bright. What a frightening thing to wear!

The boy looked up. Looked right at her as if he'd guessed what she was thinking all along. There were tiny blue lights in his eyes. The lights sparked and danced. He smiled at Mary Louise. The smile seemed to slice his face in two. Mary Louise felt a warm in her tummy. A fidget behind her knees. She grabbed her sack and ducked into the crowd.

The first floors were slow, slower than ever. At three-two-oh, one-eight-eight, everything came to a stop. Nothing moved ahead. Crowds backed up behind. People mumbled and shoved. Officer Bob came bounding up the stairs, banging his stick against the wall.

"Flatten up, everyone, flatten up," he called out. "Train coming through right now!"

"Oh no," groaned Mary Louise, and everyone else groaned, too.

Before long the train came plodding up from below. Both lanes crowded against the wall, but there was still scarcely room for the train to pass. First came a skinny little man in coal-black, gray paper stripes across his chest. He beat on a can with a wooden stick.

Clack, clack—clack-clack-clack!

Then came the train, each man moving at a slow and steady pace.

"Huh, huh—huh-huh-huh!

"Huh, huh—huh-huh-huh!"

Big heavy boxes were strapped to their backs. Their backs were broad and strong. They were built just like the boxes, chests and shoulders square and hard. Legs thick as poles, ankles the same as thighs. Mary Louise could smell the sharp and tingly sweat, the heat as hot as a stove.

"Huh, huh—huh-huh-huh!

"Huh, huh—huh-huh-huh!"

A little girl began to count. "Seventy-nine...seventy-ten... seventy-leven..."

"Hush," said the little girl's mother.

Numbers were scribbled on the boxes. Numbers as thick as the scribbles on the walls. Numbers over numbers and over numbers still. Mary Louise read them as the train rumbled past her up the stairs.

344,119

351,444

377,920

"Goodness!" Mary Louise said aloud, doing quick sums in her head. Doing numbers minus her floor from the boxes passing by. What a long way to go—what a terribly *long* way to go. Of course they got to rest, she decided. Surely they got to rest. She'd never seen a train stopped, only trains going up and going down.

One of the trains raised his head and looked right at Mary Louise. His eyes were noodle-white, his mouth a crooked nail. He said, *"indigo confection, common oversight."*

"Hello," said Mary Louise to be nice.

Officer Bob gave the signal. The crowd raised a cheer and surged ahead. Traffic began to move in both lanes.

"Why hello, Mary Louise," said Officer Bob. "How have you been I'd like to know?"

"Why I've been fine," said Mary Louise, feeling a warm on the tip of her chin. Officer Bob was tall and strong, nearly the size of some of the train. He wore a blue paper hat and kindly eyes.

"It's awfully crowded today," said Mary Louise. "I thought I'd never get to the store."

Officer Bob shook his head. Leaned in close to Mary Louise. "Stair wars," he said, so low that only Mary Louise could hear. "Real bad trouble down below."

"Oh my!" said Mary Louise.

"Now that's all down in the two-eighties, not here," Officer Bob added quickly. "But a thing like that'll back up a long ways. You have a care now, Mary Louise." He tipped his blue hat, and Mary Louise climbed the rest of the way home.

▲▼▲

Back in the safety of her own 320,193, Mary Louise locked the door and slipped the big wooden bar in its place. Tossed off her dress and didn't bother to put it away. Set the kettle on the stove and washed and scrubbed beneath the faucet till the smell of the stairs was nearly gone. Slipped on her other dress and poured a fresh cup of cabbage rose tea.

"I *guess* I'll have to drink a cup in the morning and one at night," she sighed aloud. "If I want to make it last any at all." And after that what would she do? She was nearly out of monies and couldn't think where to find any more.

"Oh well," she said, catching the last spicy drop on the tip of her tongue, "there's no use worrying about *that*." Turning back the covers, she slipped quickly into bed and in a moment she was fast asleep on her pillow.

She dreamed of drinking tea with Mrs. Wood. Mary Louise booked myce and Mrs. Wood looked at water. The water wasn't clear like water ought to be, it was the color of amethyst eyes. Mary Louise enjoyed the dream until she saw the boy's terrible clothes. Raggedy-patch clothes in awful colors that hurt her eyes. "That's *not* who you're supposed to be," said Mary Louise. The boy grinned. Lardstring noodles fell out of his mouth.

▲▼▲

Mary Louise ate and slept and drank cabbage rose tea. She wouldn't talk to Mrs. Wood. She wouldn't sit by the table and the lamp. She took her chair to the wall between the pantry and the bed. Sometimes, if she closed her eyes and listened, she could hear the singers there. They sang like bells if bells could sing. Close and far away. She could never hear the words, but she could tell when the singers were happy or sad. Sometimes she wondered where they were. Sometimes she wondered if they were anywhere at all. They were certainly much nicer than Mrs. Wood.

Someone knocked at the door. Mary Louise gave a start. She opened the little hole but didn't peek right away. That's what they liked to do. Wait until you looked, then squirt something awful inside. Or poke out your eye with a stick. This time it was only Postman Jack, and Mary Louise slid the big bolt aside and opened the door.

"Hello, Mary Louise," smiled Postman Jack, "and how are you? Like to buy a mail today?"

"Oh, I would," said Mary Louise, "but I don't have monies to spend now."

"Real sorry to hear that," said Postman Jack. He wore a brown paper hat. Gold paper buttons pinned to his coat. A shabby gray bag drooped from his shoulder to his knees. "I've got one here I can let you have cheap," he told Mary Louise. "Hardly any monies at all."

"I'm afraid that's still too much for me," sighed Mary Louise.

"This is a very special mail," said Postman Jack. "Very special mail indeed."

"Special how?" said Mary Louise.

"You'll see," said Postman Jack, "you'll see." And with that he dipped a hand into his bag and drew a mail out with a flourish. "There now," he said, with a sparkle in his eye, "what do you think of that?"

Mary Louise wanted to be polite, but she really didn't think much at all. The mail was thin as air, a pale and sallow green. It looked as if it might simply whoof and disappear.

"It doesn't look very special to me," said Mary Louise. "It looks like a mail nobody wants."

"Well now, there's two halves to every mail," winked Postman Jack, "and you haven't seen the other." He flipped the mail over and held it right before her eyes.

"Oh," said Mary Louise, bringing a finger to her lips, "oh my!"

"See," said Postman Jack, "didn't I say it was special? What do you say now, Mary Louise?"

Mary Louise knew she shouldn't, but she really wanted the mail. Before she could change her mind, she dug a hand in her pocket and came up with the marble like an eye.

"This is all I can afford," she said sadly, "and I can't really *afford* to spend that."

"I'll take it," said Postman Jack, snapping up the monies quick as air. "I'll take it, since it's you."

"Oh, thank you," said Mary Louise, pleased and surprised at her good fortune. "Thank you, Postman Jack!"

"My pleasure," said Postman Jack. He tipped his brown hat and he was gone.

▲▼▲

Mary Louise swore she'd just put the mail aside, save it for when there was nothing else to do. Since that was right now or most any time at all, she ran to the kettle and made tea, cut a piece of fatcake, and sat in the chair beneath the lamp. For a long time she looked at the pale green paper, at the paper so sheer she was certain a spider had made it. A spider as old as Mrs. Wood. Whoever had written the mail had drawn a very nice stamp to go along. It wound in sepia lines like a wispy tangle of wire that didn't end and didn't begin. Finally, she turned the mail over and looked at the tiny faded script. Caught her breath in wonder once again.

668,110

Goodness, thought Mary Louise, how could you even imagine a place so terribly far away? What was it like? How did it look? What did the people do? Mary Louise couldn't wait another moment. She carefully opened the mail. Dreamed of far adventure, strange customs and rites. The words on the paper were so delicate and tiny she could scarcely make them out, words drawn with a mite-whisker pen. She held her breath, afraid she'd blow them away. Brought the mail up close to her eyes. What the mail said was this:

Tailor John said he would make me a clothes for three monies. He is a liar and he knows it. If my legs hadn't give out bad I would go up there and tell him.

"Is that *all?*" Mary Louise cried. She stomped her feet on the floor. "Well, I'm certainly going to tell Postman Jack what I think about that!"

"What are you doing, Mary Louise?" said Mrs. Wood.

"I'm booking a mail, Mrs. Wood," said Mary Louise, then remembered she wasn't speaking to Mrs. Wood.

"My son writes me every week," said Mrs. Wood. "Even when he's out to sea."

"Out to see what?" Mary Louise said crossly.

"You are a sassy, impudent girl," said Mrs. Wood. "I doubt you have education or bearing. I expect you go naked under your clothes."

"Just go *away,* Mrs. Wood," said Mary Louise.

▲▼▲

Mary Louise booked about the boy with amethyst eyes. She slept and got up and ate sourmeal pie and drank the last of the cabbage rose tea. She fussed about the room and washed her cup and washed her spoon and listened to the traffic on the stairs. Rumble-rumble hum. Sometimes it came through the door and over the floor and went tingling up her legs. Sometimes it buzzed about in her head. Why couldn't everyone stop going up or going down? Why couldn't everyone stay where they belonged?

The knock gave her a start. "Who's there," she called out, "what do you want?"

"You're never going to know if you don't look out and see," said the voice. "You'll have to look and see, Mary Louise."

It was a very *nice* voice, thought Mary Louise. But that didn't fool her for a minute. "I can do very well without looking," she said firmly. "Now please go away and leave me alone."

The voice became a laugh. A laugh sharp as glass that cut cleanly through the heavy wooden door and rattled dishes on the shelf.

"My goodness," said Mary Louise. She opened the hole a crack. Saw a patch of yellow hair. Saw a mouth so wide it could make a laugh any size it wanted. Eyes like crackly blue hot electric lights. The eyes made a warm at the hollow of her neck. Mary Louise caught her breath and backed half a step away.

"I know who you are," she said at last. "You're the boy with the funny clothes from Grocer Bill's."

"Right you are," said the boy. "Open up and let me in, Mary Louise."

"I'll do nothing of the sort," said Mary Louise. "I don't even know you at all."

"But I know you," said the boy. "I've brought you a fine present, and my name is Artist Dan."

"What kind of a present?" Mary Louise asked cautiously.

"A present like this," said Artist Dan, and waved a fat paper sack where she could see. "Cabbage rose tea, Mary Louise, and lots of it. The finest you'll ever taste, I promise you that."

"Oh my." The sack grew larger as she looked. Of course it could be full of stones and dead spiders for all she knew, and likely was.

"You can't come in," she said boldly. "I don't know who you are, and besides your awful clothes are hurting my eyes. No one wears a clothes like *that.*"

"Not here they don't," said Artist Dan. "And there are places I've been where they don't wear pitch and soot and dead-grub yellow. Lead and drab and shadow-black and slug-dung madder. Colors dull as belly button fuzz in the dark of night."

"Well, if people dress like you somewhere," said Mary Louise, "I hope it's far away."

"Far is near and near is far," said Artist Dan.

"That's the silliest thing I've ever heard."

"Maybe so, maybe not."

"*I* have a mail from six-six-eight, one-one-oh," said Mary Louise.

"Far is where you aren't," said Artist Dan.

"See, you keep doing it," Mary Louise said sharply. "What do you art, anyway? I'll bet you art on the stairs is what you do."

"I paint," said Artist Dan,

"Paint what?" said Mary Louise.

"Paint people," said Artist Dan. "People is what I paint. I'll paint you if you like, Mary Louise."

"Well I wouldn't," Mary Louise said shortly. "I wouldn't like it at all."

"I have colors in my box you've never seen," said Artist Dan. "Bottle-green and apricot and cream. Violet and lilac and seven shades of blue. Saffron and vermilion, tangerine and pearl..."

"Go away," cried Mary Louise, "go away and leave me alone!" She snapped the hole shut, turned and leaned against the door, and heard her heart beat loudly in her ears. Pressed her head against the wood and imagined she heard him breathe. That's as foolish as it can be, she thought at once. All you can hear are the people on the stairs.

She waited long and listened, didn't breathe. What if he didn't go away? What if he stood there with all his awful colors? With his dreadful vermilions and his blues and bottle-greens? After a while she was certain he wasn't there. What she really needed now was a nice cup of cabbage rose tea. The kettle was nearly hot before she remembered the tea was gone. She tore Grocer Bill's little twisty brown paper in a hundred tiny pieces, dropped them in the drawer with the key and the broken comb. She wanted to cry, but couldn't remember how. All she wanted was some tea. What was the matter with that? And it *wasn't* tea he'd dangled before the door. It was just another trick is what it was.

▲▼▲

Mary Louise slept and ate wheat-crackle mush. Cleaned up her room and sat in her chair and booked the boy with amethyst eyes. Slammed the book shut and saw words fly this way and that. The olive coat was gone and the soot-black trousers and the fine high boots as brown as wood. The colors in her head were amber and gold and ultramarine. Cobalt and cadmium and chrome. The crisp black hair was lemon-yellow and hurt her eyes.

"Mary Louise," said Mrs. Wood, "Mary Louise?"

Mary Louise took her chair across the room. The singers were silent and wouldn't sing. She threw herself on the bed and pulled the covers over her head. She dreamed he painted indigo waves beneath her eyes, brushed silver across her lips. Circled her waist with emerald indecision, dappled crimson on her thighs. Drew a raw and florid rainbow to her toes. When she woke, her heart was louder than the hum and the mumble on the stairs. When she stood, her legs were weak and there were spiders in her head.

"Are you there, Mrs. Wood?" called Mary Louise. If Mrs. Wood was there, she didn't say. The singers were back again, but she could scarcely hear their song. She carried her chair to the far end of the room. The corners that smelled old, where the light from the lamp would never go.

She never ever came here because there was nothing here to do. No one talked or sang or said hello. There was nothing but the dust-smell, wallpaper waterstained, colors faded and gone.

And here, thought Mary Louise, is exactly where I want to be, not anywhere at all. I don't want to smell awful people on the stairs. I don't want to see bad colors or yellow hair, or blue electric eyes. I don't want dreams that leave warms in funny places. I don't even want a cup of tea. What I want is for everyone to simply leave me alone.

"Plover leech regatta," someone said, *"gainfully intact."*

"Please go away," said Mary Louise…

Ginny Sweethips'
Flying Circus

Del drove and Ginny sat.

"They're taking their sweet time," Ginny said, "damned if they're not."

"They're itchy," Del said. "Everyone's itchy. Everyone's looking to stay alive."

"Huh!" Ginny showed disgust. "I sure don't care for sittin' out here in the sun. My price is going up by the minute. You wait and see if it doesn't."

"Don't get greedy," Del said.

Ginny curled her toes on the dash. Her legs felt warm in the sun. The stockade was a hundred yards off. Barbed wire looped above the walls. The sign over the gate read:

> First Church of the Unleaded God
> & Ace High Refinery
> WELCOME
> KEEP OUT

The refinery needed paint. It had likely been silver, but was now dull as pewter and black rust. Ginny leaned out the window and called to Possum Dark.

"What's happening, friend? Those mothers dead in there or what?"

"Thinking," Possum said. "Fixing to make a move. Considering what to do." Possum Dark sat atop the van in a steno chair bolted to the roof. Circling the chair was a swivel-ring mount sporting fine twin-fifties black as grease. Possum had a death-view clean around. Keeping out the sun was a red Cinzano umbrella faded pink. Possum studied the stockade and watched heat distort the flats. He didn't care for the effect. He was suspicious of things less than cut and dried. Apprehensive of illusions of every kind. He scratched his nose and curled his tail around his leg. The gate opened up and men started across the scrub. He teased them in his sights. He prayed they'd do something silly and grand.

Possum counted thirty-seven men. A few carried sidearms, openly or concealed. Possum spotted them all at once. He wasn't too concerned. This seemed like an easygoing bunch, more intent on fun than fracas. Still, there was always the hope that he was wrong.

▲▼▲

The men milled about. They wore patched denim and faded shirts. Possum made them nervous. Del countered that; his appearance set them at ease. The men looked at Del, poked each other and grinned. Del was scrawny and bald except for tufts around the ears. The dusty black coat was too big. His neck thrust out of his shirt like a newborn buzzard looking for meat. The men forgot Possum and gathered around, waiting to see what Del would do. Waiting for Del to get around to showing them what they'd come to see. The van was painted turtle-green. Gold Barnum type named the owner, and the selected vices for sale:

Ginny Sweethips' Flying Circus
SEX*TACOS*DANGEROUS DRUGS

Del puttered about with this and that. He unhitched the wagon from the van and folded out a handy little stage. It didn't take three minutes to set up, but he dragged it out to ten, then ten on top of that. The men started to whistle and clap their hands. Del looked alarmed. They liked that. He stumbled and they laughed.

"Hey, mister, you got a girl in there or not?" a man called out.

"Better be something here besides you," another said.

"Gents," Del said, raising his hands for quiet, "Ginny Sweethips herself will soon appear on this stage, and you'll be more than glad you waited. Your every wish will be fulfilled, I promise you that. I'm bringing beauty to the wastelands, gents. Lust the way you like it, passion unrestrained. Sexual crimes you never dreamed!"

"Cut the talk, mister," a man with peach-pit eyes shouted to Del. "Show us what you got."

Others joined in, stomped their feet and whistled. Del knew he had them. Anger was what he wanted. Frustration and denial. Hatred waiting for sweet release. He waved them off, but they wouldn't stop. He placed one hand on the door of the van—and brought them to silence at once.

The double doors opened. A worn red curtain was revealed, stenciled with hearts and cherubs. Del extended his hand. He seemed to search behind the curtain, one eye closed in concentration. He looked alarmed, groping for something he couldn't find. Uncertain he remembered how to do this trick at all. And then, in a sudden burst of motion, Ginny did a double forward flip, and appeared like glory on the stage.

The men broke into shouts of wild abandon. Ginny led them in a cheer. She was dressed for the occasion. Short white skirt shiny bright, white boots with tassels. White sweater with a big red G sewn on the front.

"Ginny Sweethips, gents," Del announced with a flair, "giving you her own interpretation of Barbara Jean, the Cheerleader Next Door. Innocent as snow, yet a little bit wicked and willing to learn, if Biff the Quarterback will only teach her. Now, what do you say to *that?*"

They whistled and yelled and stomped. Ginny strutted and switched, doing long-legged kicks that left them gasping with delight. Thirty-seven pairs of eyes showed their needs. Men guessed at hidden parts. Dusted off scenarios of violence and love. Then, as quickly as she'd come, Ginny was gone. Men threatened to storm the stage. Del grinned without concern. The curtain parted and Ginny was back, blond hair replaced with saucy red, costume changed in the blink of an eye. Del introduced Nurse Nora, an angel of mercy weak as soup in the hands of Patient Pete. Moments later, hair black as a raven's throat, she was Schoolteacher Sally, cold as well water, until Steve the Bad Student loosed the fury chained within.

Ginny vanished again. Applause thundered over the flats. Del urged them on, then spread his hands for quiet.

"Did I lie to you gents? Is she all you ever dreamed? Is this the love you've wanted all your life? Could you ask for sweeter limbs, for softer flesh? For whiter teeth, for brighter eyes?"

"Yeah, but is she *real?*" a man shouted, a man with a broken face sewn up like a sock. "We're religious people here. We don't fuck with no machines."

Others echoed the question with bold shouts and shaking fists.

"Now, I don't blame you, sir, at all," Del said. "I've had a few dolly droids myself. A plastic embrace at best, I'll grant you that. Not for the likes of you, for I can tell you're a man who knows his women. No, sir, Ginny's real as rain, and she's yours in the role of your choice. Seven minutes of bliss. It'll seem like a lifetime, gents, I promise you that. Your goods gladly returned if I'm a liar. And all for only a U.S. gallon of gas!"

Howls and groans at that, as Del expected.

"That's a *cheat* is what it is! Ain't a woman worth it!"

"Gas is better'n gold, and we work damn hard to get it!"

Del stood his ground. Looked grim and disappointed. "I'd be the last man alive to try to part you from your goods," Del said. "It's not my place to drive a fellow into the arms of sweet content, to make him rest his manly frame on golden thighs. Not if he thinks this lovely girl's not worth the fee, no sir. I don't do business that way and never have."

The men moved closer. Del could smell their discontent. He read sly thoughts above their heads. There was always this moment when it occurred to them there was a way Ginny's delights might be obtained for free.

"Give it some thought, friends," Del said. "A man's got to do what he's got to do. And while you're making up your minds, turn your eyes to the top of the van for a startling and absolutely free display of the slickest bit of marksmanship you're ever likely to see!"

Before Del's words were out of his mouth and on the way, before the men could scarcely comprehend, Ginny appeared again and tossed a dozen china saucers in the air.

Possum Dark moved in a blur. Turned 140 degrees in his bolted steno chair and whipped his guns on target, blasting saucers to dust. Thunder rolled across the flats. Crockery rained on the men below. Possum stood and offered a pink killer grin and a little bow. The men saw six-foot-nine and a quarter inches of happy marsupial fury and awesome speed, of black agate eyes and a snout full of icy varmint teeth. Doubts were swept aside. Fifty-calibre madness wasn't the answer. Fun today was clearly not for free.

"Gentlemen, start your engines," Del smiled. "I'll be right here to take your fee. Enjoy a hot taco while you wait your turn at glory. Have a look at our display of fine pharmaceutical wonders and mind-expanding drugs."

In moments, men were making their way back to the stockade. Soon after that, they returned toting battered tins of gas. Del sniffed each gallon, in case some buffoon thought water would get him by. Each man received a token and took his place. Del sold tacos and dangerous drugs, taking what he could get in trade. Candles and Mason jars, a rusty knife. Half a manual on full-field maintenance for the Chrysler Mark XX Urban Tank. The drugs were different colors but the same: twelve parts oregano, three parts rabbit shit, one part marijuana stems. All this under Possum's watchful eye.

"By God," said the first man out of the van. "She's worth it, I'll tell you that. Have her do the Nurse, you won't regret it!"

"The Schoolteacher's best," said the second man through. "I never seen the like. I don't care if she's real or she ain't."

"What's in these tacos?" a customer asked Del.

"Nobody you know, mister," Del said.

▲▼▲

"It's been a long day," Ginny said. "I'm pooped, and that's the truth." She wrinkled up her nose. "First thing we hit a town, you hose 'er out good now, Del. Place smells like a sewer or maybe worse."

Del squinted at the sky and pulled up under the scant shade of mesquite. He stepped out and kicked the tires. Ginny got down, walked around and stretched.

"It's getting late," Del said. "You want to go on or stop here?"

"You figure those boys might decide to get a rebate on this gas?"

"Hope they do," Possum said from atop the van.

"You're a pisser," Ginny laughed, "I'll say that. Hell, let's keep going. I could use a hot bath and town food. What you figure's up the road?"

"East Bad News," Del said, "if this map's worth anything at all. Ginny, night driving's no good. You don't know what's waiting down the road."

"I know what's on the roof," Ginny said. "Let's do it. I'm itchy all over with bugs and dirt and that tub keeps shinin' in my head. You want me to drive a spell, I sure will."

"Get in," Del grumbled. "Your driving's scarier than anything I'll meet."

▲▼▲

Morning arrived in purple shadow and metal tones, copper, silver, and gold. From a distance, East Bad News looked to Ginny like garbage strewn carelessly over the flats. Closer, it looked like larger garbage. Tin shacks and tents and haphazard buildings rehashed from whatever they were before. Cookfires burned, and the locals wandered about and yawned and scratched. Three places offered food. Other places bed and a bath. Something to look forward to, at least. She spotted the sign down at the far end of town.

MORO'S REPAIRS
Armaments*Machinery*Electronic Shit of All Kinds

"Hold it!" Ginny said. "Pull 'er in right there."

Del looked alarmed. "What for?"

"Don't get excited. There's gear needs tending in back. I just want 'em to take a look."

"Didn't mention it to me," Del said.

Ginny saw the sad and droopy eyes, the tired wisps of hair sticking flat to Del's ears. "Del, there wasn't anything to mention," she said in a kindly tone. "Nothing you can really put your finger on, I mean. okay?"

"Whatever you think," Del said, clearly out of sorts.

Ginny sighed and got out. Barbed wire surrounded the yard behind the shop. The yard was ankle-deep in tangles of rope and copper cable, rusted unidentifiable parts. A battered pickup hugged the wall. Morning heat curled the tin roof of the building. More parts spilled out of the door. Possum made a funny noise, and Ginny saw the Dog step into the light. A Shepherd, maybe six-foot-two. It showed Possum Dark yellow eyes. A man appeared behind the Dog, wiping heavy grease on his pants. Bare to the waist, hair like stuffing out of a chair. Features hard as rock, flint eyes to match. Not bad looking, thought Ginny, if you cleaned him up good.

"Well now," said the man. He glanced at the van, read the legend on the side, took in Ginny from head to toe. "What can I do for *you*, little lady?"

"I'm not real little and don't guess I'm any lady," Ginny said. "Whatever you're thinking, don't. You open for business or just talk?"

The man grinned. "My name's Moro Gain. Never turn business away if I can help it."

"I need electric stuff."

"We got it. What's the problem?"

"Huh-unh." Ginny shook her head. "First, I gotta ask. You do confidential work or tell everything you know?"

"Secret's my middle name," Moro said. "Might cost a little more, but you got it."

"How much?"

Moro closed one eye. "Now, how do I know that? You got a nuclear device in there, or a broken watch? Drive it on in and we'll take a look." He aimed a greasy finger at Possum Dark. "Leave *him* outside."

"No way."

"No arms in the shop. That's a rule."

"He isn't carrying. Just the guns you see." Ginny smiled. "You can shake him down if you like. *I* wouldn't, I don't think."

"He looks imposing, all right."

"I'd say he is."

"What the hell," Moro said, "drive it in."

Dog unlocked the gate. Possum climbed down and followed with oily eyes.

"Go find us a place to stay," Ginny said to Del. "Clean, if you can find it. All the hot water in town. Christ sakes, Del, you still sulking or what?"

"Don't worry about me," Del said. "Don't concern yourself at all."

"Right." She hopped behind the wheel. Moro began kicking the door of his shop. It finally sprang free, wide enough to take the van. The supply wagon rocked along behind. Moro lifted the tarp, eyed the thirty-seven tins of unleaded with great interest.

"You get lousy mileage, or what?" he asked Ginny.

Ginny didn't answer. She stepped out of the van. Light came through broken panes of glass. The skinny windows reminded her of a church. Her eyes got used to shadow, and she saw that that's what it was. Pews sat to the side, piled high with auto parts. A 1997 Olds was jacked up before the altar.

"Nice place you got here," she said.

"It works for me," Moro told her. "Now what kind of trouble you got? Something in the wiring? You said electric stuff."

"I didn't mean the motor. Back here." She led him to the rear and opened the doors.

"God a'Mighty!" Moro said.

"Smells a little raunchy right now. Can't help that till we hose 'er down." Ginny stepped inside, looked back, and saw Moro still on the ground. "You coming up or not?"

"Just thinking."

"About what?" She'd seen him watching her move and didn't really have to ask.

"Well, *you* know..." Moro shuffled his feet. "How do you figure on paying? For whatever it is I got to do."

"Gas. You take a look. Tell me how many tins. I say yes or no."

"We could work something out."

"We could, huh?"

"Sure." Moro gave her a foolish grin. "Why not?"

Ginny didn't blink. "Mister, what kind of girl do you think I am?"

Moro looked puzzled and intent. "I can read good, lady, believe it or not. I figured you wasn't tacos or dangerous drugs."

"You figured wrong," Ginny said. "Sex is just software to me, and don't you forget it. I haven't got all day to watch you moonin' over my parts. I got to move or stand still. When I stand still, you look. When I move, you look more. Can't fault you for that, I'm about the prettiest thing you ever saw. Don't let it get in the way of your work."

Moro couldn't think of much to say. He took a breath and stepped into the van. There was a bed bolted flat against the floor. A red cotton spread, a worn satin pillow that said DURANGO, COLORADO and pictured chipmunks and waterfalls. An end table, a pink-shaded lamp with flamingos on the side. Red curtains on the walls. Ballet prints and a naked Minnie Mouse.

"Somethin' else," Moro said.

"Back here's the problem," Ginny said. She pulled a curtain aside at the front of the van. There was a plywood cabinet, fitted with brass screws. Ginny took a key out of her jeans and opened it up.

Moro stared a minute, then laughed aloud. "*Sensory* tapes? Well, I'll be a son of a bitch." He took a new look at Ginny, a look Ginny didn't miss. "Haven't seen a rig like this in years. Didn't know there were any still around."

"I've got three tapes," Ginny explained. "A brunette, a redhead, and a blond. Found a whole cache in Ardmore, Oklahoma. Had to look at 'bout three or four hundred to find girls that looked close enough to me. Nearly went nuts 'fore it was over. Anyway, I did it. Spliced 'em down to seven minutes each."

Moro glanced back at the bed. "How do you put 'em under?"

"Little needle comes up out the mattress. Sticks them in the ass lightnin' fast. They're out like *that*. Seven-minute dose. Headpiece is in the end table there. I get it on and off them real quick. Wires go under the floorboards back here to the rig."

"Jesus," Moro said. "They ever catch you at this, you are cooked, lady."

"That's what Possum's for," Ginny said. "Possum's pretty good at what he does. Now what's *that* look all about?"

"I wasn't sure right off if you were real."

Ginny laughed aloud. "So what do you think now?"

"I think maybe you are."

"Right," Ginny said. "It's Del who's the droid, not me. Wimp IX Series. Didn't make a whole lot. Not much demand. The customers think it's me, never think to look at him. He's a damn good barker and pretty good at tacos and drugs. A little too sensitive, you ask me. Well, nobody's perfect, so they say."

"The trouble you're having's in the rig?"

"I guess," Ginny said, "beats the hell out of me." She bit her lip and wrinkled her brow. Moro found the gestures most inviting. "Slips a little, I think. Maybe I got a short, huh?"

"Maybe." Moro fiddled with the rig, testing one of the spools with his thumb. "I'll have to get in here and see."

"It's all yours. I'll be wherever it is Del's got me staying."

"Ruby John's," Moro said. "Only place there is with a good roof. I'd like to take you out to dinner."

"Well sure you would."

"You got a real shitty attitude, friend."

"I get a whole lot of practice," Ginny said.

"And I've got a certain amount of pride," Moro told her. "I don't intend to ask you more than three or four times and that's it."

Ginny nodded. Right on the edge of approval. "You've got promise," she said. "Not a whole lot, maybe, but some."

"Does that mean dinner, or not?"

"Means not. Means if I *wanted* to have dinner with some guy, you'd maybe fit the bill."

Moro's eyes got hot. "Hell with you, lady. I don't need the company that bad."

"Fine." Ginny sniffed the air and walked out. "You have a nice day."

Moro watched her walk. Watched denims mold her legs, studied the hydraulics of her hips. Considered several unlikely acts. Considered cleaning up, searching for proper clothes. Considered finding a bottle and watching the tapes. A plastic embrace at best, or so he'd heard, but a lot less hassle in the end.

▲▼▲

Possum Dark watched the van disappear into the shop. He felt uneasy at once. His place was on top. Keeping Ginny from harm. Sending feral prayers for murder to absent genetic gods. His eyes hadn't left Dog since he'd appeared. Primal smells, old fears and needs, assailed his senses. Dog locked the gate and turned around. Didn't come closer, just turned.

"I'm Dog Quick," he said, folding hairy arms. "I don't much care for Possums."

"I don't much care for Dogs," said Possum Dark.

Dog seemed to understand. "What did you do before the War?"

"Worked in a theme park. Our Wildlife Heritage. That kind of shit. What about you?"

"Security, what else?" Dog made a face. "Learned a little electrics. Picked up a lot more from Moro Gain. I've done worse." He nodded toward the shop. "You like to shoot people with that thing?"

"Anytime I get the chance."

"You ever play any cards?"

"Some." Possum Dark showed his teeth. "I guess I could handle myself with a Dog."

"For real goods?" Dog returned the grin.

"New deck, unbroken seal, table stakes," Possum said.

▲▼▲

Moro showed up at Ruby John's Cot Emporium close to noon. Ginny had a semiprivate stall, covered by a blanket. She'd bathed and braided her hair and cut the legs clean off her jeans. She tugged at Moro's heart.

"It'll be tomorrow morning," Moro said. "Cost you ten gallons of gas."

"Ten gallons," Ginny said. "That's stealin', and you know it."

"Take it or leave it," Moro said. "You got a bad head in that rig. Going to come right off, you don't fix it. You wouldn't like that. Your customers wouldn't like it any at all."

Ginny appeared subdued but not much. "Four gallons. Tops."

"Eight. I got to make the parts myself."

"Five."

"Six," Moro said. "Six and I take you to dinner."

"Five and a half, and I want to be out of this sweatbox at dawn. On the road and gone when the sun starts bakin' your lovely town."

"Damn, you're fun to have around."

Ginny smiled. Sweet and disarming, an unexpected event. "I'm all right. You got to get to know me."

"Just how do I go about that?"

"You don't." The smile turned sober. "I haven't figured that one out."

▲▼▲

It looked like rain to the north. Sunrise was dreary. Muddy, less-than-spectacular yellows and reds. Colors through a window no one had bothered to wash. Moro had the van brought out. He said he'd thrown in a lube and hosed out the back. Five and a half gallons were gone out of the wagon. Ginny had Del count while Moro watched.

"I'm honest," Moro said, "you don't have to do that."

"I know," Ginny said, glancing curiously at Dog, who was looking rather strange. He seemed out of sorts. Sulky and off his feed. Ginny followed his eyes and saw Possum atop the van. Possum showed a wet Possum grin.

"Where you headed now?" Moro asked, wanting to hold her as long as he could.

"South," Ginny said, since she was facing that direction.

"I wouldn't," Moro said, "Not real friendly folks down there."

"I'm not picky. Business is business."

"No, sir," Moro shook his head. "*Bad* business is what it is. You got the Dry Heaves south and east. Doom City after that. Straight down and you'll hit the Hackers. Might run into Fort Pru, bunch of disgruntled insurance agents out on the flats. Stay clear away from them. Isn't worth whatever you'll make."

"You've been a big help," Ginny said.

Moro gripped her door. "You ever *listen* to anyone, lady? I'm giving good advice."

"Fine," Ginny said, "I'm 'bout as grateful as I can be."

Moro watched her leave. He was consumed by her appearance. The day seemed to focus in her eyes. Nothing he said pleased her in the least. Still, her disdain was friendly enough. There was no malice at all that he could see.

▲▼▲

There was something about the sound of Doom City she didn't like. Ginny told Del to head south and maybe west. Around noon, a yellow haze appeared on the ragged rim of the world, like someone rolling a cheap dirty rug across the flats.

"Sandstorm," Possum called from the roof. "Right out of the west. I don't like it at all. I think we better turn. Looks like trouble coming fast."

There was nothing Possum said she couldn't see. He had a habit of saying either too little or more than enough. She told him to cover his guns and get inside, that the sand would take his hide and there was nothing out there he needed to kill that wouldn't wait. Possum Dark sulked but climbed down. Hunched in back of the van, he grasped air in the shape of grips and trigger guards. Practiced rage and windage in his head.

"I'll bet I can beat that storm," Del said. "I got this feeling I can do it."

"Beat it where?" Ginny said. "We don't know where we are or what's ahead."

"That's true," Del said. "All the more reason then to get there soon as we can."

▲▼▲

Ginny stepped out and viewed the world with disregard. "I got sand in my teeth and in my toes," she complained. "I'll bet that Moro Gain knows right where storms'll likely be. I'll bet that's what happened, all right."

"Seemed like a decent sort to me," Del said.

"That's what I mean," Ginny said. "You can't trust a man like that at all."

The storm had seemed to last a couple of days. Ginny figured maybe an hour. The sky looked bad as cabbage soup. The land looked just the way it had. She couldn't see the difference between sand recently gone or newly arrived. Del got the van going again. Ginny thought about yesterday's bath. East Bad News had its points.

Before they topped the first rise, Possum Dark began to stomp on the roof. "Vehicles to port," he called out. "Sedans and pickup trucks. Flatbeds and semis. Buses of all kinds."

"What are they doing?" Del said.

"Coming right at us, hauling timber."

"Doing *what?*" Ginny made a face. "Damn it all, Del, will you stop the car? I swear, you're a driving fool."

Del stopped. Ginny climbed up with Possum to watch. The caravan kept a straight line. Cars and trucks weren't exactly hauling timber…but they were. Each carried a section of a wall. Split logs bound together, sharpened at the top. The lead car turned and the others followed. The lead car turned again. In a moment, there was a wooden stockade assembled on the flats, square as if you'd drawn it with a rule. A stockade and a gate. Over the gate a wooden sign:

FORT PRU

Games of Chance & Amusement

Term*Whole Life*Half Life*Death

"I don't like it," said Possum Dark.

"You don't like anything's still alive," Ginny said.

"They've got small arms and they're a nervous-looking bunch."

"They're just horny, Possum. That's the same as nervous, or close enough." Possum pretended to understand. "Looks like they're pulled up for the night," she called to Del. "Let's do some business, friend. The overhead don't ever stop."

▲▼▲

Five of them came out to the van. They all looked alike. Stringy, darkened by the sun. Bare to the waist except for collars and striped ties. Each carried an attaché case thin as two slices of bread without butter. Two had pistols stuck in their belts. The leader carried a fine-looking sawed-off Remington 12. It hung by a camou guitar strap to his waist. Del didn't like him at all. He had perfect white teeth and a bald head.

Eyes the color of jellyfish melting on the beach. He studied the sign on the van and looked at Del.

"You got a whore inside or not?"

Del looked him straight on. "I'm a little displeased at that. It's not the way to talk."

"Hey." The man gave Del a wink. "You don't have to give us the pitch. We're show business folk ourselves."

"Is that right?"

"Wheels of chance and honest cards. Odds I *know* you'll like. I'm head actuary of this bunch. Name's Fred. That animal up there has a piss-poor attitude, friend. No reason to poke that weapon down my throat. We're friendly people here."

"No reason I can see why Possum'd spray this place with lead and diarrhetics," Del said. "Less you can think of something I can't."

Fred smiled at that. The sun made a big gold ball on his head. "I guess we'll try your girl," he told Del. "'Course we got to see her first. What do you take in trade?"

"Goods as fine as what you're getting in return."

"I've got just the thing." The head actuary winked again. The gesture was starting to irritate Del. Fred nodded, and a friend drew clean white paper from his case. "This here is heavy bond," he told Del, shuffling the edges with his thumb. "Fifty percent linen weave, and we got it by the ream. Won't find anything like it. You can mark on it good or trade it off. Seventh Mercenary Writers came through a week ago. Whole brigade of mounted horse. Near cleaned us out, but we can spare a few reams. We got pencils too. Mirado twos and threes, unsharpened, with erasers on the end. When's the last time you saw *that*? Why, this stuff's good as gold. We got staples and legal pads. Claim forms, maim forms, forms of every sort. Deals on wheels is what we got. And *you* got gas under wraps in the wagon behind your van. I can smell it plain from here. Friend, we can sure talk some business with you there. I got seventeen rusty-ass guzzlers runnin' dry."

A gnat-whisker wire sparked hot in Del's head. He could see it in the underwriter's eyes. Gasoline greed was what it was, and he knew these men were bent on more than fleshly pleasure. He knew with androidial dread that when they could, they'd make their play.

"Well now, the gas is not for trade," he said as calmly as he could. "Sex and tacos and dangerous drugs is what we sell."

"No problem," the actuary said. "Why, no problem at all. Just an idea, is all it was. You get that little gal out here and I'll bring in my crew. How's half a ream a man sound to you?"

"Just as fair as it can be," Del said, thinking that half of that would've been fine, knowing dead certain now that Fred intended to take back whatever he gave.

▲▼▲

"That Moro fellow was right," Del said. "These insurance boys are bad news. Best thing we can do is take off and let it go."

"Pooh," said Ginny, "that's just the way men are. They come in mad as foamin' dogs and go away like cats licking cream. That's the nature of the fornicatin' trade. You wait and see. Besides, they won't get funny with Possum Dark."

"You wouldn't pray for rain if you were afire," Del muttered. "Well, I'm not unhitching the gas. I'll set you up a stage over the tarp. You can do your number there."

"Suit yourself," Ginny said, kissing a plastic cheek and scooting him out the door. "Now get on out of here and let me start getting cute."

▲▼▲

It seemed to be going well. Cheerleader Barbara Jean awoke forgotten wet dreams, left their mouths as dry as snakes. Set them up for Sally the Teach and Nora Nurse, secret violations of the soul. Maybe Ginny was right, Del decided. Faced with girlie delights, a man's normally shitty outlook disappeared. When he was done, he didn't want to wreck a thing for an hour or maybe two. Didn't care about killing for half a day. Del could only guess at this magic and how it worked. Data was one thing, sweet encounters something else.

He caught Possum's eye and felt secure. Forty-eight men waited their turns. Possum knew the caliber of their arms, the length of every blade. His black twin-fifties blessed them all.

Fred the actuary sidled up and grinned at Del. "We sure ought to talk about gas. That's what we ought to do."

"Look," Del said, "gas isn't for trade, I told you that. Go talk to those boys at the refinery, same as us."

"Tried to. They got no use for office supplies."

"That's not my problem," Del said.

"Maybe it is."

Del didn't miss the razor tones. "You got something to say, just say it."

"Half of your gas. We pay our way with the girl and don't give you any trouble."

"You forget about *him*?"

Fred studied Possum Dark. "I can afford losses better than you. Listen, I know what you are, friend. I know you're not a man. Had a CPA droid just like you 'fore the War."

"Maybe we can talk," Del said, trying to figure what to do.

"Say now, that's what I like to hear."

Ginny's fourth customer staggered out, wild-eyed and white around the gills. "Goddamn, try the Nurse," he bawled to the others. "Never had nothin' like it in my life!"

"Next," Del said, and started stacking bond paper. "Lust is the name of the game, gents, what did I tell you now?"

"The girl plastic, too?" Fred asked.

"Real as you," Del said. "We make some kind of deal, how do I know you'll keep your word?"

"Jesus," Fred said, "what do you think I am? You got my Life Underwriter's Oath!"

The next customer exploded through the curtain, tripped and fell on his face. Picked himself up and shook his head. He looked damaged, bleeding around the eyes.

"She's a tiger," Del announced, wondering what the hell was going on. "'Scuse me a minute," he told Fred, and slipped inside the van. "Just what are you doing in here?" he asked Ginny. "Those boys look like they been through a thrasher."

"Beats me," Ginny said, halfway between Nora and Barbara Jean. "Last old boy jerked around like a snake having a fit. Started pulling out his hair. Somethin' isn't right here, Del. It's gotta be the tapes. I figure that Moro fellow's a cheat."

"We got trouble inside and out," Del told her. "The head of this bunch wants our gas."

"Well, he sure can't have it, by God."

"Ginny, the man's got bug-spit eyes. Says he'll take his chances with Possum. We better clear out while we can."

"Huh-unh." Ginny shook her head. "That'll rile 'em for sure. Give me a minute or two. We've done a bunch of Noras and a Sally. I'll switch them all to Barbara Jean and see."

Del slipped back outside. It seemed a dubious answer at best.

"That's some woman," said Fred.

"She's something else today. Your insurance boys have got her fired."

Fred grinned at that. "Guess I better give her a try."

"I wouldn't," Del said.

"Why not?"

"Let her calm down some. Might be more than you want to handle."

He knew at once this wasn't the thing to say. Fred turned the color of ketchup pie. "Why, you plastic piece of shit! I can handle any woman born...*or* put together out of a kit."

"Suit yourself," Del said, feeling the day going down the drain. "No charge at all."

"Damn right there's not." Fred jerked the next man out of line. "Get ready in there, little lady. I am going to handle *all* your policy needs!"

The men cheered. Possum Dark, who understood at least three-fifths of the trouble down below, shot Del a questioning look.

"Got any of those tacos?" someone asked.

"Not likely," Del said.

Del considered turning himself off. Android suicide seemed the answer. But in less than three minutes, unnatural howls began to come from the van. The howls turned to shrieks. Life underwriters went rigid. Then Fred emerged, shattered. He looked like a man who'd kicked a bear with boils. His joints appeared to bend the wrong way. He looked whomper-eyed at Del, dazed and out-of-synch. Everything happened then in seconds thin as wire. Del saw Fred find him, saw the oil-spill eyes catch him clean. Saw the sawed-off barrels match the eyes so fast even electric feet couldn't snatch him out of the way in time. Del's arm exploded. He let it go and ran for the van. Possum couldn't help. The actuary was below and too close. The twin-fifties opened up. Underwriters fled. Possum stitched the sand and sent them flying ragged and dead.

Del reached the driver's seat as lead peppered the van. He felt slightly silly. Sitting there with one arm, one hand on the wheel.

"Move over," Ginny said, "that isn't going to work."

"I guess not."

Ginny sent them lurching through the scrub. "Never saw anything like it in my life," she said aloud. "Turned that poor fella on, he started twisting out of his socks, bones snapping like sticks. Damndest orgasm I *ever* saw."

"Something's not working just right."

"Well, I can see that, Del. Jesus, what's that!"

Ginny twisted the wheel as a large part of the desert rose straight up in the air. Smoking sand rained down on the van.

"Rockets," Del said grimly. "That's the reason they figured that crazy-fingered Possum was a snap. Watch where you're going, girl!"

Two fiery pillars exploded ahead. Del leaned out the window and looked back. Half of Fort Pru's wall was in pursuit. Possum sprayed everything in sight, but he couldn't spot where the rockets were coming from. Underwriter assault cars split up, came at them from every side.

"Trying to flank us," Del said. A rocket burst to the right. "Ginny, I'm not real sure what to do."

"How's the stub?"

"Slight electric tingle. Like a doorbell half a mile away. Ginny, they get us in a circle, we're in very deep shit."

"They hit that gas, we won't have to worry about a thing. Oh Lord, now why did I think of that?"

Possum hit a semi clean on. It came to a stop and died, fell over like a bug. Del could see that being a truck and a wall all at once had its problems, balance being one.

"Head right at them," he told Ginny, "then veer off sharp. They can't turn quick going fast."

"Del!"

Bullets rattled the van. Something heavy made a noise. The van skewed to a halt.

Ginny took her hands off the wheel and looked grim. "It appears they got the tires. Del, we're flat dead is what we are. Let's get out of this thing."

And do *what?* Del wondered. Bearings seemed to roll about in his head. He sensed a malfunction on the way.

The Fort Pru vehicles shrieked to a stop. Crazed life agents piled out and came at them over the flats, firing small arms and hurling stones. A rocket burst nearby.

Possum's guns suddenly stopped. Ginny grimaced in disgust. "Don't you tell me we're out of ammo, Possum Dark. That stuff's plenty hard to get."

Possum started to speak. Del waved his good arm to the north. "Hey now, would you look at that!"

Suddenly there was confusion in the underwriters' ranks. A vaguely familiar pickup had appeared on the rise. The driver weaved through traffic, hurling grenades. They exploded in clusters, bright pink bouquets. He spotted the man with the rocket, lying flat atop a bus. Grenades stopped him cold. Underwriters abandoned the field and ran. Ginny saw a fairly peculiar sight. Six black Harleys had joined the truck. Chow Dogs with Uzis snaked in and out of the ranks, motors snarling and spewing horsetails of sand high in the air. They showed no mercy at all, picking off stragglers as they ran. A few underwriters made it to cover. In a moment, it was over. Fort Pru fled in sectional disarray.

"Well, if that wasn't just in the nick of time," Del said.

"I hate Chow Dogs," Possum said. "They got black tongues, and that's a fact."

▲▼▲

"I hope you folks are all right," Moro said. "Well now, friend, looks as if you've thrown an arm."

"Nothing real serious," Del said.

"I'm grateful," Ginny said. "Guess I got to tell you that."

Moro was taken by her penetrating charm, her thankless manner. The fetching smudge of grease on her knee. He thought she was cute as a pup.

"I felt it was something I had to do. Circumstances being what they are."

"And just what circumstances are that?" Ginny asked.

"That pesky Shepherd Dog's sorta responsible for any trouble you might've had. Got a little pissed when that Possum cleaned him out. Five-card stud, I think it was. 'Course there might have been marking and crimping of cards, I couldn't say."

Ginny blew hair out of her eyes. "Mister, far as I can see, you're not making a lot of sense."

"I'm real embarrassed about this. That Dog got mad and kinda screwed up your gear."

"You let a *Dog* repair my stuff?" Ginny said.

"Perfectly good technician. Taught him mostly myself. Okay if you don't get his dander up. Those Shepherds are inbred, so I hear. What he did was set your tapes in a loop and speed 'em up. Customer'd get, say, twenty-six times his money's worth. Works out to a Mach seven fuck. Could cause bodily harm."

"Lord, I ought to shoot you in the foot," Ginny said.

"Look," Moro said, "I stand behind my work, and I got here quick as I could. Brought friends along to help, and I'm eating the cost of that."

"Damn right," Ginny said. The Chow Dogs sat their Harleys a ways off and glared at Possum. Possum Dark glared back. He secretly admired their leather gear, the Purina crests sewn on the backs.

"I'll be adding up costs," Ginny said. "I'm expecting full repairs."

"You'll get it. Of course you'll have to spend some time in Bad News. Might take a little while."

She caught his look and had to laugh. "You're a stubborn son of a bitch, I'll give you that. What'd you do with that Dog?"

"You want taco meat, I'll make you a deal."

"Yuck. I guess I'll pass."

Del began to weave about in roughly trapezoidal squares. Smoke started to curl out of his stub.

"For Christ's sake, Possum, sit on him or something," Ginny said.

"I can fix that," Moro told her.

"You've about fixed enough, seems to me."

"We're going to get along fine. You wait and see."

"You think so?" Ginny looked alarmed. "I better not get used to having you around."

"It could happen."

"It could just as easy *not*."

"I'll see about changing that tire," Moro said. "We ought to get Del out of the sun. You think about finding something nice to wear to dinner. East Bad News is kinda picky. We got a lot of pride around here..."

Highbrow

Will gave his weight to the sling, thrusting his feet firmly against the broad granite face. The crews worked above and to his right. The sound of chisels was swept away at once by the wind that razored the heights. He leaned half a mile into California air. The rope gave him forty feet of slack. Higher, it clipped to the A ring and the long flexible cable. The cable stretched up and out of sight to the winch station at Hairline, fifty yards above. He could lean in and snake-whip the rope and move about in an arc either way. When the angle gave out, he'd have to signal the callboy to pass the word to the winch. He decided to let it go. The kid was likely asleep. He pushed off and swung twenty feet and caught the webbing, got a sound grip and loosed himself from the sling. Hooked the sling to the webbing so the boy wouldn't decide to haul it up.

Eyebrow was twenty feet below. His crew crawled about the granite hedge, cutting and chipping furred striations. The scaffolding snaked crookedly over Eyelid, seventy-five feet to the bridge of Nose. The other brow was Mink's. Mink was perched in a sling, pretending to watch his crew on the other side. What he was doing was watching Will's people work. Will didn't care. He could look all day if he liked. All of Mink's craft was in his hands. He had no feeling for the stone. You had to feel the stone in your head and in your heart.

A shadow slid over Face. Will looked up. A steam-driven flyer clattered by. Rods pumped and thrashed, driving eight bat wings in partial accord. Streamers flew from the tail. The gondola was painted gold, hung from a fine confusion of wires and struts. Japanese tourists took pictures. Quaker, standing by the winch station above, shook his fist and waved a small red flag. The craft lurched off, leaving a trail of soot. Three weeks before, Eva Duke had mooned Norwegian balloonists. Will decided this accounted for increased aerial traffic.

Taft-Hartley wasn't looking at the flyer. He was leaning on the scaffolding, frowning out to sea. "I don't much like the weather," he told Will. "I don't plan to work up here in no storm. Quaker can ground my ass if he likes. I saw Eddie House after lightning got him working on Nose. Welded him to the rock like snot."

Will dropped goggles around his neck and sniffed the air. T.H. was right. Something was forming off the coast. A smudge on the horizon, air thickening into a haze. The sun was still bright up top, but San Clemente was a blur, a sight through dirty glass. A steamer hugged the coast, sluggishly towing barges loaded with granite into port. Will looked up and studied his work. The furrowed crest of granite was a honeycomb ridge brooding twenty-four feet out from Face to shade the Eyes. Close, it appeared to be sedimentary art, the tunnels of ants exposed, uncovered and petrified. Seen from San Clemente, the road that followed the coast, from the decks of clippers at sea, tourists and sailors marveled at the sight. The brows lived; sun and shadow worked their magic, tricks of corrugation and the subtle play of light. Stone became the stern and somber visage. The left brow and the right were in theory of equal craft, but Will knew the right had the touch. That Mink knew, too, and was totally unable to guess why.

"You'll get it," said Taft-Hartley, seemingly reading Will's thoughts. "Odds are eight to five, but I figure it'll go higher than that."

Will was irritated and showed it. There was something wrong with betting on his career. The sky was growing darker by the moment. Clouds considered wearing slate. The breeze was stiff and cool and heavy with salt.

"Get the crew started up," said Will. "I don't want anyone down here when it hits."

"I don't wager any myself, you understand," said T.H. "I'm just telling you so you'll know."

"Yeah, right." Will looked up at Mink. Mink appeared to be taking notes.

▲▼▲

Others could see the storm as well, and soon finishers and joiners, polishers and pointers, were scrambling up from Eyebrows and Nose, climbing up to Hairline to beat the threatening wind. A callboy finally dared to tell Quaker. He lurched out of the winch shack, hoisted the weather flag, and sent the steam whistle wailing over the heights. By then all but stragglers were on top. Bright crooked wires kissed the sea. Wind shivered the surface, sweeping flat water from blue to gray. San Clemente vanished as the front curled to shore in a fierce convexity of rain, slashing at coastal roads and the worktowns to the south. The first heavy drops measled granite the color of sand. Droplets formed tears, and tears coursed streams. Rain gathered to sweep down Nose across Cheeks, part and come together at the grim curve of Mouth, drawn in small rivers to the great cleft of Chin, where a rushing cascade fell to Chest. Other currents swirled from Neck and Shoulders, surged and met in a torrent past Beltline and Statesman's Cape and Trousers, gaining speed and power for some two thousand feet until a cataract drummed with a roar on the roofs of hall and cloister, gatehouse and tower, barbican and bridge, those mammoth structures carved in Greco-Brit-California splendor, nestled between colossal granite Shoes. And when this great swell of water reached the ground, it was quickly carried away in pipes and gutters, cleverly channeled and directed by engineering marvel, rushed to vast reservoirs that nourished the formal gardens and graceful fountains, which delighted Serbian tourists and retired assassin couples from as far away as Spain.

Above, Will made his way through substantial blocks of granite, the site of his future or maybe Mink's. These giant squares rested, waited to be joined and shaped and formed to crown the glory of the Work. In his heart, Will knew Quaker wouldn't fuck him up. Quaker was old and fuddled, but he was still a Master pointer. He wouldn't give the hair to Mink. Even if he didn't care for Will, he loved the Work. He'd started as a boy, a rough-shaper, worked his way to carver, then chief assistant pointer to Don Debate, and finally to Master when Debate had a seizure and fell from Mole. Fifty years on Face, and he wouldn't turn that over to Mink. Will couldn't see him doing that.

Lightning struck the tall iron beam raised above the winch station for that purpose. Will ducked. Rain blew in his eyes. The sharp crack of sound pressed his skin. He smelled burning air. The crews were huddled up before the cages. The steam engines wheezed and snaked cable. The crews waited, standing in the rain or under the narrow tin roof when there was room. Their faces were granite white, rain streaked now like weary tigers. Hammer and rasp and chisel hung heavy from their belts.

The crews kept to themselves. Mink's crew and Will's and the polishers who worked for Court. Up here they didn't talk. Down below they'd drink beer, mix, and fornicate with ease. Will couldn't see it. He didn't feel close to the others. Just his own. The others were like strangers; he didn't know their skills and didn't trust them.

Taft-Hartley nodded, and Will crowded into the next available cage. There were three elevators for the crew. Will had the clout to take Express, but that would mean riding down with Quaker. Maybe listening to Mink suck up to the old man. Will would rather swing down on a rope.

The crews squeezed into place. Tight and smelling of rain and rock and sweat. No one talked. The elevator rattled and jerked. Because of the height of the Work, each crew elevator was really a bank of five. That meant a change every four hundred feet.

T.H. punched Will, and Will glanced out the side. The elevators hugged the back of the Work, adjacent to the step-angle ramps that wound ziggurat fashion from Base to Head, a mountain of rock and soil that let the mules haul granite to the top. Will saw a mule team in trouble. They'd been caught in the downpour at Beltline, and ten-ton blocks had slipped precariously close to the edge. The crews were running about trying to figure what to do.

"Those guys are nuts," said Taft-Hartley. "I wouldn't do that for nothing."

Will didn't answer. Annie Page gave him a wink. Will nodded politely. The elevator rumbled to a halt. The engine house protested, offered death-rattle sounds. Cables seemed appeased. Will hated the ride twice a day, every day of his life. It was far safer to be at work than leave it.

"You want a beer, you're welcome to come," said T.H. "Be glad to have you." A ritual invitation, but T.H. was determined to pursue it.

"Thanks. I got to do some stuff for Pop."

"You don't want to worry about Mink. You got it for sure, Will."

Will stopped. "Just quit doing this, all right?"

"Well, sure. Okay." T.H. looked hurt, as if he had some deformity of the jaw. "The whole crew's pulling for you, is all."

"All right."

"People care, you know."

"Fine."

"Listen. I'm not going to bring this up again. I don't think you want to talk about it much."

"You see right through me, T.H."

"Well, hell, we been working together a long time, you know?"

Taft-Hartley trotted off. There was a bigger crowd than usual by the steamhouse, the taverns and stores clustered about. Rain had brought the topsiders down at the same time the grounder shift changed. Yellow jumpsuits mixed with green. Workers spilled from tunnels that led to vaulted halls and chapels, columned rooms that channeled through the vast expanse of Base. The storm was passing on. The sun was overly bright, and steam rose from the ground. Rooftops made a thousand flashing mirrors in Milhous, and the worktowns to the south.

It was then that Will saw her. Striding with a purpose through the crowd as if people were no obstruction. She appeared to be practicing for a race. He was struck by her at once. He felt a great sense of loneliness for someone he didn't know. A tall girl with bony features and a fiercely defiant chin. He longed to know in defiance of what. And then she was suddenly gone. A cropped head of hair catching the sun.

He thought about her all the way home. Imagined knowing her name and where she lived. What he would say. What she would say to him. He enjoyed small fantasies and walked with new purpose.

It was well after three, and the low roofs, the cobbled streets of Milhous were in the shadow of the Work. The rain had left the town smelling clean. Pop was in his room, the wheelchair pulled to a table and his maps. The paper shades were drawn, the wicks turned high. Charts covered the walls depicting the density of lizards in the Orocopia Range.

"I've got new thoughts on the Western Ground Gecko," said Pop. "Serious errors have been made. We know less than we think about diversity of diet. Those fuckers will scarf any spider that crawls."

"You eat anything, or just drink?" asked Will.

"Don't start on me, boy."

"Pour me one, too, you got anything left."

Pop brought a quarter bottle of gin from under the table. Two glasses followed. Will started poking through cabinets for something marginally close to supper.

"You get down before the rain?"

"Quaker's too old to know he's wet."

"Shit. I'm three years older'n him."

"My point exactly."

Pop showed restraint. Will discovered sausage, sliced a piece, and sniffed.

"You get Quaker over here and let *me* talk to him, there won't be any wonder 'bout who gets Hairline and who don't."

"Now you know I'm not about to do that."

"Me and that old fart started topside together. Worked Upper Lip and Nose. Your ma's buried just below Nostril, bless her soul. Right next to Quaker's Sarah. I'd of been Master pointer if I hadn't gone and fell, and he knows it. Where you going now?"

"Out back and clean up.

"And then where?"

"I don't know, Pop. Out."

"I thought maybe we'd talk. You know the chuckwalla's flesh was highly prized by Indians? It can use its thick tail in defensive situations."

"I won't be much late."

"Don't give a fuck if you are. Don't go thinking I do."

▲▼▲

He didn't feel he'd have trouble finding the girl. If she lived in Milhous, he'd know her. She wasn't a topsider, the green jumpsuit told him that. A carver, then, or a painter. Someone with a craft. Living in Agnew maybe, or Checkers.

He tried Checkers first, and couldn't believe his luck. A topsider he knew who'd got the dizzies named her at once from Will's description. Carrie Deeds. He said the name to himself. It sounded right. She looked like a Carrie Deeds.

At her door he had a brief moment of doubt. Up to now they were comfortably together in his head. She laughed readily and had a fairly agreeable nature. She appeared to smell faintly of cloves. She opened the door and gave him a vague, yet penetrating look. Measured him for some purpose he couldn't guess.

"I'm Will Taypes," he said. "I saw you this afternoon. You came out of Tunnel Nine."

"I didn't see you."

"I know. I was wondering if you'd like to go out."

"No."

"What?"

"No, I wouldn't like to go out." She laughed. It seemed pleasant and not demeaning at all. "I'm sorry. Didn't anyone ever turn you down before?"

"Well, sure."

"But not much."

"What's that got to do with us?"

"Listen, thanks for asking."

"You're not making this real easy."

"I guess you're right. Good night, Will Taypes."

Her image was still clear on the face of the door. He found her quite appealing. He was intrigued by contradiction. There was confidence in her eyes, which were attractively wide-set, yet he felt this masked a certain shy and vulnerable nature. A firm, yet faintly indolent chin. A sense of frailty about her face that concealed an inner strength. Possibly wanton restraint. She had clearly said *no*. But what did that mean in a woman so adept at hiding her feelings from the world?

▲▼▲

In the morning he left early and tried to catch her going to work. Waited at Tunnel 9 until the whistle blew for his shift. He was less than pleased with himself. It was not his way to let a woman trouble his sleep. The truth was, Carrie Deeds had kept him awake. He had prowled about, unearthing a cache of Pop's bad gin. Spent some time looking whomper-eyed at a poster of the eight-lined whiptail lizard.

Taft-Hartley was hung over, and several others as well. Annie was entwined with Abel Passage, looking silly. Will snagged them all on the hook of his sullen mood. Told them he could ground them as work hazards, but he'd rather give them the chance to break their necks. All appeared subdued. Will felt better as they ascended. He was sluggish on the ground, heavy and oppressed. On topside, a man was alive. He knew why Pop had taken to drink.

Mornings, the front of the Work was in shadow. The job went quickly until noon, when the sun flared over Head and started pounding white granite in the thin upper air. The fresh cuts of stone mica-bright, the Face hot as a stove. Will worked his crew hard. They cursed behind his back, sweating beer and passion. Will stalked through every hollow, T.H. at his heels, Will chalking burrs and nodulations for further work, fashioning new striations in his mind, crawling from cleft to fissure breathing stone. A finer groove with point and hammer, better delineation with the three-point chisel and the rasp. Will could see it take form, feel the crude chisel hatching, the honeycombing stone, an unfinished sketch from where he stood but something more from far away. Half a mile straight down, five miles off to San Clemente where every tourist took a picture. Clear and sharp from there and even further, past Liddy Point and out to sea. The brows had been brooding black in nature; granite is cold and undefined. Will could only capture this dark intense emotion with depth and shadow, with the play of light that changed from one moment to the next. Yet he was certain he was right. That his brow lived and breathed. That Mink had no feeling for the Work. You could look in Mink's eye and see it plain. If he wasn't too addled or disconnected, Quaker could see it, too. If he came to some decision before they started feeding him coffee with a spoon.

As if the thought had brought him to life, Will looked up and saw Mink. He sat in his sling some thirty yards away, following the feverish activity of Will's crew. Will displayed a finger. Mink would tell Quaker, who disliked perverse behavior of any sort.

He left an hour early, turning the reins over to T.H., certain this was a sign that his mind was mushy as Quaker's. If she left Tunnel 9, he didn't see her. He couldn't go to her house again. Home seemed a bad idea. Pop was out of sorts. During periods of irritation, he tended to piss on Will's socks and extra shirts. Barring that, there was gin and lizard lore. Leaving the work tunnels he started walking, taking the long road past the five-story collonaded Base. Took his time and gave a craftsman's admiring eye to the great wall of stones, slick as glass, each fashioned so carefully to the next that, like the Work far above, there was no room for the thinnest blade between. The walk took an hour. Shadow said it was likely past six. He bought a cold drink and watched tourists. Black women from King, stately and thin as wires. A green Duesenberg hitched to six matched geldings. Arabs sat in back, feeding chocolates to small Apache boys. Will found the sight faintly disturbing.

▲▼▲

Pop was drunk in his chair. A balsa-wood Gila was half complete. Will made supper, avoiding kitchen sounds. Drinking coffee out back and watching clouds play over the heights. Weather moved swiftly above Shoulder. He felt a surprising sense of relief, a lightness of the spirit that seemed wholly without reason. He realized he'd come to some decision about the girl. He'd decided not to look for her again. There were other women he wouldn't have to chase. He'd see her somewhere, but he would bring resolution into play. Stand up against her disturbing sense of motion. Forget soft distraction.

"I get supper or what?" Pop called from inside. "You here or out ruttin' around?"

Will spooned hash from the stove and brought coffee. Pop looked unsteady, erratic about the eyes. He poked food carefully with his fork, maybe looking for mines.

"I don't like the idea of being buried someplace I didn't work. 'Course that's what happens if you're fool enough to wind up a cripple. My mamma's in Lapel, and papa's close by in Knot-of-the-Tie. His pa's in Coat Button Four. My great-grandad fell from Herringbone Bend at eighty-six. Used to listen to his tales. He clearly recalled several electrical appliances. Your mother's people were prominent in the Crotch. That's sometime back, and she couldn't recall names. There was some kind of scandal, but I can't say what it was. One thing's certain, we go back on both sides down to Shoe."

"There's more of this hash."

"Be lucky to keep down what I got."

▲▼▲

Will dreamed he could see through the Work. It seemed as if stone had turned to glass. He could see every person inside. Multitudes and throngs. Legions of prone bodies facing west. The sun came up in sweet fury and set the Work afire. He saw that each body was interlinked. A tracery of veins carried blood throughout the Work. The Work moved, took a ponderous step toward the sea. Will woke and guessed he'd slept maybe an hour. He was still in his clothes. The sound that roused him came again. The moon painted a window on the floor, and when he opened the door, the same waxen light struck her face.

"I couldn't sleep," she said. "I thought we might talk. You look a little surprised."

"I guess that's what I am."

"I wouldn't go out, and you felt that was some kind of rejection."

"I think that's it."

"The truth is, I'm somewhat attracted. I just don't like topsiders who figure they can knock a girl over with their charms."

"I don't recall charming you at all."

"Well. There's that."

▲▼▲

He walked along with her through silent streets. Admired the way she moved. The quick determined stride. There was no one about. Shuttered windows, and even the taverns still. At Tunnel 9 she found a lantern. The glow lemoned her eyes. She took his hand without hesitation, a touch that seemed new and yet familiar. He didn't ask where they were going. A cool and steady draft swept through the tunnel, the smell of stone perpetually damp and clean. There were small rooms, lithic indentations on either side, places for folded canvas, scaffolding and tools, paints and other things.

She left the tunnel and led him down a short granite passage, through a wooden door. The space about him seemed hollow and immense. A high vaulted ceiling was revealed. Stone ribbing soared to dizzy heights and disappeared. Carrie Deeds drew him swiftly past fluted marble columns, carved groups, and figures. Will began to find scraps of paper, the notes of student guides.

crowned in the classical sense...
    symbolic of naval supremacy and plentiful reign...

The vaulted hall gave way to Knight's Chapel. Deep-relief sculptures of great battles and achievement. Elders, counselors, and maidens.

"Over here," Carrie whispered, a sound that fled like quick escaping birds for some time. She made the lamp brighter and held it high. "There. That's what I do. What do you think?"

A hint of challenge in her voice. A frieze done in subtle coloration. Gracious woods, the trunks of massive trees, framing stately homes and folded hills. A spaniel in the old heroic style, rampant on a lawn.

"I like it," said Will. "It's damned good work. I can almost hear that little fella bark." He meant it, and looked right at her as he spoke, knowing this was a woman who would smell idle praise in an instant, would sense any patronizing air and likely hit him with the lantern.

"I just wanted you to see," she told Will. "I wanted you to know what I do." Her words seemed to bridge something between them, words spoken and unsaid as well. She was a carver, too, and if topside was a problem, they could end whatever there was right there.

She took him past Early Years, past Piety and Truth stripped to the waist, entwined in marble and quartz. He kissed her before the high bronze gate of Funerary Hall, held her beneath brooding obsidian guards. Her breath was sweet, her body firm and yielding at once. He wanted her then, and knew she would come to him gladly. Instead, he gathered the lantern and took her quickly the way they'd come. She seemed to understand. A pulse beat patiently in her throat. She looked composed and yet intent.

Clouds had gathered to mask the moon. The steamhouse was dark, engine-dreams growling back behind. Will roused old Butz out of sleep. Butz was clearly annoyed. He had no authority to raise Express in the middle of the night. Will suggested a costly breed of gin.

"This is crazy," said Carrie Deeds. "This is crazy as it can be." She held to him tightly, her head against his shoulder, fearful of what she'd see yet curious about the ground dropping away at a rapid pace. "I got to prove myself or what? That better not be what I'm doing."

"You don't have to prove a thing. I want you up there with me."

"I asked people about you."

"What did they say?"

"That you're eight to five to get Hair."

"Me or Mink. Odds don't mean a thing to old Quaker. He'll take us on the boat one day, maybe three miles out, then he'll stand there studying on the brows, making me and Mink sweat. If he's constipated bad, he'll pick Mink. If he's thinking straight at all, he'll choose me. He knows I'm the one ought to get it."

"You ever think about if he doesn't?"

"No. Not any. Your folks carvers, too?"

"Dad is. Mom's dead. Sis is a nun at our Lady of Pat. That didn't seem the life for me."

"I wouldn't think."

"What's that supposed to mean?"

"Now don't start that. We're getting along fine."

"So you say."

▲▼▲

The elevator trembled to a stop. He led her through a maze of granite blocks. Clouds swept the moon, and planes of stone seemed to vanish and reappear. At Hairline he stopped and held back. Newcomers never understood what they would see. Carrie, though, walked boldly ahead, the high night wind sweeping her hair and snapping at her clothes. The earth below was fluid. Chalky ribbons scratched the sea.

"Lord," she said, "I didn't even imagine."

She didn't speak as he took her hand and guided her to the webbing. Snapping a safety line about his waist, he linked a shorter rope to hers. Before, he might have asked, told her how it would be. He knew, now, she would never make the descent to impress him, or show him that she could. She would do it because this was what she wanted, what she'd decided to do. She stayed close beside him on the webbing, making the fifty yards without looking above or below, the wind whipping sharply about her. Forehead seemed the curve of another moon, a luminous world fleeing in the night.

When it was over, she turned to him and smiled. A mix of emotions. Daring and hesitation. Wonder, an honest touch of fear.

"You do this every day?"

"Like falling off a log."

"I won't say you've got a way with words."

She gripped his hand as he moved from the webbing to a smooth granite fissure, a brooding hollow near the thickest point of the brow. The wind seemed to die. She rested in his arms. When he kissed her, she brought her hand between them, found the zipper at her neck. He looked into her eyes, saw bold and wicked purpose. Her skin was uncanny, another shade of moon and granite. Her features seemed lost in gentle confusion. He drew his strength from the rock itself, from the spirit of the Work. When the sweet rage consumed him, he felt as if a great stone heart beat from below. She sighed, and seemed much smaller than before. Ragged cloud tangled in her hair. He shuddered at the wonder of what had occurred. Bracing his hands on frigid granite, he saw past her to the night. The moon rippled the earth. The sea mirrored the sky. The lights of houses and small towns winked here and there, distorted by the wind.

"Come back down here," she said. "I'm cold."

He leaned against her to give her warmth.

"I think you've turned my head, Will Taypes."

"I'm doing the best I can."

"You're doing pretty good."

In the unnatural light, he could see far to the north, to the towers of Traitors' Gate, the L.A. Wall that stretched forever, and behind it nothing but dark. The Work was all there was.

"My father's obsessed with lizards. I think you ought to know."

"I can live with that. What else?"

"I don't ask a lot."

"Good. I won't do just anything you want."

"I'm not surprised to hear it."

"I'm guessing we'll get along."

Perpetuity Blues

On Maggie's seventh birthday, she found the courage to ask Mother what had happened to her father.

"Your father disappeared under strange circumstances," said Mother.

"Sorghumdances?" said Maggie.

"Circumstances," said Mother, who had taught remedial English before marriage and was taking a stab at it again. "Circumstances: a condition or fact attending an event or having some bearing upon it."

"I see," said Maggie. She didn't, but knew it wasn't safe to ask twice. What happened was Daddy got up after supper one night and put on his cardigan with the patches on the sleeves and walked to the 7-Eleven for catfood and bread. Eight months later, he hadn't shown up or called or written a card. Strange circumstances didn't seem like a satisfactory answer.

Mother died Thursday afternoon. Maggie found her watching reruns of *Rawhide* and *Bonanza*. Maggie left South Houston and went to live with Aunt Grace and Uncle Ned in Marble Creek.

"There's no telling who he might of met at that store," said Aunt Grace. "Your father wasn't right after the service. I expect he got turned in Berlin. Sent him back and planted him deep in Montgomery Ward's as a mole. That's how they do it. You wait and lead an ordinary life. You might be anyone at all. Your control phones up one day and says 'the water runs deep in Lake Ladoga' and that's it. Whatever you're doing, you just get right up and do their bidding. Either that or he run off with that slut in appliance. I got a look at her when your uncle went down to buy the Lawnboy at the End-of-Summer Sale. Your mother married beneath her. I don't say I didn't do the same. The women in our family got no sense at all when it comes to men. We come from good stock, but that doesn't put money in the bank. Your grandfather Jack worked directly with the man who invented the volleyball net they use all over the world in tournament play. Of course he never got the credit he deserved. This family's rubbed elbows with greatness more than once, but you wouldn't know it. Don't listen to your Uncle Ned's stories. And for Christ's sake, don't ever sit on his lap."

Maggie found life entirely different in a small town. There were new customs to learn. Jimmy Gerder and two other fourth graders took her down to the river after school and tried to make her take off her pants. Maggie didn't want to and ran home. After that, she ran home every day.

Uncle Ned told her stories. Maggie learned why it wasn't a good idea to sit on his lap. "There was this paleontologist," said Uncle Ned; "he went out hunting dinosaur eggs and he found some. There was this student come along with him. It was this girl with nice tits is who it was. So this paleontologist says, 'Be careful now, don't drop 'em, these old eggs are real friable.' And the girl says, 'Hey, that's great, let's fry the little fuckers.'" Uncle Ned nearly fell out of his chair.

Maggie didn't understand her uncle's stories. They all sounded alike and they were all about scientists and girls. Ned ran the hardware store on Main. He played dominoes on Saturdays with Dr. Harlow Pierce, who also ran Pierce's Drugs. On Sundays he watched girls' gymnastics on TV. When someone named Tanya did a flip, he got a funny look in his eyes. Aunt Grace would get Maggie and take her out in the car for a drive.

Maggie found a stack of magazines in the garage behind a can of kerosene. There were pictures of naked girls doing things she couldn't imagine. There were men in some of the pictures, and she guessed they were scientists, too.

Aunt Grace and Uncle Ned were dirt-poor, but they gave a party for Maggie's eighth birthday. Maggie was supposed to pass out invitations at school, but she threw them all away. Everyone knew Jimmy Gerder chased her home and knew why. She was afraid Aunt Grace would find out. Uncle Ned gave her a Phillips screwdriver in a simulated leather case you could clip in your pocket like a pen. Aunt Grace gave her a paperback history of the KGB.

Maggie loved the freedom children enjoy in small towns. She knew everyone on Main who ran the stores, the people on the streets, and the people who came in from the country Saturday nights. She knew Dr. Pierce kept a bottle in his office and another behind the tire in his trunk. She knew Mrs. Betty Keen Littler, the coach's wife, drove to Austin every Wednesday to take ceramics, and came back whonkered with her shoes on the wrong feet. She knew about Oral Blue, who drank wine and acted funny and thought he came from outer space. Oral was her favorite person to watch. He drove a falling-down pickup and lived in a trailer by the river. He came into town twice a week to fix toasters and wire lamps. No one knew his last name. Flip Gator, who ran Flip Gator's Exxon, tagged him Oral Blue. Which fit because Oral's old '68 pickup was three shades of Sear's exterior paint for fine homes. Sky Blue for the body. Royal blue for fenders. An indeterminate blue for the hood. Oral wore blue shirts and trousers. Blue Nikes with the toes cut out and blue socks.

"Don't get near him," said Aunt Grace. "He might of been turned. And for Christ's sake, don't ever sit in his lap."

Maggie kept an eye on Oral when she could. On Tuesdays and Thursdays she'd run home fast with Jimmy Gurdei on her heels and duck up the alley to the square. Then she'd sit and watch Oral stagger around trying to pinpoint his truck. Oral was something to see. He was skinny as a rail and had a head too big for his body. Like a tennis ball stabbed with a pencil. Hair white as down and chalk skin and pink eyes. A mouth like a wide open zipper. He wore a frayed straw hat painted pickup-fender blue to protect him from the harsh Texas sun. Uncle Ned said Oral was a pure-bred genetic albino greaser freak and an aberration of nature. Maggie looked it up. She didn't believe anything Uncle Ned told her.

Ten days after Maggie was eleven, Dr. Pierce didn't show up for dominoes and Ned went and found him in his store. He took one look and ran out in the street and threw up. The medical examiner from San Antone said Pierce had sat on the floor and opened forty-two-hundred pharmaceutical-type products, mixed them in a five-gallon jug, and drunk most of it down. Which accounted for the internal explosions and extreme discoloration of the skin.

Maggie had never heard about suicide before. She imagined you just caught something and died or got old. Uncle Ned began to drink a lot more after Dr. Pierce was gone. "Death is one of your alternate lifestyles worth considering," he told Maggie. "Give it some thought."

Uncle Ned became unpleasant to be around. He mostly watched girls' field hockey or Eastern Bloc track-and-field events. Maggie was filling out in certain spots. Ned noticed her during commercials and grabbed out at what he could. Aunt Grace gave him hell when she caught him. Sometimes he didn't know who he was. He'd grab and get Grace, and she'd pick up something and knock him senseless.

Maggie stayed out of the house whenever she could. School was out, and she liked to pack a lunch and walk down through the trees at the edge of town to the Colorado. She liked to wander over limestone hills where every rock you picked up was the shell of something tiny that had lived. The sun fierce-bright and the heat so heavy you could see it. She took a jar of ice water and a peanut butter sandwich and climbed up past the heady smell of green salt-cedar to the deep shade of big live oaks and native pecans. The trees here were awesome, tall and heavy-leafed, trunks thick as columns in a bad Bible movie. She would come upon the ridge above the river through a tangle of ropy vine, sneak quietly to the edge, and look over and catch half a hundred turtles like green clots of moss on a sunken log. Moccasins crossed the river, flat heads just above the water, leaving shallow wakes behind. She would eat in the shade and think how it would be if Daddy were there. How much he liked the dry rattle of locusts in the summer, the sounds that things made in the wild. He could tell her what bird was across the river. She knew a crow when she heard it, that a cardinal was red. Where was he? she wondered. She didn't believe he'd been a mole at Montgomery Ward's. Aunt Grace was wrong about that. Why didn't he come back? He might leave Mother, and she wouldn't much blame him if he did. But he wouldn't go off and leave *her*.

"I don't want you to be dead," she said aloud. "I can think of a lot of people who it's okay if they're dead, but not you."

She dropped pieces of sandwich into the olive-colored water. Fish came up and sucked them down. When the sun cut the river half in shadow, she started back. There was a road through the woods, no more than ruts for tires but faster than over the hills. Walking along thinking, watching grasshoppers bounce on ahead and show the way. The sound came up behind her, and she turned and saw the pickup teeter over the rise in odd dispersions of blue, the paint so flat it ate the sun in one bite. Oral blinked through bug spatters, strained over the wheel so his nose pressed flat against the glass. The pickup a primary disaster, and Oral mooning clown-faced, pink-eyed, smiling like a zipper, and maybe right behind some cut-rate circus with a pickled snake in a jar. He spotted Maggie and pumped the truck dead; caliche dust caught up and passed them both by.

"Well now, what have we got here?" said Oral. "It looks like a picnic and I flat missed it good. Not the first time, I'll tell you. I smell peanut butter I'm not mistaken. You want to get in here and ride?"

"What for?" said Maggie.

"Then don't. Good afternoon. Nice talking to you."

"All right, I will." Maggie opened the door and got in. She couldn't say why, it just seemed like the right thing to do.

"I've seen you in town," said Oral.

"I've seen you, too."

"There's a lot more to life than you dream of stuck on this out-of-the-way planet, I'll tell you that. There's plenty of things to see. I doubt you've got the head for it all. Far places and distant climes. Exotic modes of travel and different ways of doing brownies."

"I've been over to Waco and Fort Worth."

"That's a start."

"You just say you're a space person, don't you," said Maggie, wondering where she'd gotten the courage to say that. "You're not really, are you?"

"Not anymore I'm not," said Oral. "My ship disintegrated completely over the Great Salt Lake. I was attacked by Mormon terrorists almost at once. Spent some time in Denver door-to-door. Realized I wasn't cut out for sales. Sometime later hooked up with a tent preacher in Bloomington, Indiana. Toured the tristate area, where I did a little healing with a simple device concealed upon my person. Couldn't get new batteries and that was that. I was taken in by nuns outside of Reading, Pennsylvania, and treated well, though I was forced to mow lawns for some time. Later I was robbed and beaten severely by high-school girls in Chattanooga, where I offered to change a tire. I have always relied on the kindness of strangers. Learned you can rely on 'em to kick you in the ass." Oral picked up a paper sack shaped like a bottle and took a drink. "What's your daddy do? If I'm not mistaken, he sells nails."

"That's not my daddy, that's my uncle. My father disappeared under strange circumstances."

"That happens. More often than you might imagine. There are documented cases. Things I could tell you you wouldn't believe. Look it up. Planes of existence we can't see, or not a lot. People lost and floating about in interdimensional yogurt."

"You think my father's somewhere like that?"

"I don't know. I could ask."

"Thank you very much."

"I got this shirt from a fellow selling stuff off a truck. Pierre Cardin irregular is what it is. Dirt cheap and nothing irregular about it I can see. Whole stack of 'em there by your feet."

"They're all blue."

"Well, I know that."

"Where are we going now?"

"My place. Show you my interstellar vehicle and break open some cookies. You scared to be with me?"

"Not a lot."

"You might well ask why I make no effort to deny my strange origin or odd affiliation. I find it's easier to hide out in the open. You say you're from outer space, people tend to leave you alone. I've lived in cities and I like the country better. Not so many bad rays from people's heads. To say nothing of the dogshit in the streets. What do *you* think? You have any opinion on that? People in small towns are more tolerant of the rare and slightly defective. They all got a cousin counting his toes. I can fix nearly anything there is. Toasters. TVs. Microwave ovens. Everything except that goddamn ship. If Radio Shack had decent parts at all, I'd be out of here and gone."

Oral parked the truck under the low-hanging branches of a big native pecan. The roots ground deep in the rigid earth, squeezed rocks to the surface like broken dishes. The tree offered shade to the small aluminum trailer, which was round as a bullet. Oral had backed it off the road some time before. The tires were gone, tossed off in the brush. The trailer sat on rocks. Oral ushered Maggie in. Found Oreos in a Folger's coffee can, Sprite in a minifridge. A generator hacked out back. The trailer smelled of wine and bananas and 3-In-One oil. There was a hot plate and a cot. Blue shirts and trousers and socks.

"It's not much," said Oral. "I don't plan to stay here any longer than I have to."

"It's very cozy," said Maggie, who'd been taught to always say something nice. The trailer curved in from the door to a baked plastic window up front. The floor and the walls and the roof were explosions of colored wire and gutted home computers. Blue lights stuttered here and there.

"What's all this supposed to be?" said Maggie.

"Funky, huh?" Oral showed rapid eye movement. "No wonder they think I'm crazy. The conquest of space isn't as easy as the layman might imagine. I figure on bringing in a seat from out of the truck. Bolt it right there. Need something to seal up the door. Inner tubes and prudent vulcanizing ought to do it. You know about the alarming lack of air out in space?"

"I think we had it in school."

"Well, it's true. You doing all right at that place?"

The question took Maggie by surprise. "At school you mean? Sort of. Okay, I guess."

"Uh-huh." Oral hummed and puttered about. Stepped on a blue light and popped it like a bug. Found a tangle of wire from a purple Princess phone and cut it free. Got needle-nose pliers and twisted a little agate in to fit. "Wear this," he told Maggie. "Hang it round your waist and let the black doohickey kind of dangle over your personal private things."

"Well, I never!" Maggie didn't care for such talk.

"All right, don't. Run home all your life."

"You've been spying on me."

"You want a banana? Some ice cream? I like to crumble Oreos over the top."

"I think I better start on home."

"Go right up the draw and down the hill. Shortcut. Stick to the path. Tonight's a good night to view the summer constellations. Mickey's in the Sombrero. The Guppy's on the rise."

"I'll be sure and look."

▲▼▲

When Maggie was twelve, Aunt Grace went to Galveston on a trip. The occasion was a distant cousin's demise. Uncle Ned went along. Which seemed peculiar to Maggie, since they wouldn't *eat* together, and seldom spoke.

"We can't afford it, God knows," said Aunt Grace. "But Albert was a dear. Fought the Red menace in West Texas all his life. Fell off a shrimper and drowned, but how do we know for sure? *They'd* make it look accidental."

She left Maggie a list of things to eat. Peanut butter and Campbell's soup. Which was mostly what she got when they were home. Aunt Grace said meat and green vegetables tended to give young girls diarrhea and get their periods out of whack.

"Stay out of the ham and don't thaw anything in the fridge. Here's two dollars, that's for emergencies and not to spend. Call Mrs. Ketcher, you get sick. Lock the doors. Come straight home from school and don't look at the cable."

"I'm scared to stay alone," said Maggie.

"Don't be a 'fraidy cat. God'll look after you if you're good."

"Don't tell anyone we're gone," said Uncle Ned. "Some greaser'll break in and steal us blind."

"For God's sake, Ned, don't tell her *that*."

Uncle Ned tried to slip a paper box in the backseat. Maggie saw him do it. When they both went in to check the house, she stole a look. The carton was full of potato chips and Fritos, Cheetos and chocolate chip cookies. There was a cooler she hadn't seen iced down with Dr Peppers and frozen Snickers and Baby Ruths. There were never any chips or candy bars around the house. Aunt Grace said they couldn't afford trash. But all this stuff was in the car. Maggie didn't figure they'd be bringing any back. When the car was out of sight, she went straight to the garage and punched an ice pick hole in the kerosene can that hid Uncle Ned's stash of magazines. She did it on a rust spot so Ned'd never notice. Then she went out back and turned over flat rocks and gathered half a pickle jar of fat brown Texas roaches that had moved up from Houston for their health. Upstairs she emptied the jar where Aunt Grace kept her underwear and hose. Downstairs again she got the ice pick and opened the freezer door and poked a hole in one of the coils. In case the roasts and chickens and Uncle Ned's venison sausage had trouble thawing out she left the door open wide to summer heat.

"There," said Maggie, "y'all go fuck yourselves good." She didn't know what it meant, but it seemed to work fine for everyone else.

▲▼▲

When Maggie was thirteen, Jimmy Gerder nearly caught her. By now she knew exactly what he wanted and ran faster. But Jimmy had been going out for track. He had the proper shoes, and it was only a matter of time. Purely by chance she came across Oral's gimmick in the closet. The little black stone he'd twisted on seemed to dance like the Sony when a station was off the air. Why not, she thought, it can't hurt. Next morning she slipped it on under her dress. It felt funny and kinda nice, bouncing on her personal private things. Jimmy Gerder caught her in an ally. Six good buddies had come to watch. Jimmy wore his track outfit with a seven on the back. A Marble Creek Sidewinder rattler on the front. He was a tall and knobby boy with runny white-trash eyes and bad teeth. Maggie backed against a wall papered with county commissioner flyers. Jimmy came at her in a fifty-meter stance. His mouth moved funny; a peculiar glaze appeared. A strange invisible force picked him up and slammed him flat against the far alley wall. Maggie hadn't touched him. But something certainly had. Onlookers got away fast and spread the word. Maggie wasn't much of an easy lay. Jimmy Gerder suffered a semimild concussion, damage to several vertebrae and ribs.

She hadn't seen Oral in over a year. On the streets sometime, but not at the extraterrestrial aluminum trailer by the river.

"I wanted to thank you," she said. "I don't get chased anymore. How in the world did you do that?"

"What took you so long to try it out? Don't tell me. I got feelings, too."

Nothing seemed to have changed. There were more gutted personal home computers and blue lights, or maybe the same ones in different order.

"You wouldn't believe what happened to me," said Oral. He brought out Oreos and Sprites. "Got the ship clear out of the atmosphere and hit this time warp or something. Nearly got eat by Vikings. Worse than the Mormons. Fixed up the ship and flipped it out again. Ended up in medieval Europe. Medicis and monks, all kinds of shit. Joined someone's army in Naples. Got caught and picked olives for a duke. Look at my face. They got diseases you never heard of there."

"Oh my," said Maggie. His face didn't look too good. The bad albino skin had holes like a Baby Swiss.

"I taught 'em a thing or two," said Oral, blinking one pink eye and then the other. "Simple magic tricks. Mr. Wizard stuff. Those babies'll believe anything. Ended up owning half of Southern Italy. Olive oil and real estate. Not a bad life if you can tolerate the smell. Man could make a mint selling Soft 'n Pretty and Sure."

"I'm glad you're back safe," said Maggie. She liked Oral a lot, and didn't much care what he made up or didn't. "What are you going to do now?"

"What can I do? Try to get this mother off the ground. I'm thinking of bringing Radio Shack to task in federal court. I feel I have a case."

Maggie listened to the wind in the trees. "Do you really think you can do it, Oral? You think you can make it work again?"

"Sure I can. Or maybe not. You know what gets to me most on this world? Blue. We got reds and yellows and greens up the ass. But no blue. You got blues all over." Oral put aside his Sprite and found a bottle in a sack. "You hear from your daddy yet?"

"Not a thing. I'm afraid he's gone."

"Don't count him out. Stuck in interstellar tofu, most likely. Many documented cases."

"Daddy hates tofu. Says it looks like someone threw up and tried again."

"He's got a point."

"What's it like where you come from, Oral? I mean where you lived before."

"You said you been to Fort Worth."

"Once when I was little."

"It doesn't look like that at all. Except out past Eighth Avenue by the tracks. Looks a little like that on a good day."

▲▼▲

Maggie did fine in school after Jimmy Gerder left her alone. He cocked his head funny and walked with a limp. His folks finally sent him to Spokane to study forest conservation. By the time she reached sixteen, Maggie began to make friends. She was surprised to be chosen for the Sidewinderettes, the third finest pep squad in the state. She joined the Drama Club and started writing plays of her own. She was filling out nicely and gave Uncle Ned a wide berth.

They were still dirt-poor, but Uncle Ned and Aunt Grace attended several funerals a year. Two cousins died in Orlando not far from Disneyland, a car mishap in which both were killed outright. A nephew was mutilated beyond recognition in San Francisco, victim of a tuna-canning machine gone berserk. A new family tragedy could be expected around April, and again in late October when the weather got nice. Maggie was no longer taken in. She knew people died year round. They died in places like Cincinnati and Topeka where no one wanted to go. What Aunt Grace and Uncle Ned were doing was having fun. There wasn't much question about that. Maggie didn't like it, but there was nothing she could do about it, either.

When Maggie was eighteen, her play *Blue Sun Rising* was chosen for the senior drama presentation. It was a rousing success. Drama critic Harcourt Playce from San Angelo, Texas, told Maggie she showed promise as a writer. He gave her his personal card and the name of a Broadway theatrical producer in New York. The play was about a man who was searching for the true meaning of life on a world "very much like our own," as the program put it. There was no night at all on this world. A blue sun was always in the sky. Maggie wanted to ask Oral but was sure the principal wouldn't let him in.

Aunt Grace died a week after graduation. Maggie found her watching reruns of *M*A*S*H*. She secretly wrote a specialist in Dallas. Told him what had happened to her mother and Aunt Grace. The specialist answered in time and said there might be genetic dysfunction. They were making great strides in the field. He advised her to avoid any shows in syndication.

Life with Uncle Ned wasn't easy. With Aunt Grace gone, he no longer practiced restraint of any kind. Liquor came out of the nail bin at the store, and found its way to the kitchen. Girl and scientist magazines were displayed quite openly with *National Geographic*. Maggie began to jump when she heard a sound. There was a good chance Uncle Ned was there. Standing still too long was a mistake.

"You're going to have to stop that," said Maggie. "I mean it, Uncle Ned. I won't put up with it at all."

"You ought to get into gymnastics," said Uncle Ned. "I could work with you. Fix up bars and stuff out back. I know a lot more about it than you might think."

Maggie looked at Uncle Ned as if she were seeing him for the first time. His gaze was focused somewhere south of Houston. There seemed to be an electrical short in his face. His skin was the color of chuck roast hit with a hammer.

"I'm going to go," said Maggie. "I'm getting out of here."

"On what?" said Uncle Ned.

"I don't care on what, I'm just going. You try to stop me, you'll wish you hadn't."

"You haven't got busfare to the bathroom."

"Then I'll walk."

"You do and you'll get raped and thrown in a ditch."

"I can get that first part here. I'll worry about the ditch when I come to it."

"Don't expect any help from me. I haven't got two dimes to rub together."

"You will," said Maggie. "Some cousin'll get himself hacked up in a sawmill in Las Vegas."

"Now that's plain ignorant," said Uncle Ned. "Especially for a high-school graduate. There isn't a lot of timber in Nevada. That's something you ought to know."

"Good-bye, Uncle Ned."

It took maybe nine minutes to pack. She took *Blue Sun Rising* and a number two pencil. Left her Sidewinderette pep jacket and took a sensible cloth coat. It was the tail end of summer in Texas, but New York looked cold on *NYPD Blue*. She searched for something to steal. There were pawnshops all over New York. People stole for a living and sold the loot to buy scag and pot and ludes and whatever they could find to shoot up. There was no reason you couldn't buy food just as well. In the back of her aunt's closet she found a plastic beaded purse with eight dollars and thirty cents. Two sticks of Dentyne gum. Downstairs, Uncle Ned was watching the French National Girls' Field Hockey Finals. Maggie stopped at the front door.

"It was me poured kerosene on your magazines," she said. "I thawed all the meat out, too."

"I know it," said Uncle Ned. He didn't turn around. A girl named Nicole blocked a goal.

▲▼▲

Hitchhiking was a frightening experience. She felt alone and vulnerable on the interstate. Oral's protective device was fastened securely about her waist. But what if it didn't work? What if she'd used it up with Jimmy Gerder? A man who sold prosthetic devices picked her up almost at once. His name was Sebert Lewis, and he offered to send her to modeling school in Lubbock. He had helped several girls begin promising careers. Many were now in national magazines.

When Sebert stopped for gas, Maggie got out and ran. There were trucks everywhere. A chrome black eighteen-wheeler city. They towered over Maggie on every side. In a moment she was lost. Some of the trucks were silent. Others rumbled deep and blinked red and yellow lights. There was no one about. She spotted a café through the dark. The drivers were likely all inside. It seemed like the middle of the night. French fries reached her on a light diesel breeze.

"I don't know what to do next!" she said aloud, determined not to cry. A big red truck stood by itself. A nice chrome bulldog on the front. It wouldn't hurt to rest and maybe hide from Sebert Lewis. She wrapped her coat around her and used her suitcase for a pillow. In a moment she was asleep. Only a short time later, a face looked directly into hers.

"Oh, Lord," said Maggie, "don't you dare do whatever it is you're thinking."

"Little lady, I'm not thinking on anything at all," the man said.

"Well, all right, then. If you mean it."

He was big, about as big a man as Maggie had ever seen. Dark brown eyes nearly lost in a face like a kindly pie. "You better be glad I'm a bug on maintenance," he said. "If I'd of took off you lyin' there under the tire, I'd a squashed you flatter'n a dog on the road to Amarillo. You got a name, have you?"

"I'm Maggie McKenna from Marble Creek."

"You running away?"

"I'm going to New York City to write plays."

"You got folks back home?"

"My mother's dead and my father disappeared under strange circumstances. I'm a high-school graduate and a member of the Sidewinderettes. They don't take just everybody wants to get in. If you're thinking about calling Uncle Ned, you just forget it."

"Not my place to say what you ought to do. I'm Billy C. Mace. How'd you get to here?"

"A man named Sebert Lewis picked me up. Said he'd put me through modeling school in Lubbock."

"Lord Jesus!" said Billy Mace. "Come on, get in. Nothing's going to happen to you now."

▲▼▲

Riding in the cab of an eighteen-wheeler wasn't anything at all like a '72 Ford. You towered over the road and could see everything for miles. Cars got out of the way. Billy talked to other truckers on the road. His CB handle was Boomer Billy. He let Maggie talk to Black Buddy and Queen Louise and Stoker Fish. The truck seemed invulnerable. Nothing could possibly reach her. The road hummed miles below. There was even a place to sleep behind the driver. Billy guessed she was hungry, and before they left the stop he got cheeseburgers and onion rings to go. Billy kept plenty of Fritos and Hershey bars with almonds in the truck, and had Dr Peppers iced in a cooler. Maggie went to sleep listening to Waylon Jennings tapes. When she woke it was morning. Billy said they'd be in Tulsa in a minute.

"I've never even been out of the state," said Maggie. "And here I am already in Oklahoma."

Billy pulled into a truck stop for breakfast. And then to another for lunch. He measured the distance in meals. "Two hundred miles to lunch," he'd tell Maggie, or "a hundred seventy to supper."

Maggie read him *Blue Sun Rising* while he drove.

"I don't know a lot about plays," said Billy when she was through, "but I don't see how that sucker can miss. That third act's a doozie."

"It needs a little work."

"Not as I see it, it don't. You might want to rein in the Earth Mother symbolism a little, but that's just a layman's suggestion."

"You may be right," said Maggie.

She already knew Billy was well read. There was a shelf of books over the bunk. All the writers' names were John. John Gunther. John Milton. John D. MacDonald.

"John's my daddy's name, God rest him," said Billy. "A man named John tells you something, you can take it for a fact."

She told him about Uncle Ned and Aunt Grace. She didn't mention Oral Blue, as they had not discussed the possibilities of extraterrestrial life. Billy was livid about her experience with Sebert Lewis.

"Lord Jesus himself was looking after you," he said. "No offense meant, but a girl pretty as you is just road bait, Maggie. That modeling studio thing is likely a front. I expect this Sebert's a retired Red agent and into hard astrology on the side. Probably under deep cover for some time. I imagine there's a network of such places spread right across the country. Sebert and his cohorts cruise the roads for candidates, like yourself. Couple of days in a little room, and you're hopeless on drugs, ready to do unspeakable acts of every kind. There's a possibility of dogs. You wake up in bed with some greaser with a beard that gets military aid from this godless administration. That's where your tax dollar goes. I don't want to scare you, but you come real close to a bad end."

"I guess I don't know much, do I?" said Maggie. "I feel awful dumb."

"You learn quick enough when you drive the big rigs. There's things go on you wouldn't believe. The Russians got the news media eatin' out of their hands. I could give you names you'd recognize at once if I was to say 'em. There are biological agents in everything you eat. Those lines and numbers they got on the back of everything you buy? What that is is a code. If you're not in the KGB or the Catholic Church, you can't read it. Don't eat anything that's got three sixes. That's the sign of the beast. I wish to God I had control of my appetite. I can feel things jabbing away inside. White bread and tomatoes are pretty safe. And food isn't the only way they got you. TV's likely the worst. I can't *tell* you the danger of watching the tube."

"I already know about that," said Maggie.

▲▼▲

Billy Mace had it all arranged. As good as any travel agent could do. He left her with a Choctaw driver named Henry Black Bear in St. Louis. Henry took her to Muncie, Indiana. Gave her over to a skeletal black man named Quincy Pride. Quincy's CB handle was "Ghost." He taught her the names of every blues singer who had lived in New Orleans at any time. He played their tapes in order of appearance. At Pittsburgh she transferred to Tony D. Velotta, a handsome Italian with curly hair. Maggie thought he was the image of John Travolta.

And then very early in the morning, she woke to the bright sun in her eyes and crawled down from the bunk and Tony pointed and said, "Hey, there it is, kid. We're here."

Maggie could scarcely believe her eyes. The skyline exploded like needles in the sun. A lonely saxophone wailed offstage. She could see the trees blossom in Central Park. Smell the hot dogs cooking at the zoo. They were still in New Jersey, but they were close.

"Lordy," said Maggie, "it looks near as real as a movie."

As they sliced through upper Manhattan, Tony pointed out the sights. Not that there was an awful lot to see. He tried to explain the Bronx and Brooklyn and Queens, drawing a map with his finger on the dash. Maggie was thoroughly confused, and too excited to really care.

"So what are you going to do now? Where you going to stay?"

"I don't know," said Maggie. "I guess I'll find a hotel or something."

"How much money you got, you don't mind me asking?"

"Eight dollars and thirty cents. Now I know that's not a lot. I may have to look for work. It could take some time before I get my play produced."

"Holy Mother," said Tony. "You'd better stay with us."

"Now I couldn't do that. I'll be just fine."

"Right. For six, maybe eight minutes, tops."

▲▼▲

The Velottas lived in Brooklyn. It might as well have been Mars as far as Maggie was concerned. There were eight people in the family. Tony and his wife Carla and little Tony, who was two. Tony's father and mother, two younger brothers and a sister. They took in Maggie at once. They said she talked funny. They loved her. Carla gave her dresses. There was always plenty to eat. The Velottas had never heard of peanut butter. Maggie ate things called manicotti and veal piccata. Carla made spaghetti that didn't come out of a can. Nothing was like it was at Aunt Grace's and Uncle Ned's. The family was constantly in motion. Talking and running from one end of the house to the other. Everyone yelled at each other and laughed. Maggie tasted wine for the first time. She'd never seen a wine bottle out of a paper sack. Everyone worked in the Velotta family bakery. Maggie helped out, carrying trays of pastry to the oven.

Tony stayed a week and went back on the road. Maggie talked to Carla one evening after little Tony was in bed.

"I've got to go see my producer," she said. "You all have been wonderful to me but I can't live off you forever. The sooner I get *Blue Sun Rising* on Broadway, the better."

"Yeah, right," said Carla. She looked patient and resigned. The whole family conferred on directions. An intricate map was drawn. Likely locations of muggers and addicts were marked with an X.

"Don't talk to *anyone*," said Tony's mother. She crossed herself and gave Maggie a medal. "Especially don't talk to blacks and Puerto Ricans. Or Jews or people with slanty eyes or turbans. No turbans! Avoid men with Nazi haircuts and blue eyes. *Anyone* with blue eyes."

"Watch out for men in business suits and ties," said Papa Velotta. "They carry little black cases. Like women's purses only flat. There's supposed to be business inside but there's not. It's dope, is what it is. Everybody knows what's going on."

"Don't talk to anyone on skates with orange hair," said Carla.

"A Baptist with funny eyes will give you a pamphlet," said Papa. "Don't take it. Watch out for white socks."

"I'll try to remember everything," said Maggie.

"I'll light a candle," said Mama Velotta.

Maggie called Marty Wilde, the Broadway producer. Wilde said she had a nice voice and he liked to encourage regional talent. He would see her at three that afternoon.

"What's the name of this play?" he wanted to know.

"*Blue Sun Rising*," said Maggie.

"Jesus, I like it. You don't have an agent or anything do you?"

"I just got in town," said Maggie.

"Good. I like to work with people direct."

▲▼▲

Her first impression was right. Manhattan was as real as any cop show she'd ever seen. It was all there. The sounds, the smells, the people of many lands. There was a picture show on nearly every block. Everything was the same, everything was different. The city changed before her eyes. A man lying in the street. A kid tying celery to a cat. A woman dressed like a magazine cover, getting out of a cab. She watched the woman a long time. Maybe she'll come to see my play, Maggie thought. She looks like a woman who'd see a play.

Marty Wilde had a small office in a tall building. The building was nice outside. Inside, the halls were narrow. There was bathroom tile on the floors. A girl with carrot hair said Mr. Wilde would see her, and knocked on the wall. Marty came out at once.

"Maggie McKenna from Marble Creek, Texas," he said. "That's who you are. Maggie McKenna who wrote *Blue Sun Rising*. Hey, get in here right now."

Marty ushered her in and offered a chair. The office was bigger than a closet and had faded brown pictures on the wall. Maggie realized these were Broadway greats, people she would likely meet later. There was very little light. The window looked out on a window. Black men in *Kung Fu* suits kicked at the air. There were piles of plays in the room. Plays spilling over tables and chairs and onto the floor. This sight left Maggie depressed. If there were that many plays in New York, they might never get around to *Blue Sun Rising*.

Marty Wilde took her play and set it aside. He perched on the edge of his desk. "So tell me about Maggie McKenna. I can read an author like a page. I can see your play right on your face. A character sits down stage right. The phone rings. I can see that."

"That's amazing," said Maggie. Marty Wilde seemed worn to a nub. A turkey neck stuck out of his shirt. His eyes slept in little hammocks.

"There's not much to tell about me. I think my play's good, Mr. Wilde. If it needs any changes I'm willing to do the work."

"Every play needs work. You take your Neil Simon or your Chekhov. A hit doesn't jump out of the typewriter and hop up on the stage."

"No, I guess not."

"You better believe it. Who's this guy give you my name?"

"Harcourt Playce, he works on the San Angelo paper."

"Short little man with a clubfoot. Wears a Mexican peso on a chain. Sure, I remember."

This didn't sound like Mr. Playce, but Maggie didn't want to interrupt.

"You say you haven't got an agent."

"No, sir, I sure don't."

"Let's cut the sir stuff, Maggie. I'm older than you in years, but there's a spirit of youth pervades the stage. You're a very pretty girl. How you fixed for cash?"

"Not real good right now."

"My point exactly. Here's what I suggest. It's just an idea I'm throwing out. I take in a few writers on this scholarship thing which is, hey, my way of paying Lady Broadway back in a small way. You stay at my place, we work together. I got a friend can give you good photo work. He's affiliated with a national modeling chain. All semi-tasteful stuff. You'd know his name the minute I said it."

"You want to take my picture?"

"Just an idea. Let's get you settled in."

"This sounds a lot like girls and scientists, Mr. Wilde. I don't see what it has to do with my play."

Marty came off the desk. "I want you to be comfortable with this."

"I'm not very comfortable right now."

"So let's talk. Tell me what you're feeling."

"You just talk from over there."

"You remind me a lot of Debra Winger. In a very classical sense."

"You remind me of someone, too."

"Jesus, what a sweet kid you are. We won't try to push it. Just let it happen." He took a step closer. A strange invisible force picked him up and hurled him against the wall. Pictures of near-greats shattered. Some crucial fault gave way in the stacks of plays. Acts and scenes spilled over Marty on the floor.

"I think you broke something," said Marty. "Where'd you learn that hold? You're awful quick."

The girl with carrot hair came in.

"Call somebody," said Marty. "Get me on the couch."

"I don't think we can work together," said Maggie. "I'm real displeased with your behavior."

"I can see you don't know shit about the theater," said Marty. "You can't just waltz in here and expect to see your name in lights."

"You ought to be in jail. If you try to get in touch with me, I'll press charges."

▲▼▲

Carla said she could stay as long as she wanted. There wasn't any reason to go look for another place.

"I've got to try it on my own," said Maggie. "I believe in my play. I don't believe everyone on Broadway's like Marty Wilde."

Carla could see that she was determined. "It's not easy to get work. Tony thinks a lot of you, Maggie. We all do. You're family."

"Oh, Carla," Maggie threw her arms around her. "You're the very best family I ever had."

Carla persuaded her to wait for the Sunday *Times*. Mama Velotta filled her up with food. "Eat now. You won't get a chance to later."

▲▼▲

The room was on East Twenty-first over an all-night Chinese restaurant. Maggie shared it with three girls named Jeannie, Eva, and Sherry. They all three worked for an insurance company. Maggie got a waitress job nights at the restaurant downstairs. There was just enough money to eat and pay the rent. She slept a few hours after work and took the play around days. No one wanted to see her. They asked her to mail copies and get an agent. Maggie cut down her meals to one a day, which allowed her to make a new copy of *Blue Sun Rising* every week. She even started a new play, using Sherry's old Mac computer and the backs of paper placemats from the job. The play was *Diesel and Roses*, a psychological drama set in a truck-stop cafe. Billy Mace was in it, and so was Henry Black Bear and Quincy Pride and Tony Velotta. Carla called. There was a postal money order from Marble Creek for $175 and a note.

"It's not good news," said Carla.

"Read it," said Maggie.

"'Dying. Come home. Uncle Ned.'"

"Oh Lord."

"I'm real sorry, honey."

"It's okay. We weren't close."

The thing to do was take the money and eat and make some copies of *Blue Sun Rising*. And forget about Uncle Ned. Maggie couldn't do it. Even Uncle Ned deserved to have family put him in the ground. "I'll be back," she told New York, and made arrangements to meet Carla and get the money.

▲▼▲

The first thing she noticed was things had changed in the year she'd been away. Instead of the '72 Ford, there was a late model Buick with a boat hitch on the back. Poking out of the garage was a Ranger fishing boat, an eighteen-footer with a big Merc outboard on the stern.

"You better be dead or dying," said Maggie.

The living room looked like Sears and Western Auto had exploded. There was a brand new Sony and a VCR, and hit tapes like *Gymnasts in Chains*. The kitchen was a wildlife preserve. Maggie stood at the door but wouldn't go in. Things moved around under plates. There were cartons of Hershey bars and chips. Canned Danish hams and foreign mustards. All over the house there were things still in boxes. Uncle Ned had dug tunnels through empty bottles and dirty books. There were new Hawaiian shirts. Hush Puppies in several different styles. A man appeared in one of the tunnels.

"I'm Dr. Kraft, I guess you're Maggie."

"Is he really dying? What's wrong with him?"

"Take your pick. The man's got everything. A person can't live like that and expect their organs to behave."

Maggie went upstairs. Uncle Ned looked dead already. There were green oxygen tanks and plastic tubes.

"I'm real glad you came. This is nice."

"Uncle Ned, where'd you get all this *stuff*?"

"That all you got to say? You don't want to hear how I am?"

"I can see how you are."

"You're entitled to bad feelings. I deserve whatever you want to dish out. I want to settle things up before I go to damnation and meet your aunt. Your father had an employee stock plan at Montgomery Ward's. Left your mother well off, and that woman was too cheap to spend it. We got the money when she died and you came to us. We sort of took these little vacations. Nothing big."

"Oh Lord."

"I guess we wronged you some."

"I guess I grew up on peanut butter and Campbell's soup is what happened."

"I've got a lot to answer for. There are certain character flaws."

"That's no big news to me."

"I can see a lot clearer from the unique position I got at the moment. Poised between one plane of being and the next. When your aunt died, weakness began to thrive. I didn't mean to buy so much stuff."

"I don't suppose there's anything left."

"Not to speak of, I wouldn't think. All that junk out there's on credit. It'll have to go back. The bank's got the house. There's forty-nine dollars in a Maxwell House can in the closet. I want you to have it."

"I'll take it."

"I wish you and me'd been closer. I hope you'll give me a kiss."

"I'd rather eat a toad," said Maggie.

▲▼▲

Maggie saw Jimmy Gerder at the funeral. He still had a limp and kept his distance. She walked along the river to see Oral. It was fall, or as close as fall gets in that end of Texas. Dry leaves rattled and the Colorado was low. The log where she used to watch turtles was aground, trailing tangles of fishing line. The water was the color of chocolate milk and the turtles were gone. Oral was gone, too. Brush had sprung up under the big native pecan. The place looked empty without the multiblue pickup and the extraterrestrial trailer. Maggie wondered if he'd gotten things to work or just left. She asked around town, and no one seemed to remember seeing him go. After a Coke and a bacon and tomato at the café, she figured she had enough to get back to New York if she sold a couple of things before Sears learned Uncle Ned was dead. Put that with her forty-nine-dollar inheritance and she could do it. There was fifteen dollars left from the ticket. Even dying, Uncle Ned had remembered to pay for only one way.

▲▼▲

Winter in New York was bad. The Chinese restaurant became an outlet for video tapes. Sherry and Jeannie and Eva helped all they could. They carried Maggie on the rent and ran copies of *Blue Sun Rising* down at the insurance company. The Velottas tried to help, but Maggie wouldn't have it. She got part-time work at a pizza place on East Fifty-second. After work, she walked bone-tired to the theater district and looked at the lights. She read the names on the posters and watched people get out of cabs. There was a cold wet drizzle every night, but Maggie didn't mind. The streets reflected the magic and made it better. When the first snow fell, she sewed a blanket in her coat. The coat smelled like anchovies, and Sherry said she looked like a Chinese pilot. "For God's sake, baby, let me loan you a coat."

"I can manage," said Maggie, "you've done enough."

She could no longer afford subways or buses, so she walked every day from her room. She lost weight and coughed most of the time. The owner asked her to leave. He said customers didn't like people coughing on their pizza. She didn't tell the girls she'd lost her job. They'd want to give her money. She looked, but there weren't any jobs to be had. Especially for girls who looked like bag ladies and sounded like Camille. She kept going out every day and coming back at night. Hunger wasn't a problem. She felt too sick to eat. One night she simply didn't go home. "What's the point? What's the use pretending? No one wants to look at *Blue Sun Rising*. I can't get a job. I can't do anything at all."

The snow began to fall in slow motion, flakes the size of lemons. Broadway looked like a big Christmas tree someone had tossed out and forgot to take the lights.

"Look at the blues," said Maggie. "Oral liked the blues so much."

A man selling food gave her a pretzel and some mustard. The pretzel came up at once. A coughing fit hit her. She couldn't stop. First-nighters hurried quickly by. Maggie pulled her coat up close and looked in the steamy windows of Times Square. Radios and German bayonets were half off. There was a pre-Christmas sale on marital aids. She could still taste the mustard and the pretzel. A black man in sunglasses approached.

"You hurtin' bad, mama. You need something, I can maybe get it."

"No, thank you," said Maggie.

I can't just stand here, she thought. I've got to do something. She couldn't feel her feet. Lights were jumping about. There was a paper box in the alley. The thing to do was to sit down and try to figure things out. She thought of a good line for *Diesel and Roses* and then forgot it. A cat looked in and sniffed; there were anchovies somewhere about. Maggie dreamed of Daddy when he took her to the zoo. She dreamed of Oral under a tree and riding high with Billy Mace. The cab was toasty warm and Billy had burgers from McDonald's. She dreamed she heard applause. The cat started chewing on her coat. Oh Lord, I love New York, thought Maggie. If I can make it here, I can make it anywhere...

▲▼▲

Carla looked ethereal, computer-enhanced.

"I guess I'm dying," said Maggie. "I'm sorry to get you out in this weather."

"Oh, baby," said Carla, "hang on. Just hang on, Maggie."

Everything was fuzzy. The tubes hurt her nose. The walls were dark and needed painting. Sherry and Eva and Jeannie were there and all the Velottas. They bobbed about like balloons. Everyone had rings around their eyes.

"I want you to have *Blue Sun Rising*," said Maggie. "All of you. Equal shares. I've been thinking about off-Broadway lately. That might not be so hard. Don't see a man named Marty Wilde."

"All right, Maggie."

"She's going," someone said.

"Good-bye, Daddy. Good-bye, Oral," said Maggie.

▲▼▲

The room looked nice. There was a big window with sun coming in. The doctor leaned down close. He smelled like good cologne. He smiled at Maggie and wrote something and left. A nice-looking man got up from a chair and stood by the bed.

"Hello. You feeling like something to drink? You want anything, just ask."

"I'd like a Dr Pepper if you have one."

"You got it."

The man left and Maggie tried to stay awake. When she opened her eyes again, it was late afternoon. The man was still there. A nurse came in and propped her up. The man brought her a fresh Dr Pepper.

"You look a lot like Tony," said Maggie. He did. The same crispy hair and dark eyes. A nice black suit and a gray tie. Maybe a couple of years older. "You know Tony and Carla?"

"They ask about you every day. You can see them real soon. Everybody's been pretty worried about you."

"I guess I 'bout died."

"Yeah, I guess you did."

"This place looks awful expensive. I don't want the Velottas or anyone spending a bundle on me."

"They won't. No problem."

"Hey, I know a swell place like this isn't *free*."

"We'll talk about it. Don't worry." The man smiled at Maggie and went away.

Maggie slept and got her appetite back and wondered where she was. The next afternoon the man was back. He helped her into a wheel-chair and rolled her down the hall to a glassed-in room full of plants. There were cars outside in a circular drive. A fountain turned off for the winter. A snow-covered lawn and a dark line of trees. Far in the distance, pale blue hills against a cold and leaden sky. Men in sunglasses and overcoats walked around in the snow.

"I guess you're going to tell me where I am sometime," said Maggie. "I guess you're going to tell me who you are and what I'm doing in this place I can't afford."

"I'm Johnny Lucata," the man said. "Call me Johnny, Maggie. And this house belongs to a friend."

"He must be a friend of yours, then. I don't remember any friends with a house like this."

"You don't know him. But he's a friend of yours, too." He seemed to hesitate. He straightened his tie. "Look, I got things to tell you. Things you need to know. You want, we can talk when you feel a little better."

"I feel okay right now."

"Maybe. Only this is kinda nutsy stuff, you know? I don't want to put you back in bed or nothing."

"Mr. Lucata, whatever it is, I think I'll feel a lot better when I know what's going on."

"Right. Why not? So what do you know about olives?"

"What?"

"Olives. They got olives over in Italy. There's a place where the toe's kicking Sicily in the face. Calabria. Something like a state, only different. The man lives here, he's got a lot of the olive oil business in Calabria. Been in his family maybe four, five hundred years. You sure you want to do this now?"

"I'm sure, Mr. Lucata."

"Okay. There's this city called Reggio di Calabria right on the water. You can look and see Sicily real good. A couple of miles out of town is this castle. Been there forever, only now it's a place for monks. So what happens is a couple of months back this monk's digging around and finds this parchment in a box. It's real old and the monk reads it. What he sees shakes him up real bad. He's not going to go to the head monk because Catholics got this thing about stuff that even *starts* to get weird. But he's a monk, right? He can't just toss this thing away. He's got a sister knows a guy who's family to the man who lives here.

So the box gets to Reggio and then it gets to him." Johnny Lucata looked at Maggie. "Here's the part I said gets spooky. What this parchment says, Maggie, is that the old duke who started up the family left all the olive business to *you*."

Maggie looked blank. "Now that doesn't make sense at all, Mr. Lucata."

"Yeah, tell me. It's the straight stuff. The experts been over it. I got a copy I can show you. It's all in Latin, but you can read the part that says Maggie McKenna of Marble Creek, Texas. We got the word out, and we been looking all over trying to find you. But your uncle died and you came back to New York. We didn't know where to take it after that. Then someone in Tony's family mentions your name and it gets to us. The thing is now, the man lives here, he doesn't know what to make of all this, and he don't want to think about it a lot. He sure don't want to ask some cardinal or the Pope. What he *wants* to do is make it right for *you*, Maggie. This duke is his ancestor and he figures it's a matter of honor. I mean, he doesn't see you ought to get it *all*, but you ought to be in for a couple of points. He wants me to tell you he'd like to work it where you get maybe three, four mill a year out of this. He thinks that's fair and he knows you're pressed for cash."

Maggie sat up straight. "Are you by any chance talking about dollars? Three or four million *dollars*?"

"Five. I think we ought to say five. He kind of left that up to me. Don't worry about the taxes. We'll work a little off-tackle Panama reverse through a Liechtenstein bank. You'll get the bread through a Daffy Duck Christmas Club account."

"I just can't hardly believe this, Mr. Lucata. It's like a dream or something. No one even knew I was going to *be* back then. Why, there wasn't even a *Texas*!"

"You got it."

"This castle. There's just these monks living there now?"

"Palazzo Azzuro. Means blue palace. I been there, it's nice. Painted blue all over. Inside and out. Every kind of blue you ever saw."

"*Blue*? Oh, my goodness!"

"You okay?"

"Oral," said Maggie, "Oh, Oral, you're the finest and dearest friend I ever had!"

▲▼▲

When she was feeling like getting up and around, Johnny Lucata helped her find a relatively modest apartment off Fifth Avenue. Five mill or not, Maggie had been poor too long to start tossing money around. She did make sure there were always Dr Peppers and Baby Ruths in the fridge. And steaks and fresh fruit and nearly everything but Chinese food and pizza. Carla helped her find Bloomingdale's and Saks. Maggie picked out a new cloth coat. She sent nice perfume to Jeannie and Sherry and Eva, and paid them back triple what they'd spent to help her out. She gave presents to the Velottas and had everyone over for dinner. Johnny Lucata dropped by a lot. Just to see how she was doing. Sometimes he came in a cab. Sometimes he came in a black car with tinted windows and men wearing black suits and shades. He took her out to dinner and walks in the park. Sometimes Maggie made coffee, and they talked into night. She read him *Blue Sun Rising* and he liked it.

"You don't have to say that, just because it's me."

"I mean it. I go to plays all the time. It's *real*, Maggie. You don't have to wonder what everybody's thinking, they just say it. I want you to talk to Whitney Hess."

"Whitney Hess the producer? Do you know him?"

"Yeah, sure I know him."

"I don't want to do that, Johnny. I don't want to get help from somebody just because he's a friend of yours. That's not right. I want *Blue Sun Rising* to stand on its own."

"Are you kidding?" said Johnny. "Whitney Hess wouldn't buy a bad play from his dying mother. Besides, I want five points of this up front. You're not going to cut *me* out of a winner."

▲▼▲

Tony and Carla and Tony's brother and his sister and Mama and Papa Velotta dressed up for opening night. Johnny Lucata sent a limo to pick them up, and another to get Jeannie and Sherry and Eva. Tony got out the word, and the truckers found Billy Mace and Henry Black Bear and Quincy Pride. They all had seventh-row center seats.

Maggie thought sure she was dreaming. Her name up in lights at the Shubert Theatre. Ladies in furs and jewels dressed up for opening night. Spotlights and TV cameras and people she'd only seen in the movies. She stayed outside a long time. Standing in the very same spot where she'd thrown up pretzels in the street. Not far from the alley where she'd curled up in a box and nearly died. You just never know, she told herself. You just don't.

There was no need to wait for the reviews. After the first act, Whitney Hess said they had a smash on their hands. After the third-act curtain, even Maggie believed it was true. The audience came to its feet and shouted, "Author! Author!" and someone told Maggie they meant *her*.

Johnny hurried her out of the Shubert by the side door. He wouldn't say where they were going. A black car was by the curb around the corner. There were men in overcoats and shades.

"I want you to meet somebody," said Johnny, and opened the rear door. "This is Maggie McKenna," he said. "Maggie, I'd like you to meet my father."

Maggie caught the proper respect in his voice. She looked inside and saw an old man sitting in the corner. He was lost in a black suit, a man no more substantial than a cut-rate chicken in a sack.

"That was a nice play," he said. "I like it a lot. I like plays with a story you can't guess what's going to happen all the time. There's nothing on the television but dirt. The Reds got people in the business. They built this place in Chelyabinsk looks just like Twentieth Century Fox. Writers, directors, the works. They teach 'em how to do stuff rots out your head, then they send them over here. This is a great country. You keep writing nice plays."

"Thank you," said Maggie, "I'm very glad you liked it."

"Here. A little present from me. Your big night. You remember where you got it."

"I'm very grateful," said Maggie. "For everything." She leaned in and kissed him on the cheek.

"That's very nice. You're a nice girl. She's a nice girl, Johnny."

Johnny took her back inside, and on the way home after the big party Whitney Hess gave at the Plaza, Maggie opened her present. It was a pendant shaped like an olive. Pale emeralds formed the olive, and a ruby sat on top for the pimiento.

"It's just lovely," said Maggie.

"The old man's got a lot of class."

"Why didn't you tell me that was your father's house, Johnny? I kinda guessed later, but I didn't know for sure."

"Wasn't the right time."

"And it's the right time now?"

"Yeah, I guess it is."

"Whitney Hess wants to go into rehearsal on *Diesel and Roses* next month. I'm going to ask Billy Mace and Henry Black Bear and Quincy Pride to come on as technical advisers. There's not a thing for them to do, but I'd like to have them around."

"That's nice. It's a good idea."

"Whitney says everyone wants the movie rights to *Blue Sun Rising*. Which means we'll get a picture deal up front for *Diesel and Roses*. Oh

Lordy, I can't believe all this is really happening. Everything in my life's been either awful or as good as it can be."

"It's going to stay good now, Maggie." He leaned over and kissed her quickly. Maggie stared at the tinted glass.

"You've never done *that* before."

"Well, I have now."

Maggie wondered what was happening inside. She felt funny all over. She was dizzy from the kiss. She liked Johnny a lot, but she'd never liked him quite like this. She wanted him to kiss her again and again, but not *now*. Not wearing Oral's protective device, which she'd worn since her very first day in New York. It was something she'd never thought about before. What if you really *wanted* someone to do something to you? Would the wire and the black stone know that it wasn't Jimmy Gerder or Marty Wilde? She certainly couldn't take the chance of finding out.

The phone was ringing when they got to her apartment.

"You're famous," said Johnny. 'That'll go on all night."

"No, it won't," said Maggie, "just take it off the hook. I can be famous tomorrow. Tonight I just want to be me."

Johnny had a funny look in his eyes. She was sure he was going to kiss her right then. "Just wait right there," she said. "Don't go away. Get me a Dr Pepper and open yourself a beer." She hurried into the bedroom and shut the door. Raised up her skirt and slipped the little wire off her waist. Her heart was beating fast. "I hope you know what you're doing, Maggie McKenna."

Johnny gave a decidedly angry shout from the other room. Another man yelled. Something fell to the floor.

"Good heavens, what's that?" said Maggie. She rushed into the room. Johnny had a young man backed against the wall, threatening him with a fist. The man wore a patched cardigan sweater and khaki pants. He was trying to hit Johnny with a sack.

"Who the hell are *you*," said Johnny, "what are you doing in here!"

"Oh, my God," said Maggie. She stopped in her tracks, then ran past Johnny and threw her arms around the other man's neck. "Oh, Daddy, I *knew* you wouldn't leave me! I knew you'd come back!"

"Maggie? Is that you? Why, you're all grown up! Say, what a looker you are. Where am I? How's your mother?"

"We'll talk about that. Just sit down and rest." She could hardly see through her tears. "I'll explain," she told Johnny. "At least I'll give it a try. Oh, Oral, I hope you're wherever it is you want to be. Johnny, get Daddy a Dr Pepper." She gave him the sack. "Put this in the kitchen and you come right back."

"It's just catfood and bread," said Daddy. "I think that fella there took me wrong."

"Everything's all right now."

"Maggie, I feel like I've been floating around in yogurt. Forever or maybe an hour and a half. It's hard to say. I don't know. I'm greatly confused for the moment. I *ought* to be more than five years older'n you."

"It happens. There are documented cases. Just sit down and rest. There's plenty of time to talk." Johnny came back with a Dr Pepper. She gave it to her father and led Johnny to the kitchen.

"I don't get it," said Johnny.

"You got all that business with the monks, you can learn to handle this. Just hold me a minute, all right? And do what you did in the car."

Johnny kissed her a very long time. Maggie was sure she was going to faint.

"I'm a real serious guy," said Johnny. "I'm not just playing around. I got very strong emotions."

"I like you a lot," said Maggie. "I'm not sure I could love a man in your line of work."

"I'm in olives. I got a nice family business."

"You've got a family in overcoats and shades, Johnny Lucata."

"Okay, so we'll work something out."

"I guess maybe we will. I keep forgetting I'm in olive oil, too. Maybe you better kiss me again. Johnny, there's *so* much I want us to do. I want to show you Marble Creek. I want to show you green turtles on a log and the Sidewinderettes doing a halftime double-snake whip. I want to see every single shade of blue in that castle, and I've got a simply *great* idea for a play. Oh, Johnny, Daddy's back and you're here and I've got about everything there *is*. New York is such a knocked-out crazy wonderful town!"

Tony Red Dog

Tony learns purely by accident the Scozarri brothers have taken out a girl he liked a lot then dumped her at a pet food plant. The brothers work for the Tranalone family which is heavy into stuff like dog food and packing plants and anything that has to do with meat, so the guys who do legwork for Dominic Tranalone can drop off a stiff without driving out of town. Everybody on the street knows this is what they do, and anybody in the know buys their sausage and salami out of state. Tony figures what the brothers probably did was use the girl real bad before that. Leo and Lenny have warped ideas about social situations. Leo is mean, but Lenny's flat crazy in the head.

So Tony is mad as hell and out for blood. Nothing has pissed him off this much since the last re-make of *Geronimo*. That girl was real fine and she treated Tony nice. She didn't ever tell an Indian joke or call him chief. She had a smile on her face and her hair smelled good all the time. She didn't have to end up like that.

▲▼▲

Tony thinks about the girl all day. He can't keep his mind on the job. It isn't right. A thing like that is all wrong and he's got to set it straight. What he ought to do is drop everything and do it now. Find those assholes and get it off his mind. If he does, though, Sal will flat shit because it isn't authorized, and Mickey Ric will come down on Tony like a safe, and Tony doesn't need that. So he'll have to see Sal and Sal will have to go to Ric and Ric will have to ask the old man. Which he won't, because Mickey Ric wouldn't help Tony on a bet. If Tony Red Dog was on fire, Mickey Ricca wouldn't piss and put him out. Besides that, Bennie Fischetti's sent the word down he doesn't want any trouble with the Tranalone family right now, he don't want to rock the boat.

Which leaves Tony right where he is which is nowhere at all, and the Scozarri brothers are laughing up their sleeves. Tony gets so wound up in all this he boosts a sky-blue Caddy instead of the black he's supposed to get, which fucks up his orders for the day.

▲▼▲

Tony finds Sal where anybody can, which is at the back table of the donut shop where Sal presides twenty-two hours every day. Sal doesn't do without sleep, but at three-hundred-sixty-two pounds it is easier to nap where he is than go to bed, and there's donuts and coffee close by.

Vinnie D. and Bobby Gallo are there, and Tony says hello. Bobby and Vinnie are never real far from Sal, and Tony sees they're getting fat too. All you got to do is look at Sal, you put on maybe two or three pounds.

"I got to talk to you, Sal," Tony says. "Something's happened."

"I heard," Sal says.

"I want to do 'em," Tony says, getting right to the point. "Those bastards got it coming."

"Don't take everything personal," Sal says.

This is what Tony figured that he'd say. "Sal, I got a right. The Scozarri brothers knew I was seeing that girl. This is an embarrassment to me."

Sal blinks like an owl and licks sugar off his lips. "That's it right there," he tells Tony. "It's an embarrassment to you. It ain't business. It's a personal thing with you. You got the word same as me. No trouble. No hassle with the Tranalones."

"You could ask," Tony says, knowing how much good this will do. "It isn't just me. It's a reflection on the family. Tell Mickey Ricca that."

Sal pretends he's thinking this over, like he's making some real big decision in his head. He knows that's what a *capo* ought to do, that it lets the soldiers see he's on the ball. Sal "Hippo" Galiano is a *capo* without a lot of clout, since boosting cars and hijacking trucks now and then isn't all that big a family deal. It's not like he's Nick Cannatella who's the *caporegime* for dope, a guy even Mickey Ricca respects.

So Sal finally blinks and says, "Okay I'll make a call. I'll check it out with Ric. I ain't making no promises, you understand."

"Right," Tony says, "I appreciate it, Sal." He knows what he did before he walked in the shop. That even if Sal gets the nerve to make the call, Mickey Ricca's going to turn him down flat, that right here's as far as it's going to go. That if something gets done, Tony's got to do it on his own.

Sal is watching Tony close and he knows what's in his head. "Don't do anything stupid," he says, "You got a good job. Don't go and fuck it up. Find another broad. Take the day off. Have a little fun."

"Sure," Tony says, and even Vinnie D. can see that Tony doesn't mean that at all.

Sal looks Tony up and down. Takes in the alligator boots and the jeans, the black hair down to Tony's shoulders and the bandanna wrapped around his head. His mouth curls up like he's tasted something bad.

"Tony, listen," he says, "no fucking offense, okay? You got to dress like that? I mean, it's okay you're out in the sticks. You're attackin' the fucking wagontrain, fine. You're walking down the street here, nobody dresses like that, they got a suit. Vinnie and Bobby here, they got a suit. Anyone you see they got a suit."

Tony looks at Sal. "I'm not Vinnie D., I'm me, Sal. I got my blood. I got native ethnic pride."

"Shit, I'm an ethnic too," Sal says. "You don't see me wearing no toga and a sword, I got a suit. Everybody's got a suit." He digs in his vest and finds a bill and drops it on the table. "Here's a C, okay? Get a suit. Get a nice suit. See Harry down at Gold's and do something with the hair. Tell him that the hair's on me."

Tony picks up the bill, and Sal knows he's just tossed money down the drain, that Tony's not about to get a suit.

"Thanks," Tony says. "Ask Ric. Just ask him, okay?"

"I ain't promising a thing," Sal says.

▲▼▲

Tony's wrong about Sal. Sal calls Ric because he knows Tony's got a short fuse. He knows if Tony does something dumb that it's Sal Galiano that Ricca's going to see. So the call is to cover Sal's ass, and this tells Ric what he already knew, which is Sal can't cut it anymore. He's got to call and check, he can't handle it himself. Sal's a stand-up guy; he's got a lot of friends who moved up while Sal stayed where he was, and Ricca's got to think about that. He makes a note to find a club where Sal can put his name outside and someone else can do the work.

Tony's wrong about Mickey Ricca too. Ricca gives a lot of thought to what Tony wants to do. He knows he isn't going to let Tony make a hit. Not while the boss is trying to work this scam with the Tranalone family, which is mostly Mickey Ricca's idea. What Bennie Fischetti's telling Dominic Tranalone is they ought to squeeze the South Side blacks and split the territory up. That the black guys are getting too big and cutting into everybody's take, and not working through the families like they should. Dominic Tranalone hates blacks, so he's willing to talk to Bennie about that. What Tranalone doesn't know is that Bennie's been talking to the blacks on the side. He's going to use the blacks to squeeze the Tranalones out, and when he gets that done he'll put the black guys out of business too. So this is no time to start knocking off Tranalone guys, when everybody's supposed to be friends.

What Mickey Ricca's thinking is there ought to be a way to put Tony in the scam and also get the Indian off his back. He's got to be smart about this because it's Mickey Ricca's fault in a way that Tony Red Dog's where he is. Tony worked for Jackie Pinelli out in Phoenix, and did a favor Mickey couldn't overlook. What happened is, Charlie Franzone, who is Mickey Ricca's asshole brother-in-law, steals a car one night and rides around buck naked blowing coke. There's maybe three naked broads in the car which doesn't help. When the cops run him down, it turns out this car belongs to some big cheese up in vice. They throw the book at Charlie, and Mickey Ricca's wife is like crying all night and driving Mickey Ricca nuts. So Ricca calls Jackie Pinelli and Jackie talks to Tony Red Dog. Tony flies out to L.A. and boosts a bottle-green Jag and gets the paper and the numbers all straight, and drives it back to Phoenix the next day. The Jag goes to a guy in the D.A.'s office Jackie knows and the case against Charlie kind of falls in a hole and disappears. Ricca's wife stops crying and Ricca sends Charlie off to Texas somewhere and buys him a car wash place, which he figures even Charlie Franzone can't possibly fuck up a whole lot. He sends Jackie five grand and asks Tony what he wants. Tony wants to come back east, he's tired of working in the sticks, and Ricca says fine, come ahead.

When he sees this guy he nearly shits, but he knows he can't send the guy back. Ricca owes Tony one and a debt is a debt. Which is partly why he hates Tony's guts and wants him out. Besides that, it's embarrassing to have a fucking Apache Indian working for the family. It don't look right. Ricca sees some guy, he goes to eat, this guy makes a fucking war whoop, or sticks a couple of fingers up for feathers on his head. It's a flat humiliation is what it is, and Ricca wants to put an end to that.

So he thinks about this then he thinks a little more, and then something starts working in his head. Thinking's what got him where his is—thinking sideways and inside out until he's got every angle covered right. Now he thinks he's got something worthwhile. Something he can use. The old man doesn't like to talk a whole lot, but Ricca thinks he'll want to talk about this.

▲▼▲

Tony spends the morning boosting cars then takes the day off. With Sal's hundred bucks he buys a white leather jacket with a six-inch fringe. There's even fringe on the sleeves and some beadwork on the chest. The beadwork's Jersey Navajo but what the fuck. The jacket's worth five bills if you bought it in a store.

The rest of the day he drives around, hitting all the spots he knows where the sleazeball Scozarris might be. He drives real slow past the meat packing plants and the dives that the Tranalones own. He hits the porno shops and a string of strip joints because he knows the Scozarris have a little piece of that.

It comes to him then that he's wasting all his time. It just hits him like that and he nearly rams a cab. What a fucking dope! He's driving all over sucking gas and these guys are somewhere in the sack. There's day-time business and there's stuff you do at night. Leo and Lenny are into night, and that's when Tony's going to find them on the street. What he needs to do now is go home and sleep himself. Get a drink and a steak and go to bed. Start out again about ten.

Before he goes home he makes one more pass along the streets. He doesn't see the Scozarris but he sees something else. At a place where the Tranalone family likes to eat, he sees a black stretch limo at the curb. Tinted glass and guys in black suits, and stepping out is Tommy "Horse" Calise himself. Tony's impressed. Calise is *consigliere* to Dominic Tranalone, and one of the smartest guys around. You don't have to like a guy to admire the way he works.

Tony only gets a quick look and then Calise's inside, but he knows he's seen the Horse. You could go to a game there's maybe sixty thousand guys, you'd see the Horse right away. About six-foot-four, maybe one-forty-five soaking wet, and these eyes jammed up around his nose. Jesus, what a nose—it's a nose that could edge out any fucking nag at the track. Tony gets a look at a cute little number trailing right after Horse and he's got to laugh at that, because the nose isn't the only part that gave the Horse his name.

▲▼▲

Bennie Fischetti is sitting in the dark. The room looks like a museum, the way Ricca figures that a museum ought to look. It's maybe ninety-six inside and the old man's got a sweater and a shawl. Ricca wonders what'll happen when he dies. Bennie's son Joey is the underboss now but he don't know shit about the business. The title makes Joey feel good. What Joey knows about is girls maybe twelve or thirteen. He's forty-three he wears a suit and tennis shoes. So what's Bennie Fischetti going to do? Who's going to run the family when he's gone? Ricca knows it's got to be him, but he can't read the old man's mind. There isn't nobody on earth can do that.

"Don Fischetti, I don't wish to take your time," Ricca says, "but I feel this is something you ought to know. We've got this *soldato* works for Sal, his name's Tony Red Dog. You seen the guy once, he's got hair down to here."

The old man looks like he's awake, but Ricca isn't sure. He tells Fischetti how the Scozarris offed the girl and what Tony wants to do.

"The thing is," Ricca says, "this bimbo isn't really Tony's girl except maybe in his head. Tony sees a broad on the street he falls in love, that's his girl. What she was is a waitress turns tricks on the side out at Fatso DiCarlo's place, which is run by the Tranalone family. So the Scozarris, they were where they ought to be, and Tony's got no business in the place. What he's doing in there is sniffing after this broad. There's maybe two, three hundred places he could be, he's hanging out in a Tranalone dive. The guy's nuts."

The old man looks at Ric. He doesn't move, he just looks. "So why you bring this to me," he wants to know. "You are *consigliere.* I need to hear about an Indian? I don't need to hear about an Indian and a whore."

"Right," Ricca says quickly, "this ain't about that but it is. What I got's an idea, and that's the thing you got to hear. It's a business idea is what it is."

The old man seems to pay attention now. "Maybe I will listen," he says. "Maybe I will hear this business thing."

▲▼▲

Tony drives around all night. He wonders if Leo and Lenny are lying low. Tony doesn't think they got the sense to do that. He asks a few questions, but he can't do a whole lot of that. The guys who got answers are the guys he can't ask. He drives by the strip joints and doesn't see a thing. He tries the packing plants again. He drives by diners and cafés, and it's light when he gets into bed. Okay fine, he'll try again. There's no big rush. They got to turn up, and he'll be there when they do.

▲▼▲

It's after noon when he drops by again to see Sal. Sal doesn't ask why he isn't on the job. He sees the white jacket with the beads and he doesn't say a thing about that. He doesn't want to work Tony up, he wants to keep Tony cool.

"Hey, Tony," Sal says, "you're looking sharp. You had anything to eat? Vinnie, get Tony a couple of glazed."

"I'm fine," Tony says, and shakes his head no to Vinnie D. "So you call Ric or what?"

"I said I'd call, right?" Sal says. "So I called. Ricca says he fully understands. He says he knows how you feel."

"So it's okay or not?"

Sal forgets he's trying to be nice. Fuck it, you can't be nice to this prick. "Just listen, okay? You got no fucking manners. You got to talk, you don't listen to nobody else. Ric says he's going to get back. He says he knows you understand this ain't a good time. He says he don't like to see the Scozarris get away with this shit. He says he'll see what he can do."

"When?" Tony says.

"When what?"

"When's he going to get back?"

This burns Sal up. He doesn't like Tony's attitude at all. "Mickey Ricca gets back to you, pal, when Mickey Ricca wants to get back," he tells Tony. "That is fucking good enough for you. In the meantime, you keep your nose clean. You boost some cars for me like you're supposed to be doing right now. You don't do nothing else but that. You got that, Tony?"

"I got it, Sal."

"Fine. You got it, I'm glad to hear you got it. I'm glad I'm getting through."

"Maybe you should ought to try a smoke signal, Sal," grins Vinnie D.

"Maybe I got a signal for you," Tony says. He looks right at Vinnie D., and Vinnie doesn't smile anymore.

"Both of you, just shut the fuck up," Sal says. He flips Tony a white envelope. "From Ric. He wants you to have it."

"What is it?"

"It's a Easter card," Sal says. "What you think it is? Go on, get some work done. You got a whole half a day."

Sal watches Tony leave. He doesn't like what's going on at all. He wishes Indians would stay on the tube. He likes to watch them on the tube. They can't cause him any grief in there, they got their hands full with the Duke. What Mickey Ricca said to Sal was, "Sal, you keep that crazy Indian on ice. Give him five bills from me. Make godamn sure he don't do something me and the old man don't want to hear. I'll be in touch. You stay where I can get you on the phone."

Sal wonders where Ricca thinks he'll go. He never goes anywhere at all. So maybe Ricca thinks that's funny, it's a joke. So go fuck yourself, Sal thinks, but he doesn't think it very loud.

What Sal doesn't like about this is he knows who Ric is going to call if Tony gets out of line, and he figures that's exactly what Tony's going to do. So what's Sal going to do about that? Chase him down the street? The truth is, Tony Red Dog scares the shit out of Sal, and he figures maybe Tony knows it too.

▲▼▲

Tony doesn't go back to work. He goes to a movie instead then walks down to Otto's for a steak. The envelope he's got has three-hundred bucks from Mickey Ric. Which means Mickey Ric told Sal to give him five. Tony knows what it's for. Mickey Ricca's tossing him a bone. He's not going to do shit. He's going to tell him that he can't make the hit.

On one side of the coin, he sees maybe Mickey Ricca's right. Tony keeps his eyes open all the time. He knows more about the family business than a guy like Vinnie D. Sal sent him on a hijack deal once or twice with Daddy Jones, who's pretty high in the South Side blacks. Tony got along fine with Daddy Jones, who said he'd never seen a greaseball Indian before and even bought Tony a beer. So Tony knows the family's getting friendly with the blacks, and he knows there's got to be a reason why. Whatever that is, Tony figures the old man will end up on the top, and everyone else under that.

Tony understands all this and maybe Ricca's got a point, but it doesn't get Tony what he wants. He can't get the girl off his mind. That was an awful thing to do. About as bad as you can get. He can't let guys say the Indian's a real easy touch. You want to grind up his girl it's okay, he won't do a damn thing. Guys are talking like that, you can't show your face on the street. And if he waits for Mickey Ric, that's the way it's going to be.

While Tony is finishing off his steak, he looks up and spots a great looking broad across the room. He likes what he sees because the broad is looking right at him, too. He raises up his glass like he's seen in the movies and the girl seems to like that a lot. She likes it so much she leaves the bar and starts her way across the room. Tony likes the way she moves. She's built just right but she doesn't look cheap. She's taller than he thought and her dress is all black with no jewelry at all, like a girl in a fashion magazine. Her hair is classy too, real light blond and flipping up kind of cute on the ends.

She walks right up to his table. Just stands there and smiles. Doesn't say a thing. It hits Tony then and he stands up quick and gets her chair.

"I'm Jill," the girl says.

"Right, I'm Tony," Tony says. "What do you like to drink?"

"White wine will be fine."

Class, Tony thinks, and says, "Hey, I'll have one of those too."

She's got a little black purse like the dress. The purse is so little it couldn't hold a quarter and a dime.

"You're an Indian, right?" Jill says, this coming right out of left field. The way she says it, though, it doesn't turn him off.

"Yeah, I guess I am," Tony says.

"What kind?"

"Mescalero Apache."

"No kidding?"

"Hey, I ever lie to you before?"

The girl laughs. She's got kind of blue eyes, and one side of her mouth turns up like she's telling some joke to herself.

"I'm nuts about the jacket," Jill says.

"It's nothin'," Tony says. "I got better stuff than this. I go somewhere nice, I got a closet full of stuff. I bet I got a hundred shirts."

"So you do that a lot?"

"Do what?"

"Go somewhere nice."

Tony's getting the message straight. This doll is saying let's make a deal.

"Yeah," Tony says. "I been known to go out. I'm a fun kinda guy."

"So what do you do?" Jill says.

"I'm in cars."

"Buying or selling?"

"Just selling. No buying. And what about you?"

"I'm an actress," Jill says.

"Oh, yeah?" This is maybe going to cost a little more, Tony thinks. A girl says 'actress' she isn't some hooker walks the street, she's got a place somewhere and the price is going to go through the roof.

"So look," Tony says, "you want to take off now, you want another drink, what?"

The little smile around her mouth disappears. "Sorry," she says. "I guess I made a big mistake."

"What? How come?" Tony doesn't get this at all.

"I shouldn't ever ought to do it," Jill says. "I mean you see a guy you like and say hello, that isn't going to work. You do that, the guy's for sure going to get the wrong idea. A girl can't do that 'cause the guy's going to think something else which is just what you're thinking right now."

She reaches in her purse and gets a little gold pen and writes something on the napkin by her drink.

"Listen, I think you're a real nice guy," she tells Tony with a smile. "You change your mind, you want to think about me like you're not thinking now, you got my number there to call."

She gets up and plants a kiss on his cheek, and Tony feels her hair brush his nose. He gets a little whiff of perfume then she's gone before he knows what to do.

Jesus, what kind of broad is this? Tony follows her out the door with his eyes. The most terrific looking girl he's ever seen and now she's gone. He feels kind of dizzy and he knows he didn't drink enough for that, he knows how to hold his booze. That's a crock bout an Indian can't hold his booze, he can drink as good as anyone around. So he knows what it is, he doesn't have to think about it twice. It isn't just her bod, there's that too, but it's something more than that. He loves this girl is what it is. He doesn't even know her last name, but he knows he's got it bad.

▲▼▲

First thing in the morning, Mickey Ricca's in the old man's Caddy, wishing he was still at home in bed. Don Fischetti doesn't hardly ever sleep, so when he's got to go out which is maybe twice a year, he's up and out at six. He's got a meet at noon he doesn't care. Drive around, he tells Danny, and Danny drives around.

The Caddy's all green outside and in. The old man likes green. Fischetti and Ric are in the back. Danny Fusco drives, and Bennie's son Joey's next to him. Joey's got egg on the back of his shirt. Egg, and a little crumb of toast. How did the dummy do that? Ricca thinks. How the fuck can a guy get breakfast on his back?

"The thing with Tranalone," Bennie says, "the thing with him, he likes to talk. Dominic likes to talk. Listen, let him say what he's got to say. It don't mean a thing, you got to listen all the same."

"That's the way he is," Ric agrees. "I seen him do it all the time. He'll start on something, he's off on something else. He gets done, you don't know what he said."

"Horse," Bennie says. "Horse is the guy you want to watch. What Horse Calise says, Dominic is thinking in his head. Tranalone talks an hour and a half. Horse says maybe two words. Two words, that's all you got to know."

"The Horse is smart," Ricca says. "You got to give him that. I wouldn't put the guy down."

"You do, and you make a big mistake," Bennie says. "Anyone sees through the scam that's Horse. Dominic, he isn't going to see. You talk, you don't have the time to think."

The old man leans back and takes a nap. Danny drives around. The Caddy gets six, maybe seven miles to the gallon, so Ric figures he's got to stop for gas. Joey likes to ride; he sees some grade-school girl on a bike, and watches till she gets out of sight.

"The thing with the Indian," Bennie says.

"It's okay," Ricca says.

"I don't need a problem," Bennie says. "You got a guy he's black or maybe red. Maybe he's a Chink. You got a problem's what you got."

"You got my word, Don Fischetti," Ricca says.

"That Joey," Bennie says, giving Ric a nudge. "Always got his nose in a book. He don't read no junk he's reading high class stuff. He's reading something all the time."

Ricca's seen Joey read. Joey's got a stack of *Classic Comics* on the seat.

"Hey, you gotta be proud," Ricca says.

▲▼▲

Tony doesn't sleep at all. He knows he ought to look for the Scozarris but he sits around the room. He can't watch the TV. He doesn't want to eat. What he wants to do is call up the girl but it's the middle of the night. He wants to call her up now and tell her how he knows he's been a jerk. They can go somewhere and talk. Eat anywhere she wants. He won't try nothing funny, he won't even touch her till they know each other for a week. Jesus, he hopes she won't hold him to that.

He gets out early on the job. If he's working, he won't have to think about calling up the girl. He's afraid if he does she'll turn him down. She said he could call, but that doesn't mean she won't turn him down.

He's got a special order he's got to fill Porsches, and they got to be showroom new. This kind of car's not as common as your Chevys or your Fords, but Tony gets the job done quick. Cars are like people, Tony knows; they like to hang around their own kind. So he hits some classy tennis courts and a couple of country clubs, and by noon he's got five stashed in Dio's garage, ready for the guys to go to work. Even Dio's impressed, but Tony doesn't care about that. What he cares about is calling up the girl.

▲▼▲

Jill doesn't say no she says yes. Tony can't believe his luck. She says fine, she'll go out tonight if Tony wants, if Tony's got his act together and intends to treat her right. Tony says great, that's the way it's going to be. Jill tells him that she'll meet him at eight and tells him where.

Tony thinks about an hour what to wear. He wants to wear the white jacket with the beads but she's seen that before. He wears that, she'll think he don't have nothing else. He goes through everything he's got and ends up in his blue ostrich boots and a western-cut suit. The suit's kind of off-yellow white and there's a rattlesnake stitched on the back. The snake's got a genuine rattle sewn on with simulated ruby eyes. He looks in the mirror and he figures this will knock her on her ass.

The place where Jill says to meet her is a bar called 'A Streetcar Named Michelle.' Tony doesn't care much for bars with funny names. They usually got funny-looking people inside. Fags in tight pants and broads with purple hair. So he's glad to see this isn't that kind of place at all. There are people here in jeans and running shoes, and people in businessman suits. A girl in a waitress outfit and a guy in greasy coveralls, like the guys down at Dio's garage. There's maybe a couple of fags but not a lot of funny hair.

Jill spots him and makes her way through the crowd, and Tony goes weak in the knees. Christ, she looks great. A white woolly sweater and a skirt and nice heels. She's got something sparkly in her hair and her eyes are bright as Christmas tree lights.

"Hi," Jill says, "say I *love* those boots. Tony, you look *out*standing."

"Hey, so do you," Tony says. "Listen, you ain't seen the back of the suit." Tony turns around and Jill lets out a kind of shriek and says she's never seen anything like that before, and Tony's glad he had the sense to dress right.

Jill pulls him through the crowd and introduces him to everyone she knows, which includes some terrific looking broads. Everyone there is an actor or an actress, Jill says, only mostly they're doing something else. Tony has a few drinks, and starts to like everyone he meets. They don't talk like real people do but he likes them all the same.

And later on when they're out in the car trying to figure where to eat, Jill scoots in close and leans her head on his arm and Tony figures this is going to work. The girl's high class but she's got to come around. A nice dinner and that wine she likes to drink he's going to have her in the sack.

"So tell me about yourself," Jill says.

"There isn't anything to tell," Tony says.

"Come on, sure there is." She gives him a little toy hit that warms his heart. "Like, where'd you grow up?"

Tony doesn't like to talk about this but he does. "Arizona. On the Fort Apache Indian Reservation."

"Not good, huh?" She can tell that easy by his voice.

"It was okay, I guess."

"I don't think it was."

"Yeah, well you're right."

"So you got out of there."

"When I was fourteen, maybe fifteen. Something like that. Worked on a couple of ranches and other stuff."

"Then you got into cars."

"Right. Tucson and Phoenix. All over."

"And then you came here."

"Yeah. And then up here." Tony figures maybe that's about enough. "Look, what do you like to eat? Steak, seafood. You name it."

"Seafood's fine," Jill says.

"Terrific," Tony says, glad to talk on something that's not about him, "There's a place over on the east side, they got lobster they ship in fresh. They got 'em swimming in a tank."

"Hey, great," Jill says, "I haven't had a—*Jesus*, Tony!"

Jill has to slam her hands on the dash because Tony's suddenly turned the car around in the middle of the street. Guys are honking and yelling but Tony don't hear anyone at all. He just pulls up and stops because right there's the cream-colored Buick Lenny drives, parked at a Rodeway Inn. Christ, what's he going to do? He's got Jill in the car and everything's going real fine. If he dumps her off now he isn't going to get her back. If he waits and comes back, the Scozarris are going to maybe be gone.

"Look," he tells Jill, "I'll be right back. Sit tight, it's okay."

"What's going on?" Jill says. "What're you going to do?" She maybe looks a little scared.

Tony puts on an easy smile. "I seen a car back there. A guy owes me for the car. The guy's a deadbeat. You got to get these guys when you can."

"Yeah, right," Jill says, and doesn't look like she's buying this at all.

Tony gives her a wink and gets out and shuts the door. He stops for a minute at the trunk and gets a sawed-off pump and an old potato sack and puts the gun in the sack and walks back to the Rodeway Inn.

He doesn't know if they parked the car right before their door but his luck is running good. Leo opens up the door when Tony knocks and Tony jams the shotgun in his face.

Leo looks sick, like he might throw up.

"Inside," Tony says, and looks around fast to find Lenny. He can hear the shower going and that's another lucky break.

"It's about that fuckin' girl," Leo says.

"Sit down," Tony says, and Leo sits.

"So let's talk," Leo says.

"Let's not," Tony says. He picks up a cushion from the couch and tosses it in Leo's lap. Leo grabs the cushion and looks surprised and Tony jams the shotgun up against the cushion and there isn't hardly any noise at all. Tony pockets the empty shell and peeks in the bathroom door and the room is full of steam. He goes in and opens up the shower door. Lenny is all lathered up. He's hairy as a dog. There's a little more noise this time but not much because Lenny's pretty fat. Tony turns off the water and makes sure he's got both empties in his pocket. He wipes down the gun with a towel and leaves it on the sink and takes a look at his watch. Three, maybe four minutes. He's sorry Lenny didn't get to see who it was but Tony can't complain. One more thing to do and he's gone. Hey, the night's turning out great.

▲▼▲

It's not hardly morning when the phone wakes him up. He grabs it without even looking and Sal says, "Listen I got a message from Ric you're going to like. Ric says it ain't a good time but he thinks you got a right. This is a personal favor from Mickey Ric is what it is."

Tony sees Jill's kicked off the covers and the sun's making stripes across her back, but Sal's got his full attention now.

"You're saying Ric don't mind," Tony says. "It's okay."

"What the fuck you think," Sal says. "I gotta say it twice? A couple of the guys, they seen the car. It's at a Rodeway Inn past the loop. You get off your ass you'll catch 'em cold."

It's warm in the room, but Tony feels a chill. "Right," he says, trying to keep what he's thinking to himself. "That's great, Sal. I appreciate the call."

"So get it done," Sal says. "Do it now. I don't want to hear you complaining no more. Get it done. And hey, I want to see you here at three-forty-five."

"Why three-forty-five?" Tony says.

"Why the fuck not?" Sal says, and hangs up.

Tony sits on the bed and looks at the phone. Like maybe Sal will say something else. Something that will stop the empty feeling in his gut.

Jill sits up and stretches and looks at her watch. "My God, I got to get to work," she says. "Who was that on the phone?"

"Get up," Tony says. "Get dressed." He's still looking at the phone.

"Huh? What's with you?"

"Just do it. Hurry up." Tony's pulling on his pants and looking for his boots. Jill is standing there naked still looking half asleep. She looks great. Tony wonders why you got to do stuff that you don't want to do when you'd rather be doing something else.

"You mind telling me what?" Jill says. She looks even better with her hands on her hips.

"Let's go," Tony says. "Get somethin' on."

"Last night it was get something off."

"Last night ain't today," Tony says, and starts picking up her clothes off the floor.

▲▼▲

Tony's slamming gears and Jill is still complaining. She's got the mirror down, and trying to get her lipstick straight and Tony's taking corners like he might make the Indy this year.

"I don't care for your lousy driving style," Jill says.

"I'm driving just fine," Tony says.

"I lose my job I am moving in with you," Jill says. "I got to have some breakfast, Tony. I'm no good I don't eat. Just let me out here. Let me out I'll get a cab."

"Listen, I got a problem," Tony says. "What I got is deep shit. I got to think. I don't got the time to eat."

"Okay, fine. That's fine," Jill says. The way Tony looks, the way he talks, says now is a real good time to keep quiet and hope Tony doesn't run into a truck.

In a minute Tony stops and makes a call. Twenty minutes after that he pulls up behind the South Side Bowl-O-Lot and stops. There's another car there, a red Caddy with a lot of extra chrome. Tony doesn't say a thing to Jill. He takes the keys and gets out and walks across to the other car.

Daddy Jones is standing by the Caddy. He looks like a spider in a Panama suit. Big shades, and a lot of white teeth.

"Listen, I got trouble," Tony says.

"I expect you do," says Daddy Jones. "Going to happen, you working for the white-eyes, man. Them treaties don't mean shit."

"You want to hear this or not?" Tony says. Daddy Jones is too cool. Nothing bothers Daddy Jones and that irritates Tony a lot.

"My meter running, babe," says Daddy Jones.

Tony talks, Daddy Jones listens. After a while, Daddy Jones listens real good. When Tony's through, Daddy Jones thinks a long time.

"Keemo-sahby, this real heavy shit," says Daddy Jones.

"Tell me about it," Tony says.

"Got to talk to my man. Won't tell you a thing before I do."

"I know that. I know you got to do that."

Daddy Jones takes off his shades and looks Tony in the eye. "Man, you best be hittin' me straight. This better not be no jive."

"I am in enough shit without messing around with you," Tony says.

"I hear that," says Daddy Jones. He gives Tony a card with a number on the back. Tony goes back to his car.

Jill doesn't say a thing. She smokes and takes turns crossing one leg over the next. Tony drives a few blocks and then finds another phone. He calls Bennie Fischetti at his home. He knows Bennie doesn't take any calls, but some guy will give the old man his name.

Tony gets back in the car. He doesn't drive and he doesn't look at Jill.

"Okay, look," Tony says. "Who you doing this for? Who you supposed to call?"

For a minute Jill doesn't say a thing. Then she looks at Tony real surprised. "Tony, what are you talking about? You lost me there, hon."

Tony reaches over and holds her chin straight, not hard or anything, just enough so she doesn't turn away. "Listen," he says. "I'm not a bad guy, and maybe you'd have come on to me anyway, okay? Maybe not. But too much funny shit is happening to me, and I figure it's got to be you. I like you a lot. I'm not going to do nothing to you, all right? I ain't even mad. But you're going to have to tell me how it is."

"Oh, Jesus, Tony." Jill looks like she's going to cry. Tony lets her go.

"Sal or Mickey Ricca?" Tony says.

"Sal," Jill says. Her eyes are getting wet and she reaches up with a finger and wipes her cheek. "I hate this shit, you know? I had to. He didn't give me any choice."

"I know that," Tony says. "So what are you supposed to do?"

"Sal said it was a joke."

"Yeah it is. It's on me."

"Sal, he—all I know is he's supposed to call you this morning and tell you something to do. I don't know what. I don't know a thing about that. I guess that was him on the phone."

"He knew you'd be at my place."

Jill looks at her hands. "I wanted to be there anyway, Tony. You don't have to believe that but it's true."

"So what else?"

"He's going to call me at home. About noon. I'm supposed to tell him what I think you're going to do, anything I heard you say, which is nothing, by the way." She looks at Tony now. She's glad this is over, and Tony doesn't have to prompt her anymore. "Tomorrow night, Sal says I hit these clubs and bars and like I'm supposed to be all swacked out, you know? Boozed up. And I let on as how I was with you today and I saw you—do something. I don't even know what. Sal's supposed to tell me that."

"Jesus..." Tony lets out a breath. It's about like he figured only worse. That godamn Ricca's thought the whole thing out. Even down to Jill spreading the word at some Tranalone bar that he's hit the Scozarris. Just a little extra insurance which is Ric all the way. Whatever, the guy is going to nail it down and you got to give him that. And then Jill sort of drops out of sight like forever, only Jill doesn't know about that, which is something Sal sort of left out. Everything's falling into place and he knows why Sal said 3:45, and this burns Tony up, because this is the time Mickey Ricca gets a shave and a shine every day down at Gold's, which is close to the donut shop. The son of a bitch wants to watch. He wants to sit in his barber chair and watch Tony go, he wants the fun of doing that.

Tony thinks for a minute but he knows this is what he's got to do, that he's got to trust the girl, and he's not too worried once he tells her how Ricca don't exactly plan to keep her around.

"Okay, look," Tony says, "I'm going to lay this out on the line. Don't ask a bunch of dumb questions, just listen."

Tony tells her how he works for Sal and Ric and the Bennie Fischetti family, which he figures that she already knows, and how he had this beef with the Scozarris only Ric wouldn't let him work it out.

"So when Sal calls this morning and says fine, go ahead," Tony says, "I know right off I been fucked. If Ric says fine I'm set up and I know what Ric's going to do, I hit the Scozarris then Ric hits me. See, this makes the old man look good. The hit ain't business, so Bennie makes it up to the Tranalones and they figure how Bennie's getting old and ain't strong anymore and really wants to make peace. So the Tranalone family gets sucked in good and goes to sleep while Bennie makes a deal with the blacks. What you gotta understand is I ain't even a big player in this. What I am is a little extra angle for Mickey Ric. He looks good with the boss and he gets me out of his hair. Which is what he's been wanting all along because he don't want an Indian working for the family. This is no big news to me. This I already know."

"Oh, my God." Jill bites her lip and looks as if she might cry again. "So what are you going to do? I mean, there's got to be—" Her face brightens up like she's just had a great idea. "Tony. Tony, look—if you *don't* do anything to these Scozarri people, Ricca's plan won't work! Don't you see?" She reaches out and holds his hand tight. "I mean, you get out of town right now, Tony we could do that together, we do that and nothing's going to happen at all. Tony, I'd really like that. Honest. I really would."

"Yeah, well we got a little problem there," Tony says. He tells her how this is maybe not such a good idea since he's already done the Scozarris only nobody knows about that so it's going to be hard to back out.

"You what?" Jill looks kind of white. "When—when did you do that?"

Tony tells her when and she looks like she might get sick, either that or maybe hit him in the face.

"My God, what the hell kind of thing is that to do you got a date," she wants to know. "You take a girl out, the very first date you do that. I cannot be*lieve* this."

"Listen, it kind of came up," Tony says. "Something comes up that's what you got to do."

Jill doesn't want to talk. She turns away and looks out the front and does things with her lips, and Tony knows a broad does that there's no use trying to make her talk.

▲▼▲

Tony gets her calmed down and then stops at a drive-in spot and gets her a breakfast to go. Jill feels better after that, so he tells her what it is they've got to do. Jill listens, and it's clear she doesn't like this at all. What she'd really like to do is pack a bag and leave town. Catch a plane to L.A. or Mexico and dye her hair. Change her name to Mary Smith. She knows that's not how it's going to be. If she goes along with Sal which she doesn't want to do she's got a real short weekend ahead. With Tony Red Dog she's got a chance. Not a whole lot because Tony's full of crazy ideas that won't work but it's too late to think about that.

Tony lets her off at her apartment and makes sure he's got her phone number right.

"Take it easy," he says. "Do what you got to do you'll be fine. You're going to be just fine."

Jill gives him a look. "Don't you tell me I'll be fine. Don't you say that to me."

"Okay I won't."

Tony starts to drive off, and Jill leans in the window and plants a nice kiss on his mouth. "You're going to be just fine," Jill says.

"Yeah, right," Tony says.

He leaves her there and goes half a mile and stops at a booth to call Bennie Fischetti again. The old man won't talk, but the word will get

through that he called. Now he's got to wait. It isn't even noon he's got
to wait. Drive around and get back to Jill and check in with Daddy Jones
and then drive around some more. He thinks about Sal and Mickey Ric
and how this is going to go down, but mostly he thinks about Jill. She's
got a smile that won't quit and she's great in the sack but he isn't much in
love anymore. Some but not a lot. She really set him up good and he can
understand that, but this kind of takes the shine off of things. Like they
maybe can't really hit it off. This really brings him down and he doesn't
want to think about that, he's got a lot of shit to do.

▲▼▲

Tony pulls up at the donut shop right at 3:45. Everything looks fine.
It looks like an ordinary day. Inside, Sal is sitting in the back. He's got
donut powder on his mouth, he's got coffee down his shirt. Bobby Gallo
and Vinnie are there too. Bobby Gallo gives Tony a grin. Vinnie D. tries
to look like there's nothing going down, but Vinnie's not smart enough
for that.

"Hey, Tony," Sal says, and even Sal's got a smile. "Have a seat, you
want a glazed?"

Tony sits. He knows he's okay, it's not going to happen here.

"So listen," Sal says, and leans as close to the table as he can, "How'd
it go, you get it done?"

"Right after breakfast," Tony says.

Sal gets a kick out of this. He's shaking all over which is something
else to see.

"Jesus. Right after breakfast," Sal says. He's spitting donut powder on
his shirt. "Leo and Lenny. Like brushing your teeth, huh, Tony? Huh? Huh?"

Sal laughs and looks at Bobby and Vinnie D., and they think this
is the funniest thing they ever heard. Boy, everyone's having a lot of
fun, Tony thinks, and he sees how Bobby and Vinnie D. are kind of
edging past Sal, Vinnie pretending he's got to sneeze, and Bobby going
back for more glazed, which puts them both right behind Tony's chair.
These guys are smooth, Tony thinks. These guys are slick as Goofy
and Donald Duck.

Now Sal's not laughing anymore. Nothing's funny now that Vinnie
and Bobby Gallo are where they ought to be.

"Tony, we got to talk," Sal says.

"Fine," Tony says. "You told me to be here, Sal, so here I am."

Sal shakes his head. "Not here."

"Not here what?"

"I mean this ain't where you and me got to talk."

Tony tries to look puzzled and surprised. "Sal, just what the fuck is this? You want to tell me what? I'm not any good at playing games."

Sal looks at Tony, serious and kind of sad, only Tony knows the sad isn't real.

"You carrying, Tony?" Sal wants to know.

"No I'm not carrying," Tony says. "Should I be?"

Sal looks at Bobby Gallo, and Bobby says, "Stand up, Tony, okay?" He says it real nice.

Tony stands and lets Bobby shake him down.

"Jesus Christ, Sal." Tony tries to look scared. "You're not gonna do me. Listen, what the hell for?"

"Nothing personal, Tony," Sal says. "It's business, it's just business is all."

"Fuck that," Tony says. "Hey. Whatever this is we can work something out."

"If I could do that, Tony, I would," Sal says. "There ain't nothing I can do."

And then Tony sees something that he's never seen before. He can't hardly believe what he sees which is Sal Galiano getting up. Jesus, it's worth getting hit to see that. There probably aren't four or five guys ever seen this before. This is not your plain everyday standing up. This is a major operation. This is a dumb Jap movie where the lips and the sound don't match; this thing's coming up from the mud, it's going to fuck up Tokyo good, it's going to dump a bunch of donuts on the Japs. Tony knows it wasn't Sal's idea, that Mickey Ric told Sal he had to handle this himself, but Tony feels pretty good. How many guys have got Sal Galiano on his feet?

▲▼▲

When they get in Sal's car, Tony in back with Bobby Gallo, Sal up front with Vinnie D., Tony feels a little lump in his gut. He's felt okay until now. Now he don't feel right at all. He's thinking how he's screwed himself good. He's thinking maybe half a dozen things can go wrong, and he'll have to try to grab Bobby's piece, which Bobby's not about to let him do. He's thinking maybe Jill had the right idea: Get out of town and don't fuck with Mickey Ric. Instead here he is watching Sal take up the front seat and squeezing Vinnie out the door.

"Sal, listen," Tony says. "I got to make a call. You got to let me make a call."

This gets a laugh from up front. "You got to be kidding," Sal says.

"I'm kidding, a time like this? Sal, I got to make a call. I got to talk to Bennie Fischetti. That's who I gotta call."

"You're stalling," Sal says. "Shit, I'd do the same thing if I was you. I'd do the same thing. Tony, the old man ain't going to help. You got to learn to relax. That's what you want to do. Don't think about nothing at all. It won't take a minute, it's over like that."

"Relax," Tony says.

"That's the thing to do. That's the best thing to do."

Tony sees they're going up First, past the pawn shops and the bum hotels toward the Freeway east and out of town. He knows where they're going, he knows the way they got to take. He and Bobby Gallo and Vinnie have been out there once before, when Eddie Pliers got greedy with the skim. The Tranalone family's got their meat packing plants; Bennie Fischetti's got a marsh. The Minellis had the marsh before that, which means there's stiffs out there from like 1922, and it's not a good place to stop and fish, you don't know what you'll maybe catch.

"You got to let me call," Tony says. "Fuck, it's not going to cost you a thing. I'm paying for the call, Sal, I got to talk to the old man. I got to do that."

"What for?" Sal wants to know. Or maybe he doesn't care, he's got nothing else to do.

"I can't say what for."

"So don't."

Tony seems to think about that. "Okay. It's about Mickey Ricca. That's what it's about." They're passing Eighth. They're passing through a neighborhood's going to the dogs, half the buildings empty, a few sleazy bars, stores going out of business every day.

Sal turns his neck around as far as it will go, which is maybe half an inch. "What you want to do back there is relax," Sal says. "You don't want to be thinking up shit because it isn't going to do you no good. Okay? Just shut the fuck up. Think about a broad. Something. Don't talk."

"You hear what I gotta say," Tony says, "you're not going to say don't talk. You're going to thank me is what you're going to do. You're going to say, hey, thanks, Tony. This is what you're going to do."

"Shut the fuck up," Sal says.

"Yeah, right."

"So what about Ric?"

"Forget it. It's got to be the old man."

"Fuck you," Sal says. "We'll do a seance thing. Bobby knows a gypsy broad. You can talk to the old man then."

Vinnie thinks this is a riot, and Bobby does too. They're coming up on Seventeenth and the Freeway's six, maybe seven blocks away, and Tony's thinking, shit, this is it, it isn't coming down and I'm feeding the fish. I been set up twice, and both times by the same fucking broad. And then they pass Nineteenth and here's a Caddy pulled up by a cigar store with a window patched up with silver tape, and coming out of this store is Daddy Jones. Daddy Jones and Tommy "Horse" Calise. Daddy Jones, the Horse, and Mickey Ric.

"Holy shit, look at that!" Vinnie says, and slows the car and stares at what he sees.

"Jesus," Sal says, "keep driving. Don't stop the fucking car." Sal looks at Mickey Ric and Mickey Ric looks back, and it's hard to say who's staring harder at who. Daddy Jones ducks his head. Horse tries to turn away, tries to get back in the store, but there's no mistaking Horse. Now the car's past and there's nothing else to see and nobody says a thing. There isn't anything to say except the two *consiglieres* of the two biggest families in town are standing back there together with the number two South Side black. Standing there like asshole buddies which is not the kind of thing you want to see.

"I'm talking, you don't listen," Tony says. "I got to make a call, you say, Tony, you ain't making any call."

"Call," Sal says. "Vinnie, find a phone. The guy's got to make a call."

▲▼▲

Mickey Ricca tells the old man this is all a bunch of crap. It wasn't Horse at all it was some other guy, and anyway the colored had a piece in his hand all the time. He had a piece in his hand and Ricca couldn't do a thing. The fuckers pick him up, he's on the way to get a shine, he can't do a damn thing, and this Indian's behind all this is who it is.

Bennie Fischetti's old, he's not dumb. It could happen just the way Ricca says and it looks kind of fishy, hell it stinks is what it does, Sal and these guys they're passing by and there's Calise and the black and Mickey Ric, they just happen to walk out of this store, and who's going to buy something like that?

Only Bennie can't see how the Indian could be that stupid, he sets up a deal like this any kid could see through. An Indian's smart, he's got cunning in his blood. A deer shits somewhere he can follow it for miles. An Indian can sneak up on a fort. You don't even know he's there. And the Indian tried to call. He tried to call him all day. Bennie knows about that. And Sal Galiano, he saw the whole thing, Sal swears it was the Horse, how's a guy mistake the Horse?

And of course that's the thing, Bennie can't check it out with the Horse, he can't ask. The Horse wouldn't give Bennie the time of day. Anything's wrong in the Fischetti family, fine. That's fine with Horse Calise and Dominic Tranalone. And he can't ask the colored. What a colored's going to do he's going to lie. That's what your colored's got to do.

So Bennie don't know, he's got no way to get to the truth. What he knows is if Ric's talking straight he's let the Indian set him up. A guy fucks up once he can maybe do it twice and Bennie doesn't like to wait for that. A guy gets careless, he can bring you down quick. So maybe Ric's clean this time, he's maybe not. He's clean today so tomorrow's something else. Mickey Ric's a good man and Mickey's smart, but a guy that smart doesn't like to stay down he likes to move, and the way he likes to move is up. Besides, Bennie's thinking how Ric hasn't ever treated Joey good at all. Benny knows the kid's not bright, but Ric could show him some respect. Ric laughs at Joey and this is something Ric shouldn't ought to do.

Bennie calls in Nick Cannatella who's the *caporegime* for dope. He gives Nick a glass of wine and has a talk; when Nick leaves, he's the Fischetti family's new *consigliere*. Nick's a guy who's always treated Joey nice and he's got the whole family's respect.

Bennie sends Sal to Minnesota, where the family's getting heavy into cheese, a job where Sal won't have a whole lot to do and if he does he's got Bobby and Vinnie D. to help. Tony Red Dog gets Sal's old job, and now he's *caporegime* for hijacking trucks and heisting cars. Bennie gives Tony five Gs because he likes Tony's style, and Tony gives two of this to Jill who finds a sudden need for Caribbean sun. Tony gives a grand to the actor guy Jill dug up to play the Horse, which he did real fine, considering Horse isn't the easiest guy to do.

Bennie feels kind of bad when he's got to tell Ric the bad news; hey, a guy's got his faults, he's been around a long time he's done a job. Bennie tells Ric it's nothing personal, it's business is what it is, he wants Ric to see it that way. Bennie tells Danny Fusco to use the green Caddy, the one Bennie likes best, he wants Ric to know how he feels.

▲▼▲

The first day on his new job, Tony spots a girl named Cecile, she works in a club down the street. Cecile's got a bod that won't quit and black eyes, and Tony knows he hasn't really ever been in love before. In spite of Cecile's great shape she cashiers in the club and don't take nothing off, and Tony's got to respect her for that.

He's been the new *capo* for two, maybe three or four days, he makes sure the guys on the street know Tony Red Dog pays his debts, this is something he feels he's got to do. He's got an idea what, because something's smelling ripe in the trunk and he remembers what it is. So he takes the potato sack out and finds a box and gets some real nice paper to wrap it up, and mails the scalps he took from the Scozarris to Dominic Tranalone. Of course he checks this out with Don Fischetti first, and Bennie, who don't think a whole lot is funny, gets a real laugh out of this, and thinks the Indian guy is okay. Listen, for a red colored guy he's okay.

The Last Cardinal Bird in Tennessee

A ONE-ACT PLAY

THE TIME: *The near future*

THE SET: *The set is a shabby, dimly-lit kitchen, the reflection of a run-down high-tech world where everything is broken, and nothing gets fixed. This is tomorrow held together by a string.*

A weak beam of sunlight slants through a narrow window. The light captures dust motes in the air. The sun itself is seen occasionally through a choking industrial haze; it tells us all we need to know about the scarcities, turmoil and ecological problems of the world outside.

HOWARD is a character in the play, but he is also a part of the set. He sits in a life-support wheelchair to stage left, apart from the area of action. His chair is a patched-up array of plastic and copper tubing, wires and makeshift braces and supports. Fluids pump sluggishly through the system—and through HOWARD himself. He is totally confined within this torturous maze; only his head is wholly visible.

THE BABY is in a bottle on the kitchen shelf. Light seems to emerge from the bottle. As the play opens, the bottle is shrouded by a bird cage cover.

THE CHARACTERS: *LOUISE ANN is an overage Southern Belle. She retains her dignity by living in the past. CARLA is Puerto Rican and street-wise. She no longer remembers—or cares—which of her many "adventures" are true. It is possible that LOUISE ANN and CARLA are thirty and look forty. Or maybe they are forty and look fifty. They look a bit like bag ladies in their very best clothes. Times are hard.*

(Kitchen door opens on STAGE RIGHT. LOUISE ANN enters first, carrying a patched cloth sack of groceries. A shotgun on a frayed string is slung over one shoulder. She wears an air-filter apparatus over her nose and mouth. She removes the apparatus as she enters. CARLA comes in behind LOUISE ANN. She carries an assault rifle, and two sacks of groceries.)

CARLA: These guy, wha's he think? You hear these guy, you hear wha' he is sayin' to me? Like I am a love toy or somethin? I'm what, the flavor of the week? *(CARLA pushes her filter up on her head.)*

LOUISE ANN: *(Rolls her eyes to the ceiling as she sets her sack on a work table)* He *asked* you where the navy beans were, Carla. I believe that's what he said. *(She takes off her shotgun and leans it against the sink; she begins pawing through her sack)*

CARLA: Oh, sure. You see the guy's eyes? A man he tell you wha he is thinkin' with his eyes. He is sayin navy bean with his mouth, but he is thinkin big banana with his eyes, huh? Do I know this? Do I know wha I am sayin? I know wha I am sayin.

LOUISE ANN: *(Mouths silently along with her:)* Do I know what I am saying? I know what I am saying... *(These two have known one another a long time. They know each other's lines.)*

CARLA: *(Points to sack)* This is yours, that little one is mine. I don' buy out the whole store.

LOUISE ANN: Right there's fine. *(Glances at HOWARD)* Hi, honey, you doin all right? Ever'thing just fine?

CARLA: *(Waves, but makes no effort to look at HOWARD)* Hey, Howar', Merry Christmas.. Feliz Navidad...

LOUISE ANN: *(Pulls out pitiful twig about eight inches long, with tarnished ornaments and star)* I got the tree, Howard, isn't that nice? It's got a star and a ornament and ever'thing. I'll just put it right here. *(Walks toward HOWARD and sticks "tree" on one of his tubes)* You can see it real good, okay? You need anything? That's fine...

(All this is rhetorical. She doesn't look at HOWARD, though he makes an effort to get her attention)

(CARLA busies herself making tea, moving about)

CARLA: I don' think I am goin to do a tree. Is a lot of trouble, you know? Is just me, I don need a tree.

LOUISE ANN: Now you ought to get a tree. It just brightens things up so much.

CARLA: You got a family on the way. *(Kisses LOUISE ANN'S cheek)* Tha's a differen thing. Christmas with a little child in the house, huh?

LOUISE ANN: Howard and I are so happy. Aren't we, hon? *(Takes CARLA's hand, turns to kitchen shelf)*

CARLA: Hey, now don' wake him or nothin for me, don' do that...

LOUISE ANN: Why, it is perfectly all right. Hi, baby? Peek-a-boo. *(Lifts up bird cage cover to reveal baby in bottle)* Hi...here's your Aunt Carla come to see you.

CARLA: He*ll*o...

LOUISE ANN: He*ll*o, baby...

CARLA: He*ll*o...

LOUISE ANN: He*ll*o...

(CARLA and LOUISE ANN act "baby silly," alternately bobbing their heads toward the baby)

LOUISE ANN: Baby, you want to see the kitty? You want to see the little kitty? *(Picks up limp dead kitty on the end of a stick, waves it at baby)* Huh? Do you? Meow-meow. He just loves that ol' kitty. We couldn't keep pets at that other place.

CARLA: Meow-meow...Meow-meow...

(LOUISE ANN busies herself with sack; CARLA puts teacups on the counter)

LOUISE ANN: Shoot, couldn't do hardly anything there...and ever'thing all cramped up, nowhere to move around. Howard just hated it, didn't you, hon? *(Turns on small TV that is sitting on work table)* You start thinkin 'bout a chile, you got to think 'bout betterin yourself as well. Your lifestyle simply cannot remain the same as it was.

CARLA: *(Pause...looks at LOUISE ANN)* Louise Ann, what you think you goin to see on that thing, huh?

LOUISE ANN: *(Slightly irritated; this is a familiar routine between them)* Now they might be callin out names. They just might…

CARLA: Oh, right.

LOUISE ANN: Well they could, you don't know. It's Christmas time, Carla. They call out lots of names at Christmas. They could call out anybody's. They could call out yours, they could call out mine, they could call out someone you passed on the street…

CARLA: *(mouths silently)* …They could call out someone you passed on the street…

LOUISE ANN: You 'member Miz Toshiyama up in three-oh-nine? She's Korean or Thai or somethin, I don't know which. All those California types look alike to me…

(As LOUISE ANN is speaking, she pulls a black roach nearly three feet long from one of the sacks, and lays it on the work table)

LOUISE ANN: Anyway, she had this uncle, and they did his name right on the TV, and he doesn't live *ten* blocks away.

(As LOUISE ANN says ten, *she whacks the head off of the roach with a fierce stroke of the knife)*

LOUISE ANN: Makes you think is what it does. Ten blocks away. *(Glances at CARLA and raises a brow.)* You want to try an' think about the good things in life, you know? Attitude is ever'thing, honey. *(Finishes wrapping headless roach and puts it in the fridge.)* Plenty of trouble has come my way, and tried to intrude upon my life, and I have just said no, you will not come in, I simply will *not* allow it...

CARLA: I know these Miz Toshiyama somethin, up in three-oh-nine. Her hosbon, maybe she don't know it, but he is into suggestive talk, I tell you that. He catch me in the hall, he has these little bow, you know? He say, hey, I am really attracted to you a lot. He say, I will try to be polite at all times. Let me know, I seem to make unusual demands. I tell him, hey—you a Jap or somethin, right? Maybe you doin' somethin dirty right now, how'm I goin to know? Thas the thing, right? Focking men, they won't leave me alone, thas the truth. I arouse some kinda savage need. I gotta live with this.

(Behind CARLA's back, LOUISE ANN is mimicking her lines)

(The lights flicker, get dimmer and brighter. This is the first in a series of power failures...)

CARLA: Oh, great, here we go, right? Merry Christmas from the city to you and me. Maybe the air go out tonight. Maybe we all wake up dead Christmas Day.

(During CARLA's speech, the power failure begins to affect HOWARD's life-support system. A pipe pings, and a couple of spurts of red pulse out. HOWARD looks alarmed, but neither CARLA nor LOUISE ANN pay attention to the problem.)

LOUISE ANN: *(Peeling a wilted-looking vegetable)* You do *not* need to go

lookin for trouble, hon. Lord, when
I think. If you knew what life had in
store, I expect we'd spend all our time
in prayer.

CARLA: Me, I'm prayin all the time.
I'm sayin, Jesus, don' help me, okay?
Gimmie a break. Help somebody else
this year. Help some jerk in France.

LOUISE ANN: You can never guess
your fate, I know that. Me an' Howard
havin lunch just as nice as you please
on a Saturday afternoon? Howard
gets up and goes out, and walks right
into those terrorists at Sears. I swear,
you'd think even a bunch of Mideast
loonies'd have some respect for an
end-of-summer sale…Now him and me
both out of work and me with child.
'Course we ought to be thankful, knock
wood. *(An absent nod in HOWARD's
direction)* There's a lot worse off than
us, isn't there, hon?

*(HOWARD tries to make some sort of gesture with his mouth, but
nothing works)*

CARLA: I know these black guy, right?
He is workin in the office next to mine?
He say, listen, I had my eye on you a
long time. Like this I don' know, right?
He says, hey, les talk. He say, I gotta
quart of Idaho gin, I been savin it for
you. He say, I goin to jump-start you
battery, babe. I goin to give you sweet
content. I say, stop it, okay? You fall
inna toilet or what? The guy won't quit.
He say, I ain't talkin no plastic love,
babe. I am talkin penetration of you
sweet an' private parts. I say, right, I

am focking overcome with lust. I say, I
wan' some terminal disease, I go sit in a
crosstown bus, I don' gotta sit on you.

LOUISE ANN: Life has often dealt me
roles of quiet distress. Even before I
met Howard, my family had very little
luck shoppin discount stores. I lost
two brothers in retail accidents. Poor
Bob went out to Ward's and was set
upon by Mormons at a Fall Recliner
Sale...they said God didn't like us
leanin back...He was taken in a car
somewhere, and beaten severely about
the head. When they finally let him
go, he was captured by nuns south of
Reading, Pennsylvania, and forced to
mow lawns for some time. Bob just
wasn't right after that...My youngest
brother Will went to the Western Auto
Store and vanished out of sight. Mama
thinks he might've got into an alternate
style of life. The boy was keen on
fashion magazines.

(LOUISE ANN stops what she is doing, and leans into the TV)

LOUISE ANN: What's he sayin now?
Turn that up, Carla, he might be doin
names.

CARLA: He is doin the news, okay? He
is not doin names. You want to see the
news? You want to see a current event?
So go look out inna hall.

(LOUISE ANN reaches over and turns up the TV herself)

LOUISE ANN: He could be doin names.
That is a *part* of the news like anything
else...

(The lights flicker again. Something serious begins to go wrong with HOWARD's life-support system. A pipe breaks; a wire snaps; a little more fluid gushes free. HOWARD looks alarmed)

LOUISE ANN: *(irritated with power failure)* Oh, for Heaven's sake. I do not see why we have to put up with that. I saw last night, on the news? This man said a lady saw a whole flock of chickens. Rhode Island Reds, jus' runnin wild out on the road.

CARLA: These lady think she see a chicken, she is smokin bad shit, okay? She don' see no flock of chicken somewhere, I tell you that.

LOUISE ANN: Now she might have... you don't know that, Carla. You see the bad side of ever'thing is what you do. You got to say, now I am puttin Mr. Negative behind me...I am lookin for Mr. Good...

CARLA: *(Silently mouths LOUISE ANN's words)*

LOUISE ANN: There was this ol' lady in two-oh-five? Miz Sweeny or somethin, you recall? She swore on Jesus her sister had the last cardinal bird in Tennessee. Kept it in a hamster cage long as she could stand it. Started dreamin 'bout it and couldn't sleep. Got up in the middle of the night and stir-fried it in a wok.

CARLA: *(Shakes her head)* That was not the ol' lady's sister had these bird. That was her aunt or somethin. And it wasn' no cardinal it was a chay.

LOUISE ANN: Now I am near certain it
was a cardinal. A jay, now, if she'd had
a jay, I doubt very much she could've
kept the thing quiet. They make a
awful lot of noise.

CARLA: Hey, Louise Ann. You see
these bird you self? You don' see this,
you don' know if it hoppen or not. You
don' know somebody see a bird it's red
or blue or what.

LOUISE ANN: Well *ever*'body don't lie.
I mean I am sure there are those who
do, Carla, but I sincerely hope they are
not of my acquaintance.

CARLA: I meet these guy, couple weeks
ago? I'm workin late, he's workin late.
What he's doin, he is keeping his eye
on me. He says, listen, you ever eat a
duck? I say, no I don' ever eat a duck.
He say, I got a duck. He say, okay, I
haven' got a duck, I got somethin *tastes*
like a duck. I am lookin these guy in
the eye, I see how he is lookin at me. I
say, right, I wan' some of you duck that
ain't a duck, I got to do what? He says,
hey, you an' me, we goin to get along
fine. He say, go back to you office.
Write somethin pretty nasty on the
screen. I say, will you stop? I am real
disappointed in your behavior, man.
I say, you got no focking social grace,
you know? He say fine, so do somethin
else. I say what? He say, go back to
you office. Sit on the Xerox, okay? Fax
me you sweet little tootie, I give you
half a duck. I say, get outta here, I'm
gonna what? Expose my lovely parts
to harmful rays? He say, what do you

know, maybe it's gonna feel kinda
good. I say, hey, I'm so aroused I'm
passin out.

*(The power flickers again. HOWARD looks really concerned, as more
pipes begin to break; more fluids begin to splatter from his device)*

CARLA: *(Irritated with power failure)*
Can you believe? What is this, huh?

LOUISE ANN: Mr. Axtel in fifth grade,
he taught shop and home ec? Tried to
get me to sit on a baked potato once.
He said not many girls'd do it. I said,
well I am surely not surprised to hear
that. I related this incident to Howard
in later years. He said it smacked of
deviant behavior to him. He said he
couldn't be sure, unless he saw the
actual event. *(Raises an eyebrow in
HOWARD's direction)* Don't you try
and deny it, Howard. That is exactly
what you said. I distinctly remember
your words. *(LOUISE ANN shakes her
head and sighs; she touches CARLA 's
arm without looking up)* I shouldn't
complain, I know that. Howard and I
have had our differences, but I'd say
we've had a good life. I have found
marriage to be a tolerable condition,
in spite of the side effects. On our
very first date, Howard took my
maiden state against my will, and I
can't forgive him that. However, I do
not feel the sin's on my head, since
I had no idea what he was doin at
the time.

CARLA: Hey, this is what a man is goin
to do. He is goin to do whatever he can
get away with, right? A guy says, hey,

baby, I got these glandular needs, I am
losin all control.

LOUISE ANN: Howard may have used
some electrical device. I'm sure I
couldn't say.

CARLA: A man got somethin he wanta
do, he says, hey, that ain't perverted,
everybody doin that. Whatever it is,
this is what it's okay to do. I got this
cousin back in Puerto Rico when I'm a
kid? He tended to piss in ladies' shoes
from time to time. You step in you
Sunday school pump, you gonna get a
big surprise.

*(The power flickers once again—nothing real bad, just a little teaser
this time)*

LOUISE ANN: I only went out with
one boy before Howard. His name
was Alvin Simms. His family was
from western Illinois. First generation
up from trash is what they was. I
wouldn't let him touch me, of course,
but I'm afraid I allowed sexual
liberties over the phone. I deeply
regret doin that. Alvin's fantasies
ran to outdoor life. Badgers were
on his mind a lot. *(Shakes her head,
remembering)* When I come to think
about it, the women in my family got
no sense at all it comes to men. My
great-grandmother worked directly
with the man who invented the
volleyball net they use all over the
world in tournament play. 'Course
she never got the credit she deserved.
My family has rubbed elbows with
greatness more than once, but you

couldn't tell it from lookin at us now. You know I *try* to hold Christian thoughts in my head, Carla. But sometimes, I must admit I do not feel God is close by.

CARLA. No shit. When Is that?

LOUISE ANN: You can laugh if you like. I assure you, I am quite serious about God. Carla, now turn that up. I think they're doin names...

CARLA: He is not doin names. He's sellin somethin, okay?

LOUISE ANN: I thought he just might be doin names. Last year they did a good many names during Christmas. Not just Christmas Eve, but Christmas Day as well, and on through the entire holiday season as I recall.

CARLA: *(Speaks in a sympathetic tone. She knows when to put her cynical armor aside, and offer her friend a kind word)* They probably goin to do it real soon, right? I think that's what they goin to do.

LOUISE ANN: You might be in the bathroom or somethin, you know? I was thinkin 'bout that. You got the water on, you went out to the store? They could do it, you wouldn't even hear, you wouldn't know...

CARLA: *(Stands, gives LOUISE ANN a rough hug)* Hey, they not about to do that. I know this for sure.

LOUISE ANN: You don't have to go. I'm
pleased to have you here, you know
that. I could make some more tea.

CARLA: I got to go put up my stuff.
You lock up good. I call you in the
mornin, okay? *(Carla picks up her
assault rifle and grocery sack)* Hey,
Merry Christmas, Howard. You lookin
good, man.

*(CARLA exits. LOUISE ANN pauses a moment to watch her go. Going back
to her work, she sees something that bothers her on the TV)*

LOUISE ANN: Oh, my Lord… *(She
washes her hands quickly at the sink;
keeps her eyes on the TV)* There are a
lot of things of a disturbin nature on
the television, Howard, the situation
bein what it is and all? *(Wipes hands on
a towel)* Which is not to say one cannot
be more selective, and find somethin
more suitable for family viewin.

*(LOUISE ANN reaches up and takes the cover off the bottle containing
her baby)*

LOUISE ANN: Come on, honey. There
you are. *(Takes bottle off of the shelf,
and cuddles it to her breast)* I *see* you.
I *see* you, hon… *(Speaks as she walks
to a rocker with the bottle)* Which is
somethin I feel we should discuss
in depth, Howard. The TV and all. I
mean, we are a family now.

*(LOUISE ANN loosens her blouse and bares one breast. Her breast is
partially covered by a circle of metal and pink plastic. A clear plastic
tube is attached to the center of the circle. As she talks, LOUISE ANN
inserts the free end of the tube in the top of the bottle containing the baby)*

LOUISE ANN: ...And that means certain added responsibilities for us both. You might want to think on that, Howard, seein as how you appear to have the time...

(LOUISE ANN leans in and turns up the TV. Tinny Christmas music can be heard from the speaker. The power in the room flickers again. LOUISE ANN's face is illuminated in the light from the TV screen)

LOUISE ANN: See the man, baby? See the nice man on TV? The man *might* do names. You watch, he just might... *(LOUISE ANN rocks, and teases the baby with the "pet cat" on a stick)* He might do mama's name...he might do *daddy's* name...why, he might do *your* name, too. Yes sir, you don't know, he just might...that's what he might do...

(Everything is going wrong with HOWARD. A very sorry sight indeed)

TINNY CHRISTMAS MUSIC UP AND FADE...

CURTAIN

Hit

Artie thinks the bar was a bad idea. The place has got a 40-watt bulb, it's got sawdust on the floor. The juke plays greaser hit tunes. Pig set up the meet with this guy Jimmy Sims and Pig picked the place out, which sounded okay at the time because the dump is on the Houston ship channel and no one anybody knew is going to drop in for a beer. A cop, a cop wouldn't come within a mile. There's nothing here a cop wants to see.

The music's too loud, and Artie don't care for greaser songs. All the fucking records sound alike. A nigger or a white guy, he'll do a lot of different songs. You're driving, you listen to the spic radio, it's all the same song.

He'd like to get another beer but if he does he'll have to pee. He doesn't want to pee in here. From the window, he can see the gas flares from the Exxon place across the bay. The flares burn all day and night. There's no one else in the bar except some sailors off a ship. Artie figures the guys are Swedes. The Swedes are in a booth by the bar, feeling up a Mexican whore. The girl is maybe twelve. She's got a Minnie Mouse shirt comes down about her ass and nothing else. The Swedes like this a lot. Jesus, Artie thinks, this ain't a decent place to be.

The guy comes in the door and looks around. Right away Artie knows the guy's a goof. He's wearing wingtip shoes, black and white shoes with little holes on top, shoes big as fucking boats. Artie didn't know they sold them anymore. Wingtip shoes and a seersucker suit. A fresh haircut a white shirt. Maybe the goof sells shoes, Artie thinks. He's got a face like a guy sells shoes.

The goof is just standing there, he can't see nothing in the dark. Artie stands halfway and waves him down. The goof comes over real quick. He doesn't sit. He stands there and sticks out his hand.

"You're Mr. Smith I bet, right?" The goof gives Artie a sly little wink which Artie doesn't care for at all. "Hey-hey, all right. *Funky* place, *some*thing else. I'm Bill *Jones*, okay?"

Artie ignores the hand. "You're Jimmy Sims," Artie says. "Sit the fuck down."

The guy sits. "Hey, I thought we didn't do names."

"I do names. You don't do names. You got something to give to me."

The goof grins. "Say, right down to it. My kind of man." He reaches in the pocket of his suit and comes up with a wad of bills, the wad's big as a cantaloupe.

"Jesus," Artie says, "put that shit away."

"Hey, what's wrong?" the goof wants to know.

"You ever hear of a envelope?" Artie says. "You want to give a guy something, you use a envelope. You can buy 'em at the store, you don't hand a guy nothing like that."

"Right, you got it. My mistake. What do I know? I think I'll get a beer."

"No you won't. You get through here you can go and get a beer. What you want to do is put it on the floor."

"Do what?"

"Put the fucking money on the floor. You put it down. I pick it up."

The goof puts the wad on the floor. Artie leans down and picks it up. He gets a look at the wingtip shoes.

"You want to do some business," Artie says. "I hear you got business you tell me what you got."

"Hey, that's what we're here for, right? Let's do 'er, let's go. Ceil, we're kinda separated now I mean we sort of live apart, okay? Christ, what a looker. Miss Universe? 1986? Hey, they could be sisters, all right? Listen, nothing happens to Ceil, okay? I mean Ceil can't help it. She drives guys nuts. We're talking your love goddess, man. I mean, *Ho*ly shit, what's a guy to do. You get a look at Ceil that's it."

"Hey." Artie holds up his hand. "I don't want to hear about the wife. Your wife ain't in this I don't want to know."

"Yo, that's it," says the goof. "You got it. Button up the lip. Loose talk." The goof stops. He looks over at the Swedes. The whore's stark naked. One of the guys is wearing the Minnie Mouse shirt, he's got it stuck around his head.

"Say, what's going on over there?" The goof looks alarmed. "We got trouble, I'd say. Doesn't look good to me, is that little girl okay?"

"No," Artie says. "So what kind of business you got with me?"

"How long you been doing what you do? Wow, I'm sittin' right here, what a kick. I'm in sales myself. RVs for every need."

Artie grabs the table and leans in on the goof. "I know what you are. You're an asshole with funny looking shoes. I don't give a shit. I don't want to hear what you do. You don't want to talk about me."

"Okay, no offense. I like people, I'm a people kind of guy. So this is where we're at. This guy's giving me a hassle with Ceil. She runs this electrolysis place, you know? Unwanted hair? Where'd she meet the guy, how you figure that? Anyway she's seeing this guy, she's over at his house every night. He works all day, he's a CPA. The guy's in a wheelchair, right? The guy went to Nam he's a vet. He can't do a thing without the chair."

"This guy's in a chair," Artie says. "The guy we're talking about, he's in a chair."

"You got it. Right on. Waist down, he can't feel a thing. So he can't do anything with Ceil, I mean in a sexual manner, nothing like that. So he's got this dog to do that. Like, she goes over to see the guy, the dog gets it on with Ceil."

"Jesus," Artie says.

"Right. Listen, I don't care for this at all. I'm saying to myself, this is bad news. This is not a normal thing to do. You shouldn't ought to do it with a dog. You off the guy you want to get the dog too. Be sure and get the dog."

"Forget it," Artie says. "No dogs."

"That's extra or what? Right, okay, I can live with that."

Artie feels tired. He wishes he was back in his condo where the air works fine and nothing smells. Maybe go out and get a lobster or a steak. Christ, what kind of people are we talking about here? We're talking fucking trash.

"How do you know she's doing it with the dog?" Artie says. "How you know that?"

"Hey, I saw her, that's how, what do you think?"

"You saw her doing this."

"I look in the window she's doing it with a dog. Say, I got the right Who's the injured party here? I got a marriage on the rocks. I tell myself, hey, we can work this out."

Artie finishes off his beer. He don't want to mess with this goof but the money's okay. "Here's the way it goes," Artie says. "I need an address. I need the guy's name. You walk out of here you never saw me anywhere, that's it."

"So hey, when you think you'll do it. Real soon or what? I mean, hey, whatever you think, okay with me."

"Get the fuck out of here," Artie says.

"Right *on*. Read you loud and clear. You ever think about the RV life?"

"Get yourself a suit," Artie says. "Get some real shoes. That's what I think you ought to do."

▲▼▲

At ten the next morning, Artie leaves his car at Pig's garage and gives the Pig a grand, which is Pig's ten percent. He tells Pig he ought to give *him* an extra grand for fucking with the goof. He tells Pig about the wingtip shoes, he doesn't tell him anything else. He takes the Honda and heads out north on 45. The Honda is registered to a wino in Nacogdoches, Texas, the wino don't know he owns a car.

Artie hates to drive. The guy lives up north of Conroe, maybe thirty, forty miles. It looks real nice when you get up where the pine trees start, but the traffic's real bad before that and the people drive like fucking maniacs.

Artie's thought about the vet and figures that's okay. Screw him, a guy in a wheelchair's a guy like anybody else, he's sitting down instead of standing up. He isn't sure about the dog, he hasn't ever hit a dog. This is a pervert dog, okay, but the dog don't know about that. He gets a chance to hump something, that's what he's going to do. He's going to say what? Hey, this broad ain't a dog. I shouldn't ought to do that. The dog don't know. He sees it up there, he figures fine, that's what I need to do.

So he'll think about the dog. The goof's real hot about the dog, but it isn't up to him. The goof don't tell him what to do.

▲▼▲

The house is in a development that winds in off of 45. There's plenty of trees around, and no street lights except one at the end of every block. That's fine with Artie, he doesn't want a lot of light. He drives around in daylight to get real familiar with the streets. The neighborhood's a little run down, like everything went along fine for a while, then the people who were there when it was new moved away and the also-rans came and moved in. Some of the houses need paint and a lot of the lawns have gone to pot. Artie looks for rent-a-cop signs and he only sees two.

Three blocks from the vet he finds two empty houses in a row. All the other houses on the street are occupied. If he parks in front of the empties, no one in the houses close by is pissed off. They don't wonder why he's there, they think he's seeing someone else.

▲▼▲

Back on 45, Artie checks into the Cactus Bloom Inn, the first motel he passes on the right. He eats at a Burger King and goes back and watches

TV. There's nothing on good, he watches a bunch of soaps. Everybody looks nice. The guys are all perfect, the women are flat knocked out. The broads are mostly screwing doctors or cops or architects. Sometimes they let you see a lot then they get right where they do it and they stop. You don't get to see anymore. This one girl's great. She's got nice tits and she don't have a rash anywhere. He thinks about Angie. Angie doesn't look that great but so what? He doesn't look like a doctor in a suit.

At six Artie's driving through the neighborhood again. He goes by the guy's house once, just checking things out. He's wearing dark gray sweats and running shoes. He's got a pound of steak and a Browning 380 automatic under the seat. The Browning's got a long leather loop around the butt. When he does his jogger act he puts the loop around his neck and tucks the Browning in his waist. If the Browning comes loose it doesn't fall down his pants and maybe out on the ground. Which is hard to explain, some jerkoff is raking up the lawn.

At 6:45, Artie pulls up three houses down across the street from the vet. He keeps the motor running and has a smoke. What he wants to know is what everybody does. Like who's home from work, who has a bunch of kids and who lives next door. He likes to know who's next door. He did a guy in Tulsa one time, a guy owes the wrong people a lot of dough. He goes in through a window and waits in the dark until the guy gets home, waits maybe two, three hours, just sitting in the dark. The guy comes in, goes to the bathroom to pee, Artie shoots him in the head. He goes out the way he came in. He takes a good look and nearly does it in his pants. There hadn't been a car in the street, now there's cars everywhere, maybe twenty, thirty cars. Lights are flashing on the cars and there's cops all over the place. Artie goes back in the dead guy's house and throws up. He stays in the house all night and it's on the TV the next day, how the mayor has a stroke and kicks off, and Artie don't have to ask where.

▲▼▲

Artie sees the car in his mirror. It slows down and stops, stops right behind him maybe three feet away. He reaches for the Browning and holds it in his lap. A guy gets out, and Artie sees it's the goof. He can't fucking believe it, it's the goof. The goof just walks right up and gets in.

"Say-hey," says the goof, "is this *heavy* shit or what? It is going down, right? You're gonna *off* this dude, you're—"

Artie grabs the goof by his shirt and slams his head against the roof. "What the *fuck* are you doin' here? Huh? Huh? What the fuck!"

Artie rattles the guy good a couple of times and throws him hard against the door. "*Uh*-oh," says the goof, "*excuse* me." He holds up his hands like he's seen on TV. "You are really pissed, right? I'm saying to myself, this guy is *pissed* at *me*."

"I asked you a question, asshole. Why the fuck you following me around?"

The goof shakes his head. "Huh-unh, *no* way. I'm driving around, I'm in the neighborhood—"

"Bullshit." Artie grabs the guy again. "Get your ass out of here. Go. Don't fucking come near me again. Am I getting through to you or what?"

"Yo, I am *gone*. I am flying out today, I am hopping on the train. I am reading *you* loud and clear."

The goof jumps out. He gets in his car and whips by Artie fast. He waves all the way down the block.

Jesus. Artie can't believe the guy. Pulling up and getting right in. Artie's parked in front of the vet's, the guy jumps right in. He knows what the goof is doing. What he's doing is he's checking on his wife. He's trailing her around all day he isn't selling RVs. He's making sure she isn't fucking any dogs he doesn't know.

Artie drives off. He circles a couple of blocks to make sure the goof is gone. Back on 45 he stops off and gets a beer. It's a little after seven and he needs to kill some time. He drives up 45 for a while, turns around and comes back. When he reaches the neighborhood again it's getting dark. He passes the house and there's the van. Right behind it is a light blue Chevy so the goof's wife is in there too.

Artie keeps going. The goof's wife is early, this'll work out fine. He isn't about to do the vet until the broad is out of sight. They'll maybe find the guy the next day. Artie figures he can get back to Houston by ten. Maybe Angie's still up. He'll call her and they'll go and get a steak. They'll have a few laughs, he'll tell her about the wingtip shoes. Just the part about the shoes.

▲▼▲

There's a dog dish in the backyard and half a tub of water by the tap. There's dog shit everywhere. Artie figures the dog is in the house, he's getting ready for his date. He won't tell Angie about the dog. Angie's kinky enough the way she is. A woman likes to dump Del Monte cling peaches in the tub, she don't need to hear about a dog.

The backyard is good and dark with all the trees, and the guy's got a high cedar fence. There's a concrete slab behind the house, a little built-in patio. The back of the living room has sliding glass doors you can walk out on the slab. The curtains are pulled but there's a two-inch gap. When he stands up close, Artie can see what they're doing inside.

What he sees makes him wonder what the fuck is going on. The goof's wife is there. But there isn't just one guy, there's two. The vet is in the wheelchair, a black dude is sitting on the couch. The black guy's wearing these Ray Charles wrap around shades and he don't have any arms. All he's got are little stubs, that's all he's got. The broad's sitting by the black, she's feeding the guy a drink. Artie can't see her too well from where he is, he can only see her back. The stereo's turned up high. The black guy's flapping his stubs, he's stomping his feet on the floor. The broad feeds the guy too fast and there's booze running down the dude's front. The dude thinks this is a hoot. He laughs and waves his stubs. The goof's wife giggles on the couch. The vet says something and the broad gets up, stands up and turns around.

Artie nearly has a stroke. Christ, the goof's wife is ugly and a half. The broad's got a face would stop a train. A long pointy nose and little BB eyes. Buck teeth with nowhere to sit because her chin goes right down to her neck. She's got red high heels, a red dress, she's fucking skinny as a mop. With her hair pulled back, little kinky black wires, she looks to Artie like a rat. This is what she is. The goof's love goddess is a rat. The goof's too dumb, he don't know, he don't know he's got a rat.

The rat wobbles off to the kitchen for a drink, she can hardly stand up. The rat is fucking whacked. The heels don't work and she's walking on the sides of her shoes. Artie can't see the dog. Maybe the dog's off hiding somewhere, he don't want to do the rat.

In a minute, the rat comes out with a drink. She does a little dance and turns the music up high. She whirls around and nearly falls on her ass. She winks at the vet and plops down in his lap. She gives the guy a big kiss. He sticks his hand down the front of her dress. He don't find anything to grab but the rat thinks this is great. The rat knows what to do next. She stands up and kicks off her shoes and peels herself out of the dress. Big surprise, she's got nothing on under that. The vet yells and claps his hands. The black dude flaps his stubs. He don't know what the hell is going on but everybody's having fun.

Artie wants to leave and have a smoke but he can't take his eyes off the rat. He hasn't ever seen a broad looks worse naked but it's something more than that. The rat's got funny looking skin. Her skin's not right, it isn't pink it isn't white. She looks like she's maybe made of wax. Artie keeps looking and it comes to him at once. The rat doesn't have any hair. She don't have hair between her legs or anywhere. It isn't like she's shaved it all off, it's not there. Nothing on her arms or her toes or anywhere. Artie knows what's happened, he remembers what she does. The rat's not busy all day, she's got nothing else to do. She sits down at the shop she figures, hey, I don't guess I'm ugly enough, I'll electrocute another coupla hairs. Miss fucking Universe.

Artie doesn't want to watch what happens next, he doesn't want to see this at all. The dog's somewhere in the house, he's maybe got the night off, and Artie's got bad news for the goof. The rat's on her knees and she's going at the vet and it's clear he doesn't need the dog at all. The vet's staring at the wall he's going nuts he's going *uh! uh! uh!* He's banging on the wheelchair with his fists.

Great, Artie thinks, that's it, let's get this fucking show on the road. Artie's tired, but the rat's not through, the rat's not ready to pack it in. She's crawling around the floor. She's looking for her drink. She squints her little BB eyes and tries to focus on her watch. She looks around like there's something she forgot. She spots the black dude on the couch. Right, that's it. There's still another guy in the room she forgot about that. She picks herself up and stumbles over to his lap. The black dude grins and does his Ray Charles act. He can't see shit but he can feel. He's got a naked girl in his lap he knows that, and he don't know how she looks. He whispers something in her ear. The rat laughs and wrinkles up her nose like she's found a piece of cheese. A minute after that they're gone. She's dragged the guy off somewhere, maybe another room.

Artie backs off and has a smoke. He looks at his watch but he can't see a thing in the dark. Okay. So the rat'll go home he knows that. The goof says she never spends the night. The black guy's something else. The vet had to bring him in the van, he doesn't go nowhere by himself. Artie doesn't care for this at all. He's getting paid to do the guy and the dog. He isn't getting paid to do the black. He offs the black he'll have to do it free, the goof's not about to pay for that. Fuck it, Artie thinks. It's that or he's got to come back, he's got to make another trip, he's not about to do that.

▲▼▲

He watches while the goof's wife stumbles to her car. She lays about thirty feet of rubber and she's gone. Artie feels a lot better now. He doesn't mind work, he doesn't like to stand around and wait. The vet's in his wheelchair the black dude's on the couch. Artie thinks about a bedroom window, but he doesn't want to run into the dog. He tries the sliding door real easy. Great. The fucker isn't even locked. He leaves the

Browning where it is. There's a broken barbecue on the porch, a pile of bricks and a rusted rake. Artie feels around, and finds a length of two-inch pipe. He picks up the pipe. He slides back the door and he's in the room fast. The vet looks at him real surprised and Artie hits him once between the eyes. He goes to the black dude on the couch. The guy knows someone's in the room but that's fine. He grins and says "What's happening, man?" and that's that.

Artie works fast. He gets the two guys' wallets and takes the cash. He drops the wallets on the floor. There's a big TV and he can't take that. He takes the VCR. There's a portable TV in the kitchen, he decides to take that. He can't carry anything else. It's enough to let the cops know a burglar's been around. He opens all the drawers and dumps stuff out on the floor. He knows he ought to mess the other rooms, but he doesn't know which one holds the dog. He doesn't want to fuck with the dog. The goof wants to do the dog, he can hit him with a truck.

He leaves the house quickly, stops in the shadows to check the street. It's nearly nine. No one's anywhere about. He runs across the street. The VCR's heavy, and the TV's banging against his leg. He cuts across a lawn. Lights hit the street and he ducks behind a tree. A van turns in the vet's drive, right behind the van that's there. The lights go off. The side door opens and a big dog jumps out in the yard. A ramp slides out of the van. A guy in a wheelchair appears, and the ramp takes him down to the ground. The guy pets the dog. The dog runs around like crazy, finds a good spot and takes a dump. Another light brightens up the street. A blue Chevy pulls up to the curb. The goof's wife gets out. She runs up the driveway and gives the guy a hug. The dog sees the broad and goes nuts. He wags his tail and puts his paws up on her chest. He licks her face and starts humping on her leg.

Artie looks at the dog. He looks at the guy in the chair. What the fuck is this? Artie thinks. What the fuck is going on? He can't hang around to find out. He starts jogging for the car. In about eight minutes, the place'll be crawling with cops, and he doesn't want to wait around for that.

▲▼▲

Artie drives six or eight miles down 45. He finds a dirt road that goes off into the trees. He finds a bridge and a dried up creek where everybody stops to throw their junk. He tosses out the TV and the VCR. He hightails it back to the Cactus Bloom Inn and packs his stuff. He's trying to get a picture in his head. His head's not working right at all. There's two guys in the house. There's the guy outside and there's a dog, we got a couple of extra guys. We got the rat driving off and coming back. It don't add up. Something's wrong here, but Artie can't figure what it is. Jesus, what a fucking mess.

Artie thinks about the goof, but not much. So what's the guy going to do, call the cops, he's going to sue? There's no way he can get back to Artie, there's no way he can get back to the Pig. A guy looks for Pig, he's not there. So the goof, he's going to have to write it off.

Artie checks the room. He checks the closet and the bathroom and under the bed. He hasn't left a thing. He picks up his overnight bag and flips the lights and someone's knocking on the door. Artie stands perfectly still. He pulls the Browning from his belt and racks the slide, he goes flat against the wall beside the door. Maybe it's a maid, she wants to leave some towels. No way, it's nearly ten o'clock at night.

"Like hey, are you in there, man?" Another little knock. "Yo, let's talk, we gotta rap, okay?"

This ain't happening, Artie thinks. The goof's not out there knocking on the door. It's somebody sounds like the goof, he's not there. Artie pulls the door open fast, grabs a handful of shirt, turns the goof around, and throws him on the bed. He snaps on the lights and aims the Browning right at the goof's head.

"Say, *whoa* there," says the goof, "cool the small arms, take it easy, okay?"

"How the fuck did you find me, jerk?" Artie steps closer to the goof. "You want to find an answer real quick."

The goof grins. The guy's too stupid to worry about the gun. "Matches," says the goof. "Hey, that's all, okay? *No* problem, no big deal."

"What you mean, matches?"

"Like *matches*, man. You got matches in your car. I'm sitting in your car, you're kinda knocking me *around*, I'm saying to myself, hey-hey, matches on the dash. Cactus Bloom Inn. I'm saying, yo, everybody's gotta have a place to *stay*, that's cool. You're in the RV biz, you gotta know where everybody's at, you gotta touch 'em where they live. Mention a guy's hometown. Say something nice about his tie—"

"Shut the fuck up," Artie says. "Just shut the fuck up." Artie sits down in a chair. He looks at the goof. "Don't say nothing. Just listen. You're here, okay, I'm going to put it to you straight. Something went wrong at the house. I don't give a shit what. It ain't my problem anymore. You don't like it, okay. You keep your fucking mouth shut."

"Hey, yo, you don't have to tell *me*." The goof grabs his heart like he's going to have a stroke. "Like, I'm hearing sirens and shit, I'm thinking, whoa, what is going down, *what* is—"

"You fucking jerk." Artie sits up straight. "You're driving around. I said stay away, you're out in your fucking car."

"Say, no *way*." The goof holds up his hands. "Hey, I got the message loud and clear. What I am doing is I'm watching TV. I'm sitting there, I'm looking at the tube."

Artie frowns. "You're watching TV. You're watching TV where?"

"Like I'm in my house, man. I'm two doors down, I can hear all the racket going on, I'm thinking, hey, something is happening out there."

Artie is on his feet. He goes to the bed and slams the goof down hard and puts the Browning in his ear. "Listen, asshole," Artie says. "You are going to start making sense. I am going to count to maybe three. This guy with the dog, the dog's making out with your wife, you're living down the street."

"Okay. So it's not where I *live*. I mean it's where I kinda stay. I gotta lease, right? I got a cot, I got a TV."

"You're checking on your wife."

"Yo, I am *concerned*, okay? I got a right. You haven't seen her, man. Ceil's got the power of love. What's a guy gonna do?"

"Fuck that," Artie says. "You hear the sirens, you what?"

"I am up and *gone*, man. I am running up the street and there's Ceil, she is totally berserko, right? I take her in my arms, like wow, what a sweetie and a half. I'm saying, babe, like I want to be with *you*. She's bawling like a kid, she's saying, honey, that's where I gotta *be*."

"Jesus," Artie says.

"I'm holding on to Ceil, I'm hearing what's going down inside the house, I'm thinking, *H*oly shit, have we got a screwup here or what? I'm talking to Rick, he's the guy in the chair—listen, I meet the guy he's okay. Rick's saying, boy, like it's lucky he and Ceil weren't around. Like he's sorry but he's glad it's not them. He doesn't hardly know these guys, okay? He knew 'em at the VA hospital, right? They come through town they look him up. Rick says fine, so you guys go on to the house, I'll get there when I can. He calls Ceil, he says he won't be there until nine, he's gotta finish something up. He says there'll be a couple guys at the house, they'll have a drink, the guys'll go. He says come around nine, maybe ten, it's okay."

Right, Artie thinks. He can see the way it goes from here. The rat's got nothing to do, she's maybe whacked, she's maybe tired of doing hairs. She thinks okay, she'll maybe drop by, she'll maybe have some fun. She does her act, she leaves and drives around. She waits for the guy to get home. She hops out of the car and says, hi there, hon, here I am, how's the dog? Jesus, what a bunch of jerks.

"Get up," Artie says to the goof. "Get up off the bed."

"What for?" says the goof.

Artie grabs the goof and jerks him to his feet. He holds the goof up close and shoves the Browning in his mouth. The goof gets the picture pretty quick.

"Listen good," Artie says. "This is how it's going to be. You walk out of here, you go home. You hump Miss Universe, you watch the TV. I don't give a shit what you do. You walk out of here you don't remember me at all. You never seen me in your life. You do that, we're okay. You don't, we got a problem, you know what I mean?"

"Uhuh, wight." The goof tries to talk around the gun. Artie figures he's made a point and lets him go.

"Hey, *no* problem," says the goof. "I can see what's on your mind, okay? You're thinking, *uh*-oh, this guy maybe wants his money back, he is *not* a happy customer, right? Listen, everything is cool. Ceil and me are straight. Off into the sunset, Violin City, okay? Hey, I'm glad we got together, it's really been a kick. I mean that, right?"

"Get out of here," Artie says. "Get the fuck out of my life."

▲▼▲

Artie thinks how he'll stop and have a steak and then call and see if Angie's still up. He doesn't want to think about the goof. He doesn't want to think about the rat and how she don't have any hair. What he wants to do is get the fuck back on the road and out of town.

The only thing is, he knows there's things he's got to finish up. He knows what the goof is going to do. He knows the goof has got to tell the rat. Artie knows he's got to do that. He tells her what he did, how he did it just for her. That's what the goof is going to do. He'll tell her fucking anything to keep the rat at home, and Artie knows he can't put up with that.

It's two, maybe three, and the neighborhood's dark except for one house on the block, someone's still watching TV. There's the goof's car and the rat's blue Chevy, two doors down from the vet. It's late, and Artie doesn't want to park on the street. He turns off his lights, and pulls into an alley behind the house, where everybody leaves their garbage cans.

The house the goof's leased is built a lot like the vet's. He doesn't have a fence around the place but there's plenty of trees and shrubs. Artie stands in the back in the dark for a while, then walks up to the house. It's a two bedroom house. One on the left side, the other on the right. Artie wonders who gets the cot. You can't sleep two on a cot, there isn't any way to do that. So maybe they're sacked out on the floor.

The goof's got a patio too, and Artie figures he'll try the sliding door. He's got a small crowbar from the trunk, he can snap the lock with that. He's walking toward the house, keeping real close to the trees. He's walking toward the house when something big moves off the patio and comes at him fast across the lawn. Artie nearly pees in his pants. The thing's black as night and it doesn't make a sound. It slams paws the size of dinner plates on Artie's chest and starts humping on his leg.

"Jesus," Artie says. He tries to push the dog away. He tries to get the Browning which he's stuck inside his pants. The dog won't let him go. He's pressed in close to Artie's chest and he can't get to the gun.

"Ace don't like everyone. He don't like you, he won't come near you at all."

Artie doesn't have to ask who it is. He can see the guy now past the dog. He's sitting in a wheelchair in the dark, he's on the patio.

"You got a real nice dog," Artie says. "I been thinking about a dog. Only you got to have a yard."

"You ought to have a yard," the guy says. "You got a little dog you can keep it in the house. A big dog ought to have a yard. You and him had some business, Jimmy says."

"Jimmy said that."

"Jimmy and Ceil are okay. They ought to have a chance for romance."

"Great. I'm for that. You want to call the dog?" The dog is humping Artie's leg. Artie tries to get him off he wants to get the Browning out, but the dog doesn't want to go away.

"I might get a RV," the guy says. "Jimmy says they're great for summer fun."

"Hey, that's what you ought to do. You and the dog could take a trip." The dog starts to shake, the dog is shaking like a leaf.

"Where I'd like to maybe go is Yellowstone. You got a RV, you can camp out anywhere you like. You and me are okay, then, with Jimmy and Ceil?"

"Right. You and me are fine. You want to call the dog?"

"I'm just trying to do the right thing, you understand. That's all it is with me."

"Listen, I'm with you." The dog makes a funny little sound. "You get the dog and I'm gone, I'm out of here, I'm on my—oh, *shit*!" Something hot and wet hits Artie's leg. He hits the dog as hard as he can across the jaw. The dog yelps and drops at Artie's feet. Artie jerks the Browning from his belt, drops his arm just right and shoots the vet. The guy doesn't move. He knows he hit the guy but maybe not. Maybe the guy can't feel it, he never thought of that. All this takes a second and a half, he's squeezing off another shot. Then the guy's got something in his lap it's going *blrr-r-r-t! blrr-r-rt! blrr-r-rt!* like in fucking *Platoon, blrr-r-rt! blrr-r-rt! blrr-r-rt!* the guy's wheelchair is jerking like he's plugged it in the wall, he's knocking over shit he's going backwards everywhere. Artie's got to laugh, it's the funniest thing Artie's ever seen, this is funnier than the rat with no hair or the wingtip shoes only something's going wrong something isn't working right it isn't how it ought to be, and it doesn't seem all that fucking funny anymore...

Cush

The cars started coming in the early hot locust afternoon, turning off the highway and onto the powder-dry road, cars from towns with names like Six Mile and Santuck and Wedowee and Hawk, small-print names like Uchee and Landerville and Sprott, cars from big cities like Birmingham and Mobile and even out of state, all winding down the narrow choked-up road, leaving plumes of red dust for the other cars behind, down through the midsummer August afternoon into deep green shade under sweet gum and sycamore and pine.

The cars hesitated when they came to the bridge. The rust-iron bolt-studded sides looked strong enough to hold the pyramids, but the surface of the bridge caused some alarm. The flat wooden timbers were weathered gray as stone, sagged and bent and bowed and warped every way but straight. Every time a car got across, the bridge gave a clatter-hollow death-rattle roll like God had made a center-lane strike. Reason said that the Buick up ahead had made it fine. Caution said this was a time to reflect on mortal life. One major funeral a day was quite enough. The best way to view these events was standing up.

Aunt Alma Cree didn't give two hoots about the bridge. She stopped in the middle of the span, killed the engine, and rolled the window down. There was nobody coming up behind. If they did, why, they could wait. If they didn't want to wait, they could honk and stomp around, which wouldn't bother Alma Cree a bit. Alma had stood on the steps of Central High in Little Rock in '56, looking up at grim white soldiers tall as trees. Nine years later, she'd joined the march from Selma to Montgomery with Martin Luther King. Nothing much had disturbed her ever since. Not losing a husband who was only thirty-two. Not forty-three years teaching kids who were more concerned with street biology than reading *Moby Dick*.

She sure wasn't worried about a bridge. Least of all the one beneath her now. She knew this bridge like she knew her private parts. She knew that it was built around 1922 by a white man from Jackson who used to own the land. He didn't like to farm, but he liked to get away from his wife. Alma's grandfather bought the place cheap in '36, and the family had lived there ever since. The timber on the bridge had washed away seven times, but the iron had always held. The creek had claimed a John Deere tractor, a Chevy, and a '39 La Salle. Alma knew all about the bridge.

She remembered how she and her sister Lucy used to sneak off from the house, climb up the railing, and lean out far enough to spit. They'd spit and then wait, wait for the red-fin minnows and silver baby perch to come to lunch. They never seemed to guess it wasn't something good to eat. Alma and Lucy would laugh until their sides nearly split because spit fooled the fish every time. Didn't nobody have less sense, Mama said, than two stringy-legged nigger gals who couldn't hardly dry a dish. But Alma and Lucy didn't care. They might be dumb, but they didn't think spit was a fat green hopper or a fly.

Alma sat and smelled the rich hot scent of creek decay. She listened to the lazy day chirring in the trees, the only sound in the silent afternoon. The bottom lay heat-dazed and drugged, tangled in heavy brush and vine. The water down below was still and deep, the surface was congealed and poison green. If you spit in the water now, it wouldn't sink. The minnows and the perch had disappeared. Farther up a ways, someone told Alma a year or two before, there was still good water, still cottonmouth heaven up there, and you could see a hundred turtles at a time, sleeping like green clots of moss on a log.

But not down here, Alma thought. Everything here is mostly dead. She remembered picking pinks and puttyroot beside the creek, lady fern and toadshade in the woods. Now all that was gone, and the field by the house was choked with catbrier and nettle, and honey locust sharp with bristle thorns. The homeplace itself had passed the urge to creak and sigh. Every plank and nail had settled in and sagged as far as it could go. The house had been built in a grove of tall pecans, thick-boled giants that had shaded fifty years of Sunday picnic afternoons. The house had outlived every tree, and now they were gone, too. A few chinaberries grew around the back porch, but you can't hang a swing on a ratty little tree.

"One day, that house is going to fall," Alma said, in the quiet of the hot afternoon. One day it's going to see that the creek and the land are bone dry and Mr. Death has nearly picked the place clean. Driving up from the creek on the red-dust road, she could feel the ghosts everywhere about. Grandpas and uncles and cousins twice removed, and a whole multitude of great aunts. Papa and Mama long gone, and sister Lucy gone, too. No one in the big hollow house except Lucy's girl Pru. Pru and the baby and Uncle John Fry, dead at a hundred and three. Dead and laid out in the parlor in a box.

Lord God, Alma thought, the whole family's come to this. A dead old man and crazy Pru, who's tried to swallow lye twice. John Ezekiel Fry and Pru, and a one-eyed patchwork child, conceived in mortal sin.

"And don't forget yourself," she said aloud. "*You* aren't any great prize, Alma Cree."

▲▼▲

They couldn't all get in the parlor, but as many came in as they could, the rest trailing out in the hall and through the door and down the porch, crowding in a knot in the heat outside. The window to the parlor was raised up high so everyone could hear the preacher's message fairly clear.

Immediate family to the front, is what Preacher Will said, so Alma had to sit in a straight-back chair by her crazy niece Pru. Pru to her left, a cousin named Edgar to her right, a man she had never laid eyes on in her life.

Where did they all come from? she thought, looking at the unfamiliar faces all about. Forty, maybe fifty people, driving in from everywhere, and not any three she could recall. Had she known them in the summer as a child, had they come to Thanksgiving sometime? They were here, so they must be kin to Uncle Fry.

It was hot as an oven outside the house and in. Before the service got fully underway, a stout lady fainted in the hall. And, as a great ocean liner draws everything near it down into the unforgiving sea, Mrs. Andrea Simms of Mobile pulled several people with her out of sight. Outside, an asp dropped from a chinaberry tree down the collar of an insurance man from Tullahoma, Tennessee. Cries went out for baking soda, but Pru had little more than lye and peanut butter in the house, so the family had to flee.

▲▼▲

Preacher Will extolled the virtues of John Ezekiel Fry, noting that he had lived a long life, which anyone there could plainly see. Will himself was eighty-three, and he was certain Uncle Fry had never been inside his church at any time. Still, you had to say *some*thing, so Will filled in with Bible verse to make the service last. He knew the entire Old Testament and the New, everything but Titus and part of Malachi, enough to talk on through the summer and the fall, and somewhere into June.

Alma felt inertia settling in. Her face was flushed with heat, and all her lower parts were paralyzed. Pru was swaying back and forth, humming a Michael Jackson tune. Cousin Edgar was dead or fast asleep. Not any of us going to last long, Alma thought, and Will isn't even into Psalms.

The Lord was listening in, or some northern saint who was mindful of the heat. At that very moment, the service came abruptly to a halt. A terrible cry swept through the house, ripped through every empty hall and dusty room, through every mouse hole and weather crack, through every wall and floor. No one who heard the cry forgot. The sound was so lonely, so full of hurt and woe, so full of pain and sorrow and regret, a cry and a wail for all the grief and the misery the world had ever known, all the suffering and sin, all gathered in a single long lament.

Crazy Pru was up and on her feet, the moment the sound began, Crazy Pru with her eyes full of fright, with a mother's primal terror in her heart.

"Oh Lord God," she cried, "oh sweet Jesus, somethin's happened to my child! Somethin's wrong with little Cush!"

Pru tore through the crowd, fought to reach the hall, Aunt Alma right behind. The people gave way, parting as they came, then trailed right up the stairs, leaving Uncle John Ezekiel Fry all alone with a row of empty chairs, alone except for Leonard T. Pyne.

When Pru saw her child, she went berserk. She shrieked and pulled her hair, whirled in a jerky little dance, moaned and screamed and gagged, and collapsed in an overstuffed chair. Aunt Alma looked into the crib and thought her heart would surely stop. The child was bleeding from its single awful eye, bleeding from its mouth and from its nose, bleeding from its fingers and its toes, bleeding from its ears and from every tiny pore.

Alma didn't stop to think. She lifted up the child, this ugly little kicking screaming pinto-colored child with its possum arms and legs and its baked potato head, lifted up the child and shouted, "Get the *hell* out of my way, I'm coming through!"

Alma ran out of the room and down the hall, the child slick and wet and pulsing like a fancy shower spray. In the bathroom, she laid Cush quickly in the tub and turned the faucet on full. She splashed the child and slapped it, held it right beneath the rushing tap. The red washed away, but Alma didn't care about that. She prayed that the shock would trigger something vital inside and make the bleeding go away.

The child howled until Alma thought her ears would surely burst. It fought to get free from the water streaming down upon its head, it twisted like an eel in her hands, but she knew that she couldn't let it get away.

And then the bleeding stopped. Just like that. Cush stopped crying

and the color in the tub went from red to pink to clear, and Alma lifted
up the child, and someone handed her a towel.

"There now," Alma said, "you're going to be all right, you're going
to be just fine."

She knew this was a lie. You couldn't look at this poor little thing
with its one eye open, and one forever shut, and say everything'll be just
fine. There wasn't anything fine about Cush. There wasn't now and there
wouldn't ever be.

▲▼▲

At the very same moment the child stopped bleeding upstairs,
Uncle John Ezekiel Fry, dead at a hundred and three, farted in his cof-
fin, shook, and gave a satisfying sigh. In the time it takes a fly to bat its
wings, Fry remembered every single instant of his life, every word and
past event, every second since May 24 in 1888, things that had touched
him, and things that he didn't understand, things that he had paid no
attention to at all. He remembered the Oklahoma Run and the Panic of
'93. He remembered getting knifed when he was barely twenty-two. He
remembered Max Planck. The Sherman Silver Purchase Act. Twenty-
one-thousand, four-hundred-sixty-two catfish he'd eaten in his life. A
truckload of Delaware Punch. Sixteen tank cars of whiskey and gin.
Seven tons of pork. John Maynard Keynes. Teddy up San Juan Hill. Iwo
Jima and Ypres. Tiger tanks and Spads. A golden-skinned whore named
Caroline. Wilson got four hundred and thirty-five electoral votes, and
Taft got only eight. The St. Louis Fair in 1904. Corn bread and beans. A
girl in a red silk dress in Tupelo. Shooting a man in Mobile and stealing his silver watch. A lady in Atlanta under a lemon moon, wet from
the river, diamond droplets on her skin, and coal-black moss between
her thighs.

All this came to Uncle John Ezekiel Fry as he gripped the wooden
sides of his box and sat up and blinked his eyes, sat and blinked his eyes
and said, *"Whiskey-tit-February-cunt...Lindy sweet as blackberry pie..."*

There was no one in the room except Leonard T. Pyne. Walking hurt
a lot, so he hadn't chased the crowd upstairs. He stared at John Fry, saw
his hands on the box, saw a suit that looked empty inside, saw a face
like an apple that's been rotting in the bin for some time. Saw tar-ball
eyes that looked in instead of out, looked at things Leonard hoped to
God he'd never see.

Leonard didn't faint and didn't scream. His hair didn't stand on end.
He didn't do anything you'd think he ought to do because he didn't for a

minute believe a thing he saw. Dead men don't sit up and talk, he knew that. And if they don't, you wouldn't see them do it, so why make a fuss about that?

Leonard T. Pyne got up and walked out. He forgot he had knees near the size of basketballs. He forgot he couldn't walk without a crutch. He walked out and got into his car and drove away. He forgot he'd brought his wife Lucille. He drove back up the dirt road, across the bridge, and headed straight for New Orleans. He'd lived all his life south of Knoxville, Tennessee. He'd never gone to New Orleans, and couldn't think of any reason why he should.

▲▼▲

When the folks came down from upstairs, Uncle John Ezekiel Fry was in the kitchen, pulling open cabinets and drawers, looking for a drink. Some people fell down and prayed. Some passed out, but that could have been the heat. People who'd come from out of state said it's just like Fry to pull a stunt like this, he never gave a shit about anyone else. The next time he died, they weren't about to make the trip.

Crazy Pru, when she gathered up her wits, when the baby looked fine, or as fine as a child like that could ever be, said God worked in wondrous ways, anyone could plainly see. What if she hadn't been broke, and they'd gone and had Uncle Fry embalmed instead of laid out in a box? He'd have been dead sure, and wouldn't have a chance of waking up and coming back.

The town undertaker, Marvin Doone, could feel Preacher Will's accusing eyes, and he couldn't think of anything to say. Will had felt sorry for the family, and slipped Doone the cash to do the body up right. Which Marvin Doone had *done*, sucking out all of Uncle Fry's insides, pumping fluids in and sewing everything up, dressing the remains in a black Sears suit, also courtesy of Will. There wasn't any question in Marvin Doone's mind that Fry had absolutely no vital parts, and how could he explain that to Will?

Preacher Will never spoke to Doone again.

Doone went home and drank half a quart of gin.

Uncle John Ezekiel Fry said, *"Nipple-pussy-Mississippi-rye,"* or words to that effect, walked eight miles back to his own farm, where he ate a whole onion and fried himself some fish.

▲▼▲

"Pru, you ought to sell this place and get you and the child into town," Alma said. "There isn't anything left here for you, there's not a reason in the world for you to stay."

"Place is all paid for," said Pru. "Place belongs to me."

They were sitting on the porch, watching the evening slide away, watching the dark crowd in along the creek, watching an owl dart low among the trees. Pru rocked the baby in her arms, and the baby looked content. It played with its little possum hands, it watched Aunt Alma with its black and sleepy eye.

"Paid for's one thing," Alma said. "Keeping up is something else. There's taxes on land, and somebody's got to pay for that. The place won't grow anything, the soil's dead. Near as I can tell, stinging nettle's not a cash crop."

Pru smiled and tickled the baby's chin, though Alma couldn't see that it had a chin at all.

"Me and Cush, we be just fine," Pru said. "We goin' to make it just fine."

Alma looked straight out in the dark. "Prudence, it's not my place to say it, but I will. Your mother was my sister and I guess I got the right. That is *not* a proper name for a child. I'm sorry, but it simply is not."

"Cush, that's my baby's name," Pru said.

"It's not right," Alma said.

Pru rocked back and forth, bare feet brushing light against the porch. "Noah woke," Pru said, "and he know his son Ham seen him naked in his tent. An' Noah say, 'I'm cursin' all your children, Ham, that's what I'm goin' to do.' And lo, that's what he did. An' one of Ham's sons was called Cush."

"I don't care if he was or not," Alma said. "You want a Bible name, there's lots of names to choose, it doesn't have to be Cush."

Pru gave Alma a disconcerting look. The look said maybe-I'm-present-but-I-might-have-stepped-out.

"Lots of names, all right," Pru said, "but not too many got a *curse*.

"I figure Cush here, he oughta have a name with a curse." Alma wasn't certain how she ought to answer that.

▲▼▲

Alma found retirement a bore, just like she'd figured that she would. Her name was on the list for substitutes, but the calls that came were few and far between. She worked part-time for the Montgomery NAACP, taking calls and typing and doing what she could. She grubbed in the garden sometimes, and painted the outside of the house. She had thought for some time about a lavender house. The neighbors didn't take to this at all, but Alma didn't care. I might be into hot pink next year, she told Mrs. Sissy Hayes across the street. What do you think about *that?*

She hadn't been feeling too well since fall the year before. Getting tired too soon, and even taking afternoon naps. Something that she'd never done before. Painting the house wore her out, more than she cared to admit. I'm hardly even past sixty-five, she told herself. I'm a little worse for wear, but I'm not about to stop.

What she thought she ought to do was drop by Dr. Frank's and have a talk. Not a real appointment, just a talk. Stop by and talk about iron, maybe get a shot of B.

Dr. Frank gave her seventeen tests and said you'd better straighten out, Alma Cree. You're diabetic and you've got a bad heart. You're maybe into gout. I'm not sure your kidneys are the way they ought to be.

Alma drove home and made herself some tea. Then she sat down at the table and cried. She hadn't cried since Lucy passed away, and couldn't say when before that.

"Oh Jesus," Alma said aloud, the kitchen sun blurring through her tears. "I don't want to get old, and I sure don't want to die. But old's my first choice, I think you ought to know that."

Her body seemed to sense Alma knew she'd been betrayed. There were no more occasional aches and pains, no more little hints. The hurt came out in force with clear purpose and intent.

The pills and shots seemed to help, but not enough. Alma didn't like her new self. She'd never been sick, and she didn't like being sick now. She had to quit the part-time job. Working in the garden hurt her knees. Standing up hurt her legs and sitting down hurt everything else. What I ought to do, Alma said, is take to drink. It seems to work for everyone else.

All this occurred after Uncle Fry's abortive skirt with death and her trip down to the farm. In spite of her own new problems, Alma tried to keep in touch with Pru. She wrote now and then, but Pru never wrote back. Alma sent a little money when she could. Pru never said thanks, which didn't surprise Alma a bit. Pru's mother Lucy, rest her soul, had always been tight with a dollar, even when she wasn't dirt poor. Maybe cheap runs in Pru's blood, Alma thought. God knows everything *else* peculiar does. Lucy flat cheap, and her husband a mean-eyed drunk. No one knew who had fathered Pru's child, least of all Pru. Whoever he was, he couldn't account for Cush. Only God could take the blame for a child like Cush. Heredity was one thing, but that poor thing was something else. There weren't enough bad genes in Alabama to gang up and come out with a Cush.

▲▼▲

Alma felt she had to see Pru. She was feeling some better, and Dr. Frank said the trip would do her good. She had meant to come before, but didn't feel up to the drive. In her letters to Pru, she had mentioned that she wasn't feeling well, and let it go at that. Not that Pru likely cared—Alma wouldn't know her niece was still alive if it wasn't for Preacher Will. Will wrote every six months, the same two lines that said Pru and the child were just fine. Alma doubted that. How could they be just fine? How were they eating, how were they getting by? It had been nearly—what?—Lord, close to three years. That would make Cush about four. Who would have guessed the child would live as long as that?

As ever, Alma felt a tug from the past as she drove off the highway and onto the red dirt road. She was pleased and surprised to see the land looking fine, much better than it had the time before. The water at the creek was much higher, and running nearly clear. Wildflowers pushed up through the weeds and vines. As she watched the dark water, as she tried to peer down into the deep, a thin shaft of light made its way through the thick green branches up above, dropping silver coins in the shallows by the bank. Alma saw a sudden dart of color, quick crimson sparks against the citron-yellow light.

"Will you just look at that!" she said, and nearly laughed aloud. "Redfin minnows coming back. I'll bet you all still fool enough to eat spit!"

If her back wasn't giving her a fit, if she hadn't stiffened up from the drive, Alma would have hopped out and given spit a try. Instead, she drove through the trees and back out into the sun, up the last hill through the field and to the house.

For a moment, Alma thought that she'd gotten mixed up somehow and turned off on the wrong road. The catbrier and nettles were gone. The field was full of tall green corn. Closer to the house, the corn gave way to neat rows of cabbages, okra and tomatoes, squash and lima beans. The house was freshly painted white. All the windows had glossy black trim and new screens. A brick walk led up to the porch, and perched on the new gravel drive was a blue Ford pickup with oversize tires.

Alma felt a sudden sense of hopelessness and fear. Pru's gone, she thought. She's gone, and someone else is living here. She's gone, and there isn't any telling where that crazy girl went.

Alma parked behind the pickup truck. There wasn't any use in going in. Maybe someone would come out. She rolled the window down. A hot summer breeze dissolved the colder air at once. Alma thought about honking. Not a big honk, not something impolite, just a quick little tap.

She waited just a moment, just a small moment more. Then something in the field caught her eye, and she turned and heard the rattle of the corn, looked and saw the green stalks part and saw the scarecrow jerk-step-jiggle down the rows, saw the denim overalls faded white hanging limp on the snap-dry arms, saw the brittle-stick legs, saw the mouse-nibble gray felt hat, stratified with prehistoric sweat, saw the face like a brown paper sack creased and folded thin as dust, saw the grease-spot eyes and the paper-rip mouth, saw this dizzy apparition held together now and then with bits of rag and cotton string.

"Why, Uncle John Ezekiel Fry," Alma said, "it's nice to find you looking so spry. Think the corn'll do good this year?"

"Crowbar-Chattahoochee-suck," said Uncle Fry. *"Cling peach-sourdough-crotch..."*

"Lord God," Alma said. She watched Uncle Fry walk back into the corn. Either Uncle John Fry or a gnat got in her eye, either John Ezekiel Fry or a phantom cloud of lint. If *he's* still here, Alma thought, then Pru's around, too, though something's going on that isn't right.

At that very moment, Alma heard the screen door slam and saw Pru running barefoot down the steps—Pru, or someone who looked a whole lot like Pru, if Pru filled out and wasn't skinny as a rail, if she looked like Whitney what's-her-name. If she did her hair nice and bought a pretty pink dress and didn't look real goofy in the eyes. If all that occurred, and it seemed as if it had, then this was maybe Lucy's only daughter Prudence Jean.

"Aunt Alma, sakes alive," Pru said. "My, if this ain't a nice surprise!"

Before Aunt Alma could drag her aches and pains upright, Pru was at the car, laughing and grinning and hugging her to death.

"Say, you look fine," said Pru. "You look just as fine as you can be."

"I'm not fine at all, I've been sick," Alma said.

"Well, you sure look good to me," Pru said.

"It wouldn't hurt you much to write."

"Me and the alphabet never got along too good," said Pru. "But I sure think about you all the time."

Alma had her doubts about that. Pru led her up the brick walk across the porch and in the house. Once more, Alma felt alarmed, felt slightly out of synch, felt as if she'd found the wrong place, felt as if she might be out of state. A big unit hummed in the window and the air was icy cold. The wood floor was covered with a blue-flowered rug. There were pictures on the walls. A new lamp, a new couch, and new chairs.

"Pru," Alma said, "you want to tell me what's going on around here? I mean, everything sure looks nice, it looks fine..."

"I bet you're hot," Pru said. "You just sit and I'll get some lemonade."

I'm not hot now, Alma thought. Isn't anybody hot, you got the air turned down to thirty-two. She could hear Pru humming down the hall. Probably got a brand-new designer kitchen, too. A fridge and a stove colored everything but white.

Lord Jesus, the place painted up, a new truck and new screens and a house full of Sears! No wonder Preacher Will never said a whole lot.

Alma didn't want to think where the money came from, Pru looking slick as a fashion magazine, all her best parts pooching in or swelling out. What's a person going to think? A girl doesn't know her alphabet past *D,* she isn't working down at Merrill Lynch. What she's *working* is a Mobile dandy with a mouth full of coke-white teeth and a Cadillac to match.

It's not right, Alma thought. Looks like it pays pretty good, but it's not the thing a girl ought to do. That's what I'll say, I'll say, Pru, I know you've had a real bad time with Cush and all, but it's not the thing to do.

Pru brought the lemonade back, sat down and smiled like the ladies do in *Vogue* when they're selling good perfume.

"Aunt Alma," she said, "I bet you want to hear 'bout all this stuff I got around. I got an idea you maybe would."

Alma cleared her throat. "Well, if you feel like you *want* to tell me, Pru, that's fine."

"I sorta had good fortune come my way," Pru said. "I was workin' in the corn one day when my hoe hit somethin' hard. I dug it up and found a rusty tin can. Inside the can was a little leather sack. And inside *that,* praise God, was nine twenty-dollar gold coins lookin' fresh as they could be. I took 'em to the bank and Mr. Deek say, nine times twenty, Miz Pru, that's a hundred and eighty dollars, but I'll give you two hundred on the spot. An' I say I don't guess you will, Mr. Deek, I said I ain't near as touched as I maybe used to be. I said I seen a program 'bout coins on the public TV.

"So what I *did,* I took a bus down to Mobile an' found an ol' man cookin' fish. I say, can you read and write? He says he can, pretty good, and I say, buy me a book about coins and read me what it say. He does, and he reads up a spell and says, Lord Jesus, girl, these here coins is worth a lot. I says, tell me how much? He says, bein' mint condition like they is, 'round forty-two-thousand-ninety-three, seems to me. Well, it took some doing, but I ended up gettin' forty-six. I give the man helped me a twenty-dollar bill, and that left me forty-five, nine-hundred-eighty to the good. Now isn't that something? God sure been fine to me."

"Yes, He—well, He certainly has, Pru. I guess you've got to say that..."

The truth is, Alma didn't know what to say. She was stunned by the news. All that money from an old tin can? Money lying out in that field for more than a hundred years? Papa and Mama living rag-dirt poor, and nobody ever found a nickel till Pru. Of course, Pru could use the money, that's a fact. But it wouldn't have hurt a thing if one or two of those coins had showed up about 1942.

▲▼▲

Pru served Alma a real nice supper, and insisted she stay the night. Alma didn't argue a lot. The trip down had flat worn her out. Pru said she'd fixed up her grandma's room, and Alma didn't have to use the air.

All through the long hot brassy afternoon, while the sun tried to dig through the new weatherstripping and the freshly painted walls, Pru rattled on about the farm and Uncle Fry and how well the garden grew and this and that, talked about everything there was to talk about except Cush. Alma said maybe once or twice, how's Cush doing, and Pru said real quick Cush is doing fine. After that, Alma didn't ask. She tried to pay attention, and marvel at the Kenmore fridge and the noisy Cuisinart, but her mind was never far from the child. Pru seemed to know, seemed to feel the question there between them, felt it hanging in the air. And when she did, she hurried on to some brand-new appliance colored fire-engine red or plastic green. And that was as far as Alma got about Cush.

Then, when the day was winding down, when the heat let up and Alma sat on the porch with a glass of iced tea, Pru came up behind her and touched Alma gently on the arm.

"I know you got to see him," Pru said. "I know that's what you gotta do."

Alma sat very still for a while, then she stood and looked at Pru. "The child's my kin," Alma said. "Just because he isn't whole doesn't mean I don't love him all the same."

Pru didn't say a thing. She took Alma's hand and led her down the front steps. The chinaberry trees had grown tall. Their limbs brushed the screened-in porch by the kitchen out back. The ground all around was worn flat, like it always used to be. Worn where the cistern had stood years before, worn on the path that led out behind the house. Alma could see the twisted ghosts of peach trees inside her head. She could see the smokehouse and the outhouse after that, the storm cellar off to the right, and Papa's chicken coop. And when she turned the far corner of the house, there was Cush, sitting in a new red wagon by the steps.

Alma felt herself sway, felt her legs give way, felt her heart might come to a stop. The creature in the wagon looked nothing like a child, nothing like anything that ought to be alive. The baked potato head seemed larger than before, the warped little body parched and seared, dried and shriveled to a wisp. The patchwork pattern of his skin was thick with suppurating sores, pimples and blisters, blots and stains and spots, pustules and blotches, welts and bug bites, rashes and swellings and eruptions of every sort. Alma saw the possumlike hands were bent and twisted like a root, saw there wasn't any hair on Cush's head, saw Cush had somehow lost a leg, saw the child wore every conceivable deformity and flaw, every possible perversion of the flesh.

And then Pru sat down on the ground and said, "Cush, this here's your great-aunt Alma Cree. You was too young to recall, but you seen her once before. You want to try an' say hello, you want to try an' do that?"

Cush looked up at Alma with his black and milky eye, looked at Alma through his misery and pain, looked right at Alma Cree and smiled. The smile was something marvelous and terrible to see. One side of Cush's mouth stayed the same while the other side cut a crooked path past his cheek and past his nose, cut a deep and awful fissure up his face. When you hiccup while you try to sign your name, when the line wanders up and off the page, this is how the smile looked to Alma Cree. Cush's lips parted and secreted something white, then Cush scratched and croaked and made a sound.

"Haaalm'ah-ah...Haaalm'ah-ah," Cush said, and then the smile went away.

"Alma," Pru said with pure delight, "that's *right*. See, Aunt Alma? Cush went and said your name!"

"That's real good, Cush," Alma said, "it sure is." She felt the sky whirl crazily about, felt the earth grind its teeth and come apart. She hoped to God she'd make it to the house.

▲▼▲

"Pru, you can't take care of that child," Alma said. "You just can't do it by yourself. I know you've done all you could, but poor little Cush needs some help."

"I *got* help, Alma," said Pru, looking at her empty coffee cup. "Since I come into money, Cush has seen every kind of doctor there is. They give me all kinds of lotions, and ever' kind of pill they got. Ain't nothin' works at all, nothin' anyone can do."

"Pru," Alma said, "what happened to his leg?"

"Didn't anything happen," Pru said. "Jus' one day 'bout a year ago spring it dropped off. Cush give a little squeal an' I 'bout passed out, and that was all of that."

Tears welled in Pru's eyes. "Aunt Alma, I lay 'wake nights and I wonder just what's going on in God's head. I say, Pru, what's He thinking up there? What you figure He means to do? The farm's all shiny like Jesus reached down and touched the land. It hasn't ever been as fine before. The Lord's took the crazy from my head and got me looking real good, and give me everything there is. So how come He missed helpin' Cush, Aunt Alma? You want to tell me that? How come little Cush is somethin' Jesus flat forgot?"

"I don't know the Lord's ways," Alma said. "I wouldn't know how to answer that." Alma looked down at her hands. She couldn't look at Pru. "What I think I ought to say, what you ought to think about, is you've done about everything you can. There isn't much else you can do. You're young and you've got a life ahead, and there's places where Cush'd maybe be better off than he is…"

"No!"

The word came out as strong and solid as the hard red iron that held the bridge. "Cush is my child," Pru said. "I don't know why he's like he is, but he's mine. Alma, he isn't going anywhere but here."

Alma saw the will, saw the fierce determination in Pru, and knew at once there was nothing she could say, nothing that anyone could do.

"All right," she said, and tried her best to smile at Pru, "I guess that's the way it's got to be…"

▲▼▲

Cush liked the winter and the fall. In the summer and the spring, everything that creeped and flew and crawled did their best to seek him out. Fire ants and black ants and ants of every sort. Earwigs and stinkbugs and rusty centipedes. Sulphur butterflies made bouquets about his head to suck the sores around his eyes. Horseflies and deerflies bit his cheeks. Mosquitoes snarled about like Fokker airplanes, and black gnats clotted up his nose. Bees and yellow jackets stung his thighs. If a certain bug couldn't find Cush, Cush would somehow seek it out. With his single bent foot, he'd push his wagon down the road. A scorpion would appear and whip its tail around fast and sting his toe.

His mother tried to keep him in the house. But Cush didn't like it inside. He liked to sit out and watch the trees. He liked to watch the hawks knifing high up in the sky. There were so many wonders to see.

Every blade of grass, every new flower that pushed its way up through the soil, was a marvel to Cush's eye. He especially loved the creek. By the time he was five, he stayed there every day he could. He loved to watch the turtles poke their heads up and blink and look around. He loved to see the minnows dart about. There were more things that bit, more things around the creek that had a sting, but Cush was used to that.

Besides, staying indoors didn't help. Fresh paint and new doors and super-snug-tight screens couldn't keep the biters out. They knew Cush was there and they found a way in. Anywhere Cush might be, they wriggled in and found him out.

Cush didn't think about pain. Cush had hurt from the very first moment of his life. He didn't know there was anything else. It had never crossed his mind what *not* to hurt was like. A deaf child wonders what it might be like to hear, but he never gets it right.

Cush knew there was something different other persons felt, something that he sensed was maybe missing in his life. He didn't look like other people did, he knew that. Other people did things, and all he did was sit. Sit and look and think. Sit and get gnawed and stung and bit.

Once, in the late evening light, when Cush sat with his mother on the porch, the fan brought out from inside to try and keep the bugs at bay, Cush tried to sound a thought. That's how he looked at talk—sounding out a thought. He didn't try to sound a lot. Nothing seemed to come out right.

Still, on this night, he tried and tried hard. It was something that he knew he had to do. He worked his mouth up as best as he could and let it out.

After Pru ruled out strangulation or a stroke, she knew Cush was winding up to talk. "Hon, I'm not real sure what you're saying," Pru said, "you want to run through that again?"

Cush did. He tried again twice. Legs from old bugs, bits of vital parts, and something like liver-ripple tofu spewed out.

"Whuuuma faar?" Cush said. *"Mudd-whuum-spudoo?"*

Pru listened, and finally understood. When she did, she felt her heart would break in two. She nearly grabbed up Cush and held him tight. She hadn't tried that in three years, but she nearly did it then. "What am I *for?*" Cush had said. "Mother, what am I supposed to *do?*"

Oh Lord, thought Pru, how am I supposed to answer that? Sweet Jesus, put the right words inside my head. Pru waited, and nothing showed up that seemed divine.

"Why, isn't anything you *supposed* to do, Cush," Pru said. "God made the trees and the flowers and the sky, an' everything else there is to see. He made your Aunt Alma and he made you an' me. We're all God's children, Cush. I reckon that's about all we're supposed to be."

Cush thought about that. He thought for a very long time. He looked at his mother's words backward and forward, sideways and inside out. He still didn't know what he was for. He still didn't know what to do. Something, he was sure, but he couldn't think *what*. He was almost certain being one of God's flowers wasn't it.

▲▼▲

The trip wore Alma to a nub. She took to her bed for three days, and slept through most of two. When she finally got up, she felt fine. Hungry, and weak in the knees, but just fine. All that driving, and seeing Cush and Pru, Alma thought, that's enough to do anybody in.

She thought about Pru and the farm. How nice Pru looked and how she didn't seem crazy anymore, and how the land and the creek were all coming back again. Everything was doing fine but Cush. Even Uncle Fry. It was like Pru said. All that good flowing in, and Cush not getting his share. It didn't seem right. It sure didn't seem fair.

Alma looked at the garden and decided it was far beyond repair. She dusted the house and threw the laundry in a sack. She went to the grocery store and back. Late in the afternoon, she got a notebook out and started writing things down. Not for any reason, just something she thought she ought to do. She wrote about the funeral and Uncle John Fry. She wrote about Pru and she wrote about Cush. She wrote about how the land had changed and how the creek was full of fish. Nothing that she wrote told her anything she didn't know before, but it seemed to help to get some things down.

Two weeks back from her trip, Alma got a call. Dotty Mae Kline, who'd taught school with Alma for thirty-two years, had retired the year after Alma did. She lived in Santa Barbara now, and said, Alma, why don't you come and stay awhile?

The idea took her by surprise. Alma thought of maybe fourteen reasons why she couldn't take a trip, then tossed them all aside. "Why not?" she said, and called to see when the next plane could fly her out.

▲▼▲

Alma meant to stay a week and ended up staying four. She liked Santa Barbara a lot. It was great to be around Dotty Mae. They saw and did everything they could, and even came close to getting tipsy on

California wine. Alma felt better than she'd ever felt before. Dotty Mae said that was the good Pacific air. But Alma knew air couldn't do a whole lot for diabetes, or a heart that now and then made a scary little flop.

When she got back home, Alma found a letter in her mailbox from Pru. The postmark was two weeks old. Alma left her bags in the hall and opened Pru's letter at once. She saw the scrawly hand running up and down the page, and knew this was likely the only letter Pru had ever written in her life.

"Dir Ant Alma," it said.

"I bet yur supriz to here from me. The farm is luking fine. A agerkultr man is bout houndin me to deth. He says he don no how corn can git nin feet hi and cabig grow big as washtubs on a place like this. He says there isn no nutrunts in the soil I said I cant help that. Cush dropt a arm last week. Somethin like moss is startid growing on his hed. Otherwiz he doin fine. Uncl Fry is fine too.

Luv Pru

P.S. Friday last I wun 2 milun dollars from Ed McMahon. Alma heres a twenny dollar bill I got more than I can spend."

"Lord God," Alma said, "all that money to a dumb nigger girl!"

She crushed the letter in her fist. She was overcome with anger, furious at Pru. Things didn't *happen* like that, it wasn't right. All Pru had ever done was get herself knocked up. She hadn't done a full day's work in all her life!

Guilt rushed in to have its say, anger fighting shame, having it out inside her head. Alma was shaken. She couldn't imagine she'd said such a thing, but there it was. She'd tucked it away and out of sight, but it came right up awful quick, which meant it wasn't hiding out too deep.

The anger was there, and it wouldn't go away. Anger at Pru, who was everything she'd spent her life trying not to be. Mama and Papa and Lucy, too. Never bringing college friends home because *their* folks were black doctors and CPAs, and she didn't want anyone to know that her family was dirt-poor Alabama overall and calico black, Deep South darkies who said "Yassuh" all the time, and fit the white picture of a nigger to a tee.

She remembered every coffee-chocolate-soot-gray-sable-black face that had passed through her class. Every face for forty-three years. Her soul had ached for every one, knowing the kind of world that she had to send them to. Praying that they'd end up where she was, instead of where she'd been, and all the time saying in her heart, "I'm glad I'm me and I'm not one of *them*."

Alma sat on her couch in the growing afternoon. She looked at her luggage in the hall. She thought about smart-as-a-whip bright and funny Dotty Mae. She thought about Little Rock and Selma, and she thought about Pru.

"I'm still who I am," Alma said. "I might've let something else creep in, but I know that isn't *me*." She sat and watched the day disappear, and she prayed that this was true.

▲▼▲

In the morning, when she was rested from the trip, when the good days spent in California seemed to mingle with the pleasure and relief of coming back, when she could look at Pru's letter without old emotions crowding in, Alma got her notebook out and found a brand-new page, and wondered what she ought to say.

Alma didn't care for things she couldn't understand. She liked to deal in facts. She liked things that had a nice beginning and an end. Dotty Mae Kline had taught Philosophy and Modern English Lit. Alma Cree had been content with Geometry and French.

She looked at Pru's letter. She looked at what she'd written down before. Everything good seemed to fasten on Pru. Everything bad came to Cush. The farm was on drugs, on a mad horticultural high. Uncle Fry was apparently alive, and she didn't want to think about that. Alma tried to look for reason. She tried to find a pattern of events. She tried to make order out of things that shouldn't be. In the end, she simply set down the facts—though it went against her nature to call them that. She closed up her notebook and put it on the shelf. Completely out of sight. But not even close to out of mind.

Alma kept her quarterly appointment with Dr. Frank. Dr. Frank said, how are we doing, Alma? and Alma said we're doing just fine. Dr. Frank's nurse called back in a week. Dr. Frank wants to make a new appointment and redo some tests. What for? Alma said, and the nurse didn't care to answer that.

Alma hung up. She looked at the phone. She knew how she *felt*, she felt absolutely great. And she wasn't in California now, she was breathing plain Alabama air.

Alma knew what was wrong with the tests, she didn't have to think twice. Everything was fine inside, she didn't need a test to tell her that, and she'd never been more frightened in her life.

▲▼▲

Pru woke up laughing and half scared to death. She sat up and looked around the room, making sure everything was fine, making sure everything was sitting where it should. Pru didn't like to dream. She had real good dreams now, everything coral rose and underwater green, nice colors floating all about, and a honey-sweet sax off somewhere to the right. Real good dreams, not the kind she'd had before. Not the kind with furry snakes and blue hogs with bad breath. Good's a lot better'n bad, thought Pru, but I could do without any dreams at all.

Pru's idea of what you ought to do at night was go to sleep and wake up. Dreams took you off somewhere that wasn't real, and Pru had come to cherish *real* a lot. Once you've been crazy, you don't much want to go back. It's sort of like making out with bears, once seems just about enough.

▲▼▲

Pru drank a cup of coffee and started making oatmeal for Cush. Cush wouldn't likely touch it, but she felt she ought to try. The sun was an open steel furnace outside, and she turned all the units down to COLD. When the oatmeal was ready, she covered it with foil, found her car keys, and stepped out on the porch.

A light brown Honda was sitting in the drive. A white man was standing on the steps. Pru looked him up and down. He had blow-dry hair and a blue electric suit. He had rainwater eyes and white elevator shoes.

"What you want 'round here," Pru said. "What you doin' on my place?"

"I want to see the child," the man said.

"You ain't seein' any child," Pru said, "now git."

"God bless you," said the man.

"Same to you."

"I'll leave a few pamphlets if you like."

"What I'd *like* is you off my land now, an' you better do it quick."

The man turned and left.

"My boy isn't any freak," Pru shouted at his back. "I better not see your face again!"

She watched until the car disappeared. "Lord God," she said, and shook her head. They'd started showing up about June. She'd put a gate up, but they kept coming in. Black men in beards. White men in suits. Bald-headed men in yellow sheets. Foreign-looking men with white towels around their heads. Pru shooed them all out, but they wouldn't go away. I want to see the child, is what they said. The way they looked her in the eye flat gave Pru the creeps.

Pru stalked out to the truck. She looked for Uncle Fry. "You all goin' to leave my Cush alone," she said, mostly to herself. "I have to get me a 12-gauge and sit out on the road, you goin' to let my child be."

Uncle John Ezekiel Fry appeared, standing in the corn.

"Uncle Fry," Pru said, "you seen little Cush anywhere?"

"Goat shit," Uncle Fry said. *"Rat's ass-Atlanta, strawberry-pee..."*

"Thanks," said Pru, "you're sure a lot of help."

▲▼▲

Pru knew where to find Cush. She left the pickup on the bridge, got her oatmeal, and started down the bank. You could leave that child in the house or on the porch. You could leave him on the steps out back. Whatever you did, Cush found his way to the bridge. The bridge was where he wanted most to be.

Pru squatted down and tried to see up in the dark, up past the last gray timbers of the bridge, up where the shadows met the web of ancient iron.

"You in there, Cush?" Pru said. "You tell me if you in there, child."

"Mmmm-mupper-mudd," said Cush.

"That's good," said Pru. She couldn't see Cush, but she knew that he was there. Up in the cavern of the bank, up where the pale and twisted roots hid out from the hot and muggy day.

"I'm leavin' your oatmeal, hon," Pru said. "I'd like you to eat it if you can."

Cush wouldn't, she knew, he never did. The bowls were always where she left them, full of happy ants and flies.

▲▼▲

Pru drove up to where the highway met the road to make sure the gate was shut. The man in the Honda was gone. No one else was snooping 'round, which didn't mean they wouldn't be back. I might ought to hire someone, Pru thought. I might send up Uncle Fry. Uncle Fry just standing there would likely keep 'em out.

Driving back across the creek to the house, Pru could see the farm sprawled out in lush array. She could feel the green power there, wild and unrestrained. The air was thick with the ripe and heady smell of summer growth. Every leaf and every blade, every seed and every pod, seemed to quiver in the damp and steamy earth. Every fat green shoot pressed and tugged to reach the light, every blossom, every bud, fought to rip itself apart, fought to reach chromatic bliss.

Pru felt light-headed, slightly out of synch, like the time in Georgia when she'd found some good pot. The land seemed bathed in hazy mist. The corn and the house and the chinaberry trees were sharply etched in silver light. Everything was lemon, lavender, and pink, everything was fuzzy and obscure.

"Huh-unh," Pru said, "*no* way, I ain't havin' none of *that*."

She slammed on the brakes and ran quickly to the house. She moved through every single room and pulled all the curtains tight. She took a cold shower and changed her clothes twice. Then she went to the kitchen and made herself a drink.

Pru knew exactly where all the funny colors came from. They were leftover colors from her dream, and she didn't care for that. She didn't need pastel, she needed bright. She didn't need fuzzy, she needed flat solid and absolutely right. Primary colors are the key. Real is where it's at. Special effects don't improve your mental health.

Pru had watched a TV show that said you ought to learn to understand your dreams. Lord help us, she thought, who'd want to go and do *that?*

Pru fixed herself another drink. "I don't want to see funny colors," she said. "I don't want to know about a dream. I don't want to know 'bout *any*thing, God, I don't already know *now*...."

▲▼▲

It surprised Cush to find out who he was. Sometimes, knowing made him glad. Sometimes, it frightened him a lot. One thing it did, though, was answer the questions he'd always had burning in his head. He knew what he was for. He knew for certain now what he had to do.

Cush didn't know *how* he knew, he just did. Mother didn't tell him and he didn't think it up by himself. Maybe he overheard the minnows in the creek. Minnows whisper secrets after dark. Maybe he heard it from the trees. Trees rumble on all the time. If you listen, you can learn a whole lot. If you listen real close, if you can stand to wait them out. A tree starts a word about April twenty-six, and drags it out till June.

Now I know, Cush thought. I know what it is I have to do. He felt he ought to be satisfied with that, he felt it ought to be enough. But Cush was only five. He hadn't had time to learn the end of one question is only the beginning of the next. He knew what he was for. He knew what it was he had to do. Now maybe someone would come and tell him *why...*

▲▼▲

Cush heard the car stop on the bridge. The doors opened up and the people got out. Cush could see daylight through the planks. All the people wore white. The man and the woman and the boy, everybody spruced up, clean and shining white.

"Y'all stay here," the man said. "I'll drive up to the house."

"I'll read a verse and say a prayer," the woman said.

"Amen," said the little boy.

The man drove off. The woman sat down on a log. The little boy leaned on the railing and spat into the creek.

"Don't wander off," the woman said, "don't wander off real far."

The woman sat and read. The boy watched minnows in the creek. He heard a bird squawk somewhere in the trees. He saw a toad hop off behind a bush. Mother said toads were Satan's pets, but the boy thought toads were pretty neat. He walked off the bridge into the woods. He followed the toad down to the creek.

Stay away, Cush cried out in his head. *Stay away, little boy, don't be coming down here!*

The little boy couldn't hear Cush. The woman was heavy into John 13, and didn't know the little boy was gone. The boy saw the toad a foot away. Cush heard the cottonmouth sleeping in the brush. He heard it wake up and find the toad, heard it sense breakfast on the way.

Cush sat up with a start. Nerve ends nibbled by gnats began to quiver with alarm. Blood began to flow through contaminated pipes. He knew what was coming, what had to happen next.

Don't do it, snake, Cush shouted in his head. *Don't you bite that little boy!*

Snake didn't seem to hear, snake didn't seem to care.

Can't you see that boy's dressed up clean and white? Can't you see that's someone you shouldn't oughta bite?

Cush tried hard to push the words out of his head, tried hard to toss them out, tried to hurl them at the snake. Snake didn't answer. Snake was trying hard to figure where toad ended and little boy began.

Cush could scarcely breathe. He felt the ragged oscillation of his heart. *You want to bite something, bite me,* he thought as hard as he could. *Leave that little boy alone and bite me!*

Snake hesitated, snake came to a halt. It listened and it waited, it forgot about toad and little boy. It turned its viper will to something down below the bridge.

▲▼▲

Something white as dead feet slid down a pale vine, something black and wet moved inside a tree. Green snakes, mean snakes, snakes with yellow stripes, king snakes, ring snakes, snakes of every sort began to ripple whip and slither through the bush, began to find their way to Cush. They coiled around his leg and bit his thigh. They wound around his neck and kissed his eye. Rat snakes, fat snakes, canebrake rattlers, and rusty copperheads. Coral snakes, hog snakes, snakes from out of state. Snakes with cool and plastic eyes smelling dry and stale and sweet. White-bellied cottonmouths old as Uncle Fry, some big as sewer pipes, some near as fat as tractor tires.

Snakes hissed and snapped and curled about until Cush was out of sight. Snakes cut and slashed and tried to find a place to bite. And when the fun was all done, when the snakes had managed all the harm they could, they crawled away to find a nap.

▲▼▲

Cush lay swollen and distended like a giant Thanksgiving Day balloon, like a lacerated blimp, like a great enormous bloat. Eight brands of venom chilled his blood and couldn't even make a dent. Seventeen diseases, peculiar to the snake, battled the corruption that coursed through Cush every day, tried and gave it up and did their best to get away.

"Mom, guess what," the boy said on the bridge, "I found me a big green toad."

"Sweet Jesus," mother said, "don't touch your private parts until you wash. You do, your thing'll fall right off!"

Mother turned to Psalms 91:3. A few minutes later, the car came back down the road. The man picked his family up fast. He'd faced Pru once and didn't care to try again.

▲▼▲

Cush thought he heard the car drive away. He thought about the clean little boy. He thought about the nice white clothes. He wondered if his brand-new bites would bring the beetles and the gnats and the horseflies out in force.

▲▼▲

It was nearly ten at night when Alma got the call from Preacher Will. Alma's heart nearly stopped. Oh Lord, she thought, it's Cush. Nothing short of death would get Will to use the phone. It's Pru, Will said, and you ought to come at once. What's wrong with Pru? Alma said, and Will rambled on about bad hygiene and mental fits.

Alma hung up. She was on the road at dawn, and at the gate at ten. There were cars parked up and down the highway, RVs and campers and several dozen tents. People stood about in the red dirt road. They sat and ate lunch beneath the trees. Uncle Fry stood guard, and he wouldn't let them in.

"Uncle Fry," Alma said, "what exactly's going on? What are these people doing here, and what on earth is wrong with Pru?"

"Oyster pie," said Uncle Fry. *"Comanche-cock-Tallahassee-stew..."*

"Well, you're looking real fine," Alma said.

Uncle Fry unlocked the gate and let her in. Alma drove down the narrow dusty road toward the bridge. It hadn't been a year since she'd been to see Pru, but she was struck by the way the place had changed. It had flat been a wonder before, springing up new from a worn-out tangle of decay, to a rich and fertile farm. She had marveled at the transformation then, but the land was even more resplendent now, more radiant and alive. The very air seemed to shine. Every leaf shimmered, every blade of grass was brilliant green. There were flowers that had certainly never grown here before. Birds that had never come near the place flashed among the trees.

Alma wondered how she'd write it down. That the worst farm in Alabama state was getting prettier every day? That scarcely said a thing. She wished she'd never started taking notes. All she had accomplished was to make herself more apprehensive, more uneasy than before. Putting things down made them seem like they were real. When you saw it on paper, it seemed as if the farm and little Cush and Uncle Fry, and Prudence Jean the millionaire, were just everyday events. And that simply wasn't so. Nothing was going on that made a lick of sense. Nothing that a reasonable person who was over sixty-five liked to think about at all.

▲▼▲

"All right, I'm here," Alma said. "I want to know what's happening with Pru. I want to know what's going on. I want to know why those people are camping at the gate."

Preacher Will and Dr. Ben Shank were in the kitchen eating Velveeta cheese and ginger snaps. Oatmeal cookies and deviled ham. There were Fritos and Cheetos, Milky Ways and Mounds, dips and chips of every sort. Every soft drink known to man. Junk food stock was very likely trading high.

"Folks say they want to see the child," said Preacher Will, popping up a Nehi Orange. "More of 'em coming ever' day."

Alma stared at Will. "They want to see Cush? What for?"

"There's blueberry pie on the stove," said Will.

"You make sure those people stay out," Alma said. "Lord God, no wonder poor Pru's in a snit! What's wrong with her, Ben, besides that?"

"Hard to say," said Dr. Shank, digging in a can of cold pears. "Pixilation of the brain. Disorders of the head. Severe aberrations of the mind. The girl's unsettled somewhat. Neurons slightly out of whack."

Alma had never much cared for Ben Shank. What could you say about a man who'd spent his whole adult life working on the tonsil transplant?

"Fine," Alma said, "you want to kind of sum it up? What's the matter with her, Ben?"

"Pru's daffy as a duck."

"I wouldn't leave Satan out of this," said Will.

"Maybe *you* wouldn't, *I* would," Alma said. "Where's Pru now?"

"Up in her room. Been there for three whole days, and she won't come out."

"That girl needs care," said Dr. Shank. "You ought to keep that in mind. I know a real good place."

"The arch fiend's always on the prowl," said Will, "don't you think he's not."

"What I think I better do is see Pru," Alma said.

▲▼▲

Alma made her way through the parlor to the hall. Through cartons from Kmart, Target, and Sears. Through tapes and cassettes, through a stack of CDs, past a tacky new lamp. Coming into money hadn't changed Pru's taste a whole lot.

Pru's room was nearly dark. The windows were covered up with blankets and sheets. The sparse bit of light that seeped in gave the room an odd undersea effect.

"Pru," Alma said, "you might want to talk me in. I don't care to fall and break a leg."

"I'm not crazy anymore," Pru said. "An' I don't care what that fool preacher says, I haven't got a demon in my foot."

"I know that," Alma said. She groped about and found a chair. "What you think's the matter with you, Pru? Why you sitting up here in the dark?"

Pru sat cross-legged in the middle of her bed. Alma couldn't see her face or read her eyes.

"If I'm sittin' in the dark, I can't *see*," Pru said. "I don't want to see a thing, Alma, seeing's what messes up my head."

"Pru, what is it you don't want to see," Alma said, almost afraid to ask. "You want to tell me that?"

"I ain't going to a loony house, Alma, that's a fact."

"Now, nobody's going to do that."

"I sit right here, I'll be fine. Long as I keep out the light."

"You don't like the light?"

"I flat can't take it no more," Pru said. "I can't stand anything *pink*. Everything's lavender or a wimpy shade of green. Everything's got a fuzzy glow. I'm sick to death of tangerine. I feel like I fell into a sack of them afterdinner mints. Lord, I'd give a dollar for a little piece of brown. I'd double that for something red."

Pru leaned forward on the bed. Alma reached out and found her hands. Her eyes were big and round and her hands were like ice.

"I'm scared, Aunt Alma," Pru said. "Corn don't come in baby blue. I never seen a apricot lettuce in my life. I *know* what's going on, I know that. Them Easter egg colors is leakin' through out of my dreams. They're comin' right in and I can't hold 'em back!"

Alma felt a chill, as if someone had pressed a cold Sprite against her back. She held on to Pru real tight.

"I haven't seen any blue corn," Alma said, "but I know what you're telling me, Pru. I want you to think on that, you understand? Hon, it isn't just *you*, it's not just something in your head. I could feel it driving in, like everything's humming in the ground. Like every growing thing on the place is just swelling up to bust."

Alma gripped Pru's shoulder and looked right in her eyes. "You've got about the prettiest farm there is, but you and I know it isn't how it *ought* to be. It doesn't look right, Pru, and it isn't any wonder that you're having color problems in your head. Shoot, this place'd send van Gogh around the bend."

"Oh God, Aunt Alma, I'm scared," said Pru. "I'm scared as I can be!"

Tears trailed down Pru's cheeks, and Alma took her in her arms.

"It's going to be fine," Alma said. "Don't you worry, it'll be just fine."

"You ain't goin' to leave me here, are you?"

"Child, I am staying right here," Alma said. "I'm not going anywhere at all."

Alma held her tight. She could feel Pru's tears, she could feel her body shake. I'm sure glad you're hugging real good, Alma thought, so you won't know that I'm scared, too.

▲▼▲

Alma shooed Will and Dr. Shank out the door and started cleaning up the house. The kitchen took an hour and a half. She worked through geologic zones, through empty pizza cartons and turkey pot pies. Through Ritz Cracker boxes and frozen french fries. It might be that malnutrition was affecting Pru's head, Alma thought. A brain won't run in third gear on potato chips and Mounds.

She had the house in shape by late afternoon. Pru seemed better, but she wouldn't leave her room. Alma was alarmed to learn that Cush stayed at the creek all the time, that he wouldn't come back to the house at all.

"It isn't right," Alma said. "A little boy shouldn't live beneath a bridge."

"Might be he shouldn't," Pru said, "but I reckon that he *is.*"

▲▼▲

Alma fixed Pru supper, and took a plate up to the gate for Uncle Fry. If Uncle Fry had moved an inch since she'd left him there at ten, she couldn't tell. The cars were still there. People stood outside the gate and looked in. They didn't talk or move about. Some of the men had awful wigs. Some of the men were bald. Some of the men wore bib overalls. More than a few wore funny robes. They all gave Alma the creeps. What did they want with *Cush?* What did they think they'd *see?* As far as that goes, how did they even know that Cush was *there?*

"I don't want to think about that," Alma said as she drove back toward the creek. "I've got enough on my mind with just Pru."

▲▼▲

Alma left the car on the road and took some oatmeal down to Cush. She walked through tall sweet grass down a path beside the bridge, down through a canopy of iridescent green. The moment she saw the creek, she stopped still. The sight overwhelmed her, it took her breath away. Thick stands of fern lined the stream on either side. Wild red roses climbed the trunk of every tree. Fish darted quicksilver-bright through water clear as air. Farther toward the bend, red flag and coralroot set the banks afire.

There was more, though, a great deal more than the eye could truly see. Standing on the bank in dusky shade, standing by the creek in citron light, Alma felt totally at peace, suspended in the quiet, inconceivably serene. The rest of the farm seemed far away, stirring in the steamy afternoon, caught up in purpose and intent, caught in a fever, in a frenzy of intoxicated growth.

The creek was apart from all that. It was finished and complete, in a pure and tranquil state. Alma felt certain nothing more could happen here that could possibly enhance this magic place. She felt she was seven, she felt she was ten, she felt her sister Lucy by her side. And as she stood there caught up in the spell, lost in the enchantment of the day, her eyes seemed to draw her to the bridge, to the shadows under old and rusted iron.

Alma held her breath. Something seemed to flicker there, vague and undefined, something like a dazzle or a haze. A pale shaft dancing for an instant through the quiet. Dust motes captured in an errant beam of light. It was there and it was gone and it wasn't gone at all.

"Hello, Aunt Alma," Cush said.

Alma stood perfectly still. She felt incredibly calm, she felt frightened and alarmed, she felt totally at ease.

"Are you there, Aunt Alma, are you there?"

"I'm right here, Cush," Alma said. "I'm glad to see you're talking some better than you could." His voice was a croak, like gravel in a can. "I've brought you some oatmeal, hon. You need to eat something hot and good."

"Tell mother that I'm doing just fine," Cush said. *"You tell her that for me."*

"Now, you ought to tell her that yourself," Alma said, "that's what you ought to do. Cush, you shouldn't be staying down here. You shouldn't be out beneath a bridge."

"I'm where I ought to be," Cush said.

"Now, why you say that?"

"This is where I got to stay, this is where I got to be."

"You already told me that. What I'd like to know is *why.*"

"This is where I am, Aunt Alma. Right here's where I got to be."

He may be different, Alma thought, but he's just as aggravating as any other child I've ever known.

"Now, Cush—" Alma said, and that's as far as Alma got. Words that might have been were never said. Alma was struck by a great rush of loneliness and joy, shaken to her soul by a wave of jubilation and regret, nearly swept away by chaos and accord.

As quickly as it came, the moment passed and let her go. Let her go but held her with the faint deep whisper of the earth. Held her with a hint of the sweet oscillation of the stars. She tried to remember the universal dance. Tried her best to hum the lost chord. There were things she had forgotten, there were things she almost knew. She hung on the restive edge of secrets nearly told, a breath away from mysteries revealed. She wondered if she'd died or if she'd just come to life. She wondered why they both looked just the same.

And when she found herself again, when her heart began to stir, she looked into the shadow of the bridge. She looked, and there was Cush. Cush, or a spiderweb caught against the sun; Cush, or a phantom spark of light.

"Cush, I know you're there," Alma said. "Cush, you *talk* to me, you hear?"

Alma stood and listened to the creek. She listened to a crow call far off in the trees. She listened and she waited in the hot electric summer afternoon....

▲▼▲

Pru wasn't any better and she wasn't any worse. Pastel shades were still clouding up her head. Mint seemed the color of the day. She said she felt she had a rash, and took three or four baths before dark. She soaked herself in European soap and rubbed Chinese lotions on her skin. Every hour and a half, she completely changed her clothes.

Alma couldn't take all the bathing and the changing and the scurrying about. It made her dizzy just to watch. She prowled through the kitchen, searching for anything that wasn't in a can or in a sack. Lord God, Alma thought, there's a garden outside that would bring Luther Burbank to tears, and Pru's got a corner on Spam.

She went outside and picked several ears of corn. She yanked up carrots big as Little League bats. She made a hot supper and a salad on the side, and took it up to Pru. Pru picked around awhile and wrinkled up her nose.

"What kinda stuff is this?"

"Those are vegetables, Pru. You probably never saw one before. We grow 'em all the time on Mars."

"I ain't real hungry right now."

"Pretend you've got Froot Loops and a Coke," Alma said. "I'll leave your plate here."

▲▼▲

Alma went back downstairs and ate alone. She took a lot of time cleaning up. She did things she didn't have to do. She didn't want to think. She didn't want to think about Cush or what had happened at the bridge.

Nothing did any good at all. Cush was in her head and he wouldn't go away. "I don't even know what *happened* out there," Alma said. "I don't know if anything *did.*"

Whatever it was, it had left her full of hope and disbelief, full of doubt and good cheer, full of bliss and awful dread. She felt she was nearly in tune, on the edge of perfect pitch. She felt she nearly had the beat. That's what he did, Alma thought. He gave me a peek somewhere and brought me back. Brought me back and never told me where I'd been.

Alma left the house and walked out onto the porch. The air was hot and still. Night was on the way, and the land and the sky were strangely green. It looked like Oz, right before the wizard came clean.

Oh Lord, Alma thought, looking out into the quickly fading light, I guess I knew. I knew and I didn't want to see. I wrote it all down and I thought that'd make it go away. The farm and the money and Uncle John Fry, nothing the way it ought to be. And all of that coming out of Cush. Coming from a child with awful skin and a baked potato head.

"Who *are* you, Cush?" Alma called into the night. "Tell me who you are, tell me what you got to do!"

The cornfield shimmered with luminescent light. The air seemed electric, urgent and alive, she could feel it as it danced along her skin, she could feel the night press upon the land, she could feel the deep cadence of the earth.

"It's going to happen," Alma said, and felt a chill. "It's going to happen and it's going to happen here. *Who are you, Cush?*" she said again. *"Tell me what it is you've got to do…"*

▲▼▲

Alma tried to rest. She knew she wouldn't get away with that. Not in Pru's house, and not tonight. She dozed now and then. She made tea twice. The wind picked up and began to shake the house. It blew from the north, then shifted to the south. Tried the east and tried the west, and petered out.

A little after one, she fell asleep. At two, she woke up with a start. Pru was screaming like a cat. Alma wrapped her robe around herself and made her way back up the stairs.

"Don't turn on the light!" Pru shouted when Alma opened up the door.

"Pru, I'm getting tired of trying to find you in the dark," Alma said. She felt her way around the walls. A glow from downstairs showed her Pru. She was huddled on the floor in the corner by the bed. She was shaking like a malted-milk machine, and her eyes were fever bright.

"Pru, what's the *matter* with you, child?" Alma sat down and held her tight.

"Oh God," Pru said, "my whole insides are full of fleas. It might be fire ants or bees, it's hard to tell. They're down in my fingers and my toes. They're crawling in my knees."

Alma felt Pru's head. "I'd say you're right close to a hundred and three. I'll find you an aspirin somewhere. I'll make a cup of tea."

"I've got some Raid beneath the sink, you might bring me some of that. Oh Jesus, Aunt Alma, I'm scared. I think something's wrong with Cush. I think he needs his mama bad. I think I better go and see."

"I don't think Cush needs a thing," Alma said. "I think Cush is doing fine. Pru, you better come downstairs and sleep with me. We'll keep off all the lights."

"Don't matter," said Pru. "Dark helps some, but it don't keep the pinks from sneakin' in. I can take them limes, I can tolerate the peach, but I can't put up with pink."

"I'll get a pill," Alma said, "You try and get some sleep."

Alma helped Pru back into bed and went out and closed the door. Lord God, she thought, I don't know what to do. You can't hardly reason with a person's got decorator colors in her head.

▲▼▲

Alma's watch said a quarter after three. She didn't even try to go to bed. She sat in the kitchen and drank a cup of tea. She tried not to think about Cush. She tried not to think about Pru. Everything would work itself out. Everything would be just fine. She could hear Pru pacing about. Walking this way and that, humming a Ray Charles tune. Likely works good in the dark, Alma thought.

At exactly four o'clock, the lights began to flicker on and off. The wind came up again, this time blowing straight down. Alma knew high-school science by heart, and she'd never heard of *that*. Cups and dishes rattled on the shelves. The teapot slid across the sink. Cabinets and drawers popped open all at once. Peanut butter did a flip, and food from overseas hopped about.

Alma held on to the Kenmore stove. She knew that Sears made their stuff to last. In a moment, the rumbles and the shakes came abruptly to a halt. The wind disappeared, and Alma's ears began to pop. Something spattered on the window, something drummed upon the roof, and the rain began to fall. Alma ran into the parlor and peeked out through the blinds. Pink lightning sizzled through the corn. Every bush and every tree, every single blade of grass, was bathed in pale coronal light. Light danced up the steps and up the porch and in the house. It danced on the ceiling, on the walls, and on the floor. It crawled along the tables and the lamps.

Lord, Alma thought, this isn't going to set well with Pru. She listened, but she didn't hear a sound from upstairs. Pru wasn't singing anymore, but she wasn't up stomping or crying out.

The rain stopped as quickly as it came. Alma stepped out onto the porch. The very air was charged, rich and cool and clean. It made Alma dizzy just to breathe. The sky overhead was full of stars. The first hint of morning started glowing in the east, darts of color sharp as northern lights. And as the day began to grow, as the shadows disappeared, Alma saw them everywhere about, people standing in the road, people standing in the corn, people standing everywhere, and everyone looking past the field and through the woods, everyone looking toward the bridge.

Alma looked past the corn, past the people and the trees. Something pure and crystal bright struck her eyes, something splendid as a star, something radiant and white. Alma caught her breath. She looked at the light and she laughed and cried with joy. She felt she ought to sing. She felt goofy in the head, she felt lighter than a gnat. She felt as if someone had shot her up with bliss.

"It's going to happen," Alma said, "it's going to happen and it's going to happen here!"

Alma couldn't stay put. She couldn't just stand there with glory all about. She sprang off the porch and started running down the road. She hadn't run like that since she was ten. She ran down the road past the people, toward the bridge. The people sang and danced, the people swayed and clapped their hands. Alma passed Uncle John Ezekiel Fry. Uncle Fry grinned from ear to ear, and the light sparked off his tears.

"He's coming!" people shouted. "He's coming and he's just about here!"

"I can see him," someone said. "I can see him in the light!"

Alma was sure she heard bells, a deep sonorous toll that touched her soul and swept her clean. A noise like a thunderclap sounded overhead. Alma looked up, and the air was full of birds. Storks and cranes and gulls, hawks and terns and doves, eagles and herons, every kind of bird there was.

Alma laughed at the sky, Alma laughed at the bells, Alma laughed at the music in her head. It was Basin Street jazz, it was Mozart and Bach, it was old-time Gregorian Rock.

Alma couldn't see the road and she couldn't see the bridge. She felt enveloped and absorbed. She felt like she was swimming in the light. It dazzled and it glittered and it sang. It hummed through her body like carbonated bees. It looked like the center of a star. It looked like a hundred billion fireflies in a jar.

"I *knew* you were something special, Cush," Alma cried. "I knew that, Cush, but I got to say I never guessed *who!*"

The light seemed to flare. It drowned her in rapture, an overdose of bliss. It was much too rich, too fine, and too intense. It drove her back with joy, it drove her back with love. It lifted her and swept her off her feet. It swept her up the road and past the field and past the yard, and left her on the porch where she'd begun.

"Better not get too close," someone said. "Better not get too near the light."

"That's my grand-nephew," Alma said, "you likely didn't know that. I guess I can do about anything I please."

▲▼▲

Cush knew who he was. He knew what he was for. He knew what it was he had to do. And now, for the first time in his short and dreary life, in a life full of misery and pain, in a life filled with every dire affliction you could name, Cush knew the reason *why*. When he knew, when it came to him at last, Cush was overwhelmed with the wonder of the thing he had to do. It was awesome, it was fine, it was a marvel and a half, and Cush laughed aloud for the first time in his life.

And in that very instant, in the echo of his laugh, the spark that had smouldered in his soul, that had slept there in the dark, burst free in a rush of brilliant light. The light was the power, and Cush was the light, and Cush reached out and drew everything in. Everything wrong, everything that wasn't right. He drew in envy and avarice and doubt. He called in every plague and every blight. He called in every tumor, every misty cataract. He called in AIDS and bad breath. Ingrown toenails, anger, and regret. The heartbreak of psoriasis, the pain of tooth decay. Migraines and chilblains, heartburn and cramps. Arthritic joints and hemorrhoids. Spasms and paralytic strokes. Hatred and sorrow and excess fat. Colic and prickly heat and gout.

Cush drew them all in, every sickness, every trouble, every curse, and every pain. Cush called them down and drew them into healing light, where they vanished just as if they'd never been.

"I got it all sopped up, I did what I came to do," Cush cried. *"I got everything looking real fine!"*

Cush was the power, and Cush was the light. He was here and he was there, he was mostly everywhere. He could see Cincinnati, he could see Bangladesh. He could see Aunt Alma, see her rushing up the stairs. He could see his mother's room filled with swirls of pastel light. He could see her as she cried out with joy and surprise, see the wonder in her face, see the beauty in her smile as something blossomed inside her, blossomed for a blink and then appeared with silver eyes.

"Got it all ready for you, little sister," Cush called out from the light. *"Got it looking real fine, just as pretty as can be. I've done about all there is to do!"*

All the people standing in the road and in the field saw the light begin to quiver hum and shake, saw it rise up from the bridge, saw it rush into the early morning light.

"Hallelujah," said Uncle John Fry, standing in the tall green corn. *"hallelujah-Chattanooga-bliss...."*

Under Old New York

Stay in line and keep your goods hid, that's two things to do. That's what the kid said. No, he hadn't been up there himself, but he knew a guy who had. He told her all this and she gave him half a roll. They sat and talked in a rusted-out car. He said he came from Tennessee. He said there wasn't any work down there and he didn't think he'd ever go back. He ate the roll without chewing it at all. Hannah couldn't spare the food. But she couldn't stand to eat while the boy sat and watched with hungry eyes. The boy had a pinched-up Southern kind of look. He was skinny as a rail. He said his name was Cadillac. He liked it when she smiled at the name. This was clearly what he wanted her to do. His skin smelled bad, like soured-up milk, like something was wasted inside.

The rain came hard in the night, but the car was okay. Cadillac slept in the front. Hannah in the back. She listened to the rain. She stayed awake a long time. The boy was maybe fourteen, fifteen tops, but that was old enough. She slept with her food between her legs. She slept with an ice pick in her hand. The rain let up toward morning, but the sky was still low and hard as iron. When she woke, the boy was gone.

This was after Newark when she found out she'd come the wrong way. The old filling station map said tunnels ran into New York. The man in the store had to laugh. He said they didn't anymore. He said the niggers had stopped them all up. He said the only way over was the bridge. He said he was about to close up and she could stay on for supper if she liked. He had a place above the store. Times were hard, he knew that, and he liked to help people when he could. The big coat fit her like a tent; she knew this didn't fool the man at all. He could see right through, he could see her in his head. The store was hot and smelled of mold. Hannah said no thanks, she had to go. Her brother, who had done a lot of boxing in North Platte, Nebraska, was waiting down the street. Her brother knew right where she was, and he didn't like to wait. She bought an apple and some rolls and sliced meat. The meat had gone bad. She spent the next day doubled up sick in a culvert by the road.

That night she found the rusted-out car and Cadillac. In the morning, she ate her apple and a roll and started off again. There were plenty of people on the road. Most everyone was headed up north, but some were walking back the other way. Hannah kept to herself. She didn't talk to anyone. Cadillac had told her that, too. There are all kinds of folks out there, is what he said. You get in the line, you make friends with someone, they're going to find out what you got. What kind of food and how much. If you've got any money in your sack. You get all cozy then you get across the bridge, this friend tells a nigger what you said, something you didn't mean to say. What if I didn't say anything at all? Hannah said. Don't matter if you didn't or you did. They'll make something up and say that. There's only so many jobs over there, and folks will do anything they can to get work. This is what the guy told *him*, and he'd been across the bridge and back. He met a girl in line, and she messed him up good. Ate all his food and then stole the job that should've been his. That's just the way it is.

Hannah figured Cadillac was right or close enough. Three weeks on the road, and she'd learned a whole lot by herself. They nearly had her in Decatur, Illinois. Migrants camped out in a field. She woke in time and got away. Not a one of them was over nine or ten, kids running in a pack. Pittsburgh was good. A lot of the plants were going full. Knock on any back door, and they'd most of them fix a plate of food. It wasn't bad everywhere. Some towns were doing okay. If people had work, they'd treat you fine. They knew how it was to do without.

Around noon, the rain started up again; not the hard and steady rain that had drummed her to sleep the night before, but a rain you couldn't see, like a cloud come to earth, a dirt-cold rain that you knew could settle in, just hang there heavy for a week, until it soaked right through to the bone. Hannah drew her collar up high and pulled the woolen cap down about her ears. The rain formed a chill oily mist on her face. She licked her upper lip and tasted salt. Road dirt from West Virginia. Handout food from Indiana, wood smoke from Illinois. You stay in the shower till you're weak in the knees, till the walls begin to sweat. A million little drops sting hot against your skin. The room's full of steam, and the bathroom cabinet's full of all the white towels in the world.

Lord God, Hannah thought, when could she remember doing that? She knew exactly where and when, and thrust the picture out of her head, tossed it as far as it would go.

▲▼▲

Merchants from Newark had set up stands along the highway out of town, lean-tos and tents, makeshift counters and stands. The owners were delighted with the rain. It brought people in off the road. They huddled inside from the cold. The stalls were mostly family affairs. A husband and his wife. The man sold goods while the woman watched the customers like a hawk. Road people didn't have a lot to spend, but they all knew how to steal.

Cadillac had said buy before you get too far. Don't buy nothing on the bridge, it'll cost you an arm and a leg. Hannah looked at the pitiful display. The vegetables were wilted, the fruit was overripe. The sight made her feel helpless, helpless and angry and hungry all the same. She knew this was stuff the people couldn't sell in town. There were peaches, no bigger than limes, pulpy with the smell of sweet decay. Apples that had laid on the ground. Back home, her father had raised a few hogs, just to eat and not to sell. Hannah had taken out a bucket of scraps from the kitchen every day; every scrap in that bucket was fresher than the crap they had here.

She picked out some apples that didn't seem entirely brown. Two long loaves of hard bread. You could chew on bread and get it soft. The carrots went limp in her hand, but she bought some anyway. A bunch of green onions. One orange. She stayed away from meat. It added up to forty-eight cents, three times what everything was worth. Hannah counted out the coins she had left. Seventeen cents. Two pennies, a nickel, and a dime. Not a lot, but she would have to make do. Cadillac said you could make two dollars a day in New York, three if you had any skills.

For some time, Hannah had sensed a presence nearby. She felt vaguely ill at ease, felt the touch of curious eyes. She didn't turn around. She put the things she'd bought in a string sack she kept beneath her coat. She closed her change tightly in her fist and edged her way toward the front of the stall. An old woman blocked her path. Hannah backed off. The aisle was too narrow and there was nowhere to go.

"Excuse me," Hannah said, and tried to squeeze herself by.

The old woman looked right at her, determined not to move, looked right at her with predatory eyes, black eyes circled by halos of loose discolored flesh, looked right at her like an owl looks at a shrew.

Hannah was annoyed, startled by the dark and foreign face, by the tiny blue lips, by the nose that was sharp enough to cut.

"Listen, I have to get by," Hannah said, "you have to move."

"My husban' is dead," the woman said. "This is no matter to me, I tell you that. I can get along. I don' fock with no one, okay?"

Hannah took a deep breath, squeezed and shoved and forced her way free. She hurried through the stall into the rain. The old woman followed on her heels. Hannah looked the other way.

"Hey, I don' like to be push, okay? Is easy to push an ol' lady. What do you care?"

"Well, you just refused to let me by," Hannah said.

"My husban' is dead. He is driving this trock he falls dead."

"I'm very sorry for your loss."

"What's it to you? You got your youth, you got your looks. We live in one house thirty years. He says, I don' want to drive a trock no more. He says, I don' want to work for focking Japs. I say, what do you care? They pay, so what do you care?"

Hannah thrust her hands deep into the pockets of her coat. Everyone walked hunched up against the rain. Everyone's head disappeared. The woman was short; she scarcely came up to Hannah's chest. She took three steps to Hannah's one.

"I wish I had a egg," the woman said, "Luis, he wouldn't eat a egg. Any way you fix it, he don't touch a egg. Those apples you got, they no good. They gonna spoil plenty fast."

"I guess they'll have to do," Hannah said.

"I'm Mrs. Ortega. You don't say your name."

"Hannah," Hannah said, and wished she'd said Mary or Phyllis Ann.

"I know a Hannah once. I think she's a Jew. I guess a Jew's okay."

"That's nice," Hannah said. She wasn't listening at all.

▲▼▲

The people on the road seemed a mix. Men and women, young and old, black and white. Spanish, like Mrs. Ortega. A few Orientals now and then. Mrs. Ortega told Hannah, wanted Hannah to know, that she was Puerto Rican, that she wasn't any Mex. That her cousin by marriage owned a store in New York. Didn't just run it but owned it by himself. The cousin would meet her when she got across the bridge. That was the thing; if you knew someone who was already there, someone who would give you a job, then they wouldn't send you back. Everyone else—and Mrs. Ortega included Hannah in the lot—everyone else had to trust to their luck, had to take what they could get.

Hannah didn't care to hear this at all. It was something she had tried hard not to think about. That there were just as many people coming back along the road as going north. People who had been across the bridge. People who couldn't get a job. What kind of people did they want? Hannah wondered. Who got hired, and who got turned away? After a while, everyone seemed to look alike. They looked just like the people going north.

She guessed it was early afternoon. With the rain you couldn't tell. The world ended just beyond the road. There were buildings and houses and telephone poles on either side, all ghostly shapes behind a veil.

"A man, he give you trouble all your life," said Mrs. Ortega. "This is what a man he's gonna do. He give you trouble all your life then trouble when he's dead."

"I wouldn't know about that," Hannah said.

Horns began to blare down the road, and Hannah turned to see circles of yellow light through the rain. Everyone moved to the side. A long line of trucks lumbered by, headed north. The trucks were full of scrap iron and heavy metal drums and left the smell of oil and rust. Hannah watched them pass. Mrs. Ortega kept her eyes straight ahead, as if the trucks weren't even there.

A few minutes after that, a car came up from the south, bright lights cutting through the mist. It was long and low and black, and its tires hissed on the road. The car was moving fast. It whined past Hannah in a blur. The taillights winked and disappeared.

"Focking Japs," said Mrs. Ortega.

"Well, I don't know why you say that." Hannah knew she couldn't see inside. The windows were as black as the car.

Mrs. Ortega looked at Hannah like she didn't know anything at all. "They got a big car, it's a Jap. Take my word it's a Jap."

"I guess so," Hannah said. She let it go at that. There was no sense arguing with Mrs. Ortega. Mrs. Ortega had her own set opinion on everything there was, and didn't much care to hear yours.

And this time, Hannah had to admit, she was likely close to right. There weren't many cars on the road. You had to be rich to run a car, and there weren't a lot of poor Japanese. Not any Hannah had ever seen.

She thought about the car. About the slick black paint, about the fine black tires, about the chrome that was shiny silver bright, silver bright even in the rain. She wondered how it looked inside. It was warm and it was dry. A woman sat in back. She didn't have to wear a coat. She listened to the car radio. She had a long white dress and gold shoes. She had a ring. The ring had a big green stone. If she lost the ring, a nice-looking man would say fine, I'll get you another at the store. We'll go out to dinner somewhere, then we'll go and get a ring. They go out to dinner, and the woman has corn and fresh tomatoes and some cake. The man has a steak. Then they both order ice cream.

Hannah felt beneath her coat and found the string sack she kept inside. She pulled out two green onions, and tore off a hard piece of bread.

Mrs. Ortega shook her head. "You eat while you walk is no good. Eat when you stop. You go and eat ever'thing now, you run out."

"I won't run out," Hannah said. "And I'll eat whenever I please."

"Hah!" said Mrs. Ortega. "You don' know nothing. You don' know nothing at all."

▲▼▲

When Hannah saw the end of the line, she nearly cried. It simply wasn't right. It wasn't how she saw it in her head. In her head there was the line and the bridge and then New York City after that. Everything together, everything there where she could see. Instead, the line stretched off down the highway and vanished in a dismal shroud of rain. Everybody disappeared, just the way they had before.

"Where is it?" she said aloud. "I can't see the bridge."

"Up about a mile," someone said. "A mile or maybe two."

"A *mile*?" Hannah turned and saw the man. He was tall, he was old, or maybe young. Rain dripped off his felt hat. "Why, we've already walked about ten!"

"Ten's about it," the man said.

"Don' talk to him," said Mrs. Ortega, who had already edged past Hannah to get ahead.

"I'll talk to anyone I want," Hannah said.

The man grinned. "Your mother don't care for me at all."

"She is *not* my mother," Hannah said.

"Well then, I'd guess you're all alone. I'd say you're by yourself. Hey, you're a pretty little thing. That coat don't show it, but I bet you look fine. I'm Dutch, and I didn't get your name."

Hannah felt the color rise to her face. "Listen, I don't much care for your manners or your talk."

"So? What did I tell you?" said Mrs. Ortega. She didn't bother to turn around.

"I didn't mean no offense," said Dutch. His eyes were rimmed with red. His face was too long, and he clearly hadn't shaved in several days.

"You don't even know someone, you shouldn't ought to talk like that," Hannah said. "Even if you know this person, that is not the thing to say."

Dutch looked properly subdued. "I just figured we could talk. There's nothing else to do."

"I don't guess you and I have a thing to talk about."

"You think you'll get a job in New York?"

"I'm sure I don't know. I'll do the best I can."

"Shoot, that's all anyone can do." Dutch grinned again. "I got me a skill. I can fix things good. Anything that's broke. Something comes apart, I can put her back right." Dutch showed Hannah a wink, not the wrong kind of wink, but a wink in confidence. "See, that's the thing, you get over 'cross the bridge. You got to have a skill. That's what they want to hear. And even if you don't, if you can't do anything at all, that sure ain't what you want to say. You won't know what they're lookin' for, but you got to say a skill. That's the only chance you got."

"That seems a little risky to me," Hannah said. "I think I'd be scared to say I could do something if I can't."

Dutch looked at Hannah. "You know what scary is, girl? Scary's comin' back across the bridge with no work. You thought you had a quarter, but you don't. Isn't nothin' any scarier than that."

"No, I guess not." He didn't have to tell her that he'd done all this before. Hannah didn't have to ask. She didn't know exactly what to say. She knew she had encouraged him to talk. She wished she hadn't but she had. Now she wasn't certain how to stop.

The rain began to pound the road, much harder than before. Not straight down like a rain ought to do, but slanting in furtive and sly, cunning and cold, from here and then from there, whipping in so fast that you couldn't fight it off, couldn't duck inside your coat, couldn't hide beneath your hat. The rain swept down Hannah's collar, bit her face and stung her legs, but she was grateful for the chance to turn away, grateful not to have to talk, grateful not to have to think about coming back across without a quarter to her name.

▲▼▲

The sound came back down the line, first in a whisper like the wind from far away, then swelling to a rush, one voice drowning out the next.

The bridge! The bridge! The bridge is right ahead!

Everyone stretched for a look. The rain had slacked off, settled to a chill and steady drizzle once again. Day was winding down, and the saturated sky was a dull oppressive gray. At first Hannah couldn't see a thing. Everything was near, everything was far away. Then she saw the lights, caught her breath, saw the pale white stars strung in long and lacy patterns through the rain, saw the stars loop down in a roller coaster arc, climb again and disappear. Once she saw the lights, Hannah could pick out the towers of the bridge, two immense shadows looming high and out of sight, lost in the mist, in the fast approaching night.

"It's so big," Hannah said. "I never imagined it would look like that."

"George Washington Bridge," said Dutch. He grinned like people do when they've been somewhere before. "There she is, right there, there she is, straight ahead."

"We can see," said Mrs. Ortega. "Nobody here is blind."

"Just pointing out the sights," said Dutch.

"Watch him," said Mrs. Ortega. "I don' like his looks."

"You don't much like nothin'," said Dutch.

▲▼▲

As the line grew closer to the bridge, Hannah saw they had come upon a tangle of roads on either side, roads that passed below and overhead, roads that swept in from every side. Trucks rumbled by underneath the people road, going east toward the bridge and coming back, trucks of every shape and size and even black and shiny cars. The highways whispered and hummed. Headlights pierced the vaporous night.

Now there was a new line of people, a new line that came in from the west, a new line moving toward the bridge. The new line kept to the left side of the road, Hannah's to the right. Not a word passed between the two lines. There was nothing anyone had to say. It was clear to everyone in either line: Those people aren't the same as the people over here. They might look the same, but they aren't the same at all. They're over there and we are here. They are not in our line. People who had never said hello to whoever was behind them or ahead had something to talk about now. You might be talking to the woman or the man who would steal your job away. But at least they weren't in the other line.

Now the dark towers were directly overhead. The lines moved onto the bridge. At once, Hannah was aware of a new and greater cold, a cold that didn't come from the rain. It swept in from the north. It sang through the great webs of cable and steel. It cut through her coat like vicious darts of ice.

"Real bitch, ain't it? That's the Hudson," said Dutch. "You can't see it, but it's there."

"Mr. Guidebook," said Mrs. Ortega. "Mr. Know-It-All."

"Hey. Excuse me for livin'," said Dutch.

Hannah wondered why they didn't try to keep the bridge clean. There was garbage everywhere. Tin cans and broken glass. Scraps of food ground into the road. Cardboard boxes. Broken wooden crates. Candy wrappers, newspapers, papers of every sort, pressed wet against the rust-colored metal of the bridge.

And the smell. The smell was worst of all. A smell too strong for the wind to blow away. It came from the little tin stalls they'd set up along the sides of the road. Hannah thought about the stalls with growing dread. She had to go. She had to go real bad. She couldn't stand the thought of going *there*. But there was no place else to go.

"Listen, I'll be right back," she told Mrs. Ortega, softly so Dutch couldn't hear. Mrs. Ortega was huddled in her coat. She didn't say anything at all.

Hannah walked quickly along the line. She didn't look at anyone, she kept to the side of the bridge. She saw the flash of headlights from the trucks on the level down below. She saw a red light on the river to the south, but it quickly disappeared.

A man was selling food in a shack he'd made from cardboard and wood. He wore a hunting cap pulled down about his ears. His face was bright red from the cold. He had a flashlight hung inside the shack. Hannah could read the prices tacked up against a wall. An apple was a quarter. A sandwich was seventy-five cents. Lord God, on the road you could eat on that for a week. Still, people were lining up to buy.

Hannah tried to hold her breath inside the stall. She got out as quickly as she could. There wasn't any paper, and she tore off a piece of her filling station map and used that. Walking back along the line, she heard her name. She turned and looked and there was Cadillac. Up the line maybe twenty yards ahead. Hannah was delighted to see someone she knew. She smiled and started up to say hello. She stopped and looked at Cadillac again. He was standing between two men. One man was heavy, the other was thin. Both of the men had coats as good as new. Cadillac had a coat, too, a red plaid coat that nearly swallowed him whole, and a red cap to match. He grinned at Hannah with a big piece of chicken in his hand. Hannah hadn't tasted chicken in a month or maybe two. One of the men saw Hannah. He saw her wave at Cadillac. He looked right at her and didn't smile. He raised his hand and touched Cadillac's face, touched his face and touched his hair.

Hannah felt as if the cold had reached in and found her heart. She looked at the man. She couldn't look at Cadillac. She turned away and ran back down the line. People glanced up to watch her pass.

▲▼▲

"Wha's the matter with you?" said Mrs. Ortega. She looked Hannah up and down. "Huh? You fall ina toilet or what?"

"I am just *fine*, thank you," Hannah said. Good. Now everyone knew where she'd been.

"Okay. You don' look fine to me. You look like you eat something you ought to t'row up." Mrs. Ortega stomped her feet against the cold. "You back jus' in time. Mr. Big Shot here is telling lies. Like I don' know a lie. Like I don' live with a liar forty year."

"I didn't tell you no lie," Dutch said. "You ain't got the sense to know the truth."

"I know what I know. I don' got to hear a lie."

"Hey, ol' lady. You don't have to do nothin' but complain."

"Mrs. *Ortega—*" It suddenly occurred to Hannah that something wasn't right somewhere. That something had changed while she was gone. That the line wasn't moving anymore. That everyone had stopped. "Do you think something's wrong?" Hannah said. "Why aren't we going anywhere?"

Mrs. Ortega rolled her eyes in patience and despair. "See? You don' know nothing at all."

Dutch laughed as if Hannah had told a joke that he already knew. "The line don't go at night. Not when it's dark. It don't go nowhere in the dark."

"Well why not?"

"It just don't. They hire all day and they close her down at night. Even the niggers and the spics, they gotta sleep."

"You watch your mouth," said Mrs. Ortega.

Hannah stared at Dutch. "You mean we have to stay out here? Out here on the bridge?"

"You got it, babe."

"But there's no place to *sleep.*"

"This is the line. It ain't a hotel."

"Well, I guess I know that. I guess I've been on the road as long as you."

Hannah knew at once it was the wrong thing to say. Dutch didn't answer. He looked at her a while then hunched down in his coat and turned away. He looked beyond the bridge, past the river and the rain, as if there might be something there to see.

▲▼▲

Hannah tried to sleep, tried to huddle up against the cold. She found a piece of cardboard and folded it up across her head. It didn't do a lot of good. It kept out the rain, but it kept the smells in. The smells were there and they wouldn't go away. She thought about the garbage, the food and the trash and the paper and the glass, pressed in forever on the surface of the bridge. Like the cliff by the creek on the farm, layers of time stacked together like a cake. Her father had known all the names, what the different rocks were called. He told her the names of all the rocks and all the years. But the names were too long, and Hannah couldn't remember them at all.

She wondered if some of the smell was her. She wondered if she smelled as bad as everyone else in the line. Sometimes she'd found a river or a stream. A place far enough from the road. She had tried to get clean, tried to wash as best she could, but she was scared to take everything off. Afraid that someone might come along.

Some people slept. Some people stayed awake and talked. You weren't supposed to make a fire on the bridge, but a lot of people did. Sometimes a policeman came by and made them put the fires out. He drove a little three-wheeled car and wore a heavy leather coat. When he was gone, the people lit the fires again.

"My husban', he don't like to work for Jap," said Mrs. Ortega. "He don' like the way they look."

"I talked to a Jap feller once," said Dutch, "me and him had a drink. He gets to drinkin' real hard he says, hey, I don't like the way you look."

"I think you tell a lie. I don' think he give you any drink."

"Listen, this guy was okay. I'm cutting up scrap for this place and the Jap says, Dutch, it's gettin' hot. Stop and have a drink."

"A Jap is not gonna say that. He don' say this to you."

"Sure he did. He don't like the way I look, that's fine. Hey, you're going to work for whoever's got the pay. Don't make no difference to me, niggers, Japs, an' spics. Some guy gives me a dollar a day, I say fine. Where you want me to dig? What you like me to fix? It's all the same to me."

"You don' talk like that, Mr. Smart Aleck, you get across the bridge."

"You think I'm nuts?" Dutch laughed. "Damn right I don't. I say, good morning, Nee-grow, how you doin' Poortoe-rican, sir? Say, I'm glad you burned down the fuckin' town so ol' Dutch can get some work. I sure appreciate that."

"See, now tha's a lie," said Mrs. Ortega. "You gotta tell a lie. Nobody burn it down. Nobody doin' that."

"Right. I guess it burned down all by itself. I guess the city gets up one mornin' says look, I got nothing else to do. I guess I'll burn myself down. I guess that's what I'd like to do."

"I wish you would kindly shut up," Hannah said. "Some people don't want to talk all night. Some people like to sleep."

"So sleep," said Dutch.

"Don' listen," said Mrs. Ortega. "You don' want to listen, put somet'ing in you ear. Tha's what I think you oughta do."

▲▼▲

Hannah turned away. She pretended not to hear. She pretended that the day was just ahead and the sun was warm and bright.

"What I'm going to do," Dutch said, "I'm going to get a good job, maybe fixin' machinery and stuff. They can always use a guy can fix things up. I get this job, I'm going to eat myself sick, I'm going to sleep in a bed."

"You goin' to dream about a bed," said Mrs. Ortega. "Tha's what you goin' to do."

"This ain't no dream, ol' lady. I'm gettin' me a job. Right now it's a real good time to be going 'cross the bridge."

"Right. Tha's why ever'body coming back."

"Everybody's coming *back*," Dutch said, "'cause they haven't got a skill. See, I got a skill. What I'm thinking is, I'll maybe get on at Times Square. There's all kinds of shit going on there. That's what I'd like to do."

"Hah!" said Mrs. Ortega, "now you a liar again. They don't got a Times Square anymore. Anybody know that. My cousin, he got his own store in New York."

"Big deal," said Dutch. "Listen, they got a Times Square, okay? What they done is a bunch of rich niggers and spics, they're fixin' it up again nice. Bright lights, the whole bit. You got the bread, you can eat and see a show. A nigger, he knows how to make a buck, you gotta hand them that. Fuckin' Jap tourists'll eat it up."

"This is another big lie," said Mrs. Ortega.

"I seen it in a paper," said Dutch. "It's in the paper, it ain't a lie."

"I think you make up the paper, too," said Mrs. Ortega. "I think the paper is a lie. This is what a bum he's goin' to do."

▲▼▲

She heard the trucks and the cars as they rumbled by below. She heard the wind, she heard the rain. She heard a man singing on a boat. She heard the people talk. She slept and woke up and heard a fight. The policeman came again, riding in his three-wheeled car. He told the people not to fight. He told them not to light a fire.

Once Hannah woke to find the rain had gone away. Dutch was sleeping close against her back. His knees were tucked up against her legs. His big arm was heavy on her waist. Hannah sat up with a start. She waved her ice pick in his face.

"Look, you better not do that again," Hannah said.

"Fine. Okay," Dutch said. "Freeze your ass off. What do I care?"

▲▼▲

Dawn was bleak and ashen gray. Mist hugged the river and the cold steel heights of the bridge, and left a little open space between. Hannah itched all over. She ached everywhere. She felt her eyes were full of sand. People stood up and stirred about. People lined up for the stalls. Hannah swore she wouldn't do that again. She smelled the morning fires, smelled someone cooking food. She chewed on an onion and some bread to make the hunger go away.

Dutch looked awful. His skin was white as paste. He took a paper sack from his coat, took a long swallow, and made a face. He saw Hannah watching, grinned and wiped his mouth, and put the sack away.

Hannah reached under her coat, got half a loaf of bread, and handed it to Dutch. Dutch looked surprised. He mumbled something like "thanks," as if the word was real hard to get out. He dug past the crust for the softer bread inside.

"Don' give this bum nothing to eat," said Mrs. Ortega.

"I will if I want to," Hannah said.

"Hah! You don' get a job you don' eat. What you say then?"

The line began to move. Hannah tried to find New York, but she couldn't see the end of the bridge. At least the rain had gone away.

"Listen, last night," said Dutch. "I'm sorry 'bout that. I didn't mean nothin' wrong."

"Yes, you did," Hannah said. "Why do you say you didn't if you did?"

"You want a drink, I got a little left. It'll warm you up good inside."

"No, thank you," Hannah said.

The line stopped. Someone shouted up ahead. A woman began to scream. Someone took her off and made her stop. A crowd started to gather near the right side of the bridge.

"What's wrong," Hannah said. "Can you see what's going on?"

"What am I, a giant?" said Mrs. Ortega.

Several people ran back along the bridge. People in the line behind Dutch asked what was going on. Dutch said he didn't know. After a while, two policemen appeared in their three-wheeled cars. They told everyone to stand back. They told the line to move along. The line moved slow. Everyone had to see. Whatever it was, Hannah didn't want to look. But when she passed the place she had to look, too. There was blood on the bridge. The policemen bent over something white. The blood was dark in the somber morning light. One of the men stood and moved away.

"Oh, *God!*" Hannah said. She stumbled and brought a hand up to her face.

"Hey, so somebody's dead, it's not you," said Mrs. Ortega.

"Jesus," said Dutch. He gripped Hannah's arm.

"I'm just fine," Hannah said. She threw up her onions and her bread.

They'd cut him up bad, cut him bad everywhere. She wondered what they'd done with his clothes, with his red plaid coat and his hat. They cut him everywhere, but they didn't cut his face. His face was just fine. Were the men still on the bridge, did they go back to the end of the line? His face looked nice. Everything else was real bad, but his face was just fine.

▲▼▲

It seemed to take forever for the lines to leave the bridge. They wound down ramps and over this and under that, wound past buildings pressed one against the next, packed so tight it was hard to tell which belonged to what. Down through a grim and narrow street to a dark red building where the lines disappeared.

"Hiring hall," said Dutch before Hannah had to ask. He nodded vaguely to the left. "You don't get work, they send you out another door. You don't get to talk to nobody goin' back across the bridge."

"Why not?" Hannah said.

Dutch grinned and picked his teeth. "Shoot, they let you do that, everybody out here's all of a sudden got carpenter skills. They're plumbers or they're good at fixing trucks. Whatever the hell they're hirin' inside."

"Maybe they looking for a dronk," said Mrs. Ortega. "Maybe you get a job quick."

"Maybe you'll have a fuckin' stroke," said Dutch.

As the line drew closer to the door, Hannah was struck by a sudden sense of loss, a feeling like a shudder, like a tremble, like a quake, like a chill that swept back along the line, like a wave of dark despair. She tried to shake away the fear, tried to lose the sense of dread, tried to think good thoughts, but nothing good would come to mind. She was left with the chill and with the fear, with the image of the long walk back across the bridge.

"The line moves slow, that's a sign," said Dutch. "That means the hiring's good. It means they're takin' time to talk. You move too fast means they ain't finding anyone they want."

"It looks like we're moving fast to me," Hannah said.

"Yeah, maybe. I'd say kinda in between."

"Don' listen to him," said Mrs. Ortega. "Don' listen to a bum."

The scene inside did nothing to temper Hannah's fears. The room was immense, as wide as the building itself, a big room with harsh white lights and a concrete floor. People sat behind long and narrow desks. They wrote things down. They picked up papers and took them to a desk across the room. The papers were blue and pink and white.

You had to stop at a broad yellow line on the floor. The line was twenty feet from the desk up ahead. You couldn't see, you couldn't hear what people said. The lines were moving fast. Hannah's line and the other to her left. Hannah watched. When you didn't get a job, you went out through a door painted red. Hannah counted in her head. Seven-eight-nine-ten...nineteen-twenty-twenty-one. Hannah's heart sank. Everyone was going through the door.

"Oh, Lord," Hannah said. "They aren't hiring anyone at all!"

"Hey, you don't know, you can't never tell," said Dutch.

They hired someone at twenty-five. Another at twenty-nine. Then no one clear to forty-one. Mrs. Ortega was forty-two.

Hannah stood with her toes on the line. A black man sat behind a desk. He wore a blue shirt and blue tie. He spoke to Mrs. Ortega. Mrs. Ortega spoke to him. The man shook his head. There was a coffee cup full of yellow pencils on the desk. Mrs. Ortega picked them up, cup and all, and threw them at the man. The man stood and backed away.

"I don' need you focking job," screamed Mrs. Ortega. "I got family. I got a cousin owns a store!"

The man looked shocked and surprised. Yellow pencils rolled about the floor. Two men rushed in from the left. They picked up Mrs. Ortega and hurried her quickly across the room.

"My cousin he is coming," shouted Mrs. Ortega. Her short legs kicked at the air. "You wait. He is coming soon. My husban' is dead. He drives a Jap trock an' he is dead. My cousin owns a store."

"Oh, dear," Hannah said, "I hope she'll be okay."

"Serves her right," said Dutch.

"It does not. Don't you talk that way."

"Yeah, right."

"Next," said the man at the desk.

Hannah could scarcely move. The twenty feet seemed like a mile. The man looked her up and down. Hannah stopped before the desk. The man looked at her again. He opened his mouth to speak. Another man came up behind his chair. The man at the desk turned away. He leaned back to talk. Hannah looked at the papers on his desk. The man had them covered with his hand. Hannah looked again. There was only one word she could see. The word said ꓱ⅃⅃I. The rest lay beneath the man's thumb. The man turned back, and Hannah quickly looked away.

"Experience," said the man.

"I beg your pardon?" Hannah said.

The man pointed a pencil at her chest. "What do you do, what kind of work?"

"Oh, sorry." Hannah's mind raced. She didn't want to say tile. Not right off. Tile might give her away.

"Brick," Hannah said. "I've done a lot of work in brick."

"You work in brick?" The man seemed surprised.

"Brick, stone, tile, anything like that."

"Doing what?"

"I can lay brick good. I've made a lot of walls. I can do 'bout anything with tile."

"Let me see your hands," said the man.

Hannah held out her hands. The man ran a finger down her palm. Hannah held her breath, thankful for the first time in her life that she had grown up on a farm.

The man made a mark on a blue piece of paper and handed it to Hannah. "Table Five," he said. He didn't look up. He didn't look at Hannah again.

Hannah was stunned. She couldn't believe she had a job. She had work in New York. She didn't have to go back across the bridge. She found Table Five. It was two rows down. A black girl her own age took the paper from her hand. The girl was awfully clean.

"Here's your chits," said the girl. "The yellow's for housing, the green one's for a meal. This is your button. Put it on and don't take it off. Hang on to your button and your chits. We don't give 'em out twice. Go through the door that says Nine." The girl made a mark on the paper and gave it back.

Food. Housing, Hannah thought. Things were looking better all the time. She found Door Nine. She turned and looked back. Mrs. Ortega was in a chair across the room. The chair looked big. Or Mrs. Ortega looked small. At least she was still inside the room. She wasn't out the red door.

Hannah suddenly remembered she hadn't even thought about Dutch. She felt bad about that. She looked about the room, and couldn't find him anywhere at all. She looked at the button on her coat. It said 939. It occurred to her, then, that no one had asked her for her name.

▲▼▲

Hannah was shocked when the woman said take off your clothes, but she did as she was told. The woman handed her a towel and a bar of yellow soap. Leave your stuff here, the woman said, and Hannah did.

The shower was a pleasant surprise. The soap had a medicine smell, but the water was strong and steamy hot. There were seven other women in the showers nearby. Hannah didn't look at them and they didn't look at her. You could stay five minutes, a sign told you that Hannah wanted to spend the day. She wanted to let the water wash every mile away.

In a room off the shower, a woman gave Hannah a green jump-suit and a pair of tennis shoes. The suit wasn't new and didn't fit too well, but it was clean. It smelled just like the yellow soap. Hannah's old clothes and her button and her chits were in a sack. Her food was there, too, and her seventeen cents and her map. The ice pick was gone.

A long hall led to a big room with tables and chairs. Hannah could smell the food before she even reached the room. The smell went right to her belly, and the pain nearly brought her to her knees. She tried not to cry, but the hurt spilled over to her eyes.

The stew was hot and thick. There was fresh bread and coffee and sugar in a bowl. The sign said you could go back for more, and Hannah did. The room was half full. The women sat apart from the men. There were green jumpsuits like her own, blues and blacks and reds.

"Where you from?" said a girl at Hannah's right.

"Nebraska," Hannah said.

"South Carolina," said the girl. She had a long face. Hollow cheeks and hollow eyes. "I wish I wasn't scared. I hope it's goin' to be all right."

"I guess we'll be fine," Hannah said.

"I'm LuAnn," the girl said.

"Hannah," Hannah said.

"You ever heard of Scotia? That's in Hampton County, right close to Estill."

"I don't think I have. I've never been too far from home until now."

A loudspeaker on the wall said, "Greens to the bus. Two minutes. Give your paper to the driver outside."

"That's me," Hannah said. She wolfed down the last of her stew. "You take care, okay?"

"I'll sure try," said LuAnn.

Hannah took her bowl and her cup back to the line. The girl looked lonely and afraid. Maybe I do, too, Hannah thought. Maybe everyone here looks the same.

▲▼▲

The street signs passed in a blur. 155th...146th...Lord, who'd ever guess streets could go that high! Traffic was light. There were people everywhere, but Hannah saw few trucks or cars. The bus raced south like it was going to a fire. There was so much to see, too much to take in at one time, but Hannah tried. The broad street was called Amsterdam Avenue. Long rows of buildings stretched out on either side, grim red buildings with tiny shops and markets jammed between. A movie and a church. A park with no trees. Everyone Hannah saw was black. Sometimes a street looked shabby and dark. Sometimes it looked nice. A man selling food on a corner waved at Hannah, and Hannah waved back.

Leaden clouds still drifted overhead. Hannah thought about the people on the bridge. She wondered if Mrs. Ortega was still sitting in her chair. She wondered if Dutch was headed back.

"Hey, you like New York okay?"

Hannah nearly jumped when the girl swept into the seat beside her. "Yes. I mean I guess I like it fine."

The girl flashed a smile. She looked at Hannah's button. She thumbed through the stack of blue papers in her hand. Hannah was struck by the dark and startling beauty of the girl. Black hair and black eyes, cinnamon colored skin that seemed to shine. A new red jumpsuit that fit. Hannah touched her own hair, and wished she had a brush.

"So, a construction worker, no? Brick and tile." The girl looked at Hannah and laughed. "Boy, that is a big lot of bullshit, 939, you know that?"

"It certainly is not." Hannah was alarmed. "That's what I do."

"Right. Who cares? I'm Catana Pérez. So who are you?"

"I'm Hannah."

"Hannah what?"

"Hannah Gates."

"Gates. Like you swing in and out alla time, huh?"

"They used to tease me some in school."

"And where is that?"

"Nebraska. My father had a farm."

"Had. He don't got it now?"

"It went broke. He couldn't pay it off."

"An' your father, now he is *muerto,* he is dead."

"I didn't say that."

"You don' have to say. You are what, fifteen?"

"No! I'm seventeen, eighteen in May."

"Dios." Catana made a face. "You watch yourself, okay? The dogs, the *perros*, they gonna bark plenty at you. You're a real pretty girl. You got nice yellow hair. I guess you got tits somewhere, I don' know. See, you gonna blush a little, huh? The *perros*, they goin' to bark. You don' listen. You don' bark back, you okay. You understand what I say?"

"I think I do."

"Ah, *sí.* That's exactly what I mean. What am I gonna do with you?"

"You don't have to do a thing," Hannah said. "I'm just fine."

Catana leaned in close. Hannah smelled a light flower perfume.

"Okay. I can see what's in your head," Catana said. "This girl, she ask a lot of questions to me. Why she want to do that? Because this is what I do. I ask people stuff all day. I see you get on the bus and get where you gotta go. That's my job, that's what I do. It's better than construction work, no?"

Hannah had to smile. "Yeah, I guess so."

"You bet."

"Listen, are you a Puerto Rican? Is it all right to ask?"

"Cuban. *Cubano.* That's even better, but don't tell the PRs, they don' know."

Hannah glanced out the window again. She was surprised how things had changed. The buildings weren't so grim anymore. Most of the shops had a fresh coat of paint. The streets were fairly clean. People ate under red and white umbrellas outside. A store that sold flowers spilled its wares out on the street. It looked as if a garden had blossomed in cement.

Catana seemed to read Hannah's thoughts. "Looks a little better, right? You're out of the Heights now, girl. You on the Upper West Side." Catana touched the tip of her nose and raised it a quarter of an inch. "Pretty good place to be. Very nice."

Hannah shook her head. "I guess I'm getting real confused. Everybody says the city burned down, but it doesn't look very burned to me. Everything looks fine. You can't tell anything at all."

Catana showed no expression at all. "Hannah Gates. Hannah Gates from off the farm. I bet you milk a focking cow."

"I just asked," Hannah said.

"Yeah. Okay." Catana traced a shape like a pickle on the seat. "It don't burn up here. The fire is down there. Everything from Downtown to Midtown. Up to Central Park. On the East Side, maybe little more. Sixty-seventh, okay? On the West Side, up to fifty-ninth. That's where you gonna go. Fifty-ninth." She looked up at Hannah. "This don' mean a thing, right? You don' know where you are. You don' know where you go. You don' know what you gonna do."

"I do tile," Hannah said, "tile and brick."

"Yeah, right." Catana rolled her eyes like Mrs. Ortega. "Miss 939 tile and brick. I don't think you ever see a tile before, but that's what you gonna do. You chip and shine, you fix the subway up fine. All the tourists say, hey, everything is lookin' nice. I bet Miss 939 she been by."

"The subway?" Hannah tried not to show her alarm.

"Sure, the subway, what you think? That's why you got a green suit." Catana laughed. "You work real hard, maybe you shine all the way to Times Square. Maybe you get to see the sights."

"I know all about Times Square," Hannah said. "I read about it in a paper one time."

"Hey, she can read a paper, too. We are plenty locky you come across the bridge." Catana paused. "Listen, I tell you a couple things. Stuff you need to know. You learn where you stay. How to get to work. You don' go out after dark until you know pretty good where you are. They give you a meal tonight after work. You don' gotta have a chit. After that, buy your own food at the *bodega* where it's cheap."

Catana glanced over her shoulder, then turned to face Hannah again. "What you don' do most of all is go asking someone about the fire. That's ten, eleven years back, okay? That's gone. Don' go talking 'bout that. Nobody wants to hear."

Hannah was startled. "I just *asked*. I don't see anything wrong with that."

Something changed in Catana's eyes. "You don' see nothing wrong because you got a white face. Everybody got a white face thinks they know about the fire. They got all the answers in their head."

"I don't think anything at all," Hannah said.

"Yeah, right. So I tell you this. Then you don' gotta ask. The fire don' start up here. Where it starts is down *there*. Okay? Where everybody had a face as white as you. You think about tiles. You think about making two dollars every day."

Catana touched Hannah on the shoulder and stood. "Hey, you gonna do real good. You gonna do fine."

▲▼▲

Hannah didn't want to be mad at Catana, but she was. The girl didn't have to get up and walk away. She didn't have to leave. What did I do? Hannah thought. I asked a question is all. I asked about the fire. What's so bad about that? It isn't any secret, everybody knows about the fire. I didn't talk like Dutch. I didn't say nigger and spic. The girl tried to act pleasant after that, but she did get up and walk away.

The bus moved south. The farther south they went, the nicer things became. Traffic picked up at eighty-sixth. The bus slowed down at eighty-first. There were places to eat everywhere. The people were black and brown. A few were even white. Hannah saw a fine hotel. A place to eat Japanese food. The bus stopped again at sixty-ninth. On the corner, there were six men hanging from a pole. Six men and a girl. Hannah couldn't tell what color they had been. Everyone's face had turned black. Someone had made a sign, and hung it at the base of the pole. The sign said, *MAKE BIG MONEY IN DRUGS.* No one glanced at the people who were hanging from the pole. People bought flowers on the street, but no one looked up at the pole.

The bus moved on. Hannah saw places to eat and things to buy. People rushing everywhere about, people walking little dogs. Someone behind her said, hey, there's Lincoln Center, I read about that, and Hannah looked and saw pretty white buildings, a big opera house. But mostly she saw the people hanging on the corner with their faces turning black.

▲▼▲

The bus came to a stop, and the driver said, "Columbus Circle, everybody out."

Everyone in the bus began to talk. Hannah made her way down the aisle and outside. Catana was there and she smiled and said hello. Maybe everything was all right.

Hannah marveled at the big traffic circle, a column with a statue on the top. A tall glass building, a corner of the park. There were people everywhere, trees and grass, a man selling bright balloons. A dozen sights to see, but every eye turned to the south. To the burned and ragged spires, to the towers black as night, to the dark and ruined shells of steel and glass stark against a sullen sky.

Hannah was chilled by the grim and awesome sight. The dead city cast a charred shadow on the city still alive. It's much too close, Hannah thought. It shouldn't be as close as that. It ought to be somewhere far away. I don't want to live in a place that's all dead, I don't want to clean tiles. I don't like it here at all.

"Okay, Greens," Catana said, "line up, let's go." She laughed, as if the sound might make the shadows disappear. "Let's get under New York, let's get to work, let's make a couple dollars today."

Rhido Wars

What I do I hear this fart an a squirt an a squirt after that an then splat. Dont hardly have to wake up Im seein this big red ass with a bright blue ring round the hole where the shits comin out. He squattin maybe thirty hands off an it isnt even Light an I know its Sal Capone. You dont gotta see a face, you can see that ass, isnt any two alike. Drills are like Persons. Persons dont look or smell the same. Ever things different from ever thing else.

▲▼▲

Sal, he knowin I there, an when he all done he turn an blink his baby crap eyes. The stripes on his face is black stead of blue cause theres hardly any Light.

Sal, he not wearin nothin, not wearin anything at all. Ever thin showin, hangin, stuff stickin out. A Drill dont care bout that. Only thing he care bout, he gotta have a hat.

"You are not being sleep," Sal says. "Dark is for the sleep. Persons must sleep in the Dark and working in the Light."

I was sleepin good, Im thinkin, *then you com an shit in my yard. Im not sleepin real good after that...*

"The rain fell much in the forest last Dark," Sal says, the way they all do, like they got a sack of gravel in their craw. "The ground is being wet. Seven baskets for each of your Persons, seven by the time the sun is high. *Nine* for you, Ratch, for you are ever insolent to me. I am angered and sad that you show me disrespect, this is great sorrow and a bad thing to do.

"Be telling your Persons, a basket will not be padded with little leaves and shoots to seem full when it is not. There will be sufficient beetles and snails. Snails will be about on a wetting day as this. There will also be the grubs, Ratch, grubs of most sufficient fat.

"I should like to see voles. Not voles that are deceased, eaten by the ant. Voles are not difficult to catch. Young Lily is quick. Tell her to catch me many voles, I shall bring her honey on a stick. How is the Lily, Ratch?

She is well, I am hope. And little Macky and Dit? And the one who is bit by a snik?"

"He fine too. Hows Florence an Sil? How Miz Pain?"

"You will see that there are voles, Ratch. Voles are expected. Grasses are not."

Sal was all done. A Drill say what he got to say, thats it, he done. While they talkin an scratchin an pluckin some crawly out their fur, you maybe okay. A Drill just lookin, lookin right at you with baby crap eyes, he got some ugly in mind.

A Drills flat ugly outside, but insides ugliern that. You dont know bout ugly till you know whats in a Drills head...

▲▼▲

Its so phuckin hot you are drownin in sweat you are poundin in the head. Ever skeeto ever nat for a thousan miles aroun is crawlin in your eyes is crawlin up your ass.

The sun is up but the trees has smothered all the Light. Its Light somewhere but it isnt down here. You haven ever crawl through creepers an tanglers wrappin roun a tree, you dont know what I talkin bout here. Im talkin trees you cant even see roun, trees got snicks an stingers so big you dont want to think what maybe lookin at you there.

Im crawlin onna ground, Im turnin over rocks, I cant see dick for a phuckin foot ahead. I got a couple snails, I gota buncha grubs. Down here theres ever kinda of bug there is. Down here you a bug or a leaf. Maybe you a root. Ever thing down here squishy, ever thing wet, ever thing tangled in ever thing else. Ever thing fat bout to busting down here, an ever thing one phuckin color, ever thing *green*.

I hear Lily she off somewhere, Lily chasin voles. Dont hear Macky, an you hardly never do. Macky, he gonna spook you sometime, Macky dont make a sound at all.

Cant say that bout Dit. Know where Dit goin to be bout a hour fore he is.

A whole lotta green start shakin an here come Dit. Dit grinnin like a fool an he got a bunch of orchits in his hair. Some of em pink and some of em white, some of em colors hasnt got a name at all.

"I was you," I says, "I wouldnt let Darc Anthony see me lookin like that. Darc he likely to haul you off inna bush somewhere."

"Darc cant see no further than he nose," Dit says. "Darc isnt goin to see me."

Darc cant see real good, but Darc can smell nats phuckin half a mile away. Isnt no use telling Dit, Dit dont listen to anyone at all.

"I got some real fine grubs," Dit says, "they sweet as they can be. Been down in the dirt, hasnt ever seen the Light."

He doin that mouth-smackin shit, he holdin a grub, it squirmin an twitchin like it know what Dit goin to do. Dit hold it up bout a inch from his lips an his cheek to get holler an he suck it right in. Dit says this is a trick. What it is is somethin anyone could do, but Dit think he made it up his self.

He gets me a grub an another for his self an I dont say a thing bout this. His baskets are full, an even Sal Capone wont know if theres any gone or what.

"You see Macky," I tell him, "say he got enough snails hes to go help Lily, see if he can help her catch voles. Sals set up bout somethin, I dont know what. I dont want no trouble, so get him lots a voles."

"Set up bout what, Sal is?"

"If I know, then thats what I be sayin, now wouldnt I Dit?"

"I guess."

"Guess I would. Listen to me good, all right? When I be talkin, listen to what I got to say."

I eat another grub, an put a couple more in my cheek for later on.

"Dont eat no more," I tell Dit. "Dont think bout grubs, go think about snails. Get some more snails."

"Dont like them snails. Dont like em at all."

"Now you got it, Dit, get you ass movin, find a buncha snails..."

▲▼▲

Lily bout where I figured she be. Theres a place where chokegrass growin so high you cant see over it at all. Crawl on in theres a hollow where Light sneaks down an make goldy spots on the ground. You look at them spots an they shiver an blur an you look real long, you off somewhere, not where you think you be.

Thats where Lily is, sittin in greeny moss, sittin by the creek. She lookin awful pretty, lookin awful good. I feelin somethin funny, cause she not wearin nothin which she never do at home.

The goldys is dancing in her hair, dancing off her legs which she dippin in the creek, dancing of her little buds which is poppin out fine.

Shes found her some cappers, holdin the stems in her fingers an chewin off the tops, eatin real slow. Lily dont eat like other folks, Lily eats nice. Takin little bites like you see a critter do. I can see Mama doin that, cept Lily wouldn't know, she wouldnt member that.

I sit there watchin, which I hadnt ought to do. Its hard not to, cause a sister dont look no different than someone you isnt kin to. If you didnt know you was, youd be thinking what I was thinking too.

"You goin to sit there, Ratch, you going to take root an turn into a tree..."

I glad she isnt lookin, if she was shed of seen of me turnin a couple shades of red.

"Didnt want to scare you or nothin," I tell her, "just jumpin out a bush. Wouldnt want to do that."

Lily laugh an she do turn then, givin me a smile an her sparkle-dark eyes.

"What you talkin bout, Ratch? You couldnt scare me if you tried."

"I could, I bet. I could if I tried."

"Huh-uh, you couldn't scare me. I doubt you could even scare Macky. You might scare Dit."

"Anyone could scare Dit. A leaf could scare Dit. I bet a—a *rock* could scare ol Dit."

Lily laugh at that. She pats a place beside her an splashes her feet in the water, an I dippin mine in too. Mine are all big an crookity lookin an hers are real small. Mens an wimins are different. An it isnt just feet I talkin bout.

I try not to look at those buds. A little bit of fuzz is growin round her cut an I try not to look at that too. Even though I wearin a clothes, I fraid she might see what I tryin not to do.

"I sent Macky over, I bet he didnt come," I tell her. "I said, Dit, you tell Macky go on over an help Lily catch a buncha voles. What I bet, he didnt show at all."

"Course he didnt. You think he would?"

"I dont guess. I always thinkin, I thinkin, Ratch, why you go an open your mouth, why you say somethin it dont do any good?"

"You tryin is why," Lily says. "That's just the way you do. The way you always been."

She lookin at me then an I got to look away, got to look at somethin else. Lacers and brighters are buzzin in a beam a goldy Light. A dragun-wings dippin down quick, kissin the water an flyin on away.

"I got to be like I am, Lily. Im oldest. Its what I got to do."

"I know you do, Ratch..."

"You an older, you lookin after Famly, thats what you got to do. I gotta watch Macky, I gota watch Dit, he dont do somethin dumb. Spose he get in his head he gonna eat all his grubs? What I gonna tell Sal, Dits maybe doin that?"

"I dont think he will."

"You dont but I do. Thats what I gotta be thinkin alla time. An Macky, hes spose to help you findin voles. Whats Macky doin, what he doin now? What if you not findin voles, what Sal goin to say bout that?"

"Ratch..."

"What?"

"I got Sals ol voles, all right?"

She turn an look at me then, look at me real soft like.

"You worry bout me, Ratch, an I dont want you doing that."

"Course I do, Lily. Nothin wrong with that."

"There isnt, not if you worry the ordnary way. Not if you worryin right..."

I see right off what she talkin bout now. She look away quick an I look away too, cause I know she scared she thinkin just the way I thinking too.

I tell her I got to find Macky, I tell her I got to find Dit. See if Niks swellin has gone down where he got bit.

Im out through the chokegrass, outta there quick. Lily dont watch an Im not lookin back. I forget to give her the grub I savin in my cheek. I go head an chew it, an swallow it myself. It dont taste good like the other one did..

▲▼▲

Stay down low, not movin at all. Darc Anthony cant see shit, Dits right bout that. But there isnt nothing wrong with the ol bastards ears, he can phuckin *hear,* isnt no doubt a that.

Isnt no tellin how ol Darc is. Even if you know em, you cant never tell. Ever Drill got baby crap eyes an that ugly red muzzle pokin out. Ever one got cheeks like puckerin scars—like someone cut em, then go an paint em blue. Sometime a cheek bein purple stead of blue. Sometime they ruffs bein yellow, sometime they dirty white.

Darc I figure is oldern Sal. He isnt too ol cause he sniffin round Florence of Arabia when Sal not around. Sal likely kill him if he know bout that.

Darc, he squat there ever single day, squattin on his big black rock. Squats an shits and scratches, squats an shits again. Picks little chitters off his fur an cracks em in his teeth. Sometime he play with that big pink knobber stickin tween his legs. You see a Drill got nothin else to do, he likely doin that. Likely doin that, or lookin for a hat.

What you dont know, is while he doin that, Darc Anthony knowin where every picker is in the tangle, in the hot, in the strangle down below. What they doin down there, what they pickin, if they workin or they takin a nap. An when the days done, ol Darc tellin Sal what he seen, tellin Sal what he know.

Tellin, or keepin somethin to his self. Waitin till he got somethin good he can use on someone hadnt got sense. Someone like Dit. Then Dit got to do what Darc want him to, an wonder how he got into somethin like that.

How he did, is he dont ever listen to Ratch. Ratch spend ever minute helpin Famly, keepin ever body right. I do the best I can. Someone dont listen, what am I sposed to do...?

▲▼▲

Niks a lot worse. He burnin with fever he all swole up. A green snik got him, an theres nothing worsen that.

He not goin to make it through the night. Lily know that, but she wont give up. She keepin him cool, wipin him off, drippin water on his mouth. His lips is dry as dirt. His eyes is open, but Nik not lookin at any thing at all.

"Hes little, Ratch. He isnt hardly six. He hadnt ought to leave, you little like that."

"Little dont matter to a snik," I tell her. "A snik dont care if you six. Dont care if you seven, dont care if you ten."

"You shouldnt oughta, though. Not if you six."

"Thats what happen, Lily. You go whenever you go."

"I guess..."

I had a fire goin, nothin real big, moss an dry sticks. You not spose to, you spose to be sleepin if its Dark. Phuck it if a Drill dont like it, Little Nik goin to have a fire tonight.

▲▼▲

Macky an Dit is sleepin in the corner of the hootch.

Both of em oldern Nik, an Lily short of me. A couple of years, they start thinkin important stuff too. They will, if they dont do somethin real dumb or get bit. Lilys already smart as she can be. Wimin get smarter fastern mens. Dont know why they just do.

"Im awful sleepy," Lily says. "I dont know I can stay awake, Ratch."

"You dont have to," I tell her, "I can do that, I can watch Nik."

"You go to sleep is what you gonna do."

"I wont neither. I be watchin little Nik."

"You vow that you will?"

"I vow, now get to sleep, here?"

So she did. I did too, bout a minute after that. Didnt matter if we didnt or we did. Not to Little Nik. I waked up once an we were touchin one another, sleepin real close. Didnt do nothin, but I know she was wake a while too.

Somewhere close to Light, when the grays comin in, Lily she sit up straight, sit up shakin, making funny little sounds. I sittin up cause I hear it too, comin in soft, comin on the wind. Snortin an gruntin, shufflin about. Bumpin and pushin, stompin on the ground. Movin like they real uneasy, like somethin stir em up. Closer, too, closern they been for a spell.

"Down in the draw," I say, "down past the trees."

Dont hardly whisper, but ever body hear. No one got to tell Lily, or Macky or Dit. Ever Person, ever Famly, awake right now. Isnt no one sleepin with Rhido out there...

I reach out and take Lilys hand. Its freezin cold, like water from a spring, from way down deep somewhere.

"What they doin, Ratch, what they doin here?"

"I dont know that, Lily. Might be somebody tell us come Light. Might be we know then."

"Im kinda scared. You scared too?"

"Nothin to be scared of, far as I can see. You try an sleep now. You boys too."

Macky and Dit turn over, they eyes real bright in the last of the fire. Lily look at me, like she want me to talk for a while. I make like I sleepin. Dont wont to tell her I dont know nothin more to say...

▲▼▲

Isnt no sleepin after that, dont anybody try. Little Niks gone. Lily get him clean an I take him outside. Macky got the fire back up, Dit got us fruit an some grubs he hid from Sal.

Nobody talkin bout Rhidos or Nik or bout anything else. Talkin dont do no good. Ever day I tell Dit an Macky that. Somethin is or somethin not. Lily dont ask me nothin, even if she wantin to.

After I eat I go out an have a look. Sackers there cross the way, standin by his Famlys hooch too. I dont like him an he dont like me. Still, he know somethin goin on, same as I do.

I hear gruntin and fartin an such, an fat Mama Gass come lopin down the draw, bouncin an swayin, fatter she was the week before. Florence of Arabias right on her tail, dirty brown hair standin up on her back, muddy little eyes shiftin this way an that. Both of em wearin floppy hats with flowers stickin out.

Florence dont like me too much. She wrinkle up her muzzle, givin me a growl. I dont pay her no mind. Go back in, toss a stick on the fire, do somethin busy, walk out again. Watch the sun swellin through the trees. Macky an Dit wander out back to pee.

I know Lily, know what she thinkin in there. Long as she dont come see Little Niks not there, in her head he maybe is.

Wimin dont think the same as mens. Ever ones different from ever one else...

▲▼▲

If I hadnt shit already bet I likely would. Sal keep us waitin a hour in the sun, an that mean somethins not good. Cant be nothin youd ever want to know. Not after what we hearin, out there in the Dark.

An when I see Sal lopin up the draw, I know its goin to be awful, know its worsen that. The parts I not tellin Lily are bustin in my head, an my mouth tastin bad. I look at Sacker, an Sacker look sickern me.

Sals got a good stout pole, sharpened on the end. Got slabs of scrap-wood strapped to his forelegs, strapped to his shoulders, strapped to his chest. Ever piece he wearin got circles and jaggeds painted yeller an red. Got somethin on his head. Looks like a turtul with the innards scooped out. Looks like that, cause thats what it is.

"Persons is listening good," Sal Capone says, "persons is very much hearing what I be saying now. Anyone is not listen good, is in extreme trouble and this is not good."

With this, he pounds that stick on the ground, looks at ever hooch, looks at Sacker, Mockit an Brig, looks right at me.

"There will be no picking of foods this day. No one shall gather the kindles, no one is lifting the rocks or the stones. All Persons shall be leaving this place in orderly manners when the sun is going down. You will gather your stuffs and leave nothing behind. You will do as you are told. You will be starting this now."

Sals got nothing more to say. He turns an totters back down the draw, back to the shade. The turtul hat bounces on his head. Two hunks of wood are strapped to fit his humpy back. The wood is painted in loopy swirls of white. His asshole is ugly, purple, blue and red.

I talk to Mockit after Sals gone. Mockits Famly is two hooches down, an he bout as old as me. Mockit wants Lily, an wants to give me Dandra Bee. Mockit dont know it, but nothins ever goin to come of that.

"I heared em," Mockit tells me, "ever one did. Bicky an Dandra is real upset. The little uns is climbin up the walls. I sorry bout Nik. Pock, he lost a gurl to a big sinnerpede."

"Didnt know that."

"That was bout a week. No, it was some moren that."

Mockit looks past me to see if anyones there.

"Pock, he takes stuff down the hill. Goes right in the fort, he got a pretty a Drill might give him somethin for. He comin back late, he seen em down there."

"Seen what you an me talkin bout here."

"Rhidos. Real close by."

"Shit, I know that."

"He say a thousan, maybe a milyun, hard to see em in the Dark. Pock say they smellin, say they smellin real bad."

"Dont want to smell em. Smelled em onct before."

Mockit shakes his head. "That isnt what Pock sayin. Not that kinda smell. Pock says mad. Pock say they smellin red, like they got some kinda crazy in they heads."

"I never heard bout smellin crazy, nothin like that."

"I just sayin what he says. What you think, Ratch? What they goin to do?"

"Rhidos here, Drills wearin shit like that? What you think it goin to be?"

Mockit looks away. "Ratch, I dont want it bein that."

"Good. Then maybe it be somethin different. You dont want it to, it likely be somethin else."

I go on back, leave Mockit standin there. No use talkin, cause Mockit think like a chile sometime. A chile dont like to member nothin less its somethin good.

I member an so does he. I wasnt biggern Nik, but its clear as yesterday Somethin like that, its not about to go away...

▲▼▲

It dont take long to "gather our stuffs" like Sal Capone say. Drills, they gotta lot of stuff. Persons dont hardly have any stuff at all. What Persons do is carry stuff a Drill dont like to be haulin round they selves. Which is ever thing but they dicks an they hats.

▲▼▲

First night out, it isnt too bad. We walkin in the Dark, an we fresh, cause we dont have to work till we startin on the trail. We walk through the forest till it start thinnin out, an the land rise up to grassy hills. I been this far onct before. Haulin rock back fore they got me pickin bugs. Lily an the boys hasnt seen a lotta open, an they actin kinda scared.

"Its all right," I tell em, "it just like anyplace else."

"No it isnt, Ratch," Macky says. "Why you sayin it is when its not?"

"Dont talk back to me," I tell him, "you know better, boy."

What else I goin to say? What else I goin to tell him cept he right about that?

▲▼▲

Isnt just Macky an Lily and Dit. Lots of the younguns is whinin, an some of the older Persons too. Drills start lopin down the line, snappin they teeth, telling us we better keep em quiet, or you know what they goin to do.

I know what botherin the Drills, what make em shaky too. We cant see no Rhidos, but we surely know they there. You can hear em clear, an they not far away.

An that be somethin I member in my head. Rhidos dont like Persons. Dont like the way we smell, any moren we like the stink of them.

▲▼▲

We only stoppin onct in the Dark. We thirsty, dont got nothin to eat. What a Person do, you eat what you got, find somethin else next Light. Only we not home now, we somewhere else. Nobody think bout carryin water or somethin to eat. Isnt what we do, so nobody did.

Mockits grumblin, sayin how we oughta tell the Drills give us somethin to eat. They got plenty, they can give us some of theirs.

"Drop it," I tell him, "hush up. Get us all in plenty phuckin trouble, you start talkin like that."

Mockit mutterin some, but he keep his complainin to his self. You gotta think fore you talk. Im always tellin Dit and Macky that.

▲▼▲

The good part is, we can rest for a while. Ever body needin that. Up in the hills theres a cool wind blows in the Dark. It dont in the Light, but its nice in the Dark.

The boys is sleepin, an me an Lily is lookin at the brights. The brights an the moon is the biggest wonders ever is. The moon an the brights an specially the sun.

You can hear the Rhidos, shiftin and gruntin, some of em squealin sometimes. Moren onct, I seen a Drill go careful down there, not makin any sound at all. I seen em comin back an talkin with the rest. They not real happy, whatever they doin down there.

"We goin back, you think," Lily says, lookin up in the Dark, lookin at the brights. "I dont like it, Ratch. I like it home, dont like it out here."

Im glad its Dark, so Lily cant see me too good. Been thinkin what to say, what to tell her and Macky and Dit. Dont like em think I dont know ever thing, the Famly they countin on me.

Only, I dont know a lot moren them. Me and Mockit an the olders, wasnt much bigger than the younguns is now.

It happened.

It wasnt good, an it was somethin like this.

Somethin like this, and there wasn't any Mamas, wasnt hardly anyone bigger after that.

▲▼▲

"Dont want you thinkin bout goin back, Lily, least not yet. I think they keep on goin for a while."

"Why, Ratch? Why they want to do that? Where they want to be?"

Even in Dark, I can see a little scared in her eyes, in the way she move her mouth.

Somethin happen, Lily. Somethin fore you, somethin barely after me, an you dont want to hear bout that...

Lily does a little sniff. "You mad with me, Ratch? I dont want you doin that."

"Im not mad at you, Lily."

"Good. I dont want you to."

"There isnt no way I ever could. You gotta know that, least I hope you do."

"I do, Ratch. I surely do..."

▲▼▲

Near Light, a lot of the younguns is whinin again an we try an keep em still. Sal Capone come by with Persons from another hootch, luggin pots of water to drink. It isnt much, an he dont bring any thing to eat.

▲▼▲

Lights when it gets real bad.

I never seen any thing like that. Its Dark one minute, then the sun come blazin up hot. The sky dont have any color, its awful searin white. When you down in the tangle, in the wet and the rot, you steamin an sweatin an the bugs is bitin an crawlin up your nose. A Person, he gettin used to that. Your head start bustin you can dunk it inna creek. You can eat a grub, an you can get a drink.

Out heres nothin, out here its bare an flat. Ever tree ever bush is brittle as a bone, the juice sucked out an all the green gone. Ever things dry an ever things dead.

Theres nowhere to go, isnt nowhere to hide. Drills, they got mats whats made outa straw. Mats on sticks thats keepin off the sun. Persons dont got any mats, we walkin in the heat. Who you think made them phuckin straw mats? Persons, thats who.

Not far off, the land drop a little, makin a gully to the right. We been stayin real close ever since we hit the flats. Cant see Rhidos, all you can see is the dust they kickin up, but thats where they at. Mockit says you walk over, you can see em clear. Dont, I tell him, an keep your mouth shut. We dont need folks thinkin bout that.

▲▼▲

The suns straight high when they tell us all to sit. Why, Im thinkin, they want to stop here. Isnt nothing but dirt an a bunch of dead trees. Not enough shade for a vole or a snik. I dont know, an I not bout to ask.

We get a little water but we dont get enough. What we got we givin to the younguns, some of em lookin real bad.

Macky come over an say one of Pocks whos eight is maybe dead.

"Well he phuckin dead or not?" I ask him, "make up your mind, boy."

"I can go see," Macky says, an look at somethin else. "Don't do nothin, just stay right here."

"Whatd I do, why you mad at me?"

"He isnt mad," Lily tells him, "go sit over there with Dit."

"Sorry," I tell her. "I cant help it, Im worried bout this."

"Macky know that."

"I dont know he does or not."

"Dits bad off. I thought he was better but he gettin awful hot."

"Ill try an get water. They got to give us water an somethin to eat, they goin to have to carry this shit by they selves."

"You goin to tell em that?"

"No, Im not goin to tell em that."

"What, then?"

"I dont know yet."

"You come up with somethin. I know you always do."

And what, I thinkin, *you rekon thatll be?*

▲▼▲

Sal Capone come round with Persons bringing water, an a pot of grub soup. Just like last time, isnt near enough. I tell ever one I can dont drink all you got, an save a little soup.

Course nobody doin that.

▲▼▲

Wasnt long after we seen dust comin off the flats. When they gets closer we seen they more Drills. Only we never seen em before, this bunch is strangers, they come from far away. I seen traders, outsiders before, these Drills is nothin like that. These phuckers has clearly come to fight.

Soon as they comin in sight, a fearsome sound sweep through the Person, ever Family there. Ever body squeezin close, ever body moanin, shakin, holdin one another, coverin they faces, coverin they heads.

Dont blame em any one, its a dreadful thing to see. Even Sal Capone dont look too happy, an Sals not scared of any one.

A Drill, he walkin on his hands an he feet, dont hardly come up to your hip. Dont weigh much as a Person an a females smallern that. Weight an high, though, isnt what you want to think, you thinkin bout Drills. What you want to think bouts *mean.* What you want to think bouts strong, they strongern shit. What you want to think too, you want to think bout teeth.

Whatever you magine that phuckers thinkin, that likely isnt it. Isnt nothin inside that head cept hate an blood an killin boilin up, just waitin to bust on through. I tell a youngun that, sure as shit some Drill hops by an give him honey on a stick.

Teachin folks stuff, whats the use of that?

▲▼▲

I listen real good, they think I doin somethin else. Pickin up stuff, puttin stuff down, listenin good. The big one with the little red eyes got teeth painted black. His armor isnt plain like Sals. Its real fine wood, got a lot of shiny stones, gotta lot of pretty shells. Got feathers offa birds, skins offa lizerts an sniks. An ever inch of that armor, on his arms on his shoulders, on his knees on his chest, ever phuckin inch is covered with spines, thorns, stickers of ever sort. You get even close to this Drill he gonna punch you fulla holes.

Sides all that, he got a turtul hat an he got a wood shiel, an the shiel an the hat they fulla thorns too. He got a big spear, which is longern Sals, longern any I think I ever saw.

Theres two stays close to the big un with the thorns, an they got fine armor too. One of ems Mormon Nailer. The other ones Orangey Harding, and the main asshole, the one with the thorns, is Gandolph Scott. He tells ems all what to do, an they tell ever one else. Includin Sal Capone, who dont much care for doin that.

▲▼▲

A couple Drills from their bunch an ours go down where the Rhidos are. They gone a long time. We listen, but we dont hear anything at all.

"What they doin, you think," Mockit wants to know, "I wouldnt get close to those things you give me all the wimins there is."

Pock an me we laughin bout that. Pocks hooch right next to Mockits, an he know what goin on there.

"You dont gotta worry," Pock says, "no one goin to do that, long as them wimins can run."

Mockit dont say nothin to Pock. Pocks bout as big as me.

"They not doin nothin," Pock says. "All they doin is they goin down an look."

"Why they do that?" Mockit want to know. "You seen a Rhido, why you want to see it again?"

"Just do is all."

"Why you just do? You just sayin, you not sayin what."

"A Drill do somethin cause he want to do it," Pock say, getting tired of this, "thats why. He dont have to ask you."

"What they doin they listenin. Thats what the Drills is doin down there..."

For a minute Im thinkin isnt anyone there, then Froom, he edgin by the fire. Isnt anyone expectin that, cause Froom dont like no one an nobody like him.

"What you talkin bout," Mockit says, "listenin to *what?*"

"Rhidos," Froom says, "listenin to them."

Mockit laughs, but dont anyone else.

"Theres nothin to listen to," I tell him. "Nothin a Rhido goin to do but grunt."

"Grunt an fart some," Pock puts in. "I wouldnt listen to that."

"Its not that kinda listenin. Didnt say that."

"What kinda listenin there is?"

Froom look like he want outta there, like he wish he never come.

"I ast you somethin," says Pock.

Froom dont answer, an bout then the Drills come back. None of em talkin, just all walkin back. None of em lookin real happy at all.

"Thats Orangy Harding," Pock says, pointin to the shortest one of all. "Got a brother come to the fort one time. Got a knobber long as your arm."

"Who tol you that?"

"I seen him he was here. Brother looks just like him."

"I guess its so, Pock say it is," Mockit says.

Pock dont say nothin. In a minute Mockits gone.

▲▼▲

The worst part is, we dont stay put till Dark. Ever one gotta get up, lift your shit an go. Darc Anthony an Sal, them an Doc Cabbage, they dont like it, but they wont cross the other Drills.

Theres five, maybe six hours Light, the longest Light I ever seen. The heat come down, then it rise up again, burnin your eyes and blisterin your feet. The grounds like walkin on fire. You look anywhere an ever things wavy, ever thing poundin in your head.

The younguns is already beat, an pretty soon they droppin on the trail. A Family try to carry em on, some of em cant hardly carry theyselves. We bout lose Dit, but Im not leavin him behind. Lily cant help. She an Macky are keepin one another from fallin to the ground.

Isnt real long theres younguns by the way, covered up with dust, lookin like Persons made of clay. You walkin, you dont see bugs, dont see em anywhere. Soon as a youngun hits the ground, they swarmin ever where. Shiny black waddlers, clickin they pinchers, ants, nats an fat green flies. How they knowin, I wonder? What they eatin when we isnt there?

Florence of Arabia an fat Mamma Gass, them an little Silly Marlene, they got their hands full, lopin up an down, draggin folks off fore the bugs clean em out. Silly Marlene, she all swole up. I figure Darc, he the cause of that.

I said its the most awful Light I ever seen. You figure Dark would help, but Dark is worsen that...

▲▼▲

Near as I can tell, theres leven, maybe ten went down, might be moren that. Most of em younguns, some of em not. Sackers one, an hes old as me, close on to sixteen. Strong as he could be. Whats his Famly goin to do now?

Drills gettin all worked up just fore the sun goes down. We hadnt seen nothin in the Light. Just a buncha zeebos that run fore we even got near.

What the Drills seein now is a Leon way off neath a sticker tree. Isnt nothin get a Drill goin like a Leon will. They lopin up an down, hoppin an screamin an beatin on they chests. Some of em throwin they sticks, make em feel like they doin somethin good. Females, they havent got sticks, so they throwing lotta shit.

Drills got reason for not likin Leons much. Ever now an then, a Leon trot down to the fort, waitin for a Drill to come by. Ever now an then, a Drill not comin home at Dark.

It start gettin cool an we huddle in a little stand of rock. Sal come round with water, moren we ever got before. We can smell cookfires burnin, but all we gets fruit that the Drills wont eat no more.

Theres Persons out there, come with the other Drills. We can hear em cryin close by. I dont think they got water. I dont think they got anything to eat.

Drills got a lotta mean in they heads. Drills dont see stuff the way a Person do. They did, theyd try an keep ever one alive to do shit they dont want to. A Drill, though, he dont think bout that.

Dit, he hot an he cold, he got the fever bad. Macky give him bout all of his water an I stop him doin that. I tell him its a fine thing to do, an how he gotta quit.

Lily hear me say it. She knows its what I gotta do. All the water in the world, Dit wont make it to the Light.

"I know what happenin, Ratch," Dit tells me, the words stickin scratchy in his craw. "You dont be worry bout me."

"I always worry bout you," I tell him. "You a lot of trouble, Dit. You fillin six baskets a grubs, you bringin home two. What you figure happen to them other four?"

Dit cant hardly make a grin, but he give it a try. "Sometime I eat moren that. You just didnt ever see."

"You know what? I did the same thing, Dit. An nobody ever catch
cause Im as sly as you."

Dit too weak to answer that. I dont know if he hearin me at all.

▲▼▲

Me an Pock talk some, an Brig is there too. Mockit, he not comin
round since he aggravatin Pock. Booker an Tyro stoppin for a while.
Tyro lost two younguns on the march. Booker got a girl sick as Dit, an
figure she likely goin too.

They all leavin, its only Pock an me. Macky sleepin, Lilys watchin Dit.

Pock says, "Ratch, its somethin bad, I got a feelin inside. Dont know
what, but its bad, an likely worsen that."

"You tol me that bout a hunert times," I tell him. "Dont need to hear
it again."

"Im just sayin."

"Thats it, you sayin. Dont be sayin anymore."

"Wont, then."

"Dont."

Pock, he squattin on his heels, got him a stick, makin circles on
the ground.

"It shouldnt oughta be, you know it? Shouldnt be the way it is. You
think bout it, same as I do, same as ever one, dont say you never doin
that. I member stuff, Ratch. Just dont like to say I do."

"Good. Then dont."

"Whats the good of not talkin, you member too, you thinkin same
as me."

"Maybe I thinkin some once. Im not thinkin now."

"Might say you don't. Doesnt mean you not..."

Thats when I push him down flat. Pock look surprised, me doin that.

"Im sayin this. Whatevers in your head, keep it to yourself. Dont
want to hear what you thinkin or anyone else. Go do somethin. Dont be
sittin round here."

Pock, he dont say a thing. He put down his stick, he get up an go,
I sittin by my self.

The fire bout gone. I stick a little dead grass on, it dont do any good.

I can hear whinin where the other Persons are, I can hear Rhidos
shufflin in the Dark. Some of the Drills is movin about. A Drill dont ever
keep still, you can count on that.

Lilys asleep, Im glad she doin that. Theres nothin she can do bout
Dit. Dits goin, if he isnt gone now.

Im lookin at the sky, lookin at the brights. Theres clouds goin by real fast. Im thinkin way Pock acting, I got to watch him now. He talkin to me like that, he talkin to somebody else. Some people not thinkin, some people hasnt got a bit of sense—

I stand up quick cause I know hes right there. I see him, now, a shadow gainst the Dark. Then I see the other one, over by his self.

"I am ever having to admonish you, Ratch," Sal tells me. "There is no cause to having a fire. It is not be cooling, there is plenty of warming in the air."

Isnt a fire no more, its phuckin gone out.

"This time I am forgetting what I see. I am closing my eyes to your actions, I am seeing nothing of this. Ratch, you will have Lily rise from her sleeping. You will bring her here."

"What? What for?"

Sal dont like me sayin that. He lopes up closer an kicks my water pot. It breaks an clatters on the rocks. The ground sucks it up an thats all I got.

"Bring her, Ratch. Bring Lily here."

Somebody grunt an somebody shits, an now I can see whos up there with Sal. Somebody with a dead turtle hat, somebody with dirty little eyes. Somebody with a lotta thorns an stickers on pokin out...

▲▼▲

Im not thinkin bout Lily at all. Lily pops in I get her out quick. The more I do that, the more she poppin in again. I oughta not get ina bother but I do. No ones taken Lily off before. What I thinkin, they wouldnt for nother year or so.

Only this isnt home no more. These Drills is not the same as Sal Capone or Darc, or Lon Peron.

"I think Dit maybe goin," Macky says. "He lyin awful still."

I go look an he cold as the ground, and I say, "Macky, Im afraid he is."

▲▼▲

Florence an the others wont be checking till Light. Dont want Dit where the bugsll get him, so I cover him with dust an leave him where he is.

"You done a good job watchin," I tell Macky. "Good as anyone could."

"Not as good as Lily."

"Just bout as good. I bet she tell you herself when she gettin back here."

Macky wants to ask, wants me to tell him, but he keep it all in. He growin up good, but I wouldnt tell him that.

▲▼▲

Long before Light sets in, Drills is up gruntin an lopin about, yellin an barkin, do this an do that. Mockits Persons an Pocks is gettin up slow. All of ems hungry, thirsty an sick.

Sal come over an tell Macky come along with him. Sal don't even look at me. Macky comes back, bringin water an grubs. Macky looks scared, an he goes off again. This time he got Lily too.

I dont hardly know its her. I look at her I wanta be sick. Her skins all dirty, caked in dust, flakin like the ground when the sun dry ever thing up. She shakin awful bad. Her eyes is open an I have to shade her cause she starin at the sun.

I can see her fuzz, I can kinda see her cut, but she all scratched up on her belly down there. Theres blood an dust an I cant clean her up, theres not enough water to spare.

"Here," I tell her, "you drink some of this. You feel real better soon."

I take some water in my mouth an open her lips an let the water seep in. She chokin some, then she swallow an I know its goin in. I give her another an she try an say somethin but nothin comin out.

"She be all right, Ratch? She dont look too good."

I turn up an theres Mockit an he starin at Lily, his eyes getting bigger all the time.

"You seen enough," I tell him, "now be outa here fore I standin up."

I know what he doin an he know it too. He look off quick an go back where he come.

Im thinkin, they coulda give her a clothes, they coulda give em back. A Drill, though, they dont think bout that. Dont matter to them they got a knobber or a cut they got buds hangin out. Clothes is somethin Persons do.

I lay a little stitch I took off Dit an put it cross her parts. Wasnt anything to hide her buds, they just be pokin out. An Mockit, he can find somewhere else to look.

Me seein her now isnt like I seen her at the creek. Dont have the feelin I had bout her then. She back bein a sister an I feel good bout that.

▲▼▲

If the heat was bad before, its worsen that now. Worsen I ever mag-ined it could be. Ever one startin off sick, ever one hungry, beat an dried up from the awful Light before.

The shit we sposed to be haulin, me an Lily, Macky an Dit, is bun-dles of sticks so the Drills can have a fire. Where wes at, there isnt any sticks, isnt anything at all. Only now Dits gone, an Lily she barely on her feet. Im haulin three loads an Macky haulin one.

Same things happenin with all the others too. The younguns cryin an rollin all aroun. Ever Person can is haulin they load, but the heat is meltin us down. Isnt half a mile fore folks start droppin what they got, and fallin to the ground.

The Drills, they real upset bout that. Sal Capone an Sherbert Hoover come lopin down the line, growlin an snappin they teeth at ever one in sight. Sherb Hoover got a stick an starts hittin Persons on the back. Ever ones squealin, ever ones scared. You cant ever tell what Sherbs bout to do.

Sal tells him stop, he done enough of that. Sal gets me an Mockit and Pock an the rest of the olders an make us pick everbody up.

"It is shameful to me you are not being proper in your work," Sal says. "We have many fars to go. You must not be falling down. You must not be dropping your burdens to the ground. I am greatly disappointed. You will not be doing this again."

Sal scratches on his knobber, and turns and lopes away. Sherbert Hoover shakes his stick at me, an follows Sal down the trail. Two of the new Drills is watchin all this. Both of ems got hats. Both of em got mats on a pole to keep the sun out. One of em is Orangey Harding. The other ones Gandolph Scott, who taken Lily off. He dont even look at us, an Im glad when they both gone away.

▲▼▲

Isnt even high noon, an Macky says bout six has dropped away, but I countin moren that. I know for certain Lily cant last. She hasnt hardly spoke since Macky brung her back.

"I can pick you up," I tell her, "you dont have to walk. I know you feelin bad."

"You got plenty to carry, Ratch. You dont need to be haulin me too."

"This stuff isnt heavy. I could do it all day. Bet I could do it longern that."

"I can take some," Macky says, "I'm big enough to."

"You bout as big as a vole," I tell him. "Shit, you no biggern a ant, thats you."

"I can do it. I can do it same as you."

"You cant neither. Dont be askin me again."

I see right off the hurt in Mackys eyes. Lily lookin off, but I catch her sad too.

I wish I hadnt yell at Macky but I did. It isnt him, its ever thing else. Ever thing wrong, ever thing bad bout what we doin out here. Walkin in the sun, hungry an nothin to drink. Whats the good of that?

▲▼▲

Somethin is happenin up front. Somethin goin on, somethin givin Drills a fit. We all lookin at ever one else, wonderin what it all about. Then Darc Anthony trottin on back, barkin up a storm. Ever body gotta stop, he tell us, ever body put his stuff down, we better be still, better not make a fuss.

I look at Mockit, he lookin back. He can smell em same as me fore they even in sight. They stink blowin straight up the draw, a dry an chokin smell strong enough to gag a stone.

Its shit an dust an the smell of they parts hangin down tween they legs. Isnt nothing bad as that, isnt nothin foul an nasty as a Rhido is. You maybe not member you Mama, you may not member nothin else, you goin to member how a Rhido smell. You five maybe ten, you wakin an smell em you hear em out there, you edgin in close to you kin.

"Im scared, Ratch," Macky says, huggin the dirt next to me. "Im scared real bad. I dont wanta see em, dont want em seein me."

"They not after you, boy. They dont care bout you."

"I think I gotta pee."

"You do, better not be on me."

"You be smellin em before," Lily says, talkin best she can. "You member I tell you, that song we used to sing? You member that, Im certain that you do."

Macky too scared, dont even know his name. Theres other younguns close by hasnt ever smelled Rhido fearsome an awful as this. They howlin an whinin, the olders tryin to still em fore the Drills comin back.

"Stay down," Mockit says, an Pock tells his Persons too. "Stay down low, dont even try an look."

Im holdin Macky, he rollin his eyes, he shakin like a vole hear a snik close by. Lily too sick to hardly try.

I seein em now, keepin down an eatin dirt just raisin up my eyes. They heavin, rumblin, snortin and fartin, gruntin and poundin the ground. Isnt nothing bigger, isnt nothin ugly as a Rhido swingin his big head about, thrashin his terrible horns, thisaway and that. Phuckin horns is pointy, phuckin horns sharp, longern a chile, near longern a man.

I want to shut my eyes tight, want to be cryin like a chile. They comin so close I can see they little mouth, I can see they tiny eyes.

Theys worse, too, worsen even that. The Drills has painted white circles round the Rhidos eyes. Painted jaggy lightnin on they great saggin hides, painted moons, painted suns, all kinds a scary sights. Somes got yeller on they horns, some got stripes goin all down they sides, blackern blood, near blackern Dark...

Then ever Person there they screamin and moanin, ever one tryin to dig they selves a hole. Some of em lets they bowels go, which dont help at all.

Someone cryin, someone tearin at the ground. I look round, isnt anyone but me I shakin real bad, I tryin to breathe. What I seeins not real cause now I seein Drills too, screechin an barkin, snappin they muzzles, barin they teeth...

Gotta not be, gotta be somethin in my head. They ridin, what they doin, perched right up on the Rhidos theyselves, right on the Rhidos phuckin backs!

I think my heart goin to stop right there. Mockits eyes is rollin, Macky is throwin up spit. I never even thought about, never even magined nothing awful as this...

▲▼▲

When its over you can hear the awful quiet, so heavy it pressin on the ground. The Rhidos is gone, leavin dust an a fearful smell behind. You listen real close, you can hear em still, hear em like far off thunder, rollin off the edge of the world.

Im standin real slow. Some of the others is gettin up too. Nobody talkin, no one makin a sound. Nobody cept Mockit, Mockit cant keep from talkin too long.

"What you think they doin, Ratch? Where they goin to go?"

"Why you askin me, what the phuck I know?"

Mockits face covered up with dust. Cant see nothin but his eyes. Looks like somethin hangin from a tree, somethin livin in the Dark.

"They doin that dream," he sayin. "Whatever they done before. They doin it again."

"Wasnt any dream, Mockit. That look like a dream to you?"

Mockit dont answer. He scared an I scared too, but I wont let it show. I look out over the far. I mightve seen Rhidos, I mightve seen hot stuff risin off the flats.

One of the wimins starts wailin somewhere, then another after that. I waitin, watchin the path goes up the little draw. Waitin for a Drill maybe tell us what to do. Nobody there, nobody comin down.

What I better do, I thinkin, I better squat an wait. Squat down boilin in the sun like ever body else. Squat down waitin, ever body sick, ever body dyin, waitin for a drink.

That's what I oughta do. I oughta but I dont. Somethin happen inside me, somethin in my head. Im not squattin no more, I standin up walkin, walkin up the draw. Mockit say somethin behind me, Pock, he sayin somethin too. I keep goin, I not lookin no where.

At the top of the draw, I stop an look down. I lookin where the Drills is campin. They stuff is scattered all bout, they cookfires burnin behind a stand of rock.

Shit, I sayin to myself, isnt nobody there. Nothin but females under a little straw tent. Mama Gass an Silly Marlene, Florence of Arabia too. Dim Bassinger and little Semi More. Pain Fonda got a youngun suckin on her buds.

I turn round an start back the other way. Florence start screechin, showin her gums, gnashin her teeth. She get the others goin too.

Mockit and Pock is waitin, Pock lookin at me like I crawl out of a hole.

"What they doin," Pock say, "what they up to down there? What we spose to do now?"

"Not doin nothin, isnt nobody there."

"How we goin to get water, then, how we goin to do that?"

Him an Mockit is yappin, I walkin away. Persons is moanin, Persons is rollin on the ground.

Macky, he sittin over Lily, shakin this way an that.

"Lily she gone, Ratch. Not even breathin no more."

I gettin down to look, put a hand on her face. Her skin is burnin, her lips is swole dry.

"She sleepin, Macky. She isnt gone yet."

"She goin to be, though?"

"Try an shade her. Be doin what you can."

"We goin to get some water, Ratch? They havent brought us water in a real long time."

"Boy, you got any sense? Got any sense at all?" I standin, lookin at Macky, lookin at Lily, thinkin bout her in the mossy place, in the pretty goldy light.

"Isnt no water. Isnt goin to *be* none, either. Lily goin to die like Dit an Little Nik. I spect you an me, we goin to die too."

I turnin an I gone, Macky cryin an theres nothin I can do. Cant do nothin for Lily, cant do nothin for me. Pock say somethin I dont hardly hear. Whatever that somethin doin in my head, it doin it again...

▲▼▲

The sun, he boilin in a white an empty sky. My skin be fryin, sweat burnin in my eyes. Dont figure goin far, just far nough to see. Dont know why, just know it gotta be.

Theres a little place I can hunker down some, look past the draw an down on the flats, stretchin out below. I inchin up an look, inchin up slow. My heart near stoppin, they right there close. I could throw a rock an hit Sal an phuckin Knob Dole. I could hit Gandolph Scott, sittin on a stripy Rhido.

Isnt no use tryin to count. Theres Rhidos far as I can see, black old hides covered in the dust they feet stirrin up. Dust an shit an bout a zillion flies. Switchin they tails, shakin they pointy horns bout. Snortin, snuffin, pawin at the ground, Drills perchin on they backs.

Ratch, Im thinkin, what the phuck you doin here, get up get outta here fast. This is what part of me thinkin. Other parts thinkin what Froom is sayin, how Drills they *hearin* Rhidos, only that kinda hearins not the same...

"Ratch, you outta you head? What you doin up here?"

"Shit, Mockit, don't be doin that!"

Mockit, he come up behind me, I bout jump outta my skin.

"Get on back," I tell him, "you dont belong up here."

"Whats the matter with you? Dont no one belong up here."

"Maybe I do."

"Do what?"

"I here, you seein that plain. Maybe thats where I spose to be."

"You talkin funny now. Dont be doin that, Ratch. You kinda scarin me."

I lookin up, lookin Mockit in the eye. "You the one said it. They doin that dream out there. They done it before, they doin it again."

"Huh-uh," Mockit shakin his head. "I never said a thing like that. Even if I did, I dont know what I talkin bout, you know that."

"Mockit..."

Mockit, he stop. He hearin it too. So do the Rhidos, so do the Drills. Theres thunder way off, thunder an a awful cloud of dust. Whatever it is, its just cross the flats, comin up behind a little rise. The ground begin to tremble, like the world be comin apart. I can feel it in my belly, I can feel it in my parts. Lookin down theres little grains of sand, dancing on the dirt.

Thunder dyin, the ground not shakin, ground keepin still. Hot wind blowin cross the flats, hot wind burnin, chokin ever breath. Hot wind scorchin, soarin off the dust, showin whats hidin up there...

Mockit, he seein it first, eyes comin outta his head. Then I seein it too, seein what he see, seein what a chile be seein, wakin up cryin, wakin from a dream.

My gut wanta be throwin up, but they nothin in there, nothin it can do. *What waitin, what sittin up there is Rhidos, Rhidos standin with they heads down low, Rhidos still as they can be. Rhidos that got no color at all, Rhidos white as the moon, Rhidos pale as dead bone..!*

"Phuck phuck phuck," Mockits moanin, shakin his head, sweat drippin off his nose. Somethin wet, somethin runnin down his leg.

"Stop doin that," I tell him, "ever thing stinkin enough round here."

"Cant help it, Ratch. I likely doin somethin else too."

"Mockit, that be the last thing you do, I tellin you that."

If me an Mockit havin a dream, it getting more scary all the time. Hunkered on them Rhidos is Drills, an they isnt like Drills I ever seen. They fur is dull as dirt, they baby shit brown. They whiskers an they ruff is kinda white. They all got long pointy sticks, an the sticks got raggedy skins hangin off the end. Some got skins, an some got strings of yeller bones. Even far off, you can hear bones rattlin in the wind.

Our Drills wearin armor made of wood, stickers an dead turtle hats. These Drills isnt wearin anything at all. Nothin but snik an lizert skins wrapped about they heads.

"Isnt many of em," Mockit sayin real low, "we got moren that."

"I can see, you dont have to tell me that."

"What you gettin on me bout, Ratch? Havent done nothin to you—"

Mockit, he stop, cause somethin happenin cross the flats. One of the Rhidos movin outta line, clompin up ahead of the rest. The Drill on his back, he got his head covered with a scary lookin mask. Mask got big white teeth, got shiny red eyes, got a muzzle painted black.

The Drill standin up, start hoppin, screechin an shakin his pole at the Drills over here. The rest of his bunch, they start jumpin round too.

I leanin up an lookin down. Gandolph Scott, he be bout to have a fit. He howlin, barin his teeth. Wavin *his* pole, screamin at the Drill across the flats. He turn round, an bark at Sal Capone. Whatever he sayin, Sal sayin no. He yellin at Gandolph, Gandolph yellin back.

Then, fore you can blink, Gandolph swingin his pole, slammin Sal hard across the head. The blow lift Sal off his Rhido an knock him to the ground.

Doc Cabbage and Darc and Lon Peron is comin at Gandolph, they eyes blazin red. Gandolphs Drills is ready for that. They pokin they spears, drivin the other Drills back. Darc keeps comin, hopin over one Rhido an then the next. Orangey Harding just waitin, then he run Darc right through, his spear comin out the other side.

Sals Drills is howlin, snappin they muzzles, but theres nothin they can do. Gandolph Scott dont bother to look. He give a loud yell, raise his pole, pointin at the sky. The Rhido he ridin shake his big head, give a rumble an a snort, give a tremble an a fart. Then he start walkin, then he start to *move...*

Rhido startin real slow, trottin, clompin on his big stubby feet. Gandolph clutchin the Rhido, holdin on tight, purple ass slappin up an down.

"Phuck," Mockit sayin, diggin a hand in my back, "oh phuck, Ratch," same thing he sayin before.

Ever Rhido in the bunch, they headin after Gandolph Scott. All of em racin toward a thicket of spears, waitin just across the flat.

"Gotta get outta here, Ratch. Gotta get outta here *now.*"

"You wanta go, get."

"What? You outta you head? It happenin. The dream be happenin now. Doin it, right out there!"

"I know what they doin."

"We not spose to be here. Shouldnt be seein all this."

Ratch, things you dont member good, thats what a dreams all about...

Where that come from, what it doin in my head?

"Get back an see what you can do, Mockit. See bout your folks, an see bout Macky too. See if Lily dead. See you can get any body walkin, gettin outta here. Dont know if it do any good, but wont hurt nothin to try..."

Mockit dont answer. I turn round an Mockit isnt there.

▲▼▲

Sun fryin my back, bugs itchin ever where. Throat closin up I cant even spit.

Ever thing fast out there, ever thing blurrin, ever thing makin me dizzy in the head.

Rhidos from here is poundin cross the plain, raisin clouds of dust, getting closer all the time. Somethin on the other side, somethin not right. White Rhidos not movin, just standin there, silent an still. Like nothin wrong, nothin be goin on at all.

Gandolph seein this too, an he shakin his stick, movin his Rhidos faster still...

I wipin off sweat, slappin at a bug. When I lookin up, seein again, somethin cold, somethin scary, climbin up my neck. Wasnt but a blink he passin but ever thing different, nothin look the same. The whites, they shiftin, movin, turnin round fast, some of em left an some of em right. Baby shit Drills they hangin on tight.

Gandolph, he keep comin, eatin up dust, ridin straight in where the other Rhidos been. Gandolph see it, smell it in the air. Know somethin comin, know somethin bad, cant figure what it is. Know, in a blink, they nothing he can do. Rhidos snortin, diggin up ground, goin so fast cant nothin stop em now...

First ones to know is Rhidos headin the pack, Rhidos bigger, faster than the rest, Rhidos heavy with muscle an bone, Rhidos with awful killin horns. Best Rhidos got the meanest, ugliest phuckers on they backs, Drills with armor, stickers an barbs. Drills with big turtle hats: Gandolph Scott and Orangey Harding. Spank Sinatra, Hairyass Truman. Mormon Nailer an Phony Curtis too.

They all famous bout a second, second an a half. It happen that quick, happen in a blink. One blink they somethin, next they phuckin meat. Yellin, screechin, twitchin on the ground, bones be snappin, guts squishin out.

Hardly a one of em see what get em, most of em dead fore that. I see em though, seen they awful heads when they comin up the rise, seen they big tuskers, they little black eyes, seen they awful noses, hangin like snakes, sweepin on the ground.

Cant believe the awful things I seein, not anybody could. They biggern anything, anything they is. Coming right at you, not ever slowin down. Seen one steppin on Mormon Nailers head, smushin it flat, all the juices spurtin out. Seen one pick up Orangey Harding with his nose, lift him up an toss him flat. Orangey screamin an thrashin about.

Rhidos fightin, doin what they could. Slammin they horns at a mountain of hide. Mountain, he screechin, givin a terrible cry. Shakin, swayin, slashin his tuskers, sendin that Rhido screamin to the ground.

Rhidos turnin now, shovin one another, crazy in they heads. Ever one wantin outta there.

Drills runnin too, but there nowhere to go. Rhidos, they don't stomp em, somethin else will. Ever one of them phuckers got a bunch of baby shit Drills, hopin on they backs, barkin, howlin, tossin them bony rattle spears.

No one, nothin, got a chance of getting outta that. Isnt nothing to do out there, nothing to do but die...

▲▼▲

Im not dead, I stayin alive. Maybe I figure what for.

Got down diggin like a vole, got a half ass hole, curlin up cryin while the monsters stompin by.

Not comin out till the sun bout down. Ever thing dead now, ever thing gone. Out on the flats theres Rhidos an Drills, bodies ever where. Ever thing flat, ever thing stinkin out there. Even one of them nightmars, lyin on its back, big ol legs stickin up in the air.

Birds an jakuls they havin a feast. Some of ems eatin out the belly, some of em chewin on the nose.

First thing I dos get me a couple pointy sticks. Next thing I find me some full water pots. Lots of em broke but plenty of ems not. Ever body gone, we got lots of water now. Even got some fruits thats nearly fit to eat.

Awful thing is, you cant even tell who anybody is. Persons an Drills they all cut up, an them thats not is flat. Cant find Macky or Lily. I hope Lily dead fore any thing got back here.

I found Sal Capone. Wasnt much left but a head an a buncha broken bones.

"I require help," Sal says. "You are bringing water, Ratch, and I am needing shade."

"You be fine," I tell him, "bout a blink an a half."

▲▼▲

How they do it, Im thinkin, them Rhidos the color of bone, them baby shit Drills? What kinda creatures was that, where they comin from? I know the dream, an it never had that. Any of the younguns they gettin outta this, some of ems Mamas some day an they gotta have a new dream, they gotta member this...

▲▼▲

I walkin past the camp where the females been, Florence an Silly an the rest. Isnt nothin there to see. Everthing flat cept off behind the rocks, where they got the cookfires. Big phuckers didnt get that. Some of the spits still standin from supper the night before.

Im walkin on, down to the draw. Isnt somethin you want to bother bout. Mightve been kin, or someone you know, an no sense thinkin on that.

▲▼▲

What I be thinkin is what Puck said. Somethin most ever body thinkin now an then. How its not right. What we gotta do, way we gotta be. Itd be different there wasn't so many. If we was moren them. Seems to me thats the cause right there. Seems like thats how it is...

Slidin'

"I can see it," says Ducie, "I can see it, Laureen. I can see it real good!"

"You can't see nothing," I tell her, "there isn't anything to see, Ducie Jean. Get your pants on and hush!"

It's bad enough your baby sister's hopping 'round the like a frog. Worse still she flat looks like one, ick warts and all. 'Course, there's folks look worse than that. I got family it is hue-miliating to call 'em kin. Like ol' Jeb-Reb and Ducko Bill. Don't even talk about Grandpa Foot. 'Least Ducie's got a head, and just one, we can be thankful for that.

"Lau-reen, now leave her be," says Mattie Mom. "You know Ducie's got real good sight."

"Maybe so," I tell her. "But she don't see Dallis, Mom. Not unless she's got bye-noclars in those bug eyes of hers."

"Don't you say that," Mattie Mom says, looking' round to see if other folks are listening in. Like they weren't more'n two, three hundred people in line, squashed in ahead and behind.

"Shoot, isn't like God didn't shit out Ugly all over Texass, Mom. Isn't anyone here don't look worse than Ducie Jean."

"Lau*reen!*," Mom says, turning 'bout ten shades of red. "How can you say things like that?"

"Don't do any good to lie," I answer back, watching a girl with six tits, all of 'em biggern' mine.

Truth hurts, I say. But don't everything else?

▲▼▲

We got up early, just before the sun come boiling up mad out of Lousy Anna, sucking up yesterday's sweat, and loosing a wave of morning farts along the line. A whole new stink comes rolling in to greet the day, and I'd gag and throw up, but you got to breathe to do that.

Some retard up front says, "Likely rain be comin' this afternoon. Kinda cool things off."

God's dick, I wonder where this bugger's been? Any little kid knows *that* date in school. It hasn't rained north of Wayco or anywhere *near*

Dallis, Texass, in two hundred eighty-three years. Only, this pinhead's expecting pre-cipitation late this afternoon. Crap springs eternal, as Grandpa always says.

▲▼▲

The afternoon didn't bring rain, but it did get us on past the Trinity Ditch where a river used to be. Everyone stopped, of course, it happens every time. You'd come to a dip in the dunes and there'd be another patch of petrified mud, shrunk up tight with a million little cracks in between. It's those cracks that got to us. Told us we were looking at a place where water used to be, water and trees, critters that aren't even here anymore, the way things were Back When. If you had a drop or two you were saving, you'd forget about later, and, without even thinking, drink it right there.

A couple of kids jumped down and started hopping from one patch of dry to the next, yelling and carrying on. Their daddy jerked 'em back quick, tanning their hides and giving 'em Willie-What-For. They were kids, and didn't know better, but the crowd sure did. Most everyone there swept two fingers cross their eyes to keep the devil away. Me too, though I don't believe in much of anything at all. Still, it's not good luck to get water riled up—even if it's where water's been.

Just 'fore dark we camped outside of Old Ferrus, up on a crest that looked down a pit deep as any you'd care to see.

"See-ment," said Uncle Jeb. "That's what they was diggin' for. Way Back When in—"

"—pre-hysterical times," finished Reb. "They built stuff with it, made con-kreet's, what they—"

"—did," said Jeb, "skycrappers, silos and such. You go to—"

"—any big city—"

"—still partly—"

"—intact—"

"—you're—"

"—gonna see where—"

"—cement's come—"

"—into play most—"

"—ever'where you—"

"—look..."

Anyone tell you two heads is better'n one, they hadn't never listened to Jeb-Reb yakking away, going at it nose to nose, way into the goddamn night. Mattie Mom and me pushed Jeb-Reb's pedal-tater up near the little fire we'd built, and I got supper and water jugs out of my sack. When Jeb-Reb, Ducie, Mattie Mom and Grandpa Foot were settled in, the fire cracklin' good, I whipped out supper and waved it all around.

"Ta-da!" I said, makin' a real big show, "we got a treat tonight, folks. Sparrows-on-a-stick!"

"Aaaaah, Oooooh!" everybody said, as I passed the sticks around. Jeb-Reb clapped, one hand missing the other like it always did. Grandpa stomped himself good 'till he fell over flat.

Sometimes, kids in school make fun of me 'cause I'm kinda whole and they're not. It don't bother me. I beat 'em to the ground and they don't say nothing after that. You are what you are, like Mattie Mom says. There's no shame in having extra parts like Uncle Jeb-Reb, or not hardly any like Grandpa Foot.

"You can thank Ducie for supper tonight," I said. "She brought every one of these babies down *Zaaaap!* Just like that."

"We're proud," said Mattie Mom. "We surely are, Ducie Jean."

Ducie Jean blushed, a pretty awful shade of green. "I wish Ducko could've been here. He's real partial to bird."

"Ducie, your brother couldn't come with us, hon," Mom sighed, like she hadn't told Ducie a million times before. "Ducko don't breathe air like us. It's kinda hard to take him on a trip."

"Oh," said Ducie Jean. "I don't guess I knew that."

"Hard to imagine what else you don't know," I said.

"Laureen…" Mom gave me that look and I shut up quick. I'm a pretty tough kid, and tall for my age, but when your mother's nine-six you tend to kinda do as you're told.

A hot night breeze set a little wave of sand a'quiver and sent it rattling down the road. You could hear all the other folks up and down the line, talkin' real low, some of 'em snoring and rattling in their sleep.

"We'll be getting' in late tomorrow night," Mom told us, when we'd gotten all quiet and settled in our sacks. "Now, you're going to see something not ever'one gets to see, and I expect you to behave and do as you're told. This isn't no ordinary place we're going, I don't have to tell you that. It'd be something to tell your younguns 'bout. I mean, if you was going to have some, which, God help us, you're not."

"What's it going to look like, Mom," said Ducie, "what's it going look like, huh! Huh!"

When Ducie gets excited, her skin starts sweatin' and the icks start a'poppin an' her voice goes '*lubbuk! Lubuk!*' and Lord help any flies in the nearby vis-inity of Ducie Jean's tongue. Still, she's my semi-natural sister, and there's nothin' I can do about that.

"I could tell you," said Grandpa Foot, "but there's no way describing it, child. Not so's anyone would believe it. You can say it's like this or like that, and not come anyways close either time."

"That's not a whole lot of help, Grandpa," I said, the words popping out 'fore I could make them stop.

I've known Grandpa since I was borned, but every time he opens that ugly big toe the hair stands up on my head.

"Be right careful," he said. "Be right careful who you're talking to, child. You don't want them dreams coming back. I don't reckon you do."

Mattie Mom sucked in a breath. Even Ducie Jean got quiet.

"No, sir," I said. "I surely don't. I spoke when I oughta not to, Grandpa. It won't be happenin' again."

"Well, fine," said Grandpa. "You're a good girl, Laureen. I always said you was."

▲▼▲

I didn't sleep good. I had me a dream, all right, but it wasn't wet and nasty like the ones I get from Grandpa Foot. This was a dream I'd had before. There was dark and there was light, and the dark was good, warm and heavy like my blanket on a nice winter night. Then the light come in, all fierce and razor bright, and it gnashed and it slashed, and it swallowed up the dark and all the warm and the good inside. The world changed forever after that, and all the people in it. There was sorrow and sin, madness and blight, and nothing was ever the way it usta been.

That's the dream I had, the one I'd had before, and I never told it to a soul, not even Mattie Mom. If you're different like me, if you're cursed with Symmetry, there's things you'd best be keeping in your head.

▲▼▲

After we were up and moving, it wasn't more'n an hour or so till we hit OLD THIRTY-FIVE. You could still see the road a'peeking through, where folks had wore the sand away. Ducie found a faded white stripe from Back When. Mom made her cover it quick 'fore anyone else could get a look. There's plenty of tales 'bout THIRTY-FIVE. Granpda called it Death and Dessy-cation, whatever that is. Anyway, religion can rise up and kick you in the ass, and it's best to leave it be.

When we started up north, we hit a little rise and I looked up ahead and back south the way we'd come. There was folk as far as you could see—more than I'd ever seen before. The line seemed to wave, seemed to quiver, seemed to blur, as if it was changing, shifting into something different all the time. It wasn't, of course. That's what you call your opposite delusion, something seems like it is and isn't at the very same time. It looks that way 'cause folks are all twitching, jerking, quaking and shaking, limbs going this way and that. Too many arms, not any at all, fingers a'sprouting out of ears, out of eyes, noses where privates ought to be. Legs stuck on where they shouldn't, asses up front and tummies in the back. That's how you know we all come from south of St. Atone, north of Big Salty where the Ugly Bomb hit Back When. Two hundred eighty-three years. The very exact same day the Raggys hit Dallis, or so the Book says. That's your co-accident's, what it is: Two big Yucks occurring at the very same time...

Do I mind being different, hardly like anyone at all? Sure I do. Symmetry's what you call it, like Grandpa says. Folks like me come along now and then. It isn't my fault and it isn't how you look it's what you are inside. Uh-huh. Easy for a foot to say, old man, but I'm not about to tell him that. I got enough crazy dreams without him pokin' in.

▲▼▲

We were getting close now. If you know what happened up here it isn't hard to tell. The ground gets harder where the sand's turned to glass, crunchin' and snapping where you walk. The sun slicks the earth, leaving long, silver cuts that burn your eyes. Getting toward noon, the blisterwind howled, splitting your flesh, sucking spit and grit.

"Guess you wish you'd stayed t'home, Laureen. Guess you're not all that big on seeing Dallis now."

See, that's what Grandpa Food'd do. If there wasn't any trouble on the stove, he'd cook up a pot by hisself. I knew this was coming, knew pretty sure I'd open my yak and buy myself a woolly dream. Mattie Mom gave me a look, but it was too late for that.

"Now why in the world would you think so?" I said. "Figures I'd want to come, don't it, Grandpa? Wouldn't want to miss seein' Dallis, something near as peculiar as me..."

That tore it right there. I could feel the wet fuzzy slippin' in my head, laying there, waiting till the dark. I'd pay good like I always did, but this time I didn't mind at all. It was worth it to hear Jeb-Reb and Mattie Mom suck up a sackful of 'fraids. That, and a minute I'd never forget: Grandpa shook. The dirty gray mat that would've topped his head if he'd *had* one stirred like a bushel of snaykes. His toes all swelled and those awful black eyes tried to nail me to the ground. It was a terrible, frightening thing to see.

"Do whatever you like," I said. "I don't even care. I can't do more than a nightmare at a time."

"Maybe you can't, maybe you can. I got some doozies you haven't even thought of before."

I squatted down and looked right in his eyes:

"Folks were different, then," I whispered, singing the old time song, *"Folks was all the same..."*

Grandpa near had a stompin' fit. "Shut her up. Shut her dirty mouth 'fore I do something real awful, Mattie!"

Mattie Mom unfolded a good seven feet, leaned down and gave him a look of plain sorrow I'd never seen before.

"I don't guess I can," she said. "I guess Laureen's growing into talking for herself from here on."

And then she bent down and looked at me. "And maybe someone be talkin' so much they're forgetting 'bout honor and respect for the family that brought her into this world. Maybe that's something she ought to be thinkin' at a time like this, Miss Laureen."

I don't guess I knew a person could be so full of love and anger at the very same time. There was things, right then, I'd never known about Mattie Mom before...

▲▼▲

You could hear 'em coming, the hearing right behind the awesome quiet, silence running up and down the line, not a single heart thumping, not a whisper not a fart. And then they was there, right up on us, sitting bright and shiny, sucking in the desert sun. I'd seen 'em once before, down near Lamp-asses when I was barely six. Too dumb to run, too scared to turn away, Mattie Mom right there swooping me up, hiding my face in the folds of her dress, not moving a foot, not giving a inch away.

You had to be scared, 'cause there's nothing as grand and fearsome as a Meckstex rider, sitting there spangles a' shining, ten feet high off the ground, his great hound sniffing at the ground, black nostrils flaring, big feet pawing at the glassy earth. If I'd a looked at Grandpa then I'd have seen his toes a'quiver, seen every hair shaking. I didn't have to turn to hear Ducie's awful croak, hear the pee begin to trickle down her leg. Only thing I *didn't* hear was Jeb-Reb yakking, and if that's not a wonder, I don't know what is.

"You come to see the marvel, yes?" The voice come hollow out behind the bright helm, a voice without a face that struck the heart of every living soul there.

"This is why we've come," came the answer down the line. *"This is why we're here…"*

"You have come to see the cost of greed and lust, to look upon the tomb of awful pride, to gaze upon the shame of the world, to see for yourselves the tomb of the damned, the ruination of Man."

A groan rose up from the line, for we knew, as well as the Meckstex rider, the terrible words from the Book itself.

For a moment, there was deadly silence, only the creak of the great hounds' saddles, the scrape of steel against steel from the riders' heavy mail. There were six of them, six dark riders. Never more and never less. There might have been a dozen, a hundred, but never, could anyone recall, more than the six at any one time. Five, their armor streaked with black, scaled like beetles and hoppers and such, The leader colored red, red like clay, like rust, like the dull, blood-soil of the earth. And, as anyone knows, when the six were encountered, it was always the rider in red who spoke. Never, ever one of the five. Behind those helms these silent warriors might have been dead. And, givin' the way folks made up stuff they couldn't understand, most any fool'd tell you dead is what they was.

One of the great dogs snuffled at the ground, raising a cloud of foul air. The rider creaked and clanged, stretched in his saddle, bent real low, *then looked down at me.*

The hair stood straight up on my head. Something turned over in my belly and I knew, right then, I'd never again make fun of Ducie Jean when the pee started rollin' down her leg. In about half a second, that was going to be me.

"You," said the dark warrior, in a voice like gravel in a can, "you are of this family, you are their girl child, yes?"

"Yes, I'm th—"

Before I could get the words out, Mattie Mom was there, stretching up quick, between me and him, nearly as high as the Meckstex himself. "Yes, she's family, that's who she is," Mom said, "my girl child come out of my womb, like every true child I ever knew. I can't see your face, rider, for it's black as sin in there, so I can't say just who it is wants to know."

You could've heard the world die right then and I shut my eyes tight, waiting for Mattie Mom's guts to start spillin' on the ground. Waiting to see her blow up, see her go flying, see her vanish, see her catch on fire, waiting for her ashes to scatter on the air. When none of *that* happened, I waited for the blood-red rider to think of something awfuller than that.

"I've got respect for a mother's ire," the raider said, "I can live with that. But don't go an inch, don't go a gnat-hair further with me, old woman, for you're standing on the edge right now."

"Why, the edge is where I live, rider," Mattie Mom said, "where we all be living, 'case you didn't notice, sitting so *high* up there you can't rightly see what's crawlin' down below."

Something flashed, something glittered, something glowed behind the slit in the big golden helm, something old, something cold, like silver boiling from a star. I turned away fast, quick-quick-quick—but not before it found me, 'fore it held me in its grip, kissed the warm-warm between my thighs, turned, quick enough, 'fore it sucked my soul right out between my eyes.

Then, with a laugh, with a tortured cry from his fearsome mount, the rider was in upon us, his dog-beast flailing, thrashing, each great foot encased in clever iron spikes that defied the slick and glassy earth. The brutal thing struck, ravaged, tore at the ground, raising a deadly cloud, a fury of splintered glass all about. I heard them cry out—whine, whimper, beg for their lives: Ducie, Jeb-Reb, Grandpa Foot. And, though I hated myself for it, I cried out too. Everyone did.

Everyone, except for Mattie Mom.

Without a glance back, the leader jerked his horrid creature aside, kicked its shaggy sides and bounded off across the road, his soldiers on his heels. I could hear their laughter and curses as they echoed through their helms.

"Bastards, villains!" said Grandpa Foot. "Wretched, arrogant fellows all!"

"They are, indeed, a horrid—" said Jeb.

"—mean-spirited lot—" Reb added,

"—brutes—"

"—cut-throats and—"

"—no good—"

"—bloody band of devils!"

"Well, that's so," said Mattie Mom, holding Ducie close to quiet her fears. "It's a terrible bunch, the Meckstexers be, but far worse still would be this land without 'em."

"Huh! A devil's bad enough," said Grandpa Foot. "There's no damn need he's got to act like he is!"

▲▼▲

The night was peaceful enough, and the sky full of stars, and I lay there pretending I flew above them somehow, looking down on this blanket of lights, each a magical city spread below. My head began to swim with such thoughts and I soon grew dizzy and looked away.

I slept for a spell, but soon fell back into a dream, the dream I'd had before. Once more, I could sorta see the world the way it was in the Way Back When. Again, there was the bright and terrible light, then the darkness came and opened its terrible maw, and swallowed the light whole. The dream was real clear on that. The dark was forever, and the world and the people would never, ever be the same again.

▲▼▲

Dawn seemed to fester, like the sun wasn't sure it'd bother going through it all again. Then, when the day finally came I prayed it'd turn and go away, for it struck the glassy earth with a vengeance, with its fierce uncaring fire, and it blistered the people with its heat, seared our eyes and nearly struck us blind.

And, when we could see again, we gathered ourselves together as best we could, and climbed a steep ridge from the side road, back to 35. The ground this close to Dallis was near solid glass, now, and even the time-worn path we followed was rife with twisty turns and hidden slicks that took you off your feet and sent you falling back, bringing down the curses of those behind. Ducie carried Grandpa Foot, who muttered and squirmed all the way. Mattie Mom and me struggled and slipped with Jeb-Reb's clumsy cart. And, for once, these two old bastards had the sense to know it wouldn't take a lot of sass for Mom and me to dump them and leave them on their own.

Then we topped the ridge and there they were…just waiting, watching, patient and thoughtful as could be, every demon, every devil, every horror from a hundred hells below. Mattie Mom never said a thing, never warned us, never dropped a hint at what she knew we'd see…

They lined each side of 35, near endless rows of gallows, pikes, cages and crosses, racks and stacks, terrible devices whose awful purpose was clear enough to see. And, such instruments and means so sly, so cunning and cruel they lay beyond the ken of ordinary folk, yet each designed to torture, kill, to slash and cut, to crush and sorely maim the soul within. And, adorning each awful presentation were creatures long dead, creatures yet alive, Rag-ohs, dopers, Popers and Yids, pale Baptistos and Arkansaw Blaks. Okiehoma Gooners, Lousy-Annie Slaks. Kanuks, Frangts, people on poles, people in sacks, people festooned with hairy rats.

It was just as Mattie Mom had said, the Meckstex Rangers were a fierce and wicked bunch, but it was them that kept us free, kept us clean of them that wasn't us, them that didn't belong. "With the good goes the bad," said Grandpa Foot," and who's to say which one's which."

Ducie cried, and buried her face in Mattie Mom's skirt. Grandpa muttered to himself. It wasn't till we'd climbed the slope and left these horrors far behind that Mattie Mom stopped and told us all to gather 'round.

"What you seen's the way the world is," she said, "and no way that's going to change. There's things have to be, and that's 'cause the way things was. You all understand what I'm saying? Yesterdays ain't ever out of sight. They're *lessons* is what they are. The Lord puts knowin' in our heads so we can do right next time instead of wrong. Wrong is what you're seeing now. Wrong's what we mustn't ever, ever think about doing again."

Mattie Mom paused, and looked at me and Ducie Jean. I didn't say a thing. Ducie looked like she always did. Like someone had turned the light out behind her bulgy eyes.

"You younguns listen to your mother," said Grandpa Foot. "She's right as she can be."

"Right as rain—" said Jeb.

"—Righter'n that, she be—" said Reb.

"—Right and—"

"—proper, Mattie Mom is—"

"—couldn't have put it—"

"—any better—"

"my—"

"—self, I couldn't."

"Thanks, Jeb-Reb," said Mattie Mom. "I appreciate your support, an' I knows the girls do too."

"Hmmmmph!" said Grandpa Foot.

▲▼▲

We were getting close, now, no one had to tell me that. Not far ahead, the line had forked off to the left and the right, folks spilling over one another in great half circles, pressing against one another for a look at what there was to see.

"It's Dallis, isn't it?"

Mattie Mom didn't answer, just squeezed my hand tight.

Seemed like it took all day to really get up close. Three, four hours, maybe more'n that. The sun was harsh, and you couldn't even walk without kicking up slivers of glass.

We were so close now, we could start to see a sight that made the hairs climb right up on your head. The closer you got, the thicker they was—hundreds of 'em, maybe more than that, folks coming right at us, frozen in glass, just the way they was the very second the bomb hit Dallis in the Way Back When. Everyone's heard about Lot's Tots of course, but seeing them's something else again. Some of them was standing, one leg in the air, arms swinging this way and that. Some was lyin' on the ground, still a'running fast as they could go. You could see how they was caught, their mouths, their eyes, their faces all twisted in one last awful moment before it hit 'em and turned 'em and froze them where they stood.

"Don't look in dead faces," Mattie Mom said, jerking me aside. Wasn't any use though—couldn't anyone turn away from that.

Mattie Mom wouldn't let go. She grabbed me in one hand and Ducie in the other, and pulled us through the crowd, making her way to the front. She pushed the last lookers aside

And there we were and
oh-Lord-God-in-Heaven save
me! I thought for a minute I'd
faint dead away—

and Mattie Mom grabbed me and Ducie let out a wail. It's just like Grandpa Foot said—there isn't no way to tell about it, it's something you gotta see, and even then you don't believe it's real…

It's like a bowl, a bowl of smoky glass so big you can't see the other side. It takes in everything, everything there is, and so deep, deep, there isn't any bottom, just a great and terrible dark that dies and fades away, and the more I looked the more I wanted to see, the closer I wanted to be—

"Best not to get real near, girl…"

Something grabbed me hard and I turned around quick, looked up and saw the Meckstex rider standing so close I could smell the heat of his armor.

"What you want," I said, "get away from me!" I looked for Mattie Mom, but she was busy holding on to Ducie Jean. The rider was tall, even afoot. He held the reins of his mount, and I looked away from its awful eyes.

"You read about Dallis in the Book," the man asked. "You know the story well?"

"Reading's just words. Seeing is somethin' else again. What—what you want with me!"

The rider shook his head. "The Book tells it clear, girl. Sin rose up from the East, and the West drew its swords and swept them back…"

"I can read," I told him. "I already know all that."

"Likely know more than you think, child. For the knowledge is in your blood. I knew that when I saw you."

"You don't know me. You never see me before."

"I know what you are. I know your symmetry."

My heart nearly stopped. "I'm just like ever'one else. Looking different don't mean a thing inside."

"...and that was the year of the Sun, and the East slept in defeat, and the West put its great swords aside..."

"You got to tell me the whole Book? And keep that—*thing* on its leash. It scares the livin' daylights out of me."

"There are things you need to know. Listen to my words, girl—"

"No, you listen to me, rider!" Mattie Mom stepped right between us, tall as the man himself.

"You've no need to speak to my child. She don't need to hear anything from you!"

"She is indeed your child, woman. But truly, she is a child of us all."

I felt that chill crawling up my neck again. Mattie Mom drew herself up straight as she could be.

"Don't you even *think* such a thought as that. I know your kind. Folk know more'n you think we do."

"She is of your womb. But she is not the same."

Ducie whimpered, clutching the hem of Mom's skirt. The rider turned his hidden eyes upon her, and Ducie shrank back.

"She's *my* child, is who she is. And how she looks, she can't help that. There's others like her too."

"No. Not like her. There are others, but they are imperfect. She has the symmetry. She is cast in the mold. She—"

Mattie Mom's face went pale as ash. I felt her shudder, felt her body tense, and in that instant she reached out, jerked me roughly to her, but the rider read her clearly; he was fast, fast, his movement only a blur. He slammed me against his armored chest so hard I gasped for breath, saw bright stars swim before my eyes.

Mattie Mom loosed a terrible cry, a shriek, a moan, a sound that held all the grief in the world, and when I could see again she was shrinking, falling, falling away, then she was gone, and I was sliding, turning in a dizzy circle, down, down, down. I opened my mouth to scream and a mailed fist quickly covered my face.

"Stop that. There is no need for you to cry out, girl."

"God, you don't think so? Let me goddamn *go,* you hear? Let me *go!*"

I knew, somewhere inside my rattled brain, that wasn't a good idea, either. He held me tightly against his chest, but over his shoulder I could see the surface beneath us rushing by at a rapid pace. I thought I could see things, things down there below the cloudy glass, and I knew that couldn't be, that there was nothing down there, nothing at all to see.

"...It is written in the Book, child. The way things were, the way that things must be. Surely you can understand this is so."

I almost laughed through my fear. "What, I'm supposed to ride down this thing and we just—*die,* right? Tell me where it says that!"

"...and lo, the beaten foes slept, and when they woke they crawled out of the horror the West had left behind. And, though they had no Newks of their own, God had given them a great sea of sand, and from that sand they forged a—"

"I already *know* that," I shouted through the wind, "I'm slidin' down goddamn Dallis, I can see what they did. That was two hundred eighty-three years ago. *I* didn't do anything, what's that got to do with me?"

"It's all about you, child. All about you and the things that were and what has to be."

"You keep saying that. I don't want to hear it anymore!"

"It's about done now. There isn't much more."

"Don't. Don't you tell me that!"

I couldn't help myself. I tried to hold him close.

"I'll be there with you. That's what I'm supposed to do. And it *does* have to be, girl. You might breed, you know. And there can't be any more folks like they were before. There mustn't ever be."

I could scarcely see the sky anymore. There was nothing but the great bowl of glass, rushing by, and nothing but the fast approaching dark down below, and I *couldn't* look at that.

"What do you think it's like?" I asked the rider. "What do you think it'll be?"

"I don't know," he said. "Whatever there is, is. The way it has to be. Lo, the Book has said—"

"Goddamnit," I told him. "I already *knew* that!"

Radio Station St. Jack

One

Late in the summer afternoon, Father Mac took a lawn chair out beneath the trees to watch the war. The patio was brick, laid in a haphazard pattern that was pleasing to the eye, the surface now subdued, aged to the dark tones of earth, buckled by oaks that had been there a hundred years or more. It was a place that remained in shadowed light throughout the day. Mac liked to sit there and read old books or watch the rain sweep in from the south. There was no rain now, only an August sky seared to the color of bone.

The back of the house faced the southwestern crest of the hill, behind the radio station and the Church of Saint John.

▲▼▲

From there, Mac could see the town, the buildings and the streets through a hazy veil of blue. In spite of the smoke and several isolated fires, it appeared to be a quiet, rather orderly sort of war, and quickly winding down. The raiders had tired of small arms. They were settled in now near Hubbard and Fourth, lobbing in rounds at the Baker Hotel. The gunners seemed to lack any skill. They enjoyed the sound of mortar fire, quite unconcerned with hits. Now and then a shell would strike its mark, sending a shower of masonry to the street, drowning out the ragged cheers.

The Baker had once been fifteen stories high, a plain brick structure except for the architect's statement on top, a Spanish mission and medieval keeps. Missouri cannoneers had done the mission in proper in the spring, reducing the stories down to ten. They had stolen several horses, and beaten the town in volleyball.

Mac knew little about the present raiders. They seemed to favor red. A red hat or two, camo pantaloons. By chance or design, they'd surprised a pride of Choctaws camping on the Brazos out of town, chased them up dry Pollard Creek and into the Baker Hotel. Mac didn't know the raiders, but he knew about the Choctaw crew. They had drifted into town from Oklahoma, intent on stealing canned peaches or whatever they could find.

Sister Leah had talked to one at market and gathered several facts. The Indians were deranged, and practiced unfamiliar rites. As manhood approached, they removed the right eye and tattooed their private parts. The one Leah saw liked to hang around the alley back of Karl's Katz'n Dogs. They lurked about a lot, but did not attack the town.

Mac saw the wisdom in that. Monocular vision might limit the military arts. Whatever the reason, they never got a foray off the ground. Now they were holed up in the Baker, waiting for the red hats to tire, or run out of shells.

A shout, a hurrah, went up below. Peering through the haze, Mac saw the regular's at Hal's had brought chairs outside to watch the show. Several of the raiders wandered over for a drink. Hal set up an extra table, and went back for whiskey and ale. A round went long and dissolved an abandoned Texaco. Hal would start watering the drinks. Dilution was the rule if you came from out of town.

▲▼▲

The radio tower was etched against a cloudless afternoon. The station was a cinderblock square, painted on the sly by Brother Steve, painted while Mac was out of town, without Mac's knowledge or consent, painted a vague, El Paso service station blue with a hint of indigo, and possibly toxic to the eye.

Mac was headed for the station with regret when he caught sight of Sister Mary Jo coming down the pathway from the church. Mary Jo saw him, or possibly not, it was always hard to tell. As ever, she walked on by and didn't stop.

Mac felt a surge of irritation and desire. He picked up his pace to cut her off, to intercept perky bare feet and frizzled hair. The key to Mary Jo was awkward grace, a girl who was basically legs and collarbones. A girl, Mac thought, who ought to play guitar, who could pick sweet tunes you couldn't name.

He said hello. Waited for response of any sort.

"So," said Mary Jo. She stopped because Mac was in the way. "So how's the war?"

"I'd say it's nearly done. There wasn't much to do."

"Leah says an Indian isn't going to die the first time. Says you got to kill 'em twice."

"I don't think you do."

"Leah knows a lot of savage lore."

"Well, that's true," Mac said. He didn't press the point. Didn't tell her Indians weren't a big problem anymore, not if they'd checked in the Baker Hotel.

Mary Jo didn't move, didn't try to get away. Her eyes seemed to focus out of state. Mac was staggered by her eyes, the shape of her nose, the way she moved her mouth. The way one tooth was independent of the rest. He had let her know he cared in a dozen different ways. At first he thought her distant and aloof. Now, he knew she was simply unconcerned. With him, with the weather, with anything at all. Indifferent to love, to the state of the union, to proper dental care.

"Oh, I forgot." Mary Jo came back to life. "There's six or eight farmers in the church. They'd like to get a prayer."

"No way," Mac said, glancing at his watch, "I've got *airtime*, Mary Jo, I can't do farmers right now. I'll send over Steve."

"They don't want Steve, they want you."

"Steve'll have to do. Steve does agriculture fine."

"This big guy with a limp? He says tell you Arnie Simms."

Simms rang a bell. The name recalled baskets of freshly picked corn, tomatoes big as baby heads.

"Okay," Mac said, "I better handle this myself. Tell Steve to do the weather. Tell him *not* to do the news. Tell him not to mess with my tapes. Don' touch the CDs. You and I could have dinner if you like."

"I guess not tonight."

"I'll consider that a maybe, Mary Jo."

Mary Jo seemed unaware. He watched her walk away. There was always a slight imperfection to her dress. Today she had a T-shirt inside out, Mickey's name from right to left. Mac watched her legs, watched her ankles, watched the soles of her feet. The soft little pads were brown with dirt, the arches untouched and white as snow. A tall and skinny girl makes indolence enchanting, Mac thought, makes neglect a charming air. Lazy eyes seem to imitate desire. Which doesn't really matter, if the girl doesn't care.

▲▼▲

The church was small, made of native Texas stone. The stones were from a former local bank. They revealed ancient creatures, frozen in a Paleozoic sea. Mac came in the back door, brushed back his hair and slipped into a robe. Arnie Simms was in the front pew. His boys sat behind him, big hands resting on faded denim knees.

"Brother Simms," Mac said, grasping a hand tough as alligator hide, "it's a pleasure to see you again."

"We need rain," said Simms. "I got stock full of worms. Hoppers have near eat me out. Palo Pinto county's blowed away. That land of mine's dry as snake shit."

"Well, it hasn't been a real wet year," Mac agreed.

"Looks to me like the Lord could spare some rain. He can get all he wants, there's places not usin' it at all."

"God knows your needs, Brother," said Mac.

"Knowing and doing ain't the same, friend."

"Actually it is," Mac said, wisdom Simms didn't seem to hear.

"It might be there's something else." Simms nodded over his shoulder. "My middle boy took a Stephens County wife. A Breckenridge girl with red hair. That woman knows a lot about frogs. I figure she might've cursed the soil."

"The church doesn't hold with curses, Brother Simms. I think you know better than that."

Simms muttered something to himself. Mac looked at the four young men slouched in the second row. Pear-shaped bodies like their father, vaguely asymmetric heads. Each a year apart, each a little stranger than the next, a chart of evolutionary blight. The Breckenridge girl who liked frogs couldn't hurt. Forty-nine miles didn't seem too far to start a new genetic pool.

"I brought some seed along," said Simms, "got 'em right here." He reached beneath the pew and set a sack in front of Mac.

"My thinking is, you can bless this bunch, I'll take it back and mix it with the rest." He showed Mac a sly wink. "The good seeds'll spread the word, and they'll root out evil from the land. What you think of that?"

Mac glanced at his watch. "That just might do it, Brother Simms, sounds good to me."

He held up a hand. "You all got to be quiet, okay?" Simms and his boys bowed their heads. Mac placed his hands on the sack and closed his eyes.

"Sanctus per diem...Modus operandi...dum-de-dum-dum..."

Mac cleared his throat. Simms raised his head and looked relieved. "We sure are grateful, Father Mac. You like squash and lima beans?"

"I like 'em just fine."

"I got a basket outside. Say, we listen to you all the time. The wife can't sleep she don't hear a Ted Weems song. Shit, that woman'd whistle *Heartaches* all night."

"You need any batteries, Brother Simms, Sister Leah'll fix you up. Reasonable prices, any size you want."

"Could you play a little Hank Williams sometime? *Jesus Remembered Me? I Saw the Light?*"

"*Lost on the River*," Mac said. "*Weary Blues for Waitin'. Your Cheatin' Heart.* You got it, Brother Simms."

"Hallelujah," Simms said...

Two

Mac didn't bother with the robe. He hiked it to his knees and ran quickly up the path. Gunpowder and mesquite were in the air. Evening grackles in the trees. He thought about squash. Maybe he could trade it off in town. Good brandy might entice Mary Jo. There was still a full bottle at the house. He was saving it for something, and wasn't sure what.

At the station, he was met with funereal assault. Bach shook the cinderblock walls. *Tocata and Fugue.* A big Kraut organ gone berserk. Mac clapped his hands to his ears and burst in on Brother Steve.

"Hi, Father Mac." Steve tried a grin that didn't work.

"Don't you *ever* do organs on my station again. Not ever, boy!"

Steve colored. "I just thought—"

"It is supper time out there, Steve. Folks are trying to eat. They don't want a dirge, they want to hear something nice."

Mac picked up a stack of tapes. A Mozart requiem, Gregorian chants.

"Lord God, you got some farmer up in Jacksboro sitting down to fresh peach pie. He wants to hear a song, something with a gentle beat, you knock him right out of his chair. You got your program sheet, you got your spots. That's your job, that's it, Brother Steve."

Steve pretended to fiddle with his dials. Mac could see wheels in his head. A devastating answer, a cutting retort that would slice Mac off at the knees.

"I—got things to do," Steve said. His long limbs tangled in the chair. "Over at the church. I promised Sister Leah. Your stuff's all ready to go."

"I appreciate that," Mac said. "No offense, Brother, but you need to get a handle on religious radio. You might ought to pray over that."

"I—will, Father Mac, I'll sure do that."

Steve bobbed about like a bird, found the door and stumbled out. Mac shook his head. Steve would try. But next time or time after that, the same thing would happen again. Steve would try to follow the sheet, and start humming Hayden in his head. Arnie Simms would be waiting for the Ink Spots to go with his after-dinner snort—Brother Steve would hit him with *Dicit Dominus* and scare him half to death.

Mac had found Steve at the hardware store. He knew where everything was, he kept all the nails just right. Mac knew he should have seen it right off. The boy identified completely with the job. He had no other life at all. As soon as Mac hired him, he put all thought of nails aside. Shaved his head clean, and talked about the Essene life. He seemed to have a thing for St. Jerome. He could put up with Steve, or send him back to the hardware game. There was little you could do with a boy who liked to work, and couldn't think of anything else.

▲▼▲

Mac imagined his listeners, spread across the flat, open counties of North Texas in a hundred small towns, in farm houses ready for the night, the family gathered round the warm amber light of a battered radio; he saw them walking back through the late evening woods, shadows stretched long across their way, earphones ready for the Father Mac Show. Wise County, Parker, Erath and Cooke. Grayson and Montague and Young. Even up in Oklahoma, across the Red River into Lone Grove, Archer, Tishomingo and Durant, listeners everywhere, recovering from Brother Steve's sonic attack, ready for some sweet radio.

They were all out there, people left over from the Godawful War, people who'd made it through the times after that. People who didn't have much, people who were damned and determined to hold on tight to what they had.

Mac segued nicely into Glenn Miller's *Moonlight Cocktail,* his own familiar theme. He leaned in close, nearly tasting the mike, flipped a switch and saw the light go cherry red.

"Evening out there everybody, it's Saturday gettin' on into night. You got Father Mac on the line, and it's easy listening time. Coming right at you from the studios of Radio Station Saint John, the voice of Mineral Wells, Texas, the church on the hill with the tower on top.

"Say, whenever you're in town be sure and say hello to my good buddy Karl T. LaGrange at Karl's Katz'n Dogs. Karl's got a brand new bunch of spaniel pups, come by and pick up one you like. And, Karl's *always* got the fattest cats in town. You thinkin' steak, got a back-yard burger in mind? Pardner, you're thinkin' Karl's Katz 'n Dogs.

"Hey, how about this hot spell we got ourselves into, friends? Makes *me* want to run right over to Hal's Bar and Ready to Wear. Treat yourself to a cold one, try on a shirt while you're there. Any shade you like, long as you're partial to blue. That's Hal's Bar and Ready to Wear, next to Market Square.

"A special hello to all you raiders in town. Before you go—and hey, we're looking forward to *that*—stop by and stock up at Eddie's Guns and Ammo. If it's weapons you're after, Eddie's got 'em all.

"All right now, Brothers and Sisters, before we get into some oldies and goldies, I want to tell you we've got a *week* of fun and drama coming your way on Saint John Radio. For all you ladies out there, you don't want to miss your favorites—*Lorenzo Jones, John's Other Wife, The Guiding Light,* and Sister Leah's favorite, *The Romance of Helen Trent.* Kids, you'll want to be right here every afternoon with ol' *Tom Mix, Red Ryder, Captain Marvel* and, hey—*The Greeeeen Hornet!* After those lousy crooks, Kato! Thrills and chills on the way."

Mac leaned in close to the mike, his voice down low. "Friends, I've been saving this for last. We've got him back again, another hour of *The Jack Benny Show.* This week, the old skinflint is down in the vault where he keeps all his money locked up. He gets in a *whole* lot of trouble, and Rochester has to—I won't spoil it for you, okay? Don't miss this one, it's *all* the hi-jinks you can handle, and clean family fun.

"Right now, it's back to easy listening time with Johnny Desmond singing *This Can't Be Love...* and hey, you *know* it can't be because it *feels* so well..."

Mac leaned back to listen. The last pale fragment of the day began to fade and fall away. Seven green lizards were clinging to the window outside. Their bellies were white as tropic sand. Tiny splayed pads pressed hard against the glass. Their red throats throbbed, keeping perfect time. They couldn't hear the beat, but they could feel it in their tiny lizard souls. They dozed in the sun, made lizard love in their cinderblock holes, and came out when Mac began to play. They had a feel for swing. They liked Shep Fields, and they liked Ted Weems. Artie Shaw was God, and he'd lift them up to reptile heaven one day...

Three

The night pressed hot and heavy on the town, but it was cooler on the hill. A high breeze filtered through the trees and made it hard for gnats to fly. Mac put a steak on the grill, added one more and didn't tell himself why. He cooked Arnie Simms' lima beans. Fried an onion in a little hot sauce. Found the brandy, hidden in his socks. Thought about Duke and Les Brown, decided on sweet Jimmy Dorsey instead.

In the bedroom he found a clean shirt, kicked dirty clothes beneath the chair. *So Rare* began to drift through the house. Marmalade sax filled the night. Mac checked on the steaks. Walked in the parlor, saw candles on the table, saw one more plate than he'd need to eat alone. He'd set a voodoo trap for Mary Jo. His needs would lure her in. She would wear something summery and white.

He felt like a fool. The scene was perfect for romance, way overdone for self abuse. Mary Jo had said no. He'd said maybe, but that wouldn't make it so. He took a glass of brandy to the couch. There's no harm in fantasy, obsession helps you make it through the night. Still, Mac decided, it might be time to make repairs inside your head.

There were several nice girls in town. Willing, and adept at erotic enterprise. He thought about them one at a time. Mary Jo wouldn't go away. Reality refused to take a stand.

Mac got up and changed the tape. Benny Goodman shook the windows with *Bugle Call Rag.* He thought about music for his Monday night show. Maybe a whole Stan Kenton parade. *Peanut Vendor* and *September Song.* Move into *Artistry in Rhythm,* slide into *Laura* and *Tampico.* Would they march on the station, would they stone him if he did?

Someone knocked, and Mac spilled brandy down his shirt. Rational thought, about to take hold, gave up without a fight. Go slow, put her at ease. Show her he understood her needs. *String of Pearls, I'm Getting Sentimental Over You.*

He opened the door, and there was Sister Leah.

"Well, hi there. Hello." Mac put on a smile, rewound the story in his head. "Say, how in the world are you, Sister Leah?"

"I know it's late, Father Mac. It's after dark and I ought to be in bed. I hope I'm not disturbing you, Lord, I guess I am."

"No, no, I wasn't doing anything at all." Leah looked as if she might turn and flee. Mac backed away, blocking her view of the table set for two.

"Have a seat," he said, "how about a cup of tea?"

"Listen, don't you go to any trouble, Father Mac, don't go out of your way for me."

"No trouble, no trouble at all."

Mac quickly slid the extra tableware out of sight, hurried to the kitchen and put a kettle of water on. Returned to Sister Leah.

"I guess you think it's kinda odd, me up and wandering about."

"Sleep eludes us all sometimes," said Mac.

"You didn't have to do that, you didn't have to make tea."

"Now you take it easy, don't you worry about the tea."

Leah showed distress, uncertainty and doubt. The emotions were familiar, she wore them all the time. Possibly dimension was the cause.

Not so you'd notice, but Leah felt ugly was a cross she had to bear, and reminded somebody ever day. She was still quite young, barely sixteen. Nice blue eyes and no self regard at all. If Leah started liking herself, zits and the baby fat would go away.

"I'm real embarrassed," Sister Leah said, twisting her fingers in her lap. "I don't know what to say."

"You don't have to say a thing," Mac said. "Is everything all right in your work, are you happy here, Leah?"

Leah looked alarmed. "Oh, now, it's nothin' like that. I got the only peace here I ever had. I grew up in trouble and abuse. My folks were unkind. Slavers took me off when I was six. They sold me in Wichita Falls. I was forced to eat snake till I was nine. I've seen all the pangs of life I care to, Father Mac. I wouldn't be anywhere but here."

"Yes...of course." Mac thought they were getting to the core. Leah had something to say, and didn't know how to let it out.

The tea seemed to help. He put on some Nat King Cole and turned the volume low.

"I just love that music, Father Mac. It sounds like a river somewhere." She hummed a little off key. "Me and Mary Jo, we'll lie there and listen and fall right asleep. A body can't help drifting off."

"Well, that's good," Mac said. He felt a little flutter in his heart, tried not to think of Mary Jo in the context of *bed,* or, worse still, bed and lack of sleeping wear.

"'Course, I can't sleep at *all* you put something funny on at night. I laugh till I 'bout start to cry. *Amos and Andy, Fred Allen* and *Baby Snooks.* Jack Benny, though, he's the best of all. I swear... I guess I'm like you, Father Mac."

Mac brightened at that. "Really? Is that so?"

"Lord, yes. That ol' Maxwell car. And Rochester's always tryin' to get a raise."

"Don Wilson, Dennis Day," Mac said.

"Jack thinks he can play the violin."

"Butterfly McQueen!"

"Phil Harris and Alice Faye!"

"I guess I didn't know there was anyone else who felt the same," Mac said.

"Oh, there sure is, Father Mac, I'm here to tell you that." Leah paused and looked at her hands. "Sometimes—not to anybody else, you under-stand—sometimes just to myself, I think of the church as St. Jack." She glanced up quickly at Mac. "I don't mean any disrespect, I want to be clear about that."

Mac felt warm all over, partly from the brandy, a lot from Sister Leah.

"I know it's late for supper," he said, "but I'd be pleased if you'd join me for a bite…"

▲▼▲

Leah leaned back and closed her eyes, close to a state of final bliss. She'd barely touched the lima beans, but the steak had quickly disappeared, sizzle, grease and all.

"God love you, Father Mac. I haven't tasted horse since I was ten. I don't *remember* a meal good as that."

"I'm glad you liked it," Mac said, "it's a special treat for me as well."

"I don't guess there's a meat any better, none that I recall—" Leah drew in a breath. Elation turned quickly to alarm. "Father Mac, I know you wouldn't do nothin' wrong…"

"It's legal," Mac assured her with a grin. "Prime Appaloosa. Certified lame. Pleasure without the penance, Sister Leah. Have a little brandy with that, make the meal complete."

"Oh, now, I couldn't do that."

"Sure you could." Mac filled her glass, and another for himself. "You're dining out with your spiritual guide, as it were, and he says brandy's just fine."

▲▼▲

It wasn't quite true about the horse, Mac knew, but not false enough to make a lie. They weren't that scarce anymore, but butchering was still against the law. Karl LaGrange, at Karl's Katz'n Dogs, knew a man who could sense somehow when a horse was about to break a leg. Mac didn't know how, and didn't ask. The church couldn't cure the world's ills. Now and then, folks were bound to sin. He knew about the lame horse trade. Who was pushing nicotine, who was running pickled mice from Mexico. He knew what Hal put in his gin.

He felt the need to understand his flock. So he cut a few minor deals himself. Nothing that he felt might offend. He wouldn't smuggle choco-late, wouldn't deal in bogus hats. He did what he thought he ought to do. He knew he wasn't perfect, but no one could say that he held himself apart, that he wouldn't lend a hand.

Maybe you're baking a birthday cake, or cooking up a tart. Even if you don't go to church, Father Mac can help. He'll get you a kilo of pure cane sugar, and he'll never gouge you on the price.

▲▼▲

Brandy, Mac decided, wasn't such a good idea. It was fairly clear Leah had never touched drink of any sort. Now, she'd downed a whole Pluto glass, maybe three or four. She was sliding off the couch, one eye shut, one roaming free at will.

"Just take it easy," Mac said, "We'll get you up and get a little air."

Leah didn't answer. Mac propped her up and helped her out the door. She muttered something he couldn't hear.

"You're going to be all right," Mac said, "you're going to be fine."

"Oh Lord, we ate that horsey, Father Mac!"

"That's okay, that horsey didn't mind."

"He coulda been rompin' in a field." Tears welled up in her eyes. "I bet he liked to run and play."

"Leah, just forget about the horse."

"I been havin' bad dreams, Father Mac. I feel I'm tangled in sin, I ain't fit to be a nun."

"I don't want to hear talk like that, you're as fit as you can be. Put one foot before the other, now, we're almost there."

"God help me," Leah moaned, "Satan's got me by the foot, I been havin' dreams of TV!"

Mac looked at her. "Leah, you can't be sinning a lot. You haven't ever *seen* TV. I'm twice as old as you, and I don't recall a thing."

"I can see it in my *head,*" Leah said, sniffing in her sleeve. "I can see folks kissin', shooting one another, I can see a game show."

"You just think you can, Leah. You're not seeing anything at all."

Mac didn't care for this. Some old fart had been talking to her, putting ideas in her head. That's all I need, he thought, a visionary nun.

▲▼▲

It seemed half the night before he got her up the hill and to her door. Leah went totally limp. He felt something give in his back, something he would likely need again. Leah giggled to herself, humming the theme from the *Jack Benny Show.* He prayed Mary Jo wouldn't suddenly appear.

"We're here," Mac said quietly, "think you can make it by yourself?"

"Da-da-da-de-*dum,* de-*dum,* de-da-da-da-da-deee..."

"Fine. You get a good night's sleep."

Leah opened one eye. "Pray for me, Father Mac."

"*Semper Fidelis. Cogito, ergo,* put it in the sack, Sister Leah..."

Four

Everyone told him the Sunday service went well. He tried to remember what he'd said. Sin and redemption rang a bell. It's hard to hold a thought when your eyes are solid lead, when your head's a hollow tree.

After he steered Leah home he went back and tried to sleep. It didn't work at all. He found a fifth of Carolina gin Hal had given him for free. It packed a real punch, and left the aftertaste of eels. Events of the evening had left him out of sorts. He felt a sense of guilt. It was wrong to get teenage nuns snockered up to the gills. This was not a priestly thing to do.

He tried to read the faces in the crowd. See if he was making any sense. More than half the seats were filled; people got religion when marauders came to town.

He couldn't look at Mary Jo. He spotted Sister Leah. She looked beatific, or maybe in a trance. It was possible she didn't recall the night at all. Amen to that, he said, and brought the sermon to an end. Raised his hands and blessed the crowd, thought about what to have for lunch.

▲▼▲

Karl LaGrange and Hal and Mayor Will were waiting on the steps.

"Nice sermon," Karl said. "I like 'em when they aren't too long."

"Me too," Mac said.

"Father Mac," said Mayor Will, "I think we better talk."

"Raiders," said Hal, before Mac could ask why.

"They're talking up pillage and rape," said Will. "Sacking all the stores, burning down the town. Unlawful acts of every sort."

Mac shook his head. "Your outlaw types are going to talk like that. They get in town, they like to blow off a little steam."

"This bunch is different," Hal said. "These boys have got a bad attitude. They don't much care for volleyball. Some of 'em order funny drinks."

"Flat out mean," Karl said.

Mac considered all this. Mayor Will ran Will's Ice House and Hit Plays. He was slightly high strung and off key. He was fond of colored scarves. Hal and Karl, now, were sound as good brick and not inclined to false alarms.

"Who's running this show," Mac said, "you talk to him?"

"Doesn't *want* to talk," said Will. He glanced at the other two. "Says he wants to talk to you."

Mac was surprised. "Why me?"

"Ask him."

"He wants to see you," Karl said. "Right now is when he said."

"Well I don't want to see him. It's Sunday afternoon. I got religious stuff to do, I haven't even had lunch."

Will looked at his watch and sighed. "It's 12:45. What this guy says is he'll come up and get you, you don't come down by one."

Mac was appalled. "He wouldn't do that. This is a radio station and a church."

"I don't think he cares," Karl said. "That's what I'm reading, from the way the fella acts."

Mac muttered to himself. He was plainly irritated. Hal's import scotch was still working in his head. "All right, you tell this meat photo I'm coming. Tell him I'll be there at one or maybe not. Where's he hanging out?"

"Over near Hubbard and Oak," Hal said. "Won't let us get anywhere near."

"We're supposed to play softball at four," Will said. "I don't see how we're going to do that."

▲▼▲

Mac stalked back into the church. He was pissed, completely out of sorts. He didn't like raiders at all. Your burglar or your footpad, your average common thief, took a little pride in his craft. Every freebooter he'd known was devoid of style or class. They were prone to deceit, and had no taste in hats.

Mary Jo was sweeping up. Orange peels and nut shells and hard heels of bread. Mac wished people didn't feel compelled to bring a snack.

Brother Steve met him halfway up the aisle. "You going down there, Father Mac? You goin' to talk to this guy?"

Steve looked gaunt and full of zeal. John the Baptist in Mexican tennis shoes.

"What do you know about that, you listen at the door?"

"Shoot, everybody knows, can I go too?"

"No, you can't."

"Why not?"

"Mary Jo, you got a clean nun suit?"

"Huh? What's the matter with this?" Mary Jo leaned on her broom. Soot, dust, possibly scrambled eggs, marred her shabby dress. Mac thought she looked vaguely erotic, lazy as a snake.

"We're going into town," he told her. "You want to comb or anything, hurry up."

Steve looked disturbed. "Well why is it her and not me, I'd like to know that."

"You want something to do? Go paint. You like to paint a lot. Paint the radio tower. Anything but blue."

Steve looked aghast. "I'm n—not going up there, Father Mac!"

"You are if you keep plaguing me."

Steve scurried off and managed to disappear.

"What are we doing in town?" said Mary Jo.

"I'm going to meet this terror of the plains. I'm taking you, because I greatly admire your taste in clothes."

"There's nothing wrong with my clothes."

"They do not reflect the dignity of the church."

"Yeah, right," said Sister Mary Jo.

▲▼▲

They walked down the rough dirt road that wound through abandoned houses and a clutter of mobile homes. The road led into Sixteenth, a street still partially intact, paved here and there where grass and second growth hadn't pushed up through the cracks. The street slanted steeply toward the town. Mac could see the pockmarked ruin of the Baker Hotel, and other lesser sights.

To the east, the brickyard, the cemetery, and useless railroad tracks, the road that stretched to Parker County and beyond, where Fort Worth and Dallas used to be.

"I'd like to know why I'm going into town," said Mary Jo. "I'd sure like to hear about that."

"I don't want you sweeping out the church," Mac said. "You tend to aggravate the dust."

"I guess I already know why."

"Fine. Then you don't have to ask."

Mac decided it was better not to talk. Talk didn't work with Mary Jo. They were nearly into town, and he could smell the fresh rubble of yesterday's fight, and maybe something worse. Mary Jo stopped to watch a hawk. He admired the way the sun caught her hair. You couldn't name a color like that, it was something simply there.

Mary Jo turned too soon, before Mac could look away. "Listen, don't do that, okay?"

"Do what?"

Mary Jo rolled her eyes. "I told you last night I wasn't coming up to eat. I think I said it real clear."

"I suppose you did. Look, I'm sorry. I know you don't care for me a lot."

"Now I never said that. When did you hear me say that?"

She gave him a curious look. Didn't know what to make of it, wasn't sure he cared to try.

"Don't you ever give Leah strong drink," said Mary Jo. "I won't put up with that."

"That was a mistake."

"I'll say it was. And, hey—you didn't say we were going to have horse. You never said a thing about that."

▲▼▲

Mac turned west on Hubbard, east of the Baker Hotel. There was clearly considerable debris. Mortar rounds had exploded in the streets and demolished vacant stores. The raiders had used a lot of rounds before they found the hotel. Mac wondered if it might be prudent to bring the structure down. Blow it up and cart it off. It seemed to attract a bad crowd.

The faint smell that had reached him up the hill was a sickening presence now. Mary Jo looked at Mac with alarm and clapped a hand across her nose. Mac had an idea what lay ahead. He was sorry now that Mary Jo was there. Will was right. These weren't ordinary raiders at all.

He considered turning back, but there was no time for that. Holding her hand, he guided Mary Jo across the street. Half a block away and the source of the smell was stark and clear.

"Oh Lord," said Mary Jo.

"Don't look," said Mac.

"Thanks a lot for bringin' me along. I wish you had a thing for Steve."

"Mary Jo, I didn't figure on this."

"I think I gotta throw up."

"Don't. If you do we'll have to stop."

He tried not to look at the sight, but horror fascinates the eye, draws it and holds it there in fear. The Choctaws were strung up in a row, from Fourth past the Baker down to Oak. They were naked and devoid of private parts. Tattoos hadn't helped their cause at all.

Now Mac could see raiders up the street. A patchwork of red hats, camo pants and red athletic shoes. Hal was surely right. This bunch had a poor attitude. And bad taste on top of that.

He didn't mean to look across the street again, something simply caught his eye. Vision said a dead Indian, but his heart found a too familiar face. An awful wave of fear gripped his chest. An instant before he'd felt impersonal regret, sorrow at the useless deaths of men he didn't know. Now, he was filled with a different kind of anger, another brand of fear. He had shared the tail end of many long days with a man who was hanging from a pole, and to Mac that wasn't right. It wasn't right at all…

Five

Mac picked out the head honcho at once. A good foot taller than his men. His hat added inches to his height. A wide-brim straw dyed red, a broken feather on the top. Mac didn't fail to miss the big Colt pistol in his belt.

The raiders moved apart to let their leader through. He offered Mac a lopsided grin and a big dirty paw.

"Hi there," he said, "I bet you're Father Mac. I'm Bob the Destroyer, I hope you'll call me Bob."

"Welcome to Mineral Wells," Mac said.

"Now that's good, that's what I like to hear." Bob laughed, and cast an appraising eye on Mary Jo. "I am sure looking forward to meeting you. You'd be a stunner in red. I feel we can get to be close."

"She's leaving," Mac said. "Right now."

"Yeah? Who says?" Bob's winning smile began to fade.

"You want to talk to me, she goes."

"I think I'll put a hole in your head."

"That's going to hamper talk." Mac kept his eyes on Bob. "Go on down to Market, Mary Jo. I think they've got peaches in today. You wait for me there."

Mary Jo was scared. Mac was proud of her, she didn't let it show.

"Go on now. I'll be along in a while."

Mary Jo nodded and started up Oak. There were raiders all about. They watched her go and looked at Bob. Bob looked unconcerned, as he surely didn't care.

"I thought you and me could get along," he told Mac. "I might've been wrong."

"We can get along fine."

"I guess we ought to have a drink. There's no use talking in the sun."

Bob didn't wait for an answer. He walked off into shade. Mac watched him walk. He wasn't just tall. He looked as if he might have been stretched. His arms and his legs, every feature on his face, seemed longer than they should.

The raiders had dragged a collection of chairs, mattresses and beds, other odds and ends, and set them up beneath the awning of a vacant tire store. Bob found a bottle and glasses, and gestured Mac to sit.

"I hope you like Chinese gin," Bob said, filling Mac's glass. "I got a taste for it on a venture down south."

"You need to drop over to Hal's."

"The boys tell me it's a real nice place. You ever seen a Chink? They're peculiar as can be. Saw a bunch in New Orleans. They like to drink gin. Seem to rollerskate a lot. They've settled in good down there. When the war got done, their grandpas didn't go home. They're still tryin' to figure who won."

"So am I," Mac said. "Listen, how long you fellas plan to stay?"

"I need to burn the town. Shouldn't take a lot of time."

"You don't want to do that."

"Why not?"

"It seems real excessive to me."

Bob looked pained. "You think I'm on a summer tour? We're in the vandal trade, friend. We got to loot and terrorize."

"I understand you do. I'm not telling you how to run your business, but there's things you ought to know before all this gets out of hand."

Mac wasn't certain just how to handle this. Bob seemed reasonably sane, and had a little social grace. Still, Mac had seen marauder types before. They were all out to lunch. They had to look bad, or someone else would take their place.

"The thing is," he said, "we've got a pretty good life going here. We're not your little frogshit hamlet by the road. We've got real stores, we've got power from the dam. We got local hit plays and a volunteer band. What we are, Bob, is the county's heart and soul, and the trade comes in from all around. You burn us down, we'll be gone when you come through again. I'd like you to think about that.

"Here's what we can do. We'll work out a deal I think you'll like. We get a sort of tribute package together, the same kind of stuff you'd loot yourself. Veggies and fruit, lots of fresh meat, local arts and crafts. We'll toss in some whiskey, better than the crap you're drinking now. This kind of deal, it saves you and us trouble too. And the best part is, nobody gets hurt, everyone's happy, everyone's fine. I'll tell you what, we've had spoilers here before, and they've all been satisfied."

"What I think I'll do first," Bob said, "is drop a few rounds on your church. Violate some nuns. Torch that station up there, knock you off the air."

Mac let out a breath. "Bob, I got to take offense at that. It's not the kind of talk I like to hear."

"Don't take everything personal, Mac. You want another drink?"

"I see I'm not getting through. You're not looking at the issues, you're not facing facts. Raising cain up the hill, now that'd be a real smart move. You want to piss everybody off for a hundred miles around, that's what you ought to do. Shoot, I figured we could work this out. If you've got no respect for God and radio, I don't see how we can talk."

Bob laughed aloud. "Man, you're the best I ever heard. You make that shit up yourself? What's that little honey's name, Mary Jane?"

"*Sister* Mary Jo. I'll ask you not to mention her again. Okay, I didn't want to bring this up, but I see it's time for plain talk. No offense, Bob, but the folks in this town aren't accustomed to pillage and assault. They're not going to sit still, they're going to fight back. We'll lose a lot of people and I hate to see that. But you're going to lose a bunch, too."

Bob closed his eyes. Bob looked tired. "Is that it? Are you through?" He finished off his drink and blinked at Mac. "You and me are about done, friend. I'm glad we could sit and share a drink. I've had all the talk I can take without nailing your ass to a tree. You tell those citizens of yours that Bob the Destroyer's got a heart. That's not a good trait in illicit enterprise, but hey, that's how I am. You tell 'em they don't shoot back, I'll do the best I can. If they do, I will flat bring ruin and urination on your town. You got that clear, you with me, Father Mac?"

"Clear enough," Mac said. "And I appreciate you being frank. I'll pass the word along."

Mac stood. Bob shook his hand, and walked him to the corner up Oak.

"Thanks for coming," Bob said. "I know it's Sunday afternoon."

"Well, I didn't have a lot to do."

"Oh, listen," Bob said, started off and stopped, turned back to Mac. "We were having such fun I damn near forgot. We had a little accident. My brother, that's Fred, got to celebrating and shot himself in the foot. I'd be grateful if you'd go and get the doc."

Mac felt a surge of raw anger, so fiercely intent, that he wondered if it really came from him.

"There he is," he said, "right there." His hand shook as he pointed toward the Baker Hotel. "Fourth pole down. That's the man you want to see, he'll fix your brother up fine."

Bob looked concerned. "All those boys look Injun to me. You sure you got it right?"

"Yeah, I got it right. The man was a good friend of mine. His name was Nick Papandreou. *Doctor* Papandreou."

"Shit. I'd like to apologize for that."

"Well, it's a natural mistake. The man was kind of *dark.*"

"You're upset about this."

"You're damn right I am."

"You didn't mention this before."

"Well see, I got to kiss up to you. You're the big scare, the big cheese in town."

"There's that," Bob said. He gazed down the street. "He shouldn't have been where he was. My boys are under stress. We been after those redskins a week. They're intent on stealing meat. You know they're into carnal art?"

"I expect Doc was helping someone," Mac said. "He had a bad habit of that."

Mac wanted very much to go back up the hill and sit beneath the big tree, think about poker games and whiskey bouts at Hal's. Think about Nick. How he liked to drink too much, how he liked to dance and cry. Crying and dancing were two things Diego liked to do. He liked to do them both at once, and it was great to watch him try.

Mac looked at Bob. There was something there he'd missed before. Thinking about Diego seemed to help, seemed to make everything clear.

"That's what this is all about," Mac told him. "You son of a bitch, you don't want to talk, you don't want to deal. This is all about a *foot.* For God's sake, you could've asked anyone in town to bring the Doc. You didn't need me!"

"No way," Bob said. "They take Fred off somewhere and that's that. The town runs the show and not me. Got me over a barrel's what they got. Doctors and priests, they gotta take an oath. That foot's real bad. I think it better come off."

"Then I guess that's what you ought to do."

Bob looked appalled. "You think *I'm* going to do it? My own brother? Listen, you're out there stirring fear in everyone's heart, you don't make a lot of friends. Any one of those bastards of mine, they'd like to take me out. Fred's all I got."

Bob seemed to hesitate. Like a thought had just struck him, like Truth had found its mark. Mac wasn't fooled at all. This was clearly where Bob had been headed all along.

"That's it," Bob said, staring right at Mac. "I'm looking at a priest, I got the answer all the time. You take care of Fred's foot. Fix him up, get him on the mend."

"Stop it," Mac said, "I'm not buying this."

"You got a church, you got some nuns. You got secret healing arts. Pray, do a chant. Do whatever you got to do." Bob paused. "And get Fred another foot. I want Fred to have a foot again."

"And how am I supposed to do that?"

"The Lord works in wondrous ways. I read about that. Bradley, Bill—" Bob turned to yell up the street. "Get Fred up to the church. Father Mac here'll show you the way."

"Huh-unh, this is not a good idea," Mac said. "I know what you're doing and I won't put up with this."

Bob showed Mac a broad smile. "You fix my brother up. You get the boy a foot. Then you and me, we'll talk about pillage and rape. Burning shit down. Good folks lyin' in the streets. That, and me thinking how I might show my gratitude. Say, we caught your show Friday afternoon. Got you clear down to Morgan Hill. What you think about that?"

"We try to reach out," Mac said.

"You've got a good ear for moody brass, but I'd like to hear somethin' isn't near a hundred years old that's got *moon* in every line. Shoot, Rock and Soul is where it's at. Karen Carpenter. Barry Manilow. I got a John Denver tape doing *Rocky Mountain High*. That boy flat gives me the chills."

"That's the kind of shit brought this country to its knees," Mac said. "Bob, you listen serious to me. I can cut off your brother's foot. I can't grow him a new one, I'm just the local priest."

Bob grinned. "By damn, Mac. I sure think you better try…"

Six

Out past Mineral Wells, on the road to Palo Pinto, Mac stopped and looked, as he always did, at the enormous wicker chair, a great, towering mass of mesquite, a monument to madness, a sign of what happens to a man when the sun rots the bones, broils the flesh, bakes the brains, for close on to ninety-nine years.

Tourists

The bus wandered down through the morning countryside, down through gently rolling hills bright with lavender, pink and columbine blue. Down, down, plunging of a sudden into cool, shady forests, the road flanked with columns of redwood, cedar and loblolly pine, giants that stretched up forever into a dazzling azure sky.

A chorus of "oooohs" and "aaaahs" echoed through the bus. The morning was pleasant, and everyone rolled their windows down.

"My, how lovely," Mary Beth said. "Why, it's as lovely as can be."

"It is, indeed," said Liza Lee, leaning past her friend to see. "Oh, my, there's lily and rock moss and lady fern, too. And puttyroot and flag and merrybells by a little stream."

"Liza, I do not believe there's a flower you *don't* know, and that's as true as it can be."

"Yes, but you know birds, Mary Beth. You know birds a lot better than I."

"Oh, that's simply not so. Though I do know a few."

"More than a *few*, I'd say."

"Well, they go together, don't they? Flowers and birds? And little streams and trees? They are part of the beauty all around us, beauty for everyone to see."

The two grasped hands, and their cheery laughter echoed through the bus and made others grin, too.

As they talked, the bus broke through the trees and left the woods behind. The sun was hidden now, and the sky was a rather dreary green. Mary Beth noticed there didn't seem to be any flowers or birds—or, for that matter, anything pretty at all. Just rocks and dirt and clumps of blackened weeds.

"It's different outside, Liza Lee. There aren't any trees, and there's no little stream."

"Why, you're right, Mary Beth. There's hardly a thing out there to see."

The bus slowed then, and turned down a very narrow road, past a dark pillar of stone, over a rattling bridge and a leaden river far below. Then, just up ahead, Mary Beth saw a man squatting by the side of the road. Great beads of tallowy sweat rolled down his corpulent flesh. His skin was swollen, pocked, severely inflamed, rife with ulcerations, lesions, blisters, pustules and boils of every sort. Two scabrous crows, birds with no feathers, were perched upon his head, pecking at his flesh. An enormous serpent was sliding, slipping, slicking from an orifice between the man's legs, dropping, slopping, without ever stopping, an endless stream of moist and steamy coils, oily convolutions, hideous piles that writhed and shivered on the ground.

All this clearly caused enormous discomfort in the man. His mouth was distorted in a scream, but no sound came out at all.

"I guess we're nearly there," said Mary Beth to Liza Lee.

"Yes," said Liza Lee, "I guess we likely are..."

▲▼▲

In a moment, a new sight appeared up ahead. At first, Mary Beth assumed it was part of the landscape that stretched out as far as the eye could see—rocks, rocks, and more rocks still, rocks scattered everywhere about, rocks of every shape and size. Rocks that only came in one color, smoked, singed, sizzled, burned to a dull and basic brick.

Then, closer, she saw the stones were formed into crude, disorderly piles, stacks, heaps, lumps and little mounds. Closer still, they appeared to be dwellings of a sort—shanties, hovels and shacks, some scarcely more than holes in the ground.

Yet, there were people there, people with curious features, people without any fingers, people with nothing where their mouths ought to be. People with toes where there should have been a nose. Hoppy, jerky, clumsy people with a head and a foot, and nothing more than that. On top of these gross distortions, many people were clearly plagued by toads.

"I don't know what I expected," Mary Beth said. "They didn't tell us it would be like this."

Well, not to tell a lie, she knew that wasn't quite so. The folder *had* said there were parts of the tour where one might expect to bring to mind, imagine, recall things they scarcely remembered anymore.

"And that," Mary Beth said to herself, "is exactly what's happening now."

Hot was one thing she suddenly recalled. Another was *something really smells bad here...*

▲▼▲

"Step over here, please, gather 'round me," said Bill Jim, the bus driver, and everyone did.

"I know you've all read the rules in your handouts, but I'd like to go over them now. Just bear with me a minute and we'll get underway.

"First, stay with me at all times. That's a real important rule. There isn't any *harm* can come to you, I don't guess I have to say that."

Bill Jim showed them a cheery smile, and the passengers gave him smiles back. This showed Bill Jim people were getting in the spirit of things, and he liked to see that.

"The thing is, they've got rules here like everywhere else, and we're obliged to show 'em some respect. Okay, so don't wander off. Second, is, there's going to be folks want to come up and talk. There isn't any rule against that, but I recommend you don't

"Now. I guess we're all ready. Any questions before we start? You there, you go ahead."

"What we saw coming in?" asked Larry Lew. "Does that person *have* to do that?"

"Yes. Anyone else?"

"I was going to ask the same thing," said Mary Beth.

"Bill Jim, can I ask you why the sky's colored green?"

"Good question," Bill Jim said, for it was a question he liked a lot. "They don't do blue. They don't do blue, lavender, lilac, any colors of the purple persuasion. No sapphires, violets or plum. They do a kind of lint, bone, tallow and whey, they don't do any white. Not much yellow. I've seen a little jaundice and flax.

"As I'm sure you've noticed, most every color is your burned-up brick. They do a kind of red, but it looks black to me. Black is big here, but the tour doesn't go as far as that. If you're ready—"

"Bill Jim," said Mary Beth, "this town we're in, I guess it's got a name."

Bill Jim showed her half a grin. "I'd tell you, but then you'd have to stay."

Mary Beth knew he didn't mean that at all, but she didn't ask another question, and neither did anyone else.

▲▼▲

Mary Beth was quickly getting used to the fact that everywhere they went, everything looked much the same. Like Bill Jim said, if you didn't like brick, there weren't a lot of colors to see.

The *people* were different, though, in a way. And, in a way, they were really all the same. Like the drab, crumbly old buildings, like the hovels and little dark holes, one bodily affliction began to look much like the next. People tripped on their entrails, dropped a part or two, grew another head. It was, clearly, what everybody did.

▲▼▲

Bill Jim led them around a dark corner, into a street exactly like the one they'd left behind. Not *exactly* the same, for this street boasted a small stone fountain, a sight which surprised Mary Beth, for they'd seen nothing like it on the tour.

Water bubbled up from the center, and fell in a very pleasant spray, in a fine and sparkly mist, leaving circles of orderly ripples spreading out on every side.

A great many people were crowded about the fountain's edge, people of every shape and every size, people with every affliction you could name. Nobody moved, nobody spoke. No one did anything at all.

Bill Jim rushed them by, told them to hurry on along, told Mary Beth she was dragging behind. Mary Beth waited a moment, watching the people at the fountain, watching them stand there, gazing at the water as it bubbled and it sprayed…

▲▼▲

"You would think they could give these people something to do," Mary Beth told Liza Lee, not so loud that Bill Jim could hear. "All they do is stand around. I'm sure they would like to have jobs, or maybe take a class of some kind. I know it's not supposed to be *fun* or anything. Still…"

"Well, I don't think there's any chance of that," said Liza Lee.

A man wobbled by on his hands. His scabby legs walked clumsily behind him, held by a leash bound around the man's neck. He stuck out his tongue and said: *"Poke-drippy-slew…"* or words to that effect.

"Don't answer him or anything, just look the other way," said Liza Lee, urging Mary Beth along. "You know what Bill Jim said."

"*I* think Bill Jim finds very little happy anywhere, and doesn't like us to either, Liza Lee."

"Oh, dear." Liza Lee brought her hand up to her mouth, somewhat astonished by what her friend had said. It simply wasn't like the Mary Beth she knew.

Mary Beth was quite surprised herself. She couldn't recall saying anything about anyone that wasn't as nice as it could be.

I think I know the reason for that, she decided. *Recalling* things was something the folder warned about. The word *cool* had come to her just as she passed the fountain. Now where did that come from? And there was *thirsty,* too, then *dry,* words rushing in like that, one on top of the next.

Remembering things was the reason she had strayed from happy for a while. Being here *did* make pictures and thoughts rise up in your head. Things you hadn't remembered before, suddenly came to mind again.

And that could likely explain why she'd had a less than happy about Bill Jim. Bill Jim was a very good driver, and a very fine guide. He wasn't from Home, though, anyone could tell that. He wasn't from here, either. He came from somewhere in between. She didn't know how she knew that, but she did. It was one of the remember things again.

Which doesn't give me any right to say what I did, and I surely won't do it anymore.

▲▼▲

"Come along now," Bill Jim said, as he did most any time they came on something new. "Nothing to stop for, nothing here to see."

There was, though, and Mary Beth wasn't the only member of the tour who didn't care to be hurried along.

"Bill Jim," said Jenny Cee, "would you tell us what they're doing there, please?"

"We do wish you would," put in Johnny Dee. "I think everyone would like to know."

Mary Beth was glad someone else had asked the question first. She didn't want Bill Jim to look at her funny again.

It was, truly, a curious sight indeed, even for the sights one came across here. A long, seemingly endless line stretched down the street and out of sight. As ever, there were people of every sort about. People with knobs, nubs, creases and folds. Wrinkles and crinkles and corrugated holes. Slits, splits, clots and gaping maws.

People with people fronts, and animal behinds. People without any fronts. People with no behinds.

Many in the line were lying down, squatting, sprawling on the ground—those who had parts which allowed that sort of thing. Some had built hovels, crude piles of stone, or burrowed in the ground, as they waited in the line. Most of them weren't doing anything at all.

"There's nothing to see," Bill Jim said, "it's a line, that's all it is. Anyone can see that."

"What kind of a line?" asked Jenny Cee.

"A long line, all right?"

"And where is the head of the line, Bill Jim?"

"Down there. Somewhere down the block."

"And what do they do when they get to the front, Bill Jim?"

"They go to the *back* of the line. Is that all? Can we move along now?"

▲▼▲

Mary Beth wasn't sure when she'd drifted away. She was watching someone with a dozen heads, all of them bobbing, jerking about, none of them sure which way they ought to go. One minute the others were there, a moment later they were gone.

"Oh, my," Mary Beth said aloud, "Bill Jim is not going to like this at all."

She knew what had happened. She had started thinking again about the people in the line. One of the remember things happened, and it popped in her head there were two different kinds of people here. Well, there were no two *alike,* really, but she didn't mean that.

What she meant was, there were hangies and there were smooths. She hadn't noticed that before, and couldn't say why. When remember things were ready, they were simply there, and they weren't before that.

In that very same moment, she knew that once she had been a smooth too. Somewhere. Before she'd come Home. Now where would *that* be? Wasn't that an odd thing to recall?

Maybe that's why you wore cloze on the tour. "We do, because they *don't* do it here," she reasoned, pleased with herself for thinking something up something like that. She promised herself she'd tell the others, in case they didn't know. If, indeed, she could ever find them again.

"Goodness, I wonder just how I'm going to go about *that?*"

As ever, one street, one building, one wall looked like the ones she'd passed before. Maybe if she just stood there, Bill Jim and the others would somehow find *her?*

No, now that would never do. She had gotten into this mess, and she would find her way out.

▲▼▲

She was doing just that, or doing the best she could, when she came upon the place with the fluttery, flickery lights. Mary Beth paused to get a better look. She knew she shouldn't, but she did. The lights came from a narrow alleyway, an alley so narrow, so tight, so terribly confined, it was hard to imagine anyone could squeeze inside.

Yet, there were people in there, people packed together, people side by side, watching the shadowy blink of black and white, watching the little gray windows in the wall. As the people watched, the pale lights danced across their faces, cast dull reflections in their eyes.

Some of the people were hangies, and some of them were smooths. Nobody looked at anyone else. Nobody spoke, nobody moved. No one did anything at all.

▲▼▲

"Well, I am near certain this is where I ought to be," said Mary Beth. "I just know I have seen this place before."

The bus, she was sure, was parked just past the building ahead, the one where the squiggly crack ran up and down.

When she turned the corner, though, the bus wasn't there. What was there instead was a steep set of stairs.

A sign above the stairs in scribbly black read:

DOWN

"My word," Mary Beth said aloud, "Down doesn't help a great deal. Down where?"

"First floor, Mary Beth,..." said a voice like a rattle, like a shriek, like a clatter, like a howl inside a din, a voice that cut and cleaved the very air. *"......Pharts*
Phat
Phlegm
Phleas
Pestilence and Piss...
"Second floor,
Pigs
Puss
Puppy dogs and pain
"Third floor—"

▲▼▲

"Please," said Mary Beth, "I don't even *know* what you're talking about. I *don't* know how you know my name."

"I'm good with people," said the voice. *"People are what I do."*

"I'm afraid I don't understand that, either."

"Hey, no problem. So how do you like the tour so far?"

Mary Beth wanted to be polite, but wasn't sure what she ought to say. Mostly, she was too surprised to say anything at all. This—*person* had simply appeared, in a blink, where the stairs ought to be.

That was quite peculiar, but the man himself was the strangest thing of all. He was gaunt, pale, not very tall, and he really had a very nice smile. His face, and his bare and bony chest were covered in coils, whirls, swirls within whorls. When you tried to follow one pattern to the next, they did funny things to your head.

The eyes, though—Mary Beth had to blink twice—the eyes were two shiny bright coins, set in deep hollows in the maze, in the twisted patterns of his face. The eyes made Mary Beth want to look away, manners or not.

He sat there with a friend, sat behind a charred, scarred wooden table, sat there against something cloudy, something veiled, something dark and indistinct. The dark was hard to look at, like the man's eyes.

"Oh, just fine, thank you," Mary Beth answered finally. "The tour is really—quite nice."

"It is?" The man smiled, and winked one silver eye. *"I'll have to speak to someone about that."*

Mary Beth wasn't good at funny, but she smiled anyway.

"I don't know your name," she said, knowing that was the proper thing to do, "though you seem to know mine."

"Bob. You can call me Bob."

"That's a very good name."

"You like Steve any better? Jack? George? How about Hampton Burke-Sykes III?"

"Really. Bob's just fine with me." She had to admit, though, he didn't seem very Bob at all. She wasn't sure what would really fit.

She didn't want to ask about the friend. That, again, was the right thing to do, unless Bob said something first.

The friend was quite odd, even among the people she'd come across here. She had two pointies in front. You didn't have to see any more to know she was a smooth. Both of her eyes were sewn shut. Her ears and her nose had been cut with something sharp. Her mouth was torn in a wide and empty smile.

Mary Beth decided the smile wasn't real. This was a person who clearly didn't have any happy right now.

"Bill Jim's looking all over for you, Mary Beth. You're supposed to stay with the tour. No one ever comes here."

"I'm sorry, truly. I do apologize. I would never do anything on purpose to offend."

"Now I know that. You're a very, very good person, Mary Beth. But hey, I can overlook that."

Hoarse, cackley laughter came from the gloom, echoed from the dark behind Bob and the smooth. Mary Beth was sure she saw a host of shiny eyes before they vanished in the dark.

The man glanced over his shoulder with a smile that twisted the whorls and spirals in his face, twisted them all into something that wasn't there before. Then, he looked back at Mary Beth. Holding her in his gaze, he picked up a glass from the table, a glass so black, she couldn't guess what was inside. He drank the liquid down, smacked his lips and tossed the glass away, off into the black.

"Oh, my, manners," he said, in a voice that sounded just like Mary Beth. He turned politely to the smooth. *"You sure you won't have something? No? Not right now? Maybe later? Fine."*

The smooth didn't answer, of course. Didn't move, didn't do anything at all.

"Tell me about yourself," Bob said, though Mary Beth imagined there was much that he already knew. *"Tell me the things you like to do."*

"I like flowers and trees. I guess I like birds best of all. I guess I know the names of a zillion or two."

"That's a lot of birds, Mary Beth."

"It might not be that many. I really wouldn't know."

"What else, Mary Beth?'

"Oh, I do like to sing. I like to sing with Liza Lee. She's my best friend. I mean, I like everybody else, too."

"And you like being Home? You like it there, don't you, Mary Beth?"

"My, yes, I surely do."

"Better than you'd like being here, I suppose."

"Oh. Well…"

"Just teasing, Mary Beth. Bob's a big teaser, anyone'll tell you that. You ever see the Old Man? Ever talk to the Kid?"

"Who?" Mary Beth had to think about that for a moment, then she understood.

"Why, yes. Whenever I can, I surely do."

"When you see them, Mary Beth, will you give them this for me?"

"Now that's very nice, I—"

Bob's hand appeared in a blur, opened wide, and there was something smoky, something horrid, something vile.

"Oh. Oh—my goodness!" Mary Beth said.

Bob smiled, tried to catch her with his eyes, tried to snap her up, tried to draw her in, knew he couldn't do it, knew she was safe as safe can be, but he always had to try.

Mary Beth took a step back, felt a new remember, felt a new remember called *dread, shiver, quiver* and *afraid,* felt it for a blink before it went away. Hoped, prayed she would never remember it again.

She was gone, then, gone as quickly as she could, and she never, ever, looked back the other way...

▲▼▲

The bus had never looked so bright, so clean and so white, so cool and inviting inside. Even in the thick and fevered air, under the drear and clotted sky, the bus was as shiny and new as it could be.

Bill Jim had clearly saved up a lot to say to Mary Beth, but when the time came, he sighed, gave her a "What's the use?" look, and let the words just slide away.

Most of the group had picked up free souvenirs. Liza Lee had a cap with little horns. Johnny Dee had a scary paper mask. There were faded, raggedy shirts that read:

SURE, IT'S HOT.
BUT IT'S A *DRY* HEAT

I BEEN UP
AND I BEEN
D
O
W
N

Some of the shirts read **HARVARD, YALE,** and **M.I.T.**

Mary Beth didn't understand the shirts at all, and didn't think anybody did.

When everyone was inside again, and Bill Jim had counted them twice, the door wheezed shut, and the bus began to roll out of town.

No one said a lot as they passed the same hovels and falling-down shacks, burrows and piles of bricky stone they'd passed coming in.

"Before we get to the bridge," Bill Jim called back, "you folks will have to toss out all those souvenirs. That's the rules. You can't take anything back out of here."

Everyone did as they were told. No one really seemed to mind. Now that they were on the way Home, people were starting to chatter and gather in little groups to sing. They began to get rid of their cloze—the folder said not to do that until they got past the bridge, but a lot of people did. Mary Beth and Liza Lee joined in, and they both felt better after that.

"I am not real sure I enjoyed the tour as much as I should," Liza Lee confided to her friend. "Do you know what I mean?"

Mary Beth had to smile. "I'm supposed to be the big grouchy face here. You caught me yourself, Liza Lee."

"Oh, now I didn't mean it *that* way. It just kind of slipped out. Really, I'm doing a happy right now."

"That's good. That's what we need to do."

Mary Beth understood how Liza felt, for she still had remembers left too. Not too many, and there weren't any big ones anymore.

"Everyone, listen up a minute, please," called out Bill Jim. "We're running a little late because we didn't *all* get back in time. Now, we're going to be seeing something up ahead. As your guide, I'd advise you to talk among yourselves while we're crossing the river and the bridge. This isn't something you folks need to see, I promise you that."

Of course, the minute Bill Jim said that, *everyone* ran to the left side of the bus. No one wanted to miss anything they really shouldn't see.

They made it just in time. The other bus was coming at them fast. You had to look quickly, it was there and it was gone, whining, rushing past in a blur, going the other way.

It was dark, scarred, dented. Bashed, mashed and wantonly trashed. It was covered with dust, grime, ages and eras, millennia of rust. And, as it passed, each broken window was filled with a bare and scrawny bottom, each bum, each cheek, each gluteal lump a gallery of ancient, forgotten whorls and swirls, convolutions and knotty coils. Then the bus and its odd, unnatural rumps were far behind, and they were over the bridge at last.

"Well," said Mary Beth, "I surely don't understand that."

"I don't see any reason why we should," said Liza Lee.

▲▼▲

Past the high ridge of dark and ragged stone, up the narrow road. Once past the road, Mary Beth recalled, they would see the forest and the lovely hills again, and after that, Home.

What she hadn't remembered, hadn't recalled, was the pocked, ulcerated, quite uncomfortable man who was squatting by the side of the road.

He was there, just as he'd before, screaming in silence as the hideous, never-ending piles slicked from his body to the ground.

Everyone quickly looked away. Everyone but Mary Beth.

Why she kept looking, she really couldn't say. She didn't *want* to, but something made her stay. So she looked, and then she looked again. Looked at the man, watched him until she could scarcely see him anymore, until the bus was nearly past. Looked, looked into the twisted features, into the pale, lost and tortured eyes. And, though she knew it couldn't be, she imagined—for an instant—the man looked back.

"*William*," she said, the word just suddenly there, rising out of nowhere at all.

"*Oh, Will. Oh my, goodness me...*"

The remember flickered in, flickered out again, and, then it was gone, just as quickly as it came...

Getting Dark

John-William's mother turns the water on low and peels carrots in the sink. Wet skins slick-slick quick off the cutter and stick in a huddle where they fall. This is what skins like to do. They like to huddle up, stick with their own kind. Peel a potato and a carrot in the sink, they won't speak at all, they'll bunch up with someone they know. Like nigger-folks and whites, thinks John-William's mother. That's what Jack used to say. One's dark and one's not. One's that snake in the Garden, would've stuck it in Eve, but couldn't figure how.

John-William's mother drops carrots in a pot, puts the pot on the stove. Leaves the skins alone, leaves them where they fell. They look like bird tongues to John-William's mother, cut-cut dagger tongues, curled up at the end. She thinks about birds, big old black birds, hare-lipped fat birds without any tongues. *"weet! 'weet!"* go the birds, poor little birds without any tongues. Poke in a peel now, that'd be fine, stick a little tongue in a pointy yellow bill.

John-William's mother peers out the screen door. The birds have black ruffle necks and glitter-green eyes. They perch on phone wires just behind the house. Birds in twos now, birds in threes, birds like notes on the music at Mama Sarah's house. Note birds hop from one wire to the next. Hop down, hop up, up and down again. The birds play *Summit Ridge Drive,* play *Chatanooga Choo-choo* and *Putting on the Ritz.* When she hears those songs, John-William's mother gets a tingle where a tingle shouldn't ought to be.

"Not if you're a lady," giggles John-William's mother, "not 'less you come from the Wilcher branch of the tree."

The fan on the counter hum-hums to the left, hum-hums to the right, gives a little jerk and starts back again. John-William's mother smells Camay soap and Lipton's iced tea. Smells meatloaf and pepper and water on the stove. Flour and catsup and old coffee grounds. Summer sucks Oklahoma heat through the open screen door, mingles with the smells from inside. John-William's mother draws damp hair off her neck, pins it up back. Her dress is stuck to her skin. She pulls at her collar, lets the breeze in. Lord God, too hot for underwear in August.

Grandmaws and aunts in Shawnee and Maud can keep their corsets and their buttons and their snaps. This is Oke City, and a girl can jiggle what she likes down here.

John-William's mother peeks down for a look. They're still down there, and still looking fine. You can say what you like about your big old melons, sagging on the vine when you're still eighteen. There's not a man living doesn't have a liking for a grown-up woman's got a pair of thirty-fours poking right up like happy puppy dogs.

John-William's mother looks past her pretties, down past her tummy, feels a little shudder, feels a little warm start to grow, thinks, for an instant, why not leave the pot a'bubble, run back to bed and have a little tingle, who's going to know? Blushes at the image like a movie show flicking in her head, raises the lid off the carrots, which don't need checking at all...

...stops right there, holds the steamy lid in her hand, stops there and listens, hears it coming, hears it on the way, long before it gets there at all. Sets down the lid, drops her apron on a chair, kicks off her flats and walks out the screen door. The steps are still warm. She pulls up her skirt, leans back against the door. If some old man gets a peek, well maybe she'll let him have two.

There's no wind at all, but it's better out back than inside.

Still a little light, but the sky's turning dull pewter-gray, turning dishwater blue, like the bottom of a worn-out pan. John-William's mother doesn't like this time of day, doesn't now and never did. When she was little on the farm she'd sit on the back porch steps past Mama's kitchen door. The wood was dull gray, worn by lye soap and long dead years. Sit real still and look past the gravel back yard, past the henhouse and the barn, past the smokehouse and the dirt storm cellar with its tin door in the ground. Out past the pile where Papa put things he meant to fix and never did. A plow with no handles, busted wagon wheels, the carcass of a Ford, its rusty hide now a 12-gauge target, fine as Irish lace. Broken shovels, dull washtubs with the bottoms burned out.

And, past the orchard and the fence and the fields full of rattle-paper corn, to the land that stretched forever to the sky.

That's when John-William's mother sat still as mice and held her breath. Held it, and waited for the last pallid whisper of the light to disappear, waited for the day to give a final sigh and slide away.

You had to watch close. It happened, just like that, and it was gone. It wasn't day and it wasn't night it was something in between. Every color died and the faraway fields began to smudge against the sky. The barn, the henhouse, the rusted-out Ford began to blur, grow faint and indistinct, dull and undefined. The dark descended and sucked the day dry.

And it was then when John-William's mother, Betty Ann, heard the great stone clock, felt it strike deep, deep within the earth, felt it beat against her heart. When the time was just right, at the moment in between, she listened, and heard what the clock had come to say...

> *Not just before, Betty Ann*
> *And not just after, Betty Ann.*
> *Not quite day*
> *And not quite night,*
> *What it is, Betty Ann,*
> *Is getting dark again...*

That's when the big clock stopped for a beat, and the world grew silent and still. It seemed to Betty Ann like sorrow had come to stay, as if all the lonely had spilled out from the day. Grandmaw Wilcher said this was the moment dark came to snatch life away. "You can see it if you look real close," Grandmaw Wilcher said, "you might see a dead bird out in the yard, claw feet stickin' right up, bill wide open, sucking for a last breath of air. You might see a rock or a stick you was lookin' right at, and now it's not there. For a blink, for a wink, you're seeing things gone, things that were there a minute or so before. It might me a toad, it might be a stone, it *might* be someone you know."

Mama told Betty Ann not to listen to Grandmaw's trash, said she wasn't right in the head. And maybe that was so, but every night after, Betty Ann ran back in, safe inside before the night caught her, caught her right between the light and dark, fled to the good smell of cornbread and jelly, to the oilcloth mustard-yellow bright, to the table set with cold ham and beans, the cloth still sticky from the noon summer meal. The kerosene lamp warmed her soul, and her mother brought cool cream butter in a bowl and said, "Time you came in, Betty Ann, it's getting dark again..."

▲▼▲

In spite of the prickly sullen heat, Betty Ann, John-William's mother, feels a chill. She knows what's happened. She's waited just a beat, just a breath too long and the dark has caught her there, standing outside her kitchen door. Caught her as the night swept in and drew its cape across the yard and the trees and the house next door, and nearly got Betty

Ann, John-William's mother too. John-William's mother doesn't even look back. Looking back's like Grandmaw said, when you saw, from the corner of your eye, things that were missing, things that had been there just a blink before.

Betty Ann. John-William's mother moves quickly inside, shuts the screen door, snaps the latch, stops, pauses just a minute, listens, almost certain she can hear that great stone clock beat down-down-down, deep in the earth and far away.

Betty Ann checks the meatloaf and the carrots, pulls an Old Gold from the pack on the counter, leans in and lights it from the stove.

John-William's mother, Jack's wife Betty Ann, gets a jelly glass of water, reaches past the Sunbeam mixer and flips on the Philco radio, watches the dial begin to glow, settles in a breakfast room chair. Old familiar voices make her smile. The Kingfish tries to talk Andy into some fool scheme. Betty Ann knows exactly what'll happen next. Andy falls for it, like Andy always does. Amos has to come in and straighten the whole mess out.

Lord, they were funny. Better than Benny or Fred Allen either one. Jack wouldn't listen, wouldn't stay in the room if they were on. Said they weren't even coloreds on the show, said niggers weren't like that at all. Said they stole stuff fast as you could blink, didn't matter what it was.

The very next time Betty Ann looks up, the dark has creeped in from outside, hid the catsup and the flour in shadow. All she can see is the dim blue flame below the pot.

If I had any sense, thinks Betty Ann, I'd of opened a can of tuna fish instead of heating up the kitchen on a hot summer night. John-William didn't care, long as there were cookies or pies or something sweet in the house.

John-William's mother thinks he ought to be home right now. She doesn't like him out at night, but boys didn't know about the dark, didn't know what happens out there when the sun goes down and the day hides out of sight.

Amos 'n Andy were gone. The radio plays a song she likes a lot.

It must have been moonglow,

Way out to the sea...

She and Jack used to hear it all the time when they'd take his daddy's big Lasalle out and park. That was when they first began to date, before they even thought about getting married or anything else besides parking, feeling up and having fun. And even after that sometimes, before Jack pumped her up like a tub with John-William inside, they'd hear that song and everything would be fine. Betty Ann's father didn't trust Jack

at all. He knew what they were doing in the back of that Lasalle. Jack
didn't wear overalls, wore a Searsucker suit and a snappy bow tie. He
came from Paul's Valley, which didn't say much, even for an Oklahoma
town. Still, like Betty Ann's mother Sarah said, anyone don't have shit
on his shoes is worth looking at twice. Well that was a lie, considering
Mr. Searsucker suit didn't hang around all that long after John-William's
mother Betty Ann brought two more babies in the world who curled up
and died.

John-William's mother walks from one shadow room to the next.
The furniture is dim, like chairs and tables and beds all covered in a
ghosty kind of light, the pale green glow like the fireflies John-William's
mother used to capture in a jar.

It was the first brick house she'd ever lived in in her life. The first
time she'd lived in town except once. Betty Ann and her mother had
moved to Atoka from the farm when Mama Steck took sick and they
had to live there till she died. When it happened, Betty Ann was right
there, Betty Ann saw it, watched the night come until the room was
inky black, watched while it hovered over Mama Steck a while, then
plunged down into that dry and withered mouth and sucked her life
away. Betty Ann peed her britches right then, and never, ever, told
mother what she saw.

Jack's wife, John-William's mother walks through the dark, walks
from one room to the next. To the living room, the big bedroom where
she sleeps alone now, through the bathroom and John-William's room,
even in the closets, out through the doorway that leads to the shed that
sags against the house. Light from a half moon slants through the holes
that Jack never fixed. Truth to tell, Jack never fixed shit, never put a nail
in a wall, never fixed a leak.

Lord, what a mess, thinks John-William's mother Betty Ann. It's like
your whole life's stacked up in there, gathering dust, soaking up time,
hours used up and tossed away, moments dead and gone, rusted and
frozen where they lay. Jack's hammers and his nails and his saws and
his files and his broken axe, waiting to finish some goddamn thing he
never even started at all. John-William's bike, broken and twisted, one
wheel missing and one wheel bent. Wasn't anyone going to fix it. Why
in heaven's name was she hanging onto that?

Just too much to bother about, thinks John-William's mother, and
not enough time, not any time at all...

▲▼▲

Betty Ann, John-William's mother, perches on the edge of the tub and turns on the hot water tap. John-William's clothes are wadded in a pile. He'd ridden out for crawdads with bacon on a string, down by the creek behind the park. He'd gotten all soaked, peeled everything off, left it on the floor. John-William's mother gave him a proper scolding, the boy knew better than that. She'd scrubbed him good, tossed socks and underpants into the bin. Picked up his shirt and shook her head. His brand new Ferdinand the Bull shirt and already ruined for good.

In John-William's pockets she found a Krazy Kat button and a string from a top, a cap from a Nehi Orange and a broken lead soldier with his legs cut off above the knees. When Betty Ann was fifteen, she stayed with her cousin Helen for a while. One night they drove into Lawton for a picture show and ice cream. Helen took her daddy's new Packard. They were supposed to be back before dark. They told Helen's daddy they had a flat. What happened was they met two soldiers in town from Fort Sill. The soldiers were both nineteen. They had a pint of gin and a carton of Wings cigarettes. Helen made Betty Ann drive while she and the best-looking boy sat and giggled in the back. Betty Ann knew they were doing more than that.

Betty Ann and the other soldier spread a blanket on the grass. Helen and her friend never left the back seat. Betty Ann couldn't stand the taste of gin. She drank a little all the same and smoked a lot of cigarettes. She let the boy kiss her, and he kissed real fine. After a while she let him reach in and touch her breasts. Just on the tops and not any lower than that. She hadn't meant to but the boy was real nice and he came from out of state. He said he'd like to see her naked. Betty Ann said absolutely not. They kissed a lot more. Betty Ann was flattered he was getting so hot. The cigarettes made her too dizzy to stop. She let him get on top and rub against her through his clothes. His hardness touched her once and that was that. The boy made a noise and walked off in the grass for some time. On the way home, when they'd let the soldiers off, Helen made Betty Ann tell her everything that happened in the grass. Then Helen told Betty Ann things she hadn't even thought about before.

▲▼▲

John-William's mother lets the water run in the tub. Back in the bedroom she peels the sticky dress up over her head, drops it on the floor. Just like John-William, she thinks. Doesn't get all his bad habits from Jack. On the way back she stops, stands there in the hall. Something seems to move, something in the almost not quite corner in the dark. Something nearly there, something nearly out of sight. John-William's mother turns around fast. Gives a *little* jump, a little start. And there's Betty Ann looking back, just as surprised, just as naked as Betty Ann herself. Betty Ann knows she ought to look away, knows she shouldn't stand there staring in her birthday suit. Still, the sight in the mirror holds her fixed, holds her still, like a doe caught frightened in the light.

My lord, who's that, thinks John-William's mother. *It sure isn't me, isn't anyone that I ever knew!* It looks like her. But it can't be John-William's mother, can't be Jack's wife. Betty Ann feels sticky from the heat, from the sweat between her breasts, from the tingle in her nipples, from the heat between her knees. The woman in the mirror has beaded points of light in the dark between her thighs, has slick-silver flesh, has an opalescent glow like she's just stepped out of a moonlit sea. The woman in the mirror doesn't think about meatloaf at all, doesn't think about carrots on the stove. She thinks about the soldier and the need in his eyes and the hard thing pressed against her belly that night.

The woman in the mirror remembers every feeling, every moment with the soldier in the grass, later with a boy named Freddie and one named Alex, and Bob after that, and every single night, every morning with Jack, even the moments when he hit her too hard, when her face swelled up and she went out back to cry...

Goodness sake, thinks John-William's mother, uneasy with the thoughts in her head, and the warm spots further down than that. "Well that's what you get," she thinks out loud, "gawking at yourself like a Fort Worth floozie struttin' down Third Avenue."

▲▼▲

John-William's mother remembers the water in the tub. Lord, she'd gone and left it on. There'd be water running out the door, into the hall and onto the carpet, and Jack's wife Betty Ann running naked 'round the house with a mop and John-William's supper in the stove.

Betty Ann stops right there and frowns at the tub. She's real sure she turned the water on, but there isn't a drip or a drop, and the tub's dry as a bone. Betty Ann shakes her head, says "Well, I declare," pads in her bare feet back down the hall, back to the kitchen, back to the stove, back to the counter and the peels in the sink, back to the meatloaf in the stove. Walks to the screen to check the latch. Stops, looks out the back. Remembers where she is and has to laugh. No one walks around naked in the kitchen, bare ass naked, not a stitch at all, even in the dark. If Jack came in right then he'd think she was crazy as a loon. Which doesn't much matter, she remembers, Jack's not coming back at all.

Betty Ann stands at the screen and looks out. Doesn't seem that long ago she was watching the light slink away, waiting for the dark to slide in. She looks past the drive to the Hoopers' back yard. The walls are black, the roof has faded into night. She can see the Prewitts' fence, but the Kamps are out of sight. John-William's mother looks up as something flutters in the night. Just for an instant, it hangs there, a smudge against the inky sky. Maybe it has red eyes, she thinks. Maybe its tongue is colored orange.

A wind hot as syrup fills the night. Betty Ann's heart skips a beat. Skips two, hesitates, decides to try again. Betty Ann catches her breath, backs away from the door, leans against the sink. Lets her eyes touch the room. The garbage can, the broom, the chair and the stove. She opens the pot, peers inside. The carrots are limp, dry as brittle leaves. The pale blue flame has gone out. She opens the oven door. The meatloaf is cold, pink, with little eyes of fat. The radio is dead, the refrigerator too. The lights, the gas.

Turn on the faucet. A sputter and a cough. Betty Ann tries the phone. "Hello? Hello?" Just like in the movies. Nobody's there.

▲▼▲

Betty Ann walks naked through the gray heavy gauze of her first brick house. She'd been real scared once before, when she and John-William were alone and Jack was in Tulsa overnight. Something had scratched on the window and made wet steps on the lawn. In the morning, there was nothing there to see. The next night Jack was snoring by her side, but Betty Ann didn't sleep for a week.

"It's all right," she says, "everything's fine. Everything's *off* right now, but it'll all go on again." Her voice sounds funny in the still and empty house. She feels her way back to the kitchen, finds her Old Golds, a box of matches on the sink. Paws through the junk drawer, finds a wad of string, pencil stubs and dry fountain pens. No candles at all.

John-William's mother moves back down the hall. Looks in the mirror. Can't hardly see herself at all. Lights a kitchen match. Betty Ann naked, skin white as tallow in the flare of sudden light.

The living room carpet's black as tar. The easy chairs are blurs against the greater dark. Feels for the sofa. Can't find it anywhere at all. The match doesn't work. She tries another and another after that. Tosses the box on the floor.

Moving real slow, doesn't want to bump her toes. Opens the front door a crack. Can't see much better than she did in the back.

The houses across the street are just like hers. Stubby brick, living room, bedrooms, kitchen in the back. Arch across the porch. Now all the houses are solemn and gray, all the color drained out, the life washed away. No lights in the windows, no lights at all.

Betty Ann opens the door a little wider, a little wider still. One bare foot outside and then the next. John-William's mother, Jack's wife Betty Ann, stands naked on the hot front porch. Night wind brushes her flesh, tickles her breasts, whispers naughties in her ear.

Betty Ann stands very, very still. She can't remember when she last stood out in the night. Didn't flee, didn't run when the big clock deep in the earth warned everyone the light was dying and the dark was sweeping in, told everyone to hurry, get safe inside.

Still, it isn't so bad if you stand real still, if you don't think hard—if you don't let the dark know you're there. It can't see everything, can it? A whole world of night out there, it can't watch every leaf, every stone, every time a dog does his business on the lawn...

It comes to her then, like the secret was there all the time, like she knew it in her head. Grandmaw didn't know it all—she knew the scary part, knew about the bad, but she didn't know the rest...All you have to do is stand very, very still, listen, listen, to the great stone clock down deep-deep within the earth, listen to it tick-tick-tick away the quiet moments, the hours, the long years of the night. Don't move, don't breathe, feel the silence and the wind, feel the whisper of the dark against your skin...

John-William's mother, Jack's wife Betty Ann, peers into the dark, looks into the inky night for a very long time, and after a while she wonders if she might not be Betty Ann standing naked on the porch, she might be Betty Ann dreaming somewhere, Betty Ann back at Mama's on the farm, looking at the rusty old Ford. She might be Betty Ann having ice cream with Johnny Two Horse, who said he was pure Cherokee. She liked Johnny Two Horse a whole lot, kissed him twice till Mama found out he wasn't white, washed her mouth with soap and put a stop to that.

Johnny Two Horse kissed her again, or maybe it was only the hot breeze sliding in upon the night to sweep the dream away. And, when she peered once more into the dark, Betty Ann could see things she hadn't seen before. The houses and the lawns and the trees looked different now, like the shiny things you get when they send your pictures back. Everything that used to be black was murky gray, and everything white went just the other way. It didn't seem *wrong*, turned inside out, it seemed, to Betty Ann, the way things ought to be. Maybe the way things had been all along and were getting right again.

Up past the Harpers and the Smiths and the Roers, where the street lamp stood on the corner, something seemed to shimmer, seemed to tremble, seemed to hide behind a veil, like looking through Grandmaw's glasses where the world was all a blur. Betty Ann blinked and the blur went away.

▲▼▲

Then, for an instant, something was there and something not, something just beyond the corner, something coming, something waiting, something maybe in-between, something not quite ready, something not really there.

Betty Ann feels her mouth go dry, feels her legs go weak, backs up against the cold brick wall, backs up, finds the wall isn't there, knows, for sure, that isn't right at all. Walls stay where they are, where a wall's supposed to be. Betty Ann tries again, staggers, very nearly falls, slips through the wall, through the wires, through the wood, through the pipes and the nails, through the cobwebs and little dead spiders and bugs that huddle there.

John-William's mother, Sarah's daughter Betty Ann, walks through the curtains that trickle like powder, like snow, like ash, before her eyes, walks through the sofa that crumbles into dust, into the hall where the walls begin to vanish, into the kitchen where the stove, the mixer, and the radio sigh and fall away.

Betty Ann stands naked, looks through the screen door, where it used to be, looks for the black birds singing on the wire, black birds white now, sees them on the ground, lying on their backs with their little beaks open, claws up in the air.

"Well my goodness," says Betty Ann, "now isn't that a sight to see. Why, it's like Andy always says, You neber do knows what gon' be happ'nin' but you kin bets it will."

John-William's mother laughs at the thought, walks back through where her first brick home used to be. Stops, for a moment, glances at the mirror in the hall. The mirror's not there but someone is, someone Betty Ann thinks she ought to know. Just for an instant, just for a blink, then just as quickly gone.

Betty Ann stands outside where the porch used to be, stands there naked and watches the corner past the Smiths and the Harpers and the Roers, looks at the lamp that's black instead of white, at the murky light on the street down below. Now, the thing on the corner, the thing that seemed to shimmer, seemed to tremble, seemed to hide behind a veil, isn't something maybe there anymore, isn't something maybe not, isn't waiting in-between anymore...

John-William's mother can feel her heart pound, feel the big clock down far-far below begin to chime. Whatever wasn't there is coming on slow, dark and heavy, faint and distant, closer, closer still, hardly even there, turning, turning, past the Roers and the Smiths and the Harpers, coming right up to where John-William's mother stands naked where her first brick house used to be...

They glide down the street now, slide on in without a sound, slip on in without a hum from their engines, a whisper from their tires. One before the other, one behind the next, hazy Buicks, Franklins and Cords. Cloudy Chryslers, Lincolns and Fords. Plymouths, Packards, Porches and Rolls, dusty and obscure. Duesenbergs, Dodges, Ramblers and Olds, scarcely present, hardly there at all. Studebakers, Chevys, Rovers and nearly invisible Saabs. Bentleys, Austins, Minors and—goodness sakes, cars Betty Ann never heard about before.

They keep on coming, gliding down the street in a motion so slight they hardly stir the air. Each one black where they ought to be white, white where the black ought to be. Everything backwards, inside out. Just the way the big stone clock down down way below likes to see.

Betty Ann knows she shouldn't ought to move, shouldn't do anything at all. Ought to just mind her own business, shouldn't ought to pry. Still, she feels she's got to know, got to see what it's all about, got to know why these peculiar cars are driving by. Ought to see who, ought to see what's inside.

Betty Ann walks naked in the street, gets close to the windows, peers inside an old Franklin, looks inside a Saab. Can't see anything at all. The glass in each and every window is cold, cold, icy to the touch, covered with frost, dark and river deep.

John-William's mother wipes a little hole free and peers inside a 1930 Cadillac. And, to Betty Ann's surprise, there's Grandmaw Wilcher sitting up straight, straight as you please, hand-bones clutching the wheel, shriveled, shrunk, stiff as a board, hair hanging this way and that.

"Grandmaw Wilcher," Betty Ann says, "why you can't even drive!" Driving she is, though, nothing you can do about that.

There's no one she knows in the Lincoln or the Cord. No one in the Nash. Helen, though, is there in the back seat of the Packard, caught in what seems intimate, dark coagulation with the soldier boy from Fort Sill. Ruin and rot have set in and a coat of fuzzy green. Still, Helen looks happy as a clam, and, as Betty Ann's mother Sarah always said, happy's better than not.

Mama Steck looks not much worse than the night Betty Ann watched the dark slide in and slide out again, and suck her life away. Betty Ann can't recall anyone drove a Studebaker back then, but there's lots she can't recall.

"Jack, Jack, Jack," thinks John-William's mother, as she peeks into the Lasalle, "I got to say you do look a sight." Except for the blight and the ruin and the dent where she'd hit him with the axe. Except for that and the gross degeneration—time's going to take a toll, that and ancient ulceration of the soul—

"Told you to stop," says Betty Ann.

"Told you hit me one more time, that's it, and by God it's just what you did, you got nothing to complain about that."

Papa is in the rusted-out Ford, not looking all that good, something like tar and tallow dried on his overalls down into his shoes and some distortion of the bones.

Betty Ann thinks she might cry when she gets to the Chevy, she knew she'd find him there. That truck had hit him head on, wrapping the brand new Schwinn around him twice, penetrating bodily parts, leaving limbs twisted, badly out of whack.

Still, he did the best he could, God bless him, holding the wheel real steady, one hand sort of going this way, the other going that.

"You were my pride," says Betty Ann, "and I never forgot you, not for a minute, John-William, not for all the years that passed. I kept that Krazy Kat button and the Nehi cap as well. You tore that Ferdinand shirt real bad, but I don't guess you care about that."

Betty Ann opens the door, and slides real quiet inside. Looks at John-William, pictures in her head that he's looking back.

Just for a moment, no more than that, Betty Ann glances behind her, sees the two she lost sitting quiet, sitting still, looks there once and doesn't look back.

Nobody said it was time to drive on, but real soon everybody did. Rolling down the window, she listened to the music playing on the car radios: *Moonlight Cocktail, Twilight Time, One For My Baby, Laura, Willow Weep For Me.*

And, coming from somewhere, out of the hot and inky night, just before the clock deep-deep in the earth strikes again, a whisper in the hot night air:

> *Not just before, Betty Ann,*
> > *And not just after,*
> > > *It's not getting dark, Betty Ann,*
> *The dark's already here...*

The Heart

You can't go far in West Texas without coming on a roadside attraction that offers wondrous sights to see. It's not an easy way to make a living, and the people who run these operations know folks trying to make Amarillo or Tucumcari by dark aren't likely to slow down to 90 for a sleepy rattler or your ordinary two-headed goat. Your veteran driver's seen it all, and unless they're handing out free beer, he's going to whiz on by. When the kids were young, I'd have Judy throw a blanket over Ned and little Lou before we came to the first signs stuck beside the road. Once a child sees stuff like

GILA MONSTER, 15 MILES!
WATCH A PYTHON EAT A PIG!
HEADLESS CHICKEN COUNTS TO TEN!

you are in for trouble, pal. Now both Lou and Ned have kids and grand-kids of their own and live in civilized places like Delaware and Maine. I doubt they go in for such business up there.

I've seen everything stuffed, dried up, shrunk and fossilized there is between Taos and El Paso and I wouldn't slow down for a UFO with a flat. Still, I always stop at Harry Mack's, because Harry's the last of the old time greats, a fraud, a fake, a cheat, a first class hustler, a man who can look you in the eye and make you believe a bold-faced lie is God's unvarnished truth. And, though Harry puts on a brave, blustering face to the world, he's truly a lonely man, with neither family nor friends, and only a mutt named Buster to see him through the long nights. I try to drop by at least once a year to share a drink or two, and catch Harry up on world events, for he has no use for newspapers and what he calls "that box full crazy people yakking" and it's hard to fault him on that.

▲▼▲

The first thing you see about twenty-five miles down the road is a full-sized billboard that would put old Barnum to shame. In bold red letters higher than a stripper in six-inch heels, you're struck with a message that gets your attention even if you're sleeping at the wheel:

**** HARRY'S HOUSE OF WONDERS ****
SEE THE DEAD MAN'S HEART THAT'S STILL ALIVE
WATCH IT BEAT
BEAT
BEAT
BEFORE YOUR VERY EYES!

Now your ordinary showman would be tempted to add some real scary art—a little blood, some spooky eyes and such, but Harry's no amateur, and he knows a sign like that doesn't need any cheap distractions. The picture that's going through your head at the moment is all Harry needs to draw you in.

There's more, of course. Every mile or two. Just to let you know there's twenty-foot rattlers, man-eating gators, a four-eyed cow, cold drinks, barbecue, a petting zoo for the kiddies, and clean rest rooms. But the closer you get, the more you start seeing stuff like

IT BEATS
IT QUIVERS
IT'S ALIVE!

Harry doesn't want you to forget what you really came for. Your thoughts might wander and you find yourself at some small-time, two-bit exhibit with a cage full of house cats and tomahawks made in Taiwan.

Finally, you make it to Harry's, park, and find the little signs with arrows that show you where the rattlers and the gators and cold drinks are, and Harry hits you with his final come-on, in case you're not just dying to see that bloody thing now. From hidden speakers comes a slow and steady

Ka—BOOM. . . . .Ka-BOOM. . .Ka-Boom. . . . !

It's the heart, the great heart itself, and Harry, always thinking of others before profit for himself, has a last minute warning before he takes your three bucks for this special event (a fee he fails to mention before he's got you in.) A hand-lettered sign before the curtained door reads:

WARNING: WHILE THIS EXHIBIT IS PRESENTED FOR EDUCATIONAL PURPOSES ONLY, THE SIGHT OF THIS AMAZING HISTORICAL PHENOMENA MAY BE DISTURBING TO SOME. HARRY'S HOUSE OF WONDER CANNOT BE RESPONSIBLE FOR NAUSEA, FAINTING SPELLS OR OTHER ADVERSE REACTIONS TO THE SIGHT YOU ARE ABOUT TO BEHOLD.

Harry Mack knows there's no turning back now. What man is going to admit, in front of his wife and children, he's too chicken to go beyond that curtained door?

▲▼▲

And, at last, there it is. And, by all that's holy, it is indeed a truly awesome, incredible thing to see. People gasp, stare, shake their heads in wonder and disbelief. Logic, reason and common sense tell them what they're seeing couldn't be. Yet, there it is, a great heart pulsing at roughly sixty-three beats a minute. You could time it with your watch, but there's no need for that. The constant **Ka-Boom! Ka-Boom! Ka-Boom!** of the speakers is right in synch with the miracle before your eyes.

The room itself is dark. A tightly-focused beam from above highlights the heart itself as it floats in a ten-gallon bottle, much like those Dr. Frankenstein himself might keep around the lab. The liquid in the bottle is a pale, somewhat disturbing pink, and some device unseen keeps a stream of bubbles rising slowly past the heart itself.

There's more, though. That's not all there is to see. With Harry Mack, there's always something more. The heart doesn't simply hang suspended in its watery home. Now and then it *moves*, as if this mighty organ grows restless, and seeks to wander about. One might imagine its arteries and vessels propel it in the manner of some creature of the sea.

After a moment or so, when the crowd is mesmerized by this wonder before their eyes, the beat from the speakers grows louder for a moment, then fades, and Harry Mack, doing a fairly credible Vincent Price, comes on with his fascinating spiel. I've heard this a number of times, but for those who haven't, it's a tale as spellbinding as the living heart itself...

▲▼▲

"Thank you, ladies and gentlemen for your attention. My name is Harry Mack, and it is my privilege to be your host for this afternoon's showing of the famous Dead Man's Heart That Lives. I expect many of you will find this story most fanciful and hard to believe. I will not blame you if you do. All I can tell you is this pulsing, beating organ you see before you is as real as your own, and that the tale behind it is both strange and incredible, but absolutely true.

"It is hard to tell when Joshua Gaines first settled in Texas, but there is no doubt he was likely the first white man to build his cabin in the untamed wilds of the frontier. My family came from Tennessee in 1850, and Josh was already there. How he managed to survive in a land that swarmed with Comanches at the time is a miracle in itself, and it can come as no surprise that it was the presence of those fierce warriors that finally brought Josh down.

"My great-great grandfather told the story of that awful day, and it has been handed down to me. That brave kinsman of mine knew of what he spoke, for he was with Josh at the time. A terrible fight took place in 1857, and before it was over, old Josh knocked off several warriors and Yellow Tail himself at seven hundred yards with a buffalo rifle. Still, the odds were too great, and brave men died on both sides of the battle. Joshua Gaines himself went down with a thrust in his breast from a Comanche lance. It was an awful wound. Josh's companions were certain not a man on earth could survive a horrid puncture like that.

"Now, here's where the story takes on an almost mystical character, friends, but I don't have to tell you legend and myth have laid the foundations for many of today's most profound and respected truths.

"While Josh lay dying, an old Indian walked out of the brush. Josh's crew nearly shot him, but it was clear he wasn't a Comanche and he swore he was a friend of Josh's. He asked the others to leave him alone with Josh, and the boys helped him carry Josh's near dead body off into the mesquite.

"What happened in there remains a mystery to this day, but in the morning, the Indian was gone, and Josh walked out of the brush fit as a fiddle, his breast closed up and the wound beginning to heal. Josh never spoke of that day again, but my great-great grandfather put down in writing that Joshua Gaines was fifty years old the day he was healed.

"No great mystery to that, ladies and gentlemen, if you can believe in Indian magic and such, but the fact is that same Joshua Gaines was still alive and living in that same cabin in the year 1942. For those of you who can do sums in their head, *the man could not have been younger than one hundred and thirty-five years at that time!*"

A little mumbling from the crowd about here. Many feel they've been taken, that Harry's credibility has been stretched far beyond the limit. It is at this point that Harry's mastery of the art comes into play. For he knows that nothing on earth can top the first lie, except the second, a monstrous whopper that leaves the first one far behind.

▲▼▲

"I know," Harry goes on, "you're saying to yourself I feel like a fool falling for a tale like this. And I don't blame you a bit. I think I would too. So what I'm saying now is leave, go through that curtain and take your three bucks back, no questions asked. Or, if you want to hear the rest of the story, I invite you to stay, and hear the astonishing conclusion."

They always stay. I've never seen Harry have to give those three bucks back.

▲▼▲

"As I said, old Josh lived on and on, healthy as can be till a day in 1942. Then, Fate struck, as it is wont to do. Josh was in his local food store when a crazed bandit robbed the place and began shooting folks at random. A stray bullet struck Josh in the head. His friend Doc Ames figured he wouldn't live through the day, but Josh set him straight about that. 'I'll live, nothing but that bullet in my brain can kill me, long as I've got that heart. Still, living though I be, there'll be nothing left of me but rot and broken parts.'

"Then Josh made a startling statement, one Doc Ames could scarcely credit 'Take the heart from my breast, for it belongs to Ghost Man, a Lipan chief who borrowed it from one of their native gods to save my life. The rest of my body will die right soon, and you must promise you'll cut this heart from my bosom, as it doesn't belong to me!'

"Josh didn't die that first day, nor the second, but he perished on the third. Doc Ames pondered for some time over the task his friend had asked of him. It went far beyond his medical oath, but a promise to a friend is something else again.

"I won't go into the gruesome details of the operation that freed the heart from Josh's breast. Suffice it to say that even after that great organ was wrested from Josh's body, it remained a living thing, a heart that pulsed and throbbed with all the energy of everlasting life.

"My great uncle Herbert Mack, on hand at the time of Josh's death, can testify to the unusual events that happened next. While Doc Ames held that living organ in his hands, a noise no greater than the whispering of a night wind began whistling through the house. Then, in the blink of an eye a strange figure appeared in the doorway—an Indian warrior in the paint, war bonnet, breech-clout and moccasins of an age gone by. His dark eyes burned like fires gleaming deep under fathomless black lakes. Silently, he extended his hand, and Doc Ames dropped Joshua Gaines' heart into it. Without a word this ghostly figure from the past turned and stalked out into the night. When Doc Ames and Uncle Mack rushed out in the yard an instant later, there was no sign of anyone at all. Whoever, or whatever was there had vanished like a phantom in the night, and only something that looked like a giant black owl, with great, enormous wings, could be seen, dwindling from sight, into the rising moon."

At this point, Harry Mack paused to give his audience time to think, to ponder, and wonder how the story could end on such a note, the heart vanished in the hands of an Indian wraith, when that very same organ was right there before them, floating lazily in its jar.

▲▼▲

"It's a most peculiar tale, is it not?" Harry Mack went on, at just the proper time. "It could end right there and stand as one of the oddest events in the history of the West. But as you have likely guessed, my friends, there is still more to tell. Not a quarter hour passed before was heard the wail of Sheriff McKee's patrol car as it raced down the highway nearby. As great-uncle Herbert told it when I was still a child, he and Doc Ames had a feeling the sheriff's mission had something to do with the death of old Josh, and the strange appearance of a warrior from the past.

"Following that patrol car in Doc's old Buick, Herbert and the doctor soon came upon the sheriff's car, its headlights illuminating a big semi turned over in the middle of the road. The driver was still alive, and seemingly unhurt, at least in a physical sense, but all the blood had rushed out of the fellow's face and his body shook like he'd just been pulled from the frozen seas. It took the sheriff, Doc Ames and Uncle Herbert to keep him from shaking and breaking every bone in his body.

"The sheriff wrapped him in a blanket, and the doc gave him a generous slug from a bottle of whiskey he carried for medicinal purposes. Finally, the man was able to speak, and the story he told stunned the three who heard his tale. He was driving along when something appeared in his lights, something gigantic flying straight at him. The driver tried to swerve, but it was too late for that. All he could recall as his truck tilted over on its side was a gigantic creature, half-man and half-beast, a thing with great wings and fiery red eyes.

"None of the three could question the man's story, for a look at the front of that truck told more than words could say. 'It looked to me,' Uncle Herbert said many years later, 'as if that semi had struck a truck full of ten thousand chickens head on. There was blood, feathers and innards four feet thick from the semi's bumper to the top of the cab. And, worst of all, you could see mixed in that gruesome mess, what appeared to be the shattered bones and flesh of human remains.'

"None of the three ever spoke of this event, and certainly the driver, if indeed he kept his sanity, revealed what had happened to him that night. Later, the town fire engine came along and sprayed the place clean, and not a one of those fellows spoke of what they'd seen."

Here, Harry always paused for effect, to let his audience squirm for a moment or two. Then, as folks began to stir restlessly about, he went on.

"And that would be the end, would it not, and we'd have us a story with the tail left hanging in suspense. But there is more, my friends, as I'm certain you must have guessed. Later, in the early morning hours, my great-uncle Herbert came back to the site alone, his curiosity still aroused. Both Doc Ames and the sheriff had assumed, and reasonably so, that old Josh's heart had suffered the same fate as the phantom flying warrior when it struck the semi earlier that night. But Herbert, who shared the stubborn streak that runs in the family still, had to find out for himself. Armed with a strong, four-cell battery light, he diligently searched the roadside, the fields, and the woods around the wreck site until the first pale shades of dawn touched the horizon.

"Well, I won't keep you in suspense, for I'm sure you've guessed the answer. He found the great heart, deep in the brush some thirty yards from the road. Uncle Herbert picked the organ up and held it, raising it high in the morning light. It beat, quivered, pulsed against his hands as strong as ever. Could any power on earth, or some ethereal plane, cause this miraculous heart of an Indian god to cease its endless quest for life?

"Herbert could have shared his find with Doc Ames or others, but he was of a secret nature, and he kept his wondrous find hidden from the world, and passed its story along only to those in his family who came after."

A long pause here, as Harry Mack's voice rises to a dramatic pitch, and he points to the famous object itself, as that familiar sound **Ka-boom! Ka-boom! Ka-boom!** echoes once more through the room.

"And there it is, my friends, the heart eternal, the gift of the Ghost Man, a Lipan chief, who borrowed it from a god of his people to save his friend Joshua Gaines.

There it is before your very eyes, alive, counting off the seconds as it has since its creation, and as it well may to the very end of time!"

▲▼▲

No one ever left that room without a look of awe, even reverence on their features. And many came back year after year to see the great heart, and hear Harry Mack tell its story as only Harry ever could. I was one of those who did...

▲▼▲

"I've always wondered how you do it," I asked Harry. "I've nearly figured it a dozen times, but you've still got me fooled. There's parts of the scam I can't put my finger on at all."

We were sitting in lawn chairs out in front of Harry's house, a few yards behind the exhibit area itself. All the critters had gone silent. The cow had closed all four eyes and lain down in its stall. Even the gator had quit grunting and thrashing about and settled in for the night. The Texas sky was full of stars, Harry and I were full of barbecue, and working on the bottle of bourbon whiskey I always brought along.

"I swear, you don't ever give up trying, do you, Bob?" Harry shook his head, took another drink and leaned back in his chair. "A man tries to give folks honest, wholesome entertainment for their money, and all he gets for his trouble is mean and scurrilous talk from his friend. If this wasn't real good whiskey, I'd be inclined to wrestle you to the ground."

The idea of either of us old fools, at the age of 75, engaging in physical struggle made me groan aloud, and that brought Harry's dog Buster over to check me out, see if I'd had a stroke or what. A dog will do that kind of thing, take care of folks of the elderly persuasion. Buster was only a long-haired hound, but he had a kindness about him you won't find in a lot of human types. Being a man alone all his life, Harry had had a string of good dogs, all of them mutts, all of them much alike, and all of them carrying on the name of Buster. I think keeping the name gave Harry a sense of time not passing so swiftly by, a feeling of life remaining the same.

"It isn't so much your doubts that offend," Harry said, "a man in my business gets used to that. It's the idea you keep hanging in, wearing me down, going on and on, year in and year out." He stopped, and ran a hand through his thinning hair. "What do you figure it'd take, Bob, to shut you up for good? I mean, besides a barrel of buckshot in your rear?"

"Truth," I told him. "I think that'd do it. I believe I'd leave the topic alone after that."

I hated to do it, for I didn't want to hurt a good friend, but this business had haunted me for a good twenty years, and I simply had to let it out.

"I have to tell you, Harry, I have spent a good bit of time tracking down the story of old Joshua Gaines' heart. I know the names of nearly every pioneer who settled in Texas in those early years. I know who fought the Comanches, where the encounters took place, and when. I have to tell you there was no Joshua Gaines, no Doc Ames and, I hate to say it, no great-great grandfather with the last name of Mack—which is also yours, by the way. I have looked into every highway wreck on or around 1942, and there is no record of any such incident, much less one involving great piles of feathers, bones, innards and such.

"I'm sorry, Harry. I had no business messing in your affairs, but I just couldn't help myself. It got it in my head first time I was here, and it wouldn't go away."

For a long time, Harry just sat there, staring into his empty glass, then he stood, gave me a nod, and said, "Come on, you damn fool, I'll not have you pester me any more…"

▲▼▲

Harry unlatched the gate to the exhibit area, getting a hiss from a snake, a moan from a coyote without any teeth, and ended up at the door to the great secret itself. I must have look startled, to imagine he truly intended to go any farther than that, but it's exactly what he did. Unlocking the door, he stepped aside and ushered me in, turned on the bright light, and I stood blinking at the mighty, living heart itself.

"Okay, you got it," Harry said, folding his arms and leaning against the door. "It's a fake. A hoax. One of the best you'll ever see but as phony as a six dollar bill. One of the finest medical sculptors at the Mayo Clinic made it for me, out of rubber and plastic. It's attached to very tiny nylon wires, too small to see under that blinding light. The wires run down to the base, where a small electric motor moves the heart in a series of motions, from one side to the next. The beat, of course, comes from an inflatable rubber tube. That's the easy part.

"The damn thing cost me a fortune, but I've made back every penny of my investment, and more. There's not a con like it in the world."

"And the story," I said, "you made all that up, too?"

Harry grinned at that. "You and your search through history. I'm ashamed of you, Bob. The key to a good scam is the mix of truth and lies. No one but a stubborn old fool like you would go to the trouble to find out which settler was where and when they fought the Comanches. All that business happened over and over again and there's no telling how many names, places, battle grounds have been lost through time. As for Indians and their gods, why, there are more legends and myths out there to fill a couple of dozen libraries." Harry shook his head and laid a kindly hand on my shoulder. "I'm not angry, Bob. Really. Kind of flattered that you took the time to find me out. Let's go see if Buster drank up all our bourbon whiskey while we were gone…"

▲▼▲

I don't always sleep well at my age, but I got a good night's rest in Harry's guest room after those amazing revelations. In the morning, I packed up my overnight bag, and found Harry sitting in the same lawn chair, as if he'd never left.

"I know you went to bed," I told him. "I saw you do it, saw Buster join you."

"Oh, I got to bed," Harry said. "Just didn't get a lot of rest."

"Likely my fault," I said. "I wasn't a real good guest, mouthing off like I did."

Harry didn't answer. He offered me a hot cup of coffee, and we sat there in silence for awhile, as two old men will do when they're not sure how many mornings and evenings they have left to share. Finally, I gave Buster a pat and walked out to my car past the exhibit. Critters of all sorts were waking up, snorting and groaning and waiting for someone to bring them breakfast.

"Well, I guess this is it till next year," I said, reaching out to grab Harry's hand. Harry gave me a shake, and a real funny look to go with it.

"Never in my entire life did I imagine I'd feel guilty for conning a mark, even one who's as old a friend as you," Harry said. "But, damned if I don't, Bob. I guess a person can't always explain his feelings, even to himself."

I was some puzzled, and let it show. "I appreciate the thought, but you can lay the guilt aside now, Harry. I have to say I'm pleased you'd choose me to reveal your secrets to."

Harry sighed, looked down and scuffed his feet in the grass. "Yeah, only I didn't, Bob. I didn't do any such thing. What I did was tell you a big fat lie, and, as usual, you swallowed it whole, like any mark'd do."

"How much whiskey did you drink," I asked him. "You opened up and let it all out last night and—"

"—and snookered you again, is what I did. It *was* a lie, friend. As fantastic as it may seem, the story's just as true as it can be. It all happened, exactly the way I told it. The only thing is, it didn't happen in Texas, but in another state. Which one, I don't intend to say. All the names are changed, too. Including Joshua Gaines, the doc's—and mine."

Harry paused and looked up, the start of a weary grin at one corner of his mouth. "That's the mark of a real professional, you see, and that's no brag, just fact. What I did was hide a truth inside a lie, and a scam doesn't come much better than that. The lie is that thing pumping away in colored water. The truth is what happened to a man just like Joshua Gaines back where his family and mine come from. I just took a truth and made it into a going business, Bob. One that's treated me well, as you can see."

It took me a while to get my head working proper again, but when I did, Harry was ready, and knew I was coming.

"If the story's real, then the heart is too," I said. "And that's the part I still find hard to swallow. If there really was such a thing, where is it now? What happened to it and—"

It struck me, then, and *my* heart nearly stopped at the thought. "You got it, didn't you? By God, Harry, the Indian god's heart is in *your* chest, isn't it? I see it all now. It came down to you through your family, and all those years, no one put it to use. I expect they were afraid to even try, and I wouldn't blame them for that. But you, having more nerve and cunning than any man I've ever known, you took the chance, and it worked! The phony heart's in that shed back there, and the real one's in you!"

Harry gave me a shy, rather foolish look. "I kinda guessed you'd figure it out, Bob. You're keen as you can be, and you sniff and poke around like Buster here, until you find what's at the bottom of the hole."

"Yeah, I guess I kinda did," I said, feeling good for gigging Harry again. I gave Buster a pat, and Harry a wink, and got in behind the wheel. "No hard feelings, okay? And I will say, you nearly had me again."

Harry came up and laid his hands on the open window.

"You're a hard man to fool, Bob, I got to tell you that."

"Well, sometimes I maybe am."

"Right," Harry said. "One more thing and I'll let you get on your way, Bob." He leaned in close, out of the sun. "You really think I'm dumb enough to let some fool cut me open and slice out *my* heart and stuff that thing in? By God, I cannot let you go thinking I'm as big a sucker as you are. Uncle Herbert, which wasn't his name, of course, is the one who used the heart. And what he did was talk Doc Ames into putting that heart into the *dog* he dearly loved, who was dying in agony at the time, and was going to go anyway so why not give it a try. The dog's name was Buster, friend, and he was fifty-five years old this June. Of course you figured you were seeing new dogs all time, and so did everyone else, but there's only one Buster, and there's never been another."

Harry paused to take a breath. "Now, you got it all peeled down to the very last lie, like those little Russian dolls where you finally see there's nothing left inside. So get on your way, and drop by next year 'less you're dead or I am too. Drive careful, Bob. And don't stop at that idiot's place down the road. There's no such thing as a nine-legged calf, if there was I'd have one too..."

▲▼▲

I thought about Harry for a while, but mostly I thought about Buster, and I wondered what would happen if Harry passed on, and Buster started roaming around alone, and didn't starve or get run over and just kept wandering about, that great, eternal heart going **ka-boom! ka-boom! ka-boom!** forever in his old doggy chest. What if he just went on forever, after everything else ceased to be. Wouldn't that be something?

And one other thing, a thought I couldn't get out of my head. What if Harry still had a lie within a truth or a truth within a lie? A real con man nearly always has another trick or two up his sleeve, and Harry's the best there is, the best there'll ever be....

Limo

"There she is now," said Mr. Creel, "does she meet with your satisfaction, Mr. Bream?"

Bream leaned forward, peered out the window, breathed in the limo's brandy-flavored air, the rich, exciting scent of unborn puppy from the soft leather seats. She stood before the hotel less than a block away. The place was nothing fancy, just your standard, second-rate rip-off with bad food and a bar.

"She is quite tasteful, Mr. Creel."

"Indeed, sir."

"Well fleshed, I'd say."

"Generously endowed, Mr. Bream."

"One has to notice that."

"Stylish, but sensible shoes."

"*Cluck-Cluck!*"

"What's that again, Mr. Bream?"

"What's what?"

"You said—"

"I don't believe I said a thing, Mr. Creel."

"No, certainly not."

"She's just the right size," said Bream.

"Absolutely," said Creel.

"Not too tall or too short."

"A fine and sturdy woman, Mr. Bream."

"What's that?" Bream turned stone-dark eyes on Creel. Creel quickly glanced away. It was most discomfiting to hold such a look too long.

"Sturdy," said Bream, leaning in so close Mr. Creel could count pores, pimples, nose hairs and a speck of something on Mr. Bream's chin.

"I shall allow your unfortunate choice of words this once," said Bream, "but not again, sir, not a mote, not a smidgen more, do you hear? And not *chubby*, either, Mr. Creel. Neither chubby, chunky nor dumpy. Heavy-set bloated blowzy pudgy porky ponderous or plump. I would never tolerate a woman with a single one of those vulgar, onerous qualities. Such a woman does *not* fit my needs, and I would not hear her described in such an unwomanly manner!"

"So, what do you think of her, Mr. Bream?"

"I love this woman," said Bream. "She is magnificent. Absolutely perfect. You've done very well indeed."

"I'm grateful, Mr. Bream."

"Well of course you are, Mr. Creel."

Mr. Bream opened the door, left the brandy-flavored air and the puppy leather seats. Stepped out into the dark and dreary night, stalked across the empty avenue, left without another look back, thought about a Kansas City steak, thought about a good scotch whisky, a fine cigar. Thought of these things for scarcely a moment, then swept them from his mind, for they were merely things he needed to recall now and then, things other people did. Bream didn't drink and didn't smoke, and seldom ate anything at all.

"*Cluck! Cluck!*" said Mr. Bream.

▲▼▲

The hotel was half a block away. Bream paused for a moment and studied the girl. She stood quite primly beneath the green awning. The doorman didn't bother her at all. He knew a hooker when he saw one and clearly didn't see one now.

Comely, Bream thought. Good carriage, very nice air. Thirties, and scarcely into that. A round and pleasant face. Straw-colored hair cut just below the neck. Dark-colored skirt, a light blue blouse. A shawl of some sort held loosely over one arm, the strap of a purse across her shoulder. She stood beneath the awning for awhile, glancing up the street to her left and to her right. Impatient, thought Bream, but she scarcely let it show. A very good trait, especially in a woman these days.

Checking the street once more, she gently touched her hair, adjusted her skirt, and took a few steps forward. Paused, turned and came back again.

Bream stood perfectly still, rooted, as it were, to the street, still warm from the heat of the day. He watched as she walked, watched as she swayed one way and then the next, watched, and felt his blood begin to stir, felt the rush of that dark and turgid fluid, felt the tremble, felt the shudder through his veins. Every bone, every organ, every muscle, every bodily part begin to hum, thrum, like a finely-tuned engine, one of your fine German or Italian machines, not some crap from Detroit.

"*Cluck-cluck-cluck!*" said Mr. Bream.

Taking a deep breath, he crossed the street, stopped just before the woman, remembered what to say and then said it.

"I am Marvin Darrel Bream, ma'am. I believe you are waiting here for me."

The woman smiled, a soft and gentle smile that might have broken Bream's heart if he noticed gestures such as that.

"I'm Angelina Gorse de Sommes," the woman said. "I am your date for the evening, Mr. Bream."

"Yes," said Bream, "You are."

"It's a pleasure to meet you, Mr. Bream."

"And why is that, Ms. de Sommes?"

"It's something you say to people," Angelina said politely. "For conversation, as it were."

"Cluck! Cluck!"

"I beg your pardon?"

Bream didn't answer. He simply gripped her arm and led her gently past the doorman. The doorman smiled and tipped his cap.

Angelina looked confused, tried to keep up. "Are we having drinks here, Mr. Bream?"

"Dancing, Mr. Bream?"

"Dinner, Mr. Bream?"

"Mr. *Bream?*"

"Your breasts are sufficiently large," said Bream.

"What?" Angelina stopped. Bream tried to bring her along, but she clamped her feet firmly to the ground.

Sensible shoes, thought Bream. He suddenly jerked her hard and broke her free.

"Other parts are quite nice too," Bream muttered.

"Good buttocks, good thighs   "

"We need to *talk*, Mr. Bream. You cannot speak to me like that."

"It is conversation. Something you say to people."

"Well it certainly is not!"

Bream gripped her arm so tightly Angelina gasped. It was late, and the lobby was nearly empty. A tired bellboy gave the pair a curious look then glanced away again.

Bream shoved her roughly into an open elevator, lifted her off her feet and bounced her off the back wall.

Angelina cried out, shook her head, and wobbled dizzily to her hands and knees. Bream gave her a solid kick and sent her sprawling again.

"Cluck! Cluck! Cluck!" said Mr. Bream.

"Ping! Ping! Ping!" said the elevator and opened with a sigh. Mr. Bream grabbed Angelina by the waist and hauled her up beneath his arm. Angelina cursed and tried to kick free. Bream slapped her hard across the face.

"You have to stop that," he said. "I don't like it, it's very irritating."

Bream drew his hand away to let her breathe while he worked the plastic card into 304. Once inside, he stalked across the room, ripped the purse from her shoulder and dumped her roughly on the bed.

Angelina sprang up a lot quicker than Bream would have imagined. Standing on the bed, back against the wall, she glared at Bream, her face still stinging. She had lost one shoe, and her skirt was in disarray.

"Okay," she said, a strand of hair hanging carelessly over one brow, "That's it. I am out of here, you sick son of a bitch. This is *not* what I do!"

Bream looked puzzled. "This is what *I* do, Angelina. Please stop being unpleasant. If you continue behaving like this—"

Bream could scarcely blink before Angelina whipped the shawl off her arm and threw it at him in a blur. He flipped it aside and went at her, leaping onto the bed.

Again, Angelina was half a second faster. She went to her knees, grabbed the lamp by the bed and struck him solidly on the head.

Bream staggered back. He had read about people seeing stars and flashing lights, and now he understood what that was all about. Still, he was on his feet in an instant. Angelina was fast, but she was a woman, and a woman had never bested him yet.

Shaking the stars away, he was after her at once. She had climbed across a couch and was halfway to the door when he leaped off the floor, caught her around the waist and brought her down.

Angelina gasped for air. Too stunned to move, she knew she was being carried, saw the room swim dizzily about, then caught her breath as she hit the bed again. She reached out at once to fight him off, kicked out in a move that would drive his crotch up in his throat. Mr. Bream grabbed her, struck her once more across her face.

Angelina's defenses kicked in at once. She knew another mistake and this bastard would finish her off for good. She glanced to her left. Bream was gone. Bracing her body against the bed, she flexed her arms to bring herself erect again. This time she'd—

Nothing happened. Her arms wouldn't move. In those few seconds he'd had her stunned, he'd acted quickly and tied her wrists to the bedposts above.

"You maniac," she screamed, jerking futilely at her bonds, "let me out of here this minute. You haven't *seen* trouble until you've tangled with me, you, you freak, you—Whuh?"

Angelina stiffened as Bream suddenly leaped on her out of nowhere, pinning her legs to the bed. For a moment, she wasn't certain it was Bream it all. A parody of the man, a portrait by a drunken artist, shapes and colors gone awry. Bream in a seizure, caught in a frenzy, in a fit. His whole body quaked, quivered, shivered and shook. Most frightening of all were his eyes, great black marbles afloat in a raging red sea.

"*Cluck! Cluck! Cluuuuuuck!*" said Bream.

"Get the fuck off of me," Angelina shouted. "I'll have you beaten, chained, locked up forever in the dark!"

"Thighs," Bream sang, in very scary flats, "thighs, thighs, very fine thighs..."

With that, he drew a black marker from his pocket, lifted Angelina's skirt and began to draw little dashes across her flesh. Made another set of marks below her knees. Leaning back a moment, he droned, moaned, mumbled to himself, then ripped off her blouse, drew black dashes across one breast and then the next.

"Hey," Angelina yelled, "what the shit do you think you're doing? Get away from me!"

Bream hummed a little tune, and Angelina tried to pull herself in, make herself smaller, shrink somehow to keep this monster away.

"Breasts, breasts, full and hearty breasts," sang Mr. Bream. "Very nice indeed..."

Angelina screamed herself hoarse, arched her body to break herself free. If Mr. Bream noticed she was somewhat alarmed, he paid no attention at all. He was busy working on her arms, drawing lines of dashes just beneath her shoulders, under her armpits and back up again.

"I'll get to that lovely butt a little later," Bream said. "It might give you some displeasure if we turned you over now."

"*Cluck! Cluck! Cluck!*"

Bream hopped right off the bed, then promptly disappeared from sight. Angelina had no idea where he'd gone. That worried her a lot. The fact that he was gone simply meant he was coming *back*.

Coming back and doing what...?

It was no surprise to Angelina that Bream was a certified psycho-fruitcake-nut. He'd made that clear from the start. Just what *kind* of loony was something else. Lots of people were daft, deranged, totally out of whack. Angelina knew she was minus a screw or too herself. But *this* mother, Mr. fucking Bream, drew lines on her very private parts, and *that* wasn't right at all...

She heard him, then, stomping around somewhere to her left. She couldn't turn her head to see exactly where. Maybe in the bathroom, she thought. He couldn't be anywhere else. The bathroom or the luggage closet near the front door. And there was scarcely any room in there...

"*Cluck! Clucka-Cluck-Cluuuuck!*"

Suddenly he was back. Angelina nearly wrenched her neck to see. She hadn't eaten since lunch, and the sour taste of Tom Yum soup was crawling up the back of her throat.

Mr. Bream was naked.

Bare-assed, stripped down, nude, crude, down to his birthday suit.

"Clucka-Clucka-Claaaaawk!" said Mr. Bream. He strutted past the bed, strut-strut-strut, then shuffle-shuffle-shuffle. His head bobbed forward, forward and back, bobble-bobble-bobble like a dolly on the dash. He held his fists firmly against his chest and his arms went flap-flap-flap. And, to complete this daffy, crackbrain, freaked-out parade, Bream had stretched a red rubber glove atop his head, the fingers bobbing in a barnyard salute.

"Clucka-Clucka-Squaaaaaawk!" said Mr. Bream, waving his arms about.

"Thighs, thighs, hefty lovely thighs," he sang, strutting back and forth before Angelina's bed. *Go for a firm and juicy thigh...*

"The breast, the breast, the breast is
best is the best is the tastiest, very very
best of the rest...

"Wings, wings, precious little wings, take a bit take
a bite, a crusty wing is just right..."

Mr. Bream's eyes got big as dinner plates. He giggled, snorted and snuffed. A ropy yellow strand crawled slowly down the corner of his mouth. He shook his head, and the rubber fingers waggled back and forth.

"Try a drumstick if you will,
a drumstick's mighty fine,
one for you because there's two,
and the other one's mine..."

Bream stared at Angelina a moment, stared in wonder, as if he'd never seen her before. Then he turned away—Shuffle-Shuffle-Shuffle. Strut-Strut-Strut. Paused for a moment, stopped, as if the very heavens had opened up and struck him with a fun idea. He turned, gave Angelina a goofy grin. Marched over to the couch, reached under the cushions. Drew out a pair of the biggest wicked-looking butcher knives Angelina had ever seen.

"Cluck-Cluck-Cluuuuck!" said Bream.

Angelina drew a breath. Just looking at those gleaming blades told her they were sharpened to a razor edge, deadly as a Samurai sword.

Angelina gave him the best she had, a voice designed to set the ordinary mugger thinking twice. "Don't even think about it," she told him. "Get the hell away from me. *Now!*"

"Cluuuuuuucka-Clucka-Clooo!"

Bream came at her, swinging the gleaming knives above his head, bringing them down in a blur. They struck the bed, tore through the mattress the instant Angelina swept her legs aside. Bream shouted in a rage, raised the blades and came at her once again.

That's it, thought Angelina, *don't push it, babe...*

Before the knives struck her, she wrenched her hands free, reached up and grabbed Bream's wrists, slammed her feet into his chest and sent him sprawling off the bed.

Bream got to his feet, stared at Angelina.

"You sicko freak." Angelina shook her head and laughed. "You never learn how to tie a woman up? That is frigging pathetic, pal. It's—"

Bream's hand moved in a blur of motion. One knife struck the bedstead behind her, buried up to the hilt

Angelina drew it out and tossed it across the room.

"Fine. Now it's my turn..."

Bream growled and came at her, his other knife held out before him like a lance. Angelina leaped aside, picked up the bedside table and tossed it at Bream. Bream saw it coming and stumbled aside. Instead of going after Angelina, he jumped on the bed and jerked his other knife free. On the floor again, he stalked Angelina, coming at her slowly now.

"Good thinking," said Angelina. "You're crazy, but not entirely dumb."

She could see what he was doing, herding her to the far side of the room, trying to pin her against the wall. She quickly moved to the right. Bream moved right along with her.

"*Thighs, thighs, drumsticks and breasts,*" he sang, "*cut 'em up, slice 'em up, cook up a mess...*"

"I don't think so, not today, asshole." Bream was getting closer. Angelina kept moving to her right, then suddenly shifted to her left. Bream stomped after her, stopped, waited to see just what she'd do next.

Angelina was waiting for that. She bent low, picked up the shawl she'd tossed at Bream moments after they'd entered the room, and circled around the couch.

Bream tossed a blade right at her. It whistled and quivered in the wall.

"Now you've just got one again," said Angelina. "How's that grab you, Mr. Bream?"

Quickly, she straightened the shawl, held it by two corners, shook it, the way you snap a towel. She glanced up to check on Bream. He was crouching low, coming around the couch. Now why the hell was he doing that?

Angelina ran her hands over the edge of the shawl, found what she was looking for, drew out a pair of sagging lengths of shiny metal. Hundreds of segmented links held the instrument together. Angelina held them steady, then cracked the pair like whips. They quivered, sang, and sprang up stiff like proud chrome erections.

She heard him, tensed. Cursed herself for taking her attention away for even a moment. The blade came at her, hummed past her cheek, and clattered to the floor. Angelina moved, heading back toward the bed. Another blade came at her, and another after that. An axe buried itself in the wall.

An axe! The son of a bitch has got an arsenal stashed in that couch!

Angelina leaped over the bed, rolled over twice, came to her feet. Something with a very medieval look thunked into the floor. Angelina ducked a wave of knives, felt a keen blade slice half an inch from her heel. She wrenched in pain, shook the hurt away, felt her face redden with the sudden rage that shook her body. The bastard had cut her, *touched* her with one his nasty blades…!

She stalked toward the couch, going straight at it, not an inch to either side. Bream stood up, an axe held loosely in each hand. He frowned, looked at the shiny links of metal held at Angelina's sides. She could tell his fevered mind was trying hard to work this problem out. New things often took a little time. He knew about steaks, whiskey, Subarus, lettuce and umbrellas, the thousands of things people around him thought about every day. But the shiny things were new, and he didn't like that at all. Finally, he did what he knew how to do. He blinked, once, grinned at Angelina and raised a heavy axe.

"*Thighs, thighs, pretty pink thighs,*" he babbled, "*round, sound, lovely—*"

"Huh-uh," said Angelina. "No more. Over. Finished. All done."

She raised the two shiny links, brought them down upon him one after another. Again, again, again. On and on, without a pause, without a rest. Bream had only an instant to cry out, before the shock took him under. Angelina flailed, cut, thrashed, slashed, cleaved, sliced and diced.

She had no idea how long this bloody scourge went on, only that finally it was done, for there was nothing down there left to do.

In the bathroom, she wiped the whips clean, and thrust them back in the shawl. She found her purse and combed her hair. A tiny spot of Bream's blood had stained her dress. She dabbed a wet cloth at that, turned and walked out of the room, without looking back…

▲▼▲

"Well, Mrs. Howton, I hope everything was to your liking. It is most important to us that our clients are pleased."

"Thank you, Mr. Creel." She smiled, touched her hair, reached down and absently straightened the shawl across her arm. "Everything was fine. He was exactly what I was looking for."

"I'm so pleased to hear it, Mrs. Howton. Do let us hear from you again." He opened the door of the limo. "I think the evening's cooling off. We'll drive you back to your car. It won't take a minute."

"Thank you," she said, and placed one foot inside the car. Odd, she thought, that very nice burgundy smell is missing. Instead, there's something rather awful in here—

They were on her, then, one lean and lanky, with dead yellow teeth, skin pale as winter, eyes like the bottom of a lake. The other so fat and loathsome she shuddered and turned away. They smelled like sweat, wet earth, bad whiskey and tobacco, long since rotted and now a foul part of their souls. She screamed, then, and in an instant their hands were all over her, grabbing, probing, grunting as they found some new and lovely prize.

"Purty, purty," the fat one said, "purty as can be…"

▲▼▲

"Those two in the car," said Mr. Creel, "are you certain they'll do, sir? I have to tell you, they're a rather nasty pair."

Mr. Howard Cross Benton stood out of shadow. He looked at the limo and smiled. "They'll do nicely, Mr. Creel. Just what we're looking for."

"Well then, fine. I'm pleased, Mr. Benton. It'll just be a while…"